THE LOST SWORDS:
THE SECOND TRIAD

THE LOST SWORDS: THE SECOND TRIAD

FARSLAYER'S STORY
COINSPINNER'S STORY
MINDSWORD'S STORY

Fred Saberhagen

Published by arrangement with
Tor Books
Tom Doherty Associates, Inc.
49 West 24th Street
New York, New York 10010

Printed in the United States of America

Quality Printing and Binding by:
R.R. Donnelley & Sons Company
1009 Sloan Street
Crawfordsville, IN 47933 U.S.A.

Contents

Contents

THE FOURTH BOOK OF LOST SWORDS:
FARSLAYER'S STORY

Prologue

In the middle of the day the black-haired mermaid was drifting carelessly in a summery river, letting herself be carried slowly through the first calm pool in the Tungri below the thunder of the cataract. It was a pool that was almost big enough to be called a lake, surrounded by the greenery and bitter memories of the shores.

Her name was Black Pearl, and she had been a mermaid now for something like five years, even though she had been born with two good legs and no tail at all, into a family of fisherfolk seemingly as far removed as anyone could be from magic.

Black Pearl's pale face, now framed by the water, held an expression of intent listening, as if she might be trying to read some information from the open sky. Her black hair swirled in the water around her head, her small breasts poked above the surface. Drifting immobile now, holding her tail perfectly still, she was allowing the current to carry her out of the broad pool which was almost a lake, on a course that would take her between the two islands that were the most prominent features of this portion of the river.

To judge by the expression on Black Pearl's face, if the sky was indeed trying to tell her anything, she did not care for the message it conveyed.

Mermaids' Island, overgrown now with summer's own green magic, slid by to the mermaid's north, on her left hand as she floated on her back. Magicians' Island, somewhat smaller and stranger and somewhat less green, with a certain aura of the forbidden about it, would soon be passing to her south.

According to her own best calculation, Black Pearl had recently turned eighteen years of age, at the beginning of the summer. She knew, therefore, that she had not very many years of life remaining. Mermaids, fishgirls, of her age never did. Black Pearl's mother would be able to remember her age with accuracy, she supposed. But for years now her mother had no longer wanted to come to the shore and talk with her. If, indeed, her mother was still alive. A long time had passed since Black Pearl had tried to see any of her relatives.

As for the bitter memories—

Somewhere to the south and west of where she drifted now, no more than a few kilometers over the water, was Black Pearl's home village— though it was home to her no longer. Now, the only semblance of a home she knew was Mermaids' Island. Her only family were the two dozen or so other fishgirls inhabiting this stretch of the Tungri, and with many of them Black Pearl did not get on at all.

If she made the effort, and sent her mind groping under a cloud of black and evil magic for the appropriate memories, Black Pearl could vaguely recall being caught, lured ashore from these waters three or four years ago. Caught in a net, and sold, and carried upstream riding in a tank of water carried in a wagon driven by strangers. Upstream, she had first become part of some small traveling show. And then—

And then, somehow, she had been with that relatively innocent traveling show no more. But still she had been upstream, somewhere, so far that there the Tungri bore a different name. There she had been under the domination of a terrible and evil magician, whose face she could recall but not his name. A magician who had used her—

There were certain gates of memory beyond which she was always afraid to go.

Outside those ominous gates, memory produced another face, this one with a clear name attached, that she had known briefly in those strange days. It was the face of a young man with curly hair, and who walked upon two legs of course—as far as Black Pearl knew, nowhere in the world did there exist any young men who were equipped with tails and scales instead of legs—that fate was reserved for females. The name of this young man with curly hair and two strong legs was Zoltan, and though she still sometimes dreamed of him, in recent months such dreams were becoming rare.

Now, at the pace of the river's flow, here about that of a walking man, Magicians' Island was drawing near. With mild surprise the mermaid observed that she might actually be about to drift ashore on it, where only moments ago she had expected to pass at a good distance.

Drifting still, Black Pearl raised her head slightly from the water, looking down almost the full length of her body, white skin above the hips and silver scales below. Skin and scales alike were as magically immune to summer's sun as they were to winter's watery cold. As she raised her head, the ends of her long black hair floated about her delicate white breasts.

Once Zoltan's hand had touched her there.

Thoughts of Zoltan abruptly vanished. Only now did Black Pearl realize that there was a kind of music, Pan music, pipe music, in the air, and that for the last several minutes she had not been drifting in such perfect freedom as she had imagined. Rather the music had been drawing her unawares, influencing her ever so slowly, and gently inducing her to steer herself by subtle movements of her tail toward the island.

The music was coming—had been coming, for now it ceased—from somewhere among the greenery and rocks that made up the irregular shoreline, all strange projections and hidden coves, of Magicians' Island.

And now abruptly the musician became visible. A young man, one Black Pearl had never seen before, a well-dressed youth, stood staring at her from behind some of the tall reeds of that unpredictable shoreline. One of the young man's hands was holding the panpipe, letting it hang loosely as if it had been forgotten. Though the instrument was silent, the subtly entrancing music it had produced seemed still to be hanging in the air.

This young man was nothing at all like Zoltan. She had a good look at this one now, and his intense dark eyes returned her stare as she came drifting past him at a distance of no more than ten meters.

"I have been trying to summon up the spirits of sunlight," he called to the drifting mermaid in a rich tenor voice, at the same time holding up the panpipe carelessly for her to see. "Trying to call into being an elemental, composed of summer and the river. And, lo and behold! Success, beyond my fondest hopes! What a vision of rare beauty have I evoked to gaze upon!"

"Even in summer," Black Pearl said—and with her tail moving underwater she stopped her drifting motion gracefully—"even now the depths of the river are dark and cold, and full of hidden, ugly things. Are you sure you really wanted to raise an elemental of that kind?"

A careless wave of the panpipe in the young man's hand dismissed the idea altogether. Judging by the animated expression on his face, a busy mind was rushing forward.

"Will you sit near me for a few moments?" The question was asked of the mermaid in tones of the gravest courtesy, even though he who asked it did not bother to wait for a reply. Instead he came stepping toward her through the muddy shallows, with little concern for his fine boots or clothing. At the very edge of the current he sat himself down cross-legged on a flat rock whose top was no more than a few centimeters above the restless surface of the river, and once he was seated there gave trial of a few more notes upon the pipes of Pan.

This time, thought Black Pearl, if it was indeed a magical net that had drawn her to this island, it was a very subtle one. Not like that other time, when she had been sold upstream like so many kilograms of fish.

Curiosity overcame caution. With a surge of her body and a spray of droplets, Black Pearl came sliding lithely out of the water to sit, mermaid fashion, upon another rock, a little bigger but very similarly situated, about three meters from the one where the young piper had settled. She thought he was a few years older than herself, and now that she looked at him closely she could see by his jewelry and clothing that he possessed at least some of the outward trappings of the magician. It was a subject in which she had firsthand experience.

But if this youth was indeed a wizard, still somehow she found nothing about him frightening. "Now that you have caught me," she asked saucily, "what do you mean to do? Sell me up the river to live in a tank, for country folk to goggle at in fairs?"

"I? Sell you? No, not I." And the young man seemed not so much scornful of that idea as hardly able to comprehend it. It was as if the ideas of capturing and selling lay so far from the place where his thoughts were occupied that he could not accept them as entirely real. "And you have gray eyes," he murmured, looking at her closely.

And he raised the panpipe to his lips again and tooted on it, displaying moderate skill. He sat there on the rock wearing his ill-fitting wizard's paraphernalia, which somehow looked as if it did not truly belong to him at all. He was very handsome, and though he was almost as young as she, somehow Black Pearl had already caught the flavor or image of something tragic about him.

She said challengingly: "I've been sold up the river, you know, once already."

The dark eyes fixed on her again. "Really? I didn't know that. But I did think from my first look at you that there was something . . ." He put the silent panpipe away, letting it fall into his pocket, and made a polite gesture toward rising, which was hard to accomplish neatly on his slippery rock. He said, as if introducing himself to an equal: "My name is Cosmo Malolo."

Malolo. He was a member, then, of one of the valley's two contending clans, whose domain included her home village among others. But it had been people from the other clan, or so thought Black Pearl, who had sold her up the river before.

"My name is Black Pearl," she said in turn, remembering the manners of her childhood, those ten or twelve years in which she had been wholly human. But she stared at the young man levelly, being as ready to assume equality as he was. Mermaids were beyond, or beneath, the usual rules of social intercourse, as their families of fisherfolk were not.

She saw the young magician's gaze pass, hungrily for a moment, across her breasts, and she made no move to try to cover them with her hair. Mermaids had nothing to hide, very little to lose, and little to fear in the way of rape. Or so Black Pearl thought. She was as far beyond fear as she was beyond courtesy.

He looked away from her at last, and once more seated himself on his rock, this time settling squarely, knees up, elbows outside knees, staring at the linked fingers of his two hands, on which certain rings of power flashed in the sun.

"Let me speak to you plainly, Black Pearl," Cosmo said in a level voice, not looking directly at her. "It was not the spirits of sunlight that I sought to call with my music today, or any elemental of the river. I set out to call up a mermaid, and I have done so. But please believe that my purpose was not to capture you or sell you."

There was a pause, long enough so that at last the mermaid felt compelled to ask: "Why, then?"

"It may be no accident that you, out of all the fishgirls in the Tungri, were the one my little spell attracted. Oh, it's only a very little spell indeed. Quite gentle. You can break it at any moment, if you wish. Plunge off that rock and swim away."

"I know that. I can feel my freedom. But I am still here."

"Good. Black Pearl"—and here his dark eyes turned full upon her once again—"are you happy to be a mermaid? Or would you like to walk the land on two good legs once more?"

"That is a madman's question. What woman could ever be happy like this?" And the flatness of her tailfins smacked at the water, with a violence worthy of some much larger creature.

He looked a question at her.

Her anger quivered in her voice now. "Don't you understand? We lived on land, all of us, until we were ten or twelve years old, not knowing that this was going to happen to us, but knowing that it might. All because of some curse pronounced a hundred years ago, in that damned stupid feud between your family and those others. And then one day, like a bad dream really coming true, the curse struck me. And when that happens it is really the end of life. Because what is there for a mermaid to live for? We can never be women. We can never walk, never be away from the smell of the river and of fish. And in a few more years the curse strikes its final blow, and we die, and float down the river like so many dead fish for the turtles to eat. Have you ever seen an old mermaid? One who lived long enough to have gray hair?"

Halfway through this tirade the young man, Cosmo as he had named himself, had begun shaking his head soberly. When Black Pearl was finished he said quietly: "I believe your answer. Believe me, in turn, that I did not ask the question lightly."

"Why then do you ask it at all?"

"Because I think I may be able to help you."

"Help me how?"

"Help you to cease to be a mermaid." With a swirl of the short wizard's cape that hung from his shoulders he stood up on the rock. "How willing and able are you to keep a secret?"

Before the day was over Black Pearl had learned from the young magician of the existence of a grotto on Magicians' Island. In the island rather; it was a strange cave of a place carved out at some time in the dim past for some purpose of magic or ritual that no one any longer understood or believed in. A daring mermaid could reach this grotto easily by swimming underwater for only a few meters, from an entrance almost unfindable amid the outer limestone rocks of the island's upstream end, and emerging at last into a pool in the bottom of a roofed cave near the island's center. Here on this island, as Cosmo said in welcoming her to the grotto, the influences were favorable for good magic.

But mermaids as a rule kept clear of this small isle entirely, for there were certain frightening things, creatures of magic, who dwelt here. Black Pearl became fully aware of those powers for the first time only when, at the young magician's insistence, she was swimming through the tunnel. When the powers came buzzing invisibly around her ears, considerable determination was required for her to go on. Had she not already begun to believe Cosmo's promises to her, she would have managed to turn around somehow—no matter that the underwater tunnel was barely wide enough for her to pass straight through—and would have hurried back to the open river.

As it was, she clenched her teeth and swam on, meanwhile hearing and feeling the magic powers as they swarmed about her head and body. They were small, no more intelligent than insects, and like certain insects indifferent as to whether they moved in air or water.

But the tunnel was really very short, and the guardian powers did not sting, at least in the case of this invited visitor. Black Pearl was intrigued by what she found at the inner end of the tunnel. The small pool and its enclosing cave had rough walls of stone and appeared to be partly a natural formation. Higher up there were a couple of ways into the cave for people who breathed only air, and walked on land. Through those openings enough daylight was coming in now, on a bright day, to make the place almost cheerful.

Still Cosmo had a small oil lamp burning, at least partly for magical purposes, as Black Pearl supposed.

There was an easy, sloping ledge on each side of the little pool in which the tunnel terminated, and at the magician's invitation Black Pearl sat on one of these flanges of rock. She and the young magician talked for a while, and as the minutes passed she gradually came to feel at ease.

They discussed, among other things, her history. In general it was rare for any mermaid to come back to this valley after having been sold away. Rare, but not unheard of. And in Black Pearl's case, at least, no complaining purchaser had so far come looking for her. That had been known to happen in other cases in the past.

Cosmo expressed his own quiet outrage over the whole situation, his own quiet determination to find a way by which the mermaid curse could be ended for good and all.

Only then, when the mermaid had begun to feel fully at ease with him, did Cosmo's magical tests begin.

Words were chanted, incense was burned. By the power of the young wizard invisible forces were gathered in the air of the grotto and then dispersed again. Black Pearl's tail remained firmly in place, and she gave no sign of growing legs. The problem, said Cosmo, as he had expected from the beginning, was proving to be a difficult one, and a single session of course was not enough to develop a proper counter-spell.

Again and again, on that day of their first meeting, before Black Pearl swam away through the narrow tunnel, Cosmo pleaded and threatened and urged absolute secrecy upon her. He assured her again and again that his magical investigations, her hope of ever being cured, depended entirely upon that.

Black Pearl kept the secret until their next session on the following day. Even her friendship with the mermaid Soft Ripple was not enough to induce her to talk about this, though she had the impression that Soft Ripple sensed that something in her had changed, and was trying to puzzle out what it was.

And on the following day, during Black Pearl's second visit to the secret grotto, in a pause for rest, Cosmo said to her: "You are a strange girl, I think, even for a mermaid. Perhaps it is because of the unhappy experience you had with that magician upstream."

"He was a much stronger magician than you are."

Cosmo did not appear to be upset by the comparison. "I don't doubt it. I know that there are some whose powers exceed mine."

"But he was wicked, and I hated him from the start. And yes, I think that you are right, there has always been something out of the ordinary about me."

"Why do you say that?"

The mermaid shrugged her ivory shoulders. "I don't think my parents were even surprised when I became a mermaid. It happens only to about one of ten girls, you know, in the villages. No one knows in advance which girls the curse will strike, but I don't think anyone was surprised when it struck me."

"I admit that I have been intrigued by you, since I first saw you." Suddenly the eyes of Cosmo blazed, so that it seemed remarkable that his voice could remain steady. "Have you kept the secret of our meetings? Even from the other mermaids who sometimes swim about with you?"

"I have kept our secret," she said softly.

"See that you do. We have already progressed too far, much too dangerously far, for the secret to be revealed to anyone else."

Another day, another meeting.

Cosmo had been stroking with his fingers, making magical passes, across her shoulders and her hair. Then suddenly he let her go. "The aura, the touch, of his powers—I mean that one upstream—still clings about you."

Black Pearl shuddered slightly, through her whole body down to the tip of her scaly tail, as she lay exposed on the flat ledge of rock. "Then cleanse me of it, if you can."

"I will. I will, as much as possible. But still . . ."

"Still what?"

"I find it intriguing."

Her pink lips snarled at him. "You've said that before. His touch was evil!"

"Oh, I agree, his was an evil magic, to be sure. But now it is gone. Only the flavor, the aura, the smell of it remains. Weak enough to be attractive. Like a pungent seasoning in food."

"If you can't wash it away, don't speak of it."

"Oh, I can wash some of it away at least. I am not totally incompetent, and there is much that I can do. But let us thank all the gods that the power of that evil wizard is gone. And I am sure that it was evil. I can sense the impression that it left on you—as if you had been clamped tightly in some great, iron fist."

"Sometimes I think that I can still feel the pressure of that fist around me."

"No, the power of it is gone. But what I would learn of it are the shaping, the ingredients, that made it so powerful. So that my own magic, which is intended to do good, may be strengthened."

The mermaid, lying beside the little pool that was not much bigger than a bathtub, looked up at him doubtfully.

Cosmo asked, almost pleading: "Does it seem to you that I am a bad man?"

Despite the feelings she had begun to have for the magician, it took Black Pearl a long time to answer that. "No," she said at last.

"Then trust me. Will you trust me? It will be very hard for me to help you otherwise."

It was during that same meeting, only their third magical session in the hidden grotto, that Cosmo first slipped over Black Pearl's head the fine chain that held the amulet. She held it up before her eyes and looked at it. The amulet was plain, almost crude, a little knot of glazed clay with symbols on it.

Having put the little chain over her head, he hesitated. Then he said: "We are almost ready to make a serious attempt now; still I fear you are not ready." But even as he spoke his great dark eyes were glowing their message of compassion, of love, into her eyes, into her heart.

Cosmo moved a little closer, and with his right hand he brushed back Black Pearl's long, black hair so that he could see more clearly into her eyes. Again he repeated another warning he had already given her several times.

It was this: that the cure, even if against all odds it could be achieved this early in the course of treatment, could be no more than temporary at first.

"However successful we are at this stage, you will revert to being a mermaid again, in less than a quarter of an hour—quite possibly much less. Such a temporary alleviation of the curse would be a first step only. But it would also be proof that eventually other steps are going to be possible. Strong evidence that in time we will find a way to cure you completely, permanently. You and all the mermaid sisterhood."

The mermaid nodded.

His hand took her hand as she lay floating in the shallow water. And then, as he muttered incantations, his fingers began to stroke her hand, her arm, her shoulder.

And it was during that very treatment, what Cosmo had said would be the first serious attempt, that the miracle occurred for the first time.

Black Pearl's body, already awakened sensually by the magician's caresses even before the change he wrought had come fully upon it—her body found itself suddenly, entirely human. Completely and wholly that of a woman. Utterly female.

And Cosmo, responding to her sobs of joy with certain rather similiar sounds of his own, was right at her side when the change came. Right there to draw Black Pearl from the water, cradling her two lithe, gently kicking legs in his left arm, his right arm under her shoulders. There to swing her round with a swift motion of strong arms to the soft bed only two meters distant, where, as he said, he sometimes slept.

A quarter of an hour later, when the expected return change overtook Black Pearl, her new lover, despite all of his cautions that such a relapse was bound to happen, looked disappointed. But not for long. And she, absorbed in her new happiness, accepted the situation, too.

The sessions of magic, lovemaking, and magic again, went on. There were many such sessions, one every few days, extending over several months. Sometimes the periods of two-legged normalcy were a little prolonged—once almost to half an hour—but still the final, permanent cure eluded the researcher and his patient lover.

Each time Black Pearl swam into the grotto to meet him, Cosmo questioned her sternly as to whether she was continuing to keep their secret.

"We are now so deeply into this that everything—your own fate as well as mine—depends upon your sharing the knowledge of what we do with no one. If you fail, the powers of magic will, I fear, doom you forever to keep your mermaid shape. Indeed—I have no wish to frighten you, my darling, but I must say this—they might warp you into something truly hideous."

So Black Pearl continued to keep the secret faithfully. She would have done anything, that the burning joy of her meetings with her lover might be made permanent.

Autumn was yielding to the onset of this land's brief winter when a night came that changed everyone's life. A riverboat, whose origin Black Pearl was never to discover, came plunging down the Tungri from upstream, hurtling through the series of rapids and cascades known as the Second Cataract. The passage was extremely difficult even in bright daylight, even for an experienced crew. In wind and rain and clouds and fading daylight, the crew of this ship probably never had a chance. The bits and pieces of their upriver craft that later washed ashore were of no familiar make.

The riverboat might well have been in precipitous flight from someone or something. In any case it failed to make the passage, which only experienced boatmen who were favored by a measure of luck could ever hope to complete successfully. The craft was knocked to pieces upon the rocks within the gorge, with the loss of all hands so far as could be told.

Most of the inhabitants of the valley, the many who lived on land and the few who dwelt in water, were not aware of the wreck until hours or days later. Black Pearl, because she had just left a secret rendezvous on Magicians' Island, happened to be first to reach the scene of the disaster.

And so it was she who discovered Farslayer, one of the Twelve Swords of power and legend, lying undamaged and uncorroded on the river bottom, where the smashing of the boat had dropped it, among the deep cold boiling wells of current just below the cataract. Only a mermaid or a dolphin could have reached it swimming.

Whenever a wreck similar to this one occurred, which was not often, the mermaids as a rule came swarming round, trying to help the injured and save the drowning if they could, trying also to see what treasure and trinkets they might be able to salvage from the victims' cargo.

But here were no survivors or victims, living or dead, immediately visible. When Black Pearl first saw the Sword lying in the twilight of the river bottom, her first thought was for almost-forgotten Zoltan, because this impressive weapon so closely resembled one she'd seen him wear. She'd seen him use it too in her defense.

Much additional memory that had been almost lost came rushing back. If Zoltan had indeed been in the wrecked boat, she'd save him if she could.

Swimming and looking amid the watery thunder at the bottom of the falls, Black Pearl searched as only a mermaid could. She did indeed find one dead body, caught on the rocks nearby, but to her relief it was not Zoltan's. One other man, who was still breathing when she found him, died even as Black Pearl was trying to decide how best to carry him to shore, died without saying a word in answer to her questions.

No other survivors or casualties were discoverable at the site of the wreck. The mermaid thought to herself that there was no point in searching anymore, trying to look downriver for Zoltan; bodies and wreckage would be scattered for kilometers downstream already, and scattering farther every moment. Not even a mermaid would be able to find a single man, especially with nightfall coming on.

Black Pearl gave up thoughts of rescue, and dove back to the Sword, which lay just where she had seen it last. There was barely enough daylight still penetrating the depths to let her mermaid's vision find it once again.

When she had brought the marvelous weapon to the surface, she could see that it was not, after all, the same Sword that Zoltan had carried. His, as she remembered, had borne the symbol of a small white dragon on its black hilt, where this one showed instead the concentric rings of a small white target.

The young mermaid knew only a few fragments of the history of the Twelve Swords of Power. But she could see that this Sword, whatever its true nature, must be quite valuable.

Zoltan dropped from her mind. Black Pearl's next thought on having discovered this treasure was to take it straight to the man she loved.

Cosmo would know what to do with her find. And if there were any benefits to be had from it, Cosmo, her true love, would see that those benefits were shared with her.

Fortunately for her plan Cosmo had not yet left the grotto on Magicians' Island; there was some magical tidying-up that had had to be attended to. He was surprised to see Black Pearl back so soon, and more than surprised to see what she was carrying.

Balancing the naked Sword thoughtfully and carefully in both his hands—all magic aside, those edges, as he had already proved, were ready to cut tough leather as easily as water lilies—he agreed with her that it was probably hopeless to seek any further for survivors of the wreck tonight; tomorrow he would see to it that a party of fishermen went out from the villages on the Malolo side, to see if any might have been washed ashore alive.

But his attention had never really left the Sword. "No, Pearl, I have never seen its like before." He held the weapon in his hands up higher, the better to catch the light of his little lamp, and marveled at it. "But yes, I know what it is. Once there were eleven others like it in the world, and still there are probably nine."

"But what *is* it? Magic, surely."

"What is this one specifically? Magic such as you and I are never likely to see again. This one is Farslayer, as I can tell from the symbol on the hilt. Farslayer kills, at any distance and with absolute certainty. Hold it in your hands, and chant the name of your enemy, and swing the weapon round, and let it go—and lo! The Sword is gone to find your enemy, and he is dead. Even that evil one who once held you bound would not be able to stand against one of these. No power on earth could save him, I think—except perhaps one of the other Swords."

Black Pearl's eyes were wide with wonder. "What are you going to do with it, then?"

"Put it away in a place of safety, for now. Then I must think." And the magician opened a small locker or safe, cut right into the stone beside their couch, a safe that Black Pearl had never known was there. And Cosmo put the Sword in there, and with a word of sealing magic closed it up.

He frowned down at her as she lay in the water. "Not a word to anyone else, of course. Now there are two secrets you must keep, and this one is every bit—or almost—as big as the first."

"Of course. Not a word to anyone." And joyously she saw in Cosmo's eyes renewed evidence that she was trusted by him.

Then another thought occurred to the mermaid. "When I was swimming back here just now, I thought I saw another boat, smaller than yours, coming toward the island."

"Oh? And from which shore?"

"The north."

"That probably means Senones. Don't worry. Even if they should dare to touch shore here, I've made this ground my home, and I can make myself invisible to enemies whilst I am on it."

"Are you sure?" The Senones clan and that to which Cosmo belonged were ancient enemies.

"I'm sure. And now, besides, I have the Sword for my defense." He smiled. "The wonderful Sword that you have brought me, and for which I am very grateful. And you must be very tired. Go and rest on the other island. Or back to the wreck and look for other trinkets if you like." He seemed very loving and very confident. He added at last: "I love you, Pearl."

Black Pearl, delighted to the depths of her heart that she had been able to bring her lover such a prize, plunged obediently into the narrow tunnel and swam away.

1

HEAVY wind filled the bleak and rugged gorge of the Tungri, dragging heavy clouds through dark night. The short winter of this land was not yet over, and the freezing rain that had been falling at sundown had turned to snow some hours ago. The hermit Gelimer was snug under blankets and skins in his lonely bed, and when the half-intelligent watchbeast came to wake him he turned over with a faint groan and tried to pull the furs up over his head. Even before the hermit was fully awake, he knew what an awakening at this hour of such a night implied.

But of course Gelimer's conscience would not have allowed him to go back to sleep when he was needed on such a night, even had the anxious beast allowed it. Three breaths after he had tried to pull the covers up, the man was sitting on the edge of his simple cot, groping for the boots that ought to be just under the foot end.

He had both of his eyes open now. "All right, what is it, Geelong?"

The speechless animal, with melting sleet dripping from its fur, moved on four feet toward the single door of the one-room house, and back again. Its movement and the whole shape of its body suggested something between a large dog and a miniature bear. Geelong's front paws, capable of clumsy gripping, came ♪ in the air as the beast sat back on its haunches, and spread their digits as much as possible in the sign that the watchbeast usually employed to mean "man."

"All right, all right. I'm coming. So be it. I'm on my way."

The animal whined as if to urge the man to greater speed.

As soon as his boots were on, Gelimer rose from his cot, a strongly built man of middle size and middle age. Only a fringe of once-luxuriant dark hair remained around a pate of shiny baldness. His bearded face in the fading firelight of his hut was shedding the last traces of sleep, putting on a look of innocent determination. "Ardneh willing,

I'm on my way." Now the hermit was groping his way into his outer garments, and then his heavy coat.

He hooked a stubby battle hatchet to his belt—there were dangerous beasts to be encountered on the mountainside sometimes—and grabbed up the backpack, kept always in readiness, filled with items likely to be useful in the rescuing of stranded travelers.

Then, before Gelimer went out the door, he paused momentarily to build up the fire. Warmth and light were both likely to be needed when he got back.

The small house from which Gelimer presently emerged, with torch in hand, had been carved out of the interior of the stump of an enormous tree, easily five meters in diameter at head height above ground level. From just in front of the house, the tremendous fallen trunk was still partially in view, lying with what had been its crown downslope. So that log had lain since it was felled decades ago by a great storm, and so it would probably lie, the splintered remnants of its upper branches sticking out over the gorge of the Tungri itself, until another windstorm came strong enough to send it crashing the rest of the way down.

What he had last seen as freezing rain, a few hours ago, was now definitely snow, and had already produced a heavy accumulation. Gelimer grimaced under the hood of his anorak, and turned to a small lean-to shed built against the outer surface of the huge stump. From this shelter he pulled out a sled about the size of a bathtub. After lighting ready torches that were affixed one on each side of this vehicle, he harnessed Geelong to it. All this was quickly accomplished despite the wind and snow. A moment later the powerful watchbeast sprang away, and the hermit clinging to the rear of the sled by its handgrips had to run to keep up.

The beast ignored the thin path by which the rare intentional visitor ordinarily reached the dwelling of the hermit. Instead it struck off climbing across the rock-strewn slope above the house. Here and there along the slope grew more big trees, dimly visible now through swirling snow, rooted in pockets of soil on one broad ledge or another. Some of these trees were of the same species as that which formed the hermit's house, though none of these still-living specimens had attained the same size.

The vigorous watchbeast, anxious to do the duty it had been trained for, lumbered on, snow flying from its splayed paws.

In this direction, very nearly directly south of the hermitage, one seldom-used trail came over the mountains. It was on this slope that travelers were most likely to encounter difficulties, particularly when the weather and visibility were poor.

A few hundred meters above the hermit's dwelling, the path from the south split into two routes, one going east and the other descending in a treacherous fashion to the west. The eastern path rejoined the riverside one a few kilometers east of and above the gorge, the two paths uniting at that point to form a better-defined way that could almost be called a road. Meanwhile the western fork came down eventually to a village on the shore of Lake Abzu, where the Tungri calmed itself after the turmoil of the gorge.

The reality of the trails was much more complex than their simple goals would indicate, for in conformity with the rugged mountainside they all wound back and forth, up small slopes and down, around many boulders and the occasional tree or grove. And all of the trails were poorly marked, if marked at all, steep and treacherous at best. At night, and in a snowstorm—

The hermit's feet, accustomed better than anyone else's to these particular rocks, slipped out from under him, and he would have fallen painfully but for his tight grip on the handles of the sled. Muttering a prayer to Ardneh to grant him speed, he pressed on, crossing a small stream upon a newly formed bridge of ice and snow.

Without the aid of his beast, Gelimer could never have found the fallen man, nor, perhaps, would he have had much chance of saving him when found. But with Geelong to show the way the search, at least, was soon successful.

The body lay motionless under a new coat of snow, in moonless, starless darkness. Gelimer turned it over with a mittened hand. The fallen stranger was of slight build, his handsome face smooth-shaven, pale in the night. His forehead was marked by a little dried—if not absolutely frozen—blood. Even in the wind the hermit could hear that the man was still breathing, but he was not conscious at the moment. His fine coat, trimmed in light fur, and his well-made boots indicated that he was no peasant. Whoever he was, having fallen on a night like tonight, he was lucky to be still alive.

Another and larger mound of snow, a little way downslope, stirred when the light of the sled's torches fell upon it. That illumination, faint at the distance, now revealed the head and upraised neck of a fallen riding-beast, and a faint whinny came through the wind. Most likely a slip on ice, thought Gelimer, and a broken leg. Well, it was too bad, but beasts were only beasts, whereas men were men, and freezing to death would doubtless be as kind a death for a beast as having its throat slit in mercy. The hermit was going to have all he could handle trying to save one human life tonight.

The fallen man lay surrounded by sizable rocks, and it was impossible to maneuver the sled any closer to him than three or four meters. When Gelimer lifted the hurt one, he woke up. He was still too weak to stand unaided, or even to talk to any purpose. His mouth seemed to be forming stray syllables, but the wind whipped them away, whether there was any sense in them or not.

The man's eyes were open, and as soon as he realized that he was in a stranger's grip they widened briefly as if in terror. As if, thought the hermit, he had more fear of being caught than expectation of being rescued. But now, of course, was not the time to worry about that.

Weak and confused as the fellow was, still he was able to cling with a terrible strength to a strange pack or bundle, long as a man's leg, that he must have been carrying with him when he fell. It came up out of the snow with him, clamped in the crook of his right arm, and when Gelimer would have put the bundle aside, if only for a moment, to get the man into the sled, the object of his charity snarled weakly and gripped his treasure all the harder.

"All right, all right, we'll bring it along." And Gelimer somehow bundled the package along with its owner into the sled, and pulled up furs around them both. "Any other treasures that are worth your life to save? Evidently not. Geelong, take us home!"

In a moment the sled was moving again, first back to what with normal footing would have been a trail, and then taking a generally downhill direction, switchbacking through the altered and darkened landscape toward the hermit's house. On the return trip Geelong moved less frantically, testing with his forefeet for treacherous drifts, nosing out the limits of the trail.

Once during the ride back to the house, the man who was bundled into the sled began to thrash about. He moved his arms wildly until he again managed to locate his package, which had somehow slipped momentarily from his grip.

"Poor fellow! That bang on the head may have made you crazy. But take it easy now, you're in good hands." It was doubtful at best that the man would be able to hear him in the wind, but Gelimer talked to him anyway. He hated to miss a chance to talk when one presented itself. "We'll see you through. You're going to make it now."

Even with Geelong guiding the sled and pulling it, regaining the house was a tough struggle into the wind. The firelight within offered some guidance to the seeker, shining out in feeble chinks around the edges of the single shuttered and curtained window.

Hardly a routine night's work for Gelimer, but not an unheard-of adventure, either. This was far from being the first time he had taken in a fallen or stranded traveler, and a good many of those he'd tried to save had lived to bless him for his aid.

When they reached the hut, Geelong remained outside at first—the watchbeast was capable of unharnessing himself from the sled. Gelimer hoisted and wrestled his client, and of course the omnipresent package, out of the sled and through the small entry hall, doored and curtained at both ends for winter, that pierced the thickness of his house's circular wooden wall. Once safely inside, Gelimer let his new patient down upon the single bed, and moved quickly to build up the fire again. Indeed, both light and heat were wanted now.

Apart from the head wound, which did not look likely to be fatal, and some bruised and probably cracked ribs, there were no wounds to be discovered upon the patient's body, which was lean but still looked well nourished. The rings on his fingers suggested that he might be a magician, or at least had aspirations along that line. That crack upon the head, and exposure, would seem to be the problems here, and Gelimer thought them well within his range of competence. Despite his white robe he was no physician, but the experience of years had taught him something of the art.

Once the stranger had been undressed, examined, and tucked into a warm bed, the next step was to try him on swallowing a little water, and this was soon managed successfully. When the patient was laid flat again, his blank eyes stared up at the rough-hewn wooden ceiling of the tree-stump hut, and his limbs shivered. Then suddenly he started up convulsively, and would not lie back again until Gelimer had brought him his long package and let him hold it.

In intervals between other necessary chores, Gelimer started the soup kettle heating. Presently the patient was swallowing soup as the hermit spooned it out to him.

After he had taken nourishment, the fellow slid into what looked like a normal sleep, still without having uttered a coherent word.

Gelimer, looking at his patient carefully, decided it was now certain that he was going to live.

By this time the hermit was more than ready to go back to sleep himself, but before doing so he wished to satisfy his curiosity about something.

"Well now, and just what is this treasure of yours, that you are so reluctant to give it up? And will it perhaps provide me with some clue as to just who you are and whence you come?"

The shabby package, a bundle of coarse fabric, appeared to have been hastily made, then tied shut with tough twine. The knots in the twine were somewhere between wet and frozen, and when one of them stubbornly resisted the hermit's fingernails he went for one of his kitchen knives. The wet twine yielded to a keen edge.

When Gelimer had the package lying open on his largest table, he took one look at the leather scabbard and the black hilt he had uncovered, and turned his head to glance at his mysterious visitor once again. It was a different kind of glance this time, and he who delivered it breathed two words: "No wonder."

What had been revealed was a sword, and something about it strongly suggested that it was no ordinary weapon. The hermit, intermittently sensitive to such things, caught the unmistakable aura of strong magic in the air.

When the hermit—who had less experience than Black Pearl had had with this particular magic—had drawn the blade from the plain sheath, he turned his head again for yet another look, this one of wordless wonder, at the man who had been carrying it. The blade was a full meter long, and had been formed with supernal skill from the finest steel that Gelimer had ever seen. The polished surface of the steel was finely mottled in a way that suggested impossible depths within.

Even the plain black hilt was somehow very rich; and the hermit, turning the weapon over in his hands, noticed now that the hilt bore a small white marking, two rings concentric on a dot, making a symbolic target.

Now, for a few moments, Gelimer reveled in the sheer beauty of the thing he had discovered. But within the space of a few more heartbeats he had begun to frown again. He had a vague, only a very vague, idea of what he was holding in his hands.

In the next instant, he was rewrapping the Sword in its old covering, and wishing heartily that he could immediately put it out of his house and away from himself completely. But suppose the stranger should awaken, and find his treasure gone from his side?

He left the wrapped Sword on the table.

"I must sleep while I can," said Gelimer then to Geelong, who had come in by now and was curled on his own blanket on the far side of the room. Presently the hermit too was dozing off, a blanket over him, his body nested among extra pillows, his back against the wooden wall where it was quite warm near the tiled fireplace.

An hour passed, an hour of near silence in the house, while the storm still howled with fading energy outside. Then a piece of wood, eroded by slow fire, broke and tumbled suddenly on the hearth, making a small, abrupt noise. Gelimer, frowning, slept on. The watchbeast, sleeping, moved his ears but not his eyelids. But the eyes of the man in the bed opened suddenly, and he sat up and looked about him with something of the expression of a trapped animal, not knowing where he found himself. He looked with relief—or was it resignation?—at the package on the table beside him, then at the other human occupant of the room, and then at the dozing animal.

Then he swung his feet out of the bed, and paused, raising his hands to his face as a surge of pain swept through his skull.

The animal opened one eye, gazed at the houseguest quizzically.

Another moment and the visitor was standing, moving swiftly and stealthily, hastily pulling on such of his garments as lay within easy reach, including his damp boots that someone had left to dry at a prudent distance from the fire.

The animal had both eyes open now, but still it only looked at the stranger dumbly. To get up and dress was something that humans did all the time.

The hermit, still sleeping in exhaustion, was lying now at full length on the warm wooden floor, with his head fallen back between a pillow and a piece of firewood. The firelight gleamed on Gelimer's bald head, and he snored vigorously.

The visitor unwrapped his package, not noticing, or perhaps not caring, that the ties had earlier been cut. Then he pulled the Sword from its sheath, and shot another glance in the direction of the sleeping hermit.

The hindquarters of the watchbeast moved in a swift surge, straightening its body in a line aimed at the stranger. The animal crouched, a very low growl issuing from its throat.

But the stranger failed even to notice. His dazed mind was elsewhere, and he had no designs on his rescuer's life. Instead, he was already making for the door, the drawn blade still in his hand. With his free hand he lifted the latch silently.

Geelong subsided on his old blanket. Humans went out of doors all the time, in all kinds of weather. It was a permissible activity.

The inner door was pulled shut, very softly, behind the stranger. The small tunnel penetrating the thickness of what had been a great tree's bark was long enough to muffle the entering cold wind, muffle it enough so that Gelimer in his warm place by the fire was not awakened.

Now all was silent again inside the house except for the furtive small noises of the fire itself. A stable warmth reestablished itself in the atmosphere. Faintly, as if at a great distance, the wind howled across the upper end of the carven passage of charred wood that served as chimney.

Only a short time passed before cold air moved in again, faintly, under the inner door; and then that door opened once more. It had been left unlatched. The watchbeast raised his head again, alertly.

The stranger entered, empty-handed. His face had a newly drained and empty look, paler even than before. Mechanically, unthinkingly, he latched the door behind him. Then he moved, very wearily but still quickly, to stand over the wrappings that had once held the Sword but now lay empty and discarded on the bed.

He moved his hands over the emptiness before him, in what might have been either an abortive attempt at magic, or only a gesture of futility. His lips murmured a word, a word that might have been a name. Then he raised his eyes from the bed, and stood, swaying slightly on his feet, staring hopelessly at the curve of wooden wall little more than arm's length in front of him.

Again his lips moved, silently, as if he might be seeking the help of some divinity in prayer.

Except for that he appeared to be simply waiting.

The sound that at last awakened Gelimer impressed the hermit as enormous, and yet he could not really have said that it was loud. It was as if the human ear, sleeping or waking, could catch only the delayed afterrush of that vast howling as it faded. As if mere human sense was inevitably a heartbeat too late in its perception to receive the full screaming intensity of the thing itself.

The hermit woke up, to find himself lying in a strained position by the fire, with the strange remnants of that unearthly sound still hanging in the air. Upon the hearth the weakening fire still snapped and hissed. Across the room his watchbeast was standing up and whining softly, looking toward the bed.

Even before he looked, Gelimer knew that whatever event had awakened him was already over.

Sitting up, he turned his eyes toward the bed. And then he sprang to his feet.

His visitor, once more fully clothed or very nearly so, was now sprawled facedown and diagonally crosswise upon the narrow bed, with the toes of his wet boots still resting on the floor. Above the stranger's inert back protruded half a meter and more of beautiful steel blade, broad and mottled and glinting faintly in the firelight, beneath that black hilt with its god-chosen symbol. The blade was as motionless as the shaft of a monument; the body it had struck down was no longer breathing.

A great disconsolate whine came from the crouching watchbeast, and Gelimer without thinking could interpret the outcry: This was bad, this was very bad indeed, but there had been no way for the animal to prevent this bad thing happening.

There would have been no way for a human being to stop it either, perhaps. Gelimer glanced toward the door, and saw that it was securely latched.

The wet boots, still delicately puddling the wooden floor, would seem to mean that the man had got up, had gone outside for whatever purpose, and had come back in before he met his death.

The hermit approached the bed. There was no doubt at all that his late patient was now certainly dead. Still the hermit turned him partway over, and saw a hand-breadth or more of pointed Swordblade protruding through what must be a neatly split breastbone. Death, of course, must have been instantaneous; there was only a very moderate amount of blood, staining the cloth that had wrapped this deadly weapon and was now lying crumpled beneath the body.

With the door latched on the inside, it seemed an impossible situation.

Not knowing what else to do, and moving in something of a state of shock, Gelimer wrenched the Sword out of the stranger's body—that task wasn't easy, for the blade seemed to be held in a vise of bone—and stood for a few moments with that black hilt in hand, looking about him suspiciously, ready to meet some further attack, an attack that never came.

"Geelong, I don't suppose that you—? But of course not. You don't have any real hands, to grip a hilt, and . . . and of course you wouldn't, anyway."

The watchbeast looked at its master, trying to understand.

And certainly no man would ever be able to stab himself in such a way.

Eventually the hermit wiped the blade on the coarse cloth that had been its wrapping—the steel came clean with magical ease—and put it back into the sheath that he found lying discarded on the floor in the middle of the room. Then he went to arrange the body more neatly and decently on the bed, wadding the Sword-wrapping cloth underneath in an effort to save his own blankets. There was not going to be that much more bleeding now.

Then he decided that the only practical thing to do was to go back to sleep again, after satisfying himself that his door and his window were indeed closed tightly, and latched as securely as he could latch them. Geelong continued his whimpering, until Gelimer spoke sharply to the beast, enjoining silence.

A few moments after that the hermit was asleep by the fireside as before. The silent presence of the occupant of the bed did not disturb his slumbers. All his life Gelimer had known that it was the living against whom one must always be on guard.

In the morning, before the sun was really up, the hermit went out to dig a grave, and to see to one or two other related matters. The snow had stopped an hour ago, and by now the sky was clear. He left the sled in its shed, but he took Geelong with him.

The fallen riding-beast, as Gelimer had expected, was dead by now, already stiffened. The saddle it bore was well made, and the beast itself had been well fed, he thought, before it had started out on its last journey. There were no saddlebags; most likely the journey had been short.

With considerable effort, and with the aid of his dumb companion, Gelimer tugged the dead animal to the edge of the next cliff down, and put it over the drop, and looked after it to see where it had landed. Not all the way into the river, unfortunately; that would certainly have been best. Instead the carcass was now wedged in a crevice between rocks on the lip of the next precipice. Good enough, thought Gelimer, quite good enough. In that place, the hermit thought, the carcass should be well exposed to flying scavengers, and at the same time out of sight and smell of any human travelers who might be taking the usual trails.

Having disposed of the dead beast, the hermit now went to dig a grave for the dead man.

He dug it in the stand of trees nearest his house, where many centuries of organic growth and deposit had built up a deep soil, supported by one of the largest ledges on this side of the mountain. As soon as the sun was well up, in a brilliant sky, last night's snow began melting rapidly, and thus caused very little interference with his digging. Here the air never remained cold enough for long enough to freeze the ground solidly or to any considerable depth. Black dirt piled up swiftly atop melting snow as Gelimer plied his shovel.

When the grave had grown to be something more than a meter deep, Gelimer called it deep enough, and hiked back to his dwelling to evict its patient tenant. He noted hopefully as he walked that there was still enough snow on the ground in most places to allow him to use the sled for transport.

The trip back to the grave, with mournful Geelong pulling the burdened sled, was uneventful. Into the earth after the stranger went the bloodstained cloth that had once wrapped the Sword.

Gelimer said a devout prayer to Ardneh over the new grave just as soon as he had finished filling it in. When he opened his eyes afterward, he could see, at no great distance among the massive trunks, a place where some years ago he had laid another unlucky traveler to rest. And if he turned his head he could see, just over there, another. That grave, representing the saddest failure of all, held a young woman with her newborn babe.

After the passage of a few years these modest mounds had become all but indistinguishable from the surrounding floor of the grove, covered with dead leaves and fallen twigs under the melting snow. In a few years this new grave too would totally disappear. That is, if it was allowed to do so. That was something Gelimer was going to have to think about intensively. He still had no real clue to the identity of the man he had just buried.

Frowning, the hermit put his shovel into the sled and urged Geelong back to the hut. The Sword that awaited him there, he was beginning to think, might well pose a more difficult problem than any mere dead or dying traveler.

Now even in the shade the snow was melting rapidly, and in another hour or so all tracks made in it would be gone. That was all to the good.

Secure inside his dwelling place once more, the hermit drew the Sword out of its sheath, and looked at it even more carefully than he had before. Perhaps he should have put this treasure into the grave too, and tried his best to forget about it; he had come very near to doing just that. He foresaw that no good was likely to come of this acquisition. Yet there was no doubt that the thing was immensely valuable, and he supposed it must be the rightful property of someone. He had no right to lose the wealth of someone else.

Gelimer was still troubled by the face of the Sword's last possessor—handsome, haunted, but now finally at peace.

2

ALMOST a month passed after the stranger's burial before the hermit looked upon another human face, living or dead. Then one day he was standing inside his house, almost lost in meditation, when Geelong suddenly lumbered to the door, sniffing and whining. A moment later a completely unexpected voice called from outside, hailing whoever might be in the house.

Awaiting the hermit in his front yard, regarding him when he came out with a look of fresh and youthful confidence, was a young man of about eighteen. Curly brown hair framed a broad and honest-looking face, above a strong and blocky body, not particularly tall. The youth was clad in the gray boots and tunic of a religious pilgrim, but he still wore a short sword belted to his side—a reasonable and common precaution for any traveler in these parts.

It struck Gelimer as odd, though, that this visitor was carrying nothing at all besides the weapon, no pack or canteen.

"Good morning to you, Sir Hermit. Or do I read your white robes wrongly?" The young man's voice was as cheerful and confident as were his face and bearing.

"No, you read them properly. I have lived here alone for some twenty years, trying to serve Ardneh as best I can. My name is Gelimer." He stroked the watchbeast's ears as it crouched beside him, trying to quell the excitement inevitably produced by any visitor.

"And I am Zoltan. I come from the land of Tasavalta, which as you must know lies far to the north and east of here. My companion and I find ourselves somewhat inconveniently stranded at the moment. There was a little wind and rain last night, which confused the captain of our riverboat completely, and he succeeded in running us aground on some of the many rocks below." And the youth nodded carelessly toward the gorge, from which the faint voice of the Tungri could be heard as always.

"Ah, then no doubt you are embarked upon some pilgrimage downstream? But I am forgetting to be hospitable. You are doubtless hungry and thirsty. Come in, come in, and—"

"Thank you no, Hermit Gelimer. So far we've not lacked for food or drink."

"You mentioned a companion?"

"Yes, a lady. Being somewhat older than I am, she preferred to stay below with the boat rather than climb the cliff. But she too is well provisioned."

Still Gelimer continued to press his offer of hospitality. Presently Zoltan, who seemed at least willing to continue the conversation, accepted.

No traces of last month's visitor now remained inside the dwelling. Zoltan chose one of the two chairs and sat down, crossing his legs and making himself at ease.

"From Tasavalta, you say?" The hermit was heating water on the hearth now, starting to brew tea. Meanwhile Geelong had lain down with head on forepaws on his mat, still perturbed by the fact of another visitor in the house. The last one had not worked out at all to the watchbeast's liking.

Gelimer continued: "That is the country, is it not, where the king has so many magic Swords stocked in his treasury?"

The visitor shook his head. "The rulers of my homeland are a prince and princess, rather than a king. Prince Mark and Princess Kristin. They do possess a few of the Twelve Swords—so it is said. But I think they keep them in the armory."

"Ah yes. Of course." And Gelimer, carefully spooning out tea—a treasured gift from another traveler—took thought as to just how to proceed with his questioning. He wanted to gain knowledge without giving any of his own away.

He already knew what almost everyone else knew about the Twelve Swords, those mighty weapons that had been so mysteriously forged, more than thirty years ago, by some of the now-vanished gods. And the hermit had heard some of the stories to the effect that the Swords themselves had had more than a little to do with the strange disappearance of their powerful creators.

Each of the Twelve Blades was burdened with its own distinctive power, and according to all the testimony of witnesses there was no other force anywhere under the sun capable of standing against the power of any one of them.

"I know that there are twelve of them, or were," Gelimer went on, talking to his newest guest. "But I forget what their names are." He blinked, trying to look as holy and unworldly as he could. Sometimes he could be successful at it.

His young guest, thus encouraged and apparently finding no reason to be suspicious, was soon rattling off the names and attributes of the various magic weapons, as if he indeed might be something of an expert on the subject. From the few blades that were generally admitted to be kept in the Tasavaltan vaults, his cataloguing soon moved on to others. Presently it arrived at the one in which Gelimer had reason to be particularly interested.

"—and then there's Farslayer, which is sometimes also called the Sword of Vengeance. Though of course it can be more than that."

Gelimer blinked. "It sounds truly terrible."

"Oh, it is, believe me. You whirl it around your head, and chant—I forget just what words you're supposed to use, though my uncle did tell me once."

"Your uncle is a magician, perhaps?"

"No." Then young Zoltan for just a moment put on a look of wary intelligence, like one who realizes that he has almost said too much. Gelimer pricked up his ears. Then the youth went smoothly on: "Anyway, I'm not really sure that any of those trimmings, the whirling and chanting and so on, are really necessary. The point is, when you throw Farslayer with deadly intent, it will go on to bury itself in the heart of your chosen target, whether man, god, or demon. Even if that target is halfway around the world and you don't know where, surrounded by defenses."

"Magical or material? I mean, what if your target was enclosed by material walls?"

"Walls of stone or wood or magic, it would make no difference. Farslayer would come through 'em like so much smoke."

"Oh." And perhaps Gelimer's expression of careful vacuity changed now; but if so, the change was quickly smoothed back into blankness.

"Oh yes. There's no defense, of steel armor or of sorcery, that can save the intended victim, once Farslayer is thrown against him—or her. Two of the gods, Mars and Hermes, have died of that very blade."

"Now *that* I find hard to believe." The hermit was trying to provoke more details.

Young Zoltan was quite ready for a little good-humored argument. "I know someone who with his own eyes saw Hermes lying dead, with the wound made by Farslayer still in his back."

"That someone must have led a very adventurous life."

The young man glanced up when he heard the deliberate tone of disbelief, then calmly disregarded it. Suddenly Gelimer found the youth's implied claim of expertise considerably more convincing.

The hermit asked innocently: "And is there no possibility of defense at all?"

"None at all, I should say, apart from the other Swords. If you had Shieldbreaker in your possession, for example, you'd be able to laugh at anyone who threw Farslayer against you. Shieldbreaker's already destroyed two other Swords, Doomgiver and Townsaver, when people were foolish enough to bring them into combat directly against it."

"I see. I suppose your adventurous friend saw them destroyed also?"

"No."

The hermit saw that now he had gone too far. "Please, I did not mean to imply that I doubted your word. I only thought that perhaps some friend of yours had somewhat embellished his stories. There are many good folk who like to do that from time to time."

"But that's not what happened in this case."

"I believe you, and I am sorry. Please, go on. I find the subject of the Swords intensely interesting."

"Well—where was I?"

"You mentioned Shieldbreaker."

"Yes. Then there's Woundhealer, which can cure any wound, even a thrust of magic through the heart, if it's brought into play promptly enough. And then, maybe, Sightblinder—I don't know if Sightblinder would offer any protection against Farslayer or not. It's an interesting thought, though."

And with that the youth, his good humor apparently restored, suddenly threw back his head and began to recite:

> *Farslayer howls across the world*
> *For thy heart, for thy heart, who hast wronged*
> *me!*
> *Vengeance is his who casts the blade*
> *Yet he will in the end no triumph see.*

The youth made a good job of the recitation, putting a fair amount of feeling into it. Gelimer made himself smile in appreciation. He had heard some of the old verses about Swords before, decades ago, and over the past days those rhymes had been slowly coming back into his memory, as he continued to think and fret about the subject.

Young Zoltan cheerfully continued his cataloguing of the remaining

Swords. The hermit made sure to seem to be paying equal attention to the verses and anecdotes about Coinspinner and Soulcutter and the other Swords that followed, that his interest in the subject might not seem too particular. Meanwhile, in his concealed thoughts, he was increasingly aghast. His worst fears about the treasure he had hidden had now been confirmed, and he still had no hint as to who ought now to be considered its rightful owner.

The hermit had not been keeping count of verses, but he was just thinking that the catalogue of Swords must be nearing its end, when it was interrupted. Geelong the watchbeast sprang up suddenly on all four legs and whined loudly, facing the door. Someone else must be approaching the house.

When Gelimer went out into the front yard this time he stopped short, blinking in mild surprise.

A white-haired lady, whose age at a second look was hard to guess, was standing confronting him on the north side of his little yard, as if she had perhaps just climbed up from the river. Her erect body, clad like Zoltan's in pilgrim gray, might have belonged to a vigorous woman of forty, but her lined face looked twenty years older than that. The pilgrim gray she wore confirmed some connection with the youth, who now had followed Gelimer out of the house into the bright day of sunlight melting the last spring snow.

Zoltan quickly performed introductions.

"Lady, this is the hermit Gelimer, who has kindly offered us food and shelter should we be in need of either. Gelimer, this is the Lady Yambu, whom I serve."

"Say rather, with whom you travel." The lady's voice, like her bearing, had something regal in it. She smiled at Gelimer and stepped forward to grip him heartily by the hand.

When Zoltan had earlier informed him that his companion was a lady somewhat older than himself, several possibilities had suggested themselves to Gelimer. This lady did not appear to fit any of them very neatly.

"Yambu," repeated Gelimer aloud, and frowned in thought. "Some years ago there reigned, far to the east of here, a queen who was called the Silver Queen, and that was her name, too."

"That queen is no more," the lady said. "Or she might as well be no more. Only a pilgrim stands before you."

Smiling slightly, she shifted the direction of her gaze to Zoltan. "The captain has informed me that the *Maid of Lakes and Rivers* has now been permanently disabled," she reported. "Therefore, from here we must proceed for a time on foot. There is no need for us to return to the boat, as I have brought along all that was essential of our baggage." So saying, the lady slipped a pack of moderate size from her back and dropped it on the ground in front of Zoltan; it would be his to carry now.

Gelimer took a moment to reflect that the lady must be far from decrepit with age, to have made the steep climb up out of the gorge while carrying the pack. Then he courteously invited both of his visitors back into his humble house.

Half an hour later, the hermit was serving both the travelers some hot tea and simple food, meanwhile pausing frequently in his own mind to wonder what further questions he ought to ask them. They represented his first contact with the outside world since the Sword had come into his possession, and he thought that his next such contact might be months away.

But it would not do to stick too doggedly to the subject of Swords. When Gelimer asked the Lady Yambu politely about the object of her pilgrimage, she smiled at him lightly and told him that she was seeking truth.

"And Truth, then, is to be found somewhere downriver?"

She sipped her tea regally from its earthen cup. "I have had certain intimations that it might be."

"It might not be easy to find another boat to carry you on from here. The fishermen have boats, of course, but as a rule they don't want to go far."

The lady was unperturbed. "Then we shall walk."

Gelimer switched his attention to his other guest. "And you, young man? Do you seek Truth as well?"

"Yes," said Zoltan, and paused. "But not only that. Tell me, good hermit, do you know anything of a race of merpeople living in or near these waters? I have seen several of their kind far upstream, but no one there seems to know where they come from."

Gelimer looked at him, and thought carefully again. "Aye," he said at last. "There are mermaids in these waters. Hardly a race of them. But there have been a few such folk, whose homes are not all that far from where we sit. All maids, fish from the waist down. Their fate is a result of magic directed at certain fishing villages, by enemies."

Zoltan's eyes lit up at the discovery.

"Whose magic, and why?" Yambu asked at once. Suddenly she seemed almost as interested as the young man.

Gelimer heaved a sigh. "It is a long story," he said at last. "But if you are interested—I suppose you should hear the main points of it anyway, if you are going on downstream from here by foot—the journey, you must realize, will not be without its dangers."

"Few journeys are," said Yambu calmly. "At least among those which are worthwhile."

"When you have finished eating and enjoying your tea," said the hermit, "you must come outside, and we will climb up on a rock. From there we will be able to look downstream for many kilometers, and see the land on either side of the river; and there I will tell you something of the situation."

Presently, when their modest meal had been consumed, they were outside again. Gelimer took them to a promontory a little above his house, a place from which they could look to the south and west and see where the Tungri eventually lost itself among distant hills.

Gelimer waved his right hand to the north. "The land on the right bank is, for as far as you can see from here, under the domination of a clan called the Senones. The land on the left bank, whereon we are standing, is ruled by the Malolo clan. The two clans are bitter enemies, and have been so for many generations. The mermaids you have seen upstream were girls from one of a handful of small villages on the Malolo side, down there beyond the place where the river widens—you can barely see it from here.

"Their strange, unnatural form is a result of Senones magic, a bitter and destructive curse that was inflicted upon people in the Malolo territory several generations ago. Sometimes the girls deformed by the curse are sold into slavery as curiosities. I have heard that traveling shows and the like buy them. An evil business."

"Yes. I see," said young Zoltan. He was shading his eyes, and staring very intently and thoughtfully at the village barely visible in the distance. "And has no one ever found a cure for this particular curse?"

"It would seem that the Malolo at least have never been able to find any."

Zoltan was silent, gazing off toward the horizon. It was left to the Lady Yambu to ask their host some practical questions about the trails.

Shortly after he had imparted that information, Gelimer was again left without human companionship. His guests were on their way— long hours of sunny daylight still remained, and both pilgrims, the young man and the older woman, were eager to be gone.

The hermit, looking after them when they had vanished down the trail, still could not quite decide what was the relationship between them. The young man seemed more true companion than servant. And if that woman had really at one time been the Silver Queen . . . having talked to her now, Gelimer found he could believe she had.

Eventually the hermit, frowning, turned back to his hermitage. Hiding the Sword had really done nothing to relieve him of its burden. He still had matters of very great importance to decide.

3

THE sun had nearly disappeared from sight behind the tall trees of the valley's forest before the two pilgrims again came in sight of the small fishing village they had glimpsed from the crag above the hermit's house. Now they were walking close beside the river, and were almost on the point of entering the settlement.

At the point where the trail they had been following emerged from the forest, on the south bank, Zoltan paused and turned to look over his shoulder to the northeast. He thought that he could see that crag again, still clearly visible in the light of the lowering sun. Now, of course, those heights were much too far away for him to be able to make out whether the hermit or anyone else was standing there.

He faced forward again, and with the Lady Yambu at his side approached the village. The pair of them advanced slowly, wanting to give the inhabitants plenty of time to become aware of their arrival. Three or four of the fisherfolk were visible, garbed in heavy trousers and jackets. The place seemed quite ordinary for a settlement beside a river. It consisted of twelve or fifteen bark-roofed houses, some of them raised on stilts along the shoreline, and actually extending over the water. Thin columns of smoke from several fires ascended into the air. Just behind the village the forest rose up dense and tall, beginning to be clothed in the new growth of spring. One or two of the trees loomed impressively, being of the same gigantic species as the one that had formed the hermit's house.

The hermit Gelimer had told the travelers that this was one of the handful of villages, all within a few kilometers of each other along the Tungri, whose inhabitants lived under the mermaid curse. Those few who were now visible to the slowly approaching travelers had nothing out of the ordinary in their appearance—not, Zoltan supposed, that there was any reason to think they would. Three or four fishing boats were tied up at a dock, and only a few patches of ice were visible along the shore. At this lower altitude the ground was completely barren of snow.

"Remember, Zoltan, how the hermit warned us," admonished Yambu, watching her companion closely. "In my opinion he advised us well. You should say nothing at all about mermaids while we are among these village people, at least not until we have gained some understanding of their attitude on the subject. It must be a matter that they are not inclined to treat lightly."

"I understand. I agree," Zoltan answered shortly. He was having a difficult time trying to control his impatience, and he supposed the difficulty showed.

During their long day's hike down the mountain and through the forest he had talked at some length with Yambu about his continuing determination to seek out one particular mermaid.

"You say, my lady, that you are making this pilgrimage to seek the Truth. Well, so am I, in my own way. My goal is to find that girl—I cannot forget her. She has come to represent Truth to me."

Since leaving their native lands months ago, the two pilgrims had had this same conversation, or one very much like it, several times. By now Yambu knew almost as much as Zoltan did about the particular mermaid he was seeking. And she had learned better than to argue directly against the youth's objective. Instead she now asked him: "Exactly how many times did you really see her, in all?"

"Three times, at least. Oh, there were other occasions on the upper river when she was only a shadow, or a ripple in the water, or a movement in the leaves along the shore. But three times, later, I saw her solidly, and talked with her and even touched her."

"Given the other things that happened, we must consider that those earlier appearances were a result of evil magic."

The young man shook his head violently. "Not *her* evil. Not her magic, either."

The woman remained perfectly calm. "No. Or at least not hers primarily. But the attraction you felt and still feel for her had its root in that same evil magic."

"She was enslaved then by that ghastly wizard Wood, or one of his lieutenants!"

"True. But it seems to me that what we still do not know is to what degree, how willingly, the girl, the mermaid, went along with what the Ancient One wanted her to do."

"She did not help him willingly at all, I tell you!"

Yambu only looked sympathetically at her young companion.

Zoltan got himself under control as well as he was able. "I tell you that I saw this girl, talked to her, several times as I moved farther down the Sanzu. She was—she truly wanted to help me. She did her best to help me against the dragon at the end."

"Ah well, you were there and I was not." Yambu conceded the point. "Even so, that was three years ago. Even if you do succeed in finding her now, you ought to remember that much can change in three years, in the life of any person. Particularly in a young woman's life, whether she's half fish or not." To herself Lady Yambu was thinking how hopeless it always was to try to shield the young against their own enthusiasms.

But now, before Zoltan was required to answer, the two travelers had to put their debate behind them. Raising open hands in gestures of peace, Zoltan and Yambu were approaching the fishing village. Children came running to look at them, and then some of the adults.

As they met the inhabitants they took care to observe the little hints, given them by the hermit, as to what was locally considered proper conduct. The people spoke a variation of the common tongue, not difficult to cope with. The greetings the two travelers received from the adult villagers were tinged at first with obvious suspicion. Zoltan was not surprised by this, considering that if all the stories of the clan feud and its consequences were true, these people had every reason to be wary.

Still, Gelimer's coaching paid off. An elder appeared at last, and the two travelers were invited in and offered food and shelter for the night. The local hospitality was somewhat more cheerfully displayed when Yambu demonstrated her readiness to pay a small amount of coin.

As soon as the sun had departed from the sky the air grew chill, and mist rose from the river, which here below the rapids of the gorge widened to such an extent that it might almost have been called a lake. Both shores were heavily forested, and after sundown the cries of exotic animals, strange to Zoltan's ears, began to issue from the darkness within the nearby forest.

Against the sunset sky a fairly large building, of an ominously dark color, could be seen perched atop a denuded hill at a distance of two or three kilometers from the village.

In answer to the visitors' questions, the villagers informed them that this structure was the stronghold of the Malolo clan, and in it dwelt the overlords of this and half a dozen other settlements upon the southern shore.

After the two pilgrims had enjoyed a good supper, largely of fish and bread, Yambu turned in for the night in the House of Women, and

Zoltan went to the Dormitory of Unattached Men, which was one of the houses built out over the water on stilts. Tonight, for whatever reason, it seemed that he was going to have no more than a couple of roommates, two tired-looking village youths who had already stretched out their sleeping mats at the far end of the large room.

So far, although Zoltan had been looking and listening alertly since entering the village for anything that might suggest mermaids, he had seen and heard nothing to suggest that this place was home to them. Indeed, there was no indication that anyone here had ever heard of such creatures. Zoltan had followed Yambu's counsel, though with some difficulty, and had refrained from mentioning the subject. Now as he lay wrapped in his blanket, looking out at the misty, wintry lake and listening to the dark water lap the slender pilings below him, the thought of having to live in that water was enough to chill him to his bones. Of course real fish lived in it and prospered the year round . . . but she, the girl he sought, was not a fish. With his own hands Zoltan had touched her cool smooth shoulders, and her long black hair. Damn it, by all the gods, she was a human being like himself, even if she was burdened with a terrible curse . . . even if he did not yet know her name . . .

Zoltan slept. And then, in the middle of the night, he came awake, softly and suddenly. In the cold moonlight that fell in through a nearby window he beheld the very girl he had so long pursued. She was sitting close beside him and leaning over him, so that an amulet of some kind that she wore around her neck swung free. Her black hair fell in wet strands past her white shoulders and around her pale breasts. Below her slender, human waist, her body continued undivided and tapering, legless and silvery, scaly and graceful and terrible, down to the broad fins of her tail. In this dream—as Zoltan first believed it was—the young girl was just as he remembered her, and the three years that had passed since their last meeting might never have existed.

"Who are you?" he breathed, still more than half convinced that he was dreaming.

Her voice too was unchanged from what he remembered. "My name is Black Pearl. This is my friend, Soft Ripple. And you are Zoltan. Do you remember me?"

Only now did Zoltan realize that there was another mermaid sitting a little behind the first. The one immediately in front of him, who had called herself Black Pearl, had her silvery tail bent up gracefully beneath her, allowing her to sit in an almost completely human posture. Behind and around her, moonlight mottled empty sleeping mats, and the shadowy figure of her companion in the background. Water was dripping slowly, irregularly, from both the mermaids' hair.

"Do I—"

Suddenly the conviction was borne up in Zoltan that this was no dream. He sat up abruptly. "Do I *remember* you? I never knew your name, but I've done nothing for the past months but look for you. I've come down the river all the way from Tasavalta . . ."

He reached out suddenly to take Black Pearl by the hand. She made an effort to pull away at first, but his grip was too swift and, once anchored on her wrist, too strong. "Tell me," he pleaded. "Tell me what I can do to help you."

Down at the far end of the room one of the two bachelor youths snored, loudly and abruptly. Zoltan glanced in that direction, but as far as he could tell both of the young men were really still fast asleep.

In the stillness of the night Black Pearl's shadowy mermaid companion murmured something that Zoltan could not quite make out. Black Pearl understood what had been said, though, and ceased trying to pull free. Instead she took Zoltan's wrist in her own grip.

"We've come to bring a warning to the village. Men from the other side of the river, where the Senones live, are coming across in two boats tonight. They must be intending some hostile action."

"Men from the other side? What should I—"

"As soon as we two are gone, raise the alarm. But you must not say that my friend and I were here and told you. Otherwise the elders might ignore your warning. So please, forget we were here!"

"Very well. This place is dangerous for you, then?"

The mermaid shook her head, as if to say there was no time to explain now. "Meet me—Zoltan, meet me tomorrow night at midnight, at the edge of the lake near the mouth of the creek that flows past the Malolo stronghold. Come out in a boat if you can. If not, then watch for me from shore. Will you do that?"

"I will, I swear I will!"

Black Pearl flashed Zoltan a last look, a look that held a kind of desperation. Then in the next moments she and her silent companion were gone, as softly and swiftly as diving otters, disappearing at once through an aperture in the floor. It was the same entrance commonly used by people who arrived at the dormitory in boats. But there was no boat below the entrance now.

Only a small stain of water upon an empty sleeping mat remained to show that the visitors had not been a dream after all.

Rising silently from his blanket, Zoltan moved quickly to one of the windows on the lake side of the house and looked out. Out on the misty lake at least two large floating objects were dimly visible, holding place against the current. They had to be boats, moving silently in the moonlight, creeping in toward the village docks.

Zoltan drew in breath and shouted, as loudly as he could.

The two youths at the far end of the dormitory sprang up instantly, as if they had been prodded with sharp spears. Zoltan pointed through the window toward the boats, and shouted some more. His two roommates looked where he was pointing, and a moment later added their voices to his at full volume.

Next, drawing his short sword, Zoltan rushed outside, onto a deck built above the water. Already the uproar he had started was spreading to the other houses. Within a matter of a few moments more, it seemed that everyone in the village was awake, and all the men had sprung to arms; the small docks were swarming with defenders.

Three large boats, full of would-be attackers, could now be seen quite close to shore. The craft of this flotilla turned briefly broadside to the bank, from which position their shadowy crews launched a light volley of missiles, stones and arrows. Then the intruders dropped their weapons and plied their paddles vigorously, heading out into the concealing mists again. They were pursued by a scattered response in the form of arrows and slung stones.

In the space of half a dozen breaths the skirmish, if it could even be called that, was over. No one on shore appeared to have been injured, and there was no damage done.

Within a few minutes after the attackers had disappeared, the village leaders, gathering in torchlight among their armed and assembled people, wanted to know who had first raised the alarm. Zoltan raised his hand. He explained that he had just happened to be wakeful, and had seen the enemy approaching.

The people of the village accepted this explanation, and were quick to praise the stranger for his alertness. But Yambu, listening, looked at Zoltan strangely. Her gaze said that later, when the two of them were again alone, she would insist on being told the truth.

4

In the hours following the departure from the hermitage of the pilgrim pair, Gelimer, feeling himself unable to make headway on profound problems, decided to concentrate for the time being on simple ones. He began to take an interest in his garden, to see how the various herbs had passed through the winter, and to make somewhat belated preparations for the busy season of spring. It was a peaceful interlude. There were moments when he could almost have been convinced that the man who had brought the Sword, as well as his two most recent visitors, and all their problems including the Sword itself, were nothing but creations of his imagination.

The hermit's respite from the problem of Farslayer was brief. About noon on the day after the two pilgrims' visit, his fourth visitor of this extraordinary spring showed up.

This latest arrival was a man in his mid-thirties, dark-skinned and lean, and with a fierce, competitive eye. He had come a long way, and he had seen hard traveling, as could be told by the state of his mount and his equipment. Still he was well dressed, his riding-beast was a noble animal, and the way he wore his weapons at his belt suggested that they had most likely seen hard use at some time or other.

With an unconscious groan Gelimer straightened his back from garden chores, and calmly made this latest traveler welcome. Last night what must finally have been the last storm of the season had dusted three or four more centimeters of snow over his garden and everything else in sight, including the new grave in the grove, and the fast-disappearing carcass of the last riding-beast to have carried its master along these trails. Here in the sun the snow had already melted, but in the woods its white veil would still endure.

Since the day after the death of its last owner, the Sword itself had been hidden as well as the hermit knew how to hide anything. Gelimer doubted very much that anyone was going to find it, barring interference by some major wizard.

"Thank you for the invitation to dismount, good hermit . . . ahh!" And the formidable-looking rider, in turn, groaned with relief as he swung himself down from his saddle.

The visitor introduced himself as Chilperic. No second name. And Gelimer still did not allow his suspicions to be aroused, when, almost as soon as he had settled himself upon a chair inside the house, this newest visitor inquired: "I suppose that a fair number of travelers are fortunate enough to enjoy your hospitality, good hermit? You occupy a somewhat strategic situation here."

"This site where I live?" Gelimer looked around him, as if he could see out through his wooden walls. "It is important only in potential. Ah, 'twould be strategic indeed if there were any measurable amount of traffic up and down the river here, but the water's almost always too rough for that. Or if armies were often marching through this pass . . . but for twenty years at least that hasn't happened, either. The warmakers both upstream and down all have enough to do in their own territories without tackling more. So this is only a lonely mountainside, left to me. Often months go by without a soul appearing at my door."

"I see. Interesting. And has this past month been entirely devoid of visitors?"

Now, Gelimer was unable to accept this innocent-sounding question at face value. Indeed, he was almost convinced already that the serious search for the Sword, which he had been more than half expecting for many days, had finally arrived. For some reason it surprised the hermit at first that the searcher, if such he was, did not appear to be a local man at all. But on second thought, that was really no surprise.

Gelimer answered: "On the contrary, sir, the past month has been comparatively busy. There have actually been three other travelers before yourself." Here the hermit paused to sip his mead. Then he went on, trying to give the impression of a man who did not need to be prodded to talk to one random visitor about another, who in fact was even eager to talk on the subject, because he had something mildly unusual to tell.

"The first one who stopped here gave me the impression of a man fleeing something, or someone." And here the hermit, who had been granted time to think what he should do, went on to give a rough description of the man who had died with the Sword run through him, and of the strangely shaped bundle that man had been carrying. It was Gelimer's idea, right or wrong, that an honest owner looking for his lost treasure would come out honestly and say what he was trying to find.

Chilperic sipped at his mead, too. If the shape of the stranger's bundle had suggested anything to him, he did not say so. When he spoke again his tone indicated no more than a polite interest, though indeed the question he asked was pertinent enough: "Ah, and how long ago was this?"

The hermit allowed himself an equally polite effort to recall. "Let me see now. Was it before this past full moon, or after? But lately most of the nights have been cloudy anyway. I really cannot say with any certainty."

The other leaned forward, and spoke with evident sincerity. "I will be glad to make it worth your while to try to remember. The fact is that I have been searching for this man."

"I see. And what will happen when you find him?"

"Oh, I am not a manhunter. Nothing like that." The visitor, smiling, leaned back in his chair again. "I seek him only to satisfy my own curiosity. Nor do I really travel in search of this fellow you describe. It is only that in the course of my travels I keep encountering him—and his strange story. As an interested observer, I would like to know the ending of that tale. No, if you are kindly disposed toward the fellow, you need have no fear that he is going to suffer harm because of anything I do."

"You intrigue me."

"I should not. His story is not mine to tell."

Gelimer shrugged, doing his best to revert to an attitude of indifference. "Ardneh enjoins us to be kind to everyone. But I have no particular reason to wish this fellow well—or to wish him ill, for that matter. If you told me he was a thief, though, and that you were trying to bring him to justice, I would be inclined to believe you."

"Why so?" asked Chilperic.

"Because of the strange and jealous way he treated the peculiar bundle that he carried. As if—perhaps it had been stolen. Because of—well, because of a certain furtiveness in the fellow's manner."

"Ah, yes, you mentioned a peculiar bundle. And you said it was of an unusual size and shape?"

"Yes. Well . . ." And Gelimer gestured vaguely, measuring the air with his two hands. "A package wrapped in rough cloth. A weighty thing. It might have held a small shovel, or an axe." Surely an honest seeker would come out openly now, and say *I am looking for a Sword.*

"And I suppose you never saw the bundle opened?"

"That is correct." Ardneh was not picky about the letter of the truth, Gelimer had always thought; rather it was the underlying goal of speech that counted with the benign god. "He stayed in my house for a single night, ate sparingly, and was on his way again at first light, taking his bundle with him." That of course was the point Gelimer had been anxious to establish if he could. "Although the weather was foul at that time and the trails exceedingly dangerous, nothing I could say would induce him to delay his departure."

"You say the weather was foul, good hermit. On the night when this visitor came to you, was there in fact a notably heavy snowstorm, with enough wind to make it almost a blizzard?"

Gelimer tried his best to give the appearance of a man trying to remember, succeeding a little at a time, recovering something he had thought of small importance when it happened. "Why, I suppose that is a fair description of the weather, now that I think about it."

"And was this strange visitor traveling mounted or on foot?"

"He had a riding-beast. Yes. I didn't really notice much about the animal—but yes, that visitor traveled mounted."

"And in which direction did he go on his departure?" All pretense of a merely casual interest on the questioner's part was gradually being discarded.

"He was heading downslope, as I recall, toward the river. Of course he could easily have changed directions once he was out of my sight. He never said anything about where he was going. He did not even give me his name, which I thought odd."

"But not surprising, in his case—his name, or at least the name I have known him to use, is Cosmo Biondo, and he is a great rogue."

"A rogue, you say."

"I do. You may count yourself fortunate, Sir Hermit, that he didn't cut your throat while you were sleeping."

Gelimer, blinking to give his best impression of being mildly shocked, brought out from under his robes an amulet of Ardneh, which hung always around his neck. He held the talisman in his hand and rubbed it. "Then I truly wish that I were able to tell you more about him. I wish that yo᠎ ᠎vere indeed trying to bring him to justice."

Chilperic shook his head, dismissing that idea, and sat back in his chair once more. But presently he leaned forward again to pose another question: "As I recall, you said you have been visited by two other travelers this month as well?"

"Yes. They were two pilgrims, who came through here only yesterday. The riverboat they were traveling on, they said, had come to grief on the rocks below. The crew, I understand, were trying to tow the craft upstream again with a rope. But I really doubt that the two I met could have had anything to do with this Biondo fellow."

"Perhaps not. Headed upstream or down?"

"They said that they were going down."

"What were they like?"

Gelimer, seeing no reason not to do so, described yesterday morning's pair of visitors in some detail. But he thoughtfully omitted to mention the conversation he had had with them on the subject of Swords.

When today's visitor had finished his refreshment, and stretched, and looked about the house, he expressed a wish to be on his way while the light and the weather remained good.

Doing his best to pretend a certain reluctance to lose a temporary companion, the hermit at last bade his guest goodbye. "And good luck in your search—I would like sometime to hear the rest of this Biondo's story."

Chilperic, already mounted, looked down at Gelimer and shook his head. "It might not be safe for you to know that story, good hermit—as for me, I already know the dangerous parts of the tale, and so am free to indulge my further curiosity."

And in a moment, with a final wave, this latest visitor too was gone, having said not a word during his visit on the subject of his own goals and business. He rode downslope, in the direction of the suspension bridge that would take him across the Tungri. Would he be reporting to the Senones, then? Or perhaps seeking to question them? But it would be as easy for this traveler as for the other one to change directions once he was out of sight, and Gelimer was not minded to follow him to be sure which way he went.

5

ON the morning after their arrival at the fishing village, Zoltan and
Yambu were treated to a fine breakfast, an expression of the villagers' gratitude for Zoltan's part in last night's modest victory. Having
done justice to this homely feast of fish, beans, and the eggs of water-
fowl, the travelers thanked their hosts, bade them farewell, and pressed
forward on foot toward the hilltop stronghold or manor where dwelt
the Malolo overlords.

Patches of forest engulfed the path, between areas of cultivated land.
As they walked, Zoltan told his companion the story of his encounter
with Black Pearl during the night. She listened in silence and made no
comment. He also warned Lady Yambu that when they reached the
manor he was determined to raise the mermaid question with the au-
thorities there, in one way or another, with whatever degree of diplomacy he could manage. Now that he knew the name of Black Pearl, and
was certain that she was still alive, and here, somewhere close—well,
whatever happened, he was not going to let her get away from him
again.

"Well, of course you must make every effort to find out more, since
now you have actually seen her." Yambu sighed. She believed what the
lad had told her about last night—and she had really believed him
about the mermaid all along—but still there were things about the
business she did not like.

Zoltan persisted. "Not only to find out more. If this mermaid curse
was put upon her by some magician, then there must exist some magic
that can take it off. I mean to restore her to true womanhood."

Yambu sighed again, this time silently, at the young man's obvious
determination. "When the time comes, then, to speak to the Malolo
leaders on the subject, will you let me try my hand at the diplomacy? I
do have somewhat more experience in the field than you."

"Would you, my lady?" Zoltan cried with sincere relief. "I would be immensely grateful."

Having reached that agreement, the two trudged on in silence for a time, proceeding through the woods along a well-trodden path at the moment empty of all other traffic. Presently Zoltan spoke again. "I wonder what the leaders of this Malolo clan are like."

"It is impossible to tell until we meet them. Something like other minor lordlings elsewhere, I suppose," Yambu added with faint distaste. The lady took a dozen strides in thoughtful silence before she added: "The village leader back there gave me the impression that he thought something strange had been going on in the clan's stronghold for some time, at least a month."

"Something strange?"

"He really said nothing specific on the subject. But that was the impression I received."

Zoltan pondered this news in concerned silence.

"I wonder where everyone is?" the lady remarked suddenly in a different voice.

Indeed, the crude road which the two travelers were following had remained completely empty of other traffic, and this fact now began to take on an ominous aspect in Zoltan's eyes. At each turn, as the rutted track wound back and forth through fields and forest, he kept expecting to encounter a farmer's cart, a peddler, a goatherd, someone. But there was never anyone else in sight.

"Have all the farmers fled their lands? It should be time for planting."

Yambu shook her head. "Not a good sign."

In due time, and without ever meeting anyone, the two travelers came upon the house, which stood less than an hour's walk from the lakeside village where they had spent the night. The hill, upon which the Malolo clan had chosen to build their manor, had long ago been denuded of trees, leaving only a myriad of ancient stumps. Within a low wall, the stone and timber of the house were dark, and the grounds around the house long uncared-for and eroded. Even in the clear light of day, the whole establishment had a forbidding aspect to Zoltan.

Still no other people were in sight. And everything was silent except for the lowing of cattle, which seemed to be coming from outbuildings in the rear. The animals sounded as if they were in need of being milked.

The front entrance of the manor was protected by a small drawbridge, let down over a long-dry moat. The outer end of the drawbridge, now resting on the earth, had crushed a new spring growth of weeds beneath it. From this fact Zoltan deduced that the bridge must commonly be kept raised at least as much as it was lowered. Evidently the long-standing feud sometimes included direct assaults upon the strongholds of the chief participants.

However that might be, no one had bothered to raise the bridge today. Trudging on across its weathered timbers, the two travelers found themselves immediately before the manor's great front door. Still they had not been challenged, or even observed as far as they could tell. They had seen no one since leaving the vicinity of the village. This absence of human activity caused them to once more exchange puzzled glances.

Then Zoltan shrugged, raised his sword hilt, and rapped firmly, loudly, three times on the door.

For a time, a period of time that became noticeably extended, there was no answer.

He was just about to knock again, and louder still, when at last a small peephole, heavily protected by iron grillwork, opened near the middle of the door. "Who is it?" a crabbed and cracking tenor demanded from within.

"Two pilgrims," the lady on the doorstep answered, putting authority and volume into her voice. "The Lady Yambu and her attendant. We bring certain information that the chief of the Malolo clan should be glad to hear."

There followed a protracted and suspicious silence. Zoltan supposed that the speaker inside—he could not be sure from the voice whether it was a man or a woman—was probably using the peephole to inspect the two on the doorstep.

"You can give me the information," the voice said next, adopting now a different but still peculiar tone, somewhere between wheedling and mindless threat.

Yambu glared at the wooden barrier. "I do not conduct conversations through a door." This time no one would have doubted that a queen was speaking.

Response from inside was immediate, in the form of a tentative rattling, as of a heavy doorbar in its sockets. Then came a brief silence as of hesitation, or perhaps a consultation carried on too quietly to be audible outside. Then the bar rattled again, this time banging decisively as it was thrown aside. Bolts clattered, and a moment later the left half of the double door was creaking open.

Standing before the travelers was one man, unarmed and not very large, his gray beard and hair in wild disarray, his watery blue eyes blinking in the morning sun. The man's clothes—leather trousers, leather vest over a once-white shirt—were so stained and generally shabby that Zoltan was ready at first to take the fellow for a servant. Behind the entranceway in which he stood stretched the dim length of a great hall, where the littered condition of floor and tables, along with a few overturned chairs, suggested at first glance that a notable revel of some kind might have been held here last night.

The fellow who had opened the door looked at the Lady Yambu again, face-to-face this time, and bowed to her at once. "Welcome," he said, in a somewhat more courteous tone than before. He stood aside. "Come in, my lady, come in." But having said that much he stopped, seeming not to know how to proceed.

"Thank you, Sir Wizard," said the lady dryly, entering the house. And Zoltan, turning his head suddenly to look at the man once more, could see that the rings on his stained fingers were marked with insignia of power, and were of a richness that certainly no menial servant wore; and that a chain of thin gold encircled the man's wrinkled neck and went down inside his dirty shirt.

Yambu grabbed her companion by the sleeve and pulled him forward. "This is Zoltan of Tasavalta, who travels with me. Now may we know your name? Your public name at least?" It was a common practice for wizards of any rank to keep their true names unknown to any besides themselves.

Their reluctant host nodded abstractedly in Zoltan's direction, acknowledging the introduction. Then he turned back to his more important guest. "Call me Gesner, Lady Yambu. May I ask, what is this information that you have?"

The lady told him briefly of the incidents in the village last night. Meanwhile, not waiting for any further invitation, she moved on into the great hall, the graybeard moving at her side. Zoltan followed. Seen at closer range, the disorder was more evident than ever. And it was older—as if some feasting might have been suddenly interrupted many days ago, and only a minimum of serious housekeeping performed since. Leftover food in dishes had long since dried, and there was a smell in the air of stale drink and garbage. The ashes in the enormous hearth looked utterly cold and dead.

"And is that all, my lady?" The decrepit-looking magician sounded disappointed. "I mean—skirmishes like that are common. Why should you think my master would consider it vital news?"

Ignoring Gesner's question, Yambu looked about her and asked him in turn: "Where is your master? You are certainly not the lord of the manor here?"

A different voice replied, speaking from behind her: "No, he's not. I —I am here."

Turning to a broad stairway that came down at one end of the hall, Zoltan to his surprise saw a somewhat overweight adolescent boy, two or three years younger than himself, dressed in rich clothing but looking nervous and incompetent and frightened.

At this point two girls, also well dressed, and both somewhat younger than the boy, appeared on the stairs above him. These girls, moving like people who were reluctant to advance but still more frightened of being left behind, edged slowly downward on the stairs, keeping close behind the youth who had spoken.

And the fat boy continued his own uncertain descent of the stairs. He paused, shortly before reaching the bottom, to repeat his claim, as if he thought it quite natural that his audience should doubt him. "I am Bonar, the chief of Clan Malolo." At his side he wore a small sword, hung from a belt that did not quite appear to fit.

Yambu, the experienced diplomat, surveyed the situation, and appeared to be ready to take the young man at his word, at least for now. Addressing him politely, she related again, with more detail, what had happened in the village last night, with emphasis on how the alarm raised by Zoltan had prevented harm. This time she included the visit of the mermaids and their warning.

The lady's manner, more than the content of what she said, had a soothing and reassuring effect upon the frightened inmates of the manor. Zoltan got the impression that they were beginning to be willing, perhaps irrationally, to trust her now; that these representatives of the Malolo clan were looking for someone they could trust.

Before Lady Yambu had finished relating her story, the young people had all completed their descent of the stairs and were surrounding her and Zoltan in the great hall. The two girls, who were Bonar's sisters as Zoltan had suspected from the first, were named Rose and Violet. Now, while Gesner stood back frowning silently, the three family members bombarded the two visitors with questions.

What had Yambu and Zoltan seen on the other side of the river? What evidence was there of military activity in that direction? On these points the travelers could be reassuring, at least in a negative sense. They had not traveled on the far bank, and had not seen a living soul over there for several days. Nor had either of them observed anything at all military in that direction, unless last night's disturbance at the fishing village was to be counted. Zoltan and Yambu now related that story again, and hearing it seemed to reassure their hosts slightly.

There was a brief silence.

"What is wrong here?" Yambu asked the young people finally. "It is plain that this house has been engulfed by some crisis. Where are all the older members of this family?"

The inhabitants of the manor looked at one another. Then Bonar, nervously clenching his white hands together, suddenly blurted out what might have been the beginning of an answer: "We haven't been out of this house for days. For a good many days. Not since that man came here asking questions."

"What man was that?" Yambu inquired patiently.

"A traveler. Someone of good birth, I'm sure. He called himself Chilperic, and at first we had hopes that he was going to help us. I think he was—I don't know, a soldier of some kind. He claimed to be some kind of distant relative of ours." The speaker looked around at his companions as if for confirmation. They nodded vaguely.

"And what questions did he ask?"

Bonar and his sisters looked at each other in a silent struggle.

"But where are your own soldiers?" Zoltan demanded abruptly. Since these people were so worried about something, and since they were supposed to be engaged in a permanent feud with some other clan, it puzzled him all the more that he had not seen a sentry or armed attendant of any kind since his arrival. "Surely you have armed retainers of some kind about?"

Gesner spoke up quickly. "Of course we do. They are all on watch, at the moment."

"Most of them are out on patrol just now," said Rose, the older sister, speaking simultaneously with the wizard. Rose had fine dark hair, a face that was pleasant if somewhat long, and a figure that Zoltan under less tense conditions might have found distracting. She had come up behind her brother Bonar, and with a gesture that might have been meant as a warning laid her hand upon his arm.

Zoltan and Yambu exchanged glances.

Evidently the former queen and skilled diplomatist thought it was best to let the subject of soldiers drop for the time being. She looked at Bonar and said: "Young man, the people in the fishing village mentioned a different name than yours when they spoke to us of the chief of the Malolo."

Bonar turned paler than ever. Only the shabby magician responded verbally to the implied question. "Yes," said Gesner wearily. "Yes, no doubt they did."

An awkward silence ensued, as if the inhabitants of the house were on the verge of offering some explanation, but none of them quite dared to try.

Zoltan decided at last that diplomacy had had its chance, and he might as well attempt a blunt interrogation. "Chief Bonar—is that what we should call you?"

"It will do."

"Then, Chief, you obviously have some serious problem here. Is there some way that we can be of help?"

"We do need help," Bonar admitted at last, after having looked again at both his sisters and found none. His pale and pudgy hands were held together in front of him, and he gazed down at them as if wondering how he might be able to get the intertwined fingers apart again. "We've had . . . Well, a terrible thing has happened."

"I am not surprised to hear it. Now I invite you to tell us what it was," said Yambu, in a soft and yet commanding voice.

After much continued hesitation, the four members of the household, including Gesner, decided to hold a meeting among themselves. Having first remembered to make sure that the front door was securely closed again and locked, they withdrew to another room, with some apologies, leaving Yambu and Zoltan alone. Soon, from the other room, their muffled voices could be heard, rising now and then in argument, as they debated some matter earnestly. Zoltan and Yambu paced about, looking at each other and shrugging their shoulders.

At length the four, with the air of having come to an agreement, rejoined their visitors in the great hall. Then Bonar, the new chief of the clan, with Gesner at his back, silently motioned Yambu and Zoltan to follow him into an adjoining corridor. There the chief drew a key from inside his shirt and unlocked a door leading to a descending stair.

Zoltan went down cautiously, a hand on his sword hilt. A few moments later Bonar was escorting him and Yambu into a large vaulted room on a windowless below-ground level of the huge house. The door of this room too was doubly locked before they entered it, and it was guarded on the outside by a couple of elderly people who glared suspiciously at the intruders, and whom Zoltan had no trouble identifying as faithful old family retainers. There were a few of the same type back home at High Manor, where he had been born.

As the group of visitors filed into the vault one of the attendant servants held up a torch, revealing that they were in a windowless chamber almost as large as the great hall above.

There was a faint perception of magic in the air, and for a moment Zoltan thought that the dozen or so fully clothed people who were lying stretched out on the tables that almost filled the room were all sleeping some enchanted slumber—but only for a moment. Then he realized that all of them were dead.

Arrayed before the visitors, with some effort at neat arrangement, were eleven corpses—Zoltan quickly took an exact count. If this was a collection of combat casualties, it fit the usual pattern in that young males were in the majority. All the dead were fully clothed adults, all of them laid out on tables, or, in some cases, biers improvised from smaller furniture, chests, and chairs.

A faintly sweetish aroma hung in the air, along with the impression of simple magic in operation. Zoltan, who was no magician but who had seen more magic in his young life than many people ever saw, suspected strongly that some preservative spell was in action here, and also that the spell was neither very well designed nor very well cast. These bodies were going to have to be buried soon, or otherwise permanently disposed of.

Judging by the expression on Lady Yambu's face, and the sidelong look she cast at Gesner, she evidently shared Zoltan's thoughts. He supposed the wobbly preservative spell was the work of Gesner, who did not exactly give forth an aura of competence.

Violet, Bonar's younger sister, had begun sobbing quietly as soon as she entered the room of death. With dull brown hair and a thin body, Violet was plainer than Rose, and also had a fiercer look.

"What happened?" Lady Yambu asked, turning from the bodies to stare curiously at the young chief of the clan.

"We fought." Bonar gestured helplessly at the carnage before him. "It was about a month ago."

"Fought whom? Only among yourselves?"

"Of course not." The youth's cheeks reddened and suddenly he looked sullenly angry. "Against the damned Senones. The clan of scoundrels across the river. Our ancient enemies."

The lady looked at the crowded tables. "Would it be fair to say that your enemies won that fight?"

"I think not." Now the lad's pride was stung. "We killed as many of them as they of us."

"And where did this fight take place?" asked Zoltan, walking now between the rows of tables, looking at first one and then another of the bodies. As he inspected the dead more methodically he realized that each of them had been slain by a single thrust, through the torso, from some broad-bladed weapon. No other wounds of any kind were in evidence on any of the bodies.

Violet spoke up suddenly. "It happened here, in our house. And also in the stronghold of those scum across the river."

Yambu turned to her. "Here *and* there? I don't quite—?"

"Have you ever heard of the magical weapon called Farslayer, or the

Sword of Vengeance?" Bonar's question came out in a bitter monotone, between clenched teeth.

Zoltan had to make an effort to keep himself from flashing Yambu a sudden, almost triumphant look of understanding. But he kept his eyes on Bonar. "Yes," he said. "I have heard of it."

"Good. Then you will understand. Our two clans, neither leaving its own stronghold, fought the whole battle with that single weapon." Bonar's gesture was an aborted movement of one hand, directed toward the tables and their burdens. "My own father lies here, and two of my uncles. And—" For a moment it seemed that the new chief of the Malolo clan might be about to break down and weep.

Rose, who was now bearing up better than before, took over the job of adding details. She related in a muddled way how, a month ago, the people of this clan and those across the river, each at the time locked into their own fortress, had engaged at long range in an hour or more of terrible slaughter.

Zoltan nodded. "There's no doubt about it being Farslayer, then. Of course. And you just kept casting it back and forth . . ."

"Yes," said Bonar. "Yes. I'll see them all dead yet."

"And where is the Sword now?" the Lady Yambu asked.

"We don't know," said Violet. "We haven't seen it since that night. For a while we thought that our cousin Cosmo had taken it to the enemy. But—many days have passed now, almost a month, and no more of us have been struck down."

There was a silence in the room. Everyone was looking thoughtfully at the bodies.

"Well, if your enemies have the Sword, they are hesitating to use it," Yambu agreed at last. "But where did it come from on that night of slaughter? Did the enemy have it first, or you?"

None of the household's survivors could offer a certain explanation of how the fight had started. But when the Sword struck its first victim in this house, a number of people had been on hand who could recognize the magical weapon for what it was, and explain its dreadfully simple use to the others. Almost immediately everyone had known how to use it to strike back at the enemy.

"You hold it—so," Rose was explaining, her two delicate wrists crossed in front of her, small white fingers clenched on an imaginary hilt. "Then you spin around—in a kind of dance—" And her feet stepped daintily in dainty shoes, performing a demonstration. "Maybe the dance isn't even necessary, but most did it that way. Some of the people chanted before they threw the Sword: *For thy heart, for thy heart . . .'* and they would name a name—someone on the Senones side, you see.

"My father and brothers knew all their names over there, they knew just who they wanted to kill the most. And then, when you have chanted and spun the Sword, you just—let go."

The dainty dance came to an unsteady halt. The small white fingers opened, at the end of the extended wrists. "And then—the Sword would leap from the thrower's hands, and vanish. Each time I saw it go, it made a splash of color in the air, as pretty as a rainbow. And an ugly little howling sound, like a hurt cat.

"And then, sometimes sooner, sometimes later, it would always come back—the same way. Over there, they knew all of our names, too."

Rose sat down suddenly, rocking gently on a bench, and covered her eyes with her small white hands.

Violet and Bonar each had a few random details of that night's battle to add. So the bloody exchange of death at long range had gone on, and long before morning most of the family on each side were dead.

Zoltan took another walk among the tables, looking and thinking. This corpse must be the survivors' father, and these two—there was a family resemblance—their dead brothers. The great majority of the dead in this vaulted room were men. But not all. Evidently there had been more than one woman living in this manor who had made herself deeply hated across the water.

One, at least, of the trestled bodies was wearing a heavy steel breastplate. Probably this was the previous clan chief—had he been the first to fall that night, had he put this armor on as a decoration? If the object had been protection, the armor had done him no good, for just over his heart a broad-bladed weapon had punched through as if the steel were so much paper.

Zoltan, still walking thoughtfully among the tables, gently touched a dead arm chosen randomly. It was as stiff as wood. Gesner, now moving quietly at his side, informed him that these bodies had been here on these tables since the morning after the slaughter. Ever since then, the surviving family members, all half-demented, had been trying to think of a way to conduct a secret burial or at least a mass cremation, without giving away the extent of the clan's loss.

"We'd need help to bury or burn them all, you see. And then outsiders would be certain to find out how many were dead."

"The Lady Yambu and I are outsiders."

"We must begin to do something. Better to trust complete outsiders like yourselves than—"

A servant chose that moment to enter the vault, bringing a private message for Bonar.

Bonar, after the man had whispered in his ear, turned to his sisters. "The mercenaries are at the back door. Two of them, anyway, Koszalin and his sergeant."

6

YAMBU asked: "Mercenaries?"

Violet spoke up. "Fourteen or fifteen men and their commander, whom we've had in our pay since before the slaughter. They're camped in the woods nearby, and I'm sure they know by now that we've been seriously weakened. We've been refusing to talk to them. If those blackguards ever find out exactly how much the clan has been reduced, they'll turn on us and rob us. Then the damned Senones will attack."

"It seems to me," said Zoltan, "that if you and the Senones exchanged blow for blow with Farslayer, as you say, then your enemies can hardly be in any better shape than you are. They'll have trouble carrying out an attack."

Violet glowered. "They were a larger family than us to begin with."

Yambu indicated the bodies. "Did I understand you to say that none of these is the man Cosmo, who you say began the fight?"

The surviving family were uniformly scornful. Bonar said: "No, that coward is not here. When it should have been his turn to use the Sword, he seized it, pulled it out of a dead kinsman's body, and ran out of the house. He mounted a riding-beast and was gone before we realized what was happening."

Talk of Cosmo ended when another one of the old retainers came into the vaulted room to report fearfully that the two mercenaries at the rear door of the house were growing impatient, demanding to be admitted to present their demands.

Rose was fearful. "Demands? That's new. What demands will they have now?"

"I suppose you ought to ask them," said Yambu. Then she volunteered: "If you like, I will speak to them. I have handled a few rebellious soldiers in my time."

The offer was accepted by default; at least none of the family spoke up to reject it out of hand, and none appeared really ready to assume leadership of their own cause. So, with Zoltan at her side, and guided by a servant, the former queen proceeded through the kitchen to deal with the mercenaries. Lady Yambu took her time about getting to the door, while Bonar brought her up to date on the clan's relationship with their hired soldiers.

"You said there were fourteen or fifteen of them. Are you sure that number's accurate?" Yambu asked him.

The siblings conferred briefly among themselves. "Can't be more than a dozen," Bonar reported.

"Too many for us to overawe, I suppose. Then let us buy them off with gold, for the time being at least," Yambu suggested. "I suppose you do have some modest stock of gold available?"

"Gold?" Violet looked almost shocked. "Hardly."

"But there are pearls." This came from Rose in a fearful whisper.

"Do you mean freshwater pearls?" asked Zoltan. "Not worth much, are they?"

"These are." Violet expressed a certain indignation. "Of high quality indeed."

The other family members, after some hesitation, admitted that a few good-quality pearls were available. Urged on by a savage pounding on the door, they at last produced a small handful of pale rounded gems, which Yambu pronounced more than sufficient to buy off a dozen rascals. Shaking her head, she thrust most of the gems back into Bonar's unsteady hands. "To offer them too much at this stage would be worse than to give them too little. Now, Zoltan, attend me. Stand here, and let them see that you are armed and ready!"

When Gesner unbarred and opened the door at last, the two men outside started to push their way into the house. But then they halted on the threshold. The appearance in the kitchen of an unexpected stranger, armed and resolute, and of an unknown lady of queenly bearing, was enough to delay them momentarily. And that moment was long enough for the Lady Yambu's commanding presence to take over. In a firm voice she demanded to know just who these intruders thought they were and what they thought they wanted.

"Captain Koszalin, ma'am. I'm in charge of the defenses here. This is Shotoku, first sergeant in my company."

"Are you indeed? Those defenses seem singularly ineffective, not to say inoperative. My party was not challenged approaching the house, and I daresay that if we had been a full company bent on an attack, the result would have been the same. Were I your commanding officer, you'd be in trouble."

Zoltan grinned inwardly, in admiration of the way Yambu had managed to suggest the presence of an armed escort besides himself.

Koszalin was not a large man, but gave the impression of fierce energy, now under tight control. He and the massive Sergeant Shotoku, who stood stoically behind him, both wore scraps of armor and dirty green scarves, evidently as a kind of company insignia.

Under pointed questioning by Lady Yambu, Koszalin claimed to have twenty men at his command. He had come pounding on the door, he said, to collect the gold that was due him in back pay. But after a brief hesitation he accepted four small pearls, and then withdrew with his sergeant.

"He'll need a conference with his men now, I suppose," said Yambu when the door was closed. "Very unreliable troops, in my judgment. Doubtless the two of them will now hold a conference with their men on how best to enjoy their sudden wealth. From our point of view it will be best if they go to the nearest large town to spend it—how far is that?"

"A good day's journey," said Rose, thoughtfully.

Within a few minutes after the two mercenaries had left the house, a servant looking from an upstairs window reported that eight or ten of the ruffians, all heavily armed and moving on foot, could be seen at the bottom of the hill. They appeared to be going upon their way.

For a minute or two the members of the family were loud in their rejoicing. But the celebration was brief. First Bonar and then Violet began to voice their misgivings that the mercenaries would be likely to come back, as soon as they had spent the pearls.

Yambu nodded. "But in the meantime we can expect to enjoy a respite of about three days—that should give us the time we need to decide upon our next move."

When the servant on lookout reported that the irregular soldiers were now completely out of sight, the brother and two sisters more volubly expressed their gratitude to Yambu and Zoltan.

Meanwhile the party was drifting back into the great hall. There, some of the few active servants remaining in the household were called upon to begin a belated cleanup, and provide something in the way of hospitality for the honored guests.

But the survivors of the Clan Malolo and their visitors had not been seated long at the table before Bonar, unable to relax for any length of time, began to have doubts as to whether they might need the mercenaries after all, and before the three days were up. The damned Senones, he felt sure, were almost certain to mount a fresh attack by then.

Yambu spoke sharply to the young chief. Would he prefer that she and her companion moved on at once?

No, all three family members protested hastily. On that point all three siblings and Gesner were in agreement.

Thinking it would be hard to find a more propitious moment, Zoltan decided the time had come to let his hosts know the real reason he had come calling on them.

He cleared his throat and addressed the chief. "I wish to speak to you on a matter of some importance. To you in particular, Chief Bonar." Zoltan avoided the eyes of Lady Yambu, though he could see that her face was turned toward him.

"Of course, friend Zoltan," said Bonar in mild surprise. "What is the matter of importance?"

"It's about a mermaid."

Bonar blinked. There was a silence in the room. Lady Yambu, when Zoltan glanced her way at last, looked as if she were ready to tell him *I told you so.*

The clan chief cleared his throat. "Well, of course, if you wish to have a mermaid, friend Zoltan, we will do what we can to get one for you." Bonar sounded dubious. "Usually only entertainers and magicians find those creatures of much interest."

"I don't think you understand yet, Chief Bonar. I do want to talk about a mermaid, and the subject will not keep indefinitely. It is a particular mermaid that I wish to talk about. Black Pearl is her name."

The faces of the family members and Gesner grew even blanker than before, with incomprehension and vague anxiety. It was obvious that the name of Black Pearl meant nothing to anyone in the household. But before Zoltan could press his hosts on the topic, a renewed argument had broken out among them on the subject of the mercenaries.

He could see that it was going to be difficult to get them to think seriously on the subject of mermaids.

Turning back to face the sharp look Yambu continued to level at him, Zoltan sighed, and nodded his acquiescence. Any discussion of Black Pearl was going to have to wait.

Dinner began to arrive, piecemeal. And while the group was still at the table, Rose mentioned the subject of mermaids in passing once again. She thought vaguely that Cousin Cosmo, who had been the only current member of the clan much interested in magical research, had once tried to do something to counteract the evil spell that kept the poor fishgirls in their bondage. But all agreed with Rose that Cosmo had got nowhere in his efforts. There were just as many mermaids in the river as ever—or there seemed to be. No one was actually counting them, of course.

Gradually the remnants of the meal were cleared away, and winecups were refilled. As desultory efforts to clean up the room continued around them, talk among the surviving family members turned, as it was wont to do again and again, to that damned cowardly relative of theirs, Cosmo. Bonar and Violet were particularly incensed. That scoundrel Cosmo, instead of retaliating like a man when he'd finally had the chance to do so on the Night of Death, had stolen the Sword and run away with it like a coward.

"He ran away?" asked Yambu. "Where?"

"We don't know."

Toward the end of that terrible night, Bonar, having become clan chief by default, and pressed by the other survivors to do something, had sent a search party of mercenaries after Cosmo. At the time the only conceivable explanation of his cousin's behavior was that Cosmo had defected to the enemy. But the searchers had come back empty-handed, reporting failure to find any trace of Cosmo along the lake or river. And in the long days since then nothing had happened to confirm the supposed defection.

"I wonder if the mercenaries killed him. I wonder if they have the Sword now," said Rose, and shuddered.

"If any of those men had come into possession of the Sword," Lady Yambu sniffed, "they would have begun to kill each other over it by now. Whichever of them survived with such a treasure would take it to a city to sell. We wouldn't have seen two of them begging at your back door today."

"No," said Violet. "The Senones must have it. But they're waiting for something before they strike again."

"Waiting for what?" asked Yambu. There was no answer.

Zoltan thought to himself that there had evidently been no more active feuding of any kind since that terrible night, unless you counted the aborted attack on the fishing village. But despite that fact, the people in this stronghold were maintaining at a high level their fears that a formidable force of their enemies must still exist, and that an attack by that force must be impending at any moment.

Rose had now begun to explain how she, her brother and sister, and Gesner, had been staying in each other's company almost continuously, day and night, ever since the massacre. If at any moment the Sword should claim a new victim from among them, someone would be on hand immediately to exact revenge.

Listening to the hatred and determination in her youthful voice,

Zoltan wondered if he ought to try to argue her and her siblings into a different frame of mind. But he decided to concentrate on his own problems, at least for now.

Winecups were refilled again, and presently it began to look as if Bonar at least might be on the way to serious drunkenness. Yambu and Zoltan sipped moderately from their cups—the vintage was passable— and Bonar's two sisters drank even less than their visitors. Meanwhile Gesner, seated at the far end of a table by himself, clutched a forgotten flagon and stared at nothing, while the servitors, still looking frightened by the presence of the visitors and the authority of Yambu, continued working on their belated job of cleanup.

Wondering if the wine could be enlisted as his ally, Zoltan made one more attempt to bring up the subject of mermaids with the chief. But at his first words, Bonar gave him a single, scornful, drunken look that said: *Mermaids again? Forget it. We have more important things than that to worry about.*

Zoltan sighed, and once more abandoned his efforts. But he had already decided that if the survivors of the Malolo clan wanted his continued help, and that of the Lady Yambu, they would eventually have to help him in turn.

Yambu, drawing her young companion aside when the opportunity arose, cautioned him again against impatience. "If you want the active help of these people for your Black Pearl, there is no point in irritating them unnecessarily on the subject. Also it may be better not to let them see how important she is to you."

With that, Zoltan had to agree.

Perversely, just after this private exchange, Bonar raised the subject of mermaids yet again himself. After he had rambled on about it for a while, spilling and drinking his wine meanwhile, all of the members of the household were firmly under the impression that Zoltan wanted to rent a mermaid for some magical stunt or entertainment somewhere.

Zoltan suppressed his angry reaction to this idea. Outwardly he decided to go along with it, hoping such a plan would offer some way to get Black Pearl away. If he could not present himself convincingly to these half-mad people as a magician, maybe they would take him seriously as the proprietor of a traveling show.

Of course, Zoltan meditated, even if he were able to take Black Pearl away from here, she would still be a mermaid. So simply to take her away would be of doubtful help. If he brought her back to Tasavalta, would Old Karel or some other wizard be able to cure her?

Zoltan had no idea.

Now Bonar, who should have fallen asleep or gotten sick some time ago, was instead working himself up to a drunken effort at diplomacy. He made a formal offer of alliance to Lady Yambu.

She responded vaguely and diplomatically. Very diplomatically, Zoltan thought, considering the chief's condition.

Gradually the day had passed, and sunset was now imminent. Zoltan walked out by himself to scout the grounds before darkness fell. When he returned to the house, he found Bonar at last snoring with his head down on the table. Violet, the more diplomatic and practical sister, issued a formal invitation to the two visitors to stay indefinitely. Then Yambu and Zoltan were assigned sleeping rooms upstairs—since last month there were plenty of rooms available—and a dour servant to wait upon them.

As they were on their way upstairs to bed, Zoltan whispered privately to Yambu: "If only there were some trustworthy and halfway competent magician available, closer than Tasavalta!"

The lady only shook her head. Both of them knew there wasn't a wizard available that either of them would want to trust, not just now. Certainly not Gesner. It appeared that for the time being any direct attempt to help Black Pearl by means of countermagic would have to wait.

Zoltan looked forward to his clandestine meeting, scheduled for this very midnight, with Black Pearl.

7

Aт nightfall on that same day, just after Zoltan had finished his reconnaissance of the Malolo grounds, the man who had called himself Chilperic was making his lonely camp in a small clearing on the wooded north bank of the Tungri. Shortly before sunset Chilperic had crossed the river from south to north, making use of a rope suspension bridge that for some years had spanned the lower end of the gorge. The bridge spanned the river just above the deep pool in which the Tungri at last ceased its deadly plunging, its white self-laceration upon rocks, and widened out again into a calm flow.

Despite the feud—so Chilperic had been informed by a chance-met peasant—the bridge had remained in place for many years. Members of both feuding clans sometimes found it advantageous to have the means of a dry crossing, and so except on rare occasions both sides were willing to let the span of ropes hang there unmolested, though often they posted sentries to warn of an enemy crossing in force. Today there had not been a sentry in sight at either end.

Chilperic had been reasonably cautious in choosing a site in deep woods where his little camp would not readily be seen. With practiced and efficient movements, he erected a small shelter tent of magically thin, strong fabric in an inconspicuous place. He also took care to keep his fire small. The one visitor that he was more or less expecting would need no help in locating his bivouac. Meanwhile Chilperic's mount, also an experienced campaigner, moved about on its hobble calmly, foraging as best it could upon the new spring growth.

The man's face, as he went about the routine chores of making himself comfortable in the woods, was set in a thoughtfully attentive expression. He looked like a man who was waiting to receive some special signal, but uncertain of at just what moment or even in what form the signal might come to him.

And then Chilperic paused in the act of gathering firewood; a frown came over his face and he stared at nothing. The signal he had both feared and anticipated had arrived at last.

The first indication of his visitor's approach was neither a visual appearance nor a sound. Rather an aura of sickness began to grow in the very atmosphere Chilperic breathed, and a special gloom, which had nothing to do with clouds or sunset, seemed to fall over the earth around him. Very quickly he also began to experience a sensation of unnatural cold. His riding-beast, hardened as it was to these matters, ceased to browse and stood still and silent, quivering lightly. The cries of animals in the surrounding forest changed, and presently fell silent. Even the insects quieted.

No more than a few minutes passed from the first manifestation of the demon until the creature made its presence known in a more localized and immediate way. But somehow to the man, shivering involuntarily, the interval seemed considerably longer.

The full manifestation, as he knew well, was apt to vary substantially from one occasion to the next. On this occasion there was not very much at all in the way of an optical appearance. There was only a cloudiness that might under ordinary circumstances have been taken for a temporary blurring of vision, a little water in the eyes. And simultaneously with the cloudiness there came a strange unearthly smell and a slight sensation that the world was tilting. Had there been any lingering doubts about the nature of the presence thus establishing itself, those doubts would have been dispelled by what came next, a rain of filth falling out of nowhere into the light of the man's small fire, and into the pan of food that he had begun to prepare beside the fire.

Chilperic's expression did not change as he picked up the pan and with a snap of his wrist threw the polluted contents into the woods behind him.

"So you have come, Rabisu," he said quietly. He spoke to the ghastly thing without the least surprise, addressing it with the reluctant firmness of a man who wants to avert both his eyes and his thoughts from something horrible, even though he knows the confrontation will be even more difficult and dangerous if he fails to meet it directly and unflinchingly.

And now at last he heard the demon's voice. It sounded more in the mind of Chilperic than in his ears, and it came in the form of a noise that reminded the man of the chittering of insects, and also of the tearing of live flesh. Still, the words which modulated this noise were clear enough: "I have come to learn what you have to report to the master."

"I want you to tell our master this." As he spoke, Chilperic sat down on a log beside his fire, put his head down, let his eyes close, and rubbed his temples. He spoke in a tired voice. "Tell him all indications are that the Sword he seeks is still somewhere in this area, between the Second and Third Cataracts and near the river Tungri. But whether it will be found north or south of the river I know not."

The insect-chittering took on an ominous overtone. "There is nothing new in this report."

The man who sat by the fire frowned at the empty pan he was still holding in his right hand. Then he put it in the fire, concave side down, to cleanse it. He retained his calm. He said: "I am aware of that. The situation still holds. And tell him that the fight between the two contending clans, using Farslayer, did indeed take place just as some of his powers reported to him. Since my own last report I have visited the stronghold of the Malolo clan and made sure of that."

"A small accomplishment. And you have not visited the clan of the Senones?"

"I am on my way there now. I intend to talk with the leaders of that clan tomorrow."

"But the Sword is still missing," said the demon, as if that were the most reasonable remark in the world to make, making a point that the man might never have thought of for himself.

"I am aware that the Sword is missing." The man with an effort retained his patience. Suddenly he looked up from the fire, into the heart of the nearby aerial disturbance, as if to demonstrate that he was not afraid to do so. "That is why I am here."

"The Dark Master requires that you shall find the missing Sword for him." Again, the voice of the visitor seemed to imply that the human needed instruction on this point.

"I am aware of that, too." Fear and anger contending in him, the man still managed to control himself. "The fact that the Sword of Vengeance is missing is not my fault."

"Yet the Dark Master will require it from you." There was no doubt about it now. The power hovering over the fire, polluting the darkness among the trees, was seeking to goad Chilperic, to provoke him to some uncontrolled response. After a time its unreal-sounding voice began to repeat mechanically: "Yet the Dark Master—"

"Enough!" Chilperic stood up suddenly.

"You claim the right to give me a command?" The questioner sounded pleased at the idea.

"I do claim that right." The man drew in a deep breath, then went on in a firm voice. "If one of us two must be subordinate to the other, then know that the lowly one will not be me. I carry with me a certain thing that I would have preferred not to show to you. But I will show it now, that you may know I am not subject to your terrors."

And in his right hand the man suddenly held up a small object, a thing he had just drawn out from under his belt. It looked like a thin, folded wallet of peculiar leather, grayish and wrinkled.

He said: "Observe it closely. I have been entrusted with this by the Dark Master himself. I think you have seen it before. Whether you have seen it or not, you must know that it contains your life. If I were to hurl this little package into my fire now, or even hold it close above the flames—"

"I was but jesting, Master, when I challenged you." And the voice of the demon was suddenly clear and silvery, a joy to hear. "Surely you know that. Can you not tell when one of my poor kind is jesting?"

"Aye, I think I can tell that. Rabisu, I did not want you to know that I held your life, for I suspected the knowledge might provoke you to more dangerous and subtle tricks than these you have played for mere annoyance." Chilperic kicked his pan out of the fire.

"I, Master? To attempt to play dangerous and subtle tricks with one of your experience and wisdom? Not I, Master, never I. If—"

"Enough. Understand, evil babbler, that I keep this small pouch that holds your life close by me at all times. If you contemplate any serious action against me, I will know it, whether I am awake or asleep. That is part of the power of control our master has bestowed upon me. I will know in time to get out my knife and begin to carve—"

"Enough, Great Master! More than enough! From this moment forward I am your humble servant."

"I rejoice to hear it." The man sounded far from convinced. "But leave me now. Do not come to me again until I summon you, or the Dark Master sends you with a message."

"I hear and obey." But before the demon vanished, it caused a plate of delicious-looking and aromatic food to appear sitting on a flat rock beside the fire, just where the other food had been.

The man picked up the offering and sniffed at it briefly. The dish was, or appeared to be, of fine porcelain. The food upon it smelled delicious. But in the next moment he threw plate and all behind him into the woods.

Then patiently, squatting beside the fire, he once again began to prepare his evening meal.

The next morning Chilperic was up at dawn, busy with breaking camp. Once that routine chore was accomplished, he mounted his riding-beast and moved on to the stronghold of the Senones clan. This he had no difficulty in finding; it was a large rambling house which stood conspicuously upon a hill only a few kilometers away from where he had spent the night.

At the edge of the clearing surrounding this rural stronghold the traveler stopped briefly to survey the layout before him. Guards were in evidence, and in a few moments Chilperic had decided that these were not mercenaries, like the ones he'd encountered at the Malolo manor across the river. These looked more like conscripted locals: too poor and ineffective to be mercenaries.

They were also too nervous in their behavior, too close to the edge of fear, when there was no obvious danger in sight. Two of them, gripping their weapons spasmodically, challenged Chilperic as he rode slowly forward. Obviously the men were impressed by his clothing, his weapons, and his mount, all of which were of the highest quality. But still, to get them to do what he required, he was required to display some patience, firmness, and a certain degree of courage.

Eventually Chilperic was able to talk himself past the outer defenders of the fortified manor, by claiming to be a friend of two of the family members. Both of these people were, as Chilperic was secretly aware, very recently deceased. He of course pretended to great surprise and horror when the guards informed him that his friends were dead.

He managed also to drop a hint or two establishing himself as a bitter enemy of the Malolo.

Soon the officer of the local guards, finding himself outtalked and outthought, and not knowing what else to do, conducted this impressive visitor up to the main house. Once admitted there, Chilperic was soon able to confer with the new Tyrant of the Senones, a very young man named Hissarlik, who had taken over as head of the clan following the great slaughter.

Naturally Chilperic pretended to be greatly surprised and dismayed when he heard from Hissarlik of the carnage inflicted upon his friends and others of this household, scarcely a month ago, by the terrible Sword of Vengeance.

The two men sat talking in the main hall, on the ground floor of the manor. Two or three other surviving members of the Senones family were gathering around now to listen to the visitor, and look him over, and evaluate what he had to say.

One of the survivors present was a vengeful-sounding youth named Anselm, Hissarlik's cousin. Anselm's face tended to twitch, and he limped badly. Chilperic gathered the youth had been crippled in some atrocity performed by a Malolo gang several years ago.

Anselm's sister or cousin—Chilperic was not sure at first—a young lady named Alicia, made an appearance also.

"A dozen dead on that night," Alicia proclaimed. "And our aunt Megara still has not recovered her wits, a month later." Her eyes glittered venomously. "We owe a huge debt to those Malolo slime, and we mean to pay it."

"Your aunt Megara?" Chilperic murmured sympathetically.

"Mine, too," said Hissarlik. "She saw her father—he was the clan chief—struck down before her eyes."

"Oh, I see. Terrible, terrible." And Chilperic, looking appropriately grim, gave his head a shake.

Hissarlik, the nominal leader of this immature and yet dangerous-looking crew, seemed to have a few years to go before turning twenty, but still he gave a first impression of inward maturity. Only after Chilperic had talked with him for a while did he begin to suspect why this young man had been so far down the structure of leadership and responsibility as to be still surviving after that great exchange of Sword blows. This young fellow talked so boldly yet vaguely about the feats of arms for which he was responsible—bragging about a raid he'd ordered two nights ago against a Malolo fishing village—that Chilperic suspected that the problem, or one of the problems, might well be cowardice.

Refreshments were brought in after a while, and the talk went on. Chilperic, when he thought the proper moment had arrived, and without dropping his pretense of being an old friend of some deceased members of the family, revealed himself as an agent of the macrowizard Wood. He expected that these people, or at least their best surviving magician, would have heard of Wood, and he was not wrong.

That claim, as he had expected, somewhat perturbed and perhaps frightened his new acquaintances. Chilperic was ready to offer some kind of demonstration to back up his words. He reached inside his coat to touch the leather wallet at his belt; he was just magician enough himself to be able to detect the powerful demonic life that throbbed so vulnerably within.

As soon as he saw that Hissarlik was groping for some way of expressing polite doubt about his relationship with the famous Wood, Chilperic once more touched glossy but wrinkled leather. Muttering a few words he'd had from the Ancient One himself, he called up the demon.

This time the manifestation was much quicker, and distinctly visual. While the owners of the house shrank back, the demon appeared in their great hall in afternoon sunlight, blocking out some of the bright beams that came slanting in through the high windows. Rabisu, taking the image of a gigantic though transparent warrior—a demon could look like almost anything it chose—acquitted himself impressively, offering a demonstration of obedient power that would have gladdened the heart of any magician-master. He bent a steel bar into a loop, and caught a rat somewhere inside the wainscoting, and turned the little creature inside out, at the same time sucking it dry of life and blood, so deftly that there was hardly any mess.

It was about an hour after this demonstration when Chilperic, feeling that he had now established himself with the Senones leadership, decided to strike while the iron was hot, and began asking important questions.

Anselm, in response to a direct query, told him that the last person to be struck down by Farslayer on that night a month ago must have been some Malolo youth. Cosmo's name did not come up here directly.

Hissarlik, Alicia, and Anselm each laid claim to having killed one of the Malolo on that night, but they could not agree exactly on each other's claims. Chilperic soon lost interest in the details, and managed to switch the conversation.

An hour after that, Chilperic and his hosts were halfway through a banquet celebrating their new alliance.

Chilperic had seen to it that their talk never strayed far from the Sword for very long. Chewing thoughtfully on a tough piece of fowl, he remarked: "And it never came back into this house again."

"No." Anselm hissed a sigh of exasperation. "It appears that our enemies still have it."

His sister murmured tensely: "They're trying to break our nerves. Well, we won't break."

Their cousin Hissarlik, seated at the head of the table, shook his head slowly. "I think they may not have it after all. Their last man to be struck down may have been away from the others when it happened. It's possible that they just have never found him, or the weapon, either."

"Where else would he have been?" Alicia challenged him at once. "We searched the islands. We searched all over our side of the river, and they would have searched on theirs."

The chief could only shake his head. And Chilperic had no intention of enlightening his hosts at the moment.

The story Chilperic had heard in the Malolo stronghold was of course not about their last man to be struck down, but rather about the misfit Cosmo. Cosmo Malolo, the mysterious one in that family, misfit and leading magician as well. Cosmo, who on that night of terror had simply grabbed up the Sword and ridden off with it, effectively putting an end to the cycle of revenge. It appeared that no one, except the hermit whom Chilperic had stopped to question, had seen Cosmo since that night.

Chilperic wondered now whether he should have questioned the hermit further.

In any event, it would seem that Cosmo had not been a simple defector, bound for enemy headquarters. Or, if so, he had never reached it. It would not have been reasonable for Cosmo to stop at the hermit's at all if he intended to go no farther than the Senones manor. But then everyone agreed the weather on the night of the massacre had been terrible, the mountain trails deadly dangerous, and that might have been a factor in his whereabouts.

Chilperic was increasingly sure that the Sword had not been carried here by Cosmo, and that none of these frightened but still bitterly determined Senones fanatics had made any systematic attempt to locate Farslayer since that horrible night of slaughter. The shock had perhaps disabled them more severely than was at first apparent.

The more Chilperic talked to these people, the more their situation appeared to resemble that obtaining among the Malolo on the other side of the river. But of course Chilperic was not going to offer that comment aloud.

"But where is the Sword now?" young Hissarlik asked him, plaintively and suddenly. It sounded almost as if the question were now occurring to him for the first time, or perhaps it was that he now felt for the first time that there was some point in asking it.

"That question," responded Chilperic with slow emphasis, "is also of great interest to my master, Wood."

"I see," said Hissarlik after a pause, not really sounding as if he saw. "But I was just thinking, suppose . . . suppose that one of those poor peasants or fishermen over on the other side of the river should happen to come across this lost Sword. What would someone like that be likely to do with such a weapon?"

Anselm tried for once to be reassuring. "The peasants? People like that wouldn't know what to do with such a thing, cousin. Take my word, they'd be too frightened to do anything."

"But just suppose . . ."

Chilperic, taking every opportunity to establish himself as a useful friend, concealed his contempt for this lack of fortitude and also did his best to be comforting. "Why, sire, there are every bit as many old enmities in villages as in castles. Farslayer would be used again, and soon, depend upon it. And then any magician worth his salt—assuming of course that he was alert and looking for the Sword—should be able to tell that it had been used again. Once that happened we'd be well on our way to getting our hands on it."

The Tyrant cast a look, eloquent of hopelessness, toward his two surviving relatives, neither of whom had any magical ability at all, if Chilperic was any judge. Chilperic had already been told in further detail how the most competent magician in the clan, Hissarlik's Aunt Megara, had been paralyzed, thrown into a trance on the night of terror, and her first replacement had been among those slain by the Sword. That junior sorcerer, according to Hissarlik's description of events, had just finished casting a spell intended to stop the Sword moments before it struck him down. There had been no indication that the magician's efforts had slowed his own doom in the slightest.

"But your most competent magician—this sorceress, your aunt—was thrown into a trance, you say? Not killed?"

"Yes. Our aunt Megara," said Hissarlik with dignity. "She's been confined to her room ever since. She still exists almost as in a trance, scarcely able to talk or move about."

"Might I see her?" asked Chilperic, in his very most helpful and friendly voice. "I am of course no healer. But I have been present once or twice at similar cases, and . . ."

By now Chilperic had been accepted as an old friend of the family. Its three surviving members now conducted him upstairs. On the second floor they entered a room half-choked with incense. No doubt these fumes were somehow intended to be magically helpful, but if the air was always like this Chilperic was not surprised that the occupant of the room had remained practically comatose.

A woman lay in the single bed, between white sheets, being watched over by a faithful maid. Chilperic was surprised at first glance by the patient's obvious youth. Her face was drawn and pale, but certainly not lined. It was not uncommon, of course, for a sorceress of skill to appear much younger than she really was. But such cheating of the calendar tended to fail in such a collapse as this.

The woman in the bed ignored her visitor, though at intervals while he was there she managed to rouse herself enough to murmur a few words, usually something that sounded as if it might express some magical intention. These words never had any effect, as far as Chilperic could see.

None of the family or servants, according to Hissarlik, had been able to do much for her.

Chilperic, looking at her, was sure that he personally could not do much for her, either. But he knew someone who almost certainly could. He nodded to himself, and turned away.

"Can you be of any help?" Alicia, with her burning eyes, demanded of him at once.

"Not immediately, no, I'm sorry. But given a day or two it may very well be possible to help."

"Do you mean it?"

"Yes indeed. Can you tell me more exactly what happened? Was your aunt in the manor house with you when she was stricken? You say it happened on the night of the great slaughter, and she saw her father killed beside her?"

"No, it did not happen in the house. Rather she was found by some of our militiamen, out on Magicians' Island. There's a cave, a sort of a grotto out there, where magicians from both clans sometimes go to practice. They have warning spells or something to keep them from encountering each other. Aunt Meg was found lying unconscious with our father's body beside her, the Sword through his heart. Farslayer had struck him down from behind. He was the first victim of the treacherous Malolo on that night.

"The militia brought Megara home, along with her father's body. For a while we were all afraid that she was going to die, too. Oh gods, I was afraid we were going to have to bury her at night, under the stones out in the courtyard, with all the rest who died that night." Alicia covered her face with her hands.

"Can you help us?" This time the question came from Hissarlik.

Chilperic faced him thoughtfully. "I think I can. I certainly intend to try."

Invited to stay the night, with a strong implication that he would be welcome to remain indefinitely, Chilperic lost no time in moving his few personal effects into a snug bedroom on the manor's upper level. There a sobering number of well-furnished rooms were vacant now. As soon as he was installed, he began to plan how to convince this puny Tyrant that he and his demon could overwhelm the Tyrant's enemies—provided, of course, that the Tyrant helped Chilperic to recover the missing Sword.

In the privacy of his room, where the demon was able to visit him without disturbing other members of the household, Chilperic was able to make certain other arrangements as well.

Next morning, as he joined his hosts for breakfast, Chilperic felt confident enough to hint strongly that some real help ought soon to be available.

Hissarlik and those with him were pleased and startled at the same time. "Then you have communicated with your master during the night?"

"Of course."

"But how?"

"To a magician of the stature of my master, the great Wood, there are always means of communication." Chilperic did not say that the means employed in this case had involved several nocturnal visits to the manor by the demon, carrying messages back and forth.

"This help you mention—how long do you think it will be before it becomes truly effective?"

Chilperic smiled encouragingly. "Perhaps I will be able to do something for you, and for your poor aunt, tomorrow. Perhaps it will take a day or two longer."

"As soon as that?" The Tyrant seemed to be struggling with mixed feelings. Pleased, of course, as well he might be, but also a touch alarmed. "How near is your master himself, then?"

"Alas, the mighty Wood is still almost a continent away. But he has rapid means of transport available, when he wants to use them."

The assurance did little to allay his host's uneasiness. Still, to Chilperic, everything seemed fairly well under control.

8

HALF an hour before midnight on his first night in Malolo manor, Zoltan, having listened patiently to the last ineffective warnings Lady Yambu felt bound to deliver, slipped out of a back door of the stronghold. He went quietly over the outer wall of the compound, which was no higher than his head, then moved as silently as possible through the moonlight toward the nearby forest, intent upon keeping his rendezvous with Black Pearl. Yambu's disapproval of this midnight sortie made him uncomfortable, but a much greater degree of discomfort would have been required to keep him from going.

If the disgruntled mercenaries, Senones agents, or anyone else, were spying on the Malolo manor tonight, Zoltan observed no sign of their presence as he crossed the moonlit clearing. Once in among the trees he paused to let his eyes adjust to the deeper darkness. Then he moved along, steadily following a gradually descending slope. On his jaunt around the grounds late in the afternoon he had made certain where the creek ran near the manor house; and once he reached the creek tonight it ought to be easy to follow it downstream to the spot along the riverbank where Black Pearl had said she would meet him. Fortunately Zoltan possessed a natural talent for finding his way to any desired geographical goal.

The creek was just where he thought it ought to be, and when he had followed the path beside it for less than a kilometer, he emerged on the bank of the river. No mist had risen from the Tungri tonight, or else it had all dispersed again by this late hour, and the broad surface of the stream, a hundred meters wide, lay clear before him in the moonlight.

There was no house or dock in sight, nor had anyone been considerate enough to leave a boat where he might borrow it to go paddling out in search of his love. Zoltan found a smooth fallen log conveniently close to the water's edge, and sat on it, doing his best to quiet his impatience, preparing himself to wait.

While he was waiting, Zoltan thought over the general situation. It could have been better, but certainly it also could have been worse. The great thing was that he had now found Black Pearl, and he now knew her name. There had been moments during the past three years when such an achievement had seemed impossible.

He was almost lost in thought, enjoying in his imagination the glowing possibilities of the future, when the dark water rippled directly in his line of vision, and she was in front of him again.

Zoltan slid from his log and splashed thigh-deep into the cold, dark stream. "Black Pearl—I was afraid that you weren't coming."

Two meters farther from the shore than he, the mermaid tossed a spray of moonlit silver from her hair. Swimming without apparent effort she held her head and shoulders out of the moonlit water. It looked as if a girl with two legs was simply standing in a greater depth of water.

"Zoltan." There was great tension in the mermaid's voice. "I am pleased that you have not forgotten me."

The young man blinked at that; it seemed a quite unnatural suggestion for the object of his love to make. "Forget you? How could I ever do that?" Zoltan waded forward until the water was waist deep, and he could feel the full strength of the cold current. Reaching out with his right hand, he touched her wet hair, as before. The skin of Pearl's shoulder, when his finger only brushed against it, felt very cold. Suddenly he burst out: "And are you doomed to remain always—like this? I can't believe that, or accept it. There must be some way—"

His fingers encountered the thin chain of the amulet she wore around her neck. "Where did you get this? You didn't have this when I knew you before."

"It's nothing, many of the girls wear them. I found it on the bottom of the river, that's all." Her dark eyes held his, and she seemed to be trying to find words. "Oh, Zoltan, are you so jealous? What man would love a mermaid, and give her pretty things to wear?"

"I can love a mermaid, I've discovered. I can love you. I wish that I had pretty things to give you. I wish . . ."

The mermaid was silent for a few moments. Then she took his hand in her cold fingers, asking: "And if there should be no way for me to change, to ever be a normal woman? If I must remain like this until I die?"

"I love you," he repeated, as if that meant some means of solving any problem must exist. And if there was the slightest pause before Zoltan gave his answer, the pause might very well have been only the kind in which a speaker tries to find the most forceful words in which it was possible to express an idea.

"But you would be happier if you had two legs," he added a few seconds later, feeling that he sounded foolish. "And how can I ever love you as a man should love a woman, unless . . ."

"There might be a way for me to have two legs again," she said. "I say there *might* be. If we can find it. Often I dream I am a little girl again, with legs."

"Then when you were a little girl you were not a mermaid?"

"Oh no." Black Pearl shook her head decisively. "That happened to me later. It is a result of evil magic."

"So I have heard. Then I say there must be good magic to counteract it. Tell me what happened. Tell me how this curse ever came to fall upon your people."

Briefly the mermaid did as Zoltan asked. The feud, and the curse it brought, had fallen upon Black Pearl's people long before she was born. She could only tell Zoltan something of the early years of the feud, as she, when a small girl with two legs, had heard the story from the elders of her people. And tonight she also gave her lover an idea of what life was like for someone upon whom the curse had fallen.

All girls born in the two or three afflicted villages lived seemingly normal lives up until puberty. Then, at about the time of commencement of the menses, perhaps one out of ten of the young women underwent what could only be described as a magical seizure. There was no telling ahead of time which girls would be afflicted.

"Sometimes the change will strike by day, sometimes by night. Always it is very sudden. No one knows who will be taken and who will be spared. Except that if a girl has already been a woman for three cycles of the moon, or if she becomes pregnant, she is certain to be spared."

"Why don't the people of these villages pack up and go somewhere else when they have daughters? Just to get away from this?"

"The villages are their homes. Anyway, people say that in my grandmother's time some people tried that. The only effect was that when the change struck their daughters they were far from home, in some cases far from any river, among people who did not understand, and who wanted to burn the helpless girls as witches."

"I see."

Black Pearl looked sharply at Zoltan. "You must come in a boat next time. The water will freeze you, my poor Zoltan, your teeth are starting to chatter already."

"I'll be all right. But what about you? The water is so cold—"

Black Pearl laughed; it was a cheerful and wholly human sound. "My poor man, I live in this water all winter; it would have to turn to ice before its coldness bothered me. Next time, tomorrow night, let us meet out there." And Black Pearl, pointing out over the dark water, indicated to her lover what she called the Isle of Mermaids, and said that it was easily reachable by boat. "There are two islands. The small one is the Isle of Magicians, and we had better avoid that."

"Are there magicians on it?"

Black Pearl hesitated. "Sometimes there are. And there are other things, which can be unpleasant. The Isle of Mermaids is much nicer. Any of the maids you find there ought to be willing to pass a message on to me, if for some reason I'm not there."

"What would happen if I did go to Magicians' Island?"

Again she seemed uncertain. "Probably nothing bad. But sometimes, when people go there, there is unpleasantness."

He decided to let that subject drop for the time being. "Wouldn't it be easier for us to meet by day?"

"Yes." The mermaid's evident uneasiness remained. "But if the lords of the Malolo manor find out that you are meeting me, they will want to charge you a price for my company. You are not a wealthy man, are you?"

"No, I am not. But in any case I would not be inclined to pay them a price for that. You're not their slave, are you?" The mere thought made him angry.

"I'm no one's slave. But it will be better if you can avoid dealing with those people altogether."

"Can't do that very well," he announced cheerfully. "I'm living in their house now."

Black Pearl's confusion only increased. "If you refuse to pay them, Zoltan, then you will have to fight with them. They do consider mermaids slaves if someone else wants one of them. I have already been sold once, as you know."

"My poor girl, there aren't enough Malolo manor-lords left to fight very successfully with anyone. The Sword called Farslayer has taken care of that."

Black Pearl considered this in silence, running fingers through her long dark hair, tossing her head. She said: "Even mermaids have heard about the fight." After a pause she asked: "Which ones are dead?"

"Quite a number. I didn't get any list of their names. Why?"

"Nothing. Is there—is there a man named Cosmo among them?"

"No. Not among those still living at the manor or among their dead. He's missing. Why?"

"Why? I don't know. I don't suppose it matters."

Zoltan hesitated for a moment, trying to understand. Then he asked: "I don't suppose you can tell me anything about the Sword that killed them all? I would like very much to get my hands on it."

Black Pearl splashed water with her hands, nervously. It was a gesture that an ordinary girl might have made in swimming. "Whom do you want to kill?"

"I? No one, at the moment. No, it's a matter of seeing that certain people don't come into possession of Farslayer."

"Well, I know something, perhaps. But I am not sure that I should tell you."

"Why not? Yes, absolutely you should tell me. Where's Farslayer now? Can you tell me that?"

"No, I can't. Not right now."

He took a step toward the mermaid, but she slid effortlessly out of his reach in the water. "Black Pearl?"

"Zoltan, at our next meeting I will tell you something, I promise. Maybe that meeting will have to take place at night again."

There was a gentle disturbance in the surface of the water nearby. Another mermaid surfaced; this one had lighter hair, but in the darkness Zoltan could not otherwise distinguish her.

"It's only Soft Ripple," said Black Pearl. "You remember, she's my best friend, who came to the bachelors' hut with me."

"I remember," said Zoltan and nodded politely in the direction of the newcomer. Then he resumed his conversation with Black Pearl. "I'll seek you out again by night if need be. But if I come out here looking for you by day, I hope you don't intend to hide."

"I will not hide, by day or night. Zoltan, you have really come all this way downriver seeking me." Black Pearl's voice was gently marveling.

"Of course I have. What did you expect?"

But Black Pearl would not tell him what she had expected. Again, with Soft Ripple looking on, the lovers embraced, and this time exchanged passionate kisses. Zoltan thought he had been ready for the coldness of her mouth, but still his own nerves felt it as a shock. And another shock—though it was hardly a surprise—came when his hand, sliding down Pearl's bare back in the moment before they separated, encountered the border where smooth skin abruptly changed to scales. It felt as if her lower body were completely encased in some flexible kind of armor.

Hastily they arranged another meeting. Then, his body feeling shriveled and numb with cold from the waist down, Zoltan slowly and unhappily waded back to shore. Then he turned his steps uphill in the direction of the Malolo manor house.

Ascending the rough path that followed beside the little stream, he crossed a small clearing in bright moonlight. Looking back from the uphill end of the open space, Zoltan realized abruptly that he was being watched and shadowed. At least it looked that way. First there was one, and then, he thought, there were two dark and nimble figures just visible at the edge of moonlight at the lower end.

Zoltan wasted no time. He turned, ducked into the shadow of the trees again, and ran. The people who might be trying to follow him were not going to get any closer if he could help it. The path was very dark in stretches, but it was basically familiar to him after his trip down, and if the two figures were trying to catch up they were having no success. Now and then, looking downhill behind him, he caught a glimpse of one or another of them in moonlight, and was satisfied that they were gaining little if any distance on him.

Zoltan did not slacken his pace. Running softly, dodging among trees like a shadow, he soon drew near the cleared area around the manor. Here, to his surprise, he came close to running into several more mysterious figures. These were keeping watch on the house from the shadowed edge of the forest.

Zoltan got past these additional complications without incident. As he entered the clearing, a man's voice, its owner invisible in the darkness, called softly from somewhere off to his right. Zoltan thought that he could recognize the voice of the mercenary officer Koszalin. If this identification was correct, the mercenaries had come back from spending their pearl money sooner than expected. Or else something had happened to keep them from ever going as far as the nearest town.

Whoever the watchers at the edge of the clearing were, they must have been aware of Zoltan's passage. But they made no attempt to stop or overtake him. In a few score running paces he had reached the back door of the manor.

Lady Yambu had evidently been listening for Zoltan's return, for the moment he gave the agreed-upon signal, the door swung open to admit him to the house.

Bonar and his sisters were waiting in the kitchen along with Yambu, and the clan chief and his sister Rose were openly relieved to see that Zoltan had returned. Violet, on the other hand, immediately expressed her suspicions that he had been treating with the enemy.

Zoltan denied this flatly.

"Then where were you?"

"If I told you I was visiting a mermaid, would you believe it? I'll give you the details, if you like."

There was silence; at least the accusation of treating with the Senones was not immediately renewed. Meanwhile Yambu, not bothering to ask Zoltan what success he'd had with his mermaid, hastened to bring him up to date. For whatever reason, at least some of the mercenaries, Koszalin among them, were here instead of enjoying their binge in town. Possibly their captain had decided that much more treasure could be extracted here, and had been able to enforce patience on his men. Whatever the reason, they had returned a little after midnight, to hammer on both doors of the manor, demanding what they called their fair share of the wealth.

Zoltan, mindful of possible flanking movements, started upstairs to check on the manor's defenses there. Somewhat to his surprise, dark-haired Rose volunteered to come with him, saying that he might need help finding his way about through the darkened rooms.

"I might well need some help. Are all the windows protected with good gratings?"

"I'm almost sure they are. Let me come with you and we'll make certain."

A few moments later, as Zoltan turned to make his way out of a small bedroom whose windows were indeed securely barred, he found Rose gently but firmly blocking the narrow doorway.

Her hand came to rest on his arm; her voice was hardly louder than a whisper. "I feel safe as long as you're here. But you're wearing pilgrim clothes, and that means you don't intend to stay here very long. Doesn't it?"

"Being a pilgrim generally means not staying in one place, that's right."

"There's nothing for me here either, not really. With all the elders in the family dead, Bonar inherits the manor, the villages, everything." Rose was looking at him through narrowed eyes; in candlelight she was far from unattractive. Suddenly he realized that she must have recently put on some kind of perfume.

Just now, thought Zoltan, was not the time for him to say that he had committed his thoughts and his entire future to someone else.

Now his attractive companion, still obstructing the exit, had him by the sleeve, which she fondled as if testing the gray fabric. "Sometimes I think I'd like to be a pilgrim, too."

"Really?"

"Yes. What else is there? There's nothing else for me around here."

"The life of a pilgrim is not easy, either."

He tried to put her gently aside. Rose grabbed him, and made her plea more openly than before. "Zoltan. When you leave here, take me with you."

Zoltan was doing his best to frame an answer that would not provoke a crisis, when, to his considerable relief, another candle appeared down the dim hallway. It was Violet, in a hurry, obviously bringing some kind of news.

Violet looked at the two of them sharply, as if she suspected what her older sister was up to. Zoltan was beginning to believe that Violet tended to see everything in terms of jealousy and suspicion. She was an anti-Senones fanatic, always ready to suspect some betrayal in that direction. At the same time, Zoltan thought, she might be somewhat jealously attracted to him, too.

And in the privacy of his own thoughts he tried to imagine how outraged both women would be at the idea that any man they considered at all interesting could be as obsessively smitten as he was—with a creature they considered little more than a fish.

But the message brought upstairs by Violet allowed little time for debate. The disgruntled soldiers had renewed their pounding on the rear door. It sounded this time like a serious attempt to break it down.

The upstairs seemed secure, as far as Zoltan could tell. So he hurried back downstairs. As he arrived in the kitchen he could hear the mercenaries outside, threatening now to burn the whole manor to the ground if their demands for more treasure were not met.

The doors themselves were truly strong, and for the moment seemed secure. Gesner, the claimed magician, was at least keeping his head well, even if not contributing much beyond that. He now assured the visitors that the manor's sloping roof was of slate tiles. Most of the rest of the building was stone, and it would not be easy to burn. Gesner had now equipped himself with some serious-looking magician's paraphernalia, and announced that he intended to do what he could with fire-preventing spells. And if a fire was started by anyone outside the house, he'd attempt to make the flames snap back at and burn the fingers that had ignited them.

Yambu approved this plan. Then she and Zoltan concentrated for the moment on organizing a more mundane line of defense, ordering servants to stand by in key locations with buckets of water. A well-filled cistern on the roof offered some prospects of success.

Bonar meanwhile had unlocked an armory on the lowest level of the house, next to the improvised mortuary, and was passing out weapons to his sisters and the remaining servants, or at least to those among the servants he could persuade to take them. Violet armed herself eagerly, and Rose with some reluctance followed suit.

Entering the arsenal himself, Zoltan selected a bow and some arrows from the supply available. Thus equipped, he ran upstairs again and stationed himself in a high window that gave him a good view of the rear yard. The fools out there were getting a fire going in the rear of one of the outbuildings, and a moment later Zoltan shot a man who came running with a torch toward the manor itself. The fellow screamed so loudly when he was hit that Zoltan doubted he was mortally hurt.

Another pair of mercenaries came to drag their wounded comrade away, and Zoltan let them do so unmolested, thinking they might be ready for a general retreat. The barn, or shed, or whatever it was, was burning merrily now. Fortunately it stood just outside the compound wall, and far enough from all other buildings that the spread of the fire did not seem to present an immediate danger.

Meanwhile the fire was giving him plenty of light to aim by, which put the attackers at a definite disadvantage. But Kosazlin's shouts could be heard, rallying his men, and they were not yet ready for a general retreat. Taking shelter as best they could, they began to send a desultory drizzle of stones and arrows against the house.

When this had been going on for some time, Bonar, in a fever of martial excitement, entered the room where Zoltan was, crouched beside him and looked out. This window afforded the best view of what was going on outside.

"What's burning? Oh, the old barn, that's nothing much. How many of them have we killed?"

"None, that I know of. I hit one but I doubt he's dead. Is the rest of the house still secure?"

"The ground floor is fine, I've just made the rounds down there."

There was a sound in the hallway, just outside the bedroom, as of a servant running, calling. Then a brief scuffle.

Bonar and Zoltan both leaped up, leveling their weapons at the doorway. The door pushed open—

Zoltan found himself confronting a tall and powerful man who gripped a drawn Sword in his right hand. In the firelight that flared in through the open window Zoltan had no trouble recognizing his uncle, Prince Mark of Tasavalta.

9

ZOLTAN's hands sagged holding the half-drawn bow, and the ready arrow fell from his fingers to the floor. For a moment he could only stare at this apparition blankly, and for that moment he was sure that it must be some kind of deception, that he was facing some image of sorcery, an effect of the Sword of Stealth or some other magical disguise—and the apparition, if such it was, was lowering the Sword in its right hand.

"No need to think you're seeing visions, nephew," said the tall man, having observed the two occupants of the room carefully for a moment. He spoke in Prince Mark's familiar voice. "I would have hailed you down on the hillside, but I couldn't get close, and I didn't want to yell your name at the top of my voice. You gave us the devil of a chase uphill from the river. After we followed you to this house, we decided we'd look in to make sure that you needed no help." Now Mark sheathed his Sword.

"We?" Zoltan could only repeat the word numbly.

"Ben and I."

Behind Mark, entering from the hallway, appeared another big man. This one was indeed monstrously massive, though somewhat shorter than the prince and a few years older. Ben of Purkinje's ugly face split in a reassuring smile at the sight of the bewildered Zoltan.

And he, the prince's nephew, shaking his head in wonder and relief, at last remembered the chief of the Clan Malolo. "Bonar, put down your sword. This man is my uncle Mark, the Prince of Tasavalta."

While Bonar was managing some kind of greeting, the Lady Yambu put in her appearance, to greet both Mark and Ben with great surprise and equally great relief.

* * *

A couple of the more trustworthy servants were posted as lookouts, while a conference of explanations was conducted. Almost the first question the two newcomers were required to answer was how they had gained entrance to the house. Mark explained, and apologized, for the secret violence of their entry. The Sword he carried at his belt was Stonecutter, and he and Ben had used it to carve their way in through the solid stone wall of the manor, a process Stonecutter's magic accomplished swiftly and almost silently.

By now Rose and Violet, as well as Gesner, had joined the conference around the two newcomers, and were being introduced to them with a mixture of relief and apprehension.

Fortunately it now appeared that the mercenaries' assault, such as it had been, had abated at least for the time being.

Ben, scowling out the window, muttered: "Maybe when the fire in back dies down they'll try again."

"Maybe." The prince nodded. "That means we should use our time meanwhile to good advantage."

And now for a time the conference adjourned to the great hall of the manor, where Mark and Ben were provided with food and drink. They found this welcome, having been through some hard traveling in the past few days.

Their riding-beasts, as Ben explained, had been lost in some minor skirmish with unnamed foes "between here and the desert." Ben waved a huge hand in a generally southeast direction. For the past three days they had been on foot.

"But what brings you here?"

In answer to that question Zoltan's uncle Mark explained that he and Ben had been on their way back to Tasavalta after concluding a deal with the desert tribesman Prince al-Farabi, by which al-Farabi had been allowed to borrow the Sword Stonecutter for a time.

With that transaction concluded, and after starting home with Stonecutter, Mark had received, by winged messenger, word from his father the Emperor. In a written message the Emperor informed his son Mark that important matters, requiring almost his full attention, were developing somewhere in the extreme south of the continent.

The Emperor had warned Mark to prepare for urgent action, and to await another message which, Mark hoped, would spell out in some detail just what he was expected to do.

"That still doesn't explain how you and Ben come to be here. Did you mean to follow the river east, or—?"

Mark shook his head. "There was another part to the message. It suggested rather strongly that we might want to locate you. You, Zoltan, and you, Lady Yambu."

The two pilgrims exchanged uncertain glances. "Did the message say why?" Yambu asked.

"It did not. But it did say that a Sword was at stake here, and that Swords should not be allowed to fall into the wrong hands. So, we started for the valley of the Tungri as fast as we conveniently could. And here you are, and here we are."

Zoltan whistled his amazement softly. "My great-uncle is quite a magician."

Prince Mark sighed, but made no other comment.

Ben shrugged. "I've seen enough, that when the Emperor suggests something I'm inclined to listen."

Yambu nodded her head. Meanwhile the folk native to the manor were watching and listening in silence, though Bonar once or twice seemed on the verge of breaking in with some sharp comment.

"How did you recognize me in the dark?" Zoltan wanted to know. "I mean earlier tonight, on the hill down toward the river?"

Huge Ben snorted gently. "Who else would be talking to a mermaid?"

"Oh." Zoltan wondered if everyone in Tasavalta knew of his obsession.

Now Violet asked: "Excuse me—Your Grace? Your Majesty?—you say that the Emperor knew that your nephew and his friend were here? But how?"

Mark only shrugged. The gesture seemed to say that he did not understand his father's purposes or his father's powers. But the prince's continued smile indicated that he had learned to trust those powers; and it no longer surprised him that he did not understand.

Ben asked: "But what's going on here, Zoltan? Yambu?"

The two pilgrims told Mark and Ben of Farslayer's presence here, and how the Sword had wrought such havoc among the clanspeople on both sides of the river.

Mark nodded. "We must do what we can to get it."

A little later, when the people of the clan had left them, Mark also fretted aloud to his nephew about his ten-year-old son Adrian, who had been recently enrolled, or was about to enroll, in a new school, unspecified. There, his father hoped, he would be able safely to master the arts of magic for which he had such a natural aptitude, and which might otherwise prove such a burden to him as he grew up.

To Ben, Zoltan, and Yambu, Mark declared: "Old Karel has arranged something in the way of schooling. This time I expect it'll work out successfully."

Zoltan said: "We could use someone here right now with a little natural aptitude along the line of magic—and a little schooling, too."

No such luck.

Bonar and his sisters gawked at this royal personage when he rejoined them, and made efforts not to be overly impressed. They struggled not to be awed by his presence, or by that of the Sword he carried. Yet, at the same time, the Malolo survivors were more at ease now. If their manor was to be occupied at all, far better that it should be done by a reigning prince and his entourage.

It was easy to see that Bonar, despite his rather hollow protests that it did not matter, was somewhat perturbed by the tunnellike hole carved in the stone wall of his house, and by the ease with which these strangers had penetrated his defenses. But the physical damage could be easily enough repaired, and in the morning the huge man Ben helped the Malolo servants push back into place the blocks of stone that had been cut free.

Zoltan had already told Mark of his, Zoltan's, successful search for Black Pearl, and in the same breath had informed the prince that Black Pearl had said she knew something of the Sword's hiding place.

Bonar and his sisters repeated to Mark and Ben what they had already told Zoltan and Yambu, about the man Chilperic, who had come through here saying that he acted as the agent of the great magician Wood.

That got the prince's full attention. "What did you tell him?"

"There is little enough we can tell anyone. He went on his way dissatisfied."

Yambu and Zoltan also told Mark of the hermit.

Mark, who had of course heard of Black Pearl at great length while Zoltan was still in Tasavalta, listened sympathetically now to his nephew's continued pleas to help her, but could not promise to be of any real assistance. "You're sure it's the same wench, hey?"

"Of course!"

"Pardon, Zoltan. Of course you are. It's just that I have many other things to think of. Like Farslayer."

Still, Mark promised that if another winged messenger should come to him here from Tasavalta, he would use it to send a return message, asking Karel about magical help for mermaids.

Zoltan momentarily regretted bothering his uncle with a personal problem. But only momentarily.

An hour or two before dawn, when the fire in back had burned itself out without any renewal of the mercenaries' attack, and when most of his comrades were asleep, Mark found his way alone up to a flat portion of the manor's roof.

Here he found a comfortable seat, which for a time he occupied in silence and solitude, regarding the night sky and its mysteries. But when a quarter of an hour had passed, there came an almost inaudible whisper of wings. The expected messenger, an owlish, half-intelligent creature, whose wingspan was greater than the span of the prince's arms, came gliding down out of the stars to land beside him on a small parapet.

The prince of Tasavalta was not surprised and did not stir. "Hail, messenger," he murmured in greeting.

"Greetings to the prince of Tasavalta." The words were clearly only a memorized formula, and the thin, small voice in which they were spoken was far from human. Still, the words were clear enough.

"Do you bring me word from my father? From the Emperor?"

"Message for Prince Mark: No news from home. All goes well at home. I stand ready to bear a message back."

No news in this case was good news. The prince had been away from Tasavalta for several months now, and he tended to worry about matters at home.

True, Mark had left the affairs of Tasavalta—as well as the care of his second son, Stephen, now eight years old—in the very capable hands of his wife, Princess Kristin. But still he inevitably worried.

"Any news from the Princess Kristin? Or greetings from either of my sons?"

"No news from home. All goes well at home. I stand ready to bear a message back."

Mark sighed, and began to say the words he wanted the creature to memorize.

10

On the morning after that on which the prince conversed with a winged messenger, the hermit Gelimer was sitting on a block of wood in his dooryard, gazing in the direction of his woodpile, which had been much depleted by winter. But at the moment the hermit was hardly conscious of the wood, or anything else in the yard around him. Gelimer was enjoying the promise of an early spring sun, and thinking back over his life. He found much material there for thought, especially in the days of his youth, before he had become a hermit.

He had become an anchorite long years ago, chiefly out of a sense of the need to withdraw from evil. But from time to time it was borne in upon him that evil, along with much else from his old life, was not to be so easily avoided.

Gelimer possessed, as did many folk who were not magicians, the ability to sense the presence of magical powers. And he could sense that there was a demon in the valley now.

He thought he knew why the foul thing had come. It was the Sword, of course, like any other great material treasure a lodestone drawing all the wickedness of the world about itself. When the hermit thought of demons, and of the men and women who consorted with such creatures and tried to use them, he was tempted to reclaim the Sword from where he had hidden it, and employ it to rid the world of at least some of those evildoers. But so far he had managed to put the intrinsically repulsive thought of violence away from him.

Another aspect of the Sword's presence was inescapable. As long as he, Gelimer, knew where it was, had it virtually in his possession, he could no longer distance himself from the local political and military situation. Ordinarily he ignored the inhabitants of the valley, those of high station as well as low, and neither knew nor cared about the latest developments in the bitter feud between the clans. But now that was no longer an option; Farslayer had brought him an unwanted burden of power and responsibility.

When Gelimer had hidden the Sword, he had thought vaguely that with good luck the terrible weapon might remain where he had put it for years, for generations even, until no one any longer sought it in the valley. But already that had come to seem a foolish hope.

Very well. If he was now inescapably involved, then he must try to be involved as intelligently as possible.

By now Gelimer had logically reconstructed, at least to his own satisfaction, what must have happened in his house on the night of the storm. His visitor, Cosmo Biondo—if that had really been the man's name—must have awakened, perhaps delirious with his head injury, in the middle of the night, while Gelimer himself still slept. Then the visitor, whoever he was and whether delirious or sane, had taken the terrible Sword in hand and carried it outside. What had happened immediately after that was still uncertain, except that the Sword must have passed from the hands of the man Cosmo into the possession of someone else. Possibly, even probably, Cosmo had decided to invoke Farslayer's awful magic against someone at a distance, and had gone outside where he had room to swing the Sword, and privacy to chant whatever words he thought were necessary.

However he had rid himself of Farslayer, Cosmo had had time, before the Sword came back to him, to reenter Gelimer's house. Time to latch the door after himself, and to go to stand beside the bed—as if, having used that Sword, he might be ready to go back to sleep.

As indeed, in a sense, he had done.

Whether the violent death of Cosmo had been merited or not, Gelimer reflected that it had probably done no one any good, and settled nothing. Evil moved on through the world as before, and was now gathering in the vicinity of that hidden grave.

Even if Gelimer had been minded to take up the Sword himself and strike at that evil, he would not know where best to aim the blow. At the demon? Such creatures were notoriously difficult to kill. Gelimer had no idea whether even a Sword would be effective in such an effort, or to what physical location the Sword might go if he tried to slay a demon with it, or into whose hands the Sword of Vengeance would fall next. He knew that demons' lives, their only vulnerability, were apt to be hidden in strange places.

No, he would not try to kill the demon now roaming invisibly through the valley—at least not yet. For decades now everything—or almost everything—in the hermit's nature had shrunk from the deliberate taking of any human life. I have put all that behind me, he thought.

I am not a god, to judge and punish humans for their crimes. Even the gods did a very poor job of that when they were still around. Not you, of course, Ardneh, he added in his thoughts. You know I don't mean you. And you know which gods I do mean—the ones who created these damnable, almost indestructible Swords, thirty years ago, for the purposes of their Game. The ones who thought that the entirety of human life was no more than a game carried on for their amusement.

Well, the game of human life had swallowed up what had turned out to be the lesser reality of those gods and goddesses. What those divinities had deemed a mere amusement had destroyed them. And perhaps the limit of what human life was going to accomplish in the universe was not yet in sight.

Sitting by his woodpile now, Gelimer closed his eyes, wincing as if he felt an inner pain. He could tell that the demon had just passed, in some dimension, near him. But at the moment he stood in no immediate peril, for the thing was already gone again.

Even a nonviolent man could hardly scruple to kill a demon, by any means possible. In fact it might be thought a crime against humanity to fail to kill one if you had the power.

Despite its violence, the idea was developing a powerful attraction: *To cleanse the earth of such a foul blot—why should I not for once be willing to use the clean steel of a god-forged blade?*

But he must be very careful. He must be sure of what he was doing before he moved.

Who had the ordering of demons, who employed such difficult and deadly dangerous tools? It was certainly not likely to be any of these local fools, even though one or two of them dared to call themselves wizards. No, it would be some vastly greater power, from outside the valley. And what would bring such a power here? Certainly the Sword Farslayer, as a prize to be won, might do so.

Gelimer's thoughts kept coming back to the same conclusions, but those conclusions never brought him any nearer to knowing what to do.

Meanwhile, Chilperic on that same morning had no clear idea of where his demon was at the moment or what it was doing—filthy creature, he would like to forget that it existed, if that were only possible. Today Chilperic himself was back on the south side of the river, and in fact he was within a few hundred meters of the hermit's house. He was coming back to question the hermit again, but had decided that it would be wise to look around in the vicinity a little first.

Chilperic did not think the hermit had lied to him. But during his second night at the Senones manor, it had gradually come to him that neither Cosmo Malolo nor the Sword he had carried might ever have left these high crags. There had been a great deal of killing on that night, and there was really no reason to think that Cosmo had survived it.

And now today the sight of a scavenger bird or two, rising in bright sunlight from somewhere among the rocks that formed the lip of a precipice, suggested to Chilperic that some large creature was lying dead in that location.

To get anywhere near the place Chilperic was forced to dismount, then edge his way forward carefully on foot, until he was standing on the very brink. Forty meters or more below him, the Tungri grumbled and fumed eternally, sawing its way down through rock, day after day infinitesimally deepening its gorge.

Wrinkling his nose at the smell of death, chilly and stale in the spring air, Chilperic reached the last necessary foothold, braced himself with one arm on a rock, leaned over and looked down. Not two meters below him he saw the startling white of bone, protruding from amid coarse hair and decaying flesh. Leaning forward again, even more precariously, he was able to assure himself that the victim had not been human, but a riding-beast; there were no saddlebags, but the saddle and other tack were still in place. The discoverer could remember seeing leather worked in similar patterns when he had poked his curious nose into the Malolo stables.

Interesting. And more than that.

His heart beginning to beat faster, Chilperic looked around him carefully. He clambered back and forth along the rough brink of the cliff, probing into every nearby crevice of rock. He even managed at last to get close enough to the dead animal to move what was left of it, using his own sword as a lever. He shifted the carcass enough to see that there was no man's body, and no resplendent Sword, pinned underneath it.

Cosmo's riding-beast, quite probably. Almost certainly, if Chilperic could find Cosmo's initials or some other identification on the leather. But still the Sword of Vengeance was nowhere to be found.

Reluctantly Chilperic returned at last to his own tethered mount. He swung himself up into the saddle and sat there motionless for a moment, gazing thoughtfully down toward the thundering stream below. It might be a hopeless search down there at the bottom of the river, but then again it might not.

He could, of course, employ Rabisu in the search. But how much help the demon would be was problematical. Chilperic had for some time suspected that the foul creature might prefer, after all, that the Sword never be found. Its own life, however carefully hidden, might be as vulnerable as the life of any puny human to that blade.

Probably, Chilperic concluded, it would be best not to try to use the demon at all. It was his understanding that there were other creatures nearby, just as intelligent and much more docile, who would be even more at home along the bottom of the river.

Chilperic, on leaving the place where he had discovered the dead riding-beast, hastened to recross the river, and long before nightfall he had returned to the headquarters of the Senones clan.

Today the homegrown militia guards stationed around the perimeter of the clearing in which the Senones manor stood were not as grim and tense as they had been yesterday. And today, Chilperic noted as he handed his riding-beast over to a groom, there was more ordinary activity around the place, as if things might be beginning to return to normal.

But even before he had passed through the gate into the inner grounds, this last impression was firmly contradicted by an apparition in the sky.

Suddenly some of the people around him were gawking upward. Following the direction of their collective gaze, Chilperic beheld a marvel. Outlined against a fluffy cloud was a huge griffin, spiraling in descent. A single human figure was mounted astride the creature, which possessed the head and wings of an oversized eagle, and the four-legged body of a lion. Such creatures were extremely rare, and their flight depended more on magic than on the physical power of their wings.

The griffin's descent was quick, and not many people actually witnessed its arrival. Which was probably just as well, for most of those who did were petrified. The winged beast came down gently and peacefully enough, to land on the flat lawn immediately in front of the manor. Though not one person in a thousand among the general population ever saw one of these uncommon beasts, Chilperic was no stranger to the sight—nor was he, actually, very much surprised by the arrival of a griffin at the Senones manor just now. He had a good idea who the creature's passenger might be.

The gates in the inner wall of the manor had already been opened to admit Chilperic, and he strode in, practically unnoticed. The new Tyrant, who seemed to have been waiting on the lawn, quite possibly to welcome him, had now instead turned his back on Chilperic and the gate—for which he could scarcely be blamed—and was gaping like a yokel at the unexpected aerial arrival.

The human figure who had just arrived was at this instant in the act of dismounting from the griffin's back. This was a diminutive female with her long blond hair bound up closely, dressed in a close-fitting jacket and trousers, what looked like eminently practical garb for hurtling through the air astride a monster's back. The woman was very young—to all appearances, at least—and very pretty. She could only be the healer that Wood had promised to send.

Meanwhile the griffin was crouching on the lawn in the pose of a docile cat. Still, it managed to impress and even cow most of the local people who were quickly gathering—at a respectful distance—to behold it. Chilperic thought that the monster's presence might well worry the more thoughtful among the local people, offering as it did more evidence that whether they liked it or not they were now closely involved in the affairs of the great world.

The young woman with the neatly controlled blond hair and the small backpack immediately decided—whether through deduction or divination—which of the people present was the clan leader. For the moment she ignored everyone else, including Chilperic, and came walking straight to Hissarlik. Her movements possessed a grace that Chilperic had seldom seen matched. Genuflecting briefly before the Tyrant in a gesture of great respect, the new arrival introduced herself, in a soft voice, as Tigris, physician and surgeon.

The Tyrant, staring distractedly at this beauteous arrival—as many a more experienced man in his place would have done—murmured and mumbled something in return. Then he recovered himself sufficiently to take the young lady formally by the hand and bid her welcome.

"Thank you, my lord." The healer's eyelashes fluttered demurely, and her gaze became downcast. "Will you now have a servant show me to my quarters—my room will be next to my patient's, I pray—and provide me with a maidservant to attend me? Soon I will be ready to examine the patient."

"I, uh. Yes, of course." The Tyrant, recovering further, clapped his hands and gave the necessary orders.

Meanwhile the griffin, as if it had received some hidden signal, spread its wings again—at a closer look those limbs appeared to be more reptilian than avian—and soared suddenly into the air. The gawking crowd fell back even further, but Tigris ignored the departure of the beast completely. She had now raised her eyes and was gazing, in a way that might be thought inappropriate for a physician, at the man she had greeted as her lord.

Only when she turned away to follow the servant who was to lead her to her quarters did her gaze brush Chilperic's. It was a cool, appraising glance. He supposed it likely that the lady had come with some special orders from Wood having to do with himself. He would have to take the opportunity to meet with her alone as soon as it was practical.

Hissarlik's grim young cousin, Anselm, limped from somewhere to intercept the healer just as she was about to enter the house. At first Chilperic thought that Anselm intended to stop her from going in, but after a few moments' conversation they entered the manor together.

As for the Tyrant himself, his gleaming eyes followed his new guest until she was out of sight. Only then did he turn, with a sigh, and speak to Chilperic. "Though I have scarcely met the woman as yet, I am deeply impressed. Your master, the Ancient One, certainly fulfills his promises quickly."

"Oh, indeed he does," Chilperic assured the Tyrant. "I would not be likely to attach myself to any master who did not."

"Nor would I be."

"I see."

Now the two men, by unspoken agreement, began to stroll. They passed around the side of the sprawling house, and entered what must once have been a flower garden, though it was sadly neglected now.

As they walked, Hissarlik started to discuss his plans for the future. His only real goal, it appeared, was to determine just how, working together, he and his new friend Chilperic were going to wipe out once and for all those infamous Malolo brigands across the river.

The older man smiled at him, gently and agreeably. "Undoubtedly a very worthy objective, sire. But before I can undertake to give you assistance in such a project, there are one or two other matters that I must see to for my master."

"Oh. I see," Hissarlik said vaguely. He did not seem to be paying complete attention. His head turned away and his eyes kept straying toward the house, where certain windows on the second floor seemed likely to be those of the entranced family sorceress, next to those of the beautiful blond physician. "And what would those matters be?"

Patiently Chilperic reiterated the story of how sincerely his own dread master, Wood, wished and pined to possess the Sword of Vengeance. Once that goal had been attained, then certainly the mighty Wood would be ready to reward his friend Hissarlik even more generously than by sending a healer—provided of course that in the meantime Hissarlik had been of help in recovering the Sword.

Chilperic lowered his voice slightly when he imparted the next bit of information, which was that Wood might even have in mind something like the offer of a real partnership.

The Tyrant, now sitting at ease in a worn-out garden chair, under a leafless tree at one end of his neglected garden, scratched his head. "Well, that's all very fine, of course. If I had possession of the Sword, or anything else your master wants, I'd gladly give it to him. I hope he knows that. But the truth is I don't have Farslayer, nor do I know where it is. You don't believe I have it, do you?"

"Of course not, sire. You don't have possession of the Sword now. If you did you would already be attacking the Malolo."

"That's right."

Chilperic paused momentarily. "But I do have an idea as to where it might be found. And how, with some help you can provide, we might be able to recover it."

"Is that so?" Hissarlik still sounded cautious rather than eager. "What sort of help do you need?"

Chilperic explained briefly about his discovery, this very day, of the dead riding-beast, and his idea that the Sword might be lying at the bottom of the Tungri somewhere in that vicinity. "The water runs quite swiftly there, and I suppose that it is deep. But a creature capable of living and moving easily underwater ought not to have too much trouble in examining the bottom."

"Hmm."

"Yes." Chilperic pressed on: "Unless I'm mistaken, you Senones folk are able to call upon the local mermaids for service when you wish, though technically the creatures are supposed to be under the lordship of those fools across the river. Their grip on all their vassals, including even the fishgirls, is evidently weakening."

"Yes, we can call upon mermaids if we wish." But Hissarlik did not seem to be immediately pleased by the idea of doing so. "If you mean by magic, it was Aunt Meg who generally handled that sort of thing, of course, when she was well." Then he brightened. "What about your demon? Couldn't it conduct a search even more swiftly and surely?"

Now it was Chilperic's turn to be less than enchanted by a suggestion. "The demon has many other tasks to accomplish."

"I suppose it must have," the Tyrant agreed somewhat doubtfully.

"Tell me, my friend. Is there something you don't like about the idea of using mermaids?"

"Well, the truth is that those creatures do tend to be somewhat unreliable. They're totally lazy, of course. They can be forced magically to do some things, such as coming when they are called—though it's not always certain that they even do that. And there's no way to force them to obey perfectly when sent out on a mission. Actually they're a pretty rebellious lot, and all in all more trouble than they're worth, though we do manage to sell one once in a while."

Chilperic frowned in thought. "How long have there been mermaids in the river here? I was told their condition was the result of a spell inflicted on some villages by a Senones magician many years ago, in the course of the feud."

"Yes, that's correct." The Tyrant went on to explain that the ancestral magician, whom he claimed as his own great-grandfather, had been still in the process of perfecting the spell when he died. Great-grandfather's ultimate goal had been to develop some similar curse that might be used directly against the vile Malolo leaders, but their magical defenses had remained too strong.

"And no one since his time has devised a way to lift the spell, or to expand and perfect it as he sought to do?"

"Aunt Meg, as I say, was—is—our best magician. She's really the one you ought to talk to, as soon as she's able." Judging from his confident tone, the Tyrant had great faith in the healer Wood had sent him. "But no, friend Chilperic, as far as I know, no one on our side in modern times has been much interested in using the mermaid spell. I have the idea that somehow it's impractical. I suppose the Malolo leaders really haven't cared that much about it, either. It actually doesn't affect enough of their people to do them any harm. Having a few mermaids about is interesting, and sometimes such creatures command big prices as slaves or oddities. Sometimes the Malolo sell one, sometimes we do."

"I see."

"Yes. Now that I come to think of it, I did once hear a rumor that Cosmo, the Malolo who disappeared on the night of the big fight, was tinkering around with the curse, though I don't know why."

"It would have been Cosmo's mount that I found dead today. I think that he was carrying the Sword."

"Yes, that's what you were saying. And I have to admit Cosmo may have been the best magician on either side in modern times. But I doubt that he got anywhere trying to revoke the curse, either. People still see mermaids."

"Indeed. Where, if I may ask, did you hear this rumor about Cosmo's working on the mermaid curse?"

The Tyrant shrugged. "One hears things sometimes among the servants." It was obvious that Hissarlik was really not much interested in the subject.

Chilperic stood for a little time in silent thought. He was increasingly intrigued by the fact that this magician, Cosmo, was the same man who had so cravenly—or so wisely—terminated the Sword-throwing fight by absconding with the Sword. But Chilperic made no comment on that fact now.

"So, what about the mermaids?" he asked at last. "With your permission, my friend, I would like to have some of them searching the bottom of the river for the Sword as soon as possible."

"Very well. We can go down to the river and call some of them up for you." The Tyrant drummed with his fingers on the arms of the old chair, making no move to get up. "Boats go out to their island more or less regularly. Usually someone in the clan here takes them some food every day or two. We should take food, too. It might work better than such magic as we have available."

"Food?" Chilperic had thought of mermaids as being somehow completely self-supporting.

"Well, as I understand it, having spent their childhood ashore in villages, sleeping under roofs, and eating in most cases from some kind of plates, even when they grow tails they remain reluctant to bite raw fish and chew on snails they've just grubbed up out of the mud. At the same time, since they can't get about on land, cooking and housekeeping in the traditional ways present them with certain difficulties."

"Yes. Now that I think about it, I suppose they would."

"So, in return for some real food, or at least for certain things that pass for real food in the villages, the fishgirls provide us with a few pearls. Or other valuables if they find any. It's a sporadic kind of barter, that happens when both parties have an urge to trade. No really considerable wealth is involved."

"I see. How many mermaids do you suppose will show up when you summon them?"

Hissarlik shrugged his shoulders. "I suppose we'll get a dozen if we're lucky. As I said, there's a minor control spell that will summon them, or at last those who are within range, to attend us at the water's edge. It's related to the spell we use to call up mermaids when we want to sell or rent them out to visiting magicians, or to traveling shows. We rent them, usually. The creatures seldom live beyond the age of thirty, so there's no great bargain for a purchaser in buying one. When we have them at the shore we can give them orders, and bribe them with food. But as I warned you earlier, the magic for obedience is unreliable, and the orders we give them are seldom or never carried out just as we would wish. So, you see, the curse has never been of much value in a military way."

Chilperic brushed aside the problems associated with the regular mermaid trade. "You keep harping on the idea that they'll be unreliable as searchers."

"I'm afraid they will." Hissarlik hesitated. "And then—suppose they do find this Sword."

"Yes?"

"Well then, suppose one of them found it and instead of turning it in decided to try to use it."

"Is that what's bothering you? Consider that if Farslayer does lie at the bottom of the river, one of the fishgirls is likely to discover it there anyway."

"Oh." It was obvious from the Tyrant's sudden change of expression that he hadn't thought of that.

Chilperic pressed his new advantage. "So, it should help if I offer a reward to the fishgirl who brings it to us. And if at the same time I threaten punishment of any who try to conceal the Sword or dispose of it in any other way."

Hissarlik looked reluctantly ready to agree.

"They are at least moderately intelligent, are they not?"

"Hey?"

"The mermaids, man, the mermaids." There were limits to Chilperic's patience.

"Oh yes. As intelligent as any other peasant. Very well, then, let's go." And Hissarlik got to his feet.

Within an hour a small party, consisting of Hissarlik, Chilperic, and an escort of militia, had formed and had moved on to the riverbank, where several boats were being made available for the short jaunt to Mermaids' Island.

"Hissarlik, my friend?"

"Yes?"

"Is there any real advantage in our going out to the island? Can we not lure the creatures, and speak to them, just as successfully from here on shore?"

"Well, it might take a trifle longer that way—but yes, I suppose we can."

"Then let us do so." A handful of soldiers from the Senones Home Guard were standing by, ready to offer armed protection during the boat trip to the island, just in case some of the Malolo forces should be encountered on the island or on the water. But Chilperic, sniffing the air and eyeing suspiciously the fishing boats already on the river, had decided that he would rather not trust in the protective abilities of the Home Guard. He could of course call up the demon for protection, but his reluctance to depend entirely upon that power continued.

"I suppose we can do it just as well from shore. And perhaps we ought to wait for Megara anyway," said Hissarlik vaguely, turning away from the boat he had been about to enter.

Anselm had joined them, and was now serving as stand-in magician. He began to cast a spell. Within a quarter of an hour three or four of the underwater creatures had appeared in the water near shore, where they paddled about looking surprised, as if wondering why they had come here. Within an hour there were about a dozen, and these were all the mermaids that were likely to attend, according to Hissarlik.

A couple of the creatures sat on the muddy shoreline, while the others swam about. By now they all looked sullenly unwilling to be here.

Chilperic had to admit they were all lithe and attractive young women from the waist up. When he was assured that no more were likely to arrive, he stood up on the bank and spoke to them, describing the missing Sword, and promising to heal all of them of their affliction if one of them could bring him such a weapon. Their reaction was subdued; he could not tell to what extent his promise was believed.

So he took care, before dismissing them, and while the food from the hampers was being thrown to them, to threaten them with his demon if none of them did bring him the Sword he sought. He let them see the demon to convince them that it was no empty threat—and this time he got the reaction that he sought.

11

THE mermaid named Black Pearl had attended the gathering on the northern shore, more out of curiosity than from any compulsion by the feeble magic of Anselm Senones. She had listened to the arrogant strange man who spoke from the bank after Anselm, but she had not been much impressed by either his promises or his threats. At least not until the demon appeared to give a brief demonstration of its powers. Naturally the people on the north bank wanted the Sword, but they, or their late parents, were the same people who had sold Black Pearl into slavery, and she was not inclined to help them get anything they wanted now. Besides, if she had known where the Sword was, she would have taken it to Zoltan.

When the demon-master had finished his threats and the feeble magic of Anselm had relaxed its grip, Black Pearl had slipped away from the other mermaids, into the swift-flowing depths of the Tungri. And now she was on the south shore. Swimming and scrambling, she was struggling with great difficulty to make headway against a roaring and shallow rush of water. With hands and fins and tail she labored to ascend the rocky bed of a small stream.

This particular stream, much faster than the creek Zoltan had followed on his way to meet her, came gushing down the mountain through a narrow little canyon in the south side of the river gorge. The mouth of this brook, where it poured into the Tungri, was less than a kilometer from the hermit's house high on the irregular slope above. That house was still invisible from the place where the young mermaid squirmed and struggled.

On this spring day the little stream had been augmented by melting snow in the high country, yet still there were stretches in which its depth was insufficient to keep afloat a swimming creature of the mermaid's size. Black Pearl, in the form to which she had been condemned by enchantment, was only a little smaller than she would have been as a young woman with two legs.

Even this close to the stream's mouth she had already encountered an especially difficult spot. Here, where the water spread out into a mere corrugated sheet stretched over a rocky bed, it was impossible for any creature of her size to swim. Pausing in her efforts, lying on her side in the rushing shallows, she reached for the amulet that hung from a thin chain about her neck, and muttered a few soft words.

Almost unwillingly Black Pearl had memorized the words of the spell, after hearing Cosmo recite it countless times in the secret grotto. Perhaps he would be surprised, she thought now, to see that his magic worked for her alone almost as well as it had ever worked for him. Perhaps he would be surprised to know that it worked away from the grotto as well.

Immediately the spell had its effect. In a puff of watery mist her mermaid tail was gone, replaced by pale but very human-looking hips and legs. Shakily Black Pearl stood up, nakedly vulnerable now to the cold water and completely human. A young woman's body, perfectly normal in appearance, poised now upon two bare and very human feet.

Stepping carefully and with difficulty, yet trying to make the best speed she could, she walked forward over the rough rocks, muttering prayers to all the gods that she had ever heard of.

Barely had Black Pearl reached the next deep pool upstream before the strength of the spell she had just recited collapsed under the burden of the greater magic it labored to counteract. The forces that had for the space of a few breaths maintained her body in a normal human form abruptly dissipated. In an instant, metamorphosis reversed itself. Feet and legs were returned in the twinkling of an eye into the fishtail that she had worn for the past five years, since the age of twelve. She fell with a great splash.

But still she was able to make progress. Here, and upstream for some distance she had yet to discover, there ran a channel deep enough to support her finned body as she swam. Once more she could fight the current with her fins and tail—until she reached the next stretch where the channel disappeared.

Several times during the next few minutes of the mermaid's upstream struggle she was forced to use the secret counterspell and amulet. The trouble was that the effect of the counterspell faded rapidly with frequent repetition. The time Black Pearl was able to spend in fully human form was limited to a few minutes at most with each use of the amulet, and the power had to be carefully husbanded. Only rarely and infrequently could she escape the deforming impact of accursed Senones magic, and regain for a heartbreakingly small time the shape that would have been hers in normal life. And each interval of relief cost her more and more in psychic effort to achieve. It would be necessary to let the power in the amulet lie fallow for days, weeks, or even months before the maximum, comparatively long periods of full humanity could be attained once more. She had husbanded the power for many days before attempting this ascent, where she expected that it would be needed in its fullest form.

She was determined to tell her secrets to someone, and it certainly would not be those slave dealers on the north side of the river. Nor would it, could it, be Zoltan. Never that.

Months ago, Cosmo, lying with Black Pearl in the secret grotto upon a bed of moss and furs, with his own gift of her true woman's legs clasped round him, had murmured into her ear again and again that the secrecy was part of the spell. That if she revealed the magical power of changing to another living soul, that power might be taken from her, beyond even his wizard's power to restore it.

At that time Black Pearl had assured her lover fiercely that she would never tell. And until now she had kept the secret safe, though several times she had come close to telling Soft Ripple everything.

But today she intended to tell someone. Her confidant would not be her only real friend, Soft Ripple. Because Soft Ripple could be of no help to her, and Black Pearl desperately needed help. The secret had developed a monstrous complication.

In the intervals when Black Pearl could use her tail and swim, her progress upstream was swift. But now already she was entering yet another stretch of the stream where the water grew too shallow for swimming. A few moments later Black Pearl was on her magically restored feet again and walking. This time, while the change to normalcy still held, she took a moment to look down at herself, studying fearfully the near-flatness of her woman's belly, pale and goose-bumped now with cold.

So far the enlargement was minimal, almost undetectable. But she was more firmly convinced than ever before that she was pregnant.

Cosmo the magician, who had made this desperate upstream journey possible for Black Pearl, was—or had been—also Cosmo the man, who had made the journey necessary. The Malolo magician had been her lover for several months before the night of many killings, the night he had disappeared. Black Pearl was going to have to assume now that he was dead.

Far less than any ordinary woman did Black Pearl have any means of knowing with any certainty what went on inside her own belly, down there on the borderline of magic, the region of her body where five years ago the ancestral curse had imposed itself. Down there, where a true woman would have a womb, what did a fishgirl have? For that matter, what organs did a real fish possess? Daughter of fisherfolk as she was, she could recall no clear image. Her mind refused to think about it.

One fact was obvious. Mermaid bodies were not equipped, any more than the bodies of real fish were, for anything like human pregnancy or human birth. What was going to happen to her as her pregnancy advanced, if she did not get some effective help from somewhere, Black Pearl did not know, could only guess. But each imagined possibility that suggested itself to her was more horrible than the last. She could only be certain that the outcome was going to be monstrous, unnatural, and fatal to herself and to the unborn as well.

And one more thing was very clear to her. Never before in the history of any village, Black Pearl was quite sure, had any mermaid ever become pregnant.

For more than a month now she had been experiencing dull aching pains in her abdomen, pains that could be relieved only by her assuming the fully human form, and which returned the instant she again became half fish. She had been on the verge of telling Cosmo about her difficulty, though she feared his reaction. And then, about a month ago, on the night when manor folk had slaughtered one another across the river, he had disappeared. Terrible as it was, the only assumption she dared make was that her magician-lover was dead.

Within hours of the great slaughter, the news had spread rapidly, first in its essentials and then in its details, among the peasants and fisherfolk along both shores. From some of these legged people the story had diffused quickly to the mermaids. Black Pearl was soon aware that there was no one left in the Malolo clan who might provide effective medical help. Black Pearl didn't think there were any very capable people left in the Senones clan either, and anyway she wouldn't expect anything better from them than being sold into slavery.

So far Black Pearl had not hinted to anyone, not even Soft Ripple—and most certainly not Zoltan—of her fear that she was pregnant. Such a claim would have made no sense to either of them anyway. Neither of them had any idea that even a temporary reversal of a mermaid's condition was now possible.

Oh, if only it could be possible that Cosmo was not dead! Word passed along from the Malolo household servants had said that his body was not among those arrayed in the underground vault, where all the other dead were said to be gathered, still magically preserved. For several hours, for a few days even, that reported absence had given Black Pearl hope, and the hope had been confirmed by Zoltan. But now she realized that Cosmo's absence really proved nothing. If her lover was not dead, where was he? If he had fled the valley permanently, he might as well be dead as far as she was concerned.

With each day that passed without word from her magician-lover, Black Pearl became more and more fearfully certain that she was never going to see him again. There were still occasional moments when she nursed hopes that he was alive, but those hopes were growing more and more desperate.

In the midst of her growing despair, her thoughts had fastened on the hermit Gelimer. Black Pearl's only real hope at this point was that the hermit might be able and willing to do something to help her with her pregnancy. She wanted desperately to save the unborn child, which was Cosmo's child too, if that were at all possible. And if she could be granted some assurance that the child was not monstrous. But failing that, she still wanted at least to have a chance of saving her own life. She knew now that at least a temporary cure of her condition was attainable; and now also Zoltan had come to seek her out and had said he loved her. She had begun to forget Zoltan more than a year ago, and he had passed out of her thoughts completely for a time. Now Zoltan offered hope. But if he ever learned that she was pregnant . . .

Black Pearl had never seen the hermit Gelimer, but now she had nowhere else to turn. For all of her young life she had heard that he was a good man, one who often went out of his way to help people. The stories told in the villages said that Gelimer had more than once saved folk who were dying of cold and exposure in the mountains. In Black Pearl's mind this was good evidence that the hermit must possess some medical skills.

Now, compelled yet again to use her amulet and the weary, fading counterspell, she changed her form once more. At a place where only human hands and feet could climb, she briefly bypassed the water altogether, walking on dry land. Again the sun was warm but the breeze numbingly chill against the wet and suddenly vulnerable nakedness of her human skin.

Without warning, moments earlier than she had anticipated it, the spontaneous reversion overtook her. Abruptly deprived of feet and legs, Black Pearl fell, rolling fortunately toward the stream and landing in a small pool that was deep enough to cushion the impact of her body before it struck sharp rocks. Now suddenly the water felt comfortably warm again, on fish skin and woman skin alike.

The hazards of her journey were increasing. There was no way to exercise the least degree of control over the spontaneous relapse, no way to guess from one breath to the next exactly when it was going to strike her.

Once more the water was deep enough. She swam upstream, only to find almost immediately that her way was blocked again by a stretch of shallow water. It seemed hardly possible that any fish bigger than a minnow could swim upstream through this obstacle. She was going to have to wait here, all but helpless, letting the change-power of the amulet rest again until it had recharged itself sufficiently to let her bring her human legs back into existence. Then she would be able to rise and walk on them once more.

And, if she was pregnant, as she was sure she was, and if by some miracle she could carry the child to full term, and by some greater miracle give birth—then what kind of monster would she produce, gripped by this evil magic as she was? Perhaps the question was meaningless. But Black Pearl had had dreams of late, dreams coming to her below the surface of the river as she slept, nightmares in which she felt and saw herself giving birth to clouds of fish eggs, or to a swarm of lively tadpoles.

Even while she waited to continue her climb toward Gelimer's house, her mind sought feverishly for someone besides the hermit to whom she might turn for help. But she could think of no one. She could imagine Zoltan's reaction to the news of her pregnancy, and it would not be good. The remnants of her own leg-walking family in her home village had practically disowned her on the day, five years ago, when the evil change came upon her. It was a not uncommon reaction among mermaids' families. And even if her relatives had been willing to help her now, what could they do? They were as lacking in magical powers as they were in mundane wealth.

If only Cosmo were not dead . . . once more Black Pearl reminded herself sternly that such wishes were hopeless, useless.

But suppose that the holy hermit, when she reached him—she could not admit to herself that she might fail today to reach his house—suppose he were to refuse her help? She might be able to pay him with a pearl from a riverbottom clam, or perhaps a gemstone or even a lump of gold obtained at the same source—supposing she could work a minor miracle and find one. Such treasures failing, there was still her body that she might offer him, half-human as it was, and the few doubtful minutes for which she might be fully human. Black Pearl did not know what attitude the hermit, who had evidently chosen to live without women, might take toward an offering like that.

There was only one way to find out. Black Pearl swam and climbed, and fell and climbed again. Her capacity to change was once more almost totally exhausted. Eventually she reached a point from which she could see, still dishearteningly high and distant, what she took to be the hermit's dwelling. It was, at least, a fallen great tree with a stump that looked as if it had a shuttered window in one side, and so she had heard Gelimer's house described.

But the distance still remaining to the house was crushing. On starting upstream from the Tungri the mermaid had had no idea that the hermit's dwelling was so far up the mountainside, or she might never have attempted to reach it. But no, she'd probably have made the effort anyway. Because she had no other choice.

Now once more on the verge of despair, Black Pearl heard a whining and howling, an almost doglike yapping. Looking up in alarm, she beheld a watchbeast shuffling bearlike along a small ridge that paralleled the stream.

She recognized the breed of animal at once. Two or three times before in her short life Black Pearl had seen watchbeasts. Years ago, when she'd had legs and could walk uphill anytime she felt like it, the folk at Malolo manor had had a pair of such beasts to guard their house.

Now the beast had sighted her, or heard or scented her, which came to the same thing. Running for a little distance beside the stream, the animal howled at the unprecedented sight and at the noise of a mermaid's renewed struggling here. Then the watchbeast turned away and ran off, disappearing almost at once among the rocks and scattered vegetation of the uphill slope.

Black Pearl, still unable for the time being to use her amulet effectively, could do nothing but wait for what might happen next. Her hopes rose slightly when the watchbeast reappeared in the distance, still climbing away from her. Obviously the animal was going to the high tree-stump house, and the mermaid could hope that it was going to bring its master to her aid.

When Gelimer heard Geelong's clamor just outside his door he was considerably surprised. That particular sound had always meant a traveler was in distress, an unlikely situation in such fine weather as this.

Relatively unlikely, but of course not impossible. Hastening to follow the anxious beast, the hermit left his house and garden and soon reached the side of the pool in which Black Pearl was now resting.

The sight of a mermaid was so remote from anything the hermit had expected that for several moments he stood on the bank gazing at her stupidly, as if paralyzed. Adding something to Gelimer's difficulty was the fact that he had never spoken with a mermaid before. But her face looked not only intelligent but frightened, and he could only assume that she was much like other people. At last he spoke.

"Young woman—are you in need of help?"

She gazed up at him boldly though fearfully. "I am," she said, with the water sloshing spasmodically around her silver tail. "My need is very great. And I have come to you, come up all the way from the river, to try to get the help I need."

"You've come to me?" Gelimer, still somewhat bewildered by this unheard-of presence so far up the side of the mountain, ran a hand over his bald head. He felt himself to be at a total loss. "I will do what I can. But what can I do?"

The mermaid sat up straighter in the water, with her tail now in front, propping her torso erect on both hands extended behind her. "Sir, if you will only wait a few moments, it will be easier for you to understand my difficulty. I will demonstrate as well as explain. Wait while I rest, and then watch carefully. And I will show you a great wonder."

"Then I will wait," Gelimer said simply, and seated himself upon a handy rock.

A quarter of an hour later, Gelimer had witnessed the coming and going of the change in the young woman's body. Having seen what he would not otherwise have believed, he tended to believe the rest of the amazing story she had told him.

He had changed his position by the time the story was finished, and was seated upon a different rock, handier to the stream, with Geelong crouching contentedly near his side. Frowning in deep thought, the hermit asked: "Will you describe to me this Cosmo Malolo you say has disappeared? I seldom have any contact with the leaders of the clans, and I have never met any of the younger ones."

When he had heard the mermaid's description of her magician-lover, Gelimer's frown deepened, because now he was sure. The traveler who had called himself Chilperic had given a false name for the man that he was seeking. That man, Gelimer's tragic early visitor, was certainly the same man that this mermaid sought, no doubt with better reason.

Gelimer knew a little more of the truth now, and he knew it was his duty to tell Black Pearl that her lover was certainly dead. But as far as he could see, that truth would be of no benefit to her; it would only deprive her of hope. And if he, Gelimer, were to reveal that he knew where Cosmo lay buried, the mermaid along with other folk would justly suspect that he knew where the Sword was hidden also.

But if he dared not tell the truth to this girl who had appealed to him for help, then what could he do for her?

"I am no magician," he confessed at last. "No real healer, either. If there were any solid help that I could give you, child, I would be glad to do so. But I fear there is nothing."

For several minutes after she heard these words Black Pearl simply sat in the water, staring up at the man she had been thinking of as her last hope. Her very human cheeks had dried in the breeze since she emerged from the water, and they stayed dry; the destruction of hope had been too sudden and complete to result in tears.

The silence stretched on, until at last Gelimer could bear her empty gaze no longer. "I will try," he promised, "to find magical assistance for you somehow."

"Oh sir. Thank you, sir." The words sounded almost devoid of emotion; it was hard for Gelimer to tell if she were only being polite to him in turn, or not. "What can I give you in return?"

Gelimer thought, and sighed. "At the moment, I can think of nothing for you to give me. It may be that I will be able to give you nothing, either. I fear that it very well may be so. And yet I do pledge that I will try."

They exchanged a few more words, and the hermit promised that he would meet the mermaid, at a certain time, at a certain place at the river's edge. Years had passed since he had gone that far down into the gorge, but it was a place he could remember well enough.

Then, after bestowing Ardneh's blessing as best he could, he turned and began climbing wearily back to his house, his watchbeast moving subdued at his side.

With the edge of her despair at least somewhat blunted by the hermit's kindly attention to her troubles, and his conditional promise, Black Pearl pulled herself together as best she could, and started on her way back to the mouth of the stream. The passage downhill, with the swift current's help, was physically much easier than the ascent, and she progressed quickly.

Deep in her own thoughts, she had by now ceased to pay much attention to her surroundings, and she was within thirty meters of the two mercenaries before she saw them.

Calling to her to stop and wait for them, calling to each other to run her down, howling their lust and wonder and delight on finding her almost helpless before them, the two armed and shabby men moved on quick legs to cut her off from the broad river and freedom.

Black Pearl had not seen such men in the valley before, and the strangeness of their appearance only added to her terror. They were dressed unlike any of the native men on either side of the river, wearing scraps of alien-looking armor and green scarves round their throats, and both were well armed.

The men were trying to make their voices soft when they called to her, but the look of their faces belied the softness. In complete panic, her worries about tomorrow swallowed up in immediate terror, Black Pearl turned around and threw her tired body again into the struggle to ascend the stream. One hope, though a feeble one, lay in reaching one of the deeper pools above, where she might possibly lie concealed underwater until the men gave up their efforts and went away. Her only other hope, also a faint one, was that the hermit or the watchbeast might hear the sound of the chase and come to her aid.

At first the two men, being forced to climb or wade among sharp rocks in rushing water, fell behind a little. But then the banks of the stream opened up again, and her pursuers could run, and they gained on her rapidly.

Almost at once a fortunate curve in the stream took her temporarily out of their sight.

Black Pearl plunged into the best available pool, and lay as still as she could on the bottom, suspending her breath in mermaid fashion. She would have no problem remaining so for hours if necessary.

She thought that this was probably the deepest pool she had encountered in her struggle to ascend the stream. Still, the surface of the water was less than a meter above her head. Above her was a small greenish circle of sky; swift fluctuations in the current prevented her seeing more. Distantly she could hear her pursuers, climbing about somewhere on the bank nearby. The water was so clear that she knew she would not be invisible to them if they were to look carefully in the right place; but she would do the best she could. Quietly she turned over, lying face down now, giving them the back of her head to look at, streaming dark hair instead of a pale face.

Hardly had Black Pearl turned over before the faint gleam of something artificial on the stream's bottom caught her eye. Something in the straight and steely look of the thing caught at her memory immediately. Once before, in water vastly deeper and colder than this stream, she had made this same discovery . . .

Moving her fingers with great care in the vicinity of those suggested edges—she had had experience of their unnatural sharpness—Black Pearl brushed away the bottom sand until an ebony handle came into view.

Obviously the Sword had not been dropped here carelessly. Rather it had been buried deliberately, sunk carefully into the bottom under layers of head-sized rocks. And not only buried, but wedged firmly into place in a niche between fixed edges of stone, so that no current in the stream would ever wash it away. But fish, or some other creatures of the stream, must have been nibbling at what had once been a sheath of dark leather, which being only mundane material was almost completely gone by now. The removal of that dark covering allowed a gleam of steel to shine through.

The metal of the Sword itself was just as she remembered it, anything but mundane. There was the white target-symbol on the hilt. The mermaid had a good look at the weapon as she drew it from the hiding place. As she had expected, it showed not the slightest trace of rust or corrosion.

Now feet came stamping nearby, on the bank above her. Black Pearl could hear the voices of the two men almost clearly, and then their shouted triumph at the moment they discovered her in her inadequate hiding place.

"Look here!"

"I'll stir her out!" And a man's hands tossed in a rock that struck the scaly armor of her lower belly, just as she turned face up again; the water cushioned some of the missile's impact.

Black Pearl's head and shoulders came up out of the water, her mouth screaming, the Sword's hilt clutched in both her hands. This was not the first time she had held Farslayer in her hands. But now, for the first time, she could feel the Sword's power come suddenly to life.

The two men were standing on opposite sides of the watercourse, both of them downstream from Black Pearl, one about five meters from her, the other twice as far. When she sat up both mercenaries froze, transfixed momentarily by the impressive sight of the unexpected weapon. Then the hand of the nearer man moved to his waist, and in a moment he had drawn his own short sword.

Black Pearl screamed at him, and willed his death. The black hilt seemed to tear itself free from her clutched fingers, the weapon lunging outward of its own volition. A snarling howl of magic, louder than her own scream, resounded in the little canyon, accompanied by a brief rainbow slash of light that brushed aside the drawn blade in the man's hand. That weapon's owner, his face reflecting surprise, staggered with the Sword of Vengeance stuck clean through him. Then he toppled forward, dead before he splashed into the water.

Yelling in mortal terror, the dead man's companion turned away from the mermaid and took to his heels, bounding in panic down the mountainside.

Black Pearl was already going after the Sword again, struggling to drag her body through the shallows. Despite the thrust of current that now worked in her favor, moving those few meters seemed to take forever. Then, when she had gripped the ebony hilt again, another eternity elapsed in the course of her effort to twist and wrench Farslayer free from the lifeless body of her enemy. The victim's will seemed still alive, embodied in those dead eyes that stared alternately at her and past her with the movement of his head caused by her tugging on the steel between his ribs.

By now the mermaid was sobbing with exertion, hate, and rage. As soon as she had Farslayer free, she threw it forth again, blindly and with all her strength.

"You—you tried to kill me!" she shrieked. The surviving mercenary was probably out of range of her voice; he was already long out of sight, and at the last moment Black Pearl was sure that the effort she was making was hopeless. A reprisal against those who had threatened her was not her only goal. She felt, more strongly than any craving for revenge, the need to keep the power of this Sword for herself, to bargain with.

But the thoughts of that last moment came too late to stop the Sword. For a second time the rainbow blur of power left her hands, again she heard the weapon briefly howling in the air. In the blinking of her eyes it was gone, this time somewhere out of her sight. Though that flight had been hard to follow, she thought the weapon's path had carried it straight downstream.

And again Black Pearl hurled herself splashing and floundering after it, through water too shallow for real swimming. The Sword, as a treasure she might bargain with, represented her only hope. She would go after Farslayer and recover it yet again.

Heedless of minor injuries inflicted by rocks in the shallow current, Black Pearl hurled herself downstream. Luck was with her. The easiest way for a man on foot, running down the slope, was the faint path that almost inevitably followed such a watercourse. In this case the man in his terror-stricken flight had not deviated from the path by more than a stride or two. The mermaid found him lying facedown, Farslayer's hilt and half its blade protruding from his armored back. The Sword had overtaken him from behind. When she turned him over, she looked at his face clearly for the first time, and saw, only now, that he was still a beardless youth.

Again Black Pearl went through the ghastly process of trying to extract Farslayer from a corpse. This time not only bone but armor, a light cuirass, gripped the blade. Her lack of feet and legs with which to brace herself while pulling added considerably to the difficulty of the job; but at least this time the face was turned away.

At last the ugly job was done.

There was nothing Black Pearl could do about concealing this body, or the other one upstream; they would simply have to lie where they had fallen.

The god-forged blade rinsed clean at once in the swift stream. Carrying the Sword ahead of her, gripping the hilt in both hands most of the time, Black Pearl started once more for deep water.

She wondered, now that she had a chance to think again, just how the Sword might have come to be hidden in the stream where she had found it. Might Cosmo himself have brought it there? Or could it have been the hermit's own doing? Had Gelimer known that Farslayer was concealed in the stream she sat in, even while he was talking to her?

In any case, the hermit had offered her little help. But give him credit for honesty at least. It was up to her to help herself. So she was not going to hand this thing of power over to anyone now, except in exchange for the assistance she needed.

Zoltan would be the one to deal with. Bring him the Sword, and let him think that she was madly in love with him, let him believe whatever he already believed. Obviously it was going to take time to conclude any such arrangement. Her immediate need was to hide the Sword somewhere. Black Pearl proceeded back downstream, moving carefully. Sometimes she had to use her amulet and murmur the secret words, and stand and walk with the naked Sword held awkwardly before her naked body, both of her smallish hands grasping the black hilt. Walking, she held the weapon very carefully, that she might not fall upon it when the sudden shape change overtook her and she fell.

As she descended the long slope she pondered furiously on the question of where to hide the Sword for the time being. Immediately there came to her mind the islands, and the riverbottom. But she did not wish ever to go to Magicians' Island again if she could help it. Unless Cosmo . . .

And Mermaids' Island was generally populated by other mermaids. They, her mermaid sisters, were also forever searching the riverbottom hoping to discover things of value.

Where to hide it, then?

Now Black Pearl remembered passing, on her way uphill, a certain hollow tree, a leaning trunk all twisted and decayed but not yet fallen, that curved almost over this roaring stream down near its mouth. But a moment later she rejected the idea—inside that tree Farslayer would be far more easily accessible to walking people than to her.

When she came to the tree, however, Black Pearl had been able to think of no better place, and changed her mind again. Here the dancing brook that she was following plunged through its own miniature gorge, between high walls of rugged rock. Few people would come walking here, and none could ride.

The spot was almost gloomy even at midday. Yet another struggle was necessary for her to heave her body out of the water, getting the rounded thickness of her fishtail onto a rock, bracing herself there in a sitting position while she lifted the Sword toward the dark cavity of the gnarled bole.

Just as she did so she paused, listening intently. Someone—or something—was approaching. With the sound of a great wind.

12

WHEN the hermit had concluded his talk with the mermaid, and Black Pearl had begun her struggling return downstream, Gelimer, his forehead set in wrinkles and his mind engaged with problems, trudged back uphill toward his house. The poor ensorcelled lass on her way back to her deepwater home was going to pass right over the place where he'd hidden the Sword. Well, when he'd chosen the place in which to conceal Farslayer, he couldn't possibly have foreseen that mermaids were going to come crawling up the stream bed. This one must have passed over the Sword once already on her way upstream, and without noticing anything. Gelimer considered that he had hidden the Sword well, and he hadn't been back to look at the place since doing so. For anyone to see him taking an interest in that spot now might result in Farslayer's discovery. So, the Sword was going to have to stay where it was.

Ah, but the poor innocent child! What a terrible situation to be in. What could he do for her?

Not until after he had climbed three quarters of the way back to his house, trudging slowly, did it occur to the hermit that he might have escorted Black Pearl back down to the river. Well, too late now to think of that. She had managed the uphill struggle somehow, and doubtless she could manage going down.

Since he was no magician, it appeared to Gelimer that there was not much he could do for the mermaid's benefit, except to offer her some probably foolish hope, and let her know at least that she had a friend in the world.

As he was approaching his door, the hermit felt the demon's presence somewhere in the air, and thought that this time it was passing closer than before.

* * *

Gelimer had not been back in his house for more than a quarter of an hour when something occurred that drew him out of doors again.

The hermit had left both the inner and outer doors of his entrance standing open to the mild day, and it was a peculiar wisp of sound that entered through the doorway to draw him out. The sound was almost too faint to be heard at all, but there was a strangeness about it that caught at his attention.

Listening, waiting for the sound to come again, Gelimer stood in the doorway of his small house. He tasted the air, rubbed a hand over his bald head, and scanned the sky. A few times in his life, a very few times and long ago, he had been able to see moving across the firmament some of the powers that served the great magicians. But today he was able to see nothing magical in the sky, nothing at all but a few clouds. He called for Geelong, thinking that if there were strange sounds to be tracked down, the watchbeast would be very useful. But there was no response to the hermit's call.

He was still loitering in his doorway when the strange sound came again, a high-pitched, briefly sustained squealing. Something mechanical, the hermit thought now, a cartwheel needing grease perhaps. Of course that couldn't be right, there were never any carts on these rough trails. But—

His concern, persistent and automatic, for the Sword drew him in the general direction of that weapon's hiding place when he left the house. Gelimer called again for Geelong as he walked, and he continued to listen for the strange noise to come again.

He had not walked forty meters from his door when a shift in the direction of the wind brought the mysterious squealing sound to him more distinctly. It was a high-pitched whining, only superficially mechanical. At bottom it was much more like the cry of some great animal in agony. And at the same time he heard it, the hermit detected a new whiff of the demon's presence, which reached him through none of the usual channels of the senses.

Ignoring the deep command of instinct that urged him to run away from that presence, Gelimer began instead to run toward it. Toward the place from which the sound came also.

A hundred meters of running, moving horizontally along the great slope of the mountain, were enough to bring him to a small patch or grove of stunted thorntrees. Trotting around to the far side of this tall thicket, Gelimer came suddenly in sight of Geelong. The watchbeast had somehow been nightmarishly elevated to twice or three times Gelimer's height above the ground, and all four of his limbs were spread out and pinned on tough thorny branches. Geelong's head was twisted to one side, whether voluntarily or not, so that he looked in the direction from which his master now approached. From the animal's open mouth drooled whitish foam all mixed with blood. The creature's lolling tongue was bitten halfway through. Geelong's eyes were open, and watched Gelimer. His lower belly had been opened also, as if with a dull blade in the beginning of a disembowelment. More blood, much more, dripped from his belly, and a slender rope of gut was hanging halfway to the ground.

Gelimer struggled to find disbelief, but was unable to achieve it. He swayed on his feet, staring helplessly at the horror above him. The noise coming from Geelong's throat swelled up again into a ghastly howl.

At last able to break free of his paralysis, the hermit ran forward. As Gelimer ran he pulled from his belt the hatchet he had lately taken to carrying with him everywhere. If he could only chop free some of those small branches, the ones whose thorns were . . .

A nearby presence, which until now had managed to conceal itself, now swelled up palpably around him. It was a smothering sickness, and a physical force as well. Gelimer's hatchet fell from his hand. He fell staggering back from his first foothold on a tree, to stand choking and almost blinded.

"What do you seek here among the thorntrees, little man?" The voice, sounding like nothing so much as a deafening chorus of insects, came blasting into the hermit's ears. It surrounded him and forced its way into his mind. "You must be careful with that weapon! Otherwise you might do harm to your faithful pet."

And now Gelimer was seized by a presence that seemed to have become as material as his own body, and vastly stronger. Forces grabbed him by an arm, whirled him about effortlessly, and sent him tumbling over rocks and down a slope. Oblivious to minor damage, he stumbled to his feet, and faced uphill again.

Some force like a great wind was shaking the thorntrees now, swaying them out of phase, so that the bloody living body pinned aloft in them was wracked anew. The wound in the belly stretched and oozed and gaped. Once more the horrible noise went up from Geelong's throat, louder than before.

Dazed and blinking, Gelimer looked carefully around him, trying to recognize this world in which he found himself. He turned slowly, making a full circle on uncertain feet, questioning all the corners of the universe as to how such things could be.

He held his fingers in his ears, but that was no more effective than closing his eyes.

"Do you not like the music that your pet makes, little man?" There was no shutting that music out, or the voice of the demon, either. The question was followed by a great hideous rush of what must have been its laughter.

"Do you not like the song?"

Stumbling and choking and weeping, still trying uselessly to shut out the sounds of Geelong's agony, the man went staggering away. Now his feet, without any conscious planning on his part, were bearing him at an angle downhill, toward the place where a month ago he had concealed the Sword.

When Gelimer encountered the rushing mountain stream he tumbled into it, landing on all fours. But he lurched to his feet and went on again at once, following the stream bed downhill, unaware of the cold water and the rocks that hurt him when he fell again.

Something in him knew that the Sword was already gone, even before he looked in the place where he had hidden it. He knew, he felt the truth of the missing Sword at his first sight of the dead man. The corpse, armed and costumed like a poor mercenary, lay some ten meters downstream from the deep pool, crumpled on his side in the shallows, with his body jammed against some rocks by the rush of current.

Something in Gelimer already knew that the Sword was gone. But still he plunged heedlessly into the pool to look for Farslayer, driving his head and shoulders underwater in the deep pool, groping with both hands for the bottom—

A grip that felt like the clawed forepaws of a large dragon seized Gelimer from behind. The man was wrenched from the water, tossed rolling over and over on the hard path along the bank. Even before he stopped rolling, the demon's quasimaterial presence had let him go, had gone plunging past him into the stream. A fountain of water, a geyser of rocks and sand and mud, erupted out of the pool that had been the hiding place. But no Sword. No Sword came flying out, because Farslayer was already gone.

Gelimer was just trying to get back onto his feet when the demon like a foul wind came rushing back to once more give him its full attention. It raged and struck at him, knocked him once more spinning on the ground, so that his head rang with the impact, his arms and legs were newly bruised and bloody.

Its voice of a thousand insects shrieked at him. "What have you done with it, treacherous human? You pretended to have hidden Farslayer in this little pool, pretended to be trying to get it now, but it is not here. What have you really done with it?"

Gelimer was no longer capable of thinking clearly. Even had he wanted to answer the demon's stupid shrieking, he would hardly have been able to speak. He could only cower down and wait for what might happen to him next.

Unexpectedly, the demon-shrieking stopped. There was a silent swelling of the cheated rage surrounding the man. But before the storm of this renewed wrath could break upon him, there came a pause. A break, a distraction, as if the demon's attention had been abruptly drawn from Gelimer to something or someone else.

And in the next moment, the ghastly thing was gone.

Gone completely, to what distance or for what period of time the hermit could not have guessed. He only knew that it had let him go. Sobbing, Gelimer collapsed.

13

O N the day of Black Pearl's visit to Gelimer, and at the very time
when she reached a decision on where to hide the Sword, five
men were riding in a fishing boat out near the middle of the Tungri.
The boat was making progress steadily upstream. The two who worked
the oars were fishermen, enlisted today as rowers by the new chief of
the manor above their village, Bonar Malolo. That chief, young Bonar
himself, was sitting in the stern of the boat, beside his new guest and
acquaintance Prince Mark of Tasavalta. Up in the prow perched Zoltan,
who talked and sang almost continuously, hoping that his voice would
be heard and recognized below the surface, and that he thus would be
successful in calling up a certain mermaid from the stream.

Yesterday not much had been accomplished, besides finishing the
repair of the hole carved in the manor's wall by Stonecutter. The prince
and Ben, weary from a long journey and a night's vigil, had slept and
eaten and enjoyed the manor's hospitality.

Today the strong man Ben, along with the magician Gesner, the Lady
Yambu, and Bonar's two sisters, had remained in the Malolo manor. It
was by no means certain that the mercenaries had departed the area for
good; and Mark had wanted to leave someone he trusted in case another winged messenger should seek him there with news.

Bonar had listened doubtfully to the explanation given him early this
morning by his powerful guests, as to why it was necessary to come out
here and hunt mermaids today, but at last he had accepted it. It was
something to do with finding the Sword again, and he was all in favor
of that.

A point that had come up for discussion earlier was the question of
who was going to get the Sword if and when they did manage to
recover it. Prince Mark had already explained that he had a deep interest in retaining possession of Farslayer; in fact, that he had no intention

of accepting anything less. Mark's princely rank, his firmness even tempered as it was with courtesy, and the one Sword he already wore combined to give force to his expressed wishes. The effect was augmented by the presence at the prince's side of Ben, who when he chose to do so could look as formidable as a whole squad of mercenaries.

Bonar in fact was overwhelmed by his new allies. He pined in silence to possess the Sword again for himself, but somehow when he opened his mouth he found himself agreeing to the terms which the prince outlined for him—in return for giving up all Malolo claims upon the Sword of Vengeance, he and the remainder of his clan would receive (at some future time) wealth, prestige in the association of his house with that of Tasavalta, and perhaps, at a later date, some military aid as well.

The deal had been effectively concluded on shore some time ago, but still it rankled. Sitting in the boat Bonar took courage and began to murmur: "Still—all that may be very well, but still I think that my family and I ought to rightfully be able to retain *some* rights in that Sword for ourselves. Even if we allow it to go with you for now. When we have succeeded in finding it, that is."

Prince Mark only looked at him. But Zoltan was ready to argue the point, and at the same time he was curious.

"Sir—Chief Bonar—when your family had that Sword in their hands before, the result to them, I would say, could hardly be counted as a great benefit. What would you do with Farslayer if you had it in your hands at this moment?"

Bonar frowned at the question. Then his frown cleared up. "You mean what target would I choose? I've thought about that, this past month. I'd pick that cowardly skunk Hissarlik, beyond a doubt. We've heard that he survived the night of killing, and I have no doubt that he's now become the clan chief of the Senones dogs. And I have no doubt that he's killed several of our people. He's probably killed more of us than anyone else who still survives over there."

"How do you know how many of your people he may have killed, sir? Forgive me, but I'm curious. You mean you have some way of telling, somehow . . . ?"

Bonar was scowling at Zoltan petulantly. "Well, if Hissarlik hasn't killed very many of us yet, he's certainly getting ready to do so. He's a Senones, isn't he?"

Mark was shaking his head lightly at Zoltan, but Zoltan wasn't ready to give up the argument. "All right. Say you did have Farslayer in your hands this very moment, and you killed Hissarlik with it. Zip. Like that. What's the next thing that would happen?"

"The next thing?"

"Well. I mean, someone over there will see Hissarlik fall, or find him dead, and then immediately pick the Sword up and kill *you* with it. Isn't that the way things went a month ago?"

Bonar's eyes lighted up, the eyes of a man who at last understands a line of questioning, and has an answer ready. "Ah! Yes, you see, that's where we made our mistake before. My sisters and I have talked about that. Next time we'll manage things the clever way. First decide on a specific target, and then wait for that target to be in the proper position, or lure him into it if necessary. By proper position I mean somewhere where we can get the Sword back quickly after we use it. It means being patient. Perhaps it means setting ambushes, which is always difficult. But you're perfectly right, there's no use in making your enemy the gift of such a weapon to use against you. Not if you can help it."

Mark smiled faintly. And now Zoltan did give up, at least for the time being.

But his questioning had prompted Bonar to ask a question of his own, addressed to Mark.

"Your Majesty—uh, sir . . ."

"Just call me Mark. 'Prince' will do if you really want to use a title."

"Ah, thank you, ah Mark. If you had the Sword in *your* hands at this moment, what target would you pick? This wizard Wood you keep warning us about, I suppose. But am I not correct? Wouldn't you try to arrange some kind of ambush first, get the Sword back to use again?"

Mark, shaking his head again, took thought. Then he answered seriously and courteously. "I certainly wouldn't hurl any weapon at Wood just now. He is still in possession of Shieldbreaker, so Farslayer would probably be destroyed. One way to get rid of the damned thing, I suppose. But certainly it would fail to kill him, as long as he holds the Sword of Force."

"Is getting rid of Swords such a problem, then?" Now Bonar was enviously eyeing Stonecutter, which Mark wore at his side.

"Believe me, there are times when it seems like a good idea to destroy one, or all of them. Though it's almost impossible. Perhaps that's what your cousin Cosmo had in mind when he rode off with Farslayer."

"Do you think so?" the Chief asked doubtfully. He appeared to be having a hard time digesting that idea.

Mark turned to Zoltan and said: "I mean to have a talk with that hermit you mentioned. We'll take our search for your mermaid out to the islands first if necessary, and then—"

One of the fishermen, rowing industriously, muttered something. From under frowning, shaggy brows he looked up and around the sky.

"What did you say, man?" Mark asked him sharply. "Something about demons?"

The shaggy brows contracted further. "Aye, sir. I'm saying they have been seen in the valley. And that there's a smell in the air just now, this moment, that I don't like."

Bonar started to ask: "Does the Sword you wear, Prince, give you some protection against—"

"Wait!" Mark gestured sharply for silence. Now he too was frowning up at the cloudless sky.

The other men in the boat looked at one another. To all of them, a pall of night and gloom and sickness seemed to be descending upon the sunlit water in the middle of the day.

None of the five men spoke. There was no need. Even those among them who had never before confronted a demon were in no doubt of what this was. One of the rowers, he who had just spoken, now dropped his oar. On trembling legs the man arose, meaning to cast himself overboard. But Zoltan's hand went out and fastened on the fisherman's wrist, and after a moment the terror-stricken one sank back onto his bench.

Zoltan knew something that none of the local people did.

The horror that had just arrived was now sitting, almost fully visible, upon the surface of the water nearby, confronting the five men huddled in the boat. As none of them were any longer using the oars, the boat had now begun to drift.

It was Mark who spoke first, addressing the silent thing that hovered on the water. The confidence in his voice astonished most of his companions.

"Who are you?" he asked boldly.

"I am Rabisu." The voice was a watery gurgling, and somehow it impressed Zoltan's hearing as slime held in his hand would have impressed his sense of touch. "Rabisu. And you must now hand over to me that weapon that hangs at your belt. It will make a good addition to my collection."

"Rabisu." Mark appeared to be meditating upon the name. "I've never heard of you before." So far the prince's hand had made no move toward his Sword. He was squinting into the full horror of the thing that hovered above the water, squinting as if loathsomeness could be as dazzling as brightness.

Meanwhile, in the background, the handful of other fishing boats that had been busy on the visible stretch of the river were all making as rapidly as possible for shore, some heading toward the north bank of the river and others toward the south. The thought crossed Zoltan's mind that under ordinary conditions the fisherfolk of the two enemy camps could evidently share the river in peace.

The presence drifting above the water, just keeping up with the drifting boat, appeared to be hesitating, as if it might have been impressed by the bravery of the man who spoke to it. "You are no magician," it said to Mark at last. The statement was not quite a question.

"That is correct, I am not. Tell me, foul one, which Sword is it that you are seeking?"

On hearing such an insolent response Bonar collapsed completely. He cowered abjectly in the bottom of the boat, as many a strong man might have done in his place. Zoltan was keeping his own head up bravely. It cost him a considerable effort, even though Zoltan knew something about his uncle that the head of the Clan Malolo did not.

"Unbuckle your swordbelt and hand it to me!" roared the demon.

"What if I draw my Sword instead?" And at last Mark's hand went to the black hilt.

And still the demon hesitated to attack. "Before you can draw it, little man, you will be dead!"

"I think that I will not be dead as soon as that. In the Emperor's name, forsake this game, and begone from our sight!"

There was a disturbance above the water, and in the air above the boat, an explosion like the breaking of a knot in which the winds of a hundred storms were all entangled. Such a blast must certainly have swamped the fishing craft, but the disturbance came and went with magical swiftness, before any movement of the water or the air immediately around the boat had time to be effective. This concussion was followed instantly by a roaring bellow, uttered in a voice too loud to be human. It was the voice of the demon, no doubt about that, but in another instant the bellowing had grown faint with distance, and in an instant more it had grown fainter still.

Higher above the world, and fainter.

Gradually, but soon, it was entirely gone.

In less time than it takes to draw a breath the river around the fishing boat was once more silent, sunlit, and serene. There might never have been such things as demons in the world.

Prince Mark sat for a moment with his eyes closed. Then, leaning forward in his seat, he put a hand on the shoulder of one of the collapsed rowers. Gently he tried to shake the man out of his paralysis. But for the time being, at least, it was no use. The prince sighed, moved himself to the rowers' bench, and reached for an oar.

His nephew Zoltan had already taken the other one. With a couple of good strokes they overcame the boat's drift, and were once more headed upstream toward the islands.

Bonar, looking shamefaced, had by now managed to regain an upright position on his seat. For a time there was silence except for the creak of oarlocks. Then the chief of Clan Malolo, looking about him in all directions, asked softly and wonderingly: "Where is it?"

"The demon is gone," said Mark patiently. "It's all right now."

The young clan leader turned back and forth in his seat, gaping at the Tungri, which ran calm and undisturbed. The day was peaceful. "But gone where? Is it likely to come back?"

"It might very well come back here sometime. But there's no immediate danger. We can go on and talk to the mermaids, visit the islands as we planned."

Hearing calm human conversation around them, both of the original rowers presently revived. Seeing their three passengers serene, and the danger gone, they rather guiltily went back to work, Mark and Zoltan relinquishing their oars.

Bonar was certainly not going to let the matter rest. "But what happened to the demon? It was a real demon, wasn't it?"

Zoltan said: "Oh, it was a demon, all right. As real as they ever get. But my uncle enjoys certain powers over such creatures. Mainly the power to keep them at a distance."

Mark shrugged, under Bonar's awestricken gaze. "It's true that I'm no wizard. But I do have such a power, from my father, who happens to be the Emperor."

"Ah," said Bonar. But he did not really sound as if he understood, or was convinced of anything. Zoltan could scarcely blame him. Many if not most of the world's people thought of the Emperor as nothing more than some kind of legendary clown.

The clan chief persisted in trying to puzzle it out. "This power over demons that you say you have—indeed, that you have demonstrated. Does it never fail?"

Mark smiled grimly. "It hasn't failed me yet, or I wouldn't be here. Though I must admit I'm never completely sure it's going to work at the moment when I start to use it."

The boat was moving steadily on toward the islands. Now in the forward seat again, Zoltan talked and sang, hoping that his voice would be heard and recognized beneath the water, trying to summon up a very special mermaid.

14

HAVING done the best he could to set the mermaids searching for the Sword, Chilperic was not disposed to dawdle on the riverbank. After making sure that a couple of militiamen remained on the shore to carry news from the fishgirls should there be any, he started back to the manor as soon as possible. He was intent on keeping in close touch with the healer Tigris, and wanted to be first to hear of any change in the condition of her patient.

By the time he and Hissarlik got back to the manor, Chilperic's modest hopes of success for the mermaid project were already fading. He remembered all too well their sullen unwillingness, and he doubted the efficiency of Hissarlik's spell. Chilperic's remaining enthusiasm for that effort diminished steadily as the remaining hours of the afternoon wore on. By sunset he had virtually abandoned hope that the fishgirls were going to prove at all helpful. And he supposed that any program of underwater search they might have begun would have to be abandoned with the onset of darkness, since there was no way to provide the creatures with Old World lights, the only kind that might be used beneath the surface.

Meanwhile, Chilperic was only too well aware that time was passing and his mission here was no closer to being accomplished. The Ancient Master was not going to be pleased. Soon, Chilperic thought, he was going to have to overcome his reluctance to summon the demon, and order Rabisu to make a direct search for the Sword. There were moments when he wondered uneasily just what the demon might be up to on its own.

Just after sunset, when Chilperic was in his room alone, Tigris the healer came in secrecy to see him. The small blond woman held a finger to her lips for silence as soon as he saw her in his doorway, and she slid quickly past him into his room without waiting to be invited.

"I have news regarding my patient," was her greeting.

"She is—?"

"On the road to recovery."

"Very good!"

"The Lady Megara's conscious now, and in fact ready to have a visitor, if the visitor is careful to treat her gently."

"I certainly shall. But I must ask her some questions. Have you said anything about this recovery to any of the family yet?"

"Of course not." Tigris lifted her pretty chin. "You and I, dear Chilperic, serve the same master, and so my first report must be to you whenever that is possible."

"I should hope so. Tell me, has the woman said anything of importance to you?"

"Not really. She's asked a few questions as to how long she has been ill. I saw no point in lying to her about that."

"No, I suppose not. Anything else?"

"Not that you'd find interesting. Mainly she was curious about my identity. Natural enough. I've already warned her that I might be coming back to the room with a professional colleague, though I haven't actually said you are a physician."

"Better and better." Chilperic smiled briefly, then looked grim again. "Tell me, what exactly was wrong with her? Had it anything to do with her practicing magic?"

"In my opinion—which is valued highly, as you know, in some rather high places—"

"Yes, I concede that."

"In my opinion, the Sorceress Megara's disability was not due so much to magical backlash—though something like that may have contributed—as it was to a mere shock of a much more ordinary kind."

"A mere—?"

"Emotional trauma. Such as might be caused, for example, by the death of someone to whom she was closely attached. They tell me that her father was Farslayer's first victim, on that famous night when the feuding clans all but destroyed each other. And that she was found lying unconscious beside his body. An experience like that would be quite enough to send some people into extended shock. Perhaps to make them lie in a trance for a month." And Tigris smiled a brittle smile.

Chilperic said: "That's right. They were both found out on Magicians' Island. Evidently for some reason he'd gone out there that night to visit her. Or spy on her perhaps."

"So, having her father killed before her eyes could very well have done it. She would be standing there talking with this familiar and dependable figure—then zip! Sudden death comes in the window. Do you have any wine on hand, by any chance? Or maybe a drop of brandy?"

Chilperic had, as a matter of fact. While finding a bottle and a glass, he shook his head. He could not generate any respect for people who allowed themselves to be disabled by things that happened to others. "Well, let's go see her, then. She may know something that will help us find the Sword, and in any case we'll have to deal with her if she resumes some position of leadership here within the family. You say I can talk to her now?"

"If you try not to disturb her too much. Ah, that's very good." And Tigris set down the empty glass.

Chilperic started to open the door to the hall, then stopped in the act of doing so. "I wonder if it would be wise to bring some member of the family along to the lady's room. Naturally they'll want to know of her recovery as soon as possible."

"As you wish. Perhaps that's a good idea. It might be wiser not to confront the lady just now with two relative strangers, and no familiar face in sight."

It was just as well they had made that decision, for as soon as they went out into the corridor they encountered Hissarlik, who, as he said, was on his way to learn the latest on his aunt's condition.

A moment later the three people entered the sickroom, and the servant who had been on watch there bowed and curtsied herself back from the bed.

Aunt Megara looked a different woman from the last time Chilperic had seen her. Although he understood she must be over thirty, she now appeared hardly more than a girl. She was also much more alert than when he had seen her before, and sitting up in bed. The whole sickroom—if you could still call it that—had become a much more cheerful place. Materials used in the treatments Tigris had administered, some of them apparently intended to work on a very high plane of magic, lay scattered about.

"Aunt Meg—how are you? We were all greatly concerned." Hissarlik stepped forward to the bed.

"Better—much better." The voice of the patient still lacked life, but she raised a pale hand, readily enough, to take that of her nephew. "And you," Megara murmured. "I see that you are still alive, Hissarlik." Perhaps the discovery pleased her, but it was not doing much to cheer her up. Their hands were already separated again.

Chilperic, confident now that he would be interrupting no very fond reunion, took the opportunity of stepping forward. "Do you recognize me, Lady Megara?"

The eyes of the tired and grieving woman turned toward him. "No, I think not. Should I?"

The visitor bowed. "I am Chilperic, an associate of the physician Tigris who has so skillfully restored you. And I too have come here to be of what service to you I may."

The faded eyes fixed on him were more anxious than accusatory. "Why should you wish to do me service? You tell me your name, but who are you?"

Chilperic bowed again. "The master I have the honor to represent—as does Tigris here—wishes to establish an alliance with the worthy house of Senones. His name is Wood, and he is a wizard of some renown."

"Ah." The lady's eyes moved to those of her nephew, and back again to Chilperic.

The latter said smoothly: "You will of course want to have a family discussion about our proposal. There's no hurry. But there is one matter I fear that I must question you about at once—something about which we must be fully informed before your restoration to health can be considered complete."

Tigris was looking at him now, and Hissarlik too, but Chilperic ignored them both. He said: "I am speaking about the Sword of Vengeance, Lady Megara, the weapon that killed your father. Where did that weapon first come from, on that terrible night? Who used it against him? Above all, where is it now? Your own future, and that of your family, depends on that."

Mention of Farslayer brought renewed horror into the lady's eyes, and there was a pause. At last she shook her head. "I don't know the answer to either question. I don't remember much about that night. I was busy, practicing certain—rituals—in the cave out on Magicians' Island. My father came to visit me—in his youth he had practiced a great deal of magic himself. And then—"

"And then?"

"All I know is that the Sword was suddenly there—in my father's back." The lady closed her eyes. "As if it had come out of nowhere, through the grotto's wall somehow. And in that instant my father let out a cry, and fell—of course he was killed instantly."

Lady Megara opened her eyes again and stared at the wall. When her silence had lasted for a few moments Chilperic prodded her, gently but insistently: "What happened next?"

"Next?" Her blank gaze turned on him. "I—I don't know. I saw

Father dead, and after that I can remember nothing more." Suddenly Megara burst out: "Who else was slain that night?"

"We've talked about that before, Aunt Meg. Don't you remember?"

"Not really. Tell me again."

Hissarlik, somewhat reluctantly, began to run through the roll call of defunct relatives. To Megara, who listened to the list as if she were mesmerized, the extended roster of casualties seemed to present a generalized horror, though for some reason not a particularly acute one. Chilperic got the impression that she was listening for some name and had not heard it.

When the listing was over, she commented simply: "So many on our side were killed, then."

"I fear that is so," said her nephew calmly. Whatever grief and horror he might have felt on that night had evidently been exchanged over the past month for fear and worry. Only his craving for revenge had been retained unaltered.

"And what of the enemy?" Megara's voice grew cold and implacable. "Who among them have we killed?"

Hissarlik, taking turns with Anselm and Alicia who had now come to join the others in the sickroom, recited the names of those they had personally called on Farslayer to strike down, and the other enemy names they had heard called out by relatives who were now dead themselves. The listing sounded quite as long as that of the Senones casualties. When it was over, Megara seemed to relax a bit, apparently slumping back toward unconsciousness.

"Now leave me." It sounded very much like an order, though her voice was weak. "Now I would sleep."

In a moment, Tigris, turned physician again, was ushering Chilperic and the others out.

Chilperic had to admit that he had learned almost nothing of any value in the sickroom. And now there was nothing left for him to do, except to take the decisive step he had been vainly trying to put off. Back in his room alone he went through the few simple steps required to summon the demon.

From an inner pocket of his clothing he drew out the demon's life, caught and trapped in leather by some tricks of wizardry that were as far, or farther, beyond him as the healing skills of the physician. But to use the thing that Wood had given him was simple enough. Stroking the little wallet with his fingers, Chilperic muttered the short formula of summoning.

Then he waited, standing with his eyes almost closed, for the unspeakable presence to approach once more and establish itself inside his room.

He waited, but nothing happened.

The summoning was finished. He was sure that he had done it properly. Time stretched on, one breath after another, and still the demon did not appear.

Presently Tigris, her healing chores evidently completed for the time being, tapped at his door and came in as silently as she had done before, closing the door immediately behind her. When she saw Chilperic standing with the leather wallet in his hand, she had no need to ask what he was doing.

With Tigris watching him expressionlessly, Chilperic frowned, and rubbed again at his leather wallet, and once more uttered the proper words. He took great care to get the incantation right, rounding each syllable of it distinctly.

But still there came no response from Rabisu.

Something was definitely wrong.

Fortunately for himself, Chilperic was not a man who panicked easily. To the best of his quite limited ability, he scanned the air and earth and water around him, seeking evidence of the demon's presence, or of any interfering magic. He could find neither.

"I sense no opposition," murmured Tigris, who was evidently doing the same thing, at a level of skill doubtless much higher than his.

Chilperic sighed and nodded. So, he thought to himself, what game was this? Perhaps the creature had been called away by some direct command from Wood. Chilperic thought that unlikely, but what other explanation could there be?

In a little while Tigris, having made no comment, left him, saying that she wanted to look in again on her patient. Chilperic was still sitting alone in his room, wondering when to try the summoning again, unable to think of anything else to try, when a servant came to his door bearing a message from Hissarlik.

"My master's compliments, sir, and would you care to attend him in the great hall? Some men have arrived, claiming to be mercenaries looking for employment, and the Tyrant Hissarlik would like to consult with you on how best to deal with them."

Descending to what was optimistically called the great hall, Chilperic found lamps being lighted against the gathering dusk. Hissarlik was established in a tall chair that evidently served him as a seat of state. Two men, both strangers to Chilperic, were facing the clan chief. One of these visitors, a powerful-looking brute, was standing almost at attention, while the other, taller and much leaner, had seated himself on a table with one foot on the floor, a disrespectful position to say the least. Signs of the military profession were much in evidence in the dress and attitude of both.

The taller stranger stood up from the table when Chilperic entered, and in a moment had introduced himself as Captain Koszalin, commander, as he said, of his own free and honorable company of adventurers. Koszalin was youthful, certainly well under thirty years of age; lean, almost emaciated, with a haggard look as if perhaps he did not sleep well. His stocky comrade was his sergeant.

With Chilperic now standing at the Tyrant's right hand and giving the newcomers a stern look, Hissarlik was ready to speak out boldly from his tall chair.

He addressed Koszalin. "Well then, fellow, what use do you think you can be to us here?"

Chilperic got the impression that the youthful captain was totally unimpressed by this other youth who claimed hereditary power. But Koszalin, who appeared now to be making an effort to be pleasant, scratched his uncombed head and addressed the Tyrant.

"Why, sir, it's like this. I hear that you're on no great terms of friendship with those people across the water, the ones who call themselves Malolo." When Koszalin shifted his glance to Chilperic, his voice, perhaps unconsciously, grew more respectful. "Nor are you, sir, I suppose."

Chilperic was gradually becoming certain that these were a couple of the same mercenary scoundrels who had been hanging around the Malolo manor intermittently when he had visited there. He had had only the briefest contact with any of them then, but now he could not help wondering whether some of them might recognize him. He would have to make sure of that as soon as possible.

"Ah," said Hissarlik to the captain. "So you've had some contact with the Malolo, have you?"

"Damned unfriendly contact." The commander of the honorable company, wiry muscles working in a hairy forearm, scratched his head again; Chilperic wondered if he was going to have to ask Tigris for a minor spell to repel boarders. Koszalin went on: "Well sir, I'll tell you the exact truth. Their new chief over there, name of Bonar, said that he wanted to hire myself and my men, and then he refused to pay us. Reneged on a deal, he did. Promised pearls and then wouldn't give us nothing. We can't make our living on deals like that. I've got thirty men in my company to look after, men who look up to me like I was their father. You, sir, being a real chief yourself, will understand that kind of responsibility." The last remark was ostensibly addressed to Hissarlik, but with the words the speaker's eyes turned briefly to Chilperic to include him.

Chilperic supposed it was time he took an active part in the questioning. "When was this reneging, as you call it?"

"That's what anyone would call it, sir. It was just a couple of days ago. So, my men and I have decided to see if we can find a better reception on this side of the water."

Chilperic turned his stare briefly on the second mercenary, the powerful sergeant, who straightened up to a position even closer to military attention, but still had nothing to say.

"Well," said Chilperic to Koszalin, "suppose we do hire you. It would have to be on a trial basis. To begin with I'd expect to hear a good deal from you regarding conditions over there in the Malolo camp. We know a good bit already, mind you, and I'd expect what you told us to match in every detail with what we know already. Stand up when you're in this room, I didn't hear anyone offer you a seat."

Koszalin, who had begun to relax himself casually onto the table again, hurriedly straightened up. If he was upset by the sudden order, he gave no sign of it. Yes, undoubtedly a veteran soldier, even if his promotion to captain was quite likely self-awarded. "We could tell you a lot about them, sir. If we can reach a deal, that is, and if you can pay us something adequate on account."

"Very well." Chilperic made a motion with his head. "You and the sergeant wait outside now. We must discuss this matter first."

Koszalin saluted and turned, with his sergeant moving a step behind him.

Chilperic and Hissarlik were left alone. They were on the point of beginning their discussion when Aunt Megara, looking grim and pale, and dressed in a pale robe with a kind of turban wound round her head, surprised them by appearing in a doorway.

"Who were those men?" she demanded, sounding to Chilperic like one who might be ready to assume control.

Hissarlik explained to his aunt. He sounded ready to defend the power he had already taken.

Tigris, who entered close behind her patient, explained in a whisper to Chilperic that Aunt Megara was making good progress though she was still weak, and she had insisted on starting to get about.

"What did those men want?" Tigris added.

Chilperic explained. He was basically in favor of hiring the mercenaries, and told Tigris as much. He added that he privately intended to secure such loyalty as Koszalin and his men might be capable of for the cause of the Dark Master, Wood.

"Of course," Tigris agreed. "They don't appear very effective, but I suppose there's no one better available."

Chilperic nodded. "Soon I'll take Koszalin aside and speak to him."

Hissarlik now joined their conference, apparently without suspicion. He was also in favor of hiring Koszalin and his men, believing rightly or wrongly that they would be tougher and more reliable than his own militia when it came to combat. From what the clan chief said, it was plain that he envisioned another and final assault on the Malolo, with or without the Sword, defeating the ancient enemies of his house once and for all.

The Lady Megara listened to the discussion among the other three, and took some part in it herself. To Chilperic, observing carefully, it seemed that she was not so much interested in the question of hiring the mercenaries as she was in finding an opportunity to talk to them, once she learned they came from the south bank of the river.

15

PRESENTLY the mercenary officer and his sergeant were summoned back into the house. This time Chilperic pointedly invited Koszalin to sit down.

With Chilperic doing most of the talking, Bonar in his tall chair, and Megara standing by, an offer of employment was made to the mercenaries. Modest terms of payment were agreed upon, with the proviso that bonuses would be awarded later in the event actual combat became necessary.

When the agreement had been sealed with a round of handshakes, and the payment of a small handful of coin brought up from some subterranean Senones treasury, the Senones and Chilperic began to question the captain further.

Yes, of course, Koszalin said, everyone over on the Malolo side of the river had been talking about the Sword of great magical powers, with which last month's battle had been fought. And the people over there were all wondering where Farslayer might be. But in fact little effort was actually being made to find it.

"Then," asked Chilperic, "is it possible that the Malolo secretly have Farslayer hidden?"

"It's hard to say that anything's impossible, sir, as you know. But I don't think so."

Koszalin went on to add that the Malolo now generally thought that Farslayer was over here on the Senones side of the river.

"Well, it isn't," said Hissarlik. "And if it's not here and it's not there, where in all the hells is it?"

Naturally no one had an answer for that.

After a time, when odors of food preparation started to waft into the great hall, Hissarlik in a whispered conference with his new vizier asked whether the officer ought perhaps be invited to dine with the family tonight. Chilperic whispered back that he thought not.

Arrangements were made to feed the mercenary captain and his men outside. Before Koszalin and Sergeant Shotoku went out, they were instructed by Chilperic to make their encampment somewhere outside the grounds of Senones manor. They were also ordered sternly to refrain from bothering any of the local people.

In the morning, Chilperic awakened alone in his room, feeling reasonably well rested.

The first order of business was to try the demon-summoning again. The ritual was no more effective than before. Well, there was nothing to be done about it except to try to obtain the Sword without the demon's help; and Chilperic had to admit that he would feel a certain relief if the damned creature was really gone for good.

Descending from his room, he bypassed for the moment the great hall, where something in the way of breakfast would be served, and walked out alone into the misty morning to see how events were progressing in the matter of the mercenaries.

He soon located the small encampment, which had been established near running water as he expected. The captain, up early, came to greet him. Surveying the small handful of tents and shelters, Chilperic remarked to Koszalin: "You said last night that you had thirty men."

The other's mouth changed shape. Perhaps you could have called its new shape a smile. "Some of my men are out on patrol, sir. You see, we're already at work."

"Commendable enthusiasm," Chilperic responded dryly. "Well, until I see them back here, and have a chance to count them for myself, I won't call upon you to do any jobs that might require thirty men."

"Yes sir. That's a good idea."

Chilperic started to say something sharp, then bit the words back. After a moment of thoughtful silence, he extracted a small flask from a pocket, helped himself to a swig, and passed it over without comment.

Koszalin sniffed the flask, and then drank, politely limiting himself to a couple of swallows. "Ah," he said in tones of reverence. "That's something good, I'd say."

"I'd say so, too. Now understand me, Captain. You can tell what stories you want to that boy up in the big house, and his relatives. You can claim to have a hundred heavy cavalry at your command, and they might even believe it. But when you deal with me, I expect to hear the truth, and I can usually tell the difference. Got that?"

" 'Sir," acknowledged Koszalin, and passed the flask back with evident reluctance. He belched, almost silently. He looked at Chilperic, evidently reassessing him.

At last he said: "All right, sir. What I've really got is ten men now. Yesterday morning I had twelve, but two of 'em disappeared somewhere."

"Ten men I can believe. Understand me, now. You should do what the Tyrant Hissarlik says, unless I tell you to do something different. But between you and me, I'm the one who's really going to be giving you orders."

Koszalin demurred. "There's a certain matter of payment, sir. The payment I received did come from the Tyrant, as far as I know."

"You mean that trifle they gave you? I'll double that for you right now." And Chilperic pulled out his purse. After a quick glance around, making sure they were not observed, he handed over a small amount of gold.

Koszalin, expressionless, received the bribe and evaluated it as quickly and neatly as it was given. When it had vanished into one of his inner pockets, he assumed a position of attention. "Standing by for orders, sir," he announced. Suddenly military formality and intelligence had appeared.

"Good. Come, take a little walk with me."

Bawling an order to his sergeant to take charge of the camp for the time being, the captain readily enough joined Chilperic for a stroll through the misty woods, where it seemed probable that they could converse without being heard.

In the course of this talk Chilperic soon heard about the four strange people who had recently arrived at Malolo Manor and established themselves there as unexpected but welcome guests. This was news to Chilperic, and he pricked up his ears at once.

"Two of them are pilgrims, or at least they're wearing gray," Koszalin amplified. "A young man, who's a good shot with a bow, and an old lady. Never heard her name, but she knows how to give orders."

"Oh?" This sounded very much to Chilperic like the pair he had heard described by the hermit. And the time assigned by Koszalin for their arrival at Malolo Manor fit with that identity.

"Then, the next day, or night rather, two more men showed up. I don't know just how they got into the house. I thought we were watching both doors at the time."

"What's that?"

"Yes sir. Two more new arrivals who obviously know the first two. Both of them look like real fighters—probably some kind of officers, I'd say. And, you should know this, one of them is wearing a Sword."

Chilperic, surprised, frowned at the captain. "What do you mean, a sword?"

"What I mean is he's got one of the Twelve strapped on. Trust me, I know what I'm talking about."

"Do you know what you're saying? Which Sword?"

"You can rely on it that I know what I'm saying—sir. I've seen them before. Which Sword this is I don't know, except it can't be Farslayer that everybody's already looking for. Because everybody over there still thinks that one's over here."

Chilperic conversed with the strange young soldier a little longer, then gave him orders to stand by with his men, and turned his own steps back toward the house. Already Chilperic was turning over furiously in his own mind the feasibility of a raid on the Malolo manor—that would at least offer him a chance of getting his hands on this new Sword that seemed to have appeared on the scene. And obtaining that weapon, in turn, might very well placate the dark power that Chilperic served, in the event he failed to find Farslayer.

Before they parted, Koszalin had another suggestion. "The two strange officers who have appeared over there may be scouting in advance of their army. Commanders, high-ranking people, have been known to do such things. But if that's who they are, you can bet that their army, or its advance guard at least, isn't far behind."

When Chilperic returned from his outdoor conference with the mercenary captain, he found the Lady Megara talking with someone in the great hall. Megara was moving about the house slowly and somewhat weakly, not yet ready to go out. But obviously she was no longer going to spend most of her time confined to her room.

Megara turned at Chilperic's entrance, and asked: "Where have you been?" The question was almost a demand.

"Inspecting the defenses, my lady. It's good to see you up and about, and looking well." That was something of an exaggeration. In fact, though she was now more active, the lady indeed looked older than she had when Chilperic had first seen her. He would now estimate her age at about thirty.

"The defenses? You mean those mercenaries we hired last night. I mean to go out and talk to them myself. Later I shall—when I feel stronger."

Chilperic said nothing to discourage this plan, thinking that by doing so he would only guarantee it.

He went on to his breakfast, and managed to enjoy it. Hissarlik did not appear at the table. Soon Chilperic, this time accompanied by both Megara and Tigris, was once more closeted in his room, trying again to call his demon.

Again he drew out the leather wallet from his bosom, rubbed it, and carefully recited the words of the incantation.

This time, to his immense relief, Rabisu did respond to his summoning. Not with a physical presence, but at least the insect-chittering of the demonic voice sounded in Chilperic's mind. He thought it could probably be heard in the air around him as well.

The women could indeed hear the voice. Megara appeared largely indifferent, but Tigris frowned at Chilperic, puzzled by what she heard.

Rabisu's first response reached Chilperic in the form of an extremely attenuated whisper, as if the hideous creature were trying to make contact with him from some enormous distance. Indeed, to begin with the signal was so very faint that Chilperic could not make out what was being said.

But he persisted in his efforts at summoning, and within half an hour the voice of the demon was definitely louder, and marginally more clear. Now and then a word or two came through distinctly, but the man still found it impossible to do more than guess at the meaning of the message as a whole.

Tigris murmured to Lady Megara: "It is almost enough to make one envious, is it not?"

Megara recalled herself from some mental distance. "Envious?"

"Of the power that Wood has granted our friend here. That such a vastly inferior wizard as our friend Chilperic, no wizard at all really, should have such a superior tool as a demon placed at his command."

"I have seen demons," said Megara, still distantly. "I have felt them, too."

"My dear, I suppose we have all seen them at some time—all of us who are acquainted with the art. But to know the luxury of being able to command one . . ." Tigris let her words trail away.

Chilperic naturally had heard the conversation, though he wasn't sure what Tigris was trying to accomplish by it. Now he bowed lightly in Lady Megara's direction. "Should you ever decide to serve my master, lady, I am sure that you would be favored, too."

"Your master? I have little interest in serving any master now."

"When you are fully recovered, my lady, perhaps it will be time to speak of an alliance."

"An alliance? But why—never mind."

Chilperic went back to trying to communicate with his living tool; he was still having only very limited success in that endeavor.

He maintained his calm as well as he was able. But he had to admit to the healer-sorceress Tigris that something was still seriously wrong.

She offered to help.

But Chilperic did not know what the demon was trying to tell him, and thought that the message might well be one he wouldn't want any outsider to hear. He tried to convey this objection to Megara as delicately as possible.

"Of course. I understand perfectly."

Tigris went out with her, for which Chilperic was grateful. He supposed that she would expect a full report later.

Despite the demon's promise of a swift return, many hours had passed and night had fallen before Rabisu's voice was close and clear enough for Chilperic to be able to understand it reasonably well.

But this understanding, when he managed it, did nothing to alleviate Chilperic's growing sense of alarm. Quite the contrary.

Rabisu reported having been forced, by some overwhelming magic, to abandon his place of duty.

"Your place of duty? And where was that? I don't recall assigning you to any particular place."

"I was patrolling in the valley, lord. Trying to look out for your interests as best I could." The demon went on to report that he had been hurled away, to an almost inconceivable distance, by one of a party of men he had discovered in a fishing boat upon the Tungri.

"By a *fisherman?*"

"No, Lord Chilperic, no. Not by a fisherman at all. This man was much more than that."

"I should think he must have been. Proceed with your explanation, then. Tell me what happened."

Rabisu, in a subservient voice, continued his report. The fishing boat had come out, he thought, from the Malolo side of the river, and it had been heading for the islands. The description given by the demon of two of the boat's five passengers matched well with Koszalin's account of two of the impressive visitors who seemed to have attached themselves to the Malolo cause.

And one of these two men had been wearing a Sword.

Chilperic sighed deeply. "Was it Farslayer?"

"I do not believe that it was that Sword, sir."

"Then which was it? You are certain it was one of the Twelve?"

"To the second question I answer yes. As for the first, I regret that I do not know."

"Go on."

Rabisu related how he had caused himself to materialize directly in front of the boat, and had challenged those aboard. To his first cursory inspection, none of the men aboard the boat had seemed to be magicians at all—and Chilperic, listening to the story, knew that demons were unlikely to be wrong in such matters. But then, when Rabisu materialized, the man who wore the Sword had answered him with what seemed fearless confidence.

"And then, master, it fell on me as if from nowhere—a stroke that Ardneh himself might have delivered! I could do nothing to resist it, nothing!"

"What kind of a stroke?" Chilperic was still mystified.

"It hurled me to a vast distance. I am at a loss to give any more detailed description."

"Well, can I take it that you are successfully recovering from it now?"

"I am returning to you as fast as I am able, master. As far as I can tell, my powers are unimpaired. If I were to tell you how far that one blow hurled me—if I were to mention to you the orbit of the Moon—then you might accuse me of lying."

If the demon were a man, thought Chilperic, then he might accuse him of being drunk. As matters stood, that suspicion did not apply. He let the point pass for the time being. "And how soon will you be here again, ready to act upon my orders?"

"Within the hour, master. What will my orders be?"

"I'll make a final decision on that when you get here. Let your arrival in my room be as unobtrusive as possible."

Was it possible, Chilperic wondered, that the creature was lying to him? Wood had warned him that insubordination of that kind was a possibility with a demon, no matter what threats or punishment were used.

Probably, thought Chilperic, only Wood himself, or one of his high magical lieutenants, would be able to determine with certainty whether such a creature was telling the truth or not.

Would Tigris qualify? Perhaps.

But suppose that the tale told by the demon, however improbable it sounded, was true. That meant that he, Chilperic, now found himself facing powers that were capable of kicking Rabisu off to the end of the earth, or perhaps farther, like some troublesome puppy. Chilperic knew there were some demons in the world stronger and more powerful than Rabisu. But not very many. So any power that could do that . . .

* * *

So Chilperic now felt that whatever Wood might think, he, Chilperic, must decline to enter the lists in such a contest. Unless of course he were given substantial help. It would have to be very substantial indeed.

Frowning thoughtfully, he paced about in his little room until the demon at last arrived.

This time the demonic manifestation was quite modest: only a grinning head that might have belonged to something between a wolf and a snake, which appeared to grow out of the chamber's outer wall.

Speaking forcefully to this apparition, while he held the leather wallet in his hand for it to see, Chilperic gave orders. Rabisu was to fly to Wood, as swiftly as possible, taking word to the master of what had happened to it here. Then it was to return to Chilperic as quickly as it might, bringing whatever orders the master Wood might have for him, as well as whatever help the master might be willing to send.

Chilperic once more closed himself in his room, feeling weary, stretched out on his bed. But before he had gone to sleep, Tigris reappeared, closing the door softly behind her as usual. From the way she smiled at him, this time she was in a seductive mood.

He was not really surprised, and her evident decision to share his bed for the night was welcome, though he thought they had better keep Hissarlik from finding out.

He cautioned his companion on this subject. "The way he looked at you, he's certain to be jealous. And that certainly wouldn't help matters."

Tigris laughed her distinctive laugh. "He is only a boy, and you can manage him without trouble," she assured him.

"No doubt I can."

"Oh, by the way, I thought I should mention to you that I have very recently been in contact with our master."

"Have you indeed? Telling him what?"

"Nothing to your detriment, I assure you, dear Chilperic." Tigris had now begun to undress. "I have described our difficulties to the magnificent Wood, and he assured me that help would soon be on the way."

"Oh, in what form?"

"That he did not specify." She removed the last garment, and bounced cheerfully onto the bed. "And now, dear Chilperic, if you would like to help me with a certain personal problem, kindly place your own clothing on a chair."

On awakening, some hours later, Chilperic found his room still dark, but sensed that Tigris was up and moving about. "What are you doing?"

"I must go and check on my patient again. Go back to sleep."

"Quite a sense of duty you have." Half-consciously he felt in the darkness to make sure that the wallet holding the demon's life, and one or two other things of considerable value, was still where he wanted it to be. Then he let himself drift back to sleep.

Hissarlik, having been awakened by a light tap on his door, felt something in the center of his being hesitate for a beat when he saw the identity of his visitor. Still he was not really surprised. He was the clan leader, was he not? Still a very important person, even in these days when the clan was so sadly diminished.

"Lady Tigris."

"Indeed, it is I, my lord." She smiled at him winsomely. "Aren't you going to invite me in?"

16

MARK and Zoltan's first search for Black Pearl had been brief and unavailing. It was broken off without a landing being made on either of the islands. The small party in their boat observed a gathering of people, including what looked like a small force of militia, on the northern, Senones side of the river. There several comparatively large boats could be seen drawn up on shore in position for launching. When Bonar beheld this demonstration of enemy force he insisted on retreating, and in the circumstances Mark had to agree that might well be the wisest thing to do. Zoltan, worried about Black Pearl, reluctantly went along.

The remainder of the day and the following night passed virtually without incident at Malolo manor. The visitors divided the hours of darkness into shifts among themselves, and with the aid of Bonar and some of his servants, kept watch through the night. But neither the mercenaries nor anyone else appeared to cause trouble.

In the morning, Mark was more determined than ever to locate the mermaid who had said she knew something of the Sword's hiding place; and Zoltan was growing increasingly concerned about Black Pearl. Today therefore a stronger expedition was organized.

This morning the augmented force hiked to the fishing village in the predawn grayness. Shortly after dawn the expedition was ready, and took to the river in two boats. Ben, Lady Yambu, and the magician Gesner accompanied Mark, Zoltan, and Bonar, while Violet and Rose were left in charge of the manor.

Today's boats were larger than yesterday's, and rowed by four men each. These were all armed, so that in all thirteen armed men were taking to the river today, a force everyone agreed was probably substantial enough to face any that the Senones were likely to put in the field.

The sun was still low above the eastern stretch of river, and dew still glittered on the vegetation of Mermaids' Island, when the two boats landed there.

Exploring this scrap of land was the work of a very few minutes. None of the mermaids were to be seen, though their shore living facilities, fireplaces and simple shelters lining one of the convoluted inlets, were available for inspection. The shelters were tiny caves very close to water level, all of them now empty. The inlet was lined with steplike terraces where a mermaid could sit comfortably just in or just out of the water, and have access to the fireplaces on the next level up. Coals glowed brightly in one or two of the small, sheltered fireplaces, and someone had recently been cleaning fish. Near the fireplaces, driftwood had been piled up to dry.

Bonar and Zoltan called, but none of the fishgirls, who had presumably taken to the water nearby, responded. Bonar told his companions that the mermaids who might have been on the island moments ago had doubtless taken alarm at the size and unusual character of this invading force. They would probably be watching from somewhere in the river nearby.

Stubbornly Zoltan roamed the perimeter of the island, calling Black Pearl's name repeatedly, and waving his arms, hoping to draw the attention of underwater watchers. But he drew no response.

It was also possible to see, on the island, the places of barter where food and other necessities were sometimes left by people coming out from the mainland, in exchange for pearls and other occasional items of value left by the mermaids. Zoltan could see no reason why a direct face-to-face trade could not be conducted—perhaps, he thought, in the early years of the curse mermaids had been considered taboo, or dangerous, and this indirect method had developed.

Whatever had caused the usual inhabitants of Mermaids' Island to absent themselves today, they remained absent, which struck Zoltan as somehow ominous. After pacing from one end of the island to the other, and fruitlessly calling Black Pearl's name a dozen times more, he agreed with the prince his uncle that they had better move on and try to reach the hermit on the south shore. If fishgirls were not to be found, Gelimer seemed to represent the next most likely source of information about the Sword.

Just as they were about to embark again, Mark paused, squinting across the water. "What about Magicians' Island?"

Bonar protested that it was unsafe to visit that place, that mermaids never went there, no one ever did. Gesner, consulted for his professional opinion, admitted that wizards, himself included, visited Magicians' Island from time to time, and that the real danger to anyone had to be considered minimal.

"Then I think we ought to take a look."

The prince as usual had his way. Magicians' Island was not much more than a hundred meters from the shore base of the mermaids. But before the rowers had moved the two boats halfway there, the attention of the entire party was distracted by the sight of someone or something swimming on an interception course toward them, straight from the south.

It was a mermaid, it could be nothing else. A mermaid, just below the surface, coming toward them faster than the boats were moving, approaching at a speed that only a true fish could have matched.

She burst to the surface almost within reach of Zoltan as he crouched in the prow of one of the boats.

"Soft Ripple!" He thought he had recognized the tawny hair even before the mermaid surfaced.

Clinging to the boat, breathless with the speed of her race and with some underlying excitement, Soft Ripple babbled out an incoherent story about Black Pearl's being dead. She added something to the effect that the treacherous Cosmo was to blame.

Gesner and Bonar sat up straight in their boat at the mention of that last name.

But Zoltan had frozen in horror at what he heard.

With the clarity of dazed detachment, he saw that Soft Ripple was holding up something she now wore on a fine chain about her neck. And he could recognize the amulet that Black Pearl had been wearing the last time he saw her.

The mermaid quieted a little when she saw the unfamiliar face of Prince Mark looking over the prow at her.

Lady Yambu, coming up into the prow of the other boat, was sharply soothing, and helped the girl to get herself under control.

"Are you certain Black Pearl is dead? Have you seen her body?" It was Yambu who asked the questions.

"I am certain, lady. I have seen."

"Then show us."

Presently Soft Ripple was swimming again, more slowly this time, leading both boats in the direction of a marshy area along the south bank of the river. This marsh was not far from the outlet of the stream that Black Pearl had ascended, with such difficulty, to visit the hermit.

Before long both boats were sliding and crunching in among the tall green reeds, their rowers swearing at the difficulty, and Bonar muttering his fears of ambush to anyone who would pay attention. No one was paying attention to him for very long.

The mermaid, slithering rapidly through the reedy shallows, and calling back frequently for the boats to follow, remained always a little ahead.

Soon Zoltan saw something floating in the almost stagnant backwater ahead. With a choked cry he leaped from the boat into the waist-deep water, and went thrashing after the pale-skinned, dark-haired floating thing.

When Zoltan came within reach of the body, he felt a rush of relief, intense but brief. This body had two legs, it could not be that of a mermaid. Nor could it be Black Pearl, he thought, perhaps not even a real corpse, though the thing was floating facedown. Whatever had happened to cause death could not have left her looking so shrunken, almost waxlike and inhuman.

"This is no mermaid!"

Soft Ripple looked at him with rage and pity in her face. "It is, it is. We all of us get our legs back when we die. Did you not know that?"

He looked at her, shaking his head. He had never had any suspicion of such a thing.

Ben of Purkinje, leaning from his boat as it drifted nearer, took hold of the body with a huge hand and turned it over gently.

At the first human touch, a little swarm of almost invisible powers, like half-material insects, deserted the corpse and went whining and buzzing their way up into the empyrean.

Ben rumbled: "Aye, this is demon-death if ever I've seen it. Hard to tell how long she's been here, though."

"No!" Zoltan screamed the word. Now he had seen the face. It seemed a modeled parody of Black Pearl's.

Mark put a hand on his nephew's shoulder. Lady Yambu asked Soft Ripple sharply: "Is it really true that your kind always reverts to having legs at death?"

"It is true of all our kind in this river. I have seen it often enough; I ought to know." The bitter hatred in her glared suddenly at Prince Mark, as if he had been Black Pearl's killer. "We are allowed only a few years of life at best."

"I am sorry." Yambu's voice was kind and soft. "How did you come to find the body?"

Coaxed by Lady Yambu, Soft Ripple explained how she had come to make the discovery.

"I have been worried about Pearl for some time, and yesterday I followed her to see where she was going. I saw her start to struggle up the shallow creek here, and I wondered what her goal could possibly be. She was swimming and floundering her way upstream toward the place where the hermit is said to live. I became very worried, and thought of following her even there, but then I gave up that idea, because I thought it was really crazy for a mermaid to try to ascend such a stream.

"So I waited in the river nearby for her to come down again. After a long time, hours, a demon came roaring through the air, and I was terrified. I heard a screaming inhuman sound, and I saw a mysterious and ugly shadow hurtling across the sky. I could see it even from under the water, and I could feel the sickness that the creature brought with it. I wanted to hide, because I thought that the treacherous magician might have called a demon up to kill me—but it wasn't me that the thing was after."

"What treacherous magician?"

The mermaid spat the words. "Cosmo Malolo is the name he's known by in the world."

Bonar, shocked, demanded: "Cosmo is still alive?"

Soft Ripple ignored the clan leader's question. She said: "I didn't dare to come back here until this morning. I hadn't had any contact with Pearl all night, and I was more worried than ever. I looked for her, and I found her here—like this."

Gesner until now had been listening to the mermaid's story in silence. Now he said sharply: "Let me see that amulet that you are wearing."

Soft Ripple raised a pale hand to the chain around her throat. "I took it from Black Pearl's body. What's wrong with that? She was my friend."

Other people in both boats spoke to her more softly and courteously, asking about the amulet. At last she said: "Many of the girls in the river wear ornaments around their necks. Some wear trinkets that they find along the bottom of the river. Some are given baubles by fishermen, because the men hope that the mermaids can send them good luck in return—I don't think it ever really works that way. And some of us are given presents by our families who live on land."

Gesner asked: "But do men ever give you these? I mean, as they might give presents to a girl with legs?"

"Lacking legs and what's between them," the girl said simply, "we have no men. What man would want one who can never truly be a woman? We mermaids have only each other, and our short lives to be endured." She turned to Zoltan and flared up at him: "Why do you weep for her?" It seemed really to puzzle her that a man with legs should do so. "It is we who are still alive who are unlucky. What are you doing? Why do you want to put her body in the boat? Let her go down the river like a dead fish, and be forgotten, the way the rest of us are going."

"The point about the amulet she wears," said Gesner, "is that I can recognize cousin Cosmo's magical sign on it."

Soft Ripple stared at him. When his words had penetrated, she tore the amulet from her neck with fear and loathing, and threw it away into the river. "I never thought that it came from him!" she cried.

Zoltan was sitting now with his head down, not really paying attention to the others.

Mark reached from the boat and caught the raging girl by the hair. "There'll be time later to have a tantrum," he said, in a new and harder voice. "If you can tell me where the Sword is now, do so."

"You are wearing it at your side." But Soft Ripple said this sullenly, not as if she really believed it.

The prince released his grip. "I wear its fellow, which has a different power, and a different mark that Vulcan put on it."

"What power?" It was hard to tell how seriously the question was intended.

"That of cutting stone, swiftly and easily. Ask this Malolo chief here how I cut my way into his stronghold." And the prince's hand touched the hilt of the Sword he wore.

"Indeed." The mermaid flirted for a moment completely beneath the surface, and up again, much as a wholly human swimmer might have done.

Then, facing the prince again, she asked: "You want Farslayer to deal with your enemies, do you?"

"Yes. Especially I want to keep them from getting it. And they are your enemies as well, whether you know it or not. Chief among them is the wizard who held Black Pearl in thrall when she was far upstream."

"Very well. I know where the Sword Farslayer is now, and I will tell you."

For a moment there was silence, the people in both boats questioning whether they had heard her words aright. Then everyone burst out with questions.

The mermaid hushed them all with a small raised hand. "I know where it is because I saw the demon hide it, yesterday. I think he may have taken it from Black Pearl, though I don't know where she got it—but I did see the demon with a Sword. He hid it hastily. He knew that I was watching him, and he would have killed me, too. Except that there was something else he wanted to do, something he thought even more important than killing me to keep me quiet."

"What else?"

Soft Ripple looked at Prince Mark. "He wanted to go to you. You were sitting in a boat, a boat smaller than either of these, out near the middle of the river, with some of these same people with you. So desperate was the demon to confront you that he would not even pause to kill me first. Someday perhaps he will return and find me and kill me —but I will first tell you where the Sword is hidden."

"Where?"

"Right where he put it. Far underwater, in the deepest channel, not far from Magicians' Island."

"Take me to that Sword now. If you help me to get it, I swear by Ardneh I'll do my best to see that every mermaid in this river is given her legs again. I do not think that is impossible."

Soft Ripple looked at the prince in silence. Then she said, "Follow me," and turned and swam away.

Black Pearl's body had already been hoisted aboard one of the boats, and decently covered with a canvas sail.

Soft Ripple stopped, swimming in place, at a spot where the current was swift, within twenty meters or so of Magicians' Island. The oarsmen in both boats worked steadily to hold their craft beside her.

She said: "The Sword you seek is approximately straight below me. If any of you have the strength of a demon, and can swim like a mermaid, come down with me, and move away the rock the demon placed atop his prize to hold it safe. That rock is more than I, or a hundred like me, could move a centimeter."

Bonar was ready in a moment with the beginning of a plan to move the rock with ropes and many boats, and the help of other mermaids.

Mark instead unsheathed the Sword he was wearing at his belt.

Zoltan had by now recovered a little from the first shock of Black Pearl's death. "Give Stonecutter to me," he told his uncle, "and I'll dive with Soft Ripple, and cut up the rock. I'm a strong swimmer."

Mark, looking at him, thought that Zoltan at this moment was also somewhat reckless of his own life. "No," said Mark.

"Why not? Cutting the stone will be easy."

The mermaid was almost laughing at both of them. "No, you stay in the boat. All of you. Please, or I will have to pull you up out of the water as well. The Sword you want to find lies much too deep, and the current down there is far too swift and cold for anyone with legs to swim in it."

Then she held out her hands to Mark for Stonecutter. "Give me the Sword you wear, and I will dive alone and get the other one for you. If I can chop the boulder into little bits as easily as he says, then the rest will be easy, too."

Mark hesitated just noticeably. But then he handed over the Sword of Siege.

The mermaid smiled at him, and let Stonecutter's weight bear her down below the surface.

Time passed, slowly and intensely. The boats maintained their positions. Mark wished that he had started counting, and wondered if anyone else had. So far, he thought, no more time had passed than a skillful, breathing human diver might require to maintain herself underwater. Or not much more—

Suddenly the water erupted, revealing the head and shoulders and arms of Soft Ripple. She was tailing water strongly in the swift current, keeping herself in position to hold up a naked, gleaming Sword. On her two raised hands the mermaid offered the weapon up to Mark.

He took it from her carefully and turned the hilt to see its symbol. The Sword was Stonecutter.

Soft Ripple said: "The other one is free now. But I can carry only one up to the surface at a time."

With a flick of her tail, she dove again.

Almost absently Mark wiped dry the Sword of Siege upon his sleeve, and slowly he resheathed it. Everyone was watching the water once again, and again some were counting silently.

Ben suddenly snarled out an oath and pointed. The mermaid had reappeared, holding another Sword. But this time she was at the distance of the Isle of Magicians, where she had leaped out of the water almost like a seal, to sit upon a low, wet rock.

She waved across the water with the Sword, offering a mocking greeting to the people in the boats.

"Row! Get us over there!" the prince commanded. Oars clashed and labored. But boats were slow and clumsy, and they were not going to catch a mermaid in the water.

In fact it appeared that they were not going to catch Soft Ripple, even though she was content to remain out of the water for the time being.

"Stop her!"

The mermaid was swinging the heavy Sword slowly, tentatively, awkwardly around her head; the thin muscles of her arms and shoulders stood out with the effort.

Zoltan on hearing that last order from his prince had reached mechanically for his bow, and someone else was reaching for a sling. But both people stayed their hands. If the Sword were to fall into the water from where the mermaid held it now, it would plunge once more into the channel's hopeless depths.

Mark was cursing at the rowers: "Get us over there, quick!"

As fast as the rowers could propel them, the two fishing boats were now approaching Magicians' Island from the south. And still the mermaid, sitting safely out of everyone's reach, twirled the Sword, and still she seemed not quite able to bring herself to let it go. Perhaps for some reason she could not feel Farslayer's power—or perhaps—

Mark issued orders in a low voice: "Ben! Take your boat, land on the far side of the island. I'll take this one to where we can get close enough to argue with her from the water."

It seemed to Zoltan a very long time before the prow of the boat now carrying Ben and himself grated ashore at the nearest feasible landing spot that was just out of sight of Mark's boat, and of the mermaid on her rock.

Ben and Zoltan leaped from their boat and hit the beach running. As they did so, a small horde of minor powers took to the air around them, just as had happened when Black Pearl's body was first disturbed in the water. Zoltan had seen their like on occasion in the past, and more experienced observers than he had never been able to determine whether powerful wizards somehow created such swarming entities, or were only capable of calling them from some other plane of existence. However that might be, Zoltan knew that in a disorganized swarm like this one the miniature entities, for the most part indifferent to human beings, were hardly more dangerous than so many mosquitoes would have been.

Not that danger would have mattered to him just now. He ran forward, hoping to get into position to hurl himself at the mermaid before she threw the Sword, and drag Farslayer somehow from her grip. Still the little powers, doubtless sent here long ago to guard the island from nonmagicians, swarmed about. They were only semisentient at best. One could hear them buzzing faintly in the air, and see them like small ripples of atmospheric heat. Any human with even a minimal sensitivity to the things of magic could feel them in the air as well.

Zoltan had left ponderous Ben some strides behind. Now, approaching the hummock that concealed him from the mermaid, Zoltan slowed and raised his head cautiously over the obstacle. He could see his uncle Mark, standing in the boat, still trying to argue Soft Ripple out of throwing the Sword.

Now he could see the mermaid, too.

Zoltan eased forward, hoping to get close before she saw him. Mark continued his argument. Ben came up silently behind Zoltan, and a little to one side.

But they were all too late, or ineffective.

"If he is still alive, I kill him. If dead, let my hate follow him to hell!"

With a last hideous, obscene malediction against Cosmo Malolo, the mermaid let the bright blade fly.

17

Gelimer had just finished the painful task of burying his faithful Geelong in the cemetery grove, when the Sword of Vengeance entered his life again.

It had taken the hermit a long struggle to get the beast's mangled body down from the thorntrees, and Geelong had died well before the process could be completed; had died—for which Gelimer was thankful —even before the hermit could get into position to administer the mercy stroke himself.

After that it had been a struggle for the hermit, himself wracked by physical as well as mental pain, to get the animal's body uphill to his house. His arms and legs were bruised and every muscle in his body ached, making it a slow and painful process for him to do anything. All through the following night Gelimer, lying beside his pet's blanket-wrapped body, had tried to rest, tried to recover from the injuries caused by the demon's manhandling.

And in the morning, for the first time, he thought he knew what it felt like to be old. Moving as in a dream of pain and suffering, he had lifted the rude bundle containing his companion's mangled body, placed it on a kind of travois, and had urged his own battered body to pull the contrivance in the direction of the cemetery.

He could not have said how much time was taken by the work of pulling, selecting a gravesite, and digging. He had just finished his prayers to Ardneh over the refilled grave, had turned and started for home, when the Sword came.

Gelimer first saw the rainbow streak moving across the distant sky, coming from the north and angling to the west. Then the bright track curved, until it appeared to be coming directly at him. And now he heard and felt the all-too-familiar onrush of its approaching magic.

For just a brief moment Gelimer believed that Farslayer was coming for him, and he stood motionless and unalarmed while something in him responded with eagerness to the thought of death. But the Sword rushed by overhead. The truth was that nobody hated him, no one was his enemy, no one any longer even knew him well enough to want to waste a Sword-blow on him.

The Sword of Vengeance had not been sent to strike the hermit's heart. The rainbow streak of the Sword, swifter than any arrow Gelimer had ever seen in flight, arced close over his head, coming down directly into the cemetery grove he had just left. There, somewhere under those tall trees, it struck home with an earthen impact, dull and loud as a blow from a god's hammer.

Gelimer dropped the handle of the empty travois he had been dragging, and with his shovel still clutched in one hand hurried back under the trees. The spot of impact was impossible to miss. Something had cratered the black dirt and the spring flowers, sending earthy debris far and wide. The flying Sword had landed directly on the site of the last grave but one that he had dug.

The hermit ran forward. Regardless of the slippery mud, regardless of the protests of his own painful body, he plunged his shovel into the cratered ground and began to dig again.

Presently the smell of old death, as if at some opening of hell, came surging up to meet him. He choked on it, but persisted.

In a few moments he was sure of what had happened. He could see now that the body of Cosmo Malolo, which had been decomposing for the past month inside its crude blanket-shroud, had for a second time been pierced through the heart by the Sword of the Gods.

Gelimer threw down his shovel. His muddy fingers, trembling, closed upon that black, mud-spattered hilt. With that contact his fingers ceased to tremble. Muttering half-finished prayers of gratitude to Ardneh, and perhaps to other, darker gods as well, the hermit carried the Sword up out of the shallow, blasted pit.

Exactly who had thrown the Sword this time, and why vengeance had been wasted upon a victim already dead, were questions that did not now even cross his mind.

The grove around him was as silent and tranquil as ever. Though the day was bright, here under the trees it was almost dim with their heavy shading. Standing erect, Gelimer saluted the grave of Geelong with the Sword. Then, gripping the knurled hilt in both hands, the hermit began a ponderous, spinning dance—

His dance was carrying him, step by step, out of the grove and into the open air, where you could see for kilometers in all directions except that of the mountain whose shoulder he was standing on. He had not whirled thrice beyond the trees before there appeared to him, standing only forty or fifty meters away in sunlight, the image of the demon Rabisu. The demon came in the guise of an armored man, tall as a house, half transparent but immense, who ran forward threateningly, raising some blurred weapon—

Gelimer saw the approaching shape, and uttered a hoarse cry. In the next instant he felt the Sword fly free, tearing itself by its own power out of his grip, an instant before he would have let it go.

The blade passed straight through the demon's image as through a mirage, seeming to do no harm. Then, like an intelligent arrow, Farslayer curved its own pathway in mid-flight. But not back toward the apparition. Instead the Sword went down on the north side of the river, somewhere over the Senones stronghold.

The figure of the demon had stopped in its tracks, and turned to watch that darting descent. Now it turned back to confront Gelimer. Rabisu's assumed countenance, which had been recognizable as the semblance of a human face, was now chaotic, indescribable. The apparition stood as if paralyzed, and from its demonic throat there issued a last cry, a great howl that went on and on.

That outcry lingered in the air even after the image of the demon had disappeared.

The mermaid, Soft Ripple, had plunged into the river immediately after she threw the Sword. But she surfaced again very quickly, risking retaliation by the angry men around her, unable to resist the attraction of watching the weapon in flight. Not that there was much to see, a mere rainbow flicker toward the slope of the mountain to the south.

A moment of silence hung over the boats and the island. It was broken by another loud outcry, near at hand.

This scream had come from the throat of a woman Zoltan had never seen before. Her thin figure, wrapped in the robes of a sorceress, came tottering forward from a recess among the rocks of Magicians' Island. Facing the mermaid, this apparition halted, and uttered another hoarse scream. "Not Cosmo! No! You shall not kill him!"

Bonar raised a hand and pointed. "That is the Lady Megara Senones, the bitch-sorceress. We must take her prisoner. Gesner, can you deal with her magic?"

Gesner opened his mouth and closed it again, making no promises, not even of effort.

But Prince Mark was paying little attention to his immediate companions. "My lady," he called to the figure on the rock. "Are you in need of help?"

The woman Bonar had called Megara, the supposed sorceress, turned a distracted gaze in Mark's direction. And Zoltan, as he got his first full look at her face, took her for an old woman, even older than Yambu perhaps. At a second look he was not so sure of her age, but certain that she had been through terrible things.

Soft Ripple, thrashing in the water nearby, shrilled at her: "I know who you are, old woman. Your Cosmo is dead now! Even for you there can be no stopping that Sword. Not even you damned arrogant magicians can manage that!"

Slowly, in small jerky movements and little slumps, Megara standing on her rock relaxed from a posture of rage and anger into one of weariness and despair.

When she spoke again, she glanced toward the mermaid, and her voice was very tired. "I fear that you are right, fishgirl. If Cosmo was not dead before this . . ." Then she saw Bonar glaring at her in something like triumph. She cried to her hereditary enemy: "Will you kill me, then? Strike, if you will, there is nothing to prevent you now!"

Ben edged a little nearer Bonar, ready to restrain him from accepting this invitation.

Mark, still speaking calmly, told the lady: "We are going to the south shore, after the Sword. Come with us, if you will."

"It no longer matters to me where I go," the sorceress said after a pause. "What magic I can attempt no longer works. Except my little boat . . . yes. I accept. I'll go with you. If I could even see his body there—it would be better if I could know with certainty that he is dead."

"Cosmo Malolo?"

"Of course. He and I are lovers." The claim was made proudly but it seemed grotesque.

"Ah," said Yambu, who until now had been attending silently. "And that night, on this island, where the killing started—the two of you were discovered by your father?"

"Yes. That is what happened. And Cosmo killed him, with the Sword."

Mark had by now gone to the lady's side, and was offering her his arm, while Bonar seethed in not-quite-silent protest. His protests had no effect. Both boats were shortly under way again, Megara riding with Prince Mark aboard the one that did not hold the clan chief of the Malolo. Soft Ripple followed swimming, staying within easy earshot.

The young mermaid had more that she wanted to tell Megara about Cosmo.

"I knew what you were doing, the two of you, meeting on the island.

I watched your two boats coming and going. And I knew what he did to my friend Black Pearl. Did you know that your marvelous Cosmo screwed around with mermaids?"

Megara was sitting straight in her seat, looking straight ahead, as if she could not hear.

"Tell us about it later," Ben grumbled at the mermaid in a low voice.

"No," said the prince. "No, I think that we should hear Soft Ripple's story now."

The oarsmen worked, the two boats moved steadily toward the south shore of the river. Soft Ripple kept on talking.

"I knew Black Pearl was up to something," the mermaid said. "Finally I followed her, and I found out that she made many visits to Magicians' Island. Eventually I found an underwater tunnel there."

Soft Ripple went on to relate how she had discovered that a Malolo boat, the same one, was invariably tied up in one of the island's concealed coves when Black Pearl paid her secret visits there. Later on she became aware of another boat, one that came out to Magicians' Island from the Senones side of the river, propelled by sail and with a single occupant. It was a small craft, and Soft Ripple thought that perhaps it was partly propelled by magic. Certainly magic had somewhat protected it from observation. It had invariably come out to the island when Cosmo's craft was also there. On the first occasion this might have happened by accident, but on later occasions their meetings had obviously been planned.

Soft Ripple had at length grown curious enough to risk the secret underwater passage for herself, choosing a time when the island was otherwise deserted. Overcome by curiosity, and perhaps by jealousy, she had forced herself to go on, despite the buzzing of minor powers that generally frightened away her mermaid sisters as well as the fisherfolk of both clans.

Later, her curiosity grew so great that she even dared the passage when she knew that Meg and Cosmo were in the grotto, and she had spied on them, unsuspected, as they lay together.

"We can sometimes see quite well from underwater, did you know that? And we can hear. I saw and heard the two of you, holding up the Sword and talking about it."

Lady Megara turned finally. She changed her position so that she was looking down at the creature swimming in the water beside the boat.

Soft Ripple's eyes were glittering as she spoke. "Then, later, I spied on Black Pearl and Cosmo. He was magician enough to fix it so she grew legs, if only for a little while. Did you know that? Legs, and what's between them, too. That's what he wanted from her. That's what men always want. Yours wasn't enough for him."

"Fables and fairy stories," said Lady Megara instantly. Her voice was as soft and certain as any that Zoltan had ever heard. "Cosmo told me about you. And about the other one, Black Pearl or whatever her name was. How he had been trying to help you, out of the goodness of his heart. How you became impatient and angry when he couldn't cure you immediately, how you were starting to make up lies about him. Yes, yes indeed, he told me." And the lady in the boat nodded and smiled, almost sweetly, at the accursed creature in the water.

"Oh no. Oh no. It's you who lie." The mermaid, swimming on her back, gazed up at the people in the boat, gazed at the Lady Megara in particular. It was as if the enormity of what the lady was saying held her hypnotized. "I talked to Cosmo, yes. Why shouldn't I? I told him that I wanted legs, too. And he—he said he'd kill me if I tried to make trouble. But if I waited, and was patient, and said nothing to anyone, then maybe it would be my turn next. I knew what he meant, he meant after he was through with Black Pearl. Then he would see to it that I got legs. But I would only have had them for a few minutes at a time. Now I know he never really meant to help any of us . . ."

Lady Megara had long since ceased to listen. She said, to Mark and the others in the boats: "Cosmo showed me the Sword that he had hidden. He told me what it was going to mean for our future. Our families were both hopeless, lost in feuding. But that was not for us . . . the two of us were going to run away, taking the Sword with us. We would sell Farslayer in some great city, and that would give us the money we needed for the future.

The lady had grown animated in telling her story. "Let our families feud and kill each other if that was what they wanted. We would get away, and live our own lives, lives of peace and decency, somewhere else.

"Of course"—and her animation fled—"we would have to avoid my father at all costs."

"And then," said Lady Yambu, "one night your father caught up with you."

The two boats still made progress toward the south shore, while the mermaid continued to swim beside them. Now, reviving from the near silence of pain and despair, she once again shrieked curses against Megara and her beloved Cosmo.

Lady Meg continued to ignore her. But Zoltan, listening to Soft Ripple, believed what she said, or most of it, and thought that most of the other people in the boats believed her also. Zoltan wondered if Megara had ever suspected that her lover had been given to seducing mermaids. If so, Megara had put the idea firmly from her, and was not going to entertain it now.

Judging by Megara's expression, she was still refusing to credit such outrageous allegations, or even to think about them. Refusing to admit that such creatures as lowly fishgirls could have any important role to play in anything. That anything about them could be of any importance to the important people of the world.

But the lady in the boat was more than willing to converse with Mark, the prince who would accept her and listen to her as an equal. "I loved him," she repeated brightly, proudly, confidingly, as if she and Mark were the only people on the river. "We met on the island—the first time quite by accident. We loved each other from the first."

Again the mermaid screamed something foul.

The lady ignored the fishgirl. "And then, Cosmo showed me the marvelous Sword that he had hidden here."

At last, with an appearance of confidence, she deigned to answer the one who taunted from the water. "Yes, Cosmo told me that sometimes he caught mermaids. He was a kindhearted man, and he wanted to do something for the poor creatures. So sometimes he took them in one of his magical nets, for purposes of experimentation. It was all for their benefit. Of course I never asked their names. As for the idea that he might have had affairs with them . . ." That was obviously too absurd to deserve denial.

"He had Black Pearl. And he was going to have me next, I tell you!" Soft Ripple shrieked, her voice almost unintelligible now. Her small pale hands were pounding water into foam.

"But he never did, did he? I'm sorry for you, my dear."

"He had Black Pearl, and—and—"

Soft Ripple's voice broke, then collapsed completely in grotesque hatred, jealousy, suffering, and rage. And then suddenly she was only a young girl, weeping, drifting almost inertly beside the boat.

Mark asked the Lady Megara: "If I may, my lady, go back to the Sword for a moment. Where did Cosmo first obtain it? Did he ever tell you that?"

"He told me, freely, that he traded with a mermaid for it. And he had begun to fear that some of the creatures were developing their—their own grotesque feelings for him. That they were making up fantasies. I only know that he never . . ."

* * *

Lady Megara talked on, and now it was the mermaid's turn not to listen. Soft Ripple had fallen quite silent, gliding on her back, looking up expressionlessly at the sky. But still she swam beside the boats, as if secured to them by some invisible chain.

The woman in the boat continued speaking. "But my father grew suspicious. He must have followed me, secretly, that night. It may be that some of my magical powers were beginning to fade, because I was no longer a virgin." The Lady Megara made the declaration proudly.

"He came upon us as we lay together. He stood over us, hand on the hilt of his sword, thundering judgment, consigning us to our fates. I, the faithless, treacherous daughter, was going to spend the rest of my life in a White Temple. As for Cosmo, the Malolo seducer, a hideous death awaited him.

"But for once the judge was not allowed to enforce his sentence. He turned his back on us, and I suppose he was about to call out to his men to come in. But as soon as he did so, Cosmo pulled the great and beautiful Sword out of its hiding place, and stabbed him through the back.

"I had risen to my knees, about to try to plead with my father. When I saw Cosmo strike him, I could neither speak nor move. My father never uttered a sound. He turned partway around, with the Sword still in him, and looked at me with a great and terrible surprise; it was as if he thought that I had been the one to strike him. And in a way I had.

"Now, for once, I saw him as someone who could be hurt, someone who could need my help. He tried to speak again, but he could not.

"And then, a moment later, he fell dead."

Lady Yambu said something, so low that Zoltan could not make it out. Still the oarsmen rowed stolidly, and the boats advanced.

"Cosmo must have tried to talk to me after that. But I was paralyzed in shock.

"Perhaps I said something to him then, something terrible that made him leave me and run away. I don't remember. I don't remember. All I know is that I loved him, and I love him still."

Megara suddenly slumped over in her seat, swaying as if she might be on the brink of complete collapse. Yambu soothed her, stoically and almost silently, with memories in her own mind of some similar experience herself.

Eventually Megara raised her head and spoke again. "The next thing I remember is that my father's men had rushed into the grotto, and were trying to revive me. His body still lay there on the couch, or just beside it. Someone had already pulled out the Sword that had killed him, and I suppose had already used it again. When the men saw that my father had been struck down by Farslayer, they naturally assumed that it had come magically into the grotto from a distance—and that one of the Malolo must have thrown it. Of course none of them blamed Cosmo, or even thought of him, I suppose. If they ever thought of him at all, he was not considered dangerous.

"And so began our night of the great slaughter—but I knew no more about it. I knew nothing else very clearly for about a month."

Soft Ripple, abstracted now, continued to swim silently beside the boat.

And Bonar, riding in the other boat from Megara, confirmed how, on that night of terror, Cosmo had returned from one of his magical night outings, at about the time of the first (as the Malolo thought) Sword-death.

It had been a night of vile weather, of sleet and wind and snow. As a result, almost all members of both rival families had been gathered around their respective hearths.

There had been quite a number of eager, excitable young Malolo men on hand that night, the flower of the family youth. The same thing across the river. And the leaders on both sides had been killed quite early that night.

Cosmo on coming home that night had of course said nothing about his having been on Magicians' Island, or about the patriarch of their enemies having died there at his hand.

But Bonar could say something now about his cousin having gone to that island frequently.

He added that, on that night, Cosmo had tried to get the others to interrupt the cycle of killing. But as usual no one had paid him much attention. Cosmo had been no more highly respected by his own family than he was by their enemies. He was looked on as a failed magician, who had not been very good at anything else, either. His pleas and warnings on the night of killing had been scorned and disregarded.

Then the Sword had struck again—for what was to seem to others the last time that night—coming in through the stone walls of the Malolo manor and killing someone.

This time Cosmo had been first on the scene and had drawn the weapon from the corpse. But instead of striking back in his turn, like a true Malolo, he had seized Farslayer and run out into the night with it.

Soon the remaining family members, few, bereaved, and bewildered, discovered that he'd reclaimed the mount he'd recently left in the stables, and galloped off, the gods knew where.

Before leaving he'd said something, a few words to a stablehand, that indicated he felt responsible for some reason for the slaughter that had now overtaken his own family.

"We cannot be sure what he was thinking. But it seems that he meant to take the Sword somewhere where it could do no harm."

"A goal with which I can feel some sympathy," said Prince Mark. "In fact I can remember trying to do something like that once myself. When I was very young."

The two boats moved on steadily toward the south shore, where Mark and his friends were determined to find the hermit Gelimer.

18

H ISSARLIK, sitting on his high chair in his great hall and enjoying a solitary meal, suddenly gave a great shriek, and tumbled writhing to the floor.

Three servants, who were the only people in the room with the clan chief at the moment, became aware at that same moment of the return of a terrible visitor: the same Sword that a month ago had well-nigh depopulated the house of its owners and masters.

This time the onlookers' first glimpse of the weapon came as it fell clashing on the floor beside their wounded Tyrant. Hissarlik's clothes and the floor around him were being drenched in a steady outpouring of his blood.

Two of the servants rushed immediately to the assistance of the Tyrant. In moving the Sword out of the way, they saw that it held, impaled near its tip, a rather peculiar-looking leather wallet. The wallet was heavily spattered with Hissarlik's blood; and it was not immediately recognizable as leather, having curled up into a dry and lifeless-looking scrap of what looked like parchment.

Hissarlik was not yet dead. In fact he was not even completely disabled, though his side had been deeply gashed and blood poured from his wound. Ashen-faced, he demanded to be helped to rise. With a servant's help he got himself up on his shaky knees, and then by dint of grasping another servant's arm, hauled himself to his feet. Then, almost falling again, he bent over with difficulty to grasp the deadly Sword by its black hilt and pick it up.

The third of the servants present, who for some days now had been secretly in the pay of Tigris, had already dashed out of the room to tell her newest employer what had happened.

Meanwhile, Hissarlik, even though his eyes were glazing, had shaken free of the arms that supported him. He was holding the Sword's hilt with two hands now, and doing his staggering best to spin around.

He muttered a name, and threw the Sword, which vanished in a flash through the stone walls of the room, as magically as it had come in through them. A moment later, the latest wielder of the Sword of Vengeance had fallen again, to lie at full length on the floor. Hissarlik's eyes were glazing more rapidly now.

A door banged open. Tigris, who had been unable to stay with him at every moment, came rushing in angrily from two rooms away. She was moments too late to witness Farslayer's latest departure.

"Where is the Sword? What have you done with it? You fool, you've thrown it away, haven't you!" In a controlled rage, she knelt beside the fallen man. "Did I hear you cry out a name? That of the target, it must have been!"

The dying Hissarlik, his side still spouting blood, was trying to focus his eyes on the face of Tigris as she bent over him. He was trying to tell her something that seemed to him to be of great importance.

But she gave no indication that she was interested, or that she was about to practice any of her healing arts on him. "What's this? The demon's life, well skewered, just as I thought it might be!" In her rage she hurled the scrap of leather down. Then she gripped the dying Tyrant, and shook him angrily. "I thought the Sword might be coming to you—but why did you throw it away? Why? I needed that Sword, you fool!"

But she received no answer.

Chilperic had left the Senones manor surreptitiously before dawn, and made his way quietly to the camp of Koszalin's mercenaries. He found the captain and his men ready and waiting. Chilperic's objective today was to lead this small force against the Malolo stronghold in what he hoped was going to be a surprise attack.

They managed to cross the river under cover of darkness, but experienced some trouble with the boats, which the mercenaries handled awkwardly. As a result, the expedition landed on the south shore a great deal farther downstream than its leader had planned, and the day was well advanced before they got back within striking distance of the place he wanted to attack.

Koszalin and Chilperic had some desultory conversation en route, not all of it acrimonious. Chilperic at least felt that they had come to understand each other on several levels. But there were still problems between them.

Chilperic, checking the leather wallet in his inner pocket at frequent intervals, thought that the ten men he was leading, with a demon to back them up, had every chance of seizing the undermanned enemy fortress in a surprise attack.

Koszalin also discounted the Malolo defenses, except for those that the strange visitors might be able to provide, as consisting of no more than a handful of frightened servants.

Having seen something of the Malolo manor and its defenders first-hand, Chilperic was inclined to agree with this assessment—but not to trust it with his life.

At last, wanting to make sure that Rabisu was going to be available this time when he was needed, Chilperic overcame his distaste for the creature and tried to call it up.

As on the previous day, his first attempt got no response at all.

Chilperic muttered to himself: "What now, has the damned thing got itself banished to the orbit of the Moon again?"

But this time things were subtly worse than yesterday. Today there was not even the proper feeling of power in the leather wallet when he stroked it.

Looking carefully at the mottled, folded leather, he realized that though it was as glossy and rich-looking as usual, it was not the same wallet he had been carrying yesterday. There were subtle differences in appearance.

Looking back across the river, he swore, viciously and quietly.

He could remember all too well his nighttime visit from the damned enchantress Tigris.

Swapping passengers from one boat to another in midstream was a little chancy, but Bonar and Gesner insisted on taking over one of the boats for family affairs as soon as they had convinced themselves in discussion that the Sword had again begun to bear the deadly traffic of the feud. The mermaid had thrown it against Cosmo, alive or dead, and it had whirred off somewhere.

Just where, was a question. Mark and Ben, who had had some previous experience with the Sword of Vengeance, were not surprised that it was difficult to gauge the point of impact from a glimpse of the Sword in flight. But Cosmo alive or dead had probably not been very far away, and Farslayer would most likely be picked up again by someone involved in the affairs of the valley.

Bonar in particular was determined to reach the stronghold of his family manor as rapidly as possible, now that Farslayer had begun to fly again.

"If it is my fate now to be struck down by Farslayer," said Bonar with considerable dignity, "then I must fall where someone of my own house will be on hand to avenge me."

Mark had no wish to argue with him. But he detailed Ben of Purkinje to accompany the head of the clan and his magician back to the manor. Mark himself, with Zoltan and Yambu accompanying him, still intended to find the hermit Gelimer and search the upland where the hermit lived. That seemed to them to be the area in which the Sword had most recently come down.

The boat carrying Ben, Bonar, and Gesner pulled away, riding swiftly downstream with the current augmenting the rowers' efforts. The remaining craft, on the prince's orders, pulled straight toward the south shore. On landing, Mark detailed the four armed oarsmen to guard the boat, while Mark, Zoltan, and Yambu started uphill intending to find Gelimer.

Lady Megara climbed along with them, saying that she wished to confirm Cosmo's death and see his body. It seemed that a spot of uncertainty regarding his fate still lingered in her mind.

Aging and tired as she looked, she somehow found the energy to keep up with the other three, and the ascent went fairly swiftly. The four had not spent much time on the trail paralleling the little watercourse before they came upon the hermit.

It was Zoltan, climbing in the lead, who saw and recognized Gelimer first. The hermit was crouched over two dead bodies, one dripping wet, that were laid out side by side on the bank of the stream. When the young man got a little closer he could see that the dead men were armed and had probably been mercenaries; judging by the green scarves they both wore, they had been members of the same company that had invested Malolo manor.

Zoltan halted on the path, while Prince Mark came up silently behind his nephew and stood looking over his shoulder.

"Gelimer," Zoltan whispered.

"I surmised as much," Mark said in a low voice. "But how do two of Koszalin's people come to be lying here?"

The hermit, at last becoming aware that he had company, raised his head and stared at his visitors. Gelimer looked worn out, thought Zoltan, and perhaps a little mad. As the company of four once more approached him, he stared at them without seeming to notice whether they were friends or strangers.

"The Sword again," said Gelimer in a cracked voice. "It kills and kills, you see. You can see its mark on each of these. How many more funerals," he asked the world in general, "am I going to be required to conduct?"

"I cannot tell you that, old man," said the prince. And indeed Gelimer did seem to have aged considerably since Zoltan had seen him
last.

The hermit, for his part, now at last indicated that he recognized
Zoltan and Yambu as the two pilgrims who had dropped in on him only
a few days ago.

The hermit was introduced to Mark and Lady Megara. It was impossible to tell from Gelimer's demeanor whether he had ever heard of the
Prince of Tasavalta, or whether Megara's name meant anything to him
or not.

"I suppose that you are after it, too," he said to the prince.

No need to ask the old man what he was talking about. "I admit that
I am," said Mark. "I want it for a good reason."

"It was here, you know. Only a little while ago. I held it in these
hands." And Gelimer spread his work-worn hands and held them out
for inspection, as if they might be considered trustworthy evidence.

"Where is it now?"

"Gone again. Across the river—I think that's where it went. I sent it
after the life of the demon, and now I think that creature will trouble
the world no more." The hermit spoke with a kind of dreamy satisfaction.

"Where was the demon's life concealed, good hermit?" Mark had to
take the old man by the arm and shake him gently before he would
respond.

Gelimer blinked at him sadly. "Where was its life hidden? I don't
know. I don't understand demons. But I expect we can be sure of one
thing, that one's now dead. As dead as my Geelong."

"Geelong? Who's that?"

Yambu said: "That was the name of his pet watchbeast, I believe."

Megara, looking physically frail again after the burst of energy that
had let her climb, was growing impatient with all this talk of demons.
"Old man," she demanded. "What can you tell me of Cosmo Malolo?"

She had to repeat the question before Gelimer truly heard it. Then he
said: "Cosmo Malolo? I am sorry, my lady, but that man is dead."

"Dead?" Megara smiled gently. Zoltan, watching, thought that in the
space of a few moments the lady came to look older than the hermit.
"Yes. Yes, I thought that he was dead."

Prince Mark persisted in coming back to the subject of Rabisu. "Tell
me about the demon, Gelimer. I wonder where his life was hidden?" He
gazed intently at the hermit. "Did you say that the Sword went across
the river?"

Gelimer looked toward the north side of the river and gestured vaguely. "It went through him, right through him. And then, yes—it came down somewhere over there."

Mark muttered: "It can dart back and forth across the river faster than we can ever hope to follow it. And it probably will, assuming that the feud's still on."

Lady Yambu nodded. "I think we must assume that."

Zoltan said: "Then, if Farslayer last came down somewhere in Senones-land, the chances are its *next* target will be somewhere on this bank."

"In or near the Malolo manor," Yambu added.

"That seems likely to me," said Mark. "Well, our quickest way of getting downstream will be by boat."

"You are returning to the river?" asked the hermit. It seemed that for the moment he had forgotten completely about the two dead bodies at his feet. "I shall come down to the bank with you, if I may. I want to talk to a mermaid, you see. Black Pearl is her name."

The other two men were already moving down the trail again, and neither turned back to answer him. Yambu, falling into step beside Gelimer, explained to him that Black Pearl was dead. He heard the news without any real surprise.

While the five people were descending the hill, Gelimer told his companions a more detailed story of what Cosmo had done, and what had happened to Cosmo, on that night of many killings about a month ago.

The Lady Megara listened carefully to the story of that strange visitor, his stranger death, his burial, and his bizarre second "killing" today, by the same Sword; but it was as if these events had happened to someone she did not know.

When the party had regained the riverbank, they found the boat, which Mark had feared might be gone, still waiting for them. The oarsmen, thought Zoltan, had probably not yet had quite enough time to convince themselves that they had better desert their clients and return to their own village.

Soft Ripple was nearby in the water, and swam closer to shore at once when Gelimer began to talk to her. In turn, Gelimer heard from her the details of Black Pearl's death, and saw the mermaid's body, which was still aboard the boat.

Soft Ripple listened quietly when she was told that Cosmo had been already a month dead when she had thrown the Sword at him. Her only comment was: "I wish it could have followed him into hell!"

If Lady Megara heard this, she had nothing to say in reply. She had reached a state of imperturbable calm, and the additional confirmation of her lover's death meant nothing.

Eventually Yambu asked her friends: "But who killed Cosmo? Who actually used the Sword on him the first time? He wouldn't have carried it all the way over here from the manor, simply to throw it at one of the Senones. And even if he had, why would the Senones finally decide at that point to kill Cosmo, after having ignored him all night?"

Gelimer nodded sadly. "I have thought much about those questions. And it seems to me that that sad young man must have killed himself."

"No," said Lady Megara, softly but decisively. She had, it seemed, been listening after all.

Mark scowled. "He stabbed himself in the back, with a weapon more than a meter long? That would take some doing."

"No, he did not stab himself. I think he went outside my house, where there was more room to dance and spin. And he hurled the blade, willing his own death—vengeance on himself, for the disaster he had caused that night, including his treacherous killing of the Lady Megara's father."

And Gelimer went on to expound further on the behavior of Cosmo Malolo on that last night of his life. "Things might have gone differently, had he not fallen from his riding-beast and injured his head. Or the outcome might have been the same—who can say, now?"

"I still think," said Mark, "that Cosmo's goal when he left his manor that night must have been simply to take the Sword of Vengeance out into an empty land somewhere—such as these mountains might provide—and lose it there."

"Or perhaps," said Yambu, "to kill himself with it out there, where neither his body nor the Sword might ever be discovered."

"We'll never know."

"What's that?"

Gelimer was pointing up into the sky.

The others squinted, shading their eyes against the sun and peering.

"Some truly giant bird."

"No. No, surely that's a griffin, carrying someone."

Wood was known for using griffins. And now one of the bizarre creatures, bearing on its back a single human figure, was swiftly crossing the river from north to south, heading in the direction of Malolo manor.

19

Mark and his companions embarked again, leaving Gelimer and Lady Megara behind them on the bank. At the last moment the hermit had asked to be allowed to bury Black Pearl's body. This wish was readily granted, and the body unloaded from the boat. Zoltan made no protest; with every minute that passed, the horrible thing under the wet canvas seemed to have less and less connection with the girl he had begun to know three years ago. And in any case, he felt that duty now compelled him to go on with his uncle Mark without delay.

Lady Megara, though saying very little, had conveyed to the others that she wanted to stay with Gelimer, and to climb with him to the cemetery where Cosmo lay.

The remainder of the party got into the boat and pushed off. The prince, seated amidships, urged on his four rowers in a princely way. And those men, finding themselves now on a direct course for home, complied to the best of their ability. The boat sped downstream, headed straight for the fishing village in which Yambu and Zoltan had spent their first night in this country.

Soft Ripple, as Zoltan observed without being able to understand the fact, was still accompanying the boat. It occurred to him to wonder whether the village ahead had once been her home—and possibly Black Pearl's also.

"Are you armed?" Mark asked Yambu, when they had been under way for a minute in silence.

"Only with my wits," she answered calmly. "In this most recent epoch of my life I have forsworn the use of steel. Except of course in dire emergencies."

"Then probably you are better armed than I, my lady," Mark admitted. "Still there are times when steel has its uses."

"And such a time, you think, lies close ahead of us. I think it quite likely you are right."

Mark looked at his nephew. "If the Sword comes within reach of anyone in Malolo manor, they are likely to dispute its ownership with us. Especially if Bonar is still alive."

Zoltan nodded, and made sure that his own short sword and his knife were ready. Then he squinted ahead, looking along a western reach of river. The other boat, the one that had preceded them carrying Ben, Bonar, and Gesner, must by now be very far ahead—indeed, Zoltan, shading his eyes, was unable to see it on the river at all.

"Quite likely," said Mark, as if reading his nephew's mind, "they've already landed."

Ben, Bonar, and Gesner had indeed docked and come ashore at the fishing village. There their oarsmen had vanished at once among the huts, pausing only long enough to tie up their boat. The other inhabitants of the village, Ben noticed, were keeping out of sight also, as if perhaps they expected trouble.

Gesner, Ben, and Bonar, the latter looking around him in vague apprehension, at once started walking inland from the village, along the road that led toward Malolo manor.

Ben's presence put an obvious damper on conversation, a fact which did not bother him in the least. The three had traversed perhaps half the distance to the manor in near silence, when Gesner suddenly held up a hand, and said something to stop his companions.

Now Ben too was aware of a foretaste of magic in the air. He turned, looking high, and then he saw the rainbow flicker coming toward them.

Bonar, looking in the wrong direction, was just starting to ask a question.

Meanwhile, Chilperic and his crew of mercenaries, who had finished making their way back upstream along the southern bank, had begun to move cautiously into position for an assault. With the demon still missing—today Rabisu's absence had a kind of finality about it—Chilperic had just about abandoned the idea of attacking the manor directly, at least by daylight. Instead he hoped to be able to catch some of the enemy out in the open, or, failing that, to gain at least a good idea of the lie of the land before nightfall.

Koszalin, on Chilperic's orders, had deployed his ten men in something like a line of battle. They were combing a half-wooded area between the manor and the village. Thus Chilperic and those with him were also in position to see the Sword as it came hurtling down from the sky to land—somewhere nearby.

Chilperic cursed, knowing how difficult it was to predict, from such a brief glimpse, exactly when the Sword was going to strike its blow, what roundabout path it might follow on its way to the chosen target, or exactly who or where that target was.

Bonar was lying on his left side in the middle of the path, his arms outflung. His fingers twitched, but he was stone-dead, with Farslayer run clear through his pudgy body from front to rear. The youth had been taken unawares, cut off in mid-sentence. Actually his mouth was still open and he looked surprised. He had managed to get within a few minutes of his home before Hissarlik's dying throw reached him and struck him down.

Gesner, who had been walking close beside the youth, bent over his dead body and reached for the black hilt.

"Don't touch it, wizard."

Stopping his fingers before they reached their goal, Gesner looked over his shoulder to see Ben standing very close to him, his own utilitarian blade already drawn.

The huge man went on: "I warn you, wizard—if you really deserve that name—the Sword is mine."

Gesner, without saying anything, straightened up and moved away from his fallen leader. The magician's hands were empty—or were they? Now they appeared to be slowly curving into a gesture aimed at Ben.

Ben did not appear to be impressed. He advanced on the other man, his own drawn sword still leveled. "I've seen too much of you to have much respect for your magic at this late hour—now stand back. I mean you no harm, man."

Gesner the failed magician, now failed again, dropped his hands and stood back for the moment.

Ben had just sheathed his own sword, and started to reach for the black hilt, when Gesner's hands swept up again, and a jet of something as colorless as heat seemed to flow from his extended fingertips. Something that brought pain and tingling—

The big man had not been taken unawares, and his reaction was instantaneous and strong. He moved one long stride to Gesner, and a backhanded blow from his huge right fist knocked the small man sprawling. The slow-developing spell was broken before it could reach anything like full power.

Ben needed only a moment to twist the Sword of Vengeance free of

Bonar's ribs and backbone. Then, with Farslayer in hand, he was standing over Gesner, somewhat surprised to see that the single bare-handed blow had killed him. Gesner's head was twisted to one side in a way that indicated his neck was broken, and his eyes looked unseeingly across the litter of the forest floor.

Well, no more problems there. Ben straightened up, looking about him in the scrubby forest. He had the Sword, for Mark. Now all he had to do was get away with it.

Faint noises indicated that a number of people were coming in his direction from the west. It sounded almost like an advancing line of infantry, clumsily trying to be quiet.

Ben drew his own sword again, and dropped Farslayer into the sheath at his side. While the Sword rode there it would be impossible for him to drop and lose it; and his own blade, good weapon that it was, would serve him as well in a fight. Holding it drawn and ready, he got himself moving, away from the two fallen men, and back in the general direction of the fishing village. He knew that Mark, coming after him, would probably land there first.

Back in the great room of Malolo manor, the sisters Rose and Violet had been arguing, and had at length managed to agree that they ought to order out some of their retainers to await their brother, in case he needed aid. Now a panicked servant came running into the house, saying that he had seen the mercenary force trying to encircle the manor.

Tough, fanatical Violet was stimulated by this news, and announced that she was ready to lead a motley force of servants—if she could raise one—into the field herself. Meanwhile Rose, more resigned than frightened, threw up her hands and retired to her room.

And at the same time Chilperic, Koszalin, and their men, alerted by certain sounds indicating a brief scuffle not far ahead, changed the course of their advance. Not realizing it at first, they were starting to close in on Ben.

On first sighting the huge man, they were spurred into action at the sight of the unmistakable black hilt that rode above the scabbard at his side. They were running, spreading out to encircle him, when Tigris hurtled into view, low in the sky, riding the griffin on which she had come to Senones manor.

She skimmed close above Chilperic while he ducked and yelled threats at her, then circled him and his small force higher aloft.

"Who has it now?" she shouted down to him.

"Bitch! Treacherous bitch! Where is my demon's life? What have you done with it?"

"The life of your precious demon has been ended by the Sword—as Hissarlik's was cut short, as your own life would have been, had you still been wearing Rabisu's next to your ribs. I saved you by taking it away, you fool!"

Chilperic snarled something incoherent at her.

The griffin's beating wings hurled the air of its passage into his face. Its rider turned her head and shouted down at him: "I have authority from Wood to take command here when I see fit. And I am exercising that authority now. Do you understand me?"

Meanwhile Koszalin had been standing nearby, looking keenly from one of the disputants to the other. "Orders, sir?" he now asked of Chilperic, calmly enough.

Chilperic in rage pointed at the woman in the air. "Bring her down from that beast!" he bellowed. "Kill her, if need be!"

Koszalin shouted and gestured to his men. A ragged volley of stones and arrows combed the air around the griffin; it was hit, and perhaps hurt—Chilperic knew that the creatures were not invulnerable, though neither were they easily killed.

The rider appeared to escape injury. Spurring her flying mount into a burst of speed, Tigris escaped for the moment beyond the range of missiles.

Mark, Zoltan, and Yambu, landed at last and moving inland toward the manor, heard military-sounding voices somewhere ahead of them, and saw a griffin flying low.

After a brief conference with Mark, Yambu chose not to run into a fight, but rather to make her way around it. She would seek to reach Malolo manor and try to exert some favorable influence upon events there.

Uncle and nephew, with their weapons drawn and ready, ran on into the area where Koszalin's men had just beaten off the griffin. Mark was wielding Stonecutter—like most of the Twelve it was an impressive physical weapon, even with all magical considerations left aside.

Ben had moved a little distance toward the fishing village when he was ambushed.

Movement in a nearby thicket drew his attention and he looked closely, to behold a familiar face, altered by death. Gesner's face. Head twisted to one side, cheeks pale, eyes fixed and staring. It was a shock to see. Then the pale hands of the standing corpse curved and moved, and a wave of heat, or something akin to heat, came washing out at Ben . . .

Not to be beaten that easily, he grunted and thrust into the thicket with his sword. Gesner toppled out. Evidently there was one trick that the little wizard could do properly, and it had not worked for him.

Ben thrust again, and once more, into the body at his feet, making as sure as possible that he was going to leave Gesner dead for certain this time.

Ben had caught one glimpse of Chilperic's people already, and he was sure that they were still after him, and were likely to catch up with him again. To gain support from his friends, Ben thought he had better continue to make his way back in the direction of the river, reasoning that Mark ought soon to be approaching from that way.

If he, Ben, could establish himself near the fishing village, find a hiding place from which he could watch the path or road leading from the village to Malolo manor, he thought he would be in good shape.

He would have to be careful about his route; the open road would not do. If matters ever came to a chase in the open, he was lost; he knew he would never be able to outrun a swift pursuer. On the other hand, few if any of these ragtag mercenaries, even if they were better armed, would be anxious to challenge him one-on-one.

Yambu, meanwhile, had reached the manor, where she was recognized and admitted. Next she exchanged a few words with the sisters there, who were anxious to get her report of events on the outside.

It had proven impossible for them to get any kind of a force together to go out in aid of Bonar. All of their able-bodied servants had disappeared.

The women talked and waited. Yambu was satisfied in her own mind that for the moment there was nothing better for her to do.

As it happened, some of Koszalin's men caught up with Ben again before Mark came into sight.

Fortunately Ben had thus far sustained no wounds. Still, he had no hope of being able to outrun the enemy, much less their missiles; the only way to protect himself from their stones and arrows was by getting deep into the densest thicket he could find, which involved doing himself some damage on thorntrees.

When his breathing had quieted somewhat, Ben was able to hear his enemies on all sides of him again. Now that he was sure they knew where he was, he gave out a loud rallying cry. He had nothing to lose now by being heard.

Ben had to call three times, before he heard a distant but very welcome answer.

Zoltan and Mark, now running forward yelling, trying to sound like a whole squad of infantry, had to drive away one or two people before they came within sight of Ben.

Ben, at the moment his friends sighted him, was engaged in a one-on-one struggle, near the edge of the thicket, with powerful Sergeant Shotoku. The sergeant, a young man looking for a challenge, was the only one of the mercenaries who had been eager to go into the tangle of thorny brush after Ben.

Resistance from two or three other mercenaries prevented Mark and Zoltan from actually reaching Ben's side, and they were still some thirty or forty meters away from his position in the thicket, and only able to catch an occasional glimpse of him.

The captain himself was coming to join this skirmish.

Several of Koszalin's men had deserted him as soon as the fighting actually started. Only five or six were still obeying his orders. But these remaining men were fighters, and they still outnumbered the opposition.

Tigris chose this moment to reenter the action, daringly hovering on her griffin.

This time she chose to approach Koszalin, arguing with him, trying to get him to ally with her instead of Chilperic. She complained that the thornbushes were protecting Ben too well from above, for her to be able to fly at him with her griffin.

"What gain is there to me, sorceress, if I do switch my allegiance to your cause?"

"Name your price, soldier, if you can get me Farslayer."

Koszalin shook his head. "I think you would not pay it."

"Between my master Wood and myself we can pay much. And we will, if you bring me the Sword."

"Yonder prince has one of the Twelve, too. What about that one instead?"

"The same pay for that. And my help to you against whatever others are here. My spells are weak, now that blades are out and blood has flowed. But this is a fighting creature that I ride."

There came another small volley of missiles aimed at the griffin, on the orders of Chilperic.

Tigris's next move was a counterattack on her former partner who was trying to kill her now. First an approach as if to parley again, then a charge, striking him down, using her griffin's powerful, lionlike forepaws as her directed weapons.

Chilperic, too crafty ever to be taken by surprise, got home on the griffin with a good swordsman's thrust in the instant before he perished.

The beast reeled in midair, and almost plunged to earth; Tigris wondered if Chilperic's own sword might have had some touch of magic in its steel, to let him strike like that at a creature of such magic.

But the griffin bore the victorious Tigris up again, just before they would have crashed into a tree. Certainly, at least, something of speed and maneuverability had been lost.

In another moment or two Tigris had to admit that the situation was worse than that. The animal was going to have to land somewhere, at least until she was able to work some of her healing arts upon it. Gently she urged it down, at the same time muttering curses upon Chilperic's magically poisoned steel.

During this part of the fighting, Mark was beset by two or three opponents, and he fell, dazed by a slung stone. One of the mercenaries closed in for the kill.

Zoltan was near his uncle, but fully occupied at the moment in his own fight, unable to come to Mark's assistance.

Ben, near the edge of the thicket thirty or forty meters distant, had just overcome Sergeant Shotoku with a stranglehold. Now Ben had to throw the Sword of Vengeance at the mercenary threatening Mark if the life of the fallen prince was to be saved.

The flying Sword skewered the mercenary and knocked him down.

Koszalin bravely charged in Mark's direction.

But not to strike the helpless prince. Instead the captain seized the Sword, wrenching it free from the torso of its latest victim. Then Koszalin ran off, dodging among bushes, to get the few moments of privacy he needed.

Tigris, still on the ground tending to her griffin, was unable to keep the captain from doing what he wanted with Farslayer in the next few moments, though she probably saw him take the Sword, and guessed, and feared what he was about to do.

Some of Koszalin's men, having overheard the lady's dazzling promise of riches and other rewards, were quite ready to dispute this point with him; and Koszalin needed to kill one of them with the Sword, never letting go of its black hilt, to make his own point perfectly clear.

* * *

Koszalin was ignoring the fact that the griffin and rider had managed to become airborne again. He was ignoring his other opponents, including some who had been his own men. All of them were coming to kill him now in an effort to get Farslayer for themselves. But they were all going to be too late. The captain spun around and chanted, and launched the Sword of Vengeance on a new mission.

The recovering Mark, and others closing in on Koszalin, were able to obtain only a brief glimpse of the Sword's trajectory on this occasion. From what they could see, the indication was that the Sword of Vengeance was departing on a very long flight, headed somewhere in the general direction of the southern horizon.

Exactly who or what had been Koszalin's target was something that no one else present then understood. If any of them had heard the captain's last shouted word, which might be assumed to be the name of his chosen victim, that name had meant nothing at all to them.

But Koszalin, dying after being cut down—too late to stop the Sword's departure—was heard by several people to mutter something about a promise at last fulfilled.

Sergeant Shotoku, having survived the stranglehold, and coming to make sure that the fight was really over, had a comment to the effect that now at last his captain would be able to sleep. And indeed there was a look of peace upon Koszalin's face.

20

THE fighting and dying in the thickets and on the hillside along the road to Malolo manor had come to an end in early afternoon. Now, just a few hours later, all was quiet in the valley of the Tungri just below the Second Cataract.

With Bonar and Gesner dead, Prince Mark and his companions had no desire to try what sort of welcome they might receive from the two sisters who still occupied the manor. Lady Yambu, coming out from that house before anyone could begin to worry about her, advised against it. So when the last live mercenary had disappeared from the scene of fighting, the four instead made their way warily back to the fishing village, with whose inhabitants they considered themselves likely to be still on good terms.

At the village they were received cautiously but without open hostility. And they found Soft Ripple there, drifting in the water beside a dock, talking to some on the land who had once been her own people. Several other mermaids were gathered not far offshore, holding position effortlessly there against the current, as if they might be waiting to hear news of the day's events.

Lady Megara was nowhere to be seen, and Zoltan supposed it likely that she was still upstream somewhere with the hermit, perhaps beside Cosmo's grave.

Zoltan, feeling exhausted, stood on the bank, looking across the river to the north. What might be going on now over there, in and around the stronghold of the doomed and decimated Senones clan, was impossible to tell from this distance. But, to most of the people who were still alive on the south bank, that no longer mattered.

Yambu came up beside him. "If you wish," she said, "I will release you from any pledge of service you have made to me."

Zoltan picked up a pebble and threw it into the river. "Are you still going on downstream as a pilgrim, my lady?"

"I am. If I can find a way."

"Then I'll go with you, if you'll have me."

"Indeed, I'll have you with me, Zoltan, if I can."

"That's good, Lady Yambu. I feel an urge to see the place where this great river pours into the sea. Also I think my uncle will not mind my scouting the land downstream, and bringing him a report someday in Tasavalta."

It was the hour before sunset. Zoltan and Yambu, being still minded to continue their pilgrimage, were trying to negotiate a boat ride downstream in the morning, when a small winged messenger arrived, spiraling down out of the northern sky. The creature bore a communication for Mark, for it was able to recognize the prince among others, and settled on a branch beside him.

After exchanging greetings with the creature, the prince carefully lifted off the message pouch it had been carrying. He opened the pouch, and from among the few small items inside took out a rolled-up strip of thin and almost weightless paper.

Unrolling the message, Mark read the fine printing that it bore. Zoltan could see but not interpret the change in his uncle's weary face.

"From the Emperor?" asked Zoltan at last, unwilling to be patient.

"No, not this time. This is from home." The prince handed the parchment over to Ben, whose heavy-featured face remained expressionless while he studied the message.

"A day or two ago," said Mark, "being concerned about mermaids and what might be done to help them, I sent a message off to old Karel." That was the name of Tasavalta's wisest wizard, and a relative of Princess Kristin and family counselor as well. "Now Karel has replied, with commendable promptness. From what he has to say, it seems that mermaidism produced by magic ought to be a very easy thing to cure."

Ben suddenly began to read aloud: " 'Indeed', says Karel, 'the problem would seem to me to lie rather in sustaining such a spell than in curing it. Surely any wizard of even moderate competence ought to be able to effect a permanent cure in a reasonably short time.' Bah." And Ben, after passing the message on to Lady Yambu, turned his head away from the others and spat.

"Then," said Zoltan, woodenly, "Cosmo could have cured them all, permanently. If he had really been trying to do so."

"Or Megara could have," said his princely uncle. "Or any of the magicians in either clan, down through the years. At any time. If any of them had ever really tried."

No one said anything for a time.

"Where has Soft Ripple gone?" Mark asked at last. "Karel encloses in this pouch certain magical materials that he says ought to do the job quickly and easily."

But Zoltan was now looking at the note, where Karel had also written: "I should think that achieving a temporary cure would be actually harder than finding a permanent one." He crumpled up the note unconsciously, and let it fall from his hand. He wondered if Black Pearl's body was under the earth yet. He hoped it was. He wanted to think of her resting high on a hill and far from water.

"Where is Soft Ripple?" the prince repeated. "She must know about this. And these things must be given to the mermaids."

"She's there in the water," said Yambu. She sighed. "Give me the things, and I will talk to her. To all of them."

There was a distraction. Violet, the tough one of the Malolo sisters, with a very modest armed escort—actually it consisted of no more than one very nervous footman—came exploring, or perhaps wandering, down to the village from the manor to talk to the victors and to see what was going on.

Tough Violet did her best to put in a last claim for the Sword, saying that no agreement made with Bonar was any longer valid. She would not believe that the Sword of Vengeance was gone.

"Believe it or not, then," said Prince Mark. "As you choose."

Zoltan tried to imagine what the future would be like, here. Each of the two rival clans had now been reduced to a minimum of survivors. Perhaps the older sister was now going to inherit the manor after all, but perhaps she, Rose, still had no wish to own it. Perhaps there was no longer really anything to inherit.

Violet complained: "Anselm and Alicia are still alive over there. And they will still want to kill us."

To Zoltan it now seemed certain that at least one person, on each side, was going to try to go on with the feud, as best he or she could.

Violet had plans for the future, too. She said something about young children, distant relatives now living in distant places, who could be brought here and prepared to carry on the feud when the present generation had been totally exhausted.

Zoltan did not wish to hear any more, and walked away.

People still scanned the sky from time to time, but Tigris and her griffin were no longer to be seen. They had departed shortly after Farslayer's final disappearance. Whether Wood's lovely sorceress had gone in direct pursuit of the Sword or not was hard to say, but there seemed reason to hope that she knew no more than anyone else here of its latest destination.

At dusk, Zoltan, having heard what words of comfort could be offered him by Lady Yambu and others, went to lie down in the bachelor's quarters again, where he tried to get some rest.

Soft Ripple came to visit him one more time, and this time he did not recognize her at first. She entered the building from the land side, walking on two well-formed legs and decently clad; she startled Zoltan as he lay there, half waiting for an eruption from the water that never came.

The young woman and the young man had both, in their separate ways, loved Black Pearl; and the two of them thus had something in common.

As dusk fell, Prince Mark was still sitting outside, his bandaged face lifted to scan the dimming sky, waiting for his next message from the Emperor. Nearby, Ben, his right hand near the hilt of his sword, sat slumped over, gently snoring.

THE FIFTH BOOK OF LOST SWORDS:
COINSPINNER'S STORY

1

"I swear to you, most royal and excellent lady," declared the handsome and distinguished visitor, "I solemnly pledge, most lovely and far-seeing Princess, that if you can save the life of my Queen's consort and end his suffering, her royal gratitude and his—not to mention my own—will know no bounds."

Princess Kristin sighed. Over the course of the past two days, she had already heard the same statement a score of times from the same man, sometimes in very nearly the same words, sometimes in speech less flowery. Now once more she forced herself to attend with courtesy and patience to the representative of Culm.

As soon as the distinguished and handsome visitor had concluded his latest version of his plea, she turned half away from him, trying to frame her answer. Over the past two days she had endeavored to give the same reply in different ways. This time the Princess began her response in silence, with a gesture indicating the view beneath the balcony on which they stood.

Below the Palace, sloping away toward the sea, rank on rank of the neatly tiled, multicolored roofs of Sarykam gleamed in the bright sun of summer afternoon. Halfway between the Palace and the harbor, the mass of crowded buildings was interrupted by a tree-lined square of generous size, which held at its center the chief White Temple of the city. This structure, a pyramid of stark design and chalky whiteness, contained among other things two shrines, those of the gods Ardneh and Draffut.

Of greater practical importance to most people was the fact that the pyramid also contained, within a special coffer, the Sword called Woundhealer.

Today, as on almost every day, a line of people seeking the Sword's help had begun to form before dawn in the Temple square. Now in the middle of the afternoon that line, easily visible from the Palace balcony, was still threading its way into the eastern entrance on the harbor side of the white pyramid. The line was still long, and new arrivals kept it at an almost constant length. The people who made up the line were suffering from disease or injury of one kind or another. They were the ill, the crippled, the blind or mad or wounded, many of them needing the help of nurses or close companions simply to be here and join the line. Some of the sufferers had come from a great distance to seek Woundhealer's aid.

Even as the Princess gestured in the direction of the white pyramid, a pair of stretcher-bearers, lugging between them an ominously inert human form, were being ushered by white-robed priests toward the front of that distant queue. The priests of Ardneh who served this particular Temple were accustomed to making such decisions about priorities, thus assuming momentarily the role of gods. From the balcony there was no telling whether the body on the stretcher was that of a man, woman, or child. The Princess thought that no more than a minimum of protest would be heard from those whose turns were being thus preempted; she could see that today's line was, as usual, moving briskly, and no one in it should have to wait for very long.

Meanwhile, the most recent beneficiaries of the power of the Sword of Healing, many of them accompanied by their relieved nurses and companions, were emerging in a steady trickle from the Temple's western door. People who only moments ago had been severely injured or seriously ill, some even at the point of death, were walking out healthy and whole. From experience Kristin knew that their bandages and splints would have been left in the Temple, or were now being removed and thrown away. Stretchers and crutches, indispensable a few minutes earlier, were now being cast aside by vigorous hands. Only a few of those who had just been healed still needed help in walking, and to them strength would return in time.

For the Sword of Mercy to fail to heal was practically unheard of. As a rule every supplicant who limped or staggered or was carried into the eastern entrance of this White Temple soon came walking out, with a firm step, from the western exit. Today, as usual, some of the cured were waving their arms and shouting prayers of gratitude audible even to the two watchers on the distant balcony.

The Crown Prince Murat, tall emissary from the land of Culm, having gazed dutifully upon the distant scene as he was bidden, chose to ignore whatever inferences the Princess had meant him to draw from the sight. Instead he promptly resumed his arguments. "If, dear princess, it is a matter of some necessary payment—"

"It is not that," said Princess Kristin quickly, turning back to face her visitor fully. Kristin was about the same age as the Crown Prince, in her early thirties and the mother of two half-grown sons. But she looked a few years younger, with her fair hair, blue-green eyes, and fine features.

She said to her eminent guest: "When you paid your own formal visit to the White Temple yesterday, Prince Murat, no doubt you noted that most of those who benefit from Woundhealer's power do make some payment in the form of offerings. These funds are used to maintain the Temple and to pay its priests and guards. Others who benefit from the Sword are unable to pay; and a very few refuse to do so. But none are denied treatment on that account. If your Queen's unfortunate consort can travel here to Tasavalta, the powers of the Sword of Healing will be made available to him under the same conditions."

"Regrettably that is not possible, Princess." In the course of his brief visit Murat had already offered this explanation at least a hundred times, or so it seemed to both of them, and now it was his turn to repeat a statement slowly and patiently. "A condition of nearly total paralysis afflicts the royal consort, combined with the most fearful arthritic pain, so that even the movement required to go from one bed or one room to another is a severe ordeal for him. An overland journey of more than a thousand kilometers, only half of it on roads, is, as you can appreciate, quite out of the question. Ten kilometers would be impossible."

"Then I am truly sorry for him. And sorry for your Queen, and for all her realm." And it seemed that the Princess was speaking her true feelings. "But I am afraid that the Sword stays here, in Tasavalta. That is my final word."

A silence fell, broken only by the occasional noise, a rumbling cart or a raised voice, rising from the thronged city below. Kristin half expected her visitor to raise yet again the point that sometimes the Sword was taken out of the city of Sarykam, and carried on tour in a heavily guarded caravan that visited the outlying portions of the realm, bringing healing to those unable to reach the capital. If he did choose to raise that point again, she had her previous answer ready: Woundhealer was never allowed to go outside the borders of the realm. Her patience held; she could sympathize with Murat, though she would not yield to him.

But the persistence of the Crown Prince, not yet exhausted, this time took a different tack. He said: "Still, the journey to Culm and back with the borrowed Sword could be quickly accomplished by my troop—accompanied, of course, by any number of representatives you might choose to send with us. Our mounts are very swift, and we are now familiar with the way. My master's healing once accomplished, the Sword could be on its way back here the very same day. Within the hour. I would be willing to pledge my honor to you on that."

The soft urgency of his voice was unexpectedly hard to resist. But Kristin still said what she had to say. "I understand your arguments, Prince. I am willing to believe that you mean your pledge, and I respect it. But once your realm found itself in possession of such a treasure as Woundhealer, convincing arguments would soon be found as to why the Sword should stay there, as a policy of national health insurance."

"No, Princess, I must—"

"No, Crown Prince Murat, your request is quite impossible to meet. The Sword of Love stays here."

Before the Crown Prince could devise yet another argument, the conversation was interrupted. The door leading to the balcony, which had been standing ajar, burst open violently, and a small form came running out.

Startled and angry, the Princess turned to find herself confronting the younger of her two sons, who at ten was certainly old enough to know better than to behave in such a way.

"Well, Stephen? I hope you have some just cause for this interruption?"

The boy, as sturdy as his father had been at the same age, though somewhat darker, was flushed and scowling, evidently even angrier than his mother. But now he drew himself up, making a great effort at self-control. "Mother, you once said that I should tell you at once if I knew of anyone practicing intrigue within the Palace."

"And I suppose you have just now discovered something of the kind?" It was easy to see that the Princess was not inclined to accept the alarming implication at face value.

"Yes, Mother."

"Well?"

Stephen drew a deep breath. His anger was cooling, and now he seemed reluctant to go on.

"*Well?*"

Another deep breath. "It's my tutor, Mother. I believe he is about to come to you with false stories concerning my behavior."

And indeed the Princess, raising her gaze slightly, discovered that very gentleman now hovering inside the balcony door, irresolute as to whether he should match his pupil's daring and interrupt what looked like a state conference, simply to defend himself.

Sternly Kristin ordered her younger son to go to his room and wait there for her. The command was delivered in an incisive tone that allowed no immediate argument; it was obeyed reluctantly, in gloomy silence.

Then the Princess silently waved the tutor away, and turned to apologize to the ambassador for the interruption.

The tall man smiled faintly. "I have two children of my own at home. Youth needs no apology. And a fiery spirit may be an advantage to one who is born to rule. Indeed I suppose it must be considered a necessity."

"As are self-control, and courtesy; and those virtues my son has yet to learn."

"I'm sure he will acquire them."

"You are kind and diplomatic, Murat." The Princess sighed again, quite openly this time, and spoke for once unguardedly. "I wish his father were here."

There was a pause. It was common knowledge that Prince Mark had spent no more than ten days at home during the last half year, and that the timing and duration of his next visit home were problematical.

Murat bowed slightly. "I too wish that. I had looked forward to meeting Prince Mark. His name is known and respected even in our far corner of the world."

"Not that my husband would give you any different answer than I have given, on the subject of loaning out the Sword of Healing."

The visitor bowed again. "I must still be allowed to hope that the answer will change."

"It will not change." After a pause, the Princess added: "If you are wondering about my husband's absence, know that he is in the service of the Emperor; he is the Emperor's son, you know." In the minds of many, the Emperor was a half-mythological figure; and that a prince should believe he owed this legend service was an idea sometimes hard for outsiders to grasp.

And sometimes even the Princess, who had never seen her mysterious father-in-law, found the situation hard to understand as well.

The Crown Prince said: "I was aware of Prince Mark's parentage."

Suddenly Kristin heard herself blurting out a question. "You don't—I don't suppose that any news has come to you recently regarding his whereabouts?" A month had now gone by in which no winged messenger had brought her news of her husband. Unhappily, this was not the first time such a period had elapsed, but repetition made the stress no easier to bear.

"I regret, Princess, that I have heard nothing." Murat paused, then made an evident effort to turn the conversation to some less difficult subject. "Young Prince Stephen has an older brother, I understand."

"Yes. Prince Adrian is twelve. He's currently away from home, attending school."

Again there came interruption, this time more sedately, and welcome to both parties. It took the form of a servant, announcing the arrival of the other members of the Culm delegation. These folk had been sightseeing in the streets of Sarykam this afternoon, and some of them had visited the White Temple down the hill.

And now good manners required that the Princess and her companion come in from the balcony, to join the Culmian visitors and other folk inside the Palace.

One of the junior members of the Culmian delegation was Lieutenant Kebbi. This was Murat's cousin, a red-headed, bold-looking, and yet unfailingly courteous youth, who now showed his disappointment openly, when he heard that the Princess was standing fast in her refusal to loan out the Sword.

Lieutenant Kebbi looked as if he might want to raise an argument of his own on behalf of the Culmian cause. But Kristin turned away, not wanting to give the impetuous youth a chance. None of the arguments that she had heard so far, and none that she could imagine, were going to sway her, sympathetic as she was.

Others still importuned her. At last, beginning to show her impatience with her guests' pleading, Kristin demanded of them: "How many of my own people would die, while the Sword was absent from us?"

For that there was no answer. Even the eyes of the bold young lieutenant fell in confusion before the Princess's gaze when she turned back to him.

Once more she faced the delegation's leader. "Come, good Murat, can you number them, or tell me their names?"

The tall man only bowed in silence.

One of the several diplomats on hand quickly managed to change the subject, and talk went on until eventually the delegation from Culm withdrew to their assigned quarters. In there, servants reported, they were conversing seriously and guardedly among themselves.

In the evening, when the sun had set behind the inland mountains, the visitors from afar were once more entertained with Tasavaltan hospitality. There was music, acrobats, and dancers. To Kristin's relief the subject of the Sword had been laid to rest. This was now the third day of the Culmians' stay, and they expressed a unanimous desire to depart early in the morning.

During the evening, more than one Tasavaltan remarked to the Princess that the guests from Culm seemed to be taking their refusal as well as could be expected. Certainly they had now said and done everything they honorably could to persuade Princess Kristin to change her mind.

With some of the guests pleading weariness, and with the necessity for an early start hanging over them all, the party broke up relatively early. Before midnight the silence of the night had claimed the entire Palace, as well as most of the surrounding city.

At about dawn on the following morning—and, through a strange combination of unlucky chances, not before then—Kristin was awakened, to be informed by an ashen-faced aide that the Sword of Healing had been stolen from its place in the White Temple at some time during the night.

The Princess sat up swiftly, pulling a robe around her shoulders. "Stolen! By whom?" Though it seemed to her that the answer was already plain in her mind.

Awkwardly the messenger framed her own version of an answer. "No thief has been arrested, ma'am. The delegation from Culm reportedly departed about two hours ago. And there are witnesses who accuse them of the theft."

By this time Kristin was out of bed, fastening her robe, her arms in its sleeves. "Has Rostov been aroused? Have any steps been taken to organize a pursuit?"

"The General is being notified now, my lady, and I am sure we may rely on him to waste no time."

"Let us hope that very little time has been wasted already. If Rostov or one of his officers comes looking for me, tell them I have gone to the White Temple to see for myself whatever there may be to see."

Only a very few minutes later she was striding into the Temple, entering a scene swarming with soldiers and priests, and aglow with torches. With slight relief she saw that her chief wizard, Karel, who was also her mother's brother, was already on hand and had taken charge for the moment.

Karel was very old—exactly how old was difficult to determine, as was often the case with wizards of great power, though in this case the figure could hardly run into centuries. He was also fat, spoke in a rich, soft voice, and puffed whenever he had to move more than a few steps consecutively. This last characteristic, thought Kristin, had to be more the result of habit—or of sheer laziness, perhaps—than of disease. For Karel, like the more mundane citizens of the realm, had had the benefits of Woundhealer available to him for the past several years.

Karel reported succinctly and with deference. After a few words the

Princess was in possession of the basic, frightening facts. Last night, as usual, the Temple had been closed for a few hours, beginning at about midnight. Ordinarily a priest or two remained in the building while it was closed, ready to produce the Sword should some emergency require its healing powers; but last night, through a series of misunderstandings, none of the white-robes had been on duty.

An hour or so past midnight, the chance passage of a brief summer rainstorm had kept off the streets most of the relatively few citizens who might normally have been abroad at such a time. And so, incredible as it seemed to Kristin, apparently no one outside the Temple had witnessed the assault, or raid.

Kristin at first had real difficulty in believing this. There was always someone in that square. "And what of the guards inside the Temple?" she demanded. "Where were they? Where are they now?"

The old man sighed, and gave such explanation as he could. Inasmuch as White Temple people were notoriously poor at guarding such material treasures as came into their hands from time to time, the rulers of Tasavalta had never trusted the white-robed priests to guard the Sword. Instead, a detail of men from an elite army regiment protected Woundhealer.

At least two of these soldiers were always on duty inside the Temple's supposedly secure walls and doors. But last night, at the crucial hour, one guard of the minimal pair, though a young man, had collapsed without warning, clutching his chest in pain, and died almost at once. A few moments later the victim's partner, reaching into a dark niche to grasp the bellrope that would summon help, had been bitten on the hand by a poisonous snake, and paralyzed almost instantly. The soldier's life was still in danger. The snake was of a species not native to these parts, and so far no one had been able to explain its presence in the Temple.

Scarcely had Kristin finished listening to this most unlikely story when more news came, a fresh discovery almost as difficult to believe. A lock on one of the Temple's doors had accidentally jammed last night when the door was closed, effectively preventing the door from being secured in the usual way. The defect was a peculiar one—highly improbable, as the locksmith kept insisting—and it must have seemed to the woman who had turned the key at the hour of sunset that the door was securely locked as usual.

Karel gave a slight shrug of his heavy shoulders. "The theft was accomplished by means of magic, Princess," he said in his soft voice. "There's no doubt of that."

"And a very powerful magic it must have been." After a momentary hesitation, she asked: "A Sword?" Already she thought she knew the answer; and it would not be hard, she thought, to guess which Sword had been employed.

"Very likely a Sword." The old man nodded grimly. "I feel sure that Coinspinner has been used against us."

Once more their talk was interrupted. Now at last a witness had been discovered, one besides the poisoned guard who could give direct testimony. A shabby figure was hustled before the Princess. One of Sarykam's rare beggars, who had spent most of the night huddled in a doorway on the far side of the square, and who now swore that at the height of the rainstorm he had seen a man wearing the blue-and-orange uniform of Culm carrying a bright Sword—it had certainly been no ordinary blade—carrying it drawn and raised, into the White Temple. Meanwhile, the beggar related, others in the same livery had stood by outside with weapons drawn.

"This man you saw was carrying a Sword *into* the Temple, and not out of it? Are you quite sure?"

"Oh, oh, yes, I'm quite sure, Princess. If I'd seen a foreigner taking something out, I would've raised an alarm. Thought of doing so anyway, but—you see—I'd had a bit too much—my legs weren't working all that well—"

"Never mind that. Did you see him come out of the Temple again?"

"Yes, ma'am, I did. And then he had two Swords. I tried to raise an alarm, ma'am, like I said, but somehow—somehow—" The ragged man began to blubber.

After hearing this testimony of the sole witness, Kristin made her way into the inner sanctuary, and carried out her own belated inspection of the actual scene of the crime. There, on the very altar of Ardneh, she beheld the crystal repository in which the Sword of Healing had been kept, a fragile vault now standing broken and empty under the blank-eyed marble images of Draffut—doglike, but standing tall on his hind legs—and Ardneh, an incomprehensible jumble of sharp-edged, machinelike shapes.

The actual breaking of the crystal vault and carrying away of the Sword would have been simple, and staring at this minor wreckage told her nothing.

Leaving the Temple now, the Princess went to survey the status of the Swords still kept in the royal armory, beside the Palace and only a short walk distant.

If the Princess and her people were able to speak of Coinspinner with a certain familiarity, it was because the Sword of Chance had reposed for some time within the stone walls of the armory's heavily guarded rooms. But about seven years ago that Sword had vanished from the deepest and best-watched vault, vanished suddenly and without explanation. Under the circumstances of that disappearance there had been no need to look for thieves. One of the known attributes of the Sword of Chance was its penchant for taking itself spontaneously and unpredictably from one place to another. Forged by the great god Vulcan, like all its fellow Swords, Coinspinner scorned all obstacles that ordinary human beings might place in opposition to its powers. Coinspinner was subject to no confinement, and to no rules but its own, and exactly what those rules were no one knew. By what progression, during the last seven years, the Sword of Chance had passed from the Tasavaltan armory to somewhere in Culm would probably be impossible to determine, and would be almost certainly irrelevant to the current problem.

Deep in the vaults Kristin encountered the senior General of her armed forces. Rostov was a tall and powerful man in his late fifties, whose curly hair had now turned almost completely from black to gray. The black curve of his right cheek was scarred by an old sword-cut, which his perpetual steel-gray stubble did little to conceal.

Rostov was taking the theft personally; he was here in the armory looking for weapons of particular power to take with him in his pursuit of the thieves, who had several hours' start. A number of people could testify to that. Everyone in Sarykam had been expecting the delegation from Culm to leave this morning anyway, so no one had thought much of their moving up their departure time by a few hours. It had seemed only natural that after their unsuccessful pleading they would want to avoid anything in the nature of a protracted farewell.

Now, as Kristin ascertained with a few quick questions, three squadrons of cavalry were being made ready to take up the pursuit, which Rostov intended to lead in person. As far as she could tell, her military people were moving with methodical swiftness.

The Princess informed her General that Karel the wizard planned to accompany him; the old man had told her as much when she spoke to him in the Temple.

"Very well. If the old man is swift enough to keep up. If his wheezings as we ride do not alert the enemy." Rostov was staring at the three other Swords kept in the royal armory, and his expression showed a definite relief that these at least were still in place. Dragonslicer would probably be useless in the kind of pursuit he was about to undertake, but he now asked permission of the Princess to bring Stonecutter, and thought he would probably want Sightblinder as well.

Kristin, after granting the General her blessing to take whatever he wanted, and leaving him to his preparations, returned to the Palace. There she gave orders for several flying messengers to be dispatched from the high eyries atop the towers. The winged, half-intelligent creatures would be sent to seek out the absent Prince Mark and bear him the grim news of Woundhealer's vanishment.

By the time she had returned to the Palace, the sun was well up, but veiled in clouds. She could wish that the day were brighter. Then it would have been possible to signal ahead by heliograph, and there might have been a good chance of intercepting the fleeing Culmians at the border. But the clouds that had brought rain last night persisted, and if Coinspinner was arrayed against the realm of Tasavalta, today was not the day to expect good luck in any form.

At about this time, staring at the gray and mottled sky, Kristin began to be tormented by a truly disturbing thought: Was it possible that Murat's whole story regarding a crippled consort had been a ruse, and that the Sword was really now bound for the hands of some of Mark's deadly enemies?

The Princess's only comfort was that no evidence existed to support this theory. The fact that no attempt had been made to steal Dragonslicer, Stonecutter, and Sightblinder, or do any other damage to the realm, argued against it. Apparently the Culmian marauders had been truly interested only in obtaining the Healer.

The rain was still falling when the pursuit was launched, a swift but unhurried movement of well-trained cavalry, flowing out through the main gate of the city, every man saluting his Princess as he passed. A beastmaster with his little train of loadbeasts, carrying roosts and cages for winged fighters and messengers, brought up the rear of the procession. General Rostov and the wizard Karel rode together at its head.

2

At midday, under a partly cloudy sky and far from home, Prince Adrian, the twelve-year-old heir to the throne of Tasavalta, was standing at the top of a truncated stairway, a broken stone construction that curved up the outside of an ancient, half-ruined, and long-abandoned tower. A brisk wind blowing from the far reaches of the rocky and desolate landscape ruffled Adrian's blond hair. He carried a small pack on his back, and wore a canteen and a hunting knife at his belt. His slim body, arched slightly forward, wiry muscles tense, leaned out from the upper end of the stairs over the broken stones meters below.

The boy, tall for the age of twelve, was gazing intently, with senses far more discerning than those most folk would ever be able to call into use, across a threshold so subtle that it was all but invisible even to him. He was trying to see into the City of Wizards, inspecting the way ahead as carefully as possible before advancing any farther.

The curving stairs on which Adrian was standing came to an abrupt end halfway up the side of the moss-grown and abandoned tower. Once the steps had gone up farther, but not now. They terminated at this point in abject ruin, giving no hint to ordinary eyes of any reasonable or even visible goal that they might once have had. An observer equipped with no more than the usual complement of senses, and standing in Prince Adrian's position, would have seen nothing ahead but a bone-breaking drop to the nearest portion of the forbidding landscape.

In fact, the only other human observer on the scene had perceptions that also went beyond those of ordinary human senses—though not so far beyond as Adrian's.

Trilby, the Princeling's companion and fellow student in the arts of magic, was only two years older than he, but physically she was much more mature. With a pack on her back and a wooden staff in hand, she now came climbing the curved stairs to join him.

Reaching the top step, Trilby stood beside Adrian in momentary silence, gazing ahead to see if she could determine exactly what it was he found so fascinating; she knew that his extraordinary vision was almost always able to see more than hers. Having now shared approximately a year of study and occasional rivalry under the tutelage of old Trimbak Rao, the two young people had reached a plateau of mutual respect.

Trilby was coffee brown of skin, with straight black hair, full lips, and dark eyes that displayed a perpetually dreamy look, belying her often acutely practical turn of mind. Her shapely and rather stocky body, dressed now like Adrian's in practical traveler's clothing—loose shirt, boots, and trousers—was physically strong. A more experienced student, she was still marginally superior to Adrian in one or two aspects of magic, though after a year of cooperation and competition she suspected that he had the potential to be ultimately and overall the greatest wizard in the world.

"What d'ye see?" she asked him presently.

"Nothing special." The Prince almost whispered his reply. Then he withdrew his gaze from the distance, relaxed his pose somewhat, and spoke in a normal voice. "Just wanted to check everything out as well as I could, before we go in."

Trilby took a long look for herself. Then she said: "The road is there, am I right? Just about at the level of our feet?"

"Right." Adrian sounded confident. "As far as I can tell, it starts here, right at the place where we'll be standing when we step through to it from the top of this stairs. Then it runs in a kind of zigzag way, but free of obstacles, for a couple of kilometers, until it gets close to the tall buildings."

"That agrees with what I see." The girl paused for another careful look before continuing. "The next question is, do we go in immediately, or take a break first?" They had already hiked for half a day since leaving the studio of Trimbak Rao, early in the morning.

Adrian hesitated, not wanting to appear reluctant to get on with the test they faced. But it was uncertain what problems they might encounter immediately on entering the City, and Trilby's suggestion of stopping for food and rest soon won out in his mind.

Both of the young people were carrying canteens, as well as a modest supply of food. And each of them, if pressed, would have been able to create food by magical means. But that kind of magic was costly in time and energy; it would be much wiser to conserve both of those resources against a possible later need.

Sitting near the foot of the ruined stairs, they opened up their packs, retrieving sandwiches and fruit. There was no need for a fire, and neither explorer suggested making one.

Trilby and Adrian had taken their last meal early in the morning, before setting out on foot from the studio and workshop of Trimbak Rao. They had hiked a good number of kilometers since then, but the required path through the desolate terrain had included many turns; now, sitting at the foot of the half-ruined tower and looking back along the route they had come, they could just descry the buildings of the wizard's complex halfway up a distant hillside. These were fairly ordinary-looking buildings—now, and most of the time. But appearances here, as in much else, could be deceptive. In fact, these structures had the habit of changing their appearance drastically, depending upon the viewer's distance and angle, as well as the quality of his or her perception.

Chewing slowly on a sandwich, Adrian remarked: "I don't think we'll have any trouble actually getting in. Do you?"

Trilby shrugged. "I don't see why we should." She was not as totally confident as she sounded—she thought that perhaps Adrian wasn't either—but they had discussed the situation many times before, and she had nothing new to add at the moment.

This field trip was part of an examination marking the end of their first year of study with Trimbak Rao. Trilby and Adrian had been assigned the task of entering the chaotic and mysterious domain called the City of Wizards, obtaining a certain object there, and bringing it back to their teacher.

The object desired by Trimbak Rao was an odd-shaped ceramic tile—rather, it was any one of a number of such pieces that were to be found uniquely in the pavement of one small square in a certain parklike space within the City.

Probably—the master had been vague about background and history—the space had once been part of a real park, the grounds of some great palace perhaps, originally built in a distant location somewhere out in the mundane world. By some unspecified power of magic a portion of the palace grounds had been transported to its present location. And in the process—like most of the other components of the City—it had probably been altered drastically.

Trimbak Rao had repeatedly warned his two students, before they set out, about several potential dangers. The chief of these, if the emphasis of his warnings meant anything, was the Red Temple that adjoined the present site of the park:

"The main room of that particular Red Temple was dedicated to a particularly abominable vice. But now it should be safe enough for you to pass nearby. If you are reasonably careful." The magician hadn't clarified the statement.

Also, before he dispatched the two apprentices upon their mission, the Teacher had called their attention to the east wall of his study. Hanging there, carefully mounted in a reconstructed pattern, were a series of tiles, dull brown and unimpressive at first glance, similar to the one they were to obtain. Only the pattern, still just beginning to emerge with the growth of that series, was interesting. It seemed to depict a human body, or more probably more than one.

The number of tiles, twenty or so, already collected by the Teacher might be taken as evidence, thought Adrian, that some substantial number of Trimbak Rao's earlier students had successfully concluded missions similar to their own.

Now, while Trilby and Adrian ate some food, and rested on the bottom steps of the stairs encircling the old tower, the young Prince wondered aloud whether there might be some special reason why Trimbak Rao himself was not allowed to, or chose not to, make repeated journeys to this mysterious City park, and bring back the whole paved square if he desired it.

"And I wonder what'll happen when he has the entire pattern completed on his wall?"

"There must be some magical reason why he can't go himself," Trilby decided. She didn't know what that reason might be, and she had no opinion to offer on the subject. It was better to keep one's mind on practical matters. As the older and more experienced of the two students, she had been placed in command of this mission. But, as usual when teams were sent out, there had been a strong indication from the Teacher that all major decisions should be shared if possible.

Trilby had developed an ability to incinerate small amounts of garbage magically, and now she put that particular talent to use. Not so much a squandering of energy, she told Adrian, as a last trial to make sure that her powers were in working order.

Now, as the two advanced students busied themselves with the trivial chores of cleaning up after their meal, Adrian found he had to make a conscious effort to keep himself from reaching out with his magical perceptions to try to see what was going on with his parents and his brother at the moment.

His natural ability to maintain such occult contacts, once very strong, had been fading naturally over the past few years as he grew older. And on this subject his Teacher had counseled him: "Your parents have been making their own way in the world for some time now; you are almost old enough to do the same, and the cares of state with which they are now chiefly concerned will be yours soon enough. Right now your primary responsibility is to complete your schooling here, and to avoid unnecessary distraction."

Trilby now talked with Adrian about her parents. Her father was a middle-class merchant, her mother's family farmers in the domain of Tasavalta, with little or nothing in their background to suggest that one of their children would be extremely talented magically.

And Adrian talked of his family, and expressed his wish that he could see more of them.

Trilby assured the Prince, and not for the first time, that she did not envy him his royal status. In many ways prosperous commoners, like her own people, had things easier.

"Are we ready to go on?" the girl asked.

"Ready!" Adrian shouldered his pack again.

"On into the City, then."

Adrian, because of the superior sensitivity of his magical vision, was one step in the lead when the pair climbed again to the top of the broken stairs.

But Trilby, as the senior member of the expedition, did not forget to remind the boy that it was her duty to go first when the time actually came to cross the threshold.

This time when they reached the top of the stairs, Adrian stopped, took one more look and nodded, then let her go ahead, both of them muttering the words that Trimbak Rao had taught them.

Neither apprentice fell or even stumbled when they stepped beyond the last stair and over the subtle threshold. Both had successfully made the transition, at that point, to a somewhat different plane of existence. Both were able to establish solid footing upon the road that went on into the City, away from the tower—Adrian, turning to glance back at that structure, discovered that it existed in both planes. Here in the City it looked somewhat shorter, and did not appear to be so badly ruined after all.

The narrow road on which they now found themselves led forward crookedly, angling in long dogleg turns, toward the distant silhouette of the tall buildings clustered about the center of the City proper. The road was unpaved, of hard-packed earth, dry and yellowish, and at the moment it bore no traffic except themselves. The softer earth on either side of the way was reddish brown, stretching away in gentle undulations to a great smear of grayish dust that formed the whole circle of the horizon. Above that, the bowl of sky began as lemon yellow at the edges, and rose through shades of blue and green toward a small, gnarled cloud, quite dark and somehow hard to look at, around the zenith. The sun, thought Adrian, if it was anywhere, must be in concealment behind that cloud. The time of day, at least, had not changed greatly.

The young explorers kept walking.

"Well," said Trilby in a quiet voice when they had covered a few score meters of the road, "here we are. Looks like we've done it."

Adrian only nodded.

The explorers had now reached a point from which they could see that the thoroughfare on which they walked indeed led, after many turns, into the heart of the City proper.

And in that urban heart, which still appeared to be at least a kilometer away, they were now able to perceive in some greater detail the physical outlines of the City's crowded structures. They were a strange collection indeed, of divers styles and shapes, as if they might have been gathered here from the far corners of the world. Close behind those silhouetted buildings the peculiar sky seemed to curve down to meet the dusty earth. And Adrian thought there was a strange richness, akin to electricity, in the very air that he and Trilby now breathed.

Trilby was nudging him with an elbow. She said: "Looks like a slugpit over there."

He followed the direction of her gaze, to a place of disturbed earth some forty or fifty meters away on the right side of the road. "Yes, I see it."

They walked on without trying to investigate more closely. Both young people had been made well aware by their Teacher of certain perils in the City that had to be avoided; structures within it whose mere entry would almost certainly be fatal; snares that had to be watched for, and modes of travel that within its shadowy boundaries had to be strictly prohibited for reasons of safety. Just as Trimbak Rao had taken care to caution his advanced students about all these dangers before they set out to take their test, he had also reassured them that he considered them capable of successfully avoiding all the hazards.

Ordinary human eyes, viewing the City of Wizards from within, would have had this much in common with the eyes of the most perceptive magicians—both would perceive their surroundings as a vast jumble of ruins and intact buildings, strangely lighted under a changeable and often fantastic sky. The City's central region was streaked by open vistas of barren and abnormal earth, and marked by some grotesque and extravagant examples of whole architecture. Inside the City, or so Trimbak Rao had instructed his apprentices, sunrise and sunset were sometimes visible simultaneously, along opposite edges of the sky; and sometimes there were two moons in the sky at the same time, one full, one crescent, though otherwise looking identical to the familiar companion of Earth.

There were many viewpoints of the subject that might possibly be taken. Looking at the matter one way, the City of Wizards could scarcely be called a city at all—or, if the phenomenon was looked at in another way, it consisted of portions of several cities, and of portions of the rural world as well, normally separated in space and time, but here blended by conflicting and persistent magics into a confusing juxtaposition.

Generally, folk devoid of the skills of wizardry found it impossible to discover an entrance to the City at all—or to enter it even if they should manage to locate a threshold. People unskilled in magic might have journeyed all the continents of the mundane earth from north to south and east to west in search of the City and never have seen its gates. But to the skilled and properly initiated, many ports of entry were available.

Wizards of vastly different character and varying classes of ability came here to the City. So had they come from time immemorial, sometimes only to amuse themselves, sometimes to duel, sometimes to train their more promising apprentices. And here in the City, by the general agreement of their guilds, the more responsible among the workers in enchantment carried on many of their more dangerous experiments, researches that might otherwise do damage to some portion of the generally habitable world.

Sections and shards of the outside world, samples from a number of real cities and countrysides, had all been incorporated into the City from time to time. Houses and temples of every kind, even whole fortifications, had sometimes drifted or been hurled here, places wrenched out of their proper space-time locations by the contending or experimental forces of magic. Surprisingly, at least to Adrian, there had even been a substantial amount of original construction in the City over the centuries of its known existence, some of it carried out by human hands to the designs of human architects. But most of this deliberate building was badly designed. Much of it was never completed, and little of it endured for long.

As the Teacher had explained, both things and people judged unendurable by normal society were sometimes banished from the normal world, to end up here. Among the human inhabitants were the mad, the desperate, the fugitives, the utter outcasts of the world.

And also among the inhabitants were many who were not, and never had been, human.

3

WEST of the city of Sarykam the sky grew clear before midday, and then promptly began to cloud again with a speed that suggested the possibility of some cause beyond mere nature. The sun had moved well past the zenith, and into a fresh onrush of gray scud lower than the nearby peaks, when the Culmian Crown Prince, now riding near the rear of his fast-moving cavalcade, halted his riding-beast and turned in his saddle to look back. From this position he was able to observe a great deal of the landscape, mostly a no-man's-land of barren mountains with which his small force was surrounded. The domain of Tasavalta was physically small and narrow, and the border in this area was ill-defined. But the leader of the fleeing Culmians felt confident that he had already left it behind him.

Four or five of Crown Prince Murat's comrades in arms, all of those who had been riding near him, now stopped as well, glad of the chance of at least a brief rest for their mounts. Farther inland, the bulk of the small Culmian force had already vanished behind jagged hills. At the moment, somewhere in that direction, another trusted officer was carrying the Sword of Love steadily toward Culm.

Another Sword, Coinspinner, that Murat had secretly brought with him to Tasavalta rode openly now at his belt. And up to this point, in the adventure of Sword-stealing, the Sword of Chance had performed flawlessly for the man who wore it.

So far, all was going according to plan. It was necessary to assume that by now the theft from the White Temple had been discovered, and a determined pursuit launched. But until now none of Murat's people had actually seen anyone coming after them.

An hour ago Murat had detailed one scout to ride far in the rear for just that purpose. And he was pausing now to let that scout, Lieutenant Kebbi, catch up to report.

His timing seemed excellent. For even as the Crown Prince and his companions watched, a single rider appeared at a bend in the rearward trail, a couple of hundred meters back. The small figure in its orange-and-blue uniform waved its arm in a prearranged signal meaning that there was news to tell. Then the distant scout urged his mount forward at a good pace.

Murat, followed by the handful of people with him, spurred his own riding-beast forward along the narrow trail, and in a few moments met the scout. The lieutenant, reining in as he drew near his compatriots, reported in a somewhat breathless voice that the expected enemy pursuit had only just now come into sight.

"How far back?" the Crown Prince demanded.

"We've half an hour on them yet," said Kebbi. Then the lieutenant had a question: "Sir, what do you think will be done with the Sword of Mercy after the Royal Consort has been healed?"

Murat, mildly surprised, blinked at his relative. "I don't know," he said. "Not our problem." Then he paused. "I was quite sincere, you understand, cousin, when I pledged that Woundhealer would promptly be returned to Tasavalta." The more Murat thought about it now, the more he wondered if the lovely Princess Kristin had been right, and Woundhealer would never be returned, would never have been returned in any case.

Kebbi persisted. "I understand, sir. But I thought that your pledge was made on the condition that the Sword should be loaned to us willingly, which it most certainly was not."

"Well, as I say, it won't be our problem to worry about." The Crown Prince looked at his men gathered about him. "Ready to move on? Someone else can take a turn tail-ending."

But Kebbi spoke up quickly. "Sir, let me ride back once more—I'll be better able to judge if they're truly gaining on us or not."

"Very well, that's a good point. If your mount is tired, pick a spare." And one of the small group of riders was already leading a spare mount forward.

With several men to help, changing the lieutenant's saddle and the rest of his equipment from one animal to the other was the work of only a moment.

Meanwhile there was more information to be gained. "Can you estimate how many there are in the pursuing force?"

"Haven't got that good a look at them yet, sir. But I can let them get a little closer this time. That way I should be able to form an estimate." On a fresh steed now, Kebbi looked boldly ready to take risks.

"Wait," said Murat suddenly, and drew Coinspinner from its sheath at his belt. "This should go with the man in the position of greatest danger and greatest need."

The lieutenant stared at him wordlessly for a moment, then nodded. "Thank you, sir." In another moment, handling both the sharp blades gingerly, he and Murat had exchanged Kebbi's mundane though well-forged sword for Coinspinner.

Wasting no time, Kebbi saluted sharply with his new weapon, and turned his mount away. He appeared to be on his way to drop back again and check on the enemy's progress.

But once he had ridden away a few meters with Coinspinner still unsheathed in his grip, and had looked it over, as if he were making absolutely sure of what he had, he stopped his mount and turned back again, showing a broad grin.

Something in the posing attitude of his cousin sent the beginning of a foreboding chill down Murat's spine.

In a voice considerably louder than would have been necessary to make himself heard, the Crown Prince called out: "What are you doing, Kebbi?"

The Sword-wielder, his every movement showing confidence, edged his riding-beast back a little toward the others, as if to make sure that what he said was heard distinctly. What he said was: "I'm looking out for myself. For my own future."

"What?" demanded Murat—though in his heart he knew already. Already he understood the horror of what was happening. Certain episodes of Kebbi's childhood were replaying themselves relentlessly in Murat's memory.

His cousin smiled at him, almost benignly. "I think you understood me the first time, sir. You who have the disposal of such matters at court have pretty well arranged it that I won't have much of a future unless I do take matters into my own hands."

The little group of Murat's countrymen who sat their steeds around him were muttering now. He yelled: "What are you talking about? Have you gone mad?"

"Not in the least mad, sir." Kebbi shook his head. He had a clean-cut face, and a habitual expression that somehow managed to suggest he was supremely trustworthy. "There's just no prospect of advancement for me in the normal course of events, that's what I'm talking about. Yes, *now* I see that you look thoughtful. *Now*, with a little effort, you can remember how the case for my promotion went, when you sat on the board of review. I'm sure it was a mere detail to you, the career of a very junior officer. Oh, an extremely reliable junior officer, one who could be chosen to participate in a mission like this, and even entrusted with a Sword. But also one who could be passed over with impunity when it came time for promotions.

"No, I'm not the least bit crazy, cousin. In fact, if you stop to think about it, you'll see that my behavior makes a lot of sense. I now have a matchless treasure in my hands." He paused to swing the Sword, taking a cut or two at the air to try the balance—which was of course superb.

When the lieutenant spoke again his voice was changed, lower and calmer. "It is the real thing. We proved that beyond any doubt in the White Temple. And now that I've got this Sword in my hands, I simply prefer to keep it for myself—the matter is as uncomplicated as that."

A moment later Lieutenant Kebbi had inserted Coinspinner into the sheath at his belt. He kept his right hand comfortably on the black hilt afterward.

Murat, sitting his mount helplessly, had the feeling that his own life, his career, his sanity, were all draining out somehow from the toes of his boots, through his stirrups, to the ground. Knowing it was useless, he still had to shout again.

"Kebbi, I warn you! If this is some joke, some stupid attempt to force me to admit that you are valuable—"

The younger man was shaking his head. "That would indeed be stupid, and I'm not stupid. That's something you, dear royal cousin, are finally going to have to realize. No, no joking, cousin. I am now going to turn my steed and ride away—it would be stupid on your part to try to stop me, as I am sure you realize. Instead I would suggest that you catch up with those loyal people who are carrying the other Blade for you, and hurry home as fast as you can with that one. You can still be at least half a hero there, in royal eyes, if you arrive with a useful Sword to replace the one you've lost."

"If you are serious—then what are you attempting to do?"

"My dear Crown Prince, I am not *attempting* to do anything, as you will have to admit sooner or later. What I'm doing is an accomplished fact. I'm taking this Sword away from you, just as we took the other one from the Tasavaltans."

As Kebbi spoke, he continued to sit his mount facing the others from a distance of thirty meters or so. Now one of the Culmian sergeants, outraged beyond measure by the treachery in progress, spurred his own riding-beast forward to pass Lieutenant Kebbi, moving to cut off the unspeakable traitor's line of retreat.

That, at least, must have been the tactic the sergeant had in mind. But he was never able to perform it. He passed within half a dozen strides of his target, turned, and was just beginning to raise a mace with which to threaten or to strike when the rear hooves of his mount slipped from the narrow trail. The cavalry beast, normally surefooted, screamed in an almost human-sounding noise before it fell. A moment later the sergeant's mount had disappeared over the edge of a minor precipice.

The man himself managed to leap from his stirrups only just in time to keep from going with the animal. Instead he fell forward, awkwardly, and in landing struck his forehead on his own spiked mace. Once fallen, he lay facedown, without moving, except that the muscles of his back twitched convulsively.

"You see?" demanded Kebbi, who had been watching, as he turned back to face the others. There was a quiver of triumph in his voice. "You see? I am well protected."

The Crown Prince had nothing to say. He could only hope that he might soon awaken from this hideous dream. The only comfort he could find in the situation was the knowledge that the main body of his small force, carrying with them the Sword of Mercy, were still moving away on the road to Culm, putting distance between them and their pursuers as rapidly as possible.

As long as the band of volunteers, no more than two dozen in all, had remained closely united on this mission, then the luck carried by one man might have served to protect them all. Now the luck of the Sword of Chance was gone from them. But with the start Coinspinner had afforded, the people who were carrying Woundhealer might still be able to get away to Culm. They had their orders, and no matter what happened to Murat and his rear guard of half a dozen, they would press on.

But what was he going to do about Kebbi? It was unthinkable that the young man could simply be allowed to ride away now that he had revealed his treachery. But what could be done against a Sword?

Another officer in the small group broke the brief silence. His voice, controlled with a great effort, still quivered with his helpless fury. "What will you do now, Kebbi? Where will you go? We'll hunt you down, you know, sooner or later."

The lieutenant made a gesture, shrugging with his arms spread slightly, as if to say: *if you would hunt me, here I am.* He did not appear to be in the least perturbed by the threat. "What will I do? Why, to begin with, I believe I'll get myself out of your way here, and allow you to set up your rearguard defense—this looks like a good place to arrange an ambush. The Tasavaltans will certainly be here within half an hour. I suppose you still have some kind of a fighting chance against them, even without Coinspinner—a better chance than I had when I came up for promotion that last time."

"Traitor! Vile traitor!"

The man who was now carrying the Sword of Chance ignored the denunciation. It appeared that he could well afford to do so. In no hurry to escape, he paused to look around at the configuration of the land. "Yes, cousin, you definitely have a chance, though they must know these mountains better than you do—farewell, then." With that the treacherous lieutenant turned his mount and departed.

He was forty meters away, riding with his back to his former comrades, when one of the volunteer troopers, a dead shot with the longbow, gritting his teeth at seeing this scoundrel jog away unpunished, drew, aimed, and loosed a shaft aimed true at the center of the traitor's spine. Just at the crucial moment the renegade, who never looked back, happened to bend aside to make some minor adjustment to his right stirrup strap. The arrow missed him by several centimeters. The man with the Sword continued to ride away, superbly unaware of death's close passage. But of course the truth was that the arrow had put him in no danger of death at all.

At that same moment, no more than half a kilometer away in the direction of Tasavalta, General Rostov, having halted his advance for the moment, was grinding his teeth. All day long the General and his Tasavaltan cavalry had been suffering from bad luck, and it did not help that he knew the cause, and knew that matters were very unlikely to improve. Several landslides—none of them brought about by any sentient agency, Rostov was sure—had come down just in front of his troops, in places guaranteed to create maximum obstruction. Problems with broken harness had multiplied unbelievably for equipment that was well maintained, and a sudden attack of severe bellyache had felled one trooper who had to be left behind.

And now a rain that promised to be heavy had begun. Not that Rostov was entertaining any thought that he might be beaten. That was not his way. Nor were any of the men or women he had chosen for this pursuit resigned to defeat—at least none of them had yet been ready to admit such a thought in Rostov's hearing.

The General, knowing of a shortcut alternative to a portion of the route that the fleeing Culmians had doubtless taken, had naturally enough led the Tasavaltan force that way. Had it not been for the landslides and other delays, they would have been in time to cut their quarry off. Even as matters stood, he thought that they had gained several hours on the Sword thieves.

Rostov had not been able to catch a glimpse of the enemy since leaving Tasavalta. But during the last kilometer or two of the pursuit, fresh animal droppings and other signs indicated that the Culmians were now very close ahead.

Karel the wizard had ridden for the most part in grim silence, but certain subtle signs indicated that he was not idle. The few words uttered by the old man suggested that he was having very little luck with any of his spells today; he was not accustomed to failure, but given the overwhelming nature of the magical opposition, anything except failure would have been surprising.

Now one of Rostov's officers halted his mount beside the General's. "Sir, I wonder if the thieves will be arranging an ambush for us? There's a place just ahead that's so ideal I doubt they'll pass it up."

The General grunted. He had been thinking along the same lines, and in fact that was why he had chosen this spot to halt. So ideal was the terrain ahead for such a tactic that Rostov's instincts informed him that a Culmian ambush *must* be there, though there was no way to confirm its presence until the point was reached. A wind had sprung up in the last hour, fierce enough to ground the little flying beasts he would otherwise have used as scouts.

Having foresightedly brought Stonecutter with him, the General, after surveying the landscape more thoroughly, now put the Sword of Siege to work to open up a new trail. His intention was to bypass the probable ambush site narrowly, and, if at all possible, take the ambushers from behind.

One source of worry was the fact that Stonecutter invariably produced a pounding noise as it worked. But on reflection he thought this was not likely to prove a fatal difficulty. Out here in the open, Stonecutter's working noise would probably be unheard by people who might be waiting on the other side of a thick wall of rock. And the same howling wind that was keeping the winged scouts out of the air would tend to rush the sound away.

The wizard, for whom nothing had worked properly since setting out on this pursuit, was now beginning to adopt a fatalistic attitude. "I fear that if Coinspinner is arrayed against us . . ." Karel, with a shrug, let his words trail off.

But Rostov, as usual when going into action, was ferocious and implacable. "You tell me that the enemy has powerful weapons. I say so do we. And I also say damn their weapons. If we are in the field against them, we must find some way to attack." Almost as an afterthought, he added: "All of them won't have stayed to entertain us in an ambush. Part of their force almost certainly is bearing Woundhealer on ahead— and it's a good bet that those people will have taken Coinspinner too."

Working with Stonecutter in the driving rain, a pair of the General's men were already hacking an incline into the side of a cliff that would otherwise have been utterly impassable. They were incorporating stair-steps at the steeper parts, and making the whole wide and gently curved enough for riding-beasts to use. Naturally they had begun their labors at a spot out of sight of the enemy above. One man wielded the Sword of Siege, cutting limestone like so much butter, digging stairs rapidly out of the side of a cliff, while his helper slid the freshly carved blocks away and over the edge.

A few shock troops, with Rostov himself and Karel among them, were to climb the newly created stair and take the enemy from the rear, while the bulk of the General's three squadrons waited, mounted, ready to attack the ambush frontally at the proper moment.

And Rostov had one more weapon to bring into action. Calling a well-guarded pack-animal forward, he reached into one of its cargo panniers and pulled forth Sightblinder. The Sword of Stealth looked an exact duplicate of its god-forged brothers, save for the different symbol, in this case the sketch of a human eye, that it bore on its black hilt. At least it looked so to the one who held it; gazing at the reactions in the faces of his people looking at him now, Rostov knew that each of them was seeing something or someone even more awesome than their General.

A few moments later, halfway up the newly created path with Sightblinder still in hand, waiting for the stonecutting to be finished, Rostov was beginning to wish that he had brought dogs, to help pick up the scent when other indications of a trail were lacking. Well, it was too late to worry about that now. Beside him, Karel had his eyes closed and was muttering—trying to ward off Coinspinner's imminent counterblow, perhaps. That stroke was coming, no doubt, in some form, if the Sword of Chance was still in the possession of the ambushers. But there was nothing Rostov could do about it, and so he refused to let it worry him.

In a matter of only a few minutes the necessary rough stairs had been completed. The chunks of rock removed, sliced loose as easily as so many bits of melon, had been pushed tumbling into a depth so great that there was no need to worry about the sounds of their falling alerting the foe.

And now Rostov, disguised by the Sword of Stealth, and his handful of picked men, moving close past the pair of rock-cutters, wind and rain blasting in all their faces, were at the top of the new pathway.

No one in sight, as yet. But there was another little plateau not far above. The General, climbing ponderously and carefully, motioned sharply with his arm, and a young scout, much more agile than Rostov, clambered past him.

After peering cautiously through a notch at the top of the cliff, the lithe young soldier turned his head back and whispered: "No one in sight."

That, as Rostov understood, could mean that he had chosen exactly the right spot for his outflanking movement; or of course it could mean that no ambush had been set here after all, and he and his men were only wasting time.

Silently he gestured a command, and in silence his small party of picked men moved rapidly forward, until all were solidly established upon level ground. Armed with the Sword of Stealth, he moved ahead of them. The actual location of the supposed ambushers was still above them and in front, but each side was now shielded safely from the other by an intervening wall of rock. From the point where Rostov had now got his men, however, the supposed enemy strong point could be outflanked by an easy climb along a natural formation.

At the next level place they reached, one of the men just behind Rostov, a good tracker, paused and murmured: "A lot of hoofprints. They seem to have split up here, General. One of them at least—yes, I think only one—rode off in that direction, to the west. And what's this? An arrow, definitely Culmian, broken against a rock. It hasn't been here long, but it wasn't shot in our direction. I think it must have been aimed at the man who rode alone. Can it be that luck's deserted them?"

Rostov squinted westward through the shreds of driving mist. "Well, that western trail lies open to us if we want to follow it. But I don't think we do. Not just yet at least. No ambush there, so it's not the route they're fighting to defend."

Karel, puffing with the climb on foot, but so far keeping up, asked him: "Can it be they're splitting up in an effort to confuse us?"

"If so, it seems unlikely they'll succeed. Let's move on up the rest of the way, as quietly as we can. Then we'll be behind their ambush if there is one. We'll see how many of 'em are ready to stand and fight."

A few minutes later, the Crown Prince Murat of Culm had seen the failure of the ambush he had so carefully and, as he thought, so cleverly arranged. Howling fiends in blue and green, only slightly outnumbering his own small rear guard, but with the great advantage of surprise, had fallen upon them from the rear. And at the head of the attackers, almost crushing resistance by sheer visual shock, had moved a perfectly lifelike image of the very Queen of Culm herself. At least two of Murat's men had thrown down their weapons at the sight.

As the Crown Prince lay trying to regain his senses, after being felled by a blow to the back of his head, he could not at first understand how he had been overcome. His trap had been bypassed by people who must have somehow made their way up a sheer cliff, where he had thought that even a mountain goat would be helpless. And then, the seeming presence of the Queen—

Only when Murat saw a Sword in one of the attackers' hands, and the thought of Stonecutter occurred to him, followed by that of the Sword of Stealth, did he begin to realize the truth.

In their planning for this mission, the Culmian intelligence had failed —they had never guessed that Stonecutter and Sightblinder would still be available to their new enemies.

Victorious Rostov, proven right in his tactical predictions, was still in a grim mood. His own men had suffered only minor wounds. Five Culmians were dead, and one, their commander, was taken prisoner. But neither Coinspinner nor Woundhealer was here with the vanquished enemy.

The Crown Prince's head wound proved to be not serious. He was conscious in time to watch Rostov's cavalry squadrons come pouring relentlessly through the narrow passage he had almost died trying to defend. And presently he had recovered sufficiently to mutter a few words of anguished defiance.

Rostov, grim-visaged and surly, made little of the fact of his sole prisoner's high rank. At the General's orders, the captive was treated much as any other prisoner would have been, and as soon as he was able to stand again, he was tied into the saddle and stirrups of a captured mount.

"Where are the Swords?" Rostov then demanded of him. "I know that two at least were with you."

Murat sighed. "Woundhealer is on its way to my Queen."

"We'll see about that."

Karel, frowning, signed that he wanted to ask the prisoner a question. "And Coinspinner, Prince? I have good reason to believe that it is no longer with the other Sword."

Rostov frowned in surprise on hearing this.

Murat shook his head. There dawned on him a vague hope that these men, whose outrage and fury he could understand, and who came armed with Swords of their own, might possibly be able to avenge the treachery of Kebbi.

He drew a deep breath. "The Sword of Chance is now in a traitor's hands," he said. Briefly he confessed how he had foolishly handed over Coinspinner, with his own hands, into those of Lieutenant Kebbi, and what his cousin had done thereafter.

The fierce winds that Coinspinner had somehow caused to arise were abating now, and it had become possible for the Tasavaltan beastmaster to get his winged scouts and messengers into the air. One flyer, a magical cross between bird and mammal, was sent home to Sarykam with word for the Princess on the progress made thus far. Others were dispatched to try to locate the fleeing Culmians.

Taking several items from his mount's saddlebags, Karel went to work. Soon he was able to confirm to his own satisfaction that Coinspinner was now somewhere to the west of here, while Woundhealer lay to the south.

Wizard and General conferred briefly, and then the scar-faced Rostov turned back to his prisoner. "Well, Crown Prince. Can you ride?"

"Bound into this saddle as I am, it would seem that I have no choice."

"That is correct. Prepare to do so."

It was going to be a grim and uncomfortable ride back to Sarykam, Murat thought to himself. Though once there in the Tasavaltan capital, he vaguely supposed, things might not be too bad. Doubtless, once he was there, he would in some way be accorded special treatment because of his rank. Even a room in the Palace could be a possibility.

And whatever else happens to me, he thought, I am going to see more of that lovely, lonely Princess. Murat and his own wife had been for some time now on bad terms. Some part of him was curiously pleased that he was soon going to see Kristin again, even though she could hardly greet him with anything but the anger reserved for a treacherous enemy.

After the wizard and the General had taken counsel again, they dispatched most of their force, under Rostov's military second-in-command, armed with Stonecutter against further ambushes, in pursuit of the Culmians carrying Woundhealer. None of the Tasavaltans had much more to say to Murat for the time being. But he was not slow to realize that he was not being taken back to Sarykam, at least not immediately. Instead the two leaders, armed with Sightblinder, with himself as their prisoner, and no more than half a dozen troopers as escort, were setting out upon the trail of Lieutenant Kebbi and the other stolen Sword.

4

Who holds Coinspinner knows good odds
Whichever move he make
But the Sword of Chance, to please the gods
Slips from him like a snake.

KEBBI was singing the words of the old song to himself, in a strong tenor voice, whose musicality would probably have surprised the majority of his former comrades of Culm. Meanwhile he was allowing his riding-beast, a fast and sturdy cavalry animal, to carry him along another mountain trail, under a cheerful morning sun.

Yesterday, upon taking his leave of the Crown Prince and his small doomed force, Kebbi had traveled on until well after dark, maintaining a moderate pace in a generally northwesterly direction. He had trusted to the godly magic that he carried to guarantee that his mount was not going to step over an invisible precipice, or halt on the brink of one so suddenly that it threw him from the saddle. But the animal, doubtless unaware that it had any magical assistance to depend on, had managed but slow progress. Nor was weariness in beast or man to be cured by good fortune. Eventually, when he had fortuitously happened upon a sheltered spot beside a small stream, Kebbi had decided to make camp for the night.

He had been up with the sun and on the road again. Now, today, everything was going well—of course. And naturally—as it now seemed to him—there were no signs of pursuit.

He'd hardly bothered to make any effort at covering his trail since acquiring the Sword, but an hour ago the unexpected minor thunder of a small avalanche behind him had confirmed his expectation that his tracks were somehow going to be effectively wiped out, without any effort on his part. Or, if they weren't wiped out, it wouldn't matter.

Neither the Tasavaltans nor any outraged Culmian loyalists were going to be able to catch up with him—or if they did manage somehow to overtake him, they'd no doubt wish they hadn't.

The morning was bright and promising. Kebbi rode on, singing, with one hand resting easily upon the black hilt at his waist. He owned no land and had no real family in Culm, and most of his worldly possessions were now tied up in a modest bundle behind his saddle. Having Coinspinner, what else did he need to carry? Whenever he needed something, it would somehow be provided, he was confident.

The Sword of Fortune was now his. And unless he, like Murat, was fool enough to place it willingly in the hands of someone else, fortune was going to be his also, from now on—at least until such time as the Sword decided to take itself away.

He knew enough of Coinspinner to realize that it could be expected to do that sooner or later. Supposedly it had once rested for a few years in the Tasavaltan treasury—and then, without giving notice, the Sword had abruptly moved itself out. Simply, easily, and inexplicably it had passed through all the physical and magical barriers with which such a repository must be equipped. No one had even realized that it was gone until they came to look at it again.

So Kebbi couldn't say with any assurance how long he was likely to have the Sword, but with any luck at all—he grinned a twisted grin as that phrase passed through his mind—with even a minimum of luck, he'd possess it long enough to establish his fortune in the world. Then someone else would be welcome to take a turn at a charmed life. Kebbi wouldn't be so greedy as to object to that.

There crossed his mind the question of where he was going to rest tonight. Well, he would leave that to the currents of fortune also. Before he'd actually stolen the Sword, Kebbi had entertained, at least in passing, the idea of taking Coinspinner back to Tasavalta and thereby becoming a hero to the Princess and her people there. But when he had calculated all the possibilities as best he could, he doubted that such a double traitor could stay in very high regard elsewhere.

Oh, of course, the Sword would take care of him in Tasavalta, just as well as it would anywhere else. It was only that there were a great many other places where he would prefer to spend his future, rather than in that cool and unexciting land.

Besides, he thought, it would be harder for the Culmian folk to trace him if he took Coinspinner somewhere else, somewhere very far away most likely, for his reward. And sooner or later, whenever the Sword left him, he would become vulnerable to their revenge.

And now, even as Kebbi rode and grinned and sang, a nagging suspicion began to grow in him that he shouldn't be relying totally on the Sword's good fortune. It was never good to rely that heavily on anything outside yourself. He'd have to start using his brain again, at least. Kebbi ceased to sing, and gradually began to be more alert.

Thus most of the day passed uneventfully for the deserter. During its course he began, almost in spite of himself, to take serious thought on the subject of what his destination ought to be, if it was not to be Tasavalta again. Kebbi's plan to steal the Sword of Chance had taken form quite suddenly, only after the expedition to Sarykam was under way, and until now it had seemed to him enough, once he had his prize, to travel to some great distance from the land of Culm.

Vaguely Kebbi came to have in mind two or three cities, only one of which he had ever visited, all distant places where he thought he would be able to sell his treasure at a great profit if he chose, or where he could use the Sword somehow to obtain some of the wealth with which he would there find himself surrounded. He supposed in an uncertain way that if the Sword, or the powers behind it, just knew what he wanted, he would somehow be provided with the necessary means to reach his goal.

He took thought on the subject now, as he rode steadily along, but no better plan presented itself. Well, there was no hurry.

Toward evening he came to a place where his trail intersected another one, the latter almost large enough to be called a road. Here the fortunate traveler spied an isolated building, big enough to be more than a simple house, in front of which a dozen or more people were gathered.

In the glow of the setting sun the place looked like the poorest kind of inn. If there had not been people to be seen in front of it, he would have doubted that the dilapidated structure was in regular use. Certainly it was badly in need of maintenance and probably not far from collapse. Kebbi's first impression was that this place might well be a den of bandits. What might have been an inn's sign had fallen into ruin some time ago, and there was no deciphering it now. A couple of large tables, and some chairs and benches, all badly weathered, stood in front of the place.

Ten or twelve thuggish-looking men were standing idly about in a few small groups. Kebbi's imagination suggested that they might be only waiting for the fall of night before revealing their true identities as some breed of nocturnal monsters. As he drew nearer the men in turn looked him over quietly, for the moment having nothing to say.

In a place a little apart from the men, a few women were also waiting, for what it was hard to guess. By the look of them they might have been the dregs of Red Temple outcasts. One was lighting a fire in the open.

Kebbi, feeling the inevitable stiffness of a long day's ride, and knowing that he must show it, stopped in front of the inn and dismounted—there was no way to disguise the fact that he was riding a good and valuable animal, and he would not have been surprised to be told that some of the loungers were already trying to guess what his riding-beast might be worth if they could get it away from him.

Well, let them try it. Somewhere he'd heard that Mark, before he became Prince of Tasavalta, had been wounded—scratched, at least, and probably not too inconveniently—while carrying Coinspinner in the thick of a ferocious battle. Well, maybe that light scratch had somehow been lucky for the man who was to rise from commoner to prince—maybe it had even brought him his exalted rank. Anyhow, fate, working through the Sword of Chance, had brought Mark out of obscurity into a great position in the end, hadn't it? He, Kebbi, was ready to accept a light wound for a similar result. The gods knew he'd already had some bad ones for much less reward.

One of the younger loungers was coming toward Kebbi now, indicating with a servile smile that he was ready to act as groom for this obvious gentleman-soldier. And now, from somewhere inside the building, a villainous-looking landlord materialized to wonder aloud if the new arrival was seeking food and lodging.

"I'll take a drink first," Kebbi told the man. "Ale, if you have it. And some care for my mount. After that, we'll see about the rest." He was thinking that, magically protected as he was, he'd rather take his chances sleeping in the open at trailside than endure the bugs and noise and stench that were undoubtedly provided to every guest at this inn along with his room—or his share of floor space. The Sword's power would doubtless keep him from being murdered as long as he slept with it at his side; but he doubted whether Coinspinner's activity would condescend to reach so far into the inconsequential as to protect its owner from all vermin.

Surprisingly, the beer brought to him was pleasantly chilled, and its taste not all that bad. By the time Kebbi had swallowed a third of his first mug, a game of chance involving dice was beginning to get under way around one of the outdoor tables positioned in front of the ramshackle building. A worn blanket, once issued in someone's army, had been smoothed over the table's rough wooden surface, and on this cloth the dice were dancing. Kebbi had hardly turned his gaze in that direction before several of the players invited him, with false heartiness, to take part.

Kebbi's first impulse was to refuse—ordinarily he didn't think of himself as a gambler. But then, this would hardly be gambling, would it? And in truth he was very short of coin.

When the invitation was repeated, he nodded his head in acceptance. As he moved to take a seat on one of the curved benches that ringed the table, he noted that some of the players were aiming curious glances at the black hilt of his Sword.

"Unburden yourself, why don't you, stranger, and sit down."

Acknowledging the invitation with a smile, Kebbi shifted the burden of Coinspinner into a comfortable position. He rubbed the sheath of his weapon familiarly, with one hand. "It brings me luck," he told the company, and saw their answering grins. No one alluded to his Sword again. He wondered if any of them could possibly have recognized it for what it was. Certainly no one here would think it odd that a stranger playing in this game would want to keep his weapons handy. Perhaps, he realized suddenly, one or more of his fellow players were also using some kind of gambling magic. Well, let them try.

As might have been expected from the general appearance of the company, there was as yet no great amount of money in evidence on the blanket-covered tabletop, where now the landlord, bending over carefully, was setting down a pair of flickering and flaring lamps. The table itself was wobbly—as Kebbi had also expected—and groaned and tilted whenever someone leaned on it. The local rules, as the landlord now proclaimed, required the dice on each throw to be bounced off the rectangular base of a lamp—which lamp the thrower used was his own choice—an ancient and reasonably effective prescription against mundane manipulation.

With Kebbi sitting in, there were now six participants in the game. The remaining male loungers and the women—who for the most part remained somewhat more distant—formed a casual audience. From among the women there came the desultory sound of tambourine and drum, and eventually two of the least repulsive of them began to dance. None of the men paid much attention to the show.

When the dice came around to Kebbi, he cast them out casually, taking care only that they should strike the base of the nearest lamp. He won his first throw.

On his second throw, which followed immediately, he won again.

According to the commonly accepted rules of this game, he now had the option of letting the dice pass on, and so he chose to do.

The play went around the table, others winning or losing in their turns. So far only trivial amounts were being wagered. The rules were somewhat complicated, but every soldier knew them, and every bandit and wastrel as well.

Betting on every throw was not required. So far Kebbi had made no losing bet—he doubted it would be possible for him to do so, as long as he had Coinspinner strapped on—and the modest winnings on his first two throws remained intact.

Still, he could not manage to develop any great enthusiasm for the game. No matter what happened, Kebbi was sure, he was not going to win any important amount of money here, not from these poor-looking men. But luck had led him to this inn; and doubtless Fortune, as directed by his Sword, had some great plan for him that started in this inauspicious way. Well then, let Fortune indicate to him what she wanted him to do next.

At last he drained his mug—it had been refilled only once—set it down on the edge of the blanket with a decisive thump, and got to his feet. "Well, gentlemen," he announced cheerfully, "the road waits for me."

His announcement was greeted with unanimous scowls around the table. "Not yet it don't," a large man grumbled immediately.

"That's right," chimed in another. "How 'bout giving us the chance to get some of our money back?"

Kebbi, who had been half expecting such protests, had already decided in the interests of peace to give in to them the first time they were offered. The next time matters would be different, and no one could say he hadn't given them a chance to recoup their trivial losses. Perhaps when the protesters had lost more, they would be willing enough to see his back.

"As you wish," he said, shrugging, and resumed his seat.

"This time," announced the physically largest of his adversaries in a challenging voice, "we use my dice."

"That's all right."

A few moments later, the owner of the crooked, probably magical dice was staring at them in disbelief. His pet artifacts had obviously betrayed him; whatever spell or other trick he'd used had been overridden as if it did not exist. The pattern of the pips represented a very ordinary combination, but obviously it was not a pattern the owner had expected from these particular dice on one in a million throws.

And naturally it was a pattern that won for Kebbi yet again.

A series of muttered remarks among the locals, only partially audible to the stranger, revealed that their opinions had now begun to differ sharply. One faction was definitely ready to let the overlucky stranger go his way in peace. But another faction, fast becoming dominant, was entertaining quite different ideas.

The biggest of the local men stood up. Glowering at Kebbi, he proclaimed: "We don't need any wizards in this game."

The Culmian shook his head. "I should think your friends would pay more heed to your protest—if it didn't come from a man who brought crooked dice into the game."

As he finished speaking, Kebbi pushed back from the table and stepped free of the encumbering bench. From that position he backed away, intending to get his back near one of the scrawny trees in the inn yard. Not that he doubted the power that protected him, but somehow he saw no need to make things unreasonably difficult.

One or two players remained at the table, waiting for the interruption to be over. The rest of them came after Kebbi, unhurriedly, methodically. Now they were beginning to surround him, and some of their hands were reaching toward weapons. Their proposed victim had his right hand on the black hilt of his own blade, though he'd not actually drawn it yet.

There was a pause. So far the air of confidence displayed by the stranger was holding the others back. But none of them seemed to recognize a Sword, and Kebbi understood that in a matter of moments things were going to get really ugly.

Before the storm could break, there came an interruption.

Kebbi, his attention warily on his fellow players, was among the last to notice the arrival of a tall and handsome man, who now appeared silently, standing at the edge of the firelight, with a shadowy and much smaller attendant poised just behind him. It was as if the two of them had just arrived by walking—there had been no sight or sound of any animals they might have ridden—along the lightless road. Coinciding with the arrival of the pair, the moon emerged from behind a fragmentary cloud, and in the change of light the two figures took on a spectral look.

The tall newcomer was richly dressed. Putting up a hand, he threw back the hood of his sumptuous cape, revealing golden curls and a healthy beard to match. Simultaneously he advanced slowly toward the gaming table. The lamplight fell on clear blue eyes, muscular shoulders, large hands, and a handsome face. A long sword of some kind was belted at the newcomer's waist.

His much smaller companion followed him closely, but maintaining a certain distance like a respectful servitor. A few steps closer to the lamps and it was easy to see that she was a woman, as fair as the man, and with a delicate feminine beauty of face that more than matched his masculine good looks. Her beauty was combined with an aura of power and self-confidence, enough of both that Kebbi heard not a single mutter of lechery from any of the scum present. He thought that even had her escort not appeared so formidable, the result would have been the same.

"I hope that the game is not yet finished." The voice of the tall newcomer was powerful, and strangely accented, and he was looking steadily at Kebbi as he spoke. "Come, I am sure that it must not be finished. For I intend to play." His smile showed perfect teeth.

Kebbi said nothing in reply to this. Nor did the men who had almost surrounded him. They were leaving him alone now, and beginning to drift back in the general direction of the table. The tall blond man moved in the same direction now, and their group shattered, softly and silently, and began to disperse into the background.

The music of drum and tambourine, which had faded away when the threat of violence loomed large, now resumed slowly. Very gradually the tempo began to pick up again.

The new arrival still smiled at Kebbi across the battered table, where two lamps still flared upon brown cloth. The dice, the original dice belonging to the landlord, lay at one end unattended.

"Shall we?" The newcomer gestured toward the abundance of empty chairs.

"Why not?" As he stepped forward Kebbi had his hand on the hilt of his Sword, and he could feel the immense power so subtly playing there. Fortune had somehow found a door to open for him, even in this almost uninhabited wilderness. He returned the stranger's smile.

The former participants in the game were now drifting back again a little toward the table. Not that they had any intention of sitting down; they were glad to excuse themselves from this particular contest, but they did not want to miss seeing it, either.

The stranger was as indifferent to what these men did as he was to the indifferent women who had now resumed their dance.

Kebbi and the newcomer, as if by unspoken agreement punctiliously observing some rule of courtesy, seated themselves simultaneously.

Kebbi, feeling an intoxication much more of impending triumph than of drink, faced his single opponent across the blanket-covered table. The tall man's shadowy companion, as if she meant to protect his back, moved up close behind him, where she remained standing.

And now, moving slowly, the hand of the unknown brought forth from somewhere inside his cape a truly magnificent jewel, holding it up for all to see. The stone was the shape of a teardrop, the color of a sapphire's blood. His large, strong fingers held it up, turning it in the lamplight for Kebbi to see and admire. Still the man's attention was entirely concentrated upon Kebbi, as if he were totally indifferent as to anything that other folk might see or do.

Unhurriedly the tall man said: "I will stake this gem against the Sword you wear."

All Kebbi could think was that Fortune, the Sword's Fortune, was working even more swiftly and powerfully than he had dreamt was possible.

"One roll of the dice?" he asked.

"One roll."

"Fine. I accept."

Satisfied, the stranger nodded and looked away. Now his long arm went out to scoop up the dice where they lay at the end of the table; and now he was putting them down on the cloth in front of Kebbi.

Now, at the last moment, Kebbi felt a twinge of reluctance to stake his Sword in any wager. But Coinspinner would not, could not, have led him into this situation only to have him suffer such a loss.

Unless this could be the Sword's method of taking itself away from him? But no, according to the stories Coinspinner used no human agency for that.

Another musician, he thought vaguely, had joined in. It now seemed to him that he could hear the sound of a third drum, tapping a jarring counterpoint to the first two.

And Kebbi threw the dice against a lamp—an eight.

Now it was the stranger's turn. His large right hand cupped the landlord's dice, and threw them out with careless impatience.

Seven.

The rich jewel that Kebbi had just won came arcing toward him through the lamplight, tossed by the stranger. Kebbi automatically put up his hand and caught the bright pebble in midflight.

"Now," said the stranger, to all appearances unperturbed by such a loss. "Now, we are going to play again. Double or nothing." And between the fingers of his gloved right hand appeared two more gems, each looking exactly like the one he had just lost.

Kebbi's breath hissed out between his teeth. "I accept." His doubts had been foolish. Whatever might happen next, he was protected.

This time the stranger threw first.

Four.

Yielding to a mad twitch of bravado, Kebbi threw left-handed this time. As he did so, three fingers of his right hand were resting lightly on his sheathed Sword's hilt, and the great, strange jewel he had just won was clenched securely in the remaining two.

But there was something wrong with the result, and Kebbi could only stare at it without comprehension.

Three.

The dice read only three. A single pip on one ivory cube, two on the other. And that meant that this time, he—he and Coinspinner together —had lost.

Such a result could not be true. It could not be true. It could not be possible, or—

Struggling to make sense of the impossible, Kebbi did not notice that again only two drums beat in the background.

There had been some mistake, some error in the way the world was working. The Sword of Chance could not be beaten, least of all in a game of chance. But he could not bring himself to utter a word. How could his luck, how could the power of the Sword, have suddenly deserted him? The Sword itself was still with him. He could still feel its silent energy, seemingly unimpaired.

Kebbi was too stunned to make any effort at resistance when the tall stranger, giving up an effort to talk to him, came moving lithely around the table. He was jerked to his feet. Strong hands undid his swordbelt and pulled it away, carrying its priceless contents with it. A moment later the great jewel that had been his so briefly was torn from where his fingers still clenched it, mindlessly, against the palm of his hand. Then Kebbi was cast aside, staggering, like some emptied and discarded vessel.

A moment later the tall stranger and his diminutive attendant were in retreat, vanishing almost as suddenly as they had appeared. And already the local men, the losers in the first game, were closing in on the fallen Kebbi, determined to reclaim the few coins he had won from them.

Still too shocked to do anything, the most recent loser could already hear them arguing over who would get his riding-beast.

The tall blond man in the sumptuous cloak, hurrying away from the poor tavern with his companion and his new-won prize, had not far to go down the dark road before he was met by a griffin, a mount bigger than a warbeast, winged like a giant eagle and taloned, fanged, and muscled like a lion. The creature crouched before the man in the attitude of a submissive pet.

In the next moment the man's diminutive helper, the tiny woman of great beauty, moving like an active child, hopped aboard the beast. Then she looked down at him where he still stood gloating over the Sword he had just won.

He had drawn another Sword that looked identical to the first and was exulting with one blade in each hand.

"Master Wood?" she called, deferentially puzzled.

"One moment. With Coinspinner now in hand, I have some spells to cast. Trapping spells. Before I do anything else."

"Against Prince Mark?"

"Against his whelp. The elder one, the heir. A softer target, dear, by far."

5

As Adrian and Trilby continued their steady advance into the City of Wizards, the landscape through which they passed became even less like that of the normal world outside. Within the domain they had now entered, a glow of extra magical potential, perceptible to their trained senses, touched and transformed almost everything.

As they approached the center of the City, the architecture around them grew ever more extraordinary too. Hovels and monuments stood side by side. Segments and quarterings of palaces, disconnected from their rightful places in the outside world, loomed over shanties. Mausoleums carved with incomprehensible inscriptions bulked next to fishermen's huts, far from any water.

And that center was somewhat closer to the travelers than had at first appeared. The bizarre urban skyline ahead of them, not really as tall as they had thought, was rapidly separating itself into distinct structures as they walked toward it. And at the same time the individual structures grew more distinct, in both their normal and magical outlines. In all this the two apprentice magicians found nothing overtly alarming. But still, despite the study and preparation that had led them to expect such phenomena, the intrinsic strangeness of the place was awesome.

As the two adventurers advanced, looking around them alertly, each reminded the other at least once, in a low voice, that the most efficient way to accomplish their objective would be to obtain the desired paving tile and return to the compound of Trimbak Rao before midnight.

Their pace slowed somewhat as they found themselves, almost before they had expected it, moving right in among the taller buildings. Here the descriptions given them by Trimbak Rao continued to prove accurate. Their dog-leg road had turned into a broad paved street, not quite straight, wide in some places and narrow in others, crossed at short intervals by other thoroughfares, most of which were more dis-torted than itself.

Presently the explorers reached a distinctive intersection, marked by a triple fountain in the center. To reach their goal from here, if what their Teacher had told them was correct, it would be necessary to walk about a kilometer on a circuitous route. They could expect serious diffi-culties in ever reaching the park they were attempting to enter, Trimbak Rao had warned them, unless they approached it from the proper direction.

So far they had seen no living presence, human or otherwise, in the City besides themselves. The buildings around them appeared to be completely uninhabited, by humanity at least, and yet they certainly were not silent. At intervals there was music—of a kind. It was so unlike anything that Adrian had ever heard before, that he was unable to find words to describe it. He could tell from Trilby's expression that she was puzzled by it too. These sounds issued from unseen sources among certain of the buildings as the visitors passed. At other moments strange voices could be heard, some crying out as if in pain, some laughing, others singing or reciting gibberish. Trimbak Rao had not warned his students about these voices, and the explorers exchanged glances. But then, they had known that the City was in some sense inhabited, and there had been no reason for the Teacher to warn them of every harmless oddity they might encounter. Small waves of magical disturbance came washing across the cityscape with the voices, but still Adrian thought that most of them at least sounded human.

When he and Trilby had gone on a hundred meters from the square of the triple fountains, their pace slowed again, as by some unspoken agreement. Now something, some instinct, seemed to be telling Adrian not to hurry. Caution was essential here. Again and again he could hear the Teacher's voice, in memory, warning against undue haste.

The steps of his booted feet dragged on the cracked pavement.

Trilby appeared to be having somewhat similar thoughts, for her steps were slowing too; her eyes looked troubled when he glanced at her.

Moving at an ever more slothful pace, the explorers presently came in sight of a small, briskly flowing stream that appeared to have cut its course haphazardly between buildings. Most streets stopped abruptly at its banks, but a few had somehow acquired bridges.

Following the stream's bank, Adrian and Trilby soon entered the parklike plot of land that was their goal. At his first sight of the patch of thriving greenery, Adrian experienced a sense of anticlimax, though he was not sure how it was different from what he had been expecting.

The park was basically an expanse of grass that appeared to still be well maintained. Here and there a bank of hardy-looking flowers had been placed, as it seemed, by some gardener much given to random choices. Trees and bushes appeared in pleasingly unplanned positions, and narrow walks of fine gravel curved among them. The whole occupied not much more than an irregular hectare of land, and just beyond its hedged borders the structures of the City stood as before.

There on the park's left side stood what must be the Red Temple the Teacher had warned them about, looking very much as Trimbak Rao had described it, yet somehow not exactly as Adrian had expected. The customary Red Temple colors of red and black dominated what he could see of the structure's outer walls, which were also decorated with many statues depicting the joys of the senses.

"We'd better take a look around the perimeter of the park," said Trilby. "Before we start digging up tiles. Just to scout things out."

"Sure."

Beginning a clockwise circuit, the two young people walked closer to the Temple. As the angle from which they viewed it changed, the building began to take on a look of considerable deformity. From within the Temple's several doorways, all dark but wide open, issued sounds that made the young Prince think vaguely of some huge spinning mechanism, and also of a crowd of humanity all speaking in low and urgent voices.

Not that there was any crowd to be discovered when Trilby and Adrian peered over the hedge bordering the park, trying to see into the Temple's main entrance. Where once, no doubt, some eager throngs of customers and worshippers had passed, unmarked dust had drifted on the pavement, and small plants were growing here and there. There was no visible trace of human presence.

In the direction of the Red Temple, the indications and auras of magic, subtle and faintly ominous, were even more numerous than elsewhere in the City. But all the traces were weak and old; there was nothing that suggested clear and present danger.

They paused to study the statues and carvings on the Temple wall, showing the usual copulations and debauchery.

Adrian's companion, her head on one side, was taking time to consider the art critically.

"I intend to remain a virgin," said Trilby at last, speaking as if more to herself than to her companion. "For the foreseeable future."

Maintaining virginity was a frequent goal, Adrian knew, among both males and females who intended to devote their lives, or at least their youth, to magic. He was still a year or so too young to have to confront this as a personal decision; now he only nodded and moved slowly on.

"We'd better go slow," said Trilby, rather unnecessarily, as they turned away from the border hedge, back into the innocent-appearing parkland.

"Right. Take out time to scout this place, and do it properly." Adrian felt vaguely reassured that Trilby now shared his growing reluctance to be hurried into any aspect of their mission before they could think it out thoroughly in advance.

The park was more or less centered on a pool formed by the small river's encounter with a low dam. Over this barrier, no more than a couple of meters high, the water rushed with a continuous if muted roar.

"That's not as loud as it might be," Trilby commented.

"Magic?" Adrian asked.

"Magic?" repeated Trilby. Then with a shake of her head she answered her own question. "Well, of course it's magic. At least to some extent. Like everything else we've come across today."

Bordering on the pool was the paved square from which they were expected to remove a tile. Again things were not quite as Adrian had thought to find them. It was as if the soil had somehow been extracted from underneath, and the surface from which the tile would have to be removed was concave, with its lowest central portion under half a meter or more of standing water, at about the level of the surface of the nearby pool. This encroachment of the pool was evidently not a purely recent or temporary development. Furry-looking green plants of various sizes, thriving in this damp environment, grew over much of the exposed pavement and through the water, adding at least one more minor obstacle to the job of tile removal.

"Wow!" said Adrian suddenly, ceasing to be a coolly detached investigator.

"What is it?"

Probing with his powers as best he could into the earth directly beneath the pavement, Adrian confirmed what he had just detected there. "What a pool of energy. Could I ever raise an elemental here!"

Trilby looked at him with interest. "Are you going to try it?"

"No, not now. There wouldn't be any point. But wow, what a potential," he murmured, letting his perception range farther among the strained and troubled rocks and soil many meters beneath this fancy pavement.

* * *

Trilby was frowning lightly now, with more than concentration, Adrian thought; and he himself felt an undercurrent of slight uneasiness. Well, it was hardly astonishing if land in the vicinity of an ancient Red Temple, which had been transported magically into the City at some time in the past, should prove to be inhabited or infested by beings, powers, that seemed strange even to magicians. Perhaps yet another plane of existence, containing yet other inhabitants, was nearby.

"Well," said Trilby at last, and sighed like one unable any longer to avoid facing a distasteful job. "I suppose we ought to see about digging out our tile."

"I suppose," the Prince agreed doubtfully. "But listen, Trill—"

"What?"

"Are we really sure that this is the right place? The Teacher didn't say anything about the pavement being sunken in like this. I thought the place we wanted was going to be square and level."

"Good point. I wonder?" Trilby scraped with the toe of her boot at the green-scummed tiles of the visible portion of the floor.

And now, to Adrian, the tiles in this pavement were indeed beginning to look different than the ones he remembered in the study of Trimbak Rao. Because of the flood, the only tiles he could see clearly here were those around the edge. These were of an abstract pattern, containing no erotic figures, whereas those in the study had portrayed a scene, or several scenes . . .

"I don't know," Trilby was saying. "Remember those tiles we saw on Teacher's wall? Didn't some of them make up a scene, a figure of a woman, giving birth?"

"Yes. I can remember that. And some of them were just porn, like the Temple wall."

"No, that's not right."

The two explorers stood looking at each other in moderate puzzlement. Not that they were really concerned. Neither of them saw anything in their situation to worry about.

"The main point," said Trilby, giving her dark hair a shake, "is that we shouldn't rush things. We must make sure of what we're doing." The air seemed to be growing warmer, and she fanned herself with the hand that did not hold her staff.

Adrian had to agree. "Yes, you're right. The Teacher told us not to rush things. Over and over he told us that."

"Maybe we should scout around the area a little more."

"I think we should."

Without really thinking about it, they had turned their backs on the square of tiles, and were now standing side by side on the edge of the little pond. Its water looked deep and was almost calm, mirror-like until it began to curl into a white roar at the very edge of the dam. A small pier, wooden and moss-grown, projected from the near shoreline out into the pond, and a dugout canoe was tied at the pier's far end.

Trilby knelt down suddenly and thrust her hand into the water. "Feels cool."

Slipping off his pack, Adrian knelt beside her, cupping water in his own palms. "Sure does." Then he raised his eyes suddenly, staring at the canoe. There was something unusual about it, besides the fact that it had been carved from a single log, and finished smoothly, with exquisite skill. But for the moment he couldn't quite pin the oddity down.

Yes, something unusual, with overtones of the festive and the unpredictable . . .

"The sky's changed," Trilby informed him suddenly.

And indeed the day had now become almost normal. A bright and normal-looking sun, not too hot, was clearly visible over the building that adjoined the little park on the side opposite the Red Temple. Adrian made a mental note to himself to be sure to observe the way the sun moved as the day advanced. He still had no idea of the proper directions in this world—if indeed such an idea had any real meaning here.

At the moment, apart from the twisted architecture surrounding them, and the occasional inexplicable sounds that issued from those structures, there was hardly any indication that they were in the City at all. Or so it seemed to Adrian.

The little river maintained its muffled roar. The hot sun shimmered on the brown and gray of the pavement tiles, and glared on the surface of the pond.

The vessel resting almost motionless in the calm water drew his attention once again, and he remarked: "We have some canoes very much like that one at home. But I never saw one so neatly finished."

"We should be getting on with our job." Trilby's sudden protest began in a tone of considerable urgency, but before she had uttered half a dozen words her voice once more lacked conviction.

"I suppose we should," agreed Adrian, after taking some time to think the matter over. But even as he spoke he felt a reluctance to hurry, or to be hurried.

By now the two of them had slipped off their packs, and were sitting quietly, contentedly beside the pool, contemplating the water and the canoe that drifted lightly on its tether. It was as if they were waiting for they knew not what. All around them, beyond the borders of the park, the City seemed to have grown quieter, except for the ceaseless roaring of the stream. Even the strange sounds proceeding from the buildings came less frequently. All hints of dangerous magic were in abeyance.

Methodically, unhurriedly, Trilby pulled off her boots, and lowered her feet into the cooling water, wiggling her brown toes. The riparian ledge on which the explorers sat was just at a handy height above the pool for this maneuver.

Adrian imitated her actions. "That feels good."

"It sure does."

Trilby poked aimlessly at the water with her hiking staff, then laid it beside her on the ledge. "I wonder if we have time for a swim. I'd like a chance to really cool off."

"That sounds even better." And it did, it sounded great, except maybe there was something else they ought to be doing . . . but the thought refused to complete itself just now. Later he would come back to it . . .

Now the girl, frowning slightly, had turned her head toward him. "Adrian, I know you're not, well, you're not grown up yet, but . . ."

"Oh, sure. If you want a dip, I can take a walk." In Adrian's experience most people were fairly casual about nudity; he felt faintly surprised, and vaguely complimented that Trilby did not want him to see her with her clothes off.

She stood up. "Then it'll be your turn to swim. Or maybe we should toss to see who goes in first?"

"No, you go ahead. I'm not in any hurry."

Adrian turned his back on Trilby and started to take a walk. The hedged border of the park was only a short distance ahead of him, and beyond it rose the distorted bulk of the mysterious Red Temple, an interesting goal for exploration.

There were several openings in the boundary hedge, where little paths had been worn through, and the prince chose the nearest one. Only when he had begun to climb the broad stone stairs leading ultimately to the Red Temple did he realize that he had left his pack, canteen, and boots back at poolside. Oh, well. He climbed on barefoot, becoming interested in the configuration of the structure before him. Toward one end of the Temple, on his left, the carved figures and other elements of the design were all grotesquely flattened in one dimension, elongated in another, as if the perspective of the space in which they existed had been changed by the magical forces that had brought them to this exotic place and forced them into coexistence with other elements from elsewhere.

A selection of dark doorways, all leading into the Temple's interior, stood open ahead of him. And now that he was alone, he began to be troubled by the feeling that there was some trick, some clue, regarding their surroundings that ought to be of concern to him and Trilby but which they had not yet discovered. It wasn't a strong feeling, only a slight irritation. And it wasn't really a matter of danger, not as Adrian perceived it now. In fact he wasn't thinking of danger at all. But there was something forgotten or overlooked, maybe something that they were going to need . . .

Having progressed at a leisurely pace fully halfway up the stairs that ascended toward the distorted building, the prince on impulse stopped and turned to glance back. From here he could see over the hedge bordering the park into its interior. There was the narrow dam, the water rushing over, its muted roar still audible. And there, sure enough, was Trilby, forty or fifty meters away now, standing naked on the edge of the pool. Her brown skin was gleaming wet, and she was getting ready to dive in again.

And so he had got to see her that way after all.

She was unaware that he was looking, and indeed it didn't seem of any great importance. Yet Adrian stood very still, continuing to watch the girl. He told himself that he had a good reason for watching, that he was carefully making sure that she was still all right.

Her figure poised for a dive, and then arced out of sight. The faint sound of the splash was swallowed by the steady heavy murmur of the stream falling over the barrier. The canoe, beside its dock, bobbed gently with the waves the dive had made.

Very soon, before Trilby had resurfaced, the prince walked on, conscious of a vague feeling of uneasiness.

The nearest of the Temple's dim doorways widened around him, and he passed through it. Inside, once his eyes had adjusted from the direct glare of sun, he could see well enough. Entering the first hall he came to, Adrian discovered many empty tables and chairs, most of them tipped over now—once the instruments of gluttony, he supposed. He gave the place a perfunctory inspection upon entering, but all his senses assured him that these surroundings were perfectly safe. There was simply no danger here. Anyway, Trimbak Rao wouldn't have sent two of his favorite tender young apprentices into a place where there was real danger, would he?

Would he?

No, of course not!

Coming aimlessly outdoors again, Adrian paused, squinting upward, to check the position of the sun. By leaving the pool he had certainly changed his own position relative to the neighboring building, but there was the sun, the same angular distance above its rooftop as before.

Something to think about. Well, all in good time. He moved back into the Temple's dimness.

This time he took a different turning. Certain of the interior doorways were completely blocked, or their openings impossibly constricted, by tiers of masonry that seemed, through whim or ignorance, to have been built in the wrong place. Progress was difficult but not impossible.

The interior of this Temple was laid out according to a plan shared by a great many of its sister Temples around the world. Not that Adrian, at twelve, had ever been in any one of them before. Nor was he well acquainted with any cult of adult pleasures—but here and there he had heard stories.

This great chamber, containing a few large and strangely decorated tables, had to be the House of Luck. One wall was entirely dominated by a huge gaming wheel, wall-mounted so that the numbers as they came up could be seen clearly from any part of a large room. A number of gaming tables were in the room also.

The wheel, big enough if not sturdy enough to run a sawmill, for some reason started to turn by itself just as the boy entered the gambling hall. He paused, looking at it attentively. Music from invisible instruments, played by no human hands, was suddenly loud and clear. Adrian, turning his head in response to a different, half-heard sound, observed a pair of semi-transparent forms, of vaguely human shape, ascending a stairway. One form, now exaggeratedly female, seemed to turn back to glance at him before disappearing at the top of the stairs. Upstairs, if the stories he had heard were true, was where the House of Flesh would be.

The wheel ratcheted to a halt, at the number zero.

He continued his exploration of the ground floor. Along with the steadily increasing euphoric sense of confidence, tranquility, and well-being, though in definite contradiction to it, the undercurrent of anxiety now came back more strongly than before. It was an apparently baseless feeling that something was beginning to go wrong, something that seemed the result at least in part of sheer bad luck.

He was picking up plenty of things to think about. Yes. Well, all in good time.

But his vague uneasiness guided him outside again. As if reluctantly, shuffling on bare feet, he made his way back toward the parkland and its pool. Pausing halfway down the broad steps, at the place where he had taken a secret look at Trilby, he looked for her again. But the girl was out of sight. If she was in the pool he couldn't hear her splashing, not above the steady background roar of falling water.

Adrian moved on, still walking deliberately, heading back into the park to rejoin his companion.

Arriving at the pool, he found nothing surprising. The canoe bobbed idly, its presence suggesting . . . something. But what? And Trilby, dressed once more in shirt and trousers, was sitting where she had sat before, again contemplating the water.

She raised her head almost languidly at Adrian's arrival. "Where were you, in the Temple? Discover anything new?"

"No. Not really." He sat down beside her, just where he had been before, dipping his feet in the water again. He wondered what to say. "How was your swim?"

"Fine. Cool. The water's nice and deep, you can even dive."

"My turn, then."

"Sure." Trilby got to her feet. "And my turn to take a walk around."

"I looked inside the Red Temple, but there wasn't much. A couple of spooky-looking figures, and a gaming wheel moved. No real interaction. Maybe you can find something interesting."

Left alone, Adrian became interested in the canoe. Carved in one piece, very skillfully, from a single log of gray-brown wood, it was thin and light-looking and graceful.

But first, he felt hot and the water beckoned. In a moment, Adrian was standing, and in another he had stripped off his clothes.

The first plunge was a clean joy. Coming up from the surprising green depths, the prince drifted on his back, in water marvelously cool. Now, he thought, to see about the canoe. A few strong kicks brought him to its side.

Pulling on a gunwale to peer in, he observed a single wooden paddle, neatly carved, lying in the bottom. Yes, he was going to have to try the canoe out.

Small boats of every kind were common enough in Tasavalta, and Adrian considered himself something of an expert. Starting in deep water, you couldn't simply scramble in over the side of a canoe. He climbed first to the pier, then got himself aboard the little craft and untied the cord that held it to the dock. As he did so, he abruptly realized what was so unusual about this boat—of all the objects in sight, here in the middle of Wizards' City, it was the only one devoid of any magical aura at all.

That ought to mean something, but he wasn't sure what.

For the time being he let the paddle stay where it was. The canoe, left to its own devices, showed no immediate tendency to be carried out of the pool and over the dam.

There had been a very little water, hardly more than damp spots, in the bottom of the canoe, before he climbed in dripping. He thought it might have trickled from Trilby's naked body—she might have investigated the boat too, played around in it between swims. And when she sat in it, her bare bottom would have rested just about where his was now.

Adrian eased himself from the middle seat and lay back, stretching out as much as possible, raising his knees over the middle thwart. He let his eyes close. The sun-heated wood would have felt the same, almost too hot for comfort, on her body as on his.

. . . on her soft, smooth, brown skin. On her flesh that was so very different from his, rounded but firm with unobtrusive muscle underneath. Her big breasts, as he had seen them from a distance, bulging in the sun, their broad dark nipples seeming to turn up a little in its heat.

The canoe bobbed lightly, for no discernible reason. Adrian remembered the female figure he'd glimpsed in the Temple. With his eyes closed he could imagine he saw her walking toward him.

Opening his eyes, the boy looked down at his own bare body, wiry and immature. Most of his skin was pale, seldom touched by the sun. But his body wasn't going to stay childish much longer. Soon, in a year or two, he'd be growing, developing real muscles. And something else too.

Like the male statues carved on the Temple wall. His body would be as much a man's as any of them.

Time passed.

At last, driven by some subliminal warning, Adrian sat up abruptly. He could feel that his face was red, his ears burning, his body uncomfortable as if it had been used by alien powers. The canoe was drifting, bumping against a little bar that fortunately ran along the dam. Fortunately, because otherwise he and his boat would have gone right over. He still might, if the craft drifted only a little sideways. Grabbing up the wooden paddle, he backed water none too soon.

He had paddled back to a place near the middle of the pond, and was wondering in confusion what to do next, when he had a strong sensation that he was no longer alone. Inhuman creatures that he took at first for incubi and succubi from the Temple were standing semi-transparent on the very edge of the pool, the females clutching their transparent garments coyly round them. There were six of them, eight, ten. No, more. Numbers beyond counting. Many of the shapes were strange and indecipherable, but all were evil. Now Adrian understood that some of them might have come out of the Red Temple, but most had issued from somewhere else, only the gods knew where.

Heart pounding, throat suddenly a dry knot, the prince realized that he was surrounded by ferociously antagonistic powers, forces of hostile magic. So subtle had been their approach, so arcane the spells that shielded them from his view, that he had never perceived them until now. For hours, for days perhaps, they had been closing in on him, walling him subtly but powerfully away from the outside world.

Now he could see, he could feel, that they were on the brink of some climactic action that might destroy him. He had no time or nerve for careful thought. Acting instinctively in self-defense, his mind and his perception reached deep beneath the surface of the earth. As a drowning boy might have clutched at a log, so Adrian reached for and seized the energies of earth, molding them, prodding them into detonation.

The result was an elemental.

This particular elemental, born among the strains and heat of rocks many meters below the surface of the earth, was very powerful even of its powerful kind.

Whirling and dancing in the circle of Adrian's enemies, there were no demons, but a foul host of other hostile powers. These at first jeered at his efforts to create a counterforce, taunted him with what they supposed must be his feebleness.

It was not a matter of the Prince's unleashing the elemental at them —for he had made no effort to restrain it in the first place. This was no comparatively gentle derivative of sky or water. Rather an earth-elemental, vast and imbued with the power of gravity. Suddenly granted sentience, this creature battled its way toward the surface, sending before it from the body of the planet a deafening eruption of shattered rock, geysering water, splattering fountains of mud.

Havoc resulted. All other forces of magic blurred, within the narrow locus of the elemental's influence. This zone contained the enemy powers surrounding Adrian. Their ring was broken, the ground reshaped, and the local course of the small river temporarily disrupted.

The essence of its being invisible, having no form but that of the earth from which it had been born, the elemental reached the surface and there jerked to a stop. The canoe, with Adrian still in it, was hurled into the air, to splash back violently. Somehow, clutching hard at both gunwales, he avoided being thrown out into the water.

The small dam had already burst, or rather it had been obliterated. The water contained in the deep pool was hurled downstream, the flood carrying the boat with it.

Adrian in his canoe was carried away upon this miniature tidal wave of water, propelled by a buckling and heaving landscape. He was borne downstream, through the broken ring of the powers that would have confined and perhaps destroyed him.

The elemental, still full of life and ferocity, drove dumbly on behind its creator, and tumult swept along the riverbed. Behind its passage the crash of falling buildings partially blocked the stream, which fought a new channel through the wreckage almost at once.

Stretched out in the bottom of the canoe, clinging for his life as waves and mud poured in on him, the Prince could only close his eyes and wait. At last the thunder of the erupting earth was quiet. He could only keep clinging to the thwarts and gunwales, and allow himself to be borne along. Drained by the great effort he had made in raising the elemental, he drifted into a semiconscious state.

None of the creatures evoked by his enemy's hostile magic pursued him; for one thing their formation had been shattered, and for another they had been given no such orders. They were constrained to soothing and trapping and holding.

Still the canoe continued to be borne forward, although now at a gradually diminishing speed. The elemental was following the craft downstream, but by slow degrees the creature was ceasing to propel it forward.

The dazed boy, being swept downstream, muttered the name of Trilby once or twice. But Adrian had no way of knowing what might have happened to her. Nor, if he had known, would he have had any means of turning back to try to help her.

Once raising his head, groggily, to look back, he saw shapes of blackness, as if the shadow of the whole earth, the City's skyline visible in silhouette, were being cast upon clouds high in the sky by some great sun-light in the center of the planet. And then he slumped into unconsciousness.

On regaining full consciousness at last, and bringing his head up out of the bottom of the canoe, Adrian found that the elemental seemed to have completely dissipated. Natural darkness had overtaken him. And from the feel of his environment, he was sure that he was no longer in the City. The stream and the canoe had carried him along some natural escape route, doubtless perilous, that had brought him clean away from immediate danger.

"Trilby," he groaned again. Wherever his partner had been when the disaster struck, when the trap had tried to close on them, he realized that they might now, for all he knew, be separated by hundreds of kilometers.

The paddle was still aboard, wedged under one end of a thwart. The boy couldn't really recall putting it there. Taking up the implement again, Adrian shakily directed the craft to shore at the nearest level place. Then he got out and stood with his feet sinking into warm mud, trying to see back in the direction from which he had come. Vague, dark masses indicated heavy vegetation along both banks.

The heir to the throne of Tasavalta could be sure only that the City was now completely behind him, and that he was now standing, completely naked and utterly alone, on the bank of a strange river.

6

As soon as Wood had completed the first phase of his magical attack upon Prince Mark's son, a process that took only a few minutes, the blond and beautiful enchantress called Tigris leaped astride the griffin once again. She waited for her master to mount behind her, ready to snuggle herself provocatively against him. But this time the magician had elected to use a different means of transport. He remained at a little distance from the griffin, standing in an area shaded from the moonlight by the knotted branches of a dead tree; and by means of the flickering spots of silver light his assistant was able to observe swift changes in his physical shape. Among other alterations, Wood's body as a whole grew smaller, and his own dark pinions came sprouting from his shoulders.

Tigris, seeing how things were, whispered a command into the griffin's ear, and the great beast sprang upward, bearing her into the air. She saw her master's shadowy form rise after her.

Their flight was not a long one, and it was conducted entirely through darkness and whistling wind. Tigris was aware when, at about the halfway point, the first other powers joined them in midair. Before they landed, several airborne demons, accompanied by other powers less susceptible to ready classification, had already met her master to fawn upon him. These immaterial creatures manned the outermost line of protection of Wood's domain.

Now, as the two humans and their escort descended toward the earth again, the wind abated somewhat. Their landing was in a wild and lonely place, still well within the natural boundary of night. The griffin crouched meekly on the rocky soil, making it easy for Tigris to dismount.

She did so with a quick jump, then looked around her. By the time Wood had landed too and she had located her master on the ground, his appearance was once more that of a handsome and broad-shouldered young man.

Standing within an ancient circle of stones, evidently a place for which he felt some special preference, Wood was holding the naked Sword of Chance up in his right hand and gazing at the blade. Here, in this pool of relatively deep natural darkness, Coinspinner responded to his touch with sparks, some of which were momentarily dazzling in their brilliance.

Despite his triumph in obtaining the Sword of Chance, Wood's thoughts at this moment were troubled. Having completed—satisfactorily, he thought—the first phase of his magical attack on the young Prince, he found it necessary to reach a decision: whether or not to go immediately into the City himself, to take possession of the trapped prey.

Tigris, while her withdrawn master pondered, had perched herself seductively upon an enormous skull nearby—the unfleshed head looked like that of some mythological beast, higher than her own head when she stood before it. Only the head of a great worm, she supposed, could be so huge—but she was no expert in inhuman anatomy.

Despite the pertness of her attitude, her voice was humble in tone when next she spoke, daring to interrupt her Ancient Master's private deliberations to ask him what his next move was going to be. Somehow, during the brief interval of travel from the gaming table to this half-real wasteland, she had come to be wearing a short black skirt instead of trousers, and now there was a flash of pale thighs when she crossed her legs.

Wood, turning his head to peer out of the shadows of the tall stones, gazed at her blankly for a moment. As a rule the great wizard was not insensible of his assistant's physical attractiveness—far from it. But now other matters of greater importance had first claim on his attention.

His attack on Prince Adrian, launched with the help of Coinspinner, was only one of these, though one of the most pressing. And his decision was still not made as to whether he would go himself into the City of Wizards and collect his prey.

But now he decided that there was one other decision to be made first, one that Wood had to admit must take priority over all the rest.

Holding up the naked length of Coinspinner, he inspected the Sword more closely. Frowning at the Blade as if he could wring its secrets from it by sheer force of will, Wood twirled it, somewhat awkwardly, in his strong right hand. At the same time he was resting his left hand on the almost identical hilt of Shieldbreaker, which very rarely left his side by night or day. Touching two Swords at once, he could feel his own immersion in the godlike power of the Swords. It was like no other power he had ever encountered, either in the ancient world from which he came, or in this one. Perhaps not even Ardneh or Orcus, his enemies of thousands of years ago, would ever have been quite able to match this.

Tigris, shifting her weight restlessly on the great skull, her short skirt riding yet a little higher, persisted in her nervous questioning: "What will you do with it now, my lord?"

For a moment he blinked at her distractedly, as if he were not quite sure who this woman might be who questioned him.

But at last he answered her aloud. "With Coinspinner?" The magician held the blade up, then paused, holding it very still. "Perhaps I will destroy it."

For once his clever assistant could only stare at him without comprehension. "My lord?"

The man on the ground, he who could grow reptilian wings, or dispose of them again, whenever he chose to do so, chuckled dryly. "Do I mystify you, Tigris? But I suppose that is inescapable."

Then he twirled the Sword of Chance again, and cast it down before him forcefully, so that the point stabbed deep into the rocky earth, and the weapon remained standing upright.

His right hand, having thus emptied itself, went promptly to the other scabbard hanging at his other side. From that sheath it drew out his second Blade, equally dazzling to look at.

Now the wizard said to the young-looking, innocent-looking woman who sat above him on the great skull: "Look, here's Shieldbreaker!"

"I see it, my lord."

"Do you? Do you see that I am now granted an opportunity that may never come again? Here in my hand I now hold the Sword that blocked Coinspinner's power in tonight's game, when that power would have been used against me; this same blade can shatter the other's metal forever. Believe me, it can. It has done the same for both Doomgiver and Townsaver, in times past."

"But . . . O master, to destroy Coinspinner! Why?" Tigris was openly aghast at the thought that Wood could even consider annihilating such a magnificent weapon, an almost matchless treasure, nullifying the great advantage that he had just managed to acquire.

Actually, though the woman appeared to be taking seriously his threat to destroy the Sword, in her heart she could not really do so. Her master, for his part, could almost read her thoughts: Was this talk of destruction only some regal jest? But no, hardly that. She would know that Wood was too sober to play such games, not much of a jester at any time.

She would, he thought, probably be virtually convinced that his talk of shattering a Sword was only some kind of a test he had devised for his subordinate.

While on occasion he might arrange such tests, now he had no time or inclination for them. Nor had he much patience for giving explanations. Still, he saw that if he wanted any intelligent response from his assistant at all, something in the way of explanation was a necessity.

"I am perfectly serious, girl. Consider that this unpredictable Sword now lying at my feet will always pose an obstacle to me, or to anyone else, who seeks to attain perfect power."

"My lord?"

"But you really don't see that, do you?"

"My lord—"

He gestured impatiently. "Suppose that I managed to get into my possession every Sword, including this one, of the ten that still remain intact. Yet this one, with its cursed independence, might fly away from me at any time. It might leave me, and then it might create problems for me, only the gods know what problems, once it had arrived in the hands of someone else."

Tigris, having grasped the point as soon as it was stated plainly, was quick to be reassuring. "You'll find some clever way around that, my wise and powerful lord. Some way to bind Coinspinner's power forever to your service, and to that of no one else."

Wood answered slowly. "I might. Such magic would be a supreme challenge, but I might attempt to manage it—if only I were not so busy just now with other matters. On the other hand, if I destroy the Sword of Chance now, now while I have the certain power to do so . . ." Again he brandished Shieldbreaker. There was no other known means to destroy any of the Swords. "Then I need fear Coinspinner's power never again."

Once more Tigris shifted her shapely weight on the great skull, her pale thighs flashing as if she could not choose to be anything other than seductive. "And yet," she murmured. "And yet, my master hesitates."

The master, plunged deep in thought again, scarcely looked up at her. But he did reply. "I do. I hesitate, indeed. Whilst Coinspinner is in my grasp, I can use its power to achieve . . . great things. Yes, already it has given me advantage. Presently I'll have Prince Mark's princely whelp firmly in my grip. And then I think his father—aye, and his grandfather too—will cease to be such sharp thorns in my side."

The woman spoke cautiously. "I understand that your decision regarding this Sword must be a very difficult one, my lord."

He did look at her now, and carefully. "Do you understand, Tigris? Do you begin to grasp my problem? I wonder if you do."

And Wood closed his eyes briefly, casting abroad his inner vision, doing his best to follow the progress of the spells he had cast and the powers he had dispatched to snare young Adrian. The trouble was that the Tasavaltan whelp was guarded, better protected than Wood had ever realized . . . but yet, with Coinspinner's help, success now seemed imminent.

Oh, the overwhelming force of Chance, of Fortune, that came with this Sword was too great a power to give up!

And yet . . .

The wizard opened his eyes. He paced about, groaning intensely though almost inaudibly. Demons and spells were of no help to him now. His mind was in a frenzy, unable to come to a decision.

Then abruptly he stopped in his tracks. Suddenly he issued a sharp order. "Back to our headquarters! I will make my decision there. Wait, this time I will ride with you."

The griffin, which had dropped out of sight for a time, now appeared again as if from nowhere, spread its wings and lowered its body to make it easier for the people to get aboard. In another moment, the creature and its double human cargo had whirled into the air again.

This leg of their flight was considerably longer than the first had been, though still not long enough to bring them into daylight.

The aerial voyage terminated at Wood's headquarters. This edifice, when seen from the outside, appeared to be—and indeed was—a fortress of dark stone, sprawling along a mountain peak. It looked a forbidding place indeed, its lofty stone walls surrounding the sharp central crag that arose within them. The two arriving humans, on landing inside the high walls, entered an aspect of the place somewhat more civilized in appearance. They dismounted from the griffin at one end of a courtyard garden. This garden boasted fountains and statuary, though many of the plants that grew in it were not ordinary flowers. Blue flames, welling from some of the fountains, provided an eerie but serviceable illumination.

Nor would the statues have been of ordinary appearance, even in ordinary light. Two of the strangest among them, standing about a meter apart from each other at the lower end of the garden, were of stone carved into the shapes of squat and ugly men. This pair of grotesque carvings had been standing here before Wood built his fortress, and evidently represented a remnant of some ancient and evil shrine that had occupied these lonely heights long before he, or any other man now living, had ever seen them.

The night by now was far advanced, and overhead the sky was strange with shapes that were not ordinary clouds. An observer familiar with the City of Wizards might have been deceived into thinking that this garden and its immediate surroundings belonged to it—indeed, that this represented one of the City's more dangerous neighborhoods, remote from the much less perilous, relatively prosaic region that Trilby and Adrian had entered. But in fact this mountaintop formed no part of the City at all, though at times the magical intensity within this domain was equally great.

Wood had put down Shieldbreaker—he felt secure enough to do that here, in the middle of his own stronghold—and was now pacing about his garden with the Sword of Chance, swinging and twirling the blade in a physically inexpert way, occasionally hacking down some exotic plant. He cursed the weapon, almost steadily, because of the problem that it posed him. But yet he hesitated, not quite able to make up his mind to smite it into fragments with the overwhelming power of the Sword of Force.

At last the magician ceased to pace. Throwing back his head, he shouted at the sky: "No, I *must* use it once more!"

And once more, gripping the Sword of Chance in both hands, Wood hurled his trapping spells against the small and distant figure of Prince Adrian.

Tigris, who had followed her master on his rambling course across the garden, was perching now upon a comparatively new stone statue that bore the shape of some grotesque and probably imaginary beast. She shivered on the chill stone of her new seat, and felt a pang of anxiety as she listened to his voice call out the spells and sensed their potency. Skilled enchantress that she was, Wood's powers awed her. This man, the Ancient One, this Dark Master she now served, simply knew too much, and was more powerful than any human being ought to be. If for any reason he should ever tire of her, or decide that she was dangerous—

His new ordering of spells complete at last, Wood hastened to carry Coinspinner down to the far end of the garden where the light of the flaming fountains was dimmest, and the ugly twin statues stood. He had reason to believe those images might have a helpful influence in what he was about to do. Balancing the bare blade carefully, he set it in place with his own hands, so that Coinspinner, catching one spark of light, formed a straight and slender bridge of steel between the pair of stone grotesqueries, running from the left shoulder of one across the right shoulder of the other.

Silently, Tigris had followed her master. She was frowning worriedly, like a small girl, scuffing her bare feet in the damp, cold grass. She noted that the wind was rising. In the distance, but swiftly blowing closer, rainstorms threatened.

Having set the Sword of Chance very carefully in place, the wizard spun around, urgently commanding any of his servants who might hear him: "Now, quickly, put Shieldbreaker into my hands!"

Tigris, hopping down instantly from her latest perch, the statue of some bull-like beast, was about to run to obey. But invisible forces had heard the command also, and were ahead of her. Enslaved powers had already taken up the Sword of Force, and were now pressing the ultimate power into the hands of the magician.

Accepting the blade, Wood heard and felt the thud of energy in Shieldbreaker's black hilt. And then that energy cut off abruptly. Wood did not understand until he had turned back to the twin statues, with Sword uplifted to deliver a shattering blow.

The space between the stones, where he had placed the Sword of Chance, was empty.

The ugly, lifeless statues mocked him with their eyes, hollow sockets with stone depths illumined suddenly by distant lightning. Coinspinner had taken itself away. His luck was gone, and the gods alone, if any gods still lived, knew where.

Rain drenched him suddenly. As far as Wood could tell, the rain and lightning were completely natural.

7

Shortly after dawn, Talgai the Woodcutter, as was his daily custom, said good-bye to his small family, turned his back on their little riverside hut in its forest clearing, and with his loadbeast and his tools headed off into the deep woods to see what he could find there of value.

It was a fine morning. The woodcutter, a wiry, somewhat undersized man approaching middle age, hummed as he hiked along. Now and then he amused himself by whistling bird imitations, and sometimes he was pleased to hear an answer from the forest canopy.

For the first few hundred meters the trail he had chosen ran beside a stream, but at the first branching he turned away from the water, tugging at the little loadbeast's reins to lead it uphill.

Two hours and numerous trail branchings later, Talgai had ceased to whistle. For some time now he had been struggling along a small side trail, so little-traveled and overgrown that the intruder was forced to hack with his long brushknife at encroaching small limbs and undergrowth to force a passage. Trees in uncountable numbers, live and dead, surrounded him now, and had done so since he left home, but he only glanced at their trunks in passing and then ignored them. To earn a reasonable livelihood with the small loads that his single beast could carry, he had to, sometimes at least, find wood that was good for more than burning; and today he was determined to do just that.

Having made half a kilometer's progress along the overgrown trail, he happened to glance upward through the canopy, trying to fix the sun's height in the sky. Just as he did so his eye was caught by the gleam of something mysteriously, piercingly bright amid the greenery.

Sidestepping carefully, squinting upward for a better look, Talgai soon discovered that the bright gleam emanated from the blade of a sword, which was stuck through a treetrunk. It was a miraculously beautiful sword, looking as out of place here as something in a dream.

To the woodcutter it seemed for a moment or two as if the spectacular weapon must have been planted here just for him to find. Who else was going to be coming through here, after all?

But that, of course, was nonsense.

Now Talgai had halted, standing almost directly below this metallic apparition and staring up at it. It was certainly a glorious weapon to say the least, quite out of the class of any kind of tool that Talgai had ever seen before. And as marvelous as the presence of the thing itself were the circumstances of its presence. The bright blade was embedded in the tall tree as if perhaps some giant's arm had forced it there, so deeply that half its length came out the other side.

Talgai had never been a fighter, and was basically uninterested in weapons. Nor was he, in the ordinary sense, a treasure hunter. But the finish of that steel, even seen at a distance of several meters, and the bright straightness of that blade were far too impressive for him to simply pass it by.

There was a problem, in that the sword was well above his reach as he stood on the trail, and the tree that it transfixed was somewhat too thorny for an easy climb. The woodcutter had to remove his bundle of tools from the back of his little loadbeast, and then stand precariously balanced on the animal's back himself, to bring his right hand within reach of the black hilt.

He thought he felt a faint vibration in the Sword when he first touched it, but in a moment the sensation vanished.

Getting the Sword out of the green, tough trunk took even more wrenching and tugging than the man had expected. But eventually, with Talgai's strong grip on the black hilt, the keen blade cut itself loose.

After hopping down from the loadbeast's back, the woodcutter inspected his find with wonder. The black hilt, he now discovered, was marked with a small white symbol, depicting two dice. Talgai, who seriously disapproved of gambling, frowned. And the symbol explained nothing to him. He thought of himself as a practical man, one who stayed close to home in mind as well as in body. He had barely heard of the gods, whose disappearance a few years ago had caused much excitement in the world's more sophisticated circles. And Talgai had never heard at all of the gods' twelve magic Swords.

Well, what ought he to do now? The woodcutter looked around him rather nervously. To him the presence of any sword, especially when unsheathed, suggested combat. And surely a weapon like this must belong to some wealthy owner, who, if he was not lying slaughtered in the bushes nearby, was bound to come looking for it eventually.

Talgai was too honest to even think of keeping the weapon if he could find its owner. But he could look forward hopefully to a substantial reward.

The fact that this precious length of steel had been stuck so forcefully in a tree created in Talgai's mind the vague suggestion that other violent events might have occurred nearby. But his widening search, peering and hacking his way among the trunks and undergrowth, discovered no evidence to support this idea. His calls, first soft, then loud, all went unanswered. And no sign anywhere of recent travelers. There was in fact no indication that anyone except himself had passed this way in a long time.

Presently the woodcutter gave up the fruitless search and returned, Sword in hand, to his patient loadbeast. Standing in one of the rare beams of sunlight that reached the ground through the thick cover overhead, he fell to examining his find more closely.

The Sword's supernally keen edge did not appear to have been damaged in the least by the rough treatment it had received, and Talgai could not resist trying it out on some nearby brush. The tough twigs fell off cleanly, mown as neatly as if they had been tender grass. He whistled to himself. This was a better tool than any brushknife or machete he had ever owned!

He reloaded his other implements upon his beast and began to move along the trail again in his original direction; he could usually think better when engaged in some kind of physical action. As he walked, he slashed with his new tool at obstructing twigs and branches. Long and heavy as it was, the bright blade balanced very neatly in his hand—

And then the handle seemed to twist. His foot slipped at the same instant, and he dropped the blade.

Bending to pick it up, he thought himself lucky that he had not gashed his leg or foot with it. While he was still bent over, he happened to glance under some nearby branches, through a gap in the greenery opened by his last random slash.

Thirty meters or so away, leaves of a unique coppery color shimmered, dancing lightly in a random breeze, glowing in one of the slender, random beams of sunlight that managed to find their way down through the high green canopy above.

The woodcutter made a sound like a long sigh. He did not straighten up, lest he lose sight of what he had discovered. Instead, stooping and crawling under other branches, he maneuvered his way closer to his find. It was, as he had known from his first look, a rare tree, one of the species Talgai was always looking for. Its heartwood, highly prized as incense, made this tree worth more than any other Talgai could have found.

After making his way back to his loadbeast and his tools, Talgai needed only a brief time to hack a good path through to the tree, and a little longer to fell it with his axe and then despoil it of its central treasure.

With such a small though worthwhile cargo packed in his loadbeast's panniers, he needed work no more today—or indeed for several months. Not that he was really able to imagine such a period of inactivity, unless it should be enforced by illness or injury. But certainly he would range the forest no more today. Instead, he decided to set out at once for the nearest sizable village, where he would be able to convert his precious wood quickly to coins and food, and where he also might discover some indication of who might have lost such a valuable weapon.

Moving at an unhurried pace, Talgai did not reach the settlement until after midday. The small cluster of wooden buildings dozed as usual in the sun; a few of the inhabitants were at work in their gardens, while others rested in the shade of their verandas, or under the few ornamental trees that had survived the woodcutters' onslaughts within the town itself.

There was a river, small and generally somnolent, passing along the edge of this town, the same stream on which Talgai had his hut. The river made it easy to ship logs downstream from here to the city markets, where they were used for construction as well as fuel.

The proprietor of the local woodyard was an old acquaintance of Talgai, and greeted him in a friendly way. He was also glad to buy Talgai's cuttings of valuable heartwood for a small handful of coins, paying a price rather higher than the woodsman had expected. The townsman also marveled at the marvelous weapon Talgai was carrying with him, and at the story of how it had been found. But neither the proprietor of the woodyard nor any of the hangers-on who gathered to hear Talgai's story could offer any constructive suggestion as to who the true owner might be, or how the treasure had come to be embedded in a tree in the deep woods.

At last the businessman suggested: "If you can't find the owner, Talgai, maybe you'll be thinking of selling it?"

The woodcutter shook his head. "I'm a long way from that. I must try to find the owner first—and if I can't, this makes a marvelous brushknife. And such steel, such an edge, I believe I could even cut a tree down with it if I had to!"

"There's magic in it, then. Well, that's easy to believe."

"Yes, I suppose there is." Talgai frowned. Nothing in his small experience of magic had led him to think that it was ever quite safe or trustworthy.

Talgai was just passing out of the woodyard into the street when he turned for one more word. "You know, I think this tool has brought me good luck. I mean, it led me to find that cinnamon-wood." Then he walked on.

Not wanting to appear armed and threatening while he was in town, he had wrapped the sword in a piece of canvas, part of his usual equipment, and put it under his arm. Thus burdened, he now proceeded across the street to the single inn of the village.

The husband and wife who owned the inn were also old acquaintances of Talgai. They were glad to see him, simply as friends, and pleased to furnish him with a midday meal in return for one of the smaller of his newly acquired coins. As to the sword, they marveled at it even more than had the proprietor of the woodyard, but they could offer no more helpful comment.

A handful of other customers were at the inn, and a couple of these were travelers from afar. The first of these outlanders gazed at Talgai's prize blankly when it was unwrapped and displayed. Nor could he tell the woodcutter anything of any passing strangers, at least not of anyone who had lost a treasure and was offering a reward for it.

But the second traveler from distant places froze, a spoonful of soup halfway to his mouth, at his first glimpse of the sword. As soon as this man was ready to resume normal motion and speech, and had examined the blade more closely, he swore that he knew what it was— quickly he outlined the story of the Twelve Swords, and claimed that he had been privileged to see one of the others, twenty years ago.

"What you have there, woodcutter, is the great Sword Coinspinner— the Sword of Chance, it's also called, sometimes. By all the gods! And it was just stuck in a tree limb, in the forest? By all the gods, hard to believe, but there it is. I can believe it, though, of this one. They say Coinspinner is liable to just take itself away from anyone who has it, at any time, without rhyme or reason, and then show up where someone else can find it." The traveler shook his head. "No point in looking for the owner, I'd say. It's yours now." His tone seemed to imply that he was glad, just out of a general sense of wariness, that the Sword was not his own.

"It does seem to have brought me good luck." Talgai offered the idea cautiously.

His informant chuckled, shook his head, and chuckled again. "I should think it might do that," he said.

"May it bring you good luck forever, Talgai," the innkeeper's wife cried spontaneously.

"Talgai? Is that your name?" This came from the first far-traveler, the outsider who had been of no help in identifying the Sword. "And you say you are a woodcutter?"

"Talgai, yes sir, that's me."

"What a very remarkable coincidence! Would you believe that when I passed through Smim, two days ago, I overheard someone shouting that he wanted to get word to Talgai the Woodcutter?"

"But how can that be? Who in that town would have any message for me? I've never even been there."

"Well. It happened when I was in the town square. I heard a voice shouting, and looked up, and there was a man standing at one of the barred windows in the house of government—they have the jail cells up there, you know." Here the speaker paused, almost apologetically.

"Go on!"

"Well, there was a man up there, shouting, just calling out to anyone who'd listen to him—there were quite a few people in the square. He kept pleading for someone to take a message to his brother, who he said was Talgai the Woodcutter. It seemed—well—a somewhat mad way to attempt to send a message. But it certainly caught my attention, and I remembered. And then I suppose the poor fellow probably had no better means at his disposal."

"Did he say his name? Did he look anything like me? Was his hair the same color as mine?"

"I'm afraid I didn't notice about his hair, or what he looked like in general. Yes, he did say his name—Booglay, Barclay, what was it now?"

"Buvrai," said Talgai, in a small voice.

"That sounds like what he said. Yes, I'm sure that's it."

Everyone in the room was staring at Talgai now. He asked: "What was the message?"

"Only that he was imprisoned there—and under sentence of death."

There was a pause in which no one said anything. Then Talgai's informant went on: "In six days—I remember him calling that out into the square, over and over. In six days he was going to be hanged. There was a scaffold in the square . . ."

Talgai was standing utterly still, looking as if he had no trouble in believing any of this. He asked: "For what crime had this man been sentenced?"

The traveler, looking gloomy, said he didn't know for sure, but he thought it might have had something to do with an offense committed in a Red Temple. He did know that major offenders from a wide district around were often brought to Smim for trial and execution.

Talgai nodded sadly. "My brother was always the wild one. I haven't heard from him for many years, but . . ."

His informant, seeming embarrassed, muttered something about how those places, Red Temples, of course had a reputation for wild behavior among their customers, but still . . . anyway, the execution was going to take place in a very few days. There would just about be time for Talgai to get there before it happened.

His old friends and his several new acquaintances were all looking at the woodcutter awkwardly, and some of them at least offered condolences.

Talgai was still holding the marvelous Sword, and now he gazed at it with a peculiarly mournful expression.

The innkeeper offered: "Maybe, were it not for the lucky Sword, you wouldn't have known . . . I suppose that's good luck in a way."

Within a few minutes of having received the grim news, Talgai was moving briskly along the trail to home. Clucking to his loadbeast, he tapped its rump with a stick to make it hurry. The beast looked back at him once, in dignified and silent protest, then stepped up its pace just slightly.

Walking the trail with a good stride, Talgai brooded sadly about his brother's wasted life, and the all-too-credible news that he had just received. He would have to make good time if he was going to reach the town where his brother was imprisoned before it was too late to see him alive. But before starting on such a journey, of course, Talgai would have to go home and at least tell his wife and children what he was doing.

Some of the cash the woodcutter had obtained for the rare wood would go with him in his journey, for he knew that in large towns cash had a way of being essential. But he would leave half the money with his wife, to make life a little easier for her should Talgai be somehow delayed in his return.

Talgai had taken the tale of Coinspinner's powers with at least a grain of salt; he knew it was wise to take that attitude with travelers' tales in general, and especially with regard to tales of magical achievement. Still, considering what had happened to him, Talgai, since finding the Sword, he had to believe that it was bringing him good luck. Yes, even in the case of the bad news. If his brother was now going to die, it would be good to have at least a chance to see him first.

Talgai had already decided, without having to give the matter much thought, that he must take the Sword with him on his journey to town. What little Talgai had ever seen of prisons inclined him to fear that it might be difficult for him to see his brother even when he reached the prison. To do so he would probably have to deal with officials who were likely to want money—officials anywhere always seemed to do that—and even when given money they were likely to be difficult to deal with.

Yes, Talgai was going to need all the luck that this strange tool called Coinspinner could bring him. And as for his brother . . . well, luck probably had little to do with the predicament in which Buvrai found himself, though that scapegrace would doubtless blame everything on his bad fortune, as usual.

Coinspinner. Talgai muttered the name to himself over and over again, trying it out. He certainly couldn't say that he liked the sound of it, however lucky the Sword might be. A name like that certainly suggested gambling, and in gambling lay ruin for rich and poor alike.

An hour later, Talgai the Woodcutter had reached home, had conveyed the good news and the bad news to his wife as well as he was able, and was already saying farewell to his worried family and getting ready to start out again.

He might have chosen to travel to Smim by boat—that would have been easier than walking, and a little quicker—except that his wife might well have need of the boat while he was gone, and it was hard to say how long that was going to be.

The wizard Trimbak Rao in his studio had learned of the attempt to ensnare Adrian very shortly after it took place. Naturally the Teacher controlled powers of his own that were connected with the City. And these entities had been on the scene, in the Emperor's old park by the Red Temple, almost at once—Trimbak Rao never allowed his apprentices to enter the City entirely unwatched and unprotected.

Within an hour after the eruption of Adrian's elemental and its violent clash with the powers subservient to Wood, Trimbak Rao was on the scene himself—he had private means of getting there, much faster than any hiking apprentice. In fact, he had within his compound what amounted to a secret entrance to the City, though as part of his students' training he preferred to let them seek out their own.

As befitted his status as teacher, Trimbak Rao was suitably elderly in apperance, and in his demeanor there was often an air of mystery. Just now this air had been replaced by frantic eagerness. On his arrival in the park adjoining the Twisted Temple, the magician winced at what he saw, and stood for a moment with his eyes closed, looking like nothing more or less than a tired old man.

The land in the immediate vicinity of the park had been thoroughly devastated, though the Temple and many of the other nearby buildings remained essentially undamaged. Not so the dam, which Trimbak Rao remembered well. It no longer existed now. Much altered was the river's channel in the immediate area, particularly going downstream from this site, where a number of buildings had in fact toppled. Raw heaps of shattered rock, intermingled with soils of different colors, now covered most of the area that had been a park, and his precious square of paving tiles had been quite buried. An earth-elemental, and quite a strong one, had erupted here, no doubt of that. What else might have happened was going to take longer to determine.

Nodding to himself, the Teacher looked around. One thing at least was sure; the mighty adversary, Wood, had evidently determined not to come to the City himself just now. Or, if he had come, he was already gone again. Trimbak Rao, with a faint shudder of relief, relaxed his posture of defense, and dismissed certain powers he had brought with him. He had come ready, as ready as he could be, to fight for his apprentices, though knowing full well that such a direct encounter against Wood himself could hardly have been other than suicidal.

Exercising some more subtle powers of his own, Trimbak Rao soon managed to locate several items of great interest, including some of his apprentices' discarded clothing, packs, and weapons.

While he stood with an abandoned pack in his hands, considering, there came a minor landslide in one of the tall piles of raw earth nearby, and a sympathetic quivering of the ground beneath. One of the new mudholes was beginning to fill in. The fabric of the City was already starting to restore itself after the violent disruptions.

The Teacher persisted in his efforts to find Adrian and Trilby, but at first he was unable to find a trace of either one.

In the middle of a certain incantation, the wizard came to a pause. An idea had just struck him. Where, he thought to himself, is the canoe? He remembered full well that that vessel had been here on his last visit to the park. Well, it was hardly strange that it should be gone now, with the entire course of the river blasted. Whether it had gone with either of his apprentices was more than he could tell, but at least he could have hopes.

Two flying messengers had accompanied him from his studio, and now he dispatched them both to Tasavalta, by separate routes. It was his bitter but necessary duty to let Princess Kristin know that some kind of disaster had befallen, and the heir to the throne was missing.

* * *

With all the speed that could be managed, still more than a full day had passed before high-ranking aides of the Princess had reached the studio of Trimbak Rao, but now the Teacher and these representatives were holding an urgent conversation.

The eminent magician and teacher of magic Trimbak Rao did his best to explain to them just what had happened to Prince Adrian.

Kristin's counselors now assured Trimbak Rao that of course the Tasavaltan hunt for both Woundhealer and Coinspinner was going to be pressed firmly. Though right now it looked as if both Swords might be gone permanently out of reach.

Adrian, as all who knew him had come to agree, had the potential to someday become a true magician-king, the like of which had not been seen for a long time.

For the sake of the realm, as well as for the youngster himself, it was necessary that this potential be properly developed.

Trimbak Rao was still optimistic that Adrian was safe and could be found—though perhaps not really as optimistic as he sounded.

Trilby's fate was just as uncertain. Trimbak Rao still nursed hopes that the girl would make her own way back to her Teacher's headquarters in one piece, bringing news of what had happened.

"Your powers are still searching for her in the City?"

"Of course. Even as they search for Prince Adrian."

"And where do you place the responsibility for what has happened, wizard?"

The Teacher bowed his head. "Much of it is my own. I do not seek to evade that fact. I believe there is no doubt that the hand of Wood was behind the attack."

No one disputed that. But no one assured the magician that he himself was free of fault.

He tried to answer accusations that had not been voiced. "Apprentices who have reached the level of the Prince and this girl regularly accomplish what I was asking them to do. I saw no reason to think they would be unable to do so!"

8

ADRIAN, standing ankle-deep in mud on the bank of an unknown river, felt certain that in the course of his downstream passage in the canoe he must have passed out of the plane of existence containing the City of Wizards. But he had no idea where he was, only that the magical aura, the feel of the world around him, was blessedly familiar. He was back in the world in which he had grown up.

Trimbak Rao had warned his students of a great many of the complications involved in the several routes leading into the City and out of it, and of the danger of their getting lost if they should deviate from the course he had planned for them to the small park and back. But, thought Adrian, the Teacher had utterly failed to warn them of anything like what had actually happened.

But then he had to admit it probably wasn't the Teacher's fault. Adrian, in his new state of shocked alertness, now understood clearly that he and Trilby on entering the City must have fallen under the spell of some extremely subtle and most powerful enchantment. Whatever that enchantment's source, it had caused them to put aside all normal caution, and to forget or disregard all but one of their Teacher's warnings, the minor and routine admonition not to be too much in haste. And they had allowed themselves to be distracted from their goal by trivialities until it was almost too late for Adrian to escape the forces gathering against them there.

He wondered now whether awareness had come entirely too late for Trilby—or whether it had never come to her at all.

The naked Princeling shivered, though both the air and the mud in which he stood were quite warm. He found no reassurance in trying to take stock of his situation. Not only had he lost his clothing, but his pack and canteen and hunting knife as well.

Probing the darkness around him as best he could, with a mind now free—as far as he could tell—of enemy influences, Adrian decided that he was safe for the moment.

Of course he and Trilby had thought themselves safe in the park beside the Red Temple, too.

Once the conflict had openly erupted there, events had moved so fast that Adrian had had no opportunity to be much frightened. But fear was overtaking him now.

"Trilby? Trilby!" he called, softly at first, then louder. But he received no answer. And he had no sense, either magical or mundane, of where the girl might be.

The little river, mysterious and nameless, into whose muddy bank his feet were slowly sinking, revealed no secrets as it went murmuring on toward its unknown destination.

At least there was no sign that the threatening forces the Prince had just escaped were going to pursue him here outside the City. No immediate threats were apparent, though the magical portents for the future here were ominous, now that he looked at them carefully. He decided that he had better not stay where he was if he could help it. Certainly the physical environment afforded by this riverbank was not attractive —besides the treacherous footing, he stood confronted by a wall of growth, a great part of it thorny, dense to the point of impenetrability. Nor did anything the boy could make out upon the river's opposite shore suggest to him that conditions would be more congenial there.

The night air here, wherever he was, was really surprisingly warm, and when he had splashed ashore the water had felt warmer than he remembered it in the City. The sky was clear and looked normal, and the time here, as near as Adrian could judge it by the visible stars and planets, was an hour or two before dawn.

But he had fled the vicinity of the twisted Red Temple on near midafternoon of a sunny day, so either he had been unconscious for many hours—his own subjective feelings argued against that—or some major transformation in space or time had taken place.

The Prince's mundane senses of smell and hearing, as well as his perceptions specially attuned to the airs of magic, indicated to him the presence of some large and very likely dangerous beasts in the nearby jungle, on both banks of the river. When he tried to pick out other sounds from the murmur of the river and the noise of insects, there were occasional low growls to be heard disturbingly near at hand, and feral snufflings deep in the brush. There was also a passing odor that reminded the boy of giant cats.

His repeated calls for Trilby had slowed and faltered to a stop, but now he tried her name again. The only result was some increase in the animal noises nearby.

Fortunately he wasn't condemned to stand here until dawn; he still had his boat. Looking upstream, in the direction from which he had come, he could see nothing useful with his eyes, and in the world of magic could perceive practically nothing but a glow, distant but powerful, that could only represent the City. If he were to try going in that direction, he would have to run the risk of reentering the place from which he had just managed to escape. An ordinary person might be in no danger at all of entering the City, no matter which direction he chose to go; but Adrian, magically attuned as he was, might not be able to keep himself from entering its plane of existence once he came to the border.

Even gazing steadily in that direction was difficult for him now. When he did so he found that his senses were still half-dazzled by the power of the deadly confining magic that he had only just managed to escape, and of the elemental that had saved his life. Though at some point it had ceased to follow him downstream, that elemental was not yet dead; he could see its ongoing struggle with other, malignant, powers still mounting like a fire on the horizon.

And if he, Adrian, did reenter the City of Wizards, the next exit he managed to find—assuming that he could stay alive long enough to find one—might well deposit him in some environment very much worse than this one.

His only remaining course of action was to take his boat on downstream.

Just on the verge of pushing off again in the canoe, Adrian paused. His ears had just brought him a new sound, a somewhat distant doglike howling. There was nothing intrinsically magical or very strange about the sound, but in the lonely darkness it was ominous. Adrian heard the howl again; it was getting closer.

A moment later, wading in the shallows, he had pushed off the canoe and swung himself into it, his weight balanced between the gunwales, as it glided out into the stream. Fortunately he'd had years of experience in handling small boats, including canoes. Tasavalta abounded in mountain streams and lakes, besides bordering on the sea.

Taking up the carved paddle again, the young Prince probed the darkness alertly with all his senses, trying to hold a downstream course as close as possible to the center of the stream.

And now that he was on the water again, this time with his mind clear—as far as he could tell—and all his senses functioning, he found something strangely attractive, soothing, about the river itself.

The stars of a moonless sky shimmered in the water beneath him. The canoe swiftly answered his least touch with the paddle; who did this craft belong to, anyway, and why had it been so conveniently available for him just when he needed it? He was still unable to detect anything in the way of any magical aura left about the boat by its previous usage or users. Well, that was not strictly true, perhaps; there were a few traces, the psychic analogues of smears and smudges, but nothing meaningful.

The question and its corollaries worried him. Had the boat's availability, just when he needed it, been sheer accident? Or had it been purposefully arranged? If there had been no boat to carry him away, how might he have fared?

The howling came again, the distance at which it originated impossible to gauge. Still the Prince thought it might be following him, though he could not be sure on which bank of the narrow river it had its source.

Now Adrian remembered a brief mention by Trimbak Rao of certain carnivorous apes that infested a forest growing along one of the City's edges. Those apes were known to be dangerous to humans, and were claimed by some to be fully as intelligent as messenger birds. In darkness and loneliness it was all too easy for the boy to imagine such a creature producing just such a howling sound.

Now, as he steered and propelled the canoe downstream, Adrian tried his best to achieve some mental or magical contact with Trimbak Rao. But that proved to be impossible. The magical glow of the City behind him still dominated the air and sky, partially dazzling his extra senses. Also, he was beginning to suspect that another kind of blockage had been imposed, as if by the same deadly enemy who had tried to trap him in the City.

Trying now to reconstruct the disaster that had almost overtaken him there, Adrian found that the cause of those events was still unclear. The one thing of which he could be absolutely sure was that the near disaster had been no accident. Some enemy of enormous power and subtle, murderous cunning had set out to kill or capture him—and Trilby, possibly. And in Trilby's case the attempt might have succeeded.

Fighting down a brief renewed attack of panic, Adrian concentrated again on his progress downstream. The current was now bearing him swiftly through the darkness, and his occasional strokes of the paddle, meant to steer, added speed. But now, even as he began to take comfort in his rapid progress, the river broadened and the current accordingly slowed somewhat.

Probing the night as well as he was able, staring into a vague gap in a black shoreline, he decided that the river here was joined by some tributary stream almost as large as itself.

The psychic glare of the City at last began to fade noticeably behind him. Now Adrian, after a day's journeying and the great exertions of trying to escape from the City's dangers, found himself physically exhausted. The snug little boat, drifting in almost complete silence, provided the illusion at least of shelter and safety. Here the night air, still and damp, felt warmer than ever.

Deciding that he had better rest while he had the opportunity, he tied up his canoe to a snag, a half-sunken log protruding above the surface near midstream. Sleepily he murmured a minor spell he had found useful against marauding insects, and another intended to bring him wide awake at the approach of danger. Then he stretched himself out as comfortably as possible in the bottom of the boat and abandoned himself to slumber.

Stars and planets turned above his inert form, and gradually the sky in the east began to lighten. Once again before dawn the sound of howling came, still faint with distance, but possibly somewhat closer than before. The exhausted sleeper did not stir.

Full dawn with its bright light came at last, and with the light Adrian moved in the bottom of the boat. A moment later he sat up quickly, blinking at the day. *Now,* he thought, *at least I know which way is east.*

The morning sky, partly cloudy, looked reassuringly normal. The river here flowed chocolate brown in daylight, and was not quite as wide as he had judged it to be in darkness. The dark green jungle, shrouding each bank beyond a narrow strip of mud, still looked well-nigh impenetrable even in full daylight. Now, in the upstream direction, the extrasensory glow of the City was superimposed upon the sun in Adrian's perception. To him that glow still formed a threatening pulse of danger, tending to dominate both land and sky.

He scooped up river water in his hands and recited a short testing spell, while watching the tiny, soft mud particles beginning to settle out. There was no reaction to the spell, indicating that the water was safe to swallow.

After drinking of the river deeply—and returning to it in exchange some water of his own—Adrian untied his craft and resumed his downstream progress. He used the paddle as before, keeping the canoe away from either shore.

He was hungry now, and providing himself food by magic alone would be an undertaking somewhat more difficult and complicated than merely testing the water. He decided to try to feed himself by mundane methods alone, if that proved possible. If, without a knife, he could somehow sharpen a wooden spear, he could try some spearfishing. Or he might put a hand in the water and try magicking a fish to come within his reach.

Before he could quite decide on either effort, some recognizable wild fruit trees appeared, and he put in to shore to gather breakfast. Hunger dulled for the time being, he pushed on.

As the sun rose higher, Adrian began to feel its full heat. Digging into his memory, and applying a little thought and effort, he managed after a couple of false starts to create a spell that tanned his pale skin immediately, in such a way as to preserve him from the worst effects of the solar fire.

Hours passed. The river wound on, kilometer after kilometer, with no change in itself or in its banks. This jungle country, damp and hot, was vastly different from anything to which the boy had been accustomed, either near his home or in the vicinity of the workshop of Trimbak Rao.

Shortly after resuming his journey, Adrian thought that he heard last night's howling once again. Whether the source was closer or more distant now was hard to say.

Except for the occasional sites where fruit trees grew, he had yet to discover any place on either shore that tempted him to land. Some of the dangers were obvious, taking the shape of thorn trees and wasps' nests. Other perils were not so obvious, but Adrian had noted them. Here and there along both banks he observed the spoor of large animals, and in one tall tree he spotted a nest or crude sleeping platform such as he had heard was sometimes made by the carnivorous apes.

Still keeping the canoe near midstream most of the time, Adrian drifted, paddling as necessary. Once more he landed to pick some fruit.

About an hour after that, he came to a small island that appeared to be a safe place, supporting a few trees tall enough to cast some shade upon the water. There, Adrian tied up. With his craft all but completely concealed by the bulk of the island on one side and some overhanging branches on the other, Adrian sat cross-legged for a while in the bottom of the boat, eyes closed, first meditating to calm his mind and then trying to see into the psychic distance.

The heat of the day increased, but as he sat motionless, engaged in mental activity, he was hardly aware of it. In less than an hour he came back to himself with a start, finding his body drenched in sweat. He slipped out of the boat into the water, which was now considerably cooler than the air.

Now, even floating in the cooling water, it was impossible to relax.

His vision had made Adrian more frightened than he had been since making his escape from the City.

His psychic probing had shown him that the Sword Coinspinner had somehow been used against him at the Red Temple by his enemy, to augment by good luck the power of the spells employed. No wonder he had almost been trapped and crushed, despite his own struggles and his mentor's precautions! It would be no surprise if Trilby had been caught. The real wonder was that he, Adrian, had somehow managed to escape.

After a brief active swim, during which he was careful never to get more than a few meters from the boat, he climbed back into the canoe again and sat on the middle seat, not meditating now but simply trying to think. He was determined not to panic, despite the forces he had glimpsed arrayed against him. On his side, he had his own considerable powers. He had strong friends, who would be trying to help him. And he had time now in which to think.

On Adrian's emergence from the water, the air at first felt cool around his body, but as his skin dried it warmed again.

. . . and with the heat, fear came back with a rush, like a worried friend.

It was time now to think about Coinspinner.

Meditation and psychic probing were all very well, sometimes extremely valuable. But intelligent, reasoning thought was still more important.

The Prince in his period of silent concentration had been able to determine, at least in a very rough way, the location of the Sword of Chance—at the moment it was somewhere vaguely ahead of him, in the general direction of flow of this still-nameless river. And this discovery Adrian found puzzling.

In fact, he had just perceived several things that puzzled him; one of them was that the person who now possessed the Sword seemed to have no magic of his or her own. This person was therefore almost certainly not the mighty magician who had so powerfully attacked him.

Adrian's education, intended to fit him to rule a nation someday, had included much information about the nature and history of the Swords. He was well aware that Coinspinner had the tendency to move itself about, and that it might well have taken itself away from his enemy soon after he or she had used it.

However his enemy had lost the Sword, that deprivation had not come a moment too soon for Adrian's survival.

Now the boy pondered intently for a short time, wondering if a really powerful and learned wizard in his position would be able to make the Sword come to him, by the power of his own magic; certainly such a feat would be very difficult for anyone, if not totally impossible.

Once again sitting in a semitrance, the boy tried to send his mind, his presence, to the proper place, the present location of the Sword.

It was a daring move, and he was not entirely sure that it was the proper one to make, but he attempted it nevertheless.

In any case, the effort failed.

At the moment it seemed that neither logical thought nor psychic probing was going to get him any further. The young Prince untied his boat and let it drift downstream again. From time to time he used the paddle, mechanically, to keep the craft from drifting too near either of the shores.

The howling that had engaged his attention still persisted at irregular intervals. The Prince was growing more inclined to classify it as one of the ordinary background noises of the jungle, even though it still seemed, when he took careful note of it, to be coming closer.

As the boat drifted, he repeated his efforts to establish by means of magic some contact with his parents, or, failing that, with some of his friends and other allies or potential allies—Trimbak Rao and Trilby were of course included in these attempts. But to Adrian's disgust he discovered that, for the time being at least, he still could not even sense the direction in which any of these important people might be found.

Whenever he looked behind him, upstream, the gradually receding City still burned in its unceasing glow of complex enchantment. To a vision as sharp as Adrian's the City continued to cast its garish radiance across the sky, dazzling and dimming the capabilities of his special senses.

Still, keeping track of the location of the Sword of Chance, now moving somewhere ahead of him, was no trouble at all. Once he had found it, like a fiery brand Coinspinner had seared its image and its presence into his perception. The only difficulty Adrian experienced was to keep the brightness of that Sword from interfering with other psychic perceptions. Yes, he felt absolutely sure that Coinspinner was there ahead of him somewhere, a good many kilometers distant but not moving very quickly; and if it stayed approximately where it was now, and if the river maintained its present direction, he was sure to be carried closer to the Sword.

And Coinspinner was being borne now in innocent hands. Perhaps, he thought again, that would increase his chances of being able to get his own hands on it.

Perhaps. Well, he would try. At the moment he could establish no other reasonable goal. He was traveling in a generally westerly direction—but where was he going? He could not even guess intelligently which way he ought to go to get home.

As the day wore on, and Adrian's slow progress downstream continued, some truly giant trees came into his sight on the northern bank of the river. These towered scores of meters above the ground, standing much taller than the highest buildings of the City.

Catching his first glimpse of this soaring grove, the boy at first interpreted it as a high hill, set back somewhat from the bank. Only on coming closer had he realized that the appearance of a steep hill was produced by the grove of trees, much taller than the other species of the forest, but growing on approximately the same level of ground.

Adrian had heard of such trees, but had never seen them before. Their appearance now suggested to him that he might be entering the country of the wood-dwelling and wood-crafting Treen people, who lived in close relationship with those giant trees.

Pausing briefly at a snag near midstream, and making another psychic effort, Adrian began for the first time to get a better look at the distant presence of his chief enemy. It was Wood, undoubtedly; and he was awesomely stronger than even Adrian had expected.

It was impossible for the Prince to tell exactly where Wood was; but at least Adrian could confirm that it was not his enemy who now held the Sword of Chance.

As a well-informed heir, the Prince knew perfectly well that this deadly dangerous man could be expected to be carrying Shieldbreaker.

In light of the fact that Wood was somewhere else, the Sword of Chance now began to appear to Adrian with ever-increasing probability as an objective that he might be able to reach and take.

There was of course the chance that Coinspinner would have moved itself again, to some considerable distance, before he was able to come up with it. Whether the Sword was going to remain in the hands of its present owner for another hour, another day, another year, or many years, was beyond the power of anyone to predict, by magic or other means. Well, he could only try.

Tying up for the night at a small island, Adrian managed some magic on a sizable fish, hypnotizing and lulling his prey into the shallows until he was able to hurl it out of the water with a fierce grab. Then, after painstakingly gathering some firewood, and a successful effort at pyrokinesis, he cooked his catch whole and attacked it with a sharp stick and his teeth. By now his hunger had reached the point where the results actually tasted good.

The night passed for Adrian without incident, and his solitary journey downriver continued in the same way for most of the succeeding day. No more of the gigantic trees appeared. The unbroken walls of jungle had followed the river for so long that he had almost begun to wonder whether they were the result of some enchantment—when unexpectedly there came a change.

The first sign of human presence occurred late in the afternoon of that second day. It came in the form of a long-deceased and almost-fleshless head, dried by means of smoke or magic, and erected on a pole stuck in the mudbank just above the high-water mark. The thing was hardly more than a painted human skull, equipped with eyes of clay and shell.

If this sign was meant as a warning to intruders, one traveler at least was ready to take it to heart. Adrian put in to the opposite shore at once, and did what mental scouting he could manage of the terrain and the river just ahead. This time his extra faculties availed him little; but when he sniffed repeatedly and carefully he could detect a faint tang of woodsmoke in the damp air.

Pulling his canoe well up on the shore, he did his best to conceal the craft with some loose brush and some minor magic. Then he settled down to wait for dusk.

As soon as daylight had dimmed enough to offer good concealment, he put out and drifted once again. The small village, consisting of only a few huts, was just around the next bend.

Adrian, warned and with time to make preparations, was able to steer silently to the far side of the stream, and to use magic to keep himself from being noticed. True total invisibility would be very difficult to achieve, but in the circumstances it was not hard to make people think for a few moments that his canoe was only a drifting log.

As he passed the village, some six or eight of its inhabitants were visible around a central fire. The men and women, light bronze of skin, with straight brown hair, were wearing only loincloths, while their children ran among them naked. These head-collectors were a wiry, active, and handsome people. Adrian and his canoe went drifting by in utter silence; even had he employed no magic, it was quite likely that no one on shore would have been able to see him in the gathering night.

He was not mistaken in thinking that these were the people who had put up the warning. More prepared heads were on display within the village, mounted over doorways and on decorated poles. These effectively discouraged any faint hopes the passing traveler might have entertained of being able to land here after all.

Having thus begun traveling by night, the Prince decided that it had definite advantages. Besides, he wished to put as much distance as was feasible between himself and the skull-collectors' village. Darkness diminished physical vision, but had no effect upon Adrian's magical perceptions. He continued drifting and paddling until almost dawn, by which time he judged he might be safely out of the territory of the people who put up shriveled heads.

Hungrily prowling the deserted banks of the river for food at dawn, he found some turtle eggs and cracked and ate them raw. At this time he decided also that in future he would build fires only by day, and that he would do his best to keep them from smoking.

Having disposed of the eggs, the Prince recognized a couple of species of plants, and, using another stick, dug up an edible root or two. These, brought along in the boat, would keep him going for some time if he could also make an occasional find of fruit.

Starvation could be kept at bay indefinitely by such makeshift means as these, but still Adrian's craving was growing steadily for something like a normal diet. He considered trying to magic some food for himself out of whatever raw material he could find available, but again he decided that for the time being he had better conserve his energies for possible emergencies.

Gradually the recurrent howling had grown closer, and it was now near enoughtto become worrisome again; it sounded, after all, as if something were genuinely following him. But at the same time the sound had now been with him long enough to become familiar, and thus in a way it was no longer so alarming.

On the second day after passing the village, paddling at dawn, the Prince began to hear a roaring noise ahead. Rapidly the volume of the sound increased. Its source could not be far distant.

Cautiously he paddled around a bend, staying near the right bank. Just ahead the river plunged into a waterfall, its steady thunder giving rise to a fine watery smoke. Adrian wasted no time in getting himself and his boat out of the water.

9

Gₑₙₑᵣₐₗ Rostov and the wizard Karel, unable to decide on any entirely satisfactory way to immediately dispose of the high-ranking prisoner they had acquired in the high mountain pass, had decided to bring Crown Prince Murat with them, tied into his saddle, when they set out to follow the trail of the Culmian traitor Kebbi.

Rostov was not minded to explain any of his decisions to the treacherous thief he was compelled to drag along. But Karel, conversing with the Crown Prince at a rest stop, informed his royal captive that there had simply been no men to spare to escort the prisoner back to Sarykam. Most of the three cavalry squadrons were in hot pursuit of the Culmians who were fleeing toward their homeland with Woundhealer; only half a dozen troopers had come with the two Tasavaltan leaders on Coinspinner's track.

Their pursuit of Kebbi and the Sword of Chance had certainly begun without delay, and the pursuers kept up a brisk pace. Or rather they tried their best to do so. Hardly had the site of Murat's capture been left behind them when the first of many avalanches came down just ahead, wiping out a substantial section of the trail.

The fading thunders of this landslide could not quite drown out the voice of Rostov, as he profaned the names of many gods; when the tumult had subsided and the dust was beginning to settle, Karel, puffing, pointed out to the General with some satisfaction that this fresh obstacle represented a confirmation of his own magical divinations, a sign that they were certainly on the trail of Coinspinner.

Rostov's reply was not congratulatory.

Before the little party had worked its way around the slope rendered impassable by the first avalanche, another avalanche could be heard from the direction in which they were trying to advance. And, when that one too had been bypassed, yet another. Still they were able to make progress; both Tasavaltan leaders, and one or two of the cavalrymen among their escort, knew these mountains extremely well. And Coinspinner, perhaps, was not vitally concerned about them yet; they were still too distant from its current owner to pose him any serious threat. If and when they managed to close the gap substantially, doubtless the measures taken against them would be stronger.

Still, there was no thought of abandoning the pursuit that had just begun. Nor was it necessary, in the opinion of their most knowledgeable scout, to follow their quarry's trail very closely.

"I'll tell you how it is, sir," this trooper explained to Rostov. "A stranger here, looking to get out of the mountains in this direction, is pretty much going to have to go one way, the way we're going now. And whether he takes this branch of the trail here, or that one up there that looks like a different trail but really isn't, he's pretty certain to come out in the same place in the end. And I know where that place is. A sort of crossroads. A kind of inn stands there, or did a few years back, though it's not a place where I'd especially want to spend the night."

The General nodded grimly. "Then lead on, get us to that crossroads as best you can. Better that than try to track him along these mountainsides, with a Sword trying to bury us at every step."

Now progress became faster. Still the newly chosen route was longer, and it was necessary for the party to spend one night in a cold mountain camp before they reached the inn. Karel did his best to defend their camp with spells before he went to sleep, and all through the night a guard was posted.

Murat, still tied by the hands and by one foot, was allowed to dismount and sleep under blankets.

In the morning, progress continued to be rapid. Rostov was now carrying Sightblinder packed away behind his saddle, where it was in easy reach should he decide to call upon its powers. Before many hours of daylight had passed the small party reached the inn, and a shabby place it was.

A few men, including one who must have been the innkeeper, emerged from its dingy doorway to squint at the visitors. In silence, and with an initial lack of enthusiasm, they studied the arriving party, which consisted of nine riders, most of them Tasavaltan troopers in blue and green, and included one prisoner in orange and blue, who was bound to his saddle and stirrups.

Under Rostov's determined glare the proprietor of the inn soon began to smile, and put on an air of hospitality. "Beg your pardon, sir, but I see you have a prisoner."

"And what of it?"

"Nothing, sir, nothing at all. Except that I know the whereabouts of one other man who wears a livery of orange and blue, the same as his."

Having received the promise of some kind of a reward if he cooperated, and the threat of a very different kind of treatment if he did not, the innkeeper hastened to lead his visitors to a shed, even more ramshackle than the main building and located somewhat behind it.

A riding-beast that looked too healthy and strong to be the property of any of these locals was revealed inside the shed when the door was opened.

"One of your cavalry mounts?" asked Rostov, turning to his prisoner.

"Unbind me," said Murat, "and I will try to make the identification for you."

The General glanced at the wizard, who nodded, almost absently. Then Rostov nodded too, and in a moment a trooper had ridden up beside the Crown Prince and started to loose his hands.

In another moment Murat was able to dismount freely. Limping with cramped legs from his long confinement in the saddle, he crossed the yard and entered the shed, where he could study the riding-beast at close range.

"Yes, this is the mount Kebbi was riding when he left us."

In another moment, when the door to the next room was opened, the former lieutenant himself was discovered, immured in a dark and cell-like hole. Kebbi looked up from where he was lying on a broken cot. He was in his undergarments, and for warmth he clutched around his shoulders a coarse rag that looked as if it might have been discarded somewhere around a stable. At the sight of Murat, his face went through a whole series of expressions, all quickly suppressed except the last, a look of bright curiosity.

"Where is it, villain?" Murat demanded without preamble.

Kebbi stood up. "Where is what, traitor?"

"You dare to call me that!" A Tasavaltan trooper restrained the Crown Prince from stepping forward to strike his enemy with his fist.

Kebbi spread his hands in a gesture of innocence as he looked around at the others. "I appeal to you, gentlemen. Do I look to you like someone who has the Sword of Luck in his possession?"

"Frankly, you do not," said Karel, frowning.

At this point the proprietor of the inn cleared his throat. "Are you interested in my bondslave, here, gentlemen?" he inquired of the Tasavaltan leaders, in what was meant to be an ingratiating voice. "I can let you have him cheap."

Rostov shot one glance at the would-be salesman, who immediately fell silent.

Murat noticed that one of the hangers-on was already wearing Culmian boots that very likely had been Kebbi's. "I suppose you tried to steal something here, too?" he demanded of his cousin. "And they repaid you in kind?"

Kebbi ignored the question. He was undertaking what sounded like an earnest and sincere explanation. "General Rostov, is it not? Sir, I wish that I could hand you the Sword that our people so treacherously stole from your Princess. But alas, I cannot, though that was my intention. I would not lightly disobey the orders of my superior officer." Here he glanced at Murat. "But what he did in Sarykam was unforgivable, and would not, I am sure, have been countenanced by our Queen. Traitor is, I think, not too strong a word."

Before Kebbi had finished, Murat was almost beside himself. Experienced diplomat that he was, he found himself for once speechless with rage and indignation.

Kebbi, with an air of confident innocence, was going on to explain that he had been trying to persuade these local people to send a messenger to Tasavalta, whose leaders would assuredly be glad to ransom him.

Rostov broke in bluntly. "I don't believe you. What has happened to Coinspinner?"

"Sir, General Rostov, I was trying to bring it back to you! But now it is gone, and through no connivance of mine. These men who have been detaining me can at least assure you of that."

The General rounded on the innkeeper. "Well?"

Briefly, as Murat listened in disbelief, the events of the dice game came out.

Kebbi put forward a story that Murat had to admit sounded almost plausible. The Culmian renegade claimed simply that he had been on his way to restore the Sword of Chance to Princess Kristin, and had thought to profit enough in a small wager to provide himself with coin for the journey.

"You bet the Sword itself? To win a few coins?"

"No, sir. In that case I stood to win a huge and dazzling jewel. Ask these men here, they'll tell you. A jewel, let me hasten to assure you, I would have given to Her Majesty Princess Kristin, as compensation for—"

"Never mind the jewel for now. You threw dice, while holding the Sword of Chance—and you lost?" This time it was Karel who asked the question.

"It happened that way, sir. I can't explain it, but it did. Ask these men."

The locals, even under threat, only confirmed the Culmian traitor's tale.

"And who was this man who won Coinspinner away from you?" Again it was Karel who asked, though by now he, and Rostov at least among the Tasavaltans, had come to realize who the successful gambler must have been.

"I have no idea, sir," said Kebbi helplessly.

The General and the wizard exchanged glances.

"And I repeat, sir, that I had no notion of any plot to steal the Sword if we were denied in our appeal to borrow it. I was shocked and horrified when I realized that my commanding officer contemplated such a theft, and at the first opportunity I did what I could to make amends. I could not get my hands on Woundhealer, but I thought that the Sword of Chance might provide the Princess decent compensation."

Murat saw with satisfaction that none of the Tasavaltans appeared inclined to accept the claim. As for himself, he began to denounce it violently.

"Shut up," Rostov told him.

Murat and his cousin glared at each other in silence.

The General, fists on his hips, faced the renegade lieutenant. "I ask you once again. *Where is Coinspinner?*"

"That stranger has it, sir. I repeat, I have told you the simple truth. I thought I would need money for my journey, to pay my bill here if nothing else, and to buy food. And so I gambled—and lost. These—gentlemen here can confirm my story."

Rostov kept hammering away. "You gambled with *that* Sword in hand, and lost it?"

"I say again, that is the truth."

The General nodded slowly. Suddenly, more than a little to Murat's amazement, the Tasavaltan leaders appeared ready to concede that the story might be true.

"Tell us more about this tall stranger and his companion. Tell us every detail you can remember."

The descriptions given by Kebbi and by the locals agreed in all essentials.

"How was he armed?" pressed Karel in his soft voice.

Kebbi blinked. "Why—with a sword. Not that he even had to draw it." Realization began to dawn on him. "I don't know if it was one of the Twelve—I don't know that much about the others. The hilt at least looked like Coinspinner's or Woundhealer's."

Karel nodded to his compeer. "Shieldbreaker—and that means Wood was here. And that he has Coinspinner now."

"And the woman with him," Rostov muttered. "She'll have been that hellcat Tigris."

Kebbi, speaking up boldly, did his best to find out whether the Tasavaltans had managed to retake Woundhealer. He soon heard enough to convince him that they had not.

"Where shall we begin to look for it, sir?"

"What do you mean 'we'?"

Kebbi at first pretended to be quietly crushed at the suggestion that he was going to be taken away by the Tasavaltans in the status of a prisoner, like Murat.

Murat, since he had been unbound, had been silently considering what his chances might be of escape, and had concluded that for the time being they were not worth considering.

Argument between the two Culmians, flaring up again, was interrupted by the arrival of a winged messenger, its wings spanning about the reach of a man's arms. This creature arrived in the sky above the arguing men, uttered cries of greeting, and came spiraling right down, to perch upon the neck of Rostov's riding-beast.

With quick but steady fingers the General untied the small white packet from the bird's leg, and ripped the enclosure open. The wizard looked over Rostov's shoulder as he read, and Murat watching carefully could see both men's faces cloud. Then they raised their eyes together to look at him, in a way that gave no comfort.

"What is it?" he demanded.

"Prince Adrian," the wizard responded slowly. "An attempt had been made to kidnap the young Prince or kill him. They don't know yet in Sarykam if he has survived or not."

Kebbi, very quiet now, was watching and listening, calculating as best he could.

In his mind's eye Murat saw again the lovely Princess; in his imagination he felt the grief and shock that would be hers. "Villainous," he muttered.

"Is that what you think, then?" The General's tone was sharp.

"Of course. An attack upon a child . . ." His voice trailed off as he saw the suspicion in his captors' eyes. "You can't think that I—"

"Or that I, either—" Kebbi burst in.

"We have been given some understanding of your honor. Both of you." Old Karel glared at them for a moment. Then his head moved in a brisk nod, telling the cavalry escort to get ready to move on.

Murat for a moment hung his head in shame, feeling the justice of that last rebuke. But only for a moment. Then he began to ask urgent questions, wanting to know more details of the attempt on Adrian.

The Tasavaltan leaders ignored him, though they did not try to prevent his hearing the few details that were known, when they passed this information on to the concerned soldiers.

In the leaders' minds, trying to go to the aid of the Prince was of course going to take precedence even over trying to recover Coinspinner—that would be pretty much a lost cause anyway, if Wood still had it.

Rostov told his sergeant to make sure that the men were ready to ride. There was some suspicion, exchanged in whispers between Karel and Rostov, that the theft of Coinspinner and the assault on Adrian were somehow connected.

"We have no evidence of that as yet. Rostov, my friend, if we are to try to help Prince Adrian we must go into the City of Wizards to look for him."

"If you can get us there, my men and I are ready."

Karel informed the General that he knew a way to reach the City fairly quickly from this place—or, indeed, from almost anyplace.

"What of these two Culmian birds? I want to bring them back to Sarykam alive, eventually, if that's at all possible. But I don't want to spare the men to escort them back there now. Not if the Prince is—"

"Then I think we must bring them with us, General. Physical bonds will no longer be necessary," said the wizard. Karel waited until Kebbi's boots had been retrieved for him, and some suitable outer clothing provided. Then, when the two Culmians were already in the saddle, he proceeded, with gestures and swift words, to treat each of them to his own satisfaction. The process was completed in the space of a few breaths.

Murat felt nothing from the wizard's work. Meeting Kebbi's cold glare with his own, he wondered whether they were now really bound at all. Well, he'd test that later.

Karel and Rostov, with their two half-willing prisoners, and the determined help of their six soldiers, set out to do their best at finding Adrian.

10

THE range of mountains in which the magician Wood had chosen to establish his headquarters arose near the center of a remote wasteland, many kilometers from any permanent human habitation. Wood's fortress, constructed more by means of magic than by physical labor, was indeed forbidding.

There were moments in Wood's life in which he felt the urge to surround himself with luxury, to taste some of the softer enjoyments that he was still capable of sharing with the great mass of mankind. For this reason the gardens, and some of the interior rooms, had come into existence. But today the great wizard was much too busy to pause for such pleasures. Attended by demons, familiars, and other nonmaterial powers, he and a very few close human associates were industriously practicing their black arts.

The main thrust of today's magical effort was the continued gathering of intelligence. And so far the results had not been pleasing. Prince Adrian, the spawn of Wood's old enemy Prince Mark, had so far succeeded in completely eluding the trapping spells and powers with which Wood had sought to bind him and crush him inside the City of Wizards.

There had been several reasons, all of them seeming quite valid at the time, why Wood had chosen not to visit the site of the failure personally. For one thing, the powers that had brought him word of the failure had also assured him that Adrian was no longer in the City.

Not only had the whelp escaped, but in fact the best evidence seemed to indicate that he was still alive and free. Moreover, the elemental he had raised to break him out of the trap had, in the process, destroyed one or two of Wood's more valuable nonhuman allies.

On receipt of this disconcerting news, Wood had promptly dispatched several demons that he considered relatively trustworthy, along with certain other powers, in an attempt to locate the missing Prince. Through these and other sources he had received conflicting indications as to Adrian's probable location. But when the most likely of these several locations were checked out, the boy could be found at none of them.

The chief difficulty in pressing the search successfully was that a fugitive from the City might easily reenter the mundane world in almost any portion of a large continent.

There was a further complication. Another victim, this one a female apprentice of Trimbak Rao, had almost been ensnared within the trap. But somehow she too was still at large.

Not that the girl Trilby had any particular importance in herself. But the wizard considered that it would be interesting as well as amusing to examine her, and gather clues as to the strength of her mentor, Trimbak Rao, who someday was almost certainly going to confront Wood in open combat.

But Trilby was only an interesting detail. Wood's attention continued to be obstinately centered on Prince Adrian. The wizard was forced to admit that he himself had underestimated the youth's own abilities, which were truly incredible for one so young and necessarily so inexperienced. Well, in retrospect Wood could see that he ought to have expected something of the kind from one whose mother's family had produced the wizard Karel and a number of other adepts. And whose father's father was the Emperor.

About five years ago Wood had lost a valued human assistant, under somewhat mysterious circumstances, in the course of an abortive attempt to kidnap this same child. That episode was suddenly becoming somewhat easier to understand.

Evidently the precocious whelp had formidable defenders and allies as well as strong powers of his own. That there had been resistance really came as no surprise; but still, that Wood's best trapping spells, their effectiveness augmented by the power of Coinspinner, should have failed to snare this child was astounding.

Or else—

There was one point, however unlikely it might seem, that had to be considered. Was it remotely possible that the whelp's escape would ultimately rebound to Wood's advantage? Was it conceivable that the Sword of Chance, during the period when it was conscripted in Wood's cause, had calculated his advantage more accurately than he could do himself, and manipulated events accordingly?

Wood found that subtlety hard to believe, but he could not say that it was impossible.

An alternative explanation—and this was now beginning to seem to Wood the most probable one—was that the Sword of Chance had removed itself from his possession just as his entrapment spells were reaching the most critical point in their development.

Standing now in full daylight in his walled garden, among the variously grotesque statues, he muttered to himself: "It might have happened that way, yes. But even so, the whelp must be protected by some substantial powers of his own—or someone else's. Well, we'll see. In any case he's certainly not in the City now. And sooner or later I'll find him, and I'll have him."

It was at this point that Tigris joined her master in the garden. Today she was once more garbed in businesslike clothing, and like the other inhabitants of the stronghold she had been working hard.

"Which of our problems do you intend to confront next, my lord? And is this escaping boy truly of such great importance?"

"He is of importance, or will be, as a means of getting at his father. And at his grandfather too, I expect . . . in addition, I am growing very curious to find out just how his escape was managed. What kind of help he may have had. No, we are certainly not going to give up on him."

Here Wood turned to decisive action. Summoning another aide, he ordered the sending out of some twenty leather-winged messengers, carrying messages to certain allies of his in a number of places across the continent. The recipient of each message was near one of Adrian's possible exits from the City, and Wood's auxiliaries were bidden to seek hard for the young Prince and catch him if they could.

Then Wood and Tigris held a discussion on their best method of trying to recapture Coinspinner—and what they knew about who had it now. It was not yet possible to see this clearly; Wood thought the difficulty might be a corollary of the Sword's having recently moved itself away from him.

At about the same time that Wood and Tigris were holding their conversation in the statue garden, Karel and Rostov, along with their escort, their self-proclaimed ally Kebbi, and their original prisoner Murat, having left the vicinity of the mountain inn, were well along on their way into the City. Karel was leading them along a strange and illogical-seeming path, along which, as he commented several times, no other wizard, not even Trimbak Rao, would have been capable of guiding them.

"What about the famous Emperor?" Rostov prodded, just to see what kind of a reaction he might get. "Is he involved in this?"

Karel only grunted.

Both of the Culmian prisoners—though Kebbi claimed a higher status by right, he had not been able to achieve it—were still free from physical bondage. Entering the City, and moving about in it, would have been virtually impossible for them otherwise. But Kebbi and Murat found themselves quite effectively restricted by the brief treatment Karel had accorded them. Kebbi had said nothing about it. But Murat, whenever he turned his mount away from the wizard's, or turned his back on the old man while afoot, suddenly developed a strange leaden feeling in his soles and ankles. The sensation began to deepen into pain whenever he strayed more than a dozen paces or so from the leaders of the party. Very well, then, he was truly still bound. Later, he promised himself, he would experiment to see what the real limits were.

Rostov, his troopers, and the more-or-less willing Culmians, all under the guidance of the elderly wizard, had suddenly entered territory that was strange to them all except perhaps to Karel. Here they traversed several wildly divers kinds of landscape in rapid succession. Most members of the party found themselves seriously bewildered by sudden changes in weather, environment, and even alterations in the time of day.

The General grumbled whenever he felt like it. "Wizard, we're all convinced by now that our destination is somewhere exceedingly strange. What I want to know is, when do we arrive?"

Karel explained that they were entering the City by stages, and that although it might seem they were spending a great deal of time, even days, on the road, he planned that they should reach their goal on the same day they had left the inn.

And it was, in fact, by the best reckoning, that very same day when they arrived in the vicinity of the Twisted Temple.

"This is the place, then?" asked Rostov, staring at the peculiar streets, and the strange buildings, some of them near the little river tottering, looking about to fall. The sergeant and his five men had all, as if unconsciously, pulled their mounts somewhat closer to that of the old magician.

Murat had done the same. Meanwhile the Crown Prince of Culm had begun to wonder privately if, back in Culm, the traitor Kebbi was even now being mourned as one of the heroes who had managed to steal Woundhealer for the Royal Consort, giving up his own life in the process.

Something sly Kebbi had told him had suggested this possibility.

"We are probably both being mourned there, cousin. You more strenuously than I, of course, as befitting your higher station."

Murat, though he had said nothing on the subject, was also wondering if, indeed, the Sword of Healing would ever get to Culm. By now he had been thoroughly convinced that the military and magical forces of Tasavalta were indeed capable; and the small Culmian force trying to get away no longer possessed any Sword of their own to give them an advantage.

The Crown Prince was even beginning to feel somehow responsible for the lovely Princess's missing son, though he told himself repeatedly that there was no logical reason for him to do so.

By now he thought, or at least hoped, that he had pretty well convinced Rostov and Karel of his innocence in that regard. Indeed, he had eagerly and repeatedly volunteered to assist them in the search for the Prince, if only they would let him.

Kebbi, on hearing this, to keep up appearances at least, had hastened to volunteer also.

Murat wished very strongly that he could do something to make amends to Kristin.

11

HAVING driven his canoe solidly into shore, on the right bank of the river at a safe distance above the falls, Adrian tied up the craft and stowed the paddle. Then he made his way forward cautiously along the muddy bank, until he had come close enough to the falls to get a good look at the obstacle he now faced.

This was going to mark the end of his boating. Gazing down through a continuous mist of rising spray, the boy estimated that the drop was twenty meters in all. Not quite direct and straight, rather a complex of falls and rapids; but still more than deadly enough to eliminate any thought of riding or sending the canoe over it. But there might still be a chance—

Moving forward carefully along the bank, the Prince discovered that the rudiments of a path did make the descent beside the falls. Someone or something came up and down here with fair regularity. Patches of soil between the rocks composing the steep slope had been worn free of vegetation, but the bare spots were packed too hard to reveal any distinct tracks.

Again there was no sign of human habitation. Shading his eyes as he stood on the brink, Adrian gazed out into the distance. As far as he could follow its course toward the hazy horizon, the river below the falls was but little different from the river above. The same flat meanders resumed down there, the brown stream curving between the same dense walls of jungle, and the jungle extended away from both banks of the river, into the misty distance. No doubt about it, he was going to need the canoe if he could get it down there in one piece.

About to turn back to retrieve his canoe, he paused, taking one more look.

Kilometers away, some threads of smoke were rising, suggesting human presence.

Keep going downstream, certain Tasavaltan folk who were wise in the ways of the wilderness had taught him, *and sooner or later you'll come to a place where someone lives.*

Lugging the canoe up on shore, he dragged it to a place beside the brink, on the upper end of the descending riparian path. From here, getting down without a burden would be simple enough for an agile youth, but carrying his boat with him was going to pose a problem. Dragging the thin hull over the rough rocks was not going to do, of course; he would have to carry it cleanly.

After some meditation, and an earnest struggle with his memory, the Prince managed to recall a weight-subtracting spell he had learned for fun from a book he had discovered in his Teacher's library. Now the canoe, which had been barely liftable for a wiry twelve-year-old, became something like a manageable burden.

Once he'd got the canoe bottomside up, and himself beneath it in the proper balancing position, the job wasn't too bad. But using the lifting spell was tiring in itself, and Adrian had to stop, put down his burden, and rest several times before he was halfway down the rough descending stairs formed by uneven rocks.

When he was halfway down, he realized that someone or something was watching him. Eyes, inhuman eyes as he now realized, were focused on him from the jungle that clung to the steep slope only a few meters away.

Even as Adrian stood poised on a rock, uncertain how to react, several of the creatures came out of the greenery far enough for him to get a good look at them. From the first glimpse he had no doubt that these were the carnivorous apes he'd heard about. They were only about half the size of adult humans, lanky and almost humanoid, though moving easily on all fours in places where the footing was difficult. Their faces were not far from human, though their foreheads sloped back sharply, and their heads looked too small to contain truly intelligent brains.

Adrian set down the canoe, as carefully as he could, and pulled out the wooden paddle, the best semblance of a weapon he had available, from where it had been wedged under a seat. If worst came to worst, he'd edge his way backward, and risk a plunge into the falls. And it seemed likely that the worst was coming—club in hand, he thought he might have succeeded in standing off one of the beasts, but now there were six or eight of them confronting him.

The creatures showed their fangs and chittered at him threateningly. Surrounded on three sides by apes, and with his back to the waterfall, Adrian was on the verge of a near-suicidal plunge. The beasts closed in on him slowly, making noises that sounded like demented speech, waving their forelimbs and baring small, sharp carnivorous teeth. Their pale skins were half naked, half covered in patches of coarse fur, spotted green and brown, in a pattern that gave the beasts good camouflage against the background of the jungle.

The Prince, his mind working now in some territory beyond fear, wondered if they were accustomed to ambushing unwary travelers at this place, which seemed made to order for the tactic.

His instincts reached for magic. But there was very little in the way of magic that Adrian could perform to protect himself against animals. His most successful trick of raising an elemental was going to be no help to him now; for one thing, his energy had been temporarily depleted by the lifting spell, and for another, he sensed that the potential for raising an elemental in this particular spot was quite low.

The apes were closing in, and the boy was on the point of hurling himself desperately into the water, when something came crashing through the jungle.

Rescue, or at least a powerful distraction, had arrived in the shape of a bulky, shaggy, gigantic dog, now bounding out into the open. At first glance Adrian was almost ready to take the creature for a small bear; it looked as heavy as a big man.

Snarling and growling, the hulking, gray-furred dog charged the enemy and broke their semicircle. One of the simians, shrieking almost like a human, was killed outright by the dog's first rush, and another was caught by one leg and mangled a moment later.

This second victim, in its struggle to pull free, caught and tore one of the dog's ears with its teeth.

The remaining apes, who had not been prepared for this kind of opposition, were routed, at least for the time being.

Stooping, Adrian picked up several small rocks, which he hurled in rapid succession after the creatures as they retreated. He thought that he hit one of them at least.

Meanwhile the dog, giving its heavy gray fur a great shake, trotted growling through one last circle of the narrow and sharply sloping field of combat, as if formally establishing its dominion. Then the enormous male creature turned, sat down facing Adrian, and once more gave voice to the howl that the Prince had grown so accustomed to hearing during the days since he had left the City.

Adrian, his hands trembling and his knees now shaking in a delayed reaction to the danger, sat down also. "Here," he called, almost automatically. "Come here, boy."

Joyfully, in clumsy-looking bounds, the beast came to him with its tail wagging.

Probably, the Prince thought as he hugged and petted the shaggy bulk, there were a few other dogs in the world as big as this one or even bigger. But he could not recall ever having seen one quite this size. The massive neck bore no collar, nor any sign that it had ever worn one. There was no other mark, mundane or magical, of ownership.

Taking the torn ear gently in his fingers, he murmured a spell or two, doing what he could to stop the bleeding and promote healing; he was no great healer, but fortunately the wound appeared less serious than he had thought it would be.

"Wish I had something to feed you, dog—but at least you don't look like you're starving." Rather the opposite, in fact.

Now Adrian noticed that the beast's forepaws had a curious appearance, almost as if the forepart of each paw was incompletely divided into fingers. Or, he thought, as if the digits had once been truly divided in that way, and had now almost entirely reverted to the true canine form. The division in its present state was not complete enough to be at all useful; there was no way these paws were ever going to be used as hands.

The creature's teeth, when Adrian dared turn back a dark lip to obtain a good look at them, were truly formidable. And the eyes, large and brown, were somehow suggestive of intelligence.

Once or twice during this intrusive examination the animal again raised its head and howled. The sound was softer now, but still undoubtedly the same howl that Adrian had been hearing all the way from the City's border.

Having completed this preliminary inspection, Adrian sat down again on the edge of a rock. The dog, tail wagging, came closer, to rest its huge head and massive forepaws on the boy's leg. It crouched there looking up at him as if it hoped to be able to communicate.

He suddenly felt much less alone than he had at any time since his separation from Trilby.

"Why have you followed me all this distance, fellow? And what am I supposed to call you? No collar, no name. But you don't act wild. So, I think that you must have a name." And Adrian scratched the beast gently behind the ears.

It raised its great head slightly, obviously enjoying the treatment. It panted, dog-fashion, tongue lolling out. More than ever it seemed to want to talk to Adrian.

The first requirement was to get the canoe down the remainder of the hill, so that it could be launched in a moment if the apes returned. When Adrian had accomplished that, he seated himself to rest on another stone, as comfortably as possible, and called the dog to him again.

Then he summoned up such probing powers as he could manage on short notice, and as seemed to him appropriate. Taking his new companion's head between his hands, he set himself to looking into those very canine eyes, trying to see what might be behind them.

A few moments later, the apprentice magician was forced to blink and look away. Strange memories indeed were crashing and reverberating inside this animal's skull—of that much he was already sure. Undoglike memories, that seemed to have to do with power, among other things . . . Adrian could not be sure what kind of power was indicated, but certainly something more than mere physical ability. The vague perception had vanished almost as soon as he had tried to pin it down.

Then the boy momentarily held his breath, as he was struck by a new idea. Could this creature before him conceivably be a human being, one who had been trapped in some great shape-changing enchantment? He had heard of such things, but only as dim possibilities. He had never come close to encountering a case before.

But after thinking the idea over, and applying certain magical tests, Adrian felt sure that such was not the explanation. This being now crouching before him with lolling tongue and watchful eyes had never been human in the past, and certainly was not human now.

The Prince stroked the animal's head again. Its generous tail wagged slowly.

"Then were you once the pet or the tool of some great wizard or enchantress? That would explain much that is strange about you, dog. Though I don't see how it would explain how you come to be here now."

The animal only panted, gazing at Adrian steadily. It seemed that any further effort to find an explanation was going to have to wait.

"We'd better get moving again, downstream. You're coming with me, aren't you? Of course you are. There's no way I can force you, but I sure hope you're willing."

As soon as Adrian stood up, the dog got to its feet too, as if anxious not to be left behind. He spoke to it words of soft encouragement, still slightly worried that it might change its mind.

"I'll get the canoe in the water first, then we'll move downstream a little, away from these falls. I saw smoke, which means a village down there, and it stands to reason this whole river can't be deserted. So I'm going to need some clothes, a minimum anyway—I think I can fix that. And nothing like the clothes I was wearing when I left school—someone might be looking for those." Grasping his own hair, he pulled some of the longer strands in front of his eyes and studied them thoughtfully. Accumulated dirt, along with some side-effect of his tanning magic, had caused a definite darkening. He could probably pass as belonging to one of the riverside villages, for example that of the head-collectors.

And maybe, Adrian thought suddenly, he and his new companion would be able to work out some kind of cooperative hunting agreement. He wasn't exactly starving, but for some days now he'd been looking forward keenly to his next full meal.

When he had the canoe in the water again, at a cautious distance downstream from the tumult at the foot of the falls, the dog appeared to understand at once what he wanted it to do next. It jumped into the small craft first, landing as lightly as possible and balancing neatly amidships, while Adrian standing thigh-deep in the water held the vessel steady. Then the dog lay quietly, with its considerable weight distributed along the centerline, while he got in.

Adrian picked up the paddle and shoved off.

"You know what a Sword is, boy? No, how could you. But they're very important, and there's one of them not far ahead—I can smell it there even if you can't—and we're going to try to get our hands on it. Our paws, maybe?

"Now that I've got someone who'll listen to me, and I can tell you're listening by the way you move your—"

The Prince leaned forward, reaching out with gentle fingers. Hadn't it been the dog's right ear that was torn by the ape's teeth? No? the left one, then . . .

Neither ear showed the slightest trace of ever having been injured.

12

AT dawn of the day following the one on which he'd found the Sword, Talgai the Woodcutter was once more traveling a forest trail on foot, though this time without the company of his faithful loadbeast. He was making his way sadly and steadily toward the large town of Smim, where, as he had been told, his only brother was being held in jail, awaiting execution.

Talgai's newly acquired lucky Sword, still wrapped in its piece of ragged canvas and at the moment carried balanced on his left shoulder, was coming with him. On his back the woodcutter bore a small pack, containing a few items of spare clothing and some food. Talgai's wife, always sympathetic when she heard any tale of woe, had included several of her famous oatcakes, in an effort to do what little she could for the condemned man.

The journey might have been accomplished more swiftly and easily by water, since Talgai's hut and the town of Smim were both on the same river. But he had decided to leave his boat at home, in case his wife should need it; and anyway the road to town was reasonably safe. Particularly so, he thought, for a man carrying such a lucky Sword. With Coinspinner in hand, Talgai doubted not that he would be able to reach the town on foot, in plenty of time.

Should he fail to make good time, he could always travel by night as well as by day; but Talgai doubted that matters would come to that. As he hiked, he reflected on the bad and unhappy life led by his brother Buvrai—as far as Talgai knew, Buvrai had been in trouble almost continually since he was a boy. Not that Talgai knew much about the details of his brother's life, particularly in recent years. Nor did he wish to know more of the sad story than he did. It seemed too late to do anything about it now.

Talgai judged that he was making good time throughout the day, and as darkness approached, he found a convenient spot and stopped to rest. He dined frugally on a portion of the food he had brought with him, not forgetting to save the oatcakes for the prisoner, and augmenting his own dinner with some roadside berries. Then he wrapped himself in the cloak that his wife had insisted he bring along, and slept in the grass not far from the side of the road. This was nothing particularly unusual in the woodcutter's life, and he slept well.

Next morning he was up at dawn and off again.

During his first day's hike he had encountered several people along the way, the numbers very gradually increasing as the road broadened and the town grew nearer. But on this second day, having started on his way so early, he again had the road to himself for a time.

For a long time now he had been out of sight of the river, but now both river and road were curving in such a way as to make them run close together. Talgai took the first good chance to wash his hands and face, and get a drink. Just as he was straightening up from the water, someone nearby made a slight, throat-clearing noise.

He turned to see a wiry, long-haired boy of about twelve, and a huge gray dog, sitting together on the grass along the bank. Beside them a well-made canoe, hewed out of a single log, had been pulled ashore.

"Good morning, sir," the lad said brightly. He was wearing only a twist of bark cloth around his loins, like one of the river people, but his speech sounded very odd for one of them.

But certainly well mannered.

Talgai nodded. "Good morning to you, young sir. That's a nice canoe you have there."

"Ah—thank you." The boy was staring at Talgai's canvas bundle. "Sir, are you by any chance headed down the river? If so, I'd be glad to offer you a ride."

"Well, as a matter of fact, I am. My name is Talgai."

"And mine is Cham." All magicians adopted different names at times, and this was one that Adrian had sometimes used. Meanwhile the dog was doing his loutish best to demonstrate that he, too, approved of Talgai. The woodcutter could only marvel at the huge and impressive beast, while trying to fend off its more energetic advances.

For several hours before he encountered the woodcutter, Adrian had known that the Sword of Chance was very near.

He had put ashore in darkness, and then, with the great dog whining softly at his side, had walked slowly past the sleeping Talgai in the hour before dawn. The Prince had looked at Talgai and at his bundle—and then he had made preparations for this meeting.

Adrian had considered attempting to seize the Sword from the sleeping man—and he thought he might have succeeded, for the man was not actually in contact with Coinspinner as he slept. But the boy had hesitated, uncertain whether such a theft under these conditions would be either justifiable or wise.

The truth was that the apprentice magician, having now caught up with the Sword he had been pursuing, was having trouble trying to decide what to do next.

It was already plain to him that the man now carrying the Sword was no magician, and no warrior either. The way he casually set down the Sword of Chance in its rude canvas bundle, and turned his back on it— anyone who wanted to seize the weapon could grab it away from this incompetent, or so it seemed.

Still, Coinspinner was presumably now acting on this unsuspecting man's behalf—and it had not turned him away from this encounter with Adrian, a feat that, Adrian supposed, would have been well within the Sword's powers to accomplish. What was the meaning of this, for Adrian himself?

There were times, his father had often and solemnly told him, when it was necessary for one who bore a high responsibility to be ruthless. Still, Prince Mark was not often ruthless himself, and Prince Adrian had been raised with the ideals of simple fairness and honesty before him. He himself was in no immediate danger, as far as he could tell. How then could he justify stealing the property of this innocent and trusting man?

Another thought occurred, to confuse the Princeling further. Suppose his powerful enemy, Wood, who had almost succeeded in killing Adrian in the City, was coming after him again. Wood was known to possess Shieldbreaker, and Shieldbreaker would destroy any other Sword, indeed any weapon of any kind, that was brought into physical opposition to it. But suppose that Wood was coming after Coinspinner too—?

Adrian was no closer to solving his problem as he got into the canoe, leaving the heavier Talgai to shove off and step aboard. The new passenger, obviously skilled with boats, insisted on paddling for a while. With man, boy, and dog aboard, the canoe was now fully loaded, and riding low in the water.

A few hours later, when boy and man had agreed that the time had come for a rest stop, they beached the canoe in a likely-looking place and stepped ashore.

The dog quickly disappeared into some nearby woods, and Adrian could only hope that the beast was hunting.

Meanwhile Talgai, unpacking his own modest store of food, took the oatcakes out of his pack in the process. He was on the point of stowing them away again, and offering to share some of his plainer provisions, when he took note of the hungry look on Adrian's face.

After what looked like a brief struggle with himself, the man offered: "Here, lad, these are very good cakes. Would you like one?"

Adrian certainly would.

Before the first oatcake was completely gone, the dog had come back from the woods with a fresh-killed rabbit, which he dropped at Adrian's feet. The beast tarried to receive a pat and a word of praise, then bounded back into the trees again.

"Your dog is trained as a hunter, then! Remarkable!"

"Yes, sir, he's really a remarkable dog. I feel quite safe with him around."

Meat having now been provided, a fire was the next requirement, and to that end Adrian was already gathering some dry twigs.

Talgai had come equipped with flint and steel, so there was no need for Adrian to display, or try to hide, his fire-raising powers.

By that time a second slaughtered rabbit had been delivered, in the same way as the first; once again the dog had paused to gaze steadily at Adrian for a moment, before plunging back into the woods. Adrian got the idea that now the beast would be hunting for himself.

While the meat was starting to cook, filling the air with unbearably delicious aromas, Talgai shared more of his oatcakes.

He broke off a piece of one for himself and nibbled it, but then handed the rest over to Adrian. "I have no taste for these today. But you are too thin, your ribs are showing. Eat!"

Then, while the boy ate, the man sat back, chewing some dried fish he'd brought with him. And suddenly he began to pour out his troubles, the fact that his brother was doomed to die in a very few days. And that there seemed to be nothing that could be done about it.

"Tell me, young sir, is it really good luck to be warned of a brother's impending death? What good is a warning when there's nothing that you can do about it anyway?"

"Good luck?" Adrian, feeling that he sounded stupid, but not knowing what else to say, echoed the question.

And suddenly the woodcutter was unwrapping Coinspinner, and telling the Prince a different story, that of his lucky Sword.

The telling faltered; Talgai appeared to be somehow impressed with what must have been the strange expression on the boy's face, as Adrian stared at the Sword.

"Here, would you like to hold it? Do you think that you would be happier if you were lucky too? But be careful, the blade is very sharp indeed." And the woodcutter slid Coinspinner forward, hilt first, beside the fire.

Very cautiously indeed the Prince reached forward and took the black hilt into his own hands. Reached for it, took it into his hands, and felt the power . . .

This was not the first time that Adrian had been entrusted with a Sword to handle. Possibly—he couldn't remember with any certainty, because he had been very small—possibly his father had once even let him touch this very hilt, years ago in the royal armory at Sarykam. The Prince had no need now to try the edges of this blade with his finger to know that the simple man across from him was telling him the simple truth about their sharpness.

Good fortune, great fortune, had come, here and now, into his hands. It was evident that if a possessor of the Sword of Chance decided to give his luck away, the Sword's own powers were not going to act on his behalf to prevent his doing so.

"I could use some good luck," the Prince muttered, raising the stark beauty of the blade beside the fire, gazing at it. But even as he spoke, he knew that he was going to have to give Coinspinner back.

It didn't help to tell himself that this poor simple fellow, now smiling at him from across the fire, would actually be better off without such powerful magic. That a Sword, any Sword, would only complicate poor Talgai's life, expose him to unexpected danger, attract the attention of powerful enemies. It didn't even help to consider the possibility that Wood might even now be coming after the Sword and its possessor, whoever that might currently be.

Adrian, reluctantly, but feeling that he could do nothing else, handed back the Sword. He passed it carefully, hilt first, and Talgai took it carefully and rewrapped it in his piece of canvas and laid it by his side. Soon the rabbits were cooked, and soon after that they were eaten. By that time the great dog, with fresh blood on his muzzle and looking satisfied, had rejoined the two humans beside the fire.

Adrian listened sympathetically, and the dog appeared to do so, as Talgai repeated and elaborated upon the sad facts concerning his brother.

"He was always getting into trouble," said the woodcutter, shaking his head sadly. "Yes, even from the time when he was as young as you are. Maybe even before that. I remember well, our mother always used to say that if Buvrai kept on as he was going, he would come to something like this, sooner or later. It's just a good thing that she's not around to see it."

Adrian put in a few words now and then, expressing his sympathy as best he could. Twice he was on the point of saying something else, and twice he forbore.

It seemed that his suggestion might have been unnecessary in any case. Talgai seemed to be working his way toward the same idea on his own. Without prompting the woodcutter had fallen into a study, frowning at his canvas package.

"Of course," he said at last, thinking aloud, "of course I might try to buy his freedom. A treasure like this—it is a real treasure, even I can see that. How would I go about it, though?" He raised his eyes as if appealing to this village boy for a suggestion.

For all his schooling to be heir to a kingdom, Adrian couldn't think of what to say, or think, or do. At the moment all he could think of was that he'd had the Sword, yes, the real Sword, right in his own hands a moment ago. And then, like the damned fool idiot that he must be, he'd handed it right back again. Given it right away.

The woodcutter brightened. "Of course, the Sword itself is so lucky, maybe it would keep me from going about things in the wrong way. Until I actually handed it over to someone else. To the prison warden, or whoever. But . . . I wonder . . ."

And now it seemed to Adrian that yet another idea, this one the real step forward, had dawned at last on Talgai.

They spent one night on the journey, Adrian sleeping in the canoe, at Talgai's insistence, because it was probably a little safer there, while man and dog and lucky Sword lay all close together on the grass nearby.

The travelers were all up early and on their way, and now it was obvious, from the rapidly increasing human presence on the banks and in the river, that they were getting very close to Smim.

When Coinspinner acted next, it was a subtle move, and Adrian did not at first recognize the small event for what it was.

Talgai was taking another turn at paddling. In the midst of another lament about his brother, he turned his head, broke off in midsentence, and pointed toward something on the shore.

"What is it?" Adrian asked.

"A friend of mine. Old Konbaung, he used to be my neighbor. There he goes. But now I remember, he had a relative who worked in the court! I must catch up with him, maybe he can do something for Buvrai."

Driving hard with the paddle, Talgai turned the canoe abruptly toward the place where he was certain he had seen his old friend. There was a footpath there, following the riverbank, and one branch of it turned and angled inland, doubtless heading to town.

Running the canoe ashore, the woodcutter leaped out impetuously into the shallows. "Thank you for giving me a ride, lad. All the good gods be with you. I hope you find your parents."

Adrian stuttered something, but he was too late. The man with his back turned was already up the bank and striding rapidly inland, the Sword of Chance a nondescript bundle on his shoulder.

The dog, after bounding around irresolutely on the muddy bank for a time, whining and yapping, suddenly decided to accompany Talgai, and went running inland in pursuit. The Princeling yelled after the nameless beast, but it ignored him this time.

Now the Sword was gone, and for a moment Adrian hesitated, on the brink of running after it. That would, of course, have meant abandoning the canoe, and he felt reluctant to do that after the many difficulties the craft had borne him through.

While yet he wavered, his mind was made up for him by the appearance of two men. These were both armed and unsavory-looking, and one was strolling upstream along the bank while the other moved downstream to join him. They were going to meet at the place where Adrian was hesitating.

"Hey, kid! Nice boat you've got there. Where'd you get it?"

He might have tried some magic on them, but it had become almost instinctive to conserve energy, to use enchantment only as a last resort. Instead, Adrian pushed off the canoe again and paddled out toward midstream. The river was wide enough here for him to—

Only when he was twenty-five meters or so from shore did he become aware of the two sizable boats, big enough to hold half a dozen men each and both crowded, that were closing in on him, one from upstream and one from down.

There were several other craft on the river also, but all of those were distant, and none were concerned with what was happening here.

The two ominous boats had got within fifty meters or so of Adrian, perhaps, before he could be sure that he was the object of their interest.

At the same time, the two men on shore, of similar appearance to those in the boats, were walking along the bank, staying opposite Adrian's canoe, ready for him if he should try to land again. And the men on the bank exchanged brisk arm signals, obviously prearranged, with those in the boats.

"Let's see what you're hiding in the bottom of your boat there, lad," a voice loaded with false heartiness called out to him. It belonged to a man standing in the prow of one of the two craft closing in. On this man's shoulder there perched a winged, half reptilian-looking messenger.

Wood and his people used such creatures. Adrian felt his heart sink. "I've got nothing hidden!"

"Let's just take a look." The man grinned.

They think I've got Coinspinner with me. If only I did.

Now a middle-aged woman, something of an enchantress from the look of her, was calling out from the other boat to the male leader, telling him something about the magical aura she was able to see around Adrian. She could quite definitely confirm his identification as the missing Prince.

"Good, we've got him, then. And where's the Sword we were to look for? Has he got it there?"

"I doubt that very much," the woman called back. "If he ever had it, I think it's gone now, and no telling where."

The two boats were moving steadily closer. With many oars apiece, they could easily overtake him on the water if he tried to flee.

"That's the canoe we were told to look for, no doubt of that. And he's the right age."

The leader, smiling, spoke softly to the creature on his shoulder, whose beady eyes inspected Adrian. In a minute, the Prince thought, he's going to send it back to Wood, with word that I've been taken.

There was no way to escape—diving, trying to swim away underwater would be simply foolish.

Adrian's reaction to being trapped was the same near-instinctive reflex that had served him well before. Just as the two other boats were closing in on him, he reached with his mind into the depths of the earth, and fought for his life in the only effective way he could manage.

Call upon heat, call up pressure, evoke great density and mass and elemental toughness. The layers of rock beneath the muddy riverbed shifted, vibrated, pounded with the sudden stress of their own energies, being manipulated in a new way. Relief came with concussive force. Suddenly the materials upon which Adrian's mind was working split; a river-elemental was born almost accidentally, becoming separately objectified from the earth-elemental stirring at a deeper level.

Great pseudopods of water burst up into the air, overwhelming both large boats. Fortunately no innocent craft were near enough to be drastically affected. Gigantic geysers of rock and mud and water, flung higher than trees or houses, struck up into the air, projecting fragments high and hard enough to sting and wound the flying reptile, throwing it into a panic. It had sprung into the air from its master's shoulder at the first eruption, even as the man himself was hurled out of his boat.

One shoulder of the nearest erupting wave caught Adrian's canoe, lifted it above the river's surface, and dandled it like an infant for a moment. But the creator of the creature was able to soothe his creation successfully, and just in time; his return to the river was no worse than a splashing fall.

Unfortunately for the men and the woman in the two large boats, they were unable to take wing. Their craft were capsized, spun and hurled in midair, and men who were weighted with weapons, some of them with armor, did not fare well upon being suddenly plunged into deep water. Clinging to his own canoe as it pitched and tossed, the Prince saw with horrified fascination, how the mud and water surged and raced and spun around their bodies, turning them over again and again, sucking them under when they might have fought back to the surface.

Rock and earth hurled toward the sky splashed back into the river. Unlike the eruption in the City, this one left few visible effects a few moments after it had occurred. The great waves raised locally were quickly dying as they spread. The mud spewed up fell into muddy water. Only the drifting shapes of the two capsized boats, and the bodies of the drowned or drowning, could be seen as its results. The two men who had been standing on shore were engulfed in a huge wave, and Adrian could see one of them, covered with mud, running in panic for some nearby trees.

Adrian's canoe had not been damaged, though nearly swamped by water pouring in. Bailing frantically and not too effectively with his hands, he could not spare much attention for what was going on around him. He was aware of the flying reptile, still cawing in anguish, as it went laboring away on damaged wings.

The reaction of exhaustion came over the Prince, and he slumped in the canoe, on the point of losing consciousness. The body of a drowned man, bumping lightly against the side of the canoe, roused him to horrified new efforts.

At last, with most of the water bailed out of his craft, he was once more paddling downstream. Vaguely he had decided to go toward the docks of the town. As he paddled, he could still sense the aftershocks caused by the elemental's violence rippling through the layers of rock deep beneath the river. He could hope that what he had done wasn't going to set off a real earthquake—he continued to exert his best efforts to damp things down again.

Half dazed, the Prince found himself thinking of the great dog, and wondering what had happened to him. Well, he wasn't going to hang around to look for him.

If I had taken Coinspinner when I had the chance, and held on to it, that couldn't have happened.

Right now Adrian was obsessed with one thought only. He was grimly determined to regain his contact with the Sword.

13

TALGAI, as he trudged into the town of Smim with his lucky Sword still wrapped in canvas and still riding on his shoulder, reflected on the strange and frequently puzzling things that had happened to him in the course of his journey—and for most of which, he was sure, the Sword he carried was somehow responsible.

High on the list of oddities was the lucky meeting with the hungry lad who had happened to be paddling his canoe downstream, and who had offered him a ride. And there was the peculiar dog—peculiar to say the least—that even now was still following the woodcutter at a distance. Whenever he glanced back he could see it, coming along the path behind him, thirty or forty meters back. He didn't want to call the dog to come to him, although he would have enjoyed its company, because it belonged to the boy, after all.

And then there was the incident, less than an hour ago, that had caused Talgai to leave his benefactor and proceed on foot, trying to catch up with a man he thought he knew.

While paddling the canoe, Talgai, glancing inland, had been convinced he'd spotted an old friend. But of course the fellow, when the woodcutter had finally overtaken him, had proved to be a total stranger, though the resemblance to his old friend was indeed remarkable. By the time Talgai had discovered his mistake, however, he could see the town quite close ahead of him and there was no point in turning back to the canoe. Gripping his bundled Sword now, he made a wish that young Cham should have a safe trip and meet his parents successfully—somehow Talgai had got the notion that that was what the boy was trying to do.

A moment later, Talgai's mind was once more filled with his brother and his brother's predicament. He hastened on.

At some point since he'd last left home, the woodcutter wasn't sure just when, the idea had begun to grow in his mind that Coinspinner's magic might even be able to rescue his brother from execution. Provided, of course, that he, Talgai, could somehow contrive to get the Sword into Buvrai's possession.

Certainly Talgai could not ignore the possibility, if it offered any hope at all.

The path he had followed from the riverbank had soon joined with another, larger, one, and that in turn with a road that was considerably larger still. Traffic of all kinds came in to being and steadily increased. Presently Talgai found himself entering the busy city on the high road from the east, along with an assortment of carts, wagons, occasional mounted folk of the upper class, and other humble pedestrians like himself.

The town of Smim was busy though not particularly large, being otherwise unremarkable of its kind. But its size was great enough to be confusing to the woodsman, who tended to feel ill at ease in any settlement larger than a dozen houses.

Still he experienced no difficulty in locating the prison. Very near the center of town, this facility occupied the two upper levels of one of the largest and tallest buildings in sight. The windows of the building's two lower levels displayed rooms full of clerks puttering about, doing incomprehensible things at desks and tables.

Fearful that he might, after all, have arrived too late to help his brother, Talgai began stopping people in the street and asking whether any execution had taken place in the past several days. The answers he obtained were mainly reassuring in that regard, though one man chose to try to plunge him into despair with a tale of horrible dismemberment on the scaffold, for no reason at all that Talgai could see. But the woodcutter did manage to learn, from several sources, that a public hanging was indeed scheduled for tomorrow at dawn.

Evidently he had not arrived too late—thank the Sword for that. But certainly there was no time to waste.

After quenching his thirst at a public watering trough—for some reason several well-dressed passersby favored him with amused glances as he did this—the woodcutter walked completely around the prison and the attached administrative complex, looking things over from every angle. It was of stone construction, and it was certainly a large building, he remarked to himself unnecessarily when he had observed all sides of it. Perhaps the largest he had ever seen. The trouble was that having inspected this large building thoroughly Talgai really had no better idea of how to proceed than he had had before.

Returning to the square in front of the prison, he rather timidly observed the grim-faced guards, armed and uniformed, who were stationed at the building's doors and in its one visible courtyard. An even more disconcerting sight was the ominous-looking scaffold that had been erected twenty meters or so from the front of the prison, right in the public square. The scaffold was of logs, and it had a well-used look.

Despite their bright uniforms, the guards all looked as grim and sullen as the walls they guarded. As Talgai stared at them, and thought of the authority that they must represent, it seemed to him that any appeal for mercy was doomed to failure at the start. He might, of course, attempt to bribe someone, using the marvelous Sword he carried—he had no doubt that at least some of these people could be bribed. If only he knew better how to go about such things, or if he had more time in which to learn the proper ways—but in fact he had hardly any time at all.

Likely, the woodcutter thought, if he tried bribery he'd only approach the wrong person, or make some other mistake that he couldn't foresee, and get himself arrested. He'd hand over the Sword, and that would be that. The Sword would protect him only as long as he actually had it with him, close enough to touch. He understood that now. And once he'd handed over his lucky tool to someone else—well, there'd be no protection for himself or his brother either against these scoundrels. Whatever his brother's faults, he felt sure just from looking at the men who were about to hang him that they were scoundrels too.

Getting himself arrested wouldn't be a good idea. It wouldn't do his brother any good. And he, Talgai, had a wife and small children dependent on him.

But he was going to have to do something. He was sure of that when he stood gazing at the gallows. Just thinking of watching any execution, let alone his own brother's, made Talgai shiver. No, he wasn't going to be able to stand here and watch anything like that happen to Buvrai.

So be it. Therefore he must try to get the Sword into his brother's hands. The only question was, how to go about it?

One method of course would be to make his attempt at the last moment, when Buvrai was actually being led out to his death. But Buvrai's hands might well be bound then, Talgai supposed. And if the condemned man was unable to reach for the Sword and grasp it, make it his own, how could it do him any good?

Deep in gloomy thought, Talgai strolled aimlessly about the square before the prison. He was bothered by growing worries about the impending fate of his wife and children. Suppose he got himself into trouble that would keep him from ever seeing them again.

Standing under the gallows, he resolutely put such fears behind him. His brother's predicament was immediate and real, and therefore it had to come first.

Now, once Talgai had firmly made up his mind as to what he wanted to do, his good fortune took effect again and things began to fall his way at once.

Only moments after his decision at the scaffold, as Talgai stood looking up at the front of the prison again, he was able to identify the window of his brother's cell without any trouble. This was possible only because, fortunately, his brother came to the window and looked out while Talgai happened to be watching.

The cell window—it was heavily barred, like all the windows near it, so Talgai assumed that it opened into a cell—directly overlooked the square, providing a good view of the gallows, which at the moment was claiming Buvrai's thoughtful attention. Most of the windows in the wall were heavily barred with ironwork. Those on the ground floor opened into offices of some kind, shadowy tiled and paneled rooms where clerks and administrators sometimes appeared.

"Buvrai! It's me! Down here!"

The prisoner saw and recognized his brother gazing up at him from the street below. He shouted something back, and the two exchanged waves.

Glancing at the guards, Talgai saw that they were watching with bored expressions and a minimum of interest.

The two brothers conversed some more. Buvrai, starting to rave now, shouted that he had been imprisoned unfairly, because he had incurred the enmity of the Red Temple, who had falsely accused him of cheating in a game of chance.

"Is that all?"

"They say I killed a man. But it's all lies."

"How can I help you?"

"If you want to help me, get me out!"

The building containing the prison was no more than four stories high, and the condemned man's cell was not at the top. Still, Buvrai's window was much too far above the ground for Talgai to be able to simply walk up to it and push the Sword in between the bars. Nor did there appear to be any feasible way to climb the wall and get within reach.

"You've got to do something to get me out of here. See the governor or something. They mean to hang me tomorrow!" Buvrai went on, shouting renewed complaints against the Red Temple.

Whatever the truth of Buvrai's claims, his situation sounded bad. It sounded so bad that Talgai was beginning to have doubts again. How could good luck help against impossibility? What kind of a miracle could even Coinspinner possibly work in such a desperate case?

"Tomorrow, Talgai! Will you do something?"

"Yes, yes, I'll try!" he shouted back.

The guards were still watching and listening impassively. Probably they heard similar shouted conversations all the time.

The woodcutter couldn't imagine what good a lucky Sword was going to be in this case. But he tried as best he could to suppress his doubts. He clung as hard as possible to a simple faith that the weapon he had been carrying was going to do something effective.

Now Buvrai was shouting down more instructions for him, something about Talgai's trying to see someone who was being held in the women's cells on the ground floor. Maybe she could think of something, some way to get them both out. The woman's name sounded like Amelia.

Presently, because his brother's yelling, his concocting of desperate, half-witted schemes, was only confusing him now, and nothing was getting done, Talgai waved once more and hurried off to think, out of sight of the prisoner's window.

At last, after some agonizing minutes of indecision, trusting in Coinspinner's power but seeing no other way to harness it properly, Talgai decided that the only thing to do was to simply stand back and throw the Sword up at his brother's window.

He wondered urgently whether he ought to yell up a warning to his brother just before he threw the Sword, so that his brother would come to the window and reach out between the bars and catch it.

If anyone could catch a blade like this one, spinning in midair, without cutting off his fingers.

Well, Talgai supposed, it might be just at that point, the Sword's first contact with a new owner, where the miraculous good luck might be expected to come in. And if luck failed there—well, Buvrai, at least, had nothing to lose.

The woodcutter considered whether he ought to leave the Sword wrapped, but bind his canvas bundle tightly before he heaved it up, so it would be able to fit in between the bars when Buvrai caught it. Yes, Talgai supposed, that would be the way.

At last, with his bundle ready, and himself as ready as he could get for whatever might be going to happen, Talgai came out into the open square again, and walked steadily closer to the prison.

Buvrai was watching for him. "Well?" the prisoner shouted impatiently.

"Well," Talgai called back. "Here's all that I can do for you, brother. The best that I can do."

"Here? Where?"

"Right here. Coming up."

Talgai considered that he had a good eye for distances, and a good arm for throwing. When he threw the Sword up, with even a little luck it ought to go just about where he wanted to send it. It would almost certainly come within his brother's reach, provided that his brother was standing at the window. Maybe it would even fly right in between the bars. So, if he acted now, while his brother was at the window and presumably ready to react . . .

But Buvrai, instead of paying heed when his brother, who had evidently taken leave of his senses, appeared to be ready to throw some kind of awkward bundle up to him, just turned away from the window at the crucial moment, expressing his disgust.

Muttering the closest thing to a prayer that he had mouthed in a long time, directed indiscriminately at any god who might be willing to listen, Talgai ran forward two long steps, and with both hands, using an awkward, almost unplanned sidearm motion, heaved the Sword.

Gazing upward, holding his breath, Talgai saw the canvas-bundled Sword of Chance, spinning in midair, align itself so precisely with the configuration of the barred window that when it reached those bars it went flying neatly in between them, the bundle lacking even a centimeter to spare on either side. In a year of trying he could never, without magic, have made the cast so neatly.

In the momentary quiet that held before the watchful guards began to shout at him, he could even hear the dull clang of the muffled steel as it landed on the cell floor.

After that there was another moment, there were even several moments, in which Talgai might have tried to run away, with some chance of success. But he could not move, because he was waiting to see what was going to happen next.

Before he had thrown away the Sword he had realized that in doing so he would divest himself of its protection. Still, it came as something of a shock when rough voices shouted accusations at him, and rough hands seized him by the arm and collar.

Talgai was surrounded by outraged prison guards, who were arguing over what to do with him. One of the guards struck him on the side of the head, and others, seizing him by the arms, started to drag him into the prison building.

* * *

Meanwhile the condemned man, who had just turned away from the window following a sharp verbal exchange with his brother, looked up sharply as there was a whisper of sound from that direction, a small sound caused by the dull cloth wrapping of a flying object grazing one or more of the window bars. There was a dark shape flying in the air within the cell, followed by a dull metallic thump on his stone floor.

Gaping stupidly at the bundle that lay there now, wondering how in the world it had ever managed to get in through the bars, Buvrai was able to recognize his brother's voice, once more yelling at him from outside. But he was not able to make out the words.

Days ago, long before Talgai's appearance, the prisoner had given up the idea of ever being rescued by anything other than some superb stroke of luck. In fact he had never had any real hope of other kinds of rescue; certainly he belonged to no gang, he had no friends—except Amy, who was jailed herself—interested enough in his survival to organize a jailbreak plot. In fact it was quite possible, or at least the prisoner sometimes thought it was, that some of his own supposed friends, certain people who had once been his partners, had connived to get him into this trouble.

But luck was different. The prisoner was always ready to count upon his luck to save him somehow. And so, when Talgai had appeared, Buvrai had allowed himself to begin to hope again. Until, of course, he remembered that his brother was a fool, had always been an unlucky fool, and in the nature of things always would be.

After staring uncomprehendingly for a moment at the object now lying on the floor of his cell, the prisoner realized that this must be luck, if it was anything. In another moment he had moved to seize and unwrap the bundle. In his hands, which were now suddenly trembling and uncoordinated, the object inside the canvas felt like a weapon; it felt like a wrapped-up sword.

Talgai was not only an unlucky fool, he was absolutely crazy to think that a sword, any kind of sword, would help him fight his way out of an iron-barred stone cell. But even as Buvrai's mind acknowledged this, his fingers kept busy undoing the simple knots that held the canvas closed. There was, after all, nothing else for him to do.

Buvrai knew something of the Twelve Swords, but nothing had been further from his thoughts; and the true nature of this weapon failed utterly to dawn on him at first. The small white symbol happened to be turned away when he first looked at the black hilt.

With some flickering hope, grasping for any faint indication that Talgai must have had more in mind than just arming him with a sword,

Buvrai looked eagerly for some written message stuffed inside the canvas. But there was nothing of the kind.

Could Talgai even read and write? His brother wasn't sure. It didn't seem to matter.

Trembling between weeping and laughing hysterically at his brother's folly, Buvrai clutched the black hilt in both hands and held the weapon up. In spite of everything, the sheer quality of the blade impressed him. He even had the feeling that he ought to recognize it, recognize it as something more than—

There came now a fresh outbreak of shouting outside in the square. The prisoner, Sword clutched hard in his right fist, hurried back to his window, grabbing a bar in his left hand to pull himself up so he could see better what was happening in the square. He was just in time to see his faithful brother being dragged away toward the guardhouse in the ground level of the prison building.

Muttering profanities against a host of gods and goddesses, he turned from the window again. Talgai had sent him no message, no help, beyond the bright steel itself.

Except that now Talgai's brother was beginning to feel the sensation of magic in his hand. He was not a magician, but like many other folk he knew the feeling. Buvrai stared at the weapon in bewilderment.

Moments later, the prisoner was jarred out of his near trance by a noise at his cell door. Sword in hand, he turned to face it. Once more he wondered in a confused way, hoping against hope, whether some desperate attempt at rescue might after all be in progress, whether whoever was in charge of it had sent his brother to see to it that he was armed.

The key was being turned in his lock, and now his cell door was yanked open from outside. No rescuers stood there. Rather three guards, with their own weapons drawn, burst into the cell to confront the prisoner.

The faces of the three uniformed men were angry, but not in the least worried. They remained confident even when they saw the Sword Buvrai was holding. They no more recognized one of the Twelve than he had. Still, it was obviously a formidable weapon, on purely physical terms, and they stopped their advance at a respectful distance.

One of the guards tentatively reached out with his free hand toward the condemned man. "Come on, hand it over now!" he commanded in a threatening voice. Then he pulled his empty hand back quickly when Coinspinner's keen point shifted in his direction.

The prisoner, who did know something of the art of swordsmanship, caused the bright point to trace a slow circle in the dim prison air. "Why should I?" he demanded.

"Huh?"

"I said, why should I? What'll you do if I don't hand it over? Kill me?"

Even as Buvrai spoke, the realization was finally dawning on him that this gift that had come flying so strangely in at his window was, must be, a thing of powerful magic. How else could it have passed through the bars in such a way? And that magic, of course, was the reason Talgai, perhaps not so totally foolish after all, had given it to him.

And now at last the thought, the memory of the existence of the Twelve Swords of the gods, rose above Buvrai's mental horizon. Not that Buvrai had ever seen one of those fabulous weapons before; but what else could this be?

What he had to worry about now, the prisoner thought, was the nature of this particular blade's magic. Just what in all the hells was he supposed to do with it? He recalled that the Twelve Swords were very powerful, but what were their individual properties? Yes, he remembered now that they all bore little symbols on their hilts; but just now he was not in a good position to pause for a look at this one.

Desperately he brandished this blade of unknown potency at the three jailers, who were now advancing once more, a few centimeters at a time, scowling at him as they moved. He waited for the Sword's power, whatever that might be, to take effect. Or for the rush of some unknown friends and allies down the corridor, to take his enemies in the rear. Or for—

What actually happened next was that his three enemies charged him simultaneously.

Their charge was not coordinated, and it would not have been a well-considered move, even had the weapon in the prisoner's hand been no more than ordinary steel. The little cell lacked the latitude necessary for the attackers to bring their greater numbers into play effectively. As matters befell, at least one of the jailers handled his weapon very clumsily in the confined space, jabbing the man next to him, whose own arms involuntarily jerked sideways. Within the next moment all three of Buvrai's enemies were wounded, one of them severely; the attack collapsed without the prisoner needing to strike a blow.

In another moment his attackers were retreating in confusion from the cell, the two who were less badly hurt dragging their more seriously injured comrade with them.

Despite the jailers' confusion they did not forget to slam shut the door behind them, and the prisoner could hear the key being turned in the lock, confining him as securely as before.

What next? Bewildered as much as ever, his pulses pounding in his ears, the prisoner turned back to his window and once more looked out. At the moment, everything outside appeared discouragingly calm. In his state of dazed excitement, he forgot to examine his Sword's hilt for symbols while he had the chance.

Standing close inside the locked door, he could hear the excited voices of his adversaries out in the corridor: "Bring pikes!"

"No, someone fetch a crossbow!" And feet went scurrying away.

Magic throbbed in the prisoner's hand. He could feel it, he had had enough experience with magic to do that. But he had no idea what, if anything, this power might be able to accomplish for him.

As Buvrai waited, feeling newly helpless, he gradually became aware of a sound like distant thunder. Where was it coming from? Somewhere far away. Or was it?

Outside the window, the sun shone; out there, out in the world, it was a fine day. But inside his cell things were different. Now the rumbling came again, and the prisoner thought that he could not only hear it but feel it faintly, coming up through the floor beneath his feet . . .

Now—and there was no doubt at all about this—he could hear his enemies in the corridor quietly approaching the door again, mumbling their plans to one another. It was hopeless to try to understand what they were saying through the barrier. Quickly the prisoner slid away from the door, pressing his body into the one corner of the room where they'd have trouble hitting him if they shot through the little observation hole.

. . . and now, no possible mistake about it this time, the prisoner *could* feel the building shiver faintly, and see a fine trail of dust come trickling down from a new crack in the cell's ceiling. Whatever was going on . . .

And now the jailers were unlocking the door again, undoubtedly ready with some new way to kill him.

The door burst open once more, and with the crash the prisoner, Sword raised, leaped back into the center of the room again. His only thought now was that at least he was going to cheat the hangman.

Even as the crossbowman, crouching centered in the doorway and flanked by swords on both sides, leveled his powerful weapon, the prisoner could feel the stone floor begin to sway beneath his feet. No mere rumbling this time. Things had gone beyond that.

The stone floor lurched violently just as the guard's finger touched the trigger. The bolt, released with a harsh twang, shrieked past the prisoner's right ear to shatter itself against the quivering stone wall beside the window.

The prisoner had lost his balance with the lurching of the floor, and he fell in the opposite direction from the bowman. Buvrai in falling managed to retain his grip on the Sword, and was lucky enough not to cut himself on the keen blade. Now he started to get to his feet again. The bowman in the doorway, crazily oblivious to everything but his duty, was reloading with mechanically moving hands. The prisoner was going to have to rush him, despite the leveled blades of the other guards—

And now the earth was thundering continuously beneath them all. Around them in the building wooden beams were breaking like trees in a windstorm, although there was no wind. A large stone crashed from the ceiling, narrowly missing the sergeant of the guard. More stones came after it.

That broke the spell. With hoarse cries the three jailers abandoned their duty and turned in unison to flee for their lives, leaving the cell door open. Up and down the corridor the screams of other prisoners resounded.

My luck has changed too late, too late, thought the prisoner with a condemned man's detachment. More stones tumbled from above, driving him back away from the open door, one impact after another in front of him urging him back against the window where he could only grip the bars one-handed, for still he clutched his Sword. *Too late to do me the least damned bit of good. I'm going to die in an earthquake instead of on the—*

He had not quite time to complete that thought before, with a tremendous roar, most of his cell's floor disappeared into a sudden cloud of dust and mortar. At the same time, greater masses than ever came down from above, hurtling and crashing past his head.

Still gripping the black hilt convulsively in his right hand, the prisoner locked both arms through the window bars. He clung to their support, felt the thick iron vibrating. When one of his feet was suddenly left unsustained, this grip preserved him from a fall.

He was still alive, even unhurt, at least for the moment. And then for another moment, and another after that. With his eyes shut, he waited to be killed.

When several more moments passed and nothing violent happened to him, Buvrai opened his eyes again. Now the dust was thicker, making him cough and choke. Through its gray clouds the cries of the injured and the dying rose up as if to emphasize his luck.

Something stranger even than an earthquake was happening now. The space that had once formed the dank and shadowy interior of his cell had somehow become illuminated by the sun. In a few moments a breeze had cleared the dust a little. The prisoner could now see that he was standing on a short and narrow shelf of stone, all that remained of his cell's floor. This shelf projected from a fragment of wall, the highest part of the building that was still standing.

Now the wind, moving with unaccustomed freedom across these newly exposed stones, blew still more of the dust away. The tall, jagged remnant of intact stonework was suddenly bathed in the full sunlight.

And now the man who had been a prisoner could see, in the middle distance, other buildings that had partially or completely collapsed as well. The entire center of town was changed, and drastically. To Buvrai's ears drifted the sounds of a hundred or a thousand human voices crying out in shock, in pain and horror, uttering pleas for help.

Presently his own shock eased enough to let him move again. Carefully bending almost double, the man who had been condemned to die forced the sharpness of the Sword's blade into a small crevice in the wall, just above the tiny ledge on which he stood. Now the black hilt served as a firm handgrip, on which he could lower his weight and swing himself down. The strong blade bent a little, but he could feel, in its springy strength, that it was not going to break. And now Buvrai's extended toes, groping downward, found another foothold, in just the place where one was absolutely needed.

Slowly, moving one limb after another with numbed care, no longer really aware of any danger, he continued to clamber down the skeletal wall. Always he found the minimal handholds and footholds that were required. Always the Sword came with him, and twice again he dug it into crevices to provide himself with one more grip.

Presently Buvrai, Sword still in hand, was able to drop onto the top of a massive pile of rubble whose bulk had once represented most of the structure of the prison.

Once the former prisoner had reached that level, the rest was easy. In relative safety he scrambled down the rest of the way to the ground. Meanwhile the cries of the dying, the shocked, the injured, continued to go up all around him.

Dazedly ignoring these horrible sights and sounds, the once-condemned man began to walk away to freedom. Then he turned back, remembering something. The women's wing of the jail, a one-story wing at the eastern end of the structure, had suffered comparatively little damage. He moved unsteadily in that direction.

He had not yet got clear of the wreckage of the main body of the prison before he heard the agonized howling of a great dog. In another moment Buvrai could see the huge gray beast, digging frantically into a pile of rubble, as if it were compelled to try to rescue whoever was trapped there.

Something about the sight caused it to remain etched into Buvrai's memory. But he did not stop. Mechanically, stumbling over stones and broken timbers, he moved on toward the women's wing.

The outer door of that low structure, unguarded now, was jammed almost shut. But when Buvrai pried at it with the Sword the door sprang open. Inside was weeping and wailing chaos, but little in the way of real injury. Luckily for the women, the upper stories of the main building had not collapsed in this direction.

Taking down a ring of keys from where they hung on a handy hook, Buvrai began to open inner doors. At first he hardly recognized Amelia among the little crowd of haggard females, garbed as she was in some remnant of an unfamiliar dress, and with her hair all matted and her face devoid of makeup. When he did spot her, the other women gave his Sword plenty of room in letting him reach her. Her eyes were shocked and blank, and she said nothing. The other prisoners flowed past, and most of them were already outside by the time he got Amelia to the door.

Once outside again, he turned away across the square, tugging Amy with him. Nothing was going to stop him now. But something did, before he'd gone six steps. It was the sound of his name, called in a low, distorted voice. The voice was unrecognizable at first, sounding like that of a dying man.

But it had called his name.

Still tugging the befuddled Amelia with him by her wrist, Buvrai looked for whoever had called him. Presently he almost tripped over the head of his brother. With only his head protruding from the mass of collapsed stones and timber, Talgai appeared to be hopelessly trapped, and Buvrai thought he must be on the brink of death.

The former prisoner crouched beside his rescuer, who had now become a helpless victim. One look and Buvrai decided that there was nothing he could do.

Talgai's face and hair were gray and featureless with settled dust, his countenance was twisted in pain.

And now, after being able to exchange a few words with his brother, the woodcutter slumped into unconsciousness. His brother couldn't tell if he was alive or not.

The man who had been rescued began trying to use the Sword to pry away part of the wreckage. Luckily he inserted it into the pile of debris at a key point, and the beam pinning his brother swung and toppled away.

The great gray dog, come running up from somewhere, capered.

But the man Buvrai had managed to release still lay unconscious, and perhaps dead.

Thinking vaguely that there was nothing more that he could do for him, Buvrai stood up.

Gripping his Sword firmly, he took his woman by the arm, and started walking. Sooner or later the survivors here were going to recover from their shock, enough to remember that they still had a killing scheduled for tomorrow.

14

ADRIAN, recovering from his faintness, had left the scene of his last skirmish well behind him, and had the town docks of Smim in sight ahead. He was paddling strongly toward them when a sudden thunderous rumbling and a slowly rising column of dust turned his attention toward the center of town, which was somewhere inland, invisible behind buildings and trees. Listening as the distant screams began to arise, the Prince could only conclude that Smim was being devastated by an earthquake, or something very like one.

Waterborne as he was, Adrian could feel no vibration physically. Nor could he detect any magical disturbance. That the renewed violence in the earth might be an indirect result of his raising an elemental was a distinct possibility, but if it was so, there was nothing he could do about it.

Only somewhat later, when he had heard eyewitness reports of events in the center of Smim, did he begin to appreciate how intense, though narrowly confined, the earthquake's destruction there had been. At the time, watching from the river, Adrian saw only the light shaking of trees and buildings close to the river, a faint indication of the rolling and staggering of the ground farther inland. He could hear, mingled with the cries of humans, a number of dogs, near the town and in it, howling wildly and painfully, and he wondered for a moment if one of those howling was the great gray beast for which he had never been able to find a name.

Within the next few moments the boy became aware, even with his mundane senses, of a great tremor that came running through the river bottom, kicking up brief, strangely shaped waves. And at the same time a renewed burst of human screams, frightening though faint with distance, yells of shock and terror and pain, came carrying to Adrian across the water.

Then, almost as abruptly as it had begun, the rolling and the shaking of the earth was over. From out near the middle of the river everything on shore looked just about as before, except that now Adrian could see the plume of smoke or dust, or perhaps a mixture of the two, rising bigger than ever from some unseen source a couple of hundred meters inland. He supposed that it must be coming from somewhere near the middle of town. He hoped that the kindly woodcutter had not been hurt.

Suddenly Adrian suspected that Wood might be responsible for what was now taking on the dimensions of a real disaster. He had no real evidence, but who was more likely to initiate something that did this kind of damage?

But in the next moment the young Prince forgot almost entirely about Wood. For now the Sword of Chance, whose image had never entirely left Adrian's perception, was once more looming larger and larger in his field of mental vision.

Someone—a man—he could not tell if it was Talgai or not—was now carrying Coinspinner steadily from the interior of the town toward the waterfront. The bearer was not yet physically visible from Adrian's position, but the boy was sure that he was approaching at the pace of a swift walk.

And would the great dog be coming back with Talgai? Adrian couldn't tell. Driving hard with the paddle, he steered his small craft nearer to the docks, which were now practically deserted. Everyone at this end of town must have run to see what was happening just inland . . .

Wanting to get a better look, Adrian wished that he dared to stand up in his canoe . . . but no, there was no need. The Sword was now coming into view.

And here it came. The bright gleam of the long blade was unmistakable, borne in the right hand of a middle-sized man of about thirty years of age, who was headed toward the riverfront at a brisk walking pace. With his left hand this man clasped the arm of a young woman, and he was towing her along. She made no resistance.

From behind the couple, well inland, smoke and screams continued to go up. Adrian paddled closer.

As the couple grew nearer, the Prince could see that both of them were pale. The man, with shaggy brown hair, was roughly bearded. The woman, somewhat lighter in coloring, barefoot and wearing a cheap-looking dress, looked somewhat dazed.

The naked Sword and the figure who carried it would undoubtedly have drawn some attention in the street at any ordinary time. But just now, the one or two other folk who were visible near the docks were paying them no heed. All their attention was focused inland.

As the pale-skinned pair, still moving at a steady pace, drew still closer to the docks, Adrian could see that the woman was a few years younger than the man, and moderately attractive, though certainly no great beauty. The man's clothing hung loosely on him, as if perhaps he had recently lost weight.

Having now come right down the waterfront, the man began to pull his passive companion along the modest row of docks. He was looking for something, all right, and what he sought could hardly be anything but some quick and convenient means of getting out onto the water. There were a few clumsy-looking rowboats available, and a couple of slightly bigger craft, all of them securely tied up but unwatched at the moment.

"Going downstream, sir?" Adrian called loudly, at the same time driving his canoe right up against the dock. "Quick transportation here!"

The man looked at him without surprise, as if he had been expecting Adrian's offer, or some equivalent. He said shortly: "Don't fear the Sword, lad—I'm just carrying it for good luck. All right, here we come!"

And it was fortunate that luck came with the two passengers, for they proved to be totally ignorant of the proper ways of getting into a canoe, or riding in one; and the man at least was in too much of a hurry to even try to be careful.

"Just sit down, sir, right in the middle! Keep low, ma'am, hold as still as you can. That's it, that's it, sit toward the middle."

Then they were in, the woman forward, the man amidships. He put his heavy Sword down in the bottom of the canoe as soon as he was in —more to hide it, Adrian was sure, than to help achieve balance.

Once the load had been more or less stabilized, by means of luck and his shouted orders, the Prince, now seated in the stern, plied his paddle energetically. In silence, they headed steadily downstream. Adrian was already watching for a chance to grab the Sword, but he was determined to wait for a good chance, and so far there had been none at all.

And vaguely he continued to wonder what might have happened to Talgai, and to the great gray dog; and about what sort of disaster might have overtaken the center of the town of Smim.

Presently Adrian cleared his throat. "Something going on back there in town?" he asked at last.

A meter in front of Adrian, the man's head turned a few centimeters. "Couple of buildings fell down. Am I going to tip this damned log over if I look back?"

"No, sir, you can turn your head. Just keep your weight in the middle as much as you can. And move slow."

Shifting his body gingerly, the man turned partway around, showing Adrian his pallid face. A certain looseness of the skin around the jowls, visible through a scraggly beard, gave the impression that his face had once been plump.

The man's eyes, full now of a towering relief, and perhaps other satisfactions, settled somewhere over Adrian's shoulder, in the direction of the town they had just left. The sound of yells had faded. The Prince took a quick look back himself. Already some trees on the river bank were beginning to block the view effectively, with only the top of the drifting dust-or-smoke column visible above their crowns. Again Adrian wondered what might have happened to Talgai; of course the simple man was quite capable of handing the Sword over to someone else, to almost anyone, and getting into trouble that way.

Of course the man the woodcutter would have really wanted to give the Sword to was his brother.

Studying the pallid face in front of him, the Prince thought that perhaps he could detect a faint resemblance. And the hair of this man was practically the same color as Talgai's.

Turning forward again, the man spoke to his companion, and Adrian heard him call her Amy. Then he turned back, grinning at the Prince.

"Lad, my name's—Marland. What's yours? Never mind, I think I'll call you Mudrat."

"Whatever you like, sir," agreed Adrian, still paddling. After so many days in an open boat, days of mud and sun and magic, the description was probably not far wrong.

"I'm Amelia," said the young woman suddenly, from her place in the prow, leaning slightly sideways to look past the man at Adrian. Once more the canoe came close to tipping over. But Adrian did his best to counterbalance, Coinspinner doubtless helped, and they kept gliding along.

Evidently Amelia was starting to come out of her fog. Now she lowered her eyes to something in the bottom of the boat, the Sword no doubt. It was as if she was becoming aware of it for the first time.

"Where'd you get *that?*" she demanded of the man, lowering her voice, as if she imagined that might keep Adrian from hearing.

"My brother gave it to me," he answered shortly, not bothering to lower his.

Talgai had named his brother in Adrian's hearing, but the name certainly hadn't been Marland. Buvrai, that was it. Well, that hardly mattered. This man could only be the escaped convict—Talgai hadn't said what his brother had been convicted of.

There was a good current, making downstream progress swift and steady. Already the town of Smim had disappeared, along with almost all of the dark aerial plume that rose above its rooftops. And now even the outlying portions of Smim were gone. An occasional shack or other building still appeared near the river, but the forest had come close to reasserting its monopoly over both banks.

Now the man who had called himself Marland turned his head to Adrian again. "How far downstream you going to take us, Mudrat?" The man didn't sound threatening, or even as if he wanted to be nasty; the Prince told himself that the newly bestowed name was probably just Talgai's brother's idea of a little joke.

It seemed a safe assumption that the escapees would want to go as far as possible. "I'm going a long way, and I don't much care if I go a little farther."

"Aha. Running away?" The man could understand that, and smiled his approval. "That's the idea—see something of the world.

"Kid, do you know anything about a big city called Bihari? This river runs into it eventually, a couple hundred kilometers from here."

Anyone who knew geography at all had heard of Bihari, and certainly Adrian was familiar with the name, though he had never been anywhere near the place before. And if the man was right, the Prince now had, for the first time, a pretty good idea of where on the continent his emergence from the City of Wizards had brought him out.

"How'd you like to get a look at a real big city, kid? Yes, I can see you would. Don't worry, you'll love it. Much better than living in the jungle. Say, have we got anything to eat aboard?"

"Afraid not, sir."

The woman murmured something in a querulous tone, as if she might be ready to give up now and go back to where she might be fed. Or maybe she was only wondering what was going to happen next.

"That's all right, Amy, first things first. We're out of the jug now, and we're not going to starve. Are we, Mudrat?"

"No, sir."

"Damn right we're not. Not with"—and the man faced front again, and bent over what lay in the bottom of the canoe—"not with my little good-luck charm here."

Throughout most of the day the weather had been fair. But by late afternoon, when the canoe had made two hours of steady progress downstream from the town of Smim, the sky had clouded over heavily.

Shortly thereafter it began to rain. And shortly after that the rain began to turn to hail.

Adrian drove the canoe around a sharp bend, and there, just ahead, looming gray through the rain's curtain, was a large ruin—a fragmentary bridge. An intricate stone abutment remained standing on each shore, and four evenly spaced stone piers made a staggering progress across the river's width, but nothing remained of any of the spans between.

On the right shore, which was somewhat nearer, the broken abutment offered a sort of cavernous shelter under its thick arches.

Under a bombardment of hailstones suddenly grown painfully, dangerously large, Adrian turned the canoe's prow sharply in to shore. The three people scrambled onto the muddy bank, and with the help of Marland, whom the larger hailstones were consistently avoiding, Adrian carried the canoe and paddle up into shelter with them.

Once having reached a refuge, they paused, gasping, surveying the overhanging mass of old masonry above them.

The air had turned chilly. The rain had begun abruptly, a cold, sudden drenching that would have been commonplace in summer in the high country, but was surprising here.

"Wish we could get a fire started," muttered the man, swinging his Sword and glaring at the world.

"Maybe I can," said Adrian shortly. He was growing tired of offering politeness, undeserved and unappreciated. "Help me find some wood."

Both of his companions fell to eagerly enough, scrounging for dry chips and scraps under the arches of old stone. Neither of the adults seemed to find it surprising that their young guide thought he would be able to start a fire. Maybe they just assumed he had some ordinary means at hand. Perhaps, before they were imprisoned, they had been accustomed to having servants start fires for them. They were both certainly very impractical about boats.

Not about Swords, though. At least not the man. Of course he had no sheath for Coinspinner, no way to carry it except in his hand. But it was staying with him like an extension of his arm. Adrian, who had begun to hope that his chance to seize the Sword would come at any moment now, was forced to be patient once again. He built some of the gathered chips and twigs into a little pile.

And the man, looking in a pleased way at the freshly melted mud outside their refuge, murmured something about how any tracks they might have made were going to be washed out.

Adrian, sitting back on his heels after puffing a spark of wizard's fire up into a hungry little flame, caught Amelia looking at him with a strange expression on her face. He wondered if she'd noticed how that spark had been born, without benefit of flint and steel, or any other common means of fire-starting.

But a moment later she resumed her task of gathering, calling the man to come back and help. Actually the dry earth floor of their refuge concealed a good supply of wood fragments; over the years a great many fires must have been kindled in this shelter.

Adrian continued to build and nurse his little flame. Until Marland, in the course of his search for wood, while prying up a suspicious lump with the indestructible sharp tip of the Sword of Chance, came upon something that he found considerably more interesting.

From under a thin layer of hardened earth, he pulled up a copper scabbard. To judge by its length, it must once have been used to hold a great two-handed sword, some weapon considerably longer than Coinspinner.

Marland promptly tried the fit of his bright Sword in the old scabbard, which proved to be broad enough and considerably more than long enough for its new burden. The Sword of Chance slid in with room to spare. He frowned at this thoughtfully, smiled, and set the scabbard carefully aside. Then unhurriedly he resumed his chores, chopping up some of the larger pieces of firewood with his Sword's keen edge.

Taking note that Adrian was watching him, he misinterpreted the boy's interest.

"Well, sprout, what d'ya think? Quite a big knife, hey?"

"Yessir, it's very impressive."

"Yeah. Well, you be sure to keep your hands off it, hear me? There's a magic spell on this Sword, a curse that'll do terrible things to anyone who even touches it, except me. Unless I tell them to touch it, of course."

"Yes, sir." The warning had been spoken with impressive conviction, and the young Prince, knowing what he knew, found it not at all difficult to look suitably impressed.

A little later, when a suitable reserve of wood had been established, the man went back to pick up the scabbard again. The ancient copper was still intact, and looked quite serviceable. Of course the leather straps that had once supported it had long since deteriorated, and had crumbled away when Marland pried the thing up out of the dirt.

Originally this sheath, holding a weapon too long to be carried at a man's belt, must have been worn high on the back. The great length of a two-handed sword would have made it difficult to draw, so the scabbard was open partway down one edge, allowing for the angle required by the normal human length of arm.

The man was thoughtfully studying Coinspinner's fit in this container. "Good enough. Yes, good enough. I'll need some straps, or cords, to tie it on. Shouldn't be too hard to find. Not with a little luck." He smiled privately.

"It does look like a good fit," Adrian offered cautiously.

"I'll tell you what it really looks like. It looks like I'm carrying another sort of weapon altogether, doesn't it?" And the man who called himself Marland, sounding more and more pleased with himself, suddenly laughed.

But Amelia wasn't looking especially pleased. By now she had found the softest place in the dry dust under the ruined abutment, and now she was attempting to find a comfortable position in which to settle herself there. Adrian thought that she looked utterly weary. She lay down in the dust without flinching, like one of the very poor, or like an animal. Or, perhaps, like someone who had grown accustomed to being in prison.

Marland, turning to her to say something about his Sword, instead fell silent and stood for a moment contemplating her, rubbing his jaw. Then he shifted his gaze suddenly to Adrian. "Hey, Mudrat? Now you've got the fire going, how about you taking a little walk, and see if you can scare up something to cook?"

Adrian glanced at the world beyond the open archway. "All right." The rain still poured down, but the hail seemed to have stopped. He saw what looked like an opportunity. "Would it be all right if I borrowed your Sword? I don't have a knife or—"

"No."

"I just thought it would be a handy tool if I—"

"Forget the damned Sword. Just remember what I said about it before. Now take a walk."

Well, it had been worth a try. "All right. Maybe I can scare up some food."

"That's great, kid." Marland relaxed again. "Take your time, there's no hurry." And he turned his attention back to the woman.

The Prince walked past the upside-down canoe, and out into the rain. Now that the hail had stopped, neither rain nor air felt cold, and in his near nakedness he was indifferent to getting wet. Hailstones still lay here and there, making chilly little piles under his feet, and melting drifts of ice.

He was still standing only a few meters outside the artificial cave, wondering whether to explore upstream or down, or inland, when he heard a murmur of voices from the shelter he had just left. The voices were followed by a soft laugh from the woman, and that in turn by silence. Adrian felt a faint rush of blood to his face as he realized the most likely reason for the man's wanting to get rid of him for a time.

The Prince wasn't worried about his two passengers running off while he was gone; they did need food, and they couldn't handle the canoe. Of course with the help of Coinspinner the man could probably handle any boat he wanted to; but maybe he didn't realize that yet.

The man and woman weren't the only hungry ones. The Prince turned his steps downstream along the riverbank. He was wondering whether with a little carefully chosen dowsing magic he might uncover some turtle eggs, or maybe even catch a turtle. In one of the upland rivers with which he was familiar, this kind of mudbank would be an ideal place to look for turtles, but of course things could be different here.

There were snakes and lizards also to be considered—and there indeed was a king-sized snake, coiled upon a log just at the water's edge. Adrian had no idea whether that unfamiliar serpent might be poisonous; if so, of course it could still be good to eat. Magic might help him capture it, but he felt reluctant to use magic if it could be avoided. Magic cost energy, and it left traces in the world. And if Wood was still looking for him, the more traces of his art he left around, the easier that seeker's task would be.

Deciding to come back for the snake if nothing easier showed up, the boy moved on downstream. He had not gone far when a whiff of woodsmoke in the rainy air caught his attention. It might be smoke from his own fire, but—yes, this was another fire, cooking something.

The sun was beginning to break out now, the rainfall spattering slowly to a halt. Adrian turned inland, climbing quietly. Lances of sunlight striking at the little piles of hailstones made them steam.

On top of the first small hill, in a clearing surrounded by a little grove of trees, sat a middle-sized, middle-aged man wearing traveler's, perhaps pilgrim's, gray. He looked as dry as if no rain had ever fallen on him at all, and he was cooking something, pale-looking meat, on a spit over a small fire. Whatever it was smelled very good.

And lying comfortably near the man's feet was a familiar bulk of gray fur. The huge dog raised its head now, looking in Adrian's direction, and emitted a soft whine.

Adrian paused just beyond the ring of trees, looking things over cautiously. The little pile of offal discarded near the fire contained what looked like snakeskin, and yes, there on the ground was the serpent's neatly severed and bloody head, jaws gaping, fangs sunk helplessly into a stick of wood.

Then the man looked up at Adrian, and the Prince forgot all about the snake, and even, for the moment, about the dog.

"Hello," said the gray-eyed man, quite unsurprised. His sleeves had been rolled up somewhat for the work of butchery and cooking, revealing powerful and hairy forearms.

"Hello," said Adrian. The dog got to its feet and came to meet him, and he scratched it abstractedly behind the ears.

"You may," said the man, "have caught a glimpse of me once or twice before in the course of your brief existence. But I don't suppose you've ever had a really good look. I'm—"

And at this moment the boy felt quite certain of what two words were coming next. He was not exactly right.

"—your grandfather. I'm sure you've heard something about the circumstances of your father's birth?"

"Yes, sir, I have." Then Adrian hesitated. "But you don't . . . you don't look . . ."

"I don't look quite old enough to be your grandfather?"

Adrian nodded.

"No, I suppose I don't. Are you frightened of me?"

The Prince wanted to deny it. But under the gaze of those gray eyes he found it hard to say anything that was not true. "A little bit," he admitted at last.

"Good! Good, that's about the right attitude. You're not so frightened that you couldn't come to like me, I hope?"

Surprisingly those last words had sounded almost wistful. There was another pause, during which Adrian found himself moving, as if unconsciously, a little closer to the man. "I don't think so, sir," he said at last. "But I don't know you yet."

"I know you pretty well, though. So that's all right. All in good time." By now the boy was standing quite close to the man, and Adrian's grandfather, the Emperor, put out a strong but gentle hand and took him firmly by the chin and cheek, and turned his head a little back and forth, looking him over carefully. The inspection took only a moment, and then Adrian was released.

"When you see your father again," the Emperor said, "tell him that I am well pleased by what I see in you. So far. By the way, I'm very pleased that you didn't try to steal the Sword from the woodcutter."

"Yes, sir, thank you. It didn't seem right. Uh, Grandfather?"

"Yes."

"This dog. Did you know that he was . . ." The Prince gestured vaguely.

"With you for a time? Yes, I knew that." The Emperor reached out to thump the beast's ribs, and got a tail wag in return. "I even know his name."

"He's your dog, then? What is his name?"

"In a manner of speaking I suppose he's mine. More mine than anyone else's, perhaps. His name is Draffut."

"Sir? Oh, you mean he's named after—the god."

"No, I don't mean that at all." The grandfatherly eyes looked stern for a moment. "I mean that he once walked six meters tall on his hind legs, and had two hands, and spoke as clearly as you or I. People called him 'god,' but I think he never claimed that title for himself."

Adrian was goggling, gazing speechlessly from man to beast and back again.

"And then," the Emperor went on, "Draffut ran into a problem. He killed a man, and in his case that was especially damaging . . . but in time I think his problem can be solved." Once more he thumped the ribs, and the shaggy tail waved somewhat faster. The Emperor looked at his grandson, smiling. Subject closed, for the time being at least.

"Oh," said Adrian, at last.

"You had some other question?" his grandfather asked unhurriedly.

"Yes. Yessir, I do. What am I going to do about—?" With head and shoulder the Prince gestured toward the ruined abutment, where his canoe and his passengers waited, one of them keeping a tight grip on a Sword.

The Emperor said: "That's going to be up to you."

"Oh."

"Don't sound so disappointed. You're doing all right so far. In fact you're doing very well. And you're not as much alone as you may think. I had the canoe there for you when it was needed, didn't I?"

"Oh. Oh!" The second monosyllable was a little brighter. "The man has a Sword, Coinspinner. I expect you know that. I'm going to try to get it away from him."

"I'd be very wary about trying that. But, Adrian, son, I expect you can handle the situation, and I'm not going to take it over for you. Believe me, I have my reasons."

"Yes, sir. If you say so."

"I do say so. Now, I take it that gathering food was one of the reasons that brought you out for a walk in the rain. Have some snake, it's quite good." The point of a small dagger, whose handle had suddenly appeared in the Emperor's hand, came out to probe at the roasting meat, and with swift delicacy separated a sizable chunk from the remainder hanging on the spit.

Adrian accepted the hot gift in callused fingers, and a moment later he was chewing. "This's good. Mmm. Thanks."

"You're quite welcome. Here, have some more. I'd send you back to your—can I call them companions?—with some more of this, but I fear they might be overly curious as to where you got it. But let me show you a little trick, and you can catch another snake. All you need is a forked stick, and it's easy to avoid the fangs."

Less than half an hour later, Adrian returned to the shelter. He noticed that his small fire had been allowed to go out, but a good supply of wood remained, and with a little fakery it ought to be easy to pretend to be rekindling a surviving spark.

At Adrian's entrance, carrying a live snake, Amelia recoiled. Still lying in the dust, she stirred and pulled her dress straight, checking to see that all the fastenings were in place. But Marland, who had been squatting near her, jumped up and came forward rubbing his hands together, his eyes alight, when he saw the fat snake coiled around Adrian's arm, the fanged jaws rendered helpless by the boy's grip just below the head.

Marland got the idea at once. "Hey, Mudrat, you're a great provider!"

Coinspinner was produced, and in Marland's jealous grip did excellent mundane work in severing the serpent's head, then quickly skinning and cleaning what remained. By that time Adrian had a spit ready, and the fire going again.

Before dark their downstream journey was resumed. Marland said he wanted to travel as far as possible before camping for the night.

15

IN an effort to save time, and feeling confident in his own skills, Karel had elected to guide this small party into the City through one of its more dangerous entrances. Several times in the course of the journey, serious-looking obstacles had loomed, physical barriers or virtual walls of magic. But so far the old wizard had led them through the difficulties safely.

Karel and Rostov, their semiparoled prisoners Murat and Kebbi, and the half-dozen Tasavaltan troopers with them had now reached the area within the City of Wizards that was their goal. All of them were now contemplating their strange surroundings, made all the stranger by the devastation wrought by an earth-elemental. That at least was the agency assigned by Karel.

Whatever the cause of it might have been, Murat observed privately, it was obvious at first glance that some violence on a large scale had occurred here, not long ago. Some mighty force had smitten the surface of the earth at this point, whether from above or below he could not say, and the land was still scarred with radii of cracks that looked as if they might be healing. The land was still upthrust slightly here and there. Walls had fallen down, and trees. Many of the latter had been uprooted and their foliage was dead or dying now.

The little river that followed a crooked trench through the middle of this scene of devastation was now running calmly enough, but it was easy to see that its previous course had been somewhat disrupted. A low place, that might once have formed an extensive pond, was now a small sea of mud, drying and cracking around the edges under the pressure of the City's peculiar and sometimes multiple sun.

As the Tasavaltan wizard had several times assured his companions, time flow in the City was apt to be different from outside, so it was very difficult to judge how long they had been here already, or how long their mission was going to take. In any case, their efforts in getting here had already used up more time than the wizard had hoped they were going to have to spend.

Again, now that they were in the City, Murat and Kebbi each had a trooper assigned to him as guard. It was not, Rostov assured Karel, that the General did not trust the strength of the wizard's guardian spells. Rather it was that the Tasavaltan cavalrymen had little else to do anyway.

As for the two Culmians themselves, so far they were coexisting in an uneasy truce. They eyed each other with suspicion and spoke to each other only when absolutely necessary.

"Are we to set up a camp, then?" Rostov demanded of Karel, who sat his mount beside him. "Or can you tell at once which way we ought to go from here?"

The old wizard appeared to ignore the question. "The Emperor's Park," he muttered, as if to himself, as he looked out over the bit of pleasant greenery adjoining the distorted Red Temple.

"Why do you call it that?" asked Murat, riding a little closer. He found his question ignored, as he had more than half expected.

Rostov could doubtless have found out if he had asked, but he was not that much interested in names. "Are you sure this is the place where the Prince dropped from sight?"

"Quite sure. The remnants of Wood's magic are very strong. And there are some of Adrian's as well."

Karel now turned his attention from the tortured landscape, and focused on what looked like a most peculiar Red Temple, standing just next door. This structure was still in one piece following the recent upheaval. But still its shape was so distorted that Murat assumed it had been seriously affected.

"I have been here before," the apple-cheeked wizard was now muttering to himself. He nodded. "Yes. Several times, though my last visit was many years ago. Much has changed."

"I should think it has," said Rostov practically. "Now how do you propose that we begin our search for the Prince? Or do you wish to leave that detail to me?"

The wizard was not really ready for that question yet. Shaking his head vaguely to indicate this, he dismounted and strolled about a bit on foot. Then he paused, turning away from the Temple again to point in the general direction of the muddy depression. "There used to be a pond here. A dam, a small dock, and pleasure boats—there's what's left of the dock, at least." He indicated some planks and timbers lying forlornly in the mud.

"And this bit of land belongs to the Emperor, you say?" Murat persisted.

This time he got an answer. "Yes. Or it used to, when it occupied some portion of the mundane world. I don't know how it got to be here in the City. None of his doing, I suppose. More likely some spiteful prank by one of his enemies."

"I suppose he has many of those," offered the Crown Prince, who was not at all sure that any such being as the Emperor really existed.

Once again he got no answer. Karel, getting down to business now, called for such help as some of the others could give him, in holding certain charms and mumbling words. He was soon able to ascertain that some very powerful trapping spells had recently been used at this location—and he was pretty sure that Wood was their author.

"Trapping spells?"

"Yes. Charms to keep a person or people in one place, usually by annulling their desire to leave, or indeed to do anything but kill time. Making them forgetful of their own affairs. Such spells can be very effective when done properly—as these would certainly have been."

Rostov looked around in all directions. "No demons."

Karel agreed. "I think not. Wood may have learned not to send such creatures against the royal house of Tasavalta. But it would seem that he's adopted other methods that may work."

Returning to his survey of the site, he soon began to provide some details concerning the elemental—or, possibly, more than one—that had recently been raised here.

"That, I'm almost sure, was the lad's own work. And as soon as the elemental or elementals were raised, they came into violent conflict with the powers embodying the spells, or representing them . . . with the result that you see around you."

"And the young Prince?" asked Rostov, sticking to the point. "What happened to him?"

"As I read matters, the result of the fight was that Wood's spells were shattered, and therefore Adrian probably managed to escape with his life, somehow—we know that Trimbak Rao was here, shortly after the clash, looking the place over. I don't know if he came back later, and managed to find out something new."

"How can we be sure," Kebbi put in, "that the Prince wasn't caught after all, or killed?"

"We can't be absolutely sure."

"If he survived, if he escaped, where is he?"

"I believe he went downstream."

"Then we can follow." The renegade pointed with a brisk gesture. "That's straightforward enough."

"Not quite." Karel went on to explain that only a little way downstream the little river before them approached an exit from the City, where it split into several little rivers, each of them with as much water in it as the original, and each assuming a different course across the mundane countryside. It would be difficult for any magician, even himself or Wood, to be sure which one of those branchings Adrian had taken, assuming the boy did go downstream.

"But what gives me the most hope is, that if he had been caught, his captors would be gloating now, and I suppose demanding ransom of one kind or another." Karel paused. "Of course, as I said before, I cannot be absolutely sure that the Prince is still alive."

"Well, given all that you say, sir, how do we conduct our search?" Kebbi kept trying to promote himself out of the status of prisoner.

Before the wizard could reply, a brief disturbance interrupted the searchers' conversation. Two of the troopers were shouting for help, trying to get one of their fellows out of the hedge bordering the grounds of the Red Temple. The man refused to move, they reported, he wouldn't speak, and he looked strange.

Karel, on the spot in a moment, soon had the victim free. Some remnant, it appeared, of Wood's trapping magic was still effective, but by his art the Tasavaltan wizard had been able to push the obstacle away.

Another trooper spoke a warning: "Sir, someone's coming." The hooves of two riding-beasts were crunching through the ruins of a nearby building.

Trimbak Rao now made his appearance, a young girl riding at his side. The Tasavaltans, and Murat at least, rejoiced to hear from him that this was Trilby. Quickly Trimbak Rao reported that he had managed to locate the girl only yesterday, quite near here. She was essentially unharmed, though she had been lost for several days, wandering and hiding in the City in a state of shock and terror. She had agreed to come back to this place today, under escort, to tell Adrian's great-uncle and his loyal friends whatever she could about his disappearance and her own difficult escape.

When the girl had been introduced to everyone, she looked around, and said in a low voice: "It was—it was just very bad. I thought I was starting to know something about magic, but then—this was happening to us, and I never knew it."

Karel was grandfatherly, and very soothing. "Stronger magicians than you would have fallen under those spells in the same way, daughter. Be calm, now, and tell us what you can."

Trilby did her best.

"Once the Prince and I got this far," she said, indicating the place where they were standing, "it was like we just—stopped. We did everything but finish our business and get out. We talked about how strange things were here. We sat around talking about nothing.

"We even swam in the pool—or at least I swam, while Adrian went out exploring on his own. And then he came back, and I started out to have a look around—but I can't remember any more." She bowed her head helplessly.

"Try again, daughter. Maybe I can help you." And Karel took the girl's hands in his. He was probably capable of giving real help in this matter when even the powerful Trimbak Rao had not yet had much success.

A few moments later, the girl said: "Yes . . . wait. It's starting to come back to me now."

And now Trilby was able to remember the presence of a single canoe, drifting in the small pool above the dam, or rather tied up at the end of the little pier.

Karel appeared to find this very interesting. "What kind of a canoe was it?"

"A dugout. I remember thinking that was strange . . . and then . . . I remember thinking how odd it was, there was no magical aura about that canoe at all."

Again the old wizard nodded, as if he found this of significance.

Then Trilby went on to describe where she'd gone on her solo scouting trip. At first with Adrian, when they'd just arrived here, and later on her own, she'd examined some of the strange architectural and decorative features of the Red Temple yonder. She talked a little about those strange things now.

But right now the most important thing in her own mind was that she, who had been in command of the expedition, had failed to see it through. Trilby felt very guilty about her failure. Especially about leaving Adrian alone at poolside—

"Not your fault, daughter, not your fault. No one had any reason to suspect the kind of attack you both endured. Come now, tell us all you can remember about what happened."

The discussion continued. Meanwhile four troopers had been posted as sentries nearby, while two waited in reserve. And some of Karel's and Trimbak Rao's powers were serving in the same capacity.

Haltingly, still struggling with her emotions, the girl told the listening men how things had gone for her on that terrible day, what she'd experienced when overtaken by Wood's overwhelming assault.

"And then—then while all this foulness still held me in, it seemed like the earth was buckling up under my feet—that was Adrian's elemental, I know now—and all the while, even then, the crazy voices kept soothing me, telling me I needn't worry about any of it.

"I wanted to get away, and I couldn't. I wanted to yell, to scream for help, and then I realized that I couldn't even do that . . ."

Trilby, having finished telling the essentials, began to cry.

Karel kept after her, gently. "And you have no idea, no clue, what happened to Adrian?"

"No, no idea at all. I'm sorry."

"It's not your fault." He patted her gently. Karel could be very convincing, and his assurance seemed to be at least partially accepted.

And shortly thereafter, Trimbak Rao departed with the girl. He was taking her back to his headquarters, where some of her relatives were waiting. He and Karel had made a tentative arrangement to confer later on what magical measures ought to be taken to locate Adrian.

Murat and Kebbi had been listening to all this with Rostov and some of the troopers. Murat, having given his word of honor, was not seriously considering an escape attempt at this time.

Kebbi was a different case.

Rostov spoke. "Well, wizard? I have effectively yielded command to you, but I must persist, it seems, in prodding you to action. Where and how do we commence our search?"

"No satisfactory answer has presented itself so far. I will do my best to find out; stronger measures are going to be required."

The wizard brought out some of the impedimenta of his craft, and got down to business.

He appeared to be surprised at the first results of his divinations. "I had thought we would be directed downstream," he muttered.

"And we are not?"

"No."

"Then where?"

Karel turned his face back toward the Red Temple whose twisted bulk loomed over the little parklike area.

"There?"

"There." Karel sounded rather surprised himself.

Murat had a definite impression that the Twisted Temple, as seen from the perspective of the Emperor's Park, was growing larger and more ominous as time went by. No one else commented on any change, so he supposed that it was only in his imagination.

"I wonder if there's anyone in it now?"

"Alas, that question lacks a simple answer."

Karel, who had heard a thing or two about this particular facility, explained some of its peculiarities to his frowning listeners. This was a very special Red Temple, containing within itself access to the City from the outside. By this means certain preferred customers were brought here (at a premium price, of course) from certain of the Temple's sister establishments around the world.

Here, in a Red Temple enclave within the City of Wizards, the forces of magic could be employed in a certain, relatively economical, way, to augment the effects of pleasures available elsewhere; and, perhaps more importantly, to provide certain pleasures that were nowhere else available at any price. Or so some of the discreet advertising claimed.

Inside those misshapen walls, magic was used, almost routinely, to augment the effects of alcoholic drink and other drugs. To heighten the delights of the gourmet, and the glutton.

"And, naturally, to increase the pleasures of sex as well," Karel said. "In there, inhuman powers are capable of assuming for a time the human form, incubi and succubi more beautiful than any natural human flesh can be."

"It sounds an interesting place," the General commented dryly. "Shall we begin, then?"

16

DAYLIGHT was fading rapidly when Adrian and the two people with him finally came ashore for the night on the first day of their trip downriver from Smim. Sometime before they landed, Marland had begun to complain earnestly to his two companions about how grossly he had been maltreated by the Red Temple. Adrian at least was ready to listen, and to him the man recited many details about how the priests and guards of the pleasure palace had cheated him, and accused him falsely of cheating and of murder.

Adrian thought that Amelia probably had at least equal cause for complaint, but she was not complaining. Her resigned expression indicated that she thought complaining would be useless anyway. She seemed less disposed to seek revenge than to find some peace and quiet for herself. Adrian got the feeling that she really did not care much for Marland, but was putting up with him because he had got her out of prison, and because for the time being no one better was available.

On that first night, the three found shelter—you could hardly call what they did making camp—under a half-fallen and almost completely hollowed log, a snug and really comfortable place to which Adrian felt sure they had been led by the powers of the Sword of Chance. Marland, poking about on shore at dusk, his Sword in hand, had stumbled on the place without surprise. Already he was accepting miraculous good luck as no more than his due, and he had evidently come to trust in the Sword's powers without thinking much about them. Stretched out on the deepest drift of dead leaves available, with the black hilt clutched in one hand and the stained copper scabbard in the other, he was soon snoring.

Amelia, now evidently feeling a need to talk, stayed awake conversing with the weary Adrian for some time.

She asked the boy about his background, and he felt somewhat guilty for making up a fictitious family, a collection of cruel and demented people from whom he hoped to remain separated.

Amelia listened with half an ear. What she was really interested in was the chance to pour out some of her own troubles, which never got a very sympathetic hearing from Marland.

During this conversation the young woman revealed that she'd spent some time in the pay of the Red Temple—she didn't say specifically what her job had been, and Adrian had tact enough to refrain from asking.

It was while she had been working there that Marland—"He didn't call himself that, then"—had got to know her, and she him.

Two meters away, Marland, the copper-scabbarded Sword securely tucked under him, was snoring, dead to the world. Adrian, curious, asked Amelia: "Did he really try to swindle the Temple?"

"Hush!" hushed Amy automatically, with a glance in the direction of her sleeping man. Then, looking cynical and worn, she went on in a whisper: "What does it matter? In this world everyone tries to cheat everyone else anyway. And you know what? We're all sentenced to death already. So why not?"

Perhaps something in Adrian's face as he listened to this philosophy persuaded her not to elaborate on it. "Never mind, kid. Try to get some sleep."

And the truth was that the Prince was beginning to have great difficulty in keeping his eyes open. Remembering his grandfather's praise and encouragement gave him confidence enough to go to sleep.

He passed a comfortable and almost dreamless night. Awakening early in the morning, Adrian, lying still and doing mental calculations, decided that eight days had now passed since he and Trilby had so optimistically entered the City of Wizards. Where was she now?

The Prince's two companions were awake shortly after him. Marland was in a good mood, and allowed his guide to touch Coinspinner's hilt before beginning a hunt for food—although the man, ever cautious in matters concerning his good luck, kept gripping it at the same time. Doubtless the brief touch had some good effect, for Adrian quickly located a large clutch of birds' eggs, which were soon frying on a flat rock set next to the fire. While waiting for the eggs to cook, the three munched on some delicious fruit, just turning ripe, that happened to be growing nearby.

Again Amelia took note of Adrian's fire-starting methods. Taking advantage of a moment when Marland was absent in the woods nearby, she asked the boy straight out: "How'd you make that fire?"

The Prince had been expecting her to get around to direct questioning sooner or later, and had his answer ready. "I have a trick," he admitted openly. "It comes in handy lots of times." A fair number of people in the world had one bit of magic that they could do, some trick they had managed to perfect to the point of real usefulness.

"I bet it does." And Amelia looked thoughtful. Adrian watched to see whether she would pass this information quickly on to Marland. He couldn't be sure; but if she did, the man, to judge by his reaction, was not much interested.

Shortly after breakfast the three resumed their voyage downstream, with Adrian paddling as before. They had been underway for several hours when the Sword once more engineered the extraordinary.

The travelers were in the process of passing the junction of their river with another, slightly smaller, that came in from the direction of some hills. The onrushing tributary was fast and turbulent, even foaming from its rough plunging trip.

It was Amelia who saw the thing first, half buried in the mud, and called out to the others, and pointed. There on shore, in a minor promontory just where the rivers joined, was a squarish object of beautifully carved wood. Adrian paddled closer, beached the canoe, got out into the mud and began to dig in it with his hands.

What came to light was a tightly constructed wooden chest that must have fallen in from some bridge or boat upstream along the tributary.

"Don't open it yet." Sword still in hand, Marland took off his broken prison shoes and waded, grimacing at the mire, to join Adrian. "First let's get it solidly up on shore somewhere."

Between them that was soon accomplished, though the chest was encouragingly weighty. The next task was to get it open. The finely crafted lid was tightly closed, but secured only by a light clasp and lock that soon yielded to Coinspinner's flawless edge and steely weight.

Amelia let out a little cry in the moment after the lid went up. At first glance the chest appeared to be full of clothing, and on the top were women's dresses, all dry and unstained. As the upper contents were removed—Amelia seized them very carefully and spread them out on mud-free gravel—the receptacle proved to contain both men's and women's garments. The former fit Marland well enough for him to wear them, and most of the latter fit Amelia almost perfectly.

Her plaintive cry was for a mirror. And sure enough, that was the next item Marland, now rummaging toward the bottom of the box, managed to turn up.

Now Amelia, carrying an armload of clothes from the chest, dodged quickly into the brush out of sight of the others. There she discarded her hated prison garb, putting on a new yellow dress.

By the time she emerged, carrying a new pair of shoes—she had decided to save them for later—Marland too had changed his clothes. He had also discovered a flask of brandy, and was ready for a minor celebration.

"Well, Mudrat—looks like there's nothing here for you. That's all right, you can walk around bare-assed and nobody minds. For dear Amy and myself here, though, things are different. We're going to have to upgrade our appearance considerably, and this's a good start." Wiping his chin, he offered her a drink, which she accepted, giggling.

When the flask came back to Marland, he generously extended it to Adrian. The boy accepted, but scarcely wet his lips with the fiery stuff. Suddenly a new hope had been born. The man might now drink himself insensible, or at least into a mood where he might let his guide and servant borrow the Sword for some good reason.

But that was not to be.

Marland doubtless had his obsessions and his weaknesses, but drink did not appear to be among them. After taking a second nip himself he put the flask casually away under a thwart. When, a moment later, Amy wanted more, he watched her drink, and sternly ordered her not to take enough to make her balance in the canoe uncertain.

The ransacking of the chest went on, and Adrian was not, after all, denied all benefit from its discovery. The chest also contained some candy, some cakes—not quite as good, the Prince thought while he sampled, as those given him by Talgai—and other useful preserved food. There was even a packet of tea, and a few small pots and dishes. A small amount of money would be less immediately useful.

Marland decreed a small feast of celebration.

At the bottom of the chest they found a large cloth bag, tightly folded, in which most of the useful stuff could be carried aboard the canoe.

As for the chest itself, it was too large and awkward to come along. In the process of converting it to kindling for a fire, Coinspinner ripped open a hitherto unsuspected secret compartment, from which a couple of modestly valuable jewels came tumbling out into the light of day.

Marland grabbed them up, demonstrating more satisfaction than surprise. Now money would be available, at the next sizable town to which they came.

There was one more discovery, either in the secret compartment or a small but unhidden drawer nearby—a pair of dice. They came complete with a little cup of horn, decorated with carvings of a couple of Red Temple deities, in which to shake them before casting.

The bottom of the chest, still intact, was flat and fairly sizable. Marland set it on a flat place on the ground, and sat down suddenly in front of it, with his new dice cup in hand. The sheathed Sword was in his left hand, but the expression on his face was such that Adrian wondered suddenly whether even Coinspinner might have been temporarily forgotten.

That was not the case just yet—the man was careful to keep the Sword and scabbard in contact with his body as he sat.

"Hey," Amelia prodded. "You were in such a hurry to get on downstream?"

"Never mind. We can camp here tonight."

"Camp? In what?" She looked up at the open, partly cloudy sky.

She got no answer. Not the jewels, not the drink, not even his woman in her new dress had aroused quite the same interest in Marland's eyes as was evoked by the two little ivory cubes. While Amelia quietly retrieved the flask from the canoe and helped herself to another swig of brandy, he picked up the two dice and nursed them tenderly for a while in his fist. Then with a minor flourish he cast them out on his improvised tabletop. He scooped them up and threw them again and again, sometimes using the cup and sometimes not. His whole attention was concentrated on the results.

The Sword was now lying at Marland's feet, just barely out of contact with his body. Adrian watched both Sword and man with an almost equally concentrated attention.

He jumped when the man said suddenly: "C'mere, Mudrat. Forget about whatever it is you're doing. I want to teach you something about shooting dice."

Amelia, vaguely disapproving, and at the same time somewhat amused and interested, had settled herself on a nearby log, and was nibbling candy and looking on.

Digging into his newly acquired small hoard of petty cash, carried in one of his new pockets, the man dealt out ten small coins in front of Adrian, and set out an equal number before himself.

"Here's ten for you, boy, ten for me. Whoever loses all his coins first has to clean up the camp. Ever play dice?"

"No, sir." That wasn't exactly true, but true enough; certainly the Prince had never played in the way that this man seemed to mean.

Marland proceeded to teach the boy the rules. Actually the Prince already knew, in a hazy fashion, the game or a very similar version; but he allowed himself to be taught.

"Wait. Before we start, let me fix something." Among the men's clothes in the bountiful chest had been a couple of thin leather belts. Doing a little crude leatherwork with Coinspinner, Marland soon had these worked into a kind of harness. Presently Coinspinner's hilt, with the symbolic white dice barely visible, was peeking over the man's shoulder. Adrian glanced at it in private despair as he picked up the dice for his first turn.

It was going to be hopelessly difficult for anyone but the wearer to grab at the Sword while it rode in that position.

The Princeling threw the dice. Then Marland picked them up and threw them. Naturally enough, Adrian lost.

During the first few turns of the entirely one-sided game, the man's eyes gleamed, as if with the commencement of fever, each time he won a coin. But long before ten turns had passed, well before Adrian's row of coins was entirely gone, Marland's expression had changed. He was beginning to frown.

Adrian still had three coins in front of him when the man broke off the game in a surly fashion, and swept up all the money indiscriminately to stuff it back into his pocket.

Noting Marland's expression—anger, though fortunately not directed at him—Adrian got up without comment and busied himself with some makework tasks around the fire.

Amelia meanwhile went to her man, putting her hands on his shoulders, studying his face, trying to discover what his problem was.

She hadn't long to wait. Standing now, he smiled ruefully and reached back over his left shoulder to pat the black hilt. "As long as I wear this, I win. I can feel it now, I'm sure of it. As long as I have this with me, I'm going to win. On every turn."

"Is that so bad?"

He gave her a look that said she didn't understand. "Bad? It's—" But at that point he broke off, frowning, as if unable to explain his own feelings or even understand them. At last he said: "It isn't gambling anymore. It's like—picking up money in the street. It's good to have, but there's no kick. You ought to know what I mean."

Amelia said nothing. Watching her face, Adrian thought she was tired of listening to this man, but she kept at it.

"Of course, if I were to take this thing into a real casino . . . one of the big ones . . ." Marland brightened as this thought occurred to him, but again fell silent.

"What are you thinking of doing, Buve?" Amelia sounded worried.

If he noticed the name by which she'd called him, he disregarded it. "What am I thinking? I'm thinking that this Sword is big magic. Really big. If it could get me out of that jail the way it did . . . I'm thinking that it's bigger than anything the Red Temple can put up against it. Any Red Temple."

Now his lady friend was really growing alarmed. "Buve, what are you planning now? What are you going to get us mixed up in? Remember what happened the last time."

"That's what I remember. I remember it all too well. I want to see that those bastards remember it too." He showed his teeth in a kind of smile, and patted her arm. "Last time we didn't have the gods on our side."

But the plan, whatever it was, was put aside for the time being, withdrawn from discussion, while Marland apparently tried to perfect it in his own mind.

For sheer compulsive amusement, to have some simple fun gambling with Adrian, the man now disarmed himself temporarily. He trusted Amelia to sit close beside him, her weight on the sheathed Sword, while he and Adrian played at dice.

This time, after fickle fortune had reversed herself several times, Adrian eventually won all the small coins. The boy had not tried to cheat with magic. Used fairly, the dice had finally favored the Prince, while Marland went through several stages of emotion.

Whatever force drove Marland into this game was not satisfied until he'd lost his whole allotment of ten coins, and was tempted to dig into his pocket for more.

He drew on his capital for ten more, and ten more after those. At that point his luck finally turned and he won all of the coins back. Before that happened, Adrian was beginning to consider magical manipulation of the dice to force a win for Marland and restore him to a good temper.

The evening around the fire was drawing to a close when there came a snuffling and a rustling in the undergrowth nearby. Two greenish eyes set wide apart reflected flame, and Marland grabbed for his Sword.

After one or two preliminary howls issued out of the encircling darkness, causing Marland to jump up, a huge gray beast came bounding into the firelight to greet Adrian extravagantly. It was the great dog the Emperor had called Draffut.

Adrian, trying to fend off the creature's demonstrations, and shield it from the Sword at the same time, at last managed to explain.

Marland sheathed his Sword again. "That beast isn't going to ride in the canoe with us!"

"No, sir, he sure wouldn't fit there. He can run along on shore, and keep up."

"Well, as long as he keeps his distance most of the time." The man considered. "Actually a beast like that might help me play the part."

"What part?" asked Amelia, plainly mystified.

"That of a man who's wealthy enough to keep a giant pet. Among other extravagances."

"Then he can come with us? I promise he won't be any trouble."

"We'll see." Marland frowned. "Has he got a name?"

Adrian, with some thought in mind for the Emperor's prediliction for the truth, blurted out what he had been told: "Draffut."

Marland, appreciative of irreverence, got a good laugh out of that.

"From here on, kid," said Marland, next day, as they were pulling up to the docks of another town, "we're not going to need the canoe any longer. Don't worry, I'll pay you for it." It was never really money that concerned this man. "You're still coming with us, though. I'm going to have a job for you."

Draffut had disappeared, somewhere on shore. He had a tendency to do this, and Adrian felt reasonably confident that he was going to come back.

And he wasn't really worried about losing the canoe, either, though it was his grandfather's. Adrian expected that Grandfather could get it back if and when he really wanted it. With some vague idea, perhaps, of making such a recovery easier, the boy neglected to tie up the craft when they had got everything out of it. And there it went, riding the current on its own, turning freely with the breeze.

Having entered a sizable town, the three now began the process of rejoining civilization.

Looking for the best place to change his modest find of jewels to ready cash, Marland paced along the main street. Trivial incidents—a woman passing with a basket of laundry on her head, a baby crawling away from its mother—occurred to block him from the doorways of the first two stores he would have entered, but when he paused near the entrance of a third, a burdened loadbeast crowded him from behind, effectively nudging him inside.

Amelia and Adrian waited in the street. In what seemed like only a short time the man came out, smiling at them and jiggling a stack of coins in his fingers. "Just what the jeweler was looking for," he informed them. "It seems he's trying to construct a fancy brooch, and those little pebbles will just fit. How about something to eat?"

Having purchased sausages and pancakes from a street vendor, they stood on a corner munching.

"The more good things happen to us," said Marland, looking at Amelia, "the more afraid you look."

"I am afraid."

He snorted something, and took another bite of sausage. "You afraid, Mudrat?"

Adrian wasn't required to answer. Amelia was trying her best to argue with her man. "Look, Buve, we've got a good thing going now. A great thing. We've got some money, and—"

"*Some* money. Yeah. Hah!"

"You want more? We can get more, without—sticking our necks out again. We can go anywhere we want—"

"It's not enough. Not after what those bastards did to me—and to you—and what they almost did. I can go anywhere I want, all right, and I know where I want to go. I'm going to take it out on them."

Adrian watched as Amelia turned away. She was muttering something and he thought it might be prayers. Or maybe it was curses, or most likely some of each. She probably realized, thought the Prince, that her chances of talking Marland out of a scheme, once he'd made up his mind to it, were practically zero.

When they had finished their lunch, Marland walked ahead, strolling the street, doubtless trying to plan just what he ought to do next. Amelia and Adrian followed. They had the opportunity for another private talk, in which Amelia spelled out her fears in greater detail.

"Cham," she suggested suddenly, "your canoe's gone—he didn't pay you for that yet, did he?"

"No, ma'am."

"He will—he's not a tightwad. Where's your dog?"

"Around somewhere. He'll show up."

"Good. When he does, you might take your money and your dog and get on out of town. There's safer people than us for you to hang around with."

Adrian, wondering what to say, said nothing.

In a moment the woman continued: "Marland thinks you're lucky for him, and no gambler ever has enough luck. But whatever happens is not going to be lucky for you, kid. Or for me either. I can feel it."

"You're not running away."

"Me? No. He'd come after me, and with that lucky charm of his he'd find me. Besides, I—I had my chance a long time ago, and I didn't take it then." She seemed to feel trapped, compelled, in a way that young Adrian couldn't understand. It was foreign to his whole way of thinking.

"But you can go, sonny. He won't care about losing you that much. It'll be easy for him to recruit another helper if he thinks he needs one."

The Prince could not help feeling tempted. The overall geography was now definite enough in his mind that he felt fairly confident of being able to find his way home from here; he would have a little money, and of course his skills. But he interpreted what his grandfather had said to him as encouragement in his course of pursuing Coinspinner, though it had included a warning to be careful while he did so. And the Emperor trusted him, believed that he would be able to get the Sword, or at least do a good job of trying.

So the Prince was not going to turn his back on the Sword. Not now. "I guess I'll stick around for a while yet."

Amelia stared at him. The way she looked made him believe that she could be really nasty if she wanted to. "What do you think you're going to get out of it? Do you think he's really going to make you rich? He doesn't care about that, not really. He's going to get all three of us killed, most likely."

"I'm staying. Marland's got a lot of luck on his side."

Amelia looked at him now as if she wondered who he really was. "All right, all right. Don't say I didn't warn you."

Adrian certainly would never be able to say that. And despite his brave words and his decision he was worried. Sometimes he had definite magical indications that Wood was coming after him again.

On their first night under a roof, in the first cheap suburban inn they came to, Adrian saw Marland sleeping with the sheathed Sword pinned beneath his head and body, making a hard pillow, no doubt, but the only one that could give this man rest.

Once more the Prince, for a moment at least, contemplated trying to grab the Sword away. Grab for the black hilt, tug it from the sheath. The trick seemed safe, and almost easy. But always, knowing the Sword's power, Adrian held back. And in fact, when he looked closer, he saw that Marland had tied the hilt to the sheath with a thread or thong.

No, Adrian thought, the only way to get Coinspinner away from its owner was to have him give it freely. Of course in this case the chance of that happening was just no chance at all. Then why was he, Adrian, hanging around? Because, he supposed, he was too stubborn to give up.

As they hiked between towns next day, the gambler was ready to take his two confederates into his confidence regarding his plan to gain revenge on the Red Temple. Marland was going to have to tell both of them the plan in some detail, because he was going to need the help of both in carrying the plan out.

"The trouble is," said Marland, "that Coinspinner here is never going to let me lose. Not ever. Not even once."

"A lot of people," said Amy, "would like to have that kind of trouble."

"Shut up for a minute and let me finish. You see, the problem, my friends, is that the people who run the big casino are not idiots. They're—"

"The big casino." Amy stopped for a moment in the middle of the road. *Did you say the big casino?*

"Yes, my lady. Yes, my dearest. That's just what I said."

"O gods, I was afraid that's what you had in mind. What are they going to do when they see you come back?"

He put an arm around her shoulders and pulled her forward, set her walking down the road again. "They're not going to see me come back, my love. Because I don't want them to see me, and I'm very lucky now —haven't you noticed? Or if they do see me, they won't know me. I've lost weight since they've seen me last—a lot of weight. Plus, I have this new beard." He stroked it. Adrian thought it was looking somehow thicker and healthier in just the few days since Marland had started to become prosperous.

"They won't let you carry a weapon up to the gaming tables—will they?"

"You know something, Amy? I'm not going to ask their permission— now will you let me finish? They're not idiots, as I was starting to say, and if they find themselves up against a gambler who never loses, they're just going to close down the game, if necessary, until they find out what's wrong. And they're going to do that long before their bank is broken."

Amelia looked helpless. It was Adrian who had to ask the question: "So what are we going to do?"

The man flashed him a keen look, welcoming his eagerness. "I," said Marland, "am going to stay in the background, with the Sword. In the gaming room I'm thinking of—it's a very big room—there are little balconies, like box seats in a fancy theater, with curtains and all. I'm going to be holed up in one of those. You"—he pointed at Amelia— "are going to be bellied up to the table, a wealthy, bored lady, placing bets. And you, Mudrat"—the finger swung to Adrian—"are going to carry numbers from me to Amy. Carry them quickly and remember them carefully, without any mistakes. The numbers that I want her to bet on."

Marland paused, frowning at Adrian as they walked side by side. "We're going to have to find you a new name, Mudrat." He scowled at the boy critically, as if Adrian should have known better than to adopt a stupid name like that, or should at least stop clinging to it so stubbornly now that times were better.

"Yes, sir," said Adrian. "My name is really Cham. I think I mentioned that once before."

"All right, that'll do. Cham. Obviously we're going to have to get you some clothes, even fancy clothes, because you're going to be a page. Know what a page does? Never mind, you learn fast. We're going into the big time, kid. Maybe you'll need more than one outfit, because I don't know if we're going to be able to do all this winning in one session at the table . . . it would be better if we could."

"How much," asked Adrian, newly emboldened by being made a formal member of the enterprise, "are we going to gamble?"

Again Marland looked at him, welcoming an eager conspirator. "As much as it takes. We're going to beat them, gambling. Walk out of that place with a ton of their money—and make it look like the fairest and most honest game you ever saw. Cheating? Not us. No way. We're just lucky today." He dropped his voice, now sounding almost reverent. "It could happen that way, you know. It could happen that way, for someone, without any magic at all. All it would take would be a run of luck."

Amelia challenged him. "A run of luck like the world has never seen before!"

Marland turned to regard her, assessing the point judiciously. "No, not quite. Maybe once every hundred years, or every thousand, in the course of nature, a run of luck like this will come along. And we're going to make our run look as natural as can be."

Adrian, listening carefully, was becoming ever more intrigued with the challenge of doing such a thing and getting away with it.

The gambler was now explaining eagerly. "But we won't need a straight run. See, Amy, I'm only going to call about half the bets. The rest will be your choices, made at the table. Some will be good and some bad, just the way it works for every other player. Some of your own bets you'll win, and some you'll lose. But *all* the numbers that I pick, with the Sword, are going to be winners. Overall, our winnings are going to build up and up—and then fall back, sometimes, when you pick a loser. Sometimes we'll even lose huge amounts. So it's going to look like nothing but pure dumb, honest luck. We'll lead the house on and on, into a final wager—I don't know yet how much that'll be, I'll have to do some calculating. Think that out some more before we start. But it'll be enough to break their bank."

There was a pause of several heartbeats before Amy's voice asked, on a rising intonation: "Break the bank at the big casino?" The idea was finally getting through to her.

"That's what I'm saying."

"Won't they have their own magicians working?" Adrian, for the sake of credibility, thought he had better voice more skepticism than he felt; he had more acquaintance with the power of the Swords than Marland did.

Marland said: "Oh, they have wizards on their payroll, all right. They have some of the best in the world in their own specialty, which is anything to do with cheating at a game. But the Sword will handle them. I'll bet my life on it. Coinspinner'll slice them up like so much paper, and leave 'em standing there with their pockets empty."

Amelia, struck by a sudden thought, was fingering her new dress. It was certainly a long step up from prison garb, but still—

She demanded: "They're going to let me stand there in the big casino, at this high-powered table, and play, looking like this?"

Marland laughed. "You're not going to be looking like that, baby. Not at all. Not by the time we get to the big casino."

17

THE Crown Prince Murat, physically unbound but still manacled by leaden magic in both feet, was following Karel, as the old Tasavaltan wizard led the entire party in a lengthy inspection of the exterior of the twisted Red Temple. By reason of sortilege Karel was convinced that the most likely way to finding Prince Adrian lay here. At one point the wizard paused in his examination, to point out to the General some ceramic tiles on the side of the building, tiles Karel said were similar to those the apprentices had been sent here to obtain.

Murat was willing enough to follow the two Tasavaltan leaders, meanwhile exchanging a few desultory snarls with Cousin Kebbi. Both Culmians could not help being distracted from their feud by the sight of a multiplex sunrise/sunset. This, as Karel informed them, and Murat could well believe, was a phenomenon that could be seen only in the City of Wizards. Perhaps a dozen sun images were visible at the same time. About half of these, red and only mildly warm, were arcing slowly down toward the rim of the sky, even as the other half threatened to rise above it. All finally blended into one red glow that spread its way entirely around the horizon.

There was a mutter of satisfaction at last from Karel. But it was not caused by the celestial phenomenon, to which he had been paying little attention. "This is the way we must go in," he announced decisively, indicating one of the many dark entrances to the Red Temple.

Rostov accepted the decision, and issued the necessary orders to his handful of armed men. The General was now wearing Sightblinder once again, its hilt coming frequently in contact with his hand or arm, and his identity tended to shimmer in the eyes of his companions.

The wizard led the way. Two troopers were left outside to hold the animals. Soon all other members of the party had filed inside the Temple, and the sky and its wonders had been shut out.

But hardly had they got themselves out of sight of the entrance when the wizard called a halt.

Beside him he beheld the General's figure, going through the kalei-doscope of changes customary for one who held Sightblinder. Karel, for all his own powers, was as much subject as anyone else to the spell of images cast by the Sword of Stealth. The figures now appearing in his perception, one after another, included some from his far-distant child-hood, as well as the eidolons of Ardneh and of Draffut. The latter appeared crawling through the dark passage, under a ceiling much too low for the god's full six-meter height, displaying Draffut's unmistak-able mighty fangs, great manlike hands, and look of serene intelligence.

In addition to these figures, the cycle seen by the old magician some-times included the dread image of Wood, appearing now as a blond, handsome demigod, armed with Shieldbreaker.

I had not realized, thought Karel, *that I feared my great enemy as much as that, for the Sword of Stealth to limn him for me . . .* But he had not stopped to admire the images created by Sightblinder. He suddenly did not feel well. That was why he had come to a halt, leaning back against a wall, knowing that he must look uncharacteristically weary.

And now he understood why.

"Rostov," he said. "Get those two other men in here. The animals also."

The General gestured quickly to his sergeant before he asked the question. "What's wrong?"

"Plenty." Karel's breath was wheezing loudly now. "There's demon-smell and demon-sickness in the air. You'll be able to feel it in a min-ute. Wood is striking at us."

Murat and Kebbi exchanged uncertain glances.

"I mean the man," said Karel, looking at the renegade lieutenant, "who took your Sword from you. He goes armed with a greater weapon, Shieldbreaker. And he comes now escorted by a flight of his great pets. It will be all we can do to escape him with our lives."

The soldiers who had been left outside came into the Temple now, leading the riding-beasts.

Rostov, cursing, threw Sightblinder from him, in that instant resum-ing his own shape in the others' eyes. "If he has Shieldbreaker, this blade of mine is not going to avail us anything. But we know how to fight against the Sword of Force. What do you say, Karel? I'll tackle him barehanded, magician, if you can undertake to keep his bodyguard from killing me as I do so."

Karel shook his head. "I fear his bodyguard, as you call it, is much too strong. He is coming after us in force, with such an escort as would make any pledge of that kind on my part foolish. If worst comes to worst we may have to adopt some such plan, but before we settle for suicide let's try to get away. I hope we can make our escape in a direction that will allow us to continue our search for the Prince."

Murat was beginning to feel the demon-sickness now, deep in his guts. He'd heard of such but not experienced it before. He could tell from the faces of Kebbi and the soldiers that they were afflicted too.

"I think we can escape, but we may well be separated in the process. Before we are—" Karel dipped a hand into an inner pocket, then pushed himself away from the wall. Moving swiftly among the other members of the party, he handed each man a small object. "Each of you is now in possession of a magical token that will allow you to identify Prince Adrian if you come within sight of him. It should also serve to show you where to seek the Prince, once you are close enough."

Murat looked at the thing that had been placed in his hand. It was a tiny wooden cube.

Karel observed his puzzled look. "Part of a toy the Prince enjoyed in infancy," the wizard wheezed. "Trust me, trust the power I have given it."

Murat could feel the heaviness in his soles and ankles. He did not doubt this wizard's pledges.

Rostov stuffed his own bit of toy impatiently into his belt. He was not yet ready to give up on fighting. "What if we leave the Swords out of it entirely, wizard? And if the demons could be distracted. Could you stand against him then?"

"Stand against him, one on one? No, I cannot." Karel's face and voice were bleak. "No magician in the world, I think, can do that . . . and besides, I tell you that he does come with a host of demons. We must escape him, if we can. Here."

With a gesture, and a twist of magic, Karel did something to the wall beside him. Murat could not see just what, but whatever was done caused several stones to vanish, or move aside, opening a way into some inner recess of the Temple.

"Animals can't follow us in here, sir," the sergeant reported. Even if the newly opened entrance had been big enough, the dark passage beyond it certainly was not.

"Then leave them! Too bad, but it must be."

In a few moments the men were all inside what Murat took to be a kind of secret passage, a dimly lit narrow tunnel through constricting brickwork. They were following Karel through this, at a surprisingly swift pace, when the assault of Wood's creatures came down on them all, almost unexpectedly.

This was no mere whiff of demonic presence at a distance, but the awful thing itself. The attack fell first upon the mind and soul, rather than the body. Despite the fact that the physical masonry around him remained firmly in place, Murat had the sensation that the world was collapsing over his head.

Even worse was the inward sickness, taking possession of the bowels and bones. A fear that seemed to turn the guts to jelly . . .

The men were crawling now, rather than walking, with Karel still in the lead. The magician was muttering continuously, and it seemed that somehow he was managing to stave off complete disaster. The terrible enemy was near, but not immediately upon them.

And now the pressure of demonic presence eased a bit. Somehow, Murat thought, the old man's got them looking in the wrong place for us. So far . . .

He kept on crawling, over the body of one of the troopers, totally collapsed. The man was dead, Murat was sure of that, for he could see the flesh already shriveling, as if being dried out from within.

Another trooper died as they crawled on. Wood's onslaught came near overwhelming Karel's defenses before the Tasavaltan could guide his friends to a yet more interior level of the Twisted Temple.

When the attack of the demons first fell on them, Kebbi, two places behind his countryman in the single line, thought that his last moment had come. But in his desperation he refused to give up. Rather, Kebbi took the opportunity which presented itself, and lunged out in an effort at escape. When the wizard led them past a place where the tunnel branched, Kebbi with a gasp turned aside, and flung himself down the branch Karel and the others had not followed.

Crawling farther, he realized with a sudden surge of hope that the bond of magic that Karel had put on him had somehow been broken. The pain he had known in legs and ankles, which had increased so rapidly whenever he had distanced himself even slightly from his captors, was gone now. Karel's binding work had been dissolved, or else abandoned in the wizard's need to channel all his powers into the giants' conflict that now raged between him and Wood. The energy that had maintained the Culmians' bondage was doubtless needed elsewhere now, as the great magician fought against a greater, for his life, and the lives of his companions.

Crawling and scrambling, realizing that the physical destruction around him was actually negligible, and that the demons' attention must all be focused elsewhere, Murat's cousin got away.

Murat, as soon as he became aware that Kebbi was no longer with the survivors of the party, started grimly back into the tunnel after him. Karel, Rostov, and the troopers had all collapsed, and no one tried to stop him. If the traitor should be lying somewhere, dead and shriveled, well and good. But if he had somehow got away . . .

The Crown Prince had not gone far before he too realized that he was now freed of Karel's magical bondage.

Sensing that he was gradually leaving the battle between the demons and the magician farther and farther behind him, Kebbi kept on crawling until he saw a light.

Rostov was the first of the remaining members of the party to regain his senses. Finding himself stretched out in a small, almost lightless underground room, Sightblinder clutched in his fist, he cursed and forced himself to his feet. There was one doorway besides the one through which they had stumbled in.

Karel and the four remaining troopers were sprawled around him, all still breathing, but in various stages bordering on complete collapse. The General tried to rouse the wizard, but the old man remained practically inert; naturally the assault had fallen heaviest of all on him.

It was only at this point that Rostov realized that his two Culmian prisoners were gone.

The prostrate men seemed to be recovering, though very slowly, and none of them were able to stand unaided yet. There was nothing for the General to do but exercise patience, and in that art he had had long training. The demons were gone, and in half an hour, Rostov thought, his party might be able to get moving again.

Then came an all-too-familiar twisting in his gut, alerting him that the demons were coming back.

He could even tell the direction now. That way, through the other tunnel.

Gripping Sightblinder and setting his jaw, the General waited for his foes to show themselves.

Kebbi, pushing on alone toward the light, knew such gratitude as he was capable of when he felt the presence of the demons fall farther and farther behind him.

At about the time that presence vanished from his perception entirely, he found himself dimly able to sense some kind of threshold of magic not far ahead. He could hope, at least, that this would offer him a way of emerging from the City.

Proceeding carefully, now standing erect, he became aware of strange presences around him at varying distances. Not that they frightened him, particularly; after the demons, these ghostly half shapes were as nothing.

One moment those distant figures were insubstantial ghosts, and the next they were real forms, mundane and solid humanity.

But who?

Kebbi flattened himself against a wall in fear. As the folk approached, a dim and bulky shape came with them, and strange noises issued from it. A horrible squeaking. He had heard that demons' voices sounded like—

He could see the people clearly now. Four of them, two men, two women, in shabby garments, and they were armed with mops and brooms. The noise proceeded from the wheels of the refuse cart they pushed before them.

After that, Kebbi had little further trouble in getting out of the Temple—though on doing so he was somewhat amazed to find himself emerging from the basement door of a Red Temple quite different from the one that he had entered in the City. He was definitely not in the City of Wizards anymore.

He was certainly in some city, though. A warm and muggy place, large and heavily populated. He could see palm trees. Wherever this was, he was free.

The wizard had somehow struggled to his feet, but that was the most he could manage, and he was threatening to fall again. Supporting Karel with one arm, and with his soldiers, none more than half-conscious, huddling close to him, General Rostov waved Sightblinder at a veritable horde of hideous demonic creatures. They had come pouring in through the tunnel entrance like so many semitransparent puffs of steam or smoke. In the boldest voice that he could manage, he roared at them all to go to hell. In terms usually reserved for blundering colonels, he directed them to get their miserable, spavined, worthless carcasses out of his way, before he decided to unleash his wrath upon them.

There might have been a dozen or a score of the foul things before him, and all recoiled abjectly from his wrath. They seemed to be on the point of retreating.

From the way they were cowering now, and abasing themselves before him, Rostov was suddenly sure that they were convinced he was Wood himself.

The presence, just here and now, of their mighty human master sorely puzzled these foul creatures, and some of them raised hideous bone-rattle voices in an attempt to justify their presence; but none of them were about to dare to argue with the man they were convinced was Wood.

In another moment they were gone. And none too soon. The General, gasping, drenched with cold sweat, sank to the floor and for the first time in forty years allowed himself the luxury of nearly fainting.

Murat lost his quarry in a maze of crawling passages, but like his quarry he eventually managed to achieve his freedom. Unknown to the Crown Prince, his experiences in finding his way out were very similar to those of Kebbi. Murat, too, emerged from a different Red Temple than the one he had so hurriedly entered.

One difference in the experience of the two men was that Murat immediately knew where he was when he came out. In his early youth he had several times visited the city of Bihari.

Within an hour after the demons had been routed, Rostov, Karel, and their surviving troopers were all more or less recovered from the encounter, at least sufficiently to travel. The wizard now resumed his role of guide, and led the party on.

Long before they found their way out of the Temple, the Tasavaltans realized that they had somehow passed into a different building from the one that they had entered in the City.

For the time being at least, Wood's force of demons had been dispersed, or had lost the scent, or were reorganizing. Against the more common difficulties and snares that one Temple or another might present to a traveler in its protected regions, Karel's own powers were more than adequate protection. He could defend his several companions too.

The searchers found to their chagrin that the trail of Prince Adrian had long since disappeared, or else it had been wiped out in the most recent skirmish. Karel doubted whether even Wood would be able to track the lad this way, if this was indeed the way the Prince had come.

Either Adrian had come this way, or more likely gone boating downstream from the Emperor's Park . . . at some point on this difficult journey, the wizard realized that even if he and his companions failed to locate the Prince here, they might well be on the fastest possible track for a return to Tasavalta.

18

This was the second small suburb of Bihari that Adrian, Marland, and Amelia had entered. Walking down the first street they came to in the town, Marland made another happy discovery.

He was moving, as usual, a step or two ahead of his companions when he suddenly bent down with a little grunt of satisfaction. A moment later he had picked up a small purse that someone had dropped in the street. The color of the fine leather nearly matched that of the trodden earth, and however long the purse might have lain there, he was evidently the first to notice it.

After a reflexive look around to make sure that no one had taken any notice of his discovery, the man drew his two companions aside, under an overhanging roof, where he looked into the purse. It was just starting to rain, and the few people hurrying past on the wooden sidewalk nearby paid them no attention.

Abruptly the purse was empty, and Adrian could hear the coins jingling in Marland's quick hands, though the transition had been so neatly swift that the boy never did really see anything of them.

"Well," the man said, satisfied, not at all surprised, when his quick hidden count had been completed. "Plenty. For the time being, at least. I think I'm going to be Sir Marland from now on. A knight or baronet, from . . . well, I'll decide later where I'm from. Probably no one's going to worry about that, as long as they can see my money."

Rubbing his chin thoughtfully, he looked at Amelia. "You, of course, will be my mistress. And—"

She brushed irritably at a small stream that was trickling on her from the roof's edge, and shifted her position to avoid it. "Oh. And not your wife?"

Warned perhaps by something in Amelia's tone, Marland hesitated. Then he brightened, as if struck by a new thought. "Well, why not? It would add a touch of dull respectability to my character, and that's all to the good. All right, you'll be my wife."

He switched his gaze to Adrian. "And you, muddy one, I can't say I want to claim you as my son. Besides, as people of status we ought to have a servant. You'll be my page."

Adrian nodded agreeably. It made no difference to him. He could only hope in passing that the true owner of the purse was not going to be destroyed by its loss. The little leather bag looked to be of the finest quality, so he doubted that that would be the case.

Marland's next move was to locate a clothing shop, where he and Amelia each purchased a new outfit of somewhat better quality than the clothing they had taken from the chest. That had been a vast improvement to begin with, but the garments were now showing the effects of several days of river travel. Adrian too was at last upgraded from his loincloth to a fairly shabby but hole-free jacket and trousers, in keeping with his newly official status as a respectable servant.

After that, all three enjoyed a good meal, sitting down, though Adrian had to eat in the rear of the food shop. Having observed the behavior of a good many servants in his time, the Prince had little trouble in playing the role successfully.

On emerging from the shop's kitchen, Adrian passed a kind of notice board, contrived from the tall stump of a large tree. Among other signs tacked to the wood he saw a poster advertising a reward for a runaway twelve-year-old boy whose description matched his own appearance as it had been back in the City of Wizards.

He wasn't familiar with the amount of reward usually offered in such cases, but this one seemed unusually generous. The agency offering the reward was located in Bihari, and its name meant nothing to the Prince.

Coincidence? He doubted it. Word of his disappearance had preceded him here. Winged messengers must have been used. Had his friends or family caused the notice to be posted, or was it more of the work of Wood?

Certainly he dared not respond. Turning away from the poster thoughtfully, the Prince decided that his cover as Sir Marland's page was going to be helpful to him, and perhaps even important.

Besides, Marland had said: "I need you in my plans." And this offered Adrian enough hope of getting at the Sword to keep him keen on hanging around.

Were other such posters about, and were Marland or Amy going to see them? Even if they did, they might not connect them with their servant. But on the other hand they might.

With everyone well fed for the moment, and with Sir Marland and his new wife now rather more than just decently outfitted, in clothes that indicated at least a moderate degree of prosperity and status, and with a servant to accompany them, it was now time to seek out suitable lodging.

For their first night in this town, Marland selected a modest inn, no better than was necessary for a man of his obvious affluence. He engaged two rooms, so Adrian had a small one to himself. This was the first time he'd slept in a bed in what seemed like months, though it was really not that long.

Draffut still had not returned, and Adrian, with mixed feelings, had about given the creature up for lost.

Next day, the three traveled on by wagon-coach, on into the big resort city itself. Adrian rode in the rear, with the baggage. He was impressed by the city's size and complexity, though not so much impressed as he allowed Amelia and Buvrai to believe.

The metropolis of Bihari boasted a number of expensive inns, some large and some small, and many of them within easy walking distance of the city's huge, magnificent, and very famous Red Temple.

The Red Temple offered its own inn for guests; accommodations more luxurious than most of the others, probably more so than any of them.

But Marland rejected that choice out of hand. He wanted to be less liable to Red Temple scrutiny once the real fun started.

As he was about to begin the process of selecting one of the other hostelries for himself and his small entourage, he suddenly announced that soon, perhaps immediately, he ought to hire a bodyguard or two. Adrian supposed his decision had been brought on by a recent hue and cry after a robber in the streets.

"Not that I really need a bodyguard," he confided to Amelia, patting his Swordhilt. In the privacy of his room, using some expensive pigment, he had whitened that black hilt to something like ivory, in an effort to add to the disguising effect of the oversized scabbard. "Not with the help I've got here. But if people size me up as wealthy, which I want them to do, then it might look strange if I travel with no such protection."

Amelia sighed. "If you're really going through with this, then we must try to do it properly. Anyway, it won't hurt to have an armed man or two on our side. We could try one of the agencies," she suggested.

The man shook his head, and rubbed his Swordhilt, as if that might help him think. "I don't know. They're likely to have Temple connections. Maybe I'd better think about it for a while."

* * *

The former Lieutenant Kebbi had by now melded himself with some success into the city of resorts. Pawning a ring that he had managed to conceal from his uncouth captors at the mountain inn, he provided himself with coin sufficient to obtain cheap food and shelter for a time.

Alone in the cubicle he occupied in a lodging house, Kebbi took out the token Karel had given him, and looked at it.

Since his arrival in Bihari, he had occasionally been able to feel the little piece of wood tugging at the pocket in which he carried it. And now, when he took it out and held it in his palm, it tended to slide off in one direction. He had to tilt the flat plane of his hand up on that side to keep the fragmentary toy from falling to the floor.

The missing Prince Adrian must be here, then, and not very far away.

Kebbi no longer had a chance of getting his hands on a Sword, it seemed. But he might, he thought, be in reach of something just as valuable.

Thrusting into his belt the cheap dagger he'd acquired with almost his last coin, he started out to search for the missing Prince.

Murat had no ring to pawn in the big city, and certainly no Sword of Chance, but fortune had smiled upon him anyway. He had an old friend in Bihari, a lady—some would not have called her that—he'd known two or three years ago. Daring to call upon her, even in his disheveled condition, he had the great good luck to find her home and ready to receive him. Often nobility of rank did confer advantages.

Rising from her lounge on the terrace, she surveyed him with an expression of frank dismay. "Aphrodite and Bacchus, Murat, but where have you been?"

He made a rueful little bow. "Busy with military matters."

"At least you have survived them. And does your wife—do your people know you're here?"

"Countess, it's a long story. I shall be pleased to tell it to you one day —if after thinking things over you decide you really wish to hear it. Meanwhile, if you could advance me some money, I will be eternally grateful."

It was on the tip of his tongue to ask whether he could borrow a weapon or two from her household also. But once he had some money he could buy what he needed along that line.

Murat was also aware that the token given him by Karel was leading him to Adrian.

* * *

Kebbi, hanging around in the street outside one of Bihari's more elegant inns, was required to wait only a couple of hours before he was able to identify Prince Adrian, dressed as a pageboy in the service of a couple Kebbi had never seen before. He had no idea who they might be; certainly they did not look particularly Tasavaltan. Kebbi did not know what the Prince looked like, but if he trusted Karel's token there was no ambiguity about the boy's identity. The little wooden block almost jumped out of Kebbi's pocket when the youngster passed him.

Murat, with a substantial supply of money to help him, was content to observe matters from the middle distance. Once he'd located the inn where Prince Adrian was staying—in the guise of a servant, of all things—Murat rented a room there himself.

The young Prince's masquerade was so unlikely, although apparently voluntary, that Murat decided he had better make sure just what was going on before he attempted to interfere, and restore the heir to the Tasavaltan throne to the arms of his grateful mother.

The process of selecting a bodyguard had been concluded much faster than either Adrian or Amelia had expected—no doubt Marland's Sword had given him a hint that the young redhead calling himself Elgar was the right man for the job, though he hardly looked formidable enough to deter a robber.

That task concluded quickly, Amelia decided that she merited, deserved, needed, and wanted at least one maid.

Marland, thinking the matter over, admitted that the presence of a maid would add more realism to his character of a wealthy knight. But at the same time, the gambler said he was reluctant to acquire more servants who were not in on his plot to swindle the casino; and he was extremely reluctant to let anyone else in on it.

Amelia, getting into the spirit of things in her own way, complained: "It'll look strange if I don't have a maid, if we're supposed to be so rich. You said you didn't want to attract attention."

"That's true. But how're we going to keep her from finding out what we're up to?"

"We just won't talk about it when she's around.

"Buve, do you love me?"

"You know I do. I got you out of that hole, didn't I?"

But despite Amelia's pleas, Marland put his foot down on the subject of the maid, and none was hired.

*   *   *

After the debate on the maid had been settled, Marland grumbled about all the shopping Amelia found it necessary to do to outfit herself properly for high society. It was not the money that griped him, but the delay, when all else seemed in readiness. But the Sword he wore on his back, and in which he had great faith, was refusing to interfere with Amelia's plans. He was forced to the conclusion that they were likely to be of some benefit to his own.

He announced to his two confederates that, before attacking the big casino, he wanted to test his gambling plan in one of the many smaller establishments within this city.

When they reached the chosen place, early in the evening, neither the Sword nor the proprietors put up any obstacles to the entrance of Sir Marland and his entourage. All the rooms were crowded, as Marland had wanted and expected them to be. He and his two companions would attract no particular attention.

In these crowded conditions, the knight found it necessary to hand out a small bribe at the door to obtain for himself a table toward the rear of the room. In this relatively modest establishment, there were no private boxes, booths, or balconies such as those the main rooms of the big casino boasted.

Marland entered limping, presenting this as a silent explanation for his preference in seating. He also adopted the look of a man who had slightly too much to drink.

Adrian considered that this was putting things on too thick, and liable to draw more attention than it diverted. But the ploy seemed to work, and it was hard to argue with success.

Once the master was established at his table, where he sat growling for more drink, Adrian and the bodyguard who called himself Elgar stood by him awaiting orders, while Amelia made her way into the throng at the far end of the room, close to the big wheel.

For this evening's practice session, Adrian had garbed himself in what he considered the least embarrassing of the several page liveries that had by now been purchased for him.

Play at the table beneath the wheel was of course already in progress, with players joining in or dropping out continually. Amelia, who was no stranger to casinos, took an empty spot, and placed a modest bet or two, without having any particular luck.

Leaning his head back as if in thought, Marland made direct contact between his body and Coinspinner's hilt. Then he decided on his bet, and, beckoning Adrian to lean close, whispered it in his ear.

The boy worked his way forward through the throng until he

reached Amelia's side. So far there had been but little change in the modest stack of chips before her, but she looked uncomfortable. And worried. And glad to see Adrian arrive.

Elgar, their newly hired bodyguard, had in accordance with good professional practice taken his stand toward the rear of the room where he could supposedly keep an eye on everything. Since being hired, the man had purchased a good sword, but he still did not impress the Prince as being especially formidable. Still, as experienced fighters kept warning him, appearances could be very deceptive in such matters.

Looking around when he had the chance, the Prince, following Marland's teaching, thought that he could pick out one or two of the ubiquitous house magicians. These people looked somewhat bored, but still faithfully on duty to make sure that no would-be cheaters had any success against the house.

Marland, in sending Amelia his first chosen category—odd—of this practice run, also ordered Adrian to remind her to keep on mixing up her bets—that is, not always to use the winning, Sword-guaranteed number or category immediately, but to save it for later, so that no careful observer of the process could immediately be sure that the bets sent in by the man were invariably winners.

Adrian faithfully passed on the bets he was given. But it occurred to him how easy it ought to be for him to cross up Marland, by simply passing the wrong information to Amy. By the time the man found out, it would be too late for him to do anything about it—not too late for the Sword to do something, of course.

Murat, having followed his quarry to this casino, kept himself in the background and continued to observe. But what he saw only left him more puzzled than ever. Some kind of gambling scheme, evidently; but why should the heir apparent of Tasavalta choose to take part in it?

The Crown Prince still refrained from any effort to contact Adrian or anyone else in the party, to which Kebbi, of all people, had now somehow managed to attach himself.

Marland played for less than an hour, staking only small amounts, and then signaled his people he was ready to quit for the night. His theory of how to beat the house had been, as he considered, gloriously vindicated.

When he broke off the game he was a few thousand pieces ahead—not winnings enough to draw very much attention in a place like this. But he now had enough in his purse to stake himself solidly in the big game, day after tomorrow.

That night, in the inn, Marland was quietly jubilant. Once Elgar was safely out of earshot he announced to his two confederates that he had decided to make only a few minor changes in technique as a result of this preliminary study.

Amelia told him that was good. But she still looked as worried as ever.

19

Talking to Marland and Amelia, Adrian learned that the big casino in the Red Temple of Bihari was widely known as Sha's, after its legendary founder, not surprisingly a Red Temple priest. Sha's, or at least the inner rooms of that establishment, where the biggest games took place, had an expensive membership requirement, meant to keep out the riffraff.

The gambler had not been surprised by the requirement. As far as the Prince with his lack of experience could judge, he possessed a good familiarity with all important phases of the gambling business.

Not that he explained everything to his associates. On the day before he planned to break the bank, Marland, with Sword and scabbard strapped to his back, visited the Red Temple alone. When he rejoined his confederates he had little to say. The Prince wondered whether Marland, as an expert in the bottom line, might have been able to bypass some of the more expensive membership requirements by means of a little judicious bribery.

In any case, Marland in this environment hardly seemed like the same man who in other circumstances had often seemed clumsy and unable to cope very well.

Amy, who according to her own testimony had been in a great many gambling establishments, including this one, also seemed at home here, though she continued to worry.

She did a fairly good job of concealing her anxiety. But the Prince could tell that it was still growing.

Meanwhile Kebbi was keeping his eye on Marland's Sword, waiting for the man to get careless. The more he watched Marland, the more he realized that he might be in for a long wait. Also Kebbi continued to puzzle over why Adrian, a prince in his own land, was content to act as a servant to this gambler, who obviously had no idea of his page's true identity. Prince Adrian, as far as Kebbi could tell, was in full possession of his faculties, though he was calling himself Cham. Simply taking the opportunity to run away from home? That wouldn't be unheard of, even among royalty.

The Culmian defector bided his time, waiting to learn more.

Murat, from his room in the same inn, also maintained his observation. He also wondered about Adrian's purpose in remaining here.

When the Crown Prince of Culm, who had recently used the Sword of Chance himself, was able to identify it as the odd-looking weapon now carried by the gambler on his back, he considered that he had made real progress.

Murat remained obstinately determined to restore the young Prince to his mother, as an important means of making amends to the Princess Kristin. But, if he were later able to hand Coinspinner back to his own Queen, what a coup that would be!

Rostov, Karel, and the four surviving troopers eventually arrived in Bihari, a full day after the Culmian fugitives. The Tasavaltans' arrival in the resort city had been delayed by their difficulty with demons.

Early on the evening of the day he had chosen to consummate his revenge, Sir Marland and his two helpers, accompanied by their sturdy bodyguard Elgar, took a short walk through the streets of the resort city, made their approach to the great Red Temple of Bihari, and entered, heading directly though unhurriedly for Sha's.

Marland, as on the day of his preliminary effort, had chosen this hour deliberately, knowing that the gambling tables would be already busy, but with their busiest time still a few hours in the future.

On approaching the Red Temple complex, the young Prince was impressed. This was by far the biggest such edifice that he had ever seen; indeed he wasn't sure that any building in Sarykam was quite this large.

On entering it, Adrian was inevitably reminded of the Twisted Temple of the City of Wizards, though his visit there seemed much further in the past than the two weeks or so that it actually was. Still, there were great differences between that Red Temple and this one, besides the circumstance that this one was crowded with mundane humans and that one had long been deserted by such creatures. For one thing, there was music, live and real and mundane, almost everywhere inside this Temple, whereas that one had been haunted with ghostly sounds.

Kebbi, closely accompanying his new employer, was also inevitably reminded of his recent narrow escape from the Twisted Temple, and of the differences and similarities between that Temple and this one.

Murat, on seeing Adrian and the others leave their inn again, had followed them. The Crown Prince kept well in the background, patiently observing.

Marland at last had plenty of faces around him that he could recognize, faces whose presence would have made him indeed uneasy if he had not possessed the security of the Sword. These familiar countenances were those of Red Temple priests and other employees who had been intimately involved in his downfall only a few months previously.

One gaze in particular, tonight, caused Marland to hold his breath briefly. But the functionary, who Marland supposed might be somewhat nearsighted, looked right through him, and gave no sign of recognizing either him or Amelia.

Moments later the gambler was smiling at his own foolishness. If the Sword could extract him unharmed—as it had—from a condemned cell, a mere casino would pose no problem. With the Sword on his back now, he might have known that he was safe.

But Amelia, infinitely less sanguine, tugged urgently at his sleeve as soon as they entered the next room, and whispered that she was afraid they had been spotted.

"What makes you think so?" He hardly bothered to lower his voice.

"The croupier in the room we just left. The way he looked at us. I remember him from last time."

Marland had seen the same glance pass over them, and he was ready to assure her categorically that no recognition had occurred. On the contrary, they were practically home free already. Luck was his. He patted his woman's hand reassuringly. "I remember him too. But it's nothing. Forget it. Keep walking."

It was only natural that a good many of the dealers, clerks, croupiers, lookouts, and house magicians who had been working in Sha's then were still here now. Marland and Amelia could have called a number of them by name. But none of them were going to recognize the pair now. Marland could just feel it.

The Red Temple of Bihari, justly famous for its size and complexity, seemed to go on forever. Adrian had ceased having to play the country yokel and was beginning to gawk in earnest.

There was a strong taste of magic in the air as well. The Prince, to his own surprise, began to sense that he was no longer very far from the City of Wizards.

* * *

Marland himself had never really paid that much attention to where he was, in any physical, geographical sense. Ordinarily it made very little difference to him. The tables and games, the dice and cards, winning and losing, the risk-taking, were all he really cared about.

He, like many another gambler, had heard stories about the fabulous big game room in Sha's. Until now he had never been able to afford to enter that room, but he had determined that it would be there—though he might have been able to accomplish his goal elsewhere—that he would make his all-out effort to break the bank.

As the opulent rooms, filled with gaming tables, entertainers, customers, and food and drink, flowed by them one after another, Adrian could feel a growing sense of impending danger. There was nothing rational or logical about the apprehension, but he could not help considering, one last time, his option of abandoning the gambler and his scheme and getting away. After all, the Emperor hadn't really ordered him to stay with the gambler, or to try to take control of the Sword of Chance. That had been all his own idea.

The Prince now had a small supply of money in his pocket. He knew where he was—at least in a general way—in relation to his home, though Tasavalta was far away. And, as always, he was equipped with his own magical abilities.

But a sense of adventure held him here, and a sense that the Emperor though advising caution had somehow approved of what Adrian was doing, or what he was trying to do. Well, he still had time to decide. The sense of impending danger was not so immediate as all that.

Kebbi, meanwhile, was not having much success in formulating a plan to get his hands on Coinspinner. About all he had decided was that he had better grab the Sword as soon as he got a chance. Once he had that blade in hand, kidnapping Adrian—or anything else he decided to do—ought to be easy.

Marland, on actually arriving at the big game room, and being admitted with his party, promptly established himself in the box he had reserved. This was one of eight luxurious balconies in the rear of the huge room. All were about three meters above the floor, and Marland's was near the center, fourth from the left.

A turbaned attendant, bowing, escorted Sir Marland and his party to their box by way of a passage that ran behind all eight balconies, and was set off from them by doors and curtains. Elgar the bodyguard, at a word from his employer, assumed his station in this passage, just out-side the sole entrance to Marland's box.

The enclosure in which Adrian, Amelia, and Marland found them-selves was as big as a small room, containing a couch, a few small tables, and several chairs. Rich tapestries decorated the three closed walls, and a couple of candles on side tables shed a creamy light. Mar-land, with a sigh, pulled the most comfortable-looking chair forward to the rail and settled himself. From this position he could overlook al-most the entire huge room of games, but his face and form were largely concealed by the draperies that partially covered the front of the box.

Safe from the observation of most of the room at least, and feeling ever more confident in his tremendous luck, the gambler drew his Sword. He held Coinspinner point down on the floor, its whitened hilt clutched tight in both his hands.

Amelia had gone to one of the side tables. Several varieties of wine were provided there, courtesy of the house.

"Let's have a toast," said Marland.

Looking at him, then at Adrian, she righted three of the sparkling glasses. Opening a bottle seemingly at random, she poured the glasses full, and handed two of them to her companions.

"To victory," said Marland solemnly.

Adrian sipped from his glass. He thought he had tasted better, once or twice, in the palace at Sarykam. Marland sipped at his. Amelia hesi-tated briefly, then gulped her wine down.

A few moments later she was on her way to the gaming table, where Marland and Adrian silently watched her vanish into the crowd.

The great vertical wheel on the front wall spun twice, after her disap-pearance, before Marland dispatched Adrian with his first bet of the night: a single chip upon the category black.

The wizard Karel was at that moment entering the Red Temple of Bihari with Rostov at his side. The four troopers had been left outside, watching hired animals, including a mount for Adrian, ready to move out on a moment's notice. On entering the Temple, Karel paused for a moment. It took an effort to make himself move forward once again. His magical sense had just warned him that Wood was somewhere in the vicinity.

"Heavy magic ahead," he commented in a whisper to Rostov, who walked at his side, bearing Sightblinder muffled in a sheath but ready.

"And the Prince?" asked the General.

"He's somewhere ahead also. Ah, this way for Adrian. To our right, toward the casino."

"That way too for the heavy magic?"

"That's to our left." Karel allowed himself a brief and mirthless smile. "Not needed to augment the thrills of Sha's Casino. Gambling provides its own magic, my friend. Trimbak Rao tells me that it's an especially abominable vice."

Marland had not been alone in his box for long when Elgar put his red head in through the curtains. His eyes, as they often did, focused on the Sword in Marland's hands before rising to his employer's face.

"There's someone here says he knows you, sir."

"Really? Well, send him in. It's all right, you can stay out in the corridor."

The bodyguard stepped out again. And Marland recognized the face that appeared next, though out of habit he was careful to keep his own countenance from displaying any recognition. The newcomer was Thurso, a small man with slicked-back black hair and an artificial-looking mustache; a hanger-on in Sha's and sometimes in less opulent casinos, a sometime gambler, a doer of difficult or unpleasant tasks—for hefty fees, of course—and from time to time a blackmailer.

The heavy curtain sagged shut behind Thurso. Marland supposed that enigmatic Elgar would be doing his best to eavesdrop outside. Well, let him. It was Marland who had the Sword of Luck.

"Hello, Buvrai," said Thurso, making no effort to pitch his voice particularly low.

If he had expected to frighten Buvrai by speaking his name aloud he must have been disappointed.

"Hello yourself," said Buvrai. "But you have my name wrong. I am Sir Marland, baronet of—of somewhere out in the Far Reaches, I suppose." Confident, smiling, he toasted his visitor silently in a sip of wine. He wasn't about to ask the little swine to sit down, though.

The little man standing just inside the doorway frowned, considering this unexpected response. "I know who you are," he finally said bluntly. "It'll take more than a beard and a getup to fool me. I wonder, does the house know you're here, gambling under a false name? I rather doubt it. I rather imagine they think you went to a different world, some time ago."

The curtain at the rear of the box opened, and Adrian ducked in. He stopped short, watching the men. After glancing at him they both ignored his presence.

"Do you know something, Thurso? Someone told me that was your name. I really don't give a good fart what you imagine." Marland was still smiling.

Thurso paused, opened his mouth and closed it, then with an air of determination tried again. "All right. Play it tough. I don't know what the game is and I don't care. I could use a loan, though. Say a hundred, and I go play in the other rooms tonight. I haven't seen you and I don't know you're here."

"You're right, little man, you don't know where I am, or where you are, either, come to that. Go play wherever you like. You'll get no gold from me."

The other nodded, indicating the middle of the big room before them, beyond the half-concealing curtains. "There's Tung-Hu in his little pulpit. I could go play there, and I might profit."

"If you see a good bet there, why don't you take it?"

The other, flushing, turned away instantly. But with the curtain to the corridor raised he turned back for a last effort. "All right. But don't say I didn't give you a chance. The High Priest of the Temple will be pleased to know you're back and playing, Buvrai. And that you're in the big game this time."

Marland only chuckled. When the curtain had dropped behind Thurso, he turned eagerly in his chair to see what might be going to happen. Adrian moved up to watch over his shoulder.

Soon the dark little man was visible, approaching the floor chief of security, whose raised dais gave him a good outlook over most of the room.

Just as Thurso began to mount the steps to the dais, a startled expression flashed over his face. His arms began waving, in the manner of a man losing his balance, as he toppled from sight beyond a throng of customers. A waiter who had been hurrying past carrying an upraised tray went down also, and a crash of shattered glass was audible above the room's babble of background noise. The waiter reappeared in a moment, but the little blackmailer did not.

Security began to make a fuss around the spot, and presently the heads and shoulders of two guards could be seen carrying something heavy away between them.

Thurso was not seen again. Marland glanced at Adrian, then sighed and said nothing. Adrian was still staring out over the crowd. Obviously the great majority of the people in the huge room were not aware that anything of importance had happened. With unobtrusive efficiency, servants and security people were now cleaning something up. The Prince wondered if it might be blood.

His sense of adventure was suddenly much diminished, and fear was starting to take over. He had thought himself free at any time to walk out on Marland. But now he had grave doubts that the Sword would allow it.

Carrying Marland's next bet down to Amy at the table, Adrian thought that her nerves were getting worse, though she maintained her position at the table and continued to play. A catastrophic failure of her nerves, thought Adrian, had become a distinct possibility. He wanted to say something encouraging to her, but the right words were hard to find.

Since entering the great Temple of Bihari, Adrian had been aware of all types of entertainers, almost everywhere in sight, performing for the customers or pleading for the chance to do so. Here, in Sha's Casino, the entertainers were less obtrusive than elsewhere in the Temple. Here in Sha's, so Marland had informed him, were also to be found the best house wizards in the world, and the worst chances of cheating. These wizards were superbly good at their very specialized job, which was primarily to make sure that none of the customers were ever able to cheat the house.

The legend, which the management of the casino took pains to propagate, was that no one in all the centuries of its operation had ever managed to succeed in that endeavor. Marland said that it was very possibly true.

Each day the house wizards, having made sure that their reputation with regard to their primary responsibility would remain untarnished, next did their best to keep the customers from cheating one another. In this they were often successful, though here their record was not unblemished.

And naturally this evening, after the man in Box Four started winning strongly, some of the house magicians began to take notice. It was barely possible that something strange was up. But security's preliminary look discovered nothing, no reason to harbor the faintest suspicion of Marland or his people.

The chief of floor security in the big room, the wizard named Tung-Hu, frowned, catching the shadow of a potential magical disturbance of quite a different kind. But the shadow had come and gone before Tung-Hu could even attempt to identify it.

Wood was the source. But he was able to soothe away the nervous apprehension of the house magicians almost as well as if he had been armed with one of the subtle Swords.

* * *

In the casino only Karel, and through him Rostov, were certainly aware of the Ancient One's ominous approach.

At the entrance to the great private room, Sightblinder, invisible but powerful in Rostov's fist, caused the attendants to back away in confusion. Several of them hastened to wave the General and his companion in.

On entering the big game room, Rostov thought it was high enough to allow the great god Draffut to stand upright. He also observed that the huge gaming wheel on the far wall took up most of the height with its diameter.

"The Prince is here?" he whispered to the wizard beside him, sheathing the Sword of Stealth again.

"Adrian is here. Somewhere in this room. Be ready."

Before the eccentric knight in the curtained box had been an hour at play, he, and the nervous lady at the table who was so obviously his partner, had established themselves as considerable winners.

Observers could readily see that there was rarely time enough for the young page, who served this couple as messenger, to make his way from the box to Amelia's side and back again between successive spins of the great wheel. The great wheel made a distinctive noise, and on some spins, when particularly great sums were known to be at stake, the huge room grew so quiet that that noise could be distinctly heard to its far corners.

Play continued, with the winnings of the mysterious man in the box steadily mounting. Amy's own, unaided luck was not bad tonight, and as usual the Sword was invincible.

Such success attracted yet again the attention of the guardians of the house. Still the interest they were taking in Marland was hardly more than routine; during the last month Sha's had survived one or two bigger winners.

But when two more lucky numbers had come in for Marland, Tung-Hu decided it would be a good idea to listen in on what the young messenger was saying.

Word was passed down from the security chief. One of the floor agents of the house, who circulated continually among the crowd, and looked like nothing but another harried player, managed to do this. He heard Adrian tell Amy only that her next bet should be on red.

She acknowledged the message with a nod, and placed her bet.

And red happened of course to win.

* * *

Marland was less happy at his impending victory than he had anticipated. Coinspinner was with him, what could possibly go wrong? The
bank here, of course, had huge reserves. But he had already mentioned
to his confederates the probability that as soon as it became obvious
that he was on a really tremendous winning streak, other bettors would
flock to ride his choices, piling their wagers atop the winning categories
or digits enforced by Coinspinner.

This, if the house allowed it to happen, would break even the biggest
bank in short order.

Marland slumped in his chair, staring at the dyed hilt of his Sword.
He hoped that nothing really fatal had happened to Thurso. He hadn't
really wanted to kill the little bastard, after all.

A wave of noise, almost of applause, swept through the crowd in the
room beyond the curtains of his box. Someone had won big.

Marland was bored.

And in fact no crisis of this magnitude had confronted Sha's in many
years. Tung-Hu had already communicated with his superiors, who
were seriously considering suspending play for a time. By doing this
the house would risk having to write off its already very serious losses.

But for the moment the luck of the house took a twist for the better.
It was Amelia's turn to place her bet unaided, and a fortune was swept
away from her.

The security investigation of course was ordered stepped up. The
next step called for the infiltration of some agent into Marland's box to
get a firsthand look at whatever might be going on there. Somehow the
draperies, or some other obstruction, always prevented anyone looking
up from seeing very much.

Usually probes of this type were most successfully carried out by one
of the dancing girls who roamed the Temple, performing on request or
with apparent spontaneity. Besides gathering information, there was
the chance that the presence of such a girl might stir up some jealousy,
and rob this strange Sir Marland of the full cooperation of the lady who
now represented him at the table. At the very least it might distract the
gambler from his endeavors.

Tung-Hu ordered that a certain girl be brought to him at once. Somehow his orders went astray.

Without waiting for the girl's arrival, the suspicious house wizard
next tried his most skillful and subtle magical method of scanning the
interior of the box without making a physical approach. He could be-

hold the result before him in a crystal globe. Yes, there was the gambler, seated, holding both hands clenched before him in a rather awkward-looking position, as if they were resting on something. But there was nothing under them. Irrelevant. Everything in Box Four looked clean. Tung-Hu's most accomplished powers assured him that there was nothing magical for him to worry about.

"Even so, it seems imperative that we investigate the matter more intensely." The High Priest of the local Red Temple himself was now standing beside Tung-Hu on the security dais. The High Priest was beginning to be desperate, though in keeping with his dignity he expressed it in a restrained way. This stranger's winnings were once more mounting to the point where it would be more than embarrassing for the casino if things went on this way.

Wood had now entered the big room, secretly, and was standing inconspicuously against a wall while he conferred with Tigris. The Ancient One had disdained to adopt any special disguise for this occasion, wearing his usual appearance of a youthful demigod.

With the hilt of Shieldbreaker under his hand, Wood was able to see and recognize at a glance Rostov carrying Sightblinder, and Karel beside him; the odd behavior of others in the vicinity of the General proved which Sword Rostov was carrying. Neither Tasavaltan had spotted Wood as yet.

Wood was also able to identify Adrian without any trouble. But now he was no longer content with the idea of kidnapping Prince Mark's whelp. Not when there were two other Swords besides his own in this room.

"We must," he whispered to Tigris, "get at least one of those two into our grasp as well."

"How, my lord?"

"As to Coinspinner, getting this mysterious man into a special game, and then challenging him to bet his Sword, would seem to be the way to go."

"You will go right to his box, and challenge him?"

"Or somehow bring him to the table, and meet him there. Of course that will draw dear Rostov, with his Sword, as well."

"*I* could go to his box," said Tigris, "and tempt him to the table. Or to anywhere you like."

Her master, hesitating again, hardly seemed to hear her. "Or would it be better not to win the Sword of Chance again, but to destroy it now? I wasted one opportunity to do so, and now here's another; who can say if I shall ever gain another?"

Still, as before, Wood was tempted to keep the Sword of Chance and use it for himself—anyone, any being, human or otherwise, who managed to get Coinspinner and Shieldbreaker in hand at the same time would be very powerful indeed.

And Sightblinder was here, too, in the same room. The Sword of Stealth, with either of the other two Swords present, would also form a very powerful combination.

"Will you call upon the demons, sir?" asked Tigris.

"I think not. Many of them are still scattered. And I'd be surprised if the damned young whelp there lacks the power his father and grandsire seem to share against my pets."

Suddenly the master wizard was decisive. "It will be the gaming table. Save your efforts, I'll get him out of his box myself."

Adrian, coming to the table with another bet chosen by Marland, in his hurry and concentration did not at first recognize Wood among the crowd.

Once Wood had reached the table, he observed Amelia's next bet. Then Wood, having provided himself with the necessary tokens, placed his own wager in direct opposition.

There was, as on other crucial turns, a silence as the wheel spun. This time the silence was broken only by a sound as of a single drum, doubtless held by one of the musicians. Then came a gasp from the crowd. The lady had lost, a huge sum this time.

Marland, who had been watching closely, hurriedly left his seat. His first thought was that either Amy or Adrian had blundered. His second was that one or both of them were deliberately betraying him for some reason.

Only at the last moment did Marland remember to sheathe and conceal his Sword before he plunged into the crowd. He pushed his way through the crowd and toward the table.

Kebbi, seeing his employer rush out of the box in an agitated state, hastily followed.

Murat, still patiently observing from the post where he had established himself on the floor of the big room, decided that matters were somehow coming to a head, and started toward the table also.

Adrian had turned from the table when the noise of the crowd made him look back. Coinspinner's choice had lost. For a moment the Prince could only gape. Then he realized that Shieldbreaker must somehow be arrayed against Marland.

And Shieldbreaker must mean that Wood was present. A moment

later, the boy saw and recognized the Ancient One among the crowd that pressed around the table.

Wood smiled evilly in Adrian's direction.

There would be no raising an elemental here. Not against this man's effortless power. Adrian now realized that he was lost. There was only one way out. There was only one way, as every heir to a warrior's throne must know, to fight against Shieldbreaker. Barehanded.

Resisting the impulse to run away, Adrian began to work his way through the crowd directly toward Wood.

Wood saw him coming, smirked at him at first, then frowned. Against an unarmed opponent, even one physically much weaker, there was only one way for the holder of the Sword of Force to win, and that was to rid himself of his peerless weapon as quickly as possible.

Adrian, having committed himself, darted forward with the speed of desperation. Wood, still fumbling to draw his Sword, could only jump aside. It was almost a panicked move, that of a powerfully built man avoiding in desperation the attack of a mere child.

Still in the act of drawing Shieldbreaker in order to throw it away, Wood attracted the full attention of the armed guards who had been steadily reinforcing the security presence near the table.

The guard nearest to Wood was extremely good at his trade. He had his short sword fully drawn, menacing this troublemaker, even before Shieldbreaker in Wood's clumsy hand had finally and fully cleared the scabbard. But against the handiwork of Vulcan, mere human skill was futile. The drum-note of the Sword of Force was sounding now, and it laid a slight emphasis upon one single beat. The guard's weapon was shattered into flying bits of steel that stung and bit at everyone they struck.

Wood paused, shuddering. Shieldbreaker was fully drawn now, hilt nestled in his right hand. It would begin, it was already starting, to meld itself into that hand. In another moment he would not be able to cast the Sword away, and it would mean his doom if he were attacked in that state by some unweaponed foe.

Meanwhile howling confusion, panic, had exploded in the room, following the blast of shrapnel from the shattered sword. Many here were armed, and weapons were now coming out. Accidental wounds were being inflicted in the crowd.

Rostov, Sightblinder in his right hand, was trying to fight his way toward his struggling Prince, but the General could make little headway against the mob of bodies. Half of the people surrounding Rostov saw him as some loved one, the other half as a dread enemy.

Tigris found herself bewildered by the simultaneous appearance of two Woods, who shouted contradictory commands. The enchantress had long known in a theoretical way what the Sword of Stealth might do to her, but the actual event was still difficult to deal with.

Before she could decide which of the images of Wood was genuine, she found Karel's magic surrounding her, the old man's craft blocking her own magic, at every turn.

Marland, stumbling amid the sudden melee around the table, tripped and fell softly to the carpet, just as the wild swing of someone's fist passed through the space vacated by his head. He was just starting to crawl, trying to distance himself from the fighting, when a surge of struggling bodies against the far side of the table tipped it over in his direction.

Missed me, he thought, *of course.* And then he saw Amy.

The fallen table, now turned completely upside down, had not missed her, and in fact she was pinned under it. For just a moment, in the way that the mind will twist things sometimes, Buvrai thought he saw his brother Talgai once again, head gray with dust protruding from the rubble of a fallen building.

But it was Amy. She lay so pale and still, prone, with the edge of the table across her back. Buvrai scrambled closer.

While a horde of people stamped and struggled around him, the guards trying to overcome mass panic and quell fights among the customers, Buvrai pulled Coinspinner from its sheath and wrapped her inert fingers around the hilt. "Amy, don't. Don't be dead. Amy, I love you." Then he let go of the Sword himself.

In the next moment he felt himself grabbed from behind, hauled to his feet in the grasp of a brawny security man.

"I recognize you! You're the one who was sentenced—" The guard broke off, let go of Marland, rolled his eyes and fell.

Kebbi, fulfilling his duty as bodyguard until he could learn from Marland what had happened to the Sword, had smashed the fellow in the head from behind with the hilt of his own weapon.

Meanwhile Wood, struggling desperately to rid himself of Shieldbreaker, tried instinctively to hack at Adrian. It was a mistake. Of course the slashes of the Sword of Force had no effect upon the unarmed youth.

Then Wood by a supreme effort managed to discard the Sword of Force just before it immovably attached itself to his right hand.

After that Wood, relying on his own powers, managed to make his getaway. Adrian saw him vanish.

Murat had hurled himself into the melee with the idea of rescuing Adrian. Then to his utter astonishment the Crown Prince suddenly beheld Princess Kristin before him—and restrained himself only in the nick of time from grabbing General Rostov with some idea of carrying him to safety.

Murat plunged back into the fray, helped lift a heavy table off a young woman who was screaming too loudly to be seriously injured. A few moments after that, the Crown Prince pulled out Adrian, still intact, from amid the struggling bodies and upended furniture.

Minutes passed before the fighting ended. When peace had finally been enforced by the house guards, the last bets were still required to be honored, by house and customers alike. On the last play the house had in fact won back a substantial portion of its night's losses. And if, according to the strict rules, any money was still due to the mysterious Sir Marland, payment would be suspended until he could be found. The High Priest breathed a sigh of relief when it became apparent that the suspension of payment might well be permanent. Rumors now rapidly spreading from several sources indicated that the man calling himself Sir Marland was really someone else.

As order was being finally restored in Sha's, Adrian was just outside, getting into the saddle of a riding-beast. Escorted by an accomplished wizard, a determined General still armed with Sightblinder, and four Tasavaltan troopers, the Prince was preparing himself for the long journey home to Sarykam.

For some minutes now there had been no sign of either Murat or Kebbi, and neither Adrian nor his escort expected either Culmian to make an appearance now.

Karel had been the last Tasavaltan out of the casino. Before very quietly taking himself away, the old man had searched as best he could, with eyes and magic, for both Shieldbreaker and Coinspinner. He had had no success. Wood or Tigris might have recovered Shieldbreaker, he supposed—but if so, why had they fled the scene?

And Coinspinner? Sighing, the old man reflected that the Sword of Chance had most likely simply taken itself away again, no one knew where. Or had someone else simply picked it up in the confusion? There was no way to be sure.

THE SIXTH BOOK OF LOST SWORDS:
MINDSWORD'S STORY

1

BETWEEN two lofty jagged mountain spines the rocky land declined in frozen swirls that bottomed in a deep depression, forming at its lowest point a narrow and almost circular hollow shielded from human observation by tall crags on every side. Around noon on a summer day a man alone was climbing toward this hidden place. He had begun climbing far below, and he was headed directly for the unseen hollow with fierce determination, as if he knew that it was there.

The climber was a strong and active man, though without any particular skill or experience in the art of ascending mountains; more than once today he had come near falling to his death when a handhold or foothold betrayed him. Dogged resolution had so far sustained him in his effort, though several times in the past two hours he had come near despairing of his survival.

The one fighting his way upward with such dedication was tall, dark of hair and beard, handsome in his own dark careless way. His age was approaching forty, and at the moment, breathing hard in the thin mountain air, he was keenly aware of every year.

The man's lean body had been worn leaner by much recent travel and other difficulties. He was dressed in the clothes of a soldier or a hunter; his jacket, much faded but still faintly blue and orange, might have been part of a uniform when it was new. He wore a small pack on his back; at the left side of his belt swung an empty sheath of a size to hold a long sword, balanced on the right side by a long practical knife. Despite the difficulties of the ascent, the climber evidently considered none of these items dispensable.

At the altitude where he had begun his long climb, the day was warm and sunny, but up here on the high slopes, somewhere around timberline, the summer afternoon was beginning with a light, cold drizzle, spiced with an occasional stinging pellet of snow or hail. Gusts of wind dragged rolling mists across the mountain's face, more often than not obscuring the climber's view of what lay ahead of him and above. Nevertheless he pressed on.

Already at many points in his ascent the climber had paused to rest. Now he did so once more, clinging in a brief truce to the nearly vertical rock. While catching his breath he examined his surroundings carefully, as if he expected to see something out of the ordinary. Also, he seemed to be listening intently, in hopes of picking up the sound of something more meaningful than wind.

Soon he advanced again, with unflagging determination.

His hopes, whatever their foundation, were soon justified, for presently he was granted evidence that his goal was near. As the climber's line of sight topped the next stony barrier he was able to see, no more than thirty meters above him and ahead, the notched entrance to a circular pit, which he knew must be the bottom of the hidden depression between crests.

At this sight the man paused, nodding to himself. Because of certain clues he had been given before he began to climb, he felt certain of what he was going to discover in that desolate place. And if any confirmation were needed that he was very near his goal, he had it now. Because now he was beginning to hear the voices.

The voices, which sounded more in his mind than in his ears, were strange to him, not just unfamiliar but extremely odd. In truth, as the explorer knew, they were not really vocal sounds. But he could not help hearing them and thinking of them as voices, these songs and cries that were so much more than the noise of the wet wind. There surged around him an utterance as of a multitude at worship, singing a polyphonic paean above the gusts.

The climber moved forward another step, and now a new sign appeared to assure him that he was on the right track, and had not far to go. The rocks ahead of him remained properly dead and motionless whenever he gazed straight at them. But all the landscape near the corners of his vision had now begun to move. The effect was such that the entire mountainside around him appeared to be on the verge of swirling away in an ecstatic dance.

Rendered momentarily dizzy by the illusion of dancing rocks, the seeker paused again, closing his eyes. The mountainside beneath his hands and feet felt stable, and with his intellect he knew it was. He understood perfectly well that the dance and the ecstasy were in his mind; but that rendered them no less rhythmic or ecstatic.

Having moved a little closer to his goal, the climber was able now to hear the magic voices more clearly, though still the words were indistinguishable. Some of the voices sounded human and some did not, but all of them were shrieking together in a great chorus of triumph and rapture.

The one who sought opened his eyes and studied the way ahead.

Although much of the mountainside was obscured by blowing mist, he knew that, physically, the worst of the climb was over. From where he stood, the surface he had still to negotiate angled more and more back toward the horizontal. Within the space of a few breaths the tall dark man, standing erect now and moving up on legs alone, was almost on the threshold of the notched entrance to the hollow in the rocks.

As he drew steadily nearer to that point, the fanciful—or perhaps not so fanciful—idea crossed the climber's mind that perhaps no other human being had set eyes upon these cracked and moss-grown stones since the old mountains had thrust upward from the earth.

Once more he felt himself rendered a touch unsteady by the superhuman power of magic that loomed ahead. Once more he paused to close his eyes, trying to regain an inner balance. Standing there with eyes closed and arms outstretched, the man thought that now he could *feel* the mountain dancing. It was as if the whole earth around him were acting out the joy of certain victory, of success extended to eternity . . . though what victory, or what success was being celebrated, was more than any mere mortal in his place could tell.

Opening his eyes, the adventurer found himself still groping like a blind man. Trying to make his mind a blank, he forced himself to forge on, one shuffling step after another.

And now at last he had reached the very threshold of the entrance to the secret place, a point from which he could see directly into the hollow before him.

Ahead, through swirling mist and wind, he beheld a broad cup of dark rock, irregular in shape, some forty meters across here at the sculpted bottom. The whole bottom of the cup was deeply littered by an age-old detritus of stones and rough soil eroded from the surrounding cliffs. Tough grass and other small plants, only enough of them to emphasize the barrenness, grew very sparsely in that soil.

In almost the precise middle of this desolate hollow, surmounting a natural cairn of tumbled stones, an upright Sword was poised.

The cruciform dull black hilt stood uppermost, over a long blade. The metal of that blade, straight as a ray of sun, and as naked as the surrounding rock, appeared unnaturally bright in the dull, cloud-filtered daylight. It flashed intermittently, sending forth momentary gleams as brilliant as the sun that hid itself above the wind-rushed clouds.

Considering the Sword's position, the discoverer surmised that it must at some time have fallen—or been cast—from somewhere high on one of the surrounding cliffs. The weapon had landed point first atop the rockpile, wedging itself indestructibly in some fine crevice, or perhaps cracking open its own niche with the force of its falling weight behind that unbreakable point.

But it was very hard to think, or plan. In the visitor's ears and through his mind, the voices that were not voices roared and sang unceasingly.

For a moment the tall man tilted back his head, the wind whipping his dark hair and beard, his eyes squinting up into the rolling, rushing clouds as if he hoped to be able to gather from them some sign, some trace, concerning the one who had discarded or accidentally dropped this god-forged weapon here.

How long might the Sword of Glory have been here, waiting to be claimed? The visitor could not be sure, but it might well have been for years. He could picture how in winter that bright Blade would stand here meters deep in drifted snow, and how in spring and summer it must be washed in floods of snowmelt and of rain. But not the smallest spot of rust showed on that steel; and the man who stood before it now would have been willing to wager his existence that this weapon had not lost the faintest increment of keenness from either of its long, finely tapered edges.

Possibly, he thought, the Blade had worn a sheath when it fell—or was hurled—into its present position. That it stood entirely naked now was easily explained—over a period of months or years, any covering of cloth or leather could have been nibbled away by the sharp teeth of scavengers, small mindless creatures unaffected by the magic they uncovered.

The absence of a covering, however, created certain problems for an approaching human being.

Hesitantly, advancing step by step with many pauses, the climber continued his progress toward the matchless treasure. As much as possible he kept his eyes averted from that gleaming Blade, and he tried without success to close his mind against the glare, the influence, that poured so boundlessly, like some effortless reflection of a melting sun, from the thing atop the mound of rock, the artifact that had been wrought at a god's forge from magic and meteoric metal.

The discoverer knew—but the knowledge was of little help—that the glare afflicting him was not really in his eyes. He reminded himself as he advanced—though the suggestion did him little good—that the roaring voices, those of beings forever balancing upon the brink of some orgasmic triumph, were not really in his ears.

Useless efforts to protect himself, useless. The finder knew an almost overpowering urge to fall on his knees and worship—not the Sword itself, no, but someone, something, he knew not who or what, except that the object must be transcendent, and the Sword called him to it.

By now the man, gasping and trembling more in his excitement than from physical effort, was almost near enough to reach out and touch that dull black hilt. But some basic instinct of survival, justified or not, warned him that he must not do so yet.

When he dared to peer more closely at the hilt, he saw the small white symbol that he had known must be there, the device of a waving banner.

"It *is* the Mindsword, then," the trembling explorer whispered to himself. "It can be nothing else."—As if there could have been any doubt. But the mere sound of his own voice, which he could still manage to hold steady, his own words, which he could still contain within the bounds of rationality, helped him to master his excitement and his nameless fear.

He knew that many people, standing this close to this uncovered Blade, would have turned and fled in helpless terror. Many others would have fallen down in mindless worship of they knew not what. The discoverer, being a proud, able, and determined man, did neither. With tremendous stubbornness he had forced his way here, risking his life, to take possession of this prize. And he was not going to be deprived of it now.

But at the same time he feared that he might be unable to collect his treasure without help.

Yet again the adventurer squeezed shut his eyes, trying to establish some measure of composure. Closed lids shut out the sight of the Sword, but could not banish its majestic, insistent presence. In the depths of his mind and soul he could feel how the universe swirled around him. Half-born emotions only partially his own, fledgling hopes, stillborn ambitions, washed over him in a bewildering torrent. The man's brain echoed with the redoubled roar of a vast multitude of voices, some human and some not. All of them were praying, praising, worshiping—who? Or what?

He thought that it would prove impossible for him, strong man that he was, to remain for an hour within a hundred meters of this naked Blade when he did not control it. He had to possess his prize quickly, before it drove him mad or forced him into flight. And before he could touch it directly he had to cover it with something, muzzle its powers, put a sheath on it somehow.

The difficulty was not entirely unexpected; it was no accident that an empty sheath of the required size hung at the discoverer's belt. But he could not slip a sheath on the weapon in its present position, and he still dared not perform the simple act of reaching out to pluck the Mindsword from the rocks.

Surges of unidentifiable longing swept through the adventurer as he hesitated. He felt stabbed by pangs of deathly devotion to some overwhelmingly great but tantalizingly unspecific cause. Bright barbs that might have been sun-twinkles from the metal came dashing against his sanity like crests of poisoned foam.

Moving a half-step closer, he stretched out a hand toward the naked Sword—and then at the last moment dared not touch it.

Groaning, snatching back his trembling arm, the man fell back a step. And then another step, and yet another.

But this man was not going to give up. There might be another way. With unsteady fingers he began to unfasten the empty sheath from his Swordbelt.

With the detached sheath clutched in his left hand, the man gave a sound like a despairing giggle, and bent to pick up some small rocks. These he tossed, one after another, in the direction of the black hilt, trying to knock it over. At last one of his small missiles struck the Sword, which tilted but did not topple under the impact.

Laughing madly now, the man threw bigger stones, pitching them harder and harder, knowing that no rock he could ever throw, nothing he could ever do, could crack even the thinnest extremity of those sharpened edges.

At last he lobbed a larger stone that hit the Sword directly. The treasure fell, anticlimactically, making a slight noise. Obligingly its blade had now assumed a tilted position on the rockpile, the bright point uppermost, angled some degrees above the horizontal. And now the Sword's capturer could approach, sheath in hand, and—without needing to touch his prize directly—could begin to bind and tame his quarry, to hood it like a falcon with the mundane empty leather.

Slowly and carefully he got the point started into the sheath, then worked the sheath along the blade. In its new position the Mindsword rocked, slowly and precariously, with every indirect pressure from his hand.

The madness in the air, and in the rock, began to weaken.

The man could not have said how long the task occupied him, but eventually it was done. The simple covering was effective. The world was stable again, the many voices muted into—almost—perfect silence.

Now the latest possessor of the Mindsword could freely grasp the hard black pommel, feeling in it no more than the subtle power that any thing of great magic might be expected to possess, the sense of tremendous forces bound and coiled and waiting. Now he could pick up his great prize and buckle it on tightly at his belt. And now the world around him was perfectly worldly once again, consisting of little more than rocks and wind and rain. Somewhere birds were crying in the moving mist. He had not noticed until now that there were birds nesting and flying and hunting amid these lofty rocks.

For a quarter of an hour after the Sword was sheathed the newly armed adventurer sat on a small ledge, resting with his treasure at his side, experiencing a reaction of weakness.

Then he was on his feet again, and briskly on his way. The hardest part of the long descent, down to where he'd left his riding-beast, must be completed before nightfall. Early in the morning he'd ride on, in the direction of Sarykam. He had a great gift now to give. A truly worthy gift, to place in the lovely hands of the Princess Kristin.

2

In a small village at the foot of the Ludus Mountains, not many kilometers from the spot where the adventurer had very recently obtained his Sword, but at a considerably lower altitude, a blind albino man sat huddled in one corner of the small main room of a solidly built though sparsely furnished hut.

Few people could have determined the blind man's age by looking at him, but certainly his youth was decades past. His angular body, now slumped and blanket-covered in a crudely constructed peasant's chair, would still have been very tall but for the fact that he never stood fully erect. Long ringlets of unclean white hair hung past his bony shoulders, entering into confusion with a once-white beard now colorless with old stains of food and drink.

No mask or bandage concealed the empty sockets of his eyes; long-lashed lids sagged over spots of raw softness in a face that was otherwise all harsh masculine planes and angles.

The blind man had lived in this hut, or in another very similar dwelling nearby, for the past fourteen years, rarely stirring out of doors for any purpose. Apart from his blindness he was not physically crippled, though his lack of deliberate movement, together with occasional nervous tremors in his limbs, suggested that he might be lame. Actually the chief cause of his immobility lay in a disability of his will. For fourteen years he had been obsessed with certain events in the ever-receding past.

This afternoon two visitors were standing in the blind man's hut. Both callers were men, and both wore the humble dress—common furs and homespun cloth—of inhabitants of the nearby village. Half an hour ago the pair of visitors had tapped at the unlocked door of the blind man's house, waited with habitual patience for an answer that never came, and at last had let themselves in, calling loudly to announce their arrival. Since then they had been standing deferentially in front of the albino, waiting for him to show some awareness of their presence.

At last the one who sat huddled in the chair deigned to acknowledge, by a certain stillness of his body, a cessation of the long-continued nervous movements of his hands and feet, that he had perceived his callers' existence.

Seizing the opportunity the moment it arrived, the elder visitor spoke softly.

"Lord Vilkata?"

There was no immediate response, even when the quiet salutation was repeated. For some time the man slumped in the chair pretended not to hear his callers. They did not take offense at such behavior; it was only the Lord Vilkata's way. Since their rescue of the blind man from deep snow at the foot of a nearby cliff some fourteen winters ago, many if not quite all of the villagers had been convinced that he was one of the vanished race of gods, in fact the last survivor of that august company. Therefore, his hosts believed, his presence in their village was certain sooner or later to bring them inestimable benefits. True, their life so far had remained as harsh as ever despite the albino's presence; but at least no disaster beyond the ordinary had befallen, and who knew what might have happened were the Lord not here?

The blind man for his part had accepted deferential treatment, and the regular satisfaction of his bodily wants, as no more than his due. Beyond that he had made few demands upon his hosts. Some of the demands he did make were quite incomprehensible and never met. Others were quite clear. From the first day the guest had insisted that his rescuers call him by what he said was his proper name. So long as the villagers did that, and fed him as well as they could, and kept him warm, and allowed him from time to time the company in bed of one or two of their more comely daughters—then he would deign to speak to them.

Sometimes he even listened to them as well.

"Grandfather?" This was the younger visitor, trying out a theory of his own, that after all these years the eminent guest might be ready to answer to a simpler title.

The experimenter might have saved his breath. The Lord Vilkata took no notice of him.

The senior of the two visitors said nothing for a while, and remained impassive. He had been perfectly sure that the experiment would fail.

After a while the senior tried again, sticking to his own kind of patient communication. "Lord Vilkata?"

"Yes, what is it?" This time the snappish answer came at once, sooner than the elder had expected. Something out of the ordinary was perturbing the blind god-man today.

The elder visitor asked gently, deferentially, what the honored one's trouble was.

The reply was quick and petulant: "My trouble stems from the Sword, of course. What else?"

They were back to the incomprehensible. The two visitors, standing before the huddled figure in the chair, silently exchanged glances. It was nothing new for dear Grandfather—everyone called him that, outside his hut—to talk about the Sword, though none of his hearers knew what "the Sword" might be.

For some time after his rescue, long years ago, the honored guest had talked of almost nothing else but this strange Sword of enormous importance, and the elders of the village in those days had expended much effort and time in a useless attempt to discover just what he meant. For hours on end, sometimes seemingly for days, their guest and prisoner and lucky charm had harangued the people who had saved his life in an effort to get them to organize search parties, go out into the mountains, and find this mysterious weapon that so obsessed him.

During the first few years after their guest's arrival the people had listened to these tirades patiently—taking shifts when necessary—and tried to understand. Of course the villagers knew in a general way what swords were like, but really they knew and cared nothing about them beyond that—they had their spears and slings and clubs for hunting, and for those rare other occasions when weapons were essential. They harkened tolerantly to the blind man's urgent mumblings, and sometimes to soothe him they pretended to search, but really they made no effort. Only madmen would waste strength and time combing the mountains for objects that were not needed and perhaps did not exist.

Before he had been three years among them, the villagers reached a consensus that their honored Grandfather was quite mad. They accepted the fact that he was mad, as holy men and old men sometimes were, but his madness did not diminish his holiness or his importance to the village. The value of a resident lord, or god—the distinction was not a profound one for the villagers—really did not depend on anything he said, or anything he did overtly. They soothed their guest and prisoner as best they could, and told him pleasant lies to keep him quiet. Yes, Great Elder, excuse us, Lord Vilkata, soon the weather will improve, and then we will climb back up into the high country and resume the search. Next time we will certainly find your Sword.

Eventually the honored one had seemed to forget about the mysterious Sword, or at least he spoke of it less and less frequently. Instead he spent what strength he had in other lamentations, chiefly for his lost youth and fame and power.

But today the older of the pair of visiting elders was growing worried that those early days of fiery obsession might have come back. Because:

"Someone," Old Grandfather was croaking now, "has found the Sword, and is carrying it away. Taking it away, farther and farther, while we sit here and do nothing."

Once more the two men who stood before him exchanged glances. "What Sword would that be, Grandfather?" the younger visitor asked, quite innocently. In the early years of the god's visit this man had been only a simple villager and not an elder, too young to pay any attention to talk about some unessential Sword. So his question now was no attempt at mockery. But still it was too much for the albino, who lapsed into incoherent abuse.

Where once high intelligence had ruled, inside the skull of Vilkata the survivor, now stretched a ravaged mental wasteland illuminated only intermittently by flashes of his former intellect. The mind of the quondam Dark King ached in its concentration on a bitter craving for revenge upon the world in general. Revenge, for the impertinence of the world, in having dared to escape his domination! A sharper and more localized craving for vengeance was centered upon Prince Mark and Princess Kristin of Tasavalta—and to a slightly lesser degree upon the Tasavaltan people—for what Vilkata considered good and sufficient reason.

Inextricably mixed with these cravings for revenge there persisted a monumental regret for the Mindsword's loss. Somehow, on that last day of Vilkata's power, that very nearly peerless weapon had slipped out of his possession.

On that day, in staggering retreat with a band of fugitive gods, crossing the mountains at no very great distance from this hut, Vilkata had been either carrying the Mindsword or wearing it at his belt—he could not now remember which. That black day had seen the Dark King in full flight from his last battlefield, where Soulcutter in the hands of the Silver Queen had finally snuffed out his bid to rule the world. And then within hours he'd somehow lost his own Sword—condemning himself to spend the next fourteen years trying to remember exactly where and how.

He seemed to remember that, at one point during the disastrous retreat, the god Vulcan had been carrying him on his back . . . but that might have been only a dream, or nightmare.

By the time the Dark King had lost his Sword, he'd already been half mad, suffering the psychic pain of terminal defeat, and on top of that, the acid despair engendered by that other Sword, Soulcutter. That output of the Sword of Despair had begun on the battlefield to eat into Vilkata's innermost being.

On that day, on that particular field of combat, the dull dead force of Soulcutter had proven even stronger than the Mindsword's blazing, dazzling call to glory. Vilkata's host, thousands of warriors fanatically loyal to him and ferociously triumphant, had in a frighteningly short span of time degenerated into something less than a mob. His large and powerful army had become little more than an assembly of lethargic bodies. The warriors were slumping to the ground, all their blood still in their veins and their bones unbroken, but their strength melting in a lunatic inertia. The great mass of helpless men had been slain or taken captive before they could recover. Only those few who remained physically close to Vilkata, deep inside the zone of the Mindsword's power, had been able to survive. And even those survivors were badly shaken.

But since he'd fled the battlefield he'd seldom thought about the battle. Ever since that day, most of the Dark King's conscious thought had been expended in a fruitless effort to recall just how and where and when during the terrible retreat he'd lost his Sword. He'd been separated from it somewhere in these very mountains, of that much he was certain. The region was thinly populated, and wherever he'd dropped the treasure, it might still be there.

Alas, these local people, his faithful rescuers, had proven useless in this urgent quest. Vilkata was beginning to wonder, though, if they might not know more than they pretended. It was quite possible, he had recently begun to realize, that they wanted his great Sword for themselves. Might they have already found it, and lied to him of continued failure?

No. In his clearer hours he knew that his mind had tended to wander since his loss, but rationality still prevailed. He'd have known, he'd have felt the change, if anyone had picked the Mindsword up. And, as the remnants of his once-mighty magic had continued to assure him, no one had done so.

Not until today.

Today someone else *had* seized his treasure. The full horror of the fact was slowly being borne in upon the man who had been the Dark King. He could even, behind his sightless eyesockets, conjure up and nurse a fragmentary vision of the one who held it now. . . .

Suddenly screaming renewed abuse, he drove the pair of village elders from him. If they could not comprehend his problem, at least they must be made to leave him alone so he could think. When the two men were gone, some of the women who usually tended to him still remained in the hut—he could hear them moving about in the next room—but they would know better than to bother him.

Vilkata lapsed back into his dark solitary thoughts. The nervous, unconscious movements of his hands and feet soon resumed.

By sunset, the women had also departed, save for one girl, the youngest of several who currently took turns sleeping in an outer room against the possibility that their guest-god should awaken and require something during the night. When the older women looked in on him before leaving, the blind man had let them know in a few savage words that tonight, as on most nights, he preferred to sleep alone.

Though his empty sockets were utterly dead to light, Vilkata was always able to tell when sunset arrived. There were certain changes in the faint sounds of village life that drifted into his small house from time to time, alterations in the sound of birds and insects, and a subtly different feeling in the air.

On this particular evening, the sun was not long gone before another change occurred. This alteration began very subtly, and was almost impossible to define at first. Only one long skilled in magic could have noticed it as soon as the blind man did.

It was also completely unexpected, and it caused him to hold his breath for a full half minute when he first became aware of it.

But there was no mistake. A very different sort of visitor was soon going to arrive.

Vilkata's senses, long trained to the implements and materials of enchantment, had been able to detect the approach of this caller from afar, though he doubted very strongly that anyone else in the village had the least inkling of who—or what—was coming.

Not the least doubt now. There was a subtle smell of sickness in the air, a feeling like an uneasy shifting of the world beneath the blind man's chair, so he could easily have imagined himself perched on the mast of some ship far out of sight of land on the great sea, with storms surrounding him. This evening there was for a little while a more unusual manifestation, a heavy throbbing as of a distant drum. This last Vilkata was able at once to recognize as no mere human sound, and indeed it proceeded from a source that was ordinarily well beyond the reach of human ears.

From the moment when the man who had been the Dark King first detected his approaching visitor, he entertained no doubts about its nature. Most humans would have been terrified, but Vilkata was not altogether dismayed. The time had been when he, by choice, had spent more hours of each day with demons than with human beings.

The knowledge that a demon was swiftly approaching, the first such visitation he had experienced in fourteen years, was not now the total surprise that it would have been a day ago, or on any day when no one had laid hands upon his Sword. Still the event shocked Vilkata into a mental state more closely approaching normality.

The drumming sound soon faded and disappeared, but the other manifestations grew rapidly in strength. This evening the first overt sign of the newcomer's immediate presence was—happy surprise!—a welcome return of vision to the blind man. Not ordinary vision, no, rather a lurid and distorted approximation, more colorful than ordinary human eyesight and keener in some respects. Despite this seeming acuity, Vilkata knew well that the demonic mode of sight was even less trustworthy than that enjoyed by common folk.

"I can see," he suddenly whispered aloud, into what had been the unrelieved darkness of his hut. Now the stark outlines of walls and furniture, the colors drab, were plain in lightless night. His first reaction was that of a man awakening from dull sleep to horror and ugliness. Was *this* the room in which he spent his days, and years? This shabby hovel, cramped and dirty—

Before Vilkata could complete the thought he heard the demon's voice. The syllables sounded in the man's ears as any human might have heard them, light desiccated sounds evoking thoughts of dead leaves swirling among dry bones.

"Receive and enjoy my humble gift of sight, Dark King," the demon said—and its tone was reassuringly deferential, as of old.

Vilkata thought that he recognized—or rather that he ought to recognize—this particular demon. In the old days he had known many of the foul things—many. He ought to remember this one's name. . . .

The man mumbled his response, as if he were speaking to himself, unaccustomed to any real conversation.

"I can see my room now—but not my visitor." Still the thing's name eluded him, still its individual presence hovered tantalizingly on the brink of recognizability.

"I hesitate to show myself," the dry bones scraped.

"I know your nature, visitor. That would indeed be hard to mistake. What can you have to fear from me? Be bold and show yourself, assume whatever form you choose. What is your name?"

Without further hesitation the demon took form in Vilkata's vision, appearing as if from nowhere, adopting a shape utterly incompatible with its voice—or with its real nature. The chosen form was that of a naked woman. Vilkata was not surprised. In all the dealings he'd had with demons in the days of his power, naked humanity was one of the most common illusions they projected.

Distrustfully he stared at this almost-convincing semblance of a female human body, lusty and youthful. The woman-face was blurred in detail, as usual in these visions, but what did that matter? The rest of the body, the sexual regions in particular, was very clear. Long black hair fell around full breasts. The firmly rounded thighs were slightly parted, the painted eyelids half lowered, the red lips smiling. The nameless female, archetype of a palace courtesan, sprawled wantonly in a crude chair across the room, her body unadorned save for a long string of pearls.

The Dark King knew well that as a rule these erotic images lacked substance. He commanded sharply: "Put on a different shape, I do not care for that one."

"As you wish, Lord Vilkata." The woman's lips moved to form the dry demon's voice, and even as they moved, they changed. In a twinkling her shape had become that of a male human, an anxious-looking, honest, sturdy yeoman of early middle age, unarmed and clothed for rough service, standing beside the chair in which the woman had been sitting. Briefly the yeoman's shoulders sprouted rudimentary wings, which disappeared again the moment Vilkata frowned at the manifestation.

The eyeless man who was no longer blind prodded, in a suddenly strong voice: "I asked you your name."

"I am Akbar, Lord Vilkata," said the yeoman in humble tones, going down on one knee in the center of the shabby, uncarpeted wooden floor. "Perhaps you remember me."

"Akbar. Yes, of course. I do remember now." The demon of that name had been one of the most cowardly and otherwise contemptible of the host who had served the Dark King—though by no means the least powerful. "You may rise."

The figure of the yeoman bounced up briskly to his feet, capable-looking hands clasped before him. "Long have I sought to find you, Dark King. I am anxious to serve you again, and I promise to do so as faithfully as before."

Well, Vilkata could believe that kind of promise; because no demon, least of all the dastardly Akbar, had ever served anyone with any kind of faith. But all of their race were very powerful, and if you had the power and skill in magic to control demons, knew their limitations—and were willing to accept the risks—they could be very useful.

Suddenly the man in the crude chair frowned. "Why have you come seeking me now, after all this time? It must have something to do with the Sword."

The yeoman bowed. "My master is as clever as always."

"Ha. Perhaps I am still clever, perhaps not. But there are certain things a man does not forget—what is it, then? What do you want?"

"It is with great humility, Master, that I propose—dare I use the word?—a partnership."

"Say on."

Vilkata listened carefully as the thing went on, always speaking with great deference, to suggest what their relationship should be: from now on it would stay with Vilkata, or at least be in touch with him frequently, and help him. His magically renewed vision would persist indefinitely, even when the demon itself was elsewhere. Akbar could also provide the aging man with new strength and energy, perhaps even some change in appearance, physically renewed youth—and, a matter of even greater importance, it would take him near the Sword he sought to recover.

"Take me near it? Does that mean, in plain language, that you will help me get it back?"

"Of course . . . and there is revenge, Master! I do not forget what is most important. I can help you attain the revenge you seek to have upon your bitterest enemies."

Suddenly Vilkata was aware of a pulse beating in his own head. Blood returning, as it seemed, after years of almost-suspended life. "Yes? And what then?"

"What then, Master? My poor intellect does not permit me to follow—"

"I mean, what do you intend to gain from this partnership of ours?"

The thing's dry, androgynous voice continued to be fawning, soothing, in contrast with the sturdy, honest yeoman's figure: "All I ask in return from you, Great Master, is that you give me certain preferential treatment. When you have regained the power that once was yours—and, if and when the Sword of Glory is yours again, that you should appoint me as your second in command over whatever forces of human beings and demons you then command. Your viceroy, over whatever lands you may then rule."

The albino's voice had become as dry as the demon's own. "No thoughts of having the top place for yourself, I suppose?"

"Above yourself? Not I! No, no. Never! Remember, Great Lord, was I not content to be subordinate in the old days? When you ruled a kingdom, Master, and that Sword was yours before?" The yeoman spoke so earnestly; what a fine, sturdy peasant he seemed! "Was I not content?"

The thing seemed to be asking the question seriously, really hoping for an answer.

"I suppose you were," Vilkata grudgingly acknowledged. "That is to say, I don't recall any particular effort at rebellion." In fact, as this conversation progressed he had gradually come to remember more and more about Akbar. Yes, definitely a cowardly sort of demon. Self-effacing, forever trying to avoid risk and responsibility, always seeking first of all to evade the pain of magical punishment and the possibility of destruction. One of the more easily managed demons, certainly. The very one he might have chosen to meet, had the choice been his, in his current state of weakness.

"There you are, my lord. I see that you do remember me. Why should you not, with my help, be able to regain your Sword?"

Wind whined, stirring the dry leaves; for a moment the yeoman's face was blurred into a caricature. "You were a fine master, a great and intelligent master. I am not clever enough to be a master over clever men and demons—not without direction from above—but you assuredly are."

The thing was waiting for an answer.

"Of course I will accept your offer," the Dark King said after a moment. What choice had he, really? It would be pointless, he thought, for him to issue warnings, to say anything of his abiding suspicions. At one time his magic had been quite capable of managing demons, including creatures vastly more formidable, because less cowardly, than this one. His powers might be shaky now—but fortunately there was no need to try to establish magical control over Akbar just yet. The demon was coming to him willingly, and Vilkata saw no reason, given time and a chance to regain his physical and psychic strength, why his powers of control should not eventually be dominant again. Gradually, subtly, he would regain the upper hand. . . .

"Our pact is concluded, then?" the sturdy, hearty yeoman asked him anxiously.

"Our pact is made, and sealed. Where is the Mindsword now?"

"It is not far from here at all, Master. Not very far. Allow me to show you, Master, what I see."

And in a moment, by means of his demonically provided vision, just as on occasion in the old days, Vilkata was once more able to behold a physically distant scene. This picture was of a rider traveling alone, wearing the Mindsword at his side. Magic and symbolism informed the vision, so that the Dark King perceived the weapon of the gods as a pillar of billowing flame, long as a spear.

"Take me to it!"

"I shall, Master, I shall! Never fear. But that Sword, as you know, is very powerful. We must take no chances. We must have a plan."

"You mean the fellow might detect us when we get near him, or even as we approach, and use the Sword on us? Is he a magician, then?"

"Perhaps he is not . . . but consider that he has managed to obtain possession of a Sword that other magicians have sought for many years, and failed to find."

"Indeed he has done that . . . and he might well get wind of us, and draw the Sword at an untimely moment—yes, there is that."

Vilkata had no wish to spend the rest of his life in the abject adoration, the selfless service, of any other being.

"There is that, Master, as you say. We would not want him to draw the Sword when we were near. The danger is very real."

Impatiently the Dark King waved a hand before his face, and the wraith of that distant, unknown rider vanished. He, Vilkata, was once more gazing with eyeless and demonic vision at his immediate surroundings, the dark, drab, ugly room of his long exile.

"Of course," he said. "And I—wait." His voice turned sharp, and he directed his vision toward the small room's only door, which now stood closed. "Who's there?"

He knew, even as he spoke, that the person outside must be only the village girl who had stayed for the night, roused to a fatal curiosity by the sound of a strange voice in the Lord Vilkata's room. But it would certainly be best to make sure.

There was a whisper and a blurring in the air. Without visibly occupying the intervening space, the figure of the yeoman, moving with inhuman speed and silence, was already standing at the door, pulling it quickly open.

Just outside, the slight figure of the young girl stood revealed, her face startled, empty hands beginning to rise before her as if in an effort to ward something off.

The yeoman holding the door open bowed lightly toward Vilkata.

"A pleasant morsel, Master," the dry leaves rasped, "for the two of us to share tonight. For each of us to enjoy, in his own way. What remains will be appropriate as a small present for these villagers. A token of your appreciation of their years of hospitality."

Vilkata began to laugh. His mirth rose louder and harder, as he had not laughed in years. Meanwhile the girl seemed to be petrified.

"Bring her in," the Dark King commanded presently.

But the yeoman only bowed himself aside, out of deference, it seemed. "Nay, you, Master, shall of course be first."

Vilkata looked at his new partner. Then he arose from his crude chair, on limbs and joints that had suddenly regained something of their youthful suppleness and strength, and stalked toward the door.

The girl screamed at his approach, and broke free of her paralysis. She ran into the little kitchen behind her. There was no door leading directly outside from the kitchen, and she went for the only window.

The man who had once been the Dark King, and now would be again, caught her from behind; the back of her simple dress tore in his grip as he pulled her back into the room. Now she slumped in his grip, and seemed to have no voice for screaming left.

But a moment later the girl broke free, with a spasmodic effort. Careening against the table in the center of the room, she snatched up a kitchen knife.

The demon blurred into action once more; one of the yeoman's hands, suddenly sharp-taloned at the end of an arm unnaturally elongated, swung forward past Vilkata's shoulder to strike.

The knife fell from the girl's hand. Her face, suddenly bloody, grew blurred in the Dark King's demonic vision, as she slumped forward into his ready grasp.

3

CROWN Prince Murat's destination on his lonely ride was Tasavalta. Slightly more than a year had passed since his first visit to that realm. In the course of that visit he had met Princess Kristin for the first time. Murat had spent only a few days in her presence, and had not laid eyes on her since his hasty departure from her land. But throughout the intervening months the image of her lovely face had never completely left him; the impression of grace and beauty inspired by her chastely clothed body had endured.

Now, on the first day after Murat had found the Sword, Kristin's presence was brighter and clearer than ever in his mind's eye as he rode alone toward her homeland, traversing the desolation of the southern foothills of the Ludus Mountains.

Around midday the Crown Prince was roused from certain improbable daydreams concerning himself and the Princess by the discovery that he was being followed. Glancing back along the way he had come, he caught a glimpse of a single rider on his track, no more than two hundred meters behind him.

Setting all daydreams aside for the moment, Murat began to concentrate intently on matters at hand. Guiding his riding-beast into a maze of tumbled, almost house-sized boulders, he circled back to intercept his own trail, and at a carefully selected point of vantage waited to surprise the man who followed him. Disdaining to draw in his own defense the weapon he was carrying as a gift for the Princess, Murat instead unholstered an ordinary battle-ax from its place beside his saddle. Then he waited, listening to the approaching sound of hooves, ready for whoever might be coming.

Moments later a young man, armed, rode into sight, almost within arm's length. Murat drew back his ax—

"Father! Don't strike!"

The weapon was lowered, as the man who wielded it recoiled. Then the Crown Prince leaned forward in his saddle, staring with the stupidity of total astonishment into the eyes of his only son. Only in the last year or two had the youth grown into his full stature, and for a moment his father had failed to recognize him.

"Carlo!"

"Father!"

The ax was quickly reholstered, by a fumbling hand. After a moment or two of awkwardness—father and son had not seen each other for many months—they dismounted and embraced.

"You are looking well," Murat commented at last, holding his son at arm's length. Carlo, dark and round-faced, well dressed and well armed, was not as tall as his father, but in a year or two he would probably be physically stronger.

"And you," the lad responded, "are looking tired."

In the next moment explanations, and demands for news, poured out on both sides.

Carlo had left Culm only a month ago, and could report on what was happening there. Unfortunately the conditions that had turned his father into a semivoluntary exile still obtained. The aged Queen, Murat's stepmother, still ruled, with her sickly consort at her side. And the royal couple, like many others in the homeland, still blamed Murat for failing to bring home the healing Sword of Love.

Without being asked, Carlo added to his report the information that his own mother and his sister were now living with his mother's relatives. "I told Mother that I meant to find you, Father."

"And had my dear wife any message for me?"

Carlo, suddenly downcast, had to admit that she had not.

Murat, having expected no other answer, shrugged; years ago his wife's feelings and opinions had largely ceased to interest him. Then, seeing his son's sad face, he smiled and tried to cheer him up. "I am glad that you came looking for me."

Carlo brightened at that. He began to explain how, with considerable difficulty, he had managed to track down his father.

Then he asked, in a puzzled voice, and in the manner of one who really wanted to know, what his father was doing.

The older man gazed on his son with quiet satisfaction. "I have been on a quest of my own."

"A successful quest?"

"Indeed! Very successful!" Murat, clutching the black hilt at his side, in his turn explained something—not all—about his search for, and recovery of, the Sword.

"But that's wonderful!" Carlo was suitably impressed. "And where are you going now, Father? Back to Culm?"

"To Tasavalta."

The youth shook his head, uncomprehending. "Tasavalta again! But why?"

"For a very good reason. On my last visit to that land, a year ago, I did someone a great wrong. Now at last I am able to do something to set the matter right."

Carlo was frowning. He didn't understand. "But—the Tasavaltans will want to throw you in prison, won't they? Or worse?"

"Princess Kristin will listen to me. Especially when I present her with this Sword as a gift."

"You intend to give it away? To the Princess in Sarykam?" The young man's perplexity grew worse.

"Yes, that's what I mean to do. Come, if you're ready, let us ride on."

The two remounted. As they rode on, side by side, Murat's son was silent for a time. Then, still looking troubled, he said, "I hear that Prince Mark has a short temper. If they really believe that you have wronged them—" Carlo broke off, looking worried.

"Mark is generally away on some adventure. If he happens to be at home, well, I'm not afraid to face him. Short-tempered or not, he is said to be a fair man, and he will listen to me."

Actually the Crown Prince spoke with somewhat more confidence than he felt. It had already occurred to him that in the unlikely event that Kristin's clod of a husband was on hand when he, Murat, arrived in Sarykam, his welcome could well be unpleasant. But Murat had determined to take the chance.

Carlo, riding beside him, kept turning his head to look at the black hilt. At last the youth asked: "May I hold the Mindsword, Father? In the sheath, I mean. I won't draw it, of course."

His father considered the request seriously, then solemnly shook his head. "I think not. I have pledged not to draw it, nor to give it to anyone except the Princess herself."

"I'm sorry, Father, but I still don't understand why you intend to give it to Princess Kristin and Prince Mark."

An edge crept into Murat's voice. "I thought I had explained. A year ago I stole the Sword Woundhealer from that lady's treasury. In doing so I wronged her greatly, though at the time I had convinced myself that what I was doing was the proper course of action. Now I am determined to make amends."

Carlo was silent. Murat wondered suddenly if he was thinking that his father had wronged others also, in times past, and never made amends in such grand style.

At last the youth spoke again. "Isn't there some other way for you to right the wrong you feel you have committed against Princess Kristin?"

"This is the way I choose," Murat said shortly, and tapped the black hilt with his palm.

Carlo, well acquainted with that tone, did not argue.

Shortly before sunset the two travelers stopped to make camp for the night. The subject of Swords was not discussed again between them before they slept, Murat lying with the sheathed Sword as close to him as a lover's body.

In the morning father and son traveled on companionably toward Tasavalta, speaking of peaceful matters, using the time to renew their acquaintance.

Early on the second day after Carlo had joined Murat, the pair became aware that they were being followed. No such luck as a single stalker this time, but rather a band of eight, who definitely had the look of bandits. When father and son tried to outdistance their pursuers, four more riders appeared ahead, posted in just the right spot for tactical advantage, efficiently cutting off the travelers' escape.

Father and son slowed their hard-breathing mounts to a walk, and presently to a halt. A ravine to their right and a rock wall to their left formed practically impassable barriers. The two found themselves trapped, effectively surrounded by a dozen mounted men who were poorly clothed, heavily armed, and plainly devoid of good intentions.

Murat had not yet voiced to his son his worst fear: that these might not be merely ordinary brigands, but the agents of some great magician or other potentate who had somehow learned that he, Murat, now possessed the Mindsword, meant to have it from him, and felt confident of being able to achieve that end. The Crown Prince had been aware all along that his finding might well have shaken the threads of several complicated wizard-webs.

"Father?" Carlo awaited orders. The young man was pale, but bearing himself well; he had already drawn his own sword and looked ready to fight to the death if his father should command it.

Murat had as yet unsheathed no weapon. The pledge he had made to himself, in his own mind, never to draw the Sword for his own benefit, was indeed a solemn one. But now circumstances were gravely altered. Now not only was his own life at stake but his son's as well, and not only their lives but possession of the Princess Kristin's treasure.

While Murat hesitated, the band of ruffians were closing in calmly and efficiently to their front and rear, little by little improving their already overwhelming position, edging their riding-beasts momentarily closer and closer still—except for three who remained well out of sword-range, holding bows and arrows ready.

Until now the highwaymen had gone about their business without wasting breath on words. But now at last the bandit leader, one of the four who waited ahead, called out to his victims, demanding that the pair dismount and hand over all their worldly possessions. As he pronounced this ultimatum, the robber's voice and attitude were rather cheery. If, he said, the surrounded pair surrendered their material possessions without fuss, he would graciously allow them to keep their lives.

Murat, his right hand resting lightly on the black hilt, replied in a firm princely voice. "I think that we will hand over nothing."

"Oh, no?" The bandit leader sounded neither angered nor surprised by Murat's defiance, but suddenly tired and rather sad. He was a squat man, with a long graying mustache, who occupied his saddle as if he might have been born there. "Well, then, your fate be on your own heads." But still the brigand delayed, giving his men no command to attack, squinting at Murat now as if trying to settle some new doubt in his own mind. Presently he added: "Your clothing will be worth more to us if we can get it without holes or bloodstains. I grant you one last chance to reconsider."

"Instead," said the Crown Prince, raising his royal voice once more, "I propose a rather different arrangement. If you and your men will let us pass, and go promptly and peacefully on your way, I will refrain from drawing my Sword."

There was no immediate reply from the mustached man. A great many people knew about the gods' Twelve Swords, and quite a few had seen at least one of them at some time. For a moment the bandit leader did not appear to react at all. Then he said in the same tired voice: "Anyone can craft a sword with such a dull black hilt."

Murat did not respond.

With a gesture the weary-looking robber ordered his archers to nock their arrows.

And Murat, feeling a profound reluctance mixed with an unexpected fiery anticipation, drew the Mindsword from its plain sheath.

His own first sensation was one of surprise. The naked Sword now in his grip and control had much less effect on him than it had had when he approached the unclaimed weapon. Now the vast power of the gods' magic went flowing outward, away from the Sword's holder in all directions.

The bandits' riding-beasts, as well as Carlo's, exploded in rearing and plunging excitement. This was caused, Murat supposed, by the sudden turmoil gripping their masters' minds and bodies. One or two men in the enemy ranks were thrown, but no one save Murat, not even the victims themselves, paid much attention to this fact. Each of the men caught in the web of magic had to respond in his own way to the wrenching internal change imposed from without. Some of the bandits cast down their weapons violently, some sheathed them with great care. Several of those who were not thrown dismounted voluntarily, while others went galloping in little circles, shouting incoherently like drunken men or lunatics.

Among the bandits only their leader remained physically almost motionless. He bowed his head for a long moment, and his rough hands gripping the reins went white-knuckled.

His shoulders heaved. Moments later, he raised a tear-stained face to plead with Murat. "Forgive me, lord!" the robber cried in a breaking voice. "I did not know you—I could not see you clearly when we approached, I did not realize—"

"You are forgiven," Murat called back mechanically. His chief emotion was relief that the armed threat had disappeared, that his life and his son's life were safe. And at the same time he knew horror at what he had been forced to do. The Sword in his right hand felt very heavy; on drawing the Blade he had raised it overhead, but now he let his right arm sag down slowly to his side.

Suddenly remembering Carlo, the Crown Prince reined his riding-beast around. His son, sword still drawn in his right hand, was just bringing his own plunging mount under control. And with a pang Murat saw that Carlo, like the bandit leader, was weeping.

The young man stretched out a hand toward him, and choked out words. "Father . . . are you all right?"

"Yes, of course I am. And you?" Hastily Murat sheathed the radiant steel in his right hand.

Carlo sobbed. "If—if any of them had hurt you, I'd—I'd have—I don't know what."

Deeply moved, and vaguely alarmed, Murat rode closer to his son. "Put up your sword, Carlo. It's all right now, they can't hurt either of us."

Meanwhile the bandits, all of them now dismounted and empty-handed, were prostrating themselves among a litter of discarded weapons, groveling before the Crown Prince.

"Lead us, Master!" one of them cried.

"Lead you?" he whispered, startled as if he did not understand at first. Later he was to wonder why he had not understood at once.

Instantly the plea became a chorus. "Lead us!"

"Take us with you, wherever you are going! Don't abandon us here!" shouted another bandit. It was a cry from the very bottom of the heart.

Murat cast one more look around him, while his left hand, trembling, sought out the black hilt once more. The Mindsword's radiant power was sheathed, quenched for the time being, but its presence persisted strongly in the surrounding light and air, as the sun's heat might linger in low country after the sun had set.

Gradually the men who were prostrate on the ground, and Carlo weeping in his saddle, managed to regain full control of themselves.

"Get to your feet," Murat curtly ordered his new devotees, as soon as he judged that they were calm enough to listen to him. Being an object of worship was already making him uncomfortable.

Now instantly obedient, his former enemies got to their feet only to advance on their new lord with empty hands raised in supplication. They clustered timidly yet eagerly around the Crown Prince, daring to clutch gently at his boots and stirrups, relentlessly importuning him to become their leader.

The gray-mustached man who had been their leader before the Sword was drawn now came pushing his way through and ahead of the others, pleading as fervently as any.

"Master, allow me to introduce myself. I am called Gauranga of the Mountains, and I place myself and my poor company of villains entirely at your service. I am their leader, and the only one with any skill at all in magic. We are not much, perhaps, but we are the most accomplished and successful band of brigands for many kilometers around."

Murat could not help feeling a certain sympathy for the poor outcasts, despite their recent murderous intentions. But other concerns still dominated his thoughts.

"Are you sure you're all right, Carlo? The Sword's influence fell upon you also. I didn't want that to happen but as things were I couldn't help it. I'm sorry—"

"I'm fine, Father," the lad interrupted. And really he now looked perfectly well. Then his young face clouded again. "It was only when I thought—when I feared that they might hurt you—"

"Yes. Well, they didn't." The Crown Prince turned his head to speak sharply to one of his new devotees. "Let go of my stirrups, you, and stand back a little—that's better. They didn't hurt either of us."

Murat, inspecting his son, felt reassured. It was unlikely, after all, that Carlo could have taken any real harm. Historically the Sword's effects were very often only temporary; and what was more natural, after all, than that a son should honor and love his father?

The condition of the bandits was another matter. A few minutes ago, they had all been thieves and murderers—and they had hardly changed in that respect, Murat realized. They would grab up their weapons instantly if he were to point out to them someone he wished robbed or murdered; grab up their weapons and fight for him, win, or die in the attempt.

In a few more moments he and Carlo were ready to move on. But a dozen men on foot still surrounded them, begging not to be left behind.

"What do you want of me?" Murat demanded of them irritably. But he realized it was a foolish question even before the words had left his lips.

"Be our leader!" the bandits clamored eagerly, almost in unison.

Now Gauranga, the former leader of the robbers, spoke up again, enthusiastically offering for Murat's consideration a scheme his band had long contemplated. There was a certain walled village that the robbers knew of, a settlement so large and strongly defended that the risks of attacking it had been judged unacceptable. But now, in the service of their glorious new leader, they would gladly stake their lives in such an effort.

"But the lord must not risk his own life!" Another bandit broke in, suddenly aware of the peril implicit in his former leader's proposition. "Our new lord must stay in a place of safety!" Others growled their agreement.

Before Murat could decide how best to placate the gang and get them out of his way, another bandit had the floor and was arguing that the lord would be in no real danger even if he were to join in the attack.

"The Sword he carries will open the eyes of the villagers, even as it did ours." And then, as the elated bandit went on to explain, all the inhabitants' treasure, their food and drink, their gold and their daughters, would become instantly available for plundering. Once the whole village belonged to the lord, he could distribute its wealth among his followers as he chose.

At this prospect a joyful babble arose, only to die out again as soon as Murat broke in firmly. "No! No, I am not going to attack any village, and neither are you. I command you all: from this moment forward, attack no one unless I give you permission."

There was a murmur of surprise at this, though nothing that could have been called an objection. Briefly the Crown Prince regained the quiet, respectful attention of the group.

Then a question burst from one of the worshipers. "What is your name, Lord?"

Another pleaded: "Will you tell us your name?"

Again a general clamor mounted. From the exaggerated tones of pleading and worship in the men's voices, someone just arriving on the scene might have thought that they were mocking the silent man in their midst. But he, who had experience of the Swords, knew better.

It was Carlo, his adoring son, who shouted out his title—Crown Prince of Culm—and then with huge pride claimed the Crown Prince as his father.

A disproportionately loud cheer arose from the small group.

"See?" one of the thieves demanded triumphantly of his fellows. "I knew it all along! Real nobility!"

"The greatest!"

With a quick, reluctant salute Murat acknowledged the newest round of cheers. He felt weary. He needed time to think. "Very well, you may come with me, for the time being."

Renewed cheering answered him. The Crown Prince was thinking that this was certainly the quickest way out of the situation, and such an escort ought at least to discourage other bandits from attacking. The presence of this gang would reduce his chances of having to go through this all over again.

While he thought of it, he sternly ordered his recruits to protect, obey, and honor his son as well.

"He shall be second only to yourself, sir."

"And," Murat reiterated, "there must be no more robbery and murder. Not while you serve me."

Still the men raised no objection, though now several of them looked thoughtful. Murat could imagine their concern: if robbery was now forbidden them, what were they to do from now on, how were they to survive?

One man cried out—it was not an objection but a plea for help—that they faced an immediate food shortage.

Murat and Carlo exchanged looks. Together, their two packs did not contain enough surplus food to provide more than one meal for so many.

"Enough!" Murat shouted into a fresh murmuring, and once more obtained instant silence.

"I have changed my mind," he said. "I order you to go on about your business. Depart from my son and me. Obtain food as best you can, but kill no one for it." It seemed to him a reasonable compromise, under the circumstances.

He ought to have known better, but the reaction caught him completely by surprise. Stricken faces turned toward him. One howled to know why they were being so hideously punished. One or two others swore that they must kill themselves if their sublime master disowned them in this way.

Others, Gauranga among them, objected more rationally: "Go about our business? But Lord, you have forbidden us our business!"

Murat looked at Carlo. Carlo looked back at him, waiting in happy expectancy, ready to be delighted with whatever his glorious Father should decide.

The Crown Prince closed his eyes for a moment, feeling a great weariness. In time, he repeated to himself, people tended to recover from what the Mindsword did to them. At least they recovered if they wanted to recover, if they were not exposed to the Sword's continued influence, if other pressures were in place to have some contrary effect on them.

He had no intention of ever drawing this particular damned Blade again. That being the case, he relented.

"Very well, those of you who want to follow me may do so, for the time being. But sooner or later you must all go your own ways. I do not need your services."

Gauranga and his men looked sad on hearing this. Sad but determined, Murat decided. Some of them at least were certain to try to prove their worth as followers. And at least an immediate mass excommunication had been avoided.

4

Murat and his son, attended by their new retinue of ragged but faithful followers, continued their cross-country progress at a somewhat slower pace. As the hours passed, and time came to stop for the night, the Crown Prince came to find the presence of the bandits, or former bandits, less ominous and worrisome. It was, after all, pleasant to be able to fall asleep knowing that his life and his son's were guarded by sentinels of fanatical loyalty.

The next day Murat was able to obtain food—to almost everyone's surprise, he insisted on paying for it—from a village whose alarmed inhabitants were fortunate enough to enjoy a modest surplus. Murat intended to feed the former bandits, if he could, as long as they were with him, but beyond that he really felt no responsibility to them. After all, these men when in possession of their free will had been perfectly willing to kill him and his son. Nor was the Crown Prince willing to assume any responsibility, in his own mind, for what the current members of his armed escort might do after he eventually sent them away. Then they would be free men once more, and their conduct would be entirely up to them.

By afternoon of the second day of his escorted journey, Murat started to find some amusement in the robbers' continued adulation—they were often unintentionally entertaining, as drunken men or lunatics could sometimes be.

Chuckling, he commented on this fact to his son, who worshipfully agreed.

It was very fortunate, the Crown Prince thought to himself as they rode on, that he himself, instead of some raw youth—Carlo, for example, or almost anyone of Carlo's age—had recovered the Sword of Glory. Much better for such dangerous power to repose in the hands of one like himself, an experienced man of the world, someone able to take such things in stride. In happier times he as Crown Prince had already received—perhaps, he thought, sometimes even deserved—his share of adulation. A man in his position learned to accept praise and devotion graciously, and not to allow such things to warp his judgment.

As the odd group progressed southward the landscape grew hour by hour less barren, rugged, and desolate. More farms and villages appeared, and the trail they were following turned into a real road on which moved other travelers. These unanimously gave Murat and his rough escort a wide berth.

Near sunset of their third day on the road together, the Crown Prince and his retinue came upon a blind beggar sitting at the wayside, a pale abandoned-looking man, some fifty years of age to judge by appearances, who raised his thin voice in a moaning plea for alms. In the red evening light the beggar's clothes were gray as a pilgrim's, so worn and tattered that their material and original design were hard to discern. The wooden begging bowl at the wretch's side had nothing in it, as Murat saw when he reined near to toss in a small coin.

A grimy bandage covered the mendicant's eyes. His beard and curly hair might have been shiny black, just touched with gray, had they not been dull with dirt.

At the sounds of the coin clinking in his bowl, and of the hooves of a large party stopping, the beggar raised his sightless face and turned it from side to side, as if to hear better.

"Thank you, Master," croaked the beggar at last, hearing no more coins.

"I have not given you very much." Murat raised his head to glance ahead and behind along the almost deserted road. "And you seem to have chosen a spot where you can expect but little more."

Now words poured from the beggar rapidly; evidently he was eager to talk to anyone who'd listen. "You see before you, kind Master, a victim of malignant fate. A persecution almost beyond belief has toppled me from a position of great respect and brought me here."

In Murat's experience, most mendicants had some heart-rending story to tell, and some of their tales were doubtless true. But here was an oddity to intrigue the curiosity of the Crown Prince: this fellow's speech was that of an educated man, a rare attribute in one of his profession.

Meanwhile, the blind man was spinning out his tale of troubles. "Ah, if only my blessed mistress knew to what a state I have been reduced!"

"And who's your mistress, fellow?"

The answer came firmly, and without hesitation: "I was honored to be able to serve the glorious Princess Kristin, who still rules in Tasavalta—if only word of my plight could reach her!"

Murat paused, staring at the man. "I see—on good terms with royalty, are you?" A laugh went up from those of his armed retainers who were listening.

The wretch, as if he were truly capable of injured feelings, seemed to be trying to summon up his dignity. "Sir, for years I served faithfully the royal house of Tasavalta. You will not believe the old blind beggar, sir, and for that no one can blame you—but these hands have many a time held the little Princess, when she was only a child, and bounced her on this knee."

Murat paused again, longer this time, wondering.

"Are you lying to me, fellow?" he asked at last, in a quiet voice. "About knowing the Princess? If so, admit it now, and no harm shall come to you. I'll even give you another coin." He jingled his purse temptingly.

The blind man was silent for a moment; but then he had risen to his feet, and was lifting his angular face toward the Crown Prince, and shaking his head ever so slightly from side to side, as if he might be straining to use the sense that he no longer possessed.

At last he blurted out: "I am not lying, Lord. Great Lord, if you can bring me to the palace at Sarykam, blessed be your name, and granted be all your wishes." And with that he fell on his knees before Murat.

Murat turned to look at his son. But since his exposure to the Mindsword, Carlo had ceased to offer him any advice or argument. Now, whatever happened, Murat's son only waited worshipfully to see what his lord and master and father would decide.

Sighing, Murat turned to one of his new followers, and gave orders that the strange beggar be given food and drink, and one of the bandits' spare mounts.

Then he faced the trembling beggar again. "Fellow, I take it you are able to ride? Of course if I present you to the Princess, and she looks at you like the piece of rotten meat that you appear to be, and does not know you, I'll look quite a fool. If that proves to be the case, I'll see to it that you don't slip away forgotten."

But the fellow only raised his quivering arms, his repulsive face almost radiant with apparent joy. "A million blessings on you, glorious Master!"

Murat nodded absently. Already he half regretted his decision. "What is your name, by the way?"

"I was called Metaxas, Lord."

When a riding-beast was led to the fellow, he groped for saddle and stirrup and managed to get himself aboard. Meanwhile Murat had noticed one of the bandits picking the forgotten coin out of the bowl, and stuffing it away in his own pocket. Well, why not? thought the Crown Prince. The one wretch probably deserved it as much as the other.

"Ride on!" Murat commanded, and signaled the advance.

That night, while Murat's eager servants were making camp for him and Carlo, Murat strolled over to the former beggar, intending to question him further. But he was distracted from his questions by the fellow's greeting: "I see, Master, that you carry a great treasure with you. I see also that you have suffered much, but that in the future you will be rewarded as you deserve."

Murat was not impressed. He supposed that the man might well have overheard some talk among the bandits about the Sword. He said: "For one without eyes, you claim to see a great deal."

Metaxas only bowed in his new clothing—new to him—cheap worn stuff, but still a vast improvement.

The Crown Prince turned away from the beggar, but he had not gone far when he was approached, humbly, by Gauranga of the Mountains, the former leader and acting wizard of the bandit group.

"What is it?"

"Master," gray-mustached Gauranga whispered, "I sense something wrong about this ugly foundling."

"Wrong? In what way?"

"I don't know, Master." Gauranga shook his head. "But there's something I do not like. A bad smell, and I don't mean the kind of stink that can be removed by scrubbing. Beware of him!"

Murat cast a look over his shoulder at the beggar, who looked about as unthreatening as a man could look. "I will, my friend. Thank you for your warning. The old wretch seems harmless enough to me, but keep an eye on him just in case."

Again the Crown Prince walked on. A few minutes later, Carlo, frowning suspiciously in the direction of the blind man who was well out of hearing, approached his father and volunteered his first advice in days. "It would be good, I think, Father, to hear this beggar's history in more detail, to test if his claim is genuine."

The father shook his head. "I assumed at first that he was probably lying when he said he knew the Princess Kristin. But when I offered to bring him to Sarykam, he accepted at once, with what appeared to be unfeigned joy. Either he's an excellent actor, or he may be speaking the truth after all, in which case the Princess will be pleased to have me bring her an old family retainer I've rescued from disaster. Of course, it's still possible that our newest recruit has deluded himself with dreams of a happy past."

"That may be the answer, Father. And I was wondering, has it occurred to you . . . ?"

"What?" Murat demanded impatiently.

"Well—that Woundhealer would have been used to cure him of his blindness, empty eyesockets or not, had he really been a favorite at the Tasavaltan court during the years when that Sword was there."

The older man frowned. "We'll see. Certainly we'll have to clean the fellow up further before we can bring him near the Princess. Remind me to have a couple of the men see to it tomorrow, when we reach running water somewhere."

"If you were to use your Sword now, Father, to make the blind man your loyal servant, then you could be sure of him at once."

Murat darted a sharp look at his son. "I told you that I am not going to use the Princess's Sword again."

Next day Murat took time to see that the blind man was cleaned up more thoroughly, dressed in somewhat better clothing, and his eyes— or rather the holes where his eyes had been—covered with a clean bandage. There could be at least no doubt about his blindness.

Within another day or two Murat, Carlo, and their crew of converted bandits, bringing with them Metaxas the sightless beggar, were closely approaching the frontier of Tasavalta. This boundary ran unmarked over vast stretches of country, but the robbers assured Murat they knew exactly where it lay.

"What will you do, Father," Carlo was asking now, "if Her Highness does not welcome you as a friend?"

"I thought I had explained that. I will talk to her. I believe she is as reasonable as she is beautiful, and she will listen."

"But suppose she doesn't?"

Murat looked steadily at his son. "I can assure you of this much. Whatever problem of credibility I might face when we reach Sarykam, there can be no question of my using the Sword to persuade Kristin to see me as a friend. Is that what you were going to suggest?"

"I wasn't planning to suggest that, Father. I was just—"

"Good."

Carlo was silent.

"This power," his father continued, thumping the black hilt, "is going to remain safely muffled in its sheath, until I can hand over the sheath and all to Princess Kristin. I wish to be fairly reconciled with the Princess, not win her over in a one-sided contest of magic."

Still, from time to time during the day, Carlo continued to express his doubts about his father's plan.

"I don't see, Father, why you are so reluctant to draw the Sword in her presence—or in anyone's. Now having experienced the effects for myself, I can testify that the Sword of Glory does not deceive—at least it doesn't when *you* are holding it. In your hands, it only enables the object of its influence to see the truth about its holder." After noting the way his father looked at him, the young man shook his head and dared to argue further. "It's true, Father! You really are a great man, and worthy of great devotion!"

The Crown Prince smiled, shook his head, and rode on.

Murat had heard that long stretches of the borders of Tasavalta were usually left not only unmarked but unguarded, so that more often than not it was possible to cross back and forth without being seen or challenged. Again, some of his magically reformed bandits confirmed this, though otherwise they had little good to say about the land they were about to enter.

But this time fortune decreed that they were not to achieve an unseen crossing. Scarcely had Murat's little party set foot inside the realm of Princess Kristin than it encountered a Tasavaltan cavalry patrol.

5

THE land in the vicinity of the encounter was relatively flat and almost treeless; it was quite possible that the patrol had been a kilometer or more away when they caught sight of Murat's party crossing the border. However they had made the discovery, the Tasavaltans were now riding quickly to intercept the intruders.

"No doubt we are a suspicious-looking crew," muttered the Crown Prince to his son. "To the border patrol, we can hardly appear to be anything but bandits."

"What are we going to do, Father?"

"We are certainly not going to run away."

Ordering his followers not to flee, nor to begin a fight, Murat led them slowly forward. As the riders in green and blue drew near, the thuggish-looking members of Murat's escort closed ranks protectively about their leader and his son.

Sternly the Crown Prince ordered his bandit-escort to lower their weapons, and move into an open formation, so he could see the Tasavaltans and they would have a good view of him. Then he continued to ride forward, raising empty hands in a peaceful gesture. Carlo followed of his own accord, keeping a little behind his father.

When Murat had come within fifty or sixty meters of the patrol, some of the troopers began pointing toward him, and calling to their officer. The Crown Prince, when he thought about it, was not surprised; he supposed that probably the whole Tasavaltan army must have been alerted to watch for last year's most notorious villain, the foreign potentate who had been royally entertained by the Princess, and then had treacherously repaid Tasavaltan hospitality by stealing Woundhealer.

Finally the patrol's commanding officer shouted: "Ho, there! You are Crown Prince Murat of Culm?"

Murat reined his animal to a halt, and called back in a firm voice: "I am the man you name. I come in peace, Lieutenant, with my son beside me, to speak to your most honored Princess. I will require an escort to your capital, and I ask that you provide it."

The officer was very young, and his uniform impeccable, even after what must have been several days in the field. He glared at Murat in triumph. "As to the matter of escorts, you'll get one, all right. I have my orders as to what to do, should you ever be caught trespassing within our boundaries. And I intend to carry out my orders. If your son and the rest of your gang wish to depart now, they'll save themselves some trouble. I have no orders concerning them."

The officer, thought Murat, must have felt confident that the ragtag ruffians before him would take to their heels rather than confront regulars at equal odds, the moment he gave them leave to do so. But instead Murat's fanatical bandits, enraged at the very idea of their lord made captive, gripped their weapons and surged forward. Only the Crown Prince shouting at them made them stop.

Startled, the cavalry officer yelled commands at his men, quickly deploying them in readiness for combat. Then, his face reddening, he informed Murat that he and all his escort were prisoners, and that they had better throw down their arms at once.

Murat, struggling to control his restive riding-beast, could feel his anger escalating and the situation slipping away from him. "I have told you that I come in peace—"

The patrol commander interrupted, ordering his archers to nock arrows.

Murat's fanatical defenders bristled; they were not disciplined troops, whom he would have been able to hold in check. His veteran judgment warned him that whatever sway he still held over the situation was rapidly disappearing. Now it seemed that everyone was shouting, so his own conciliatory words had no chance of being heard. A fight was on the verge of breaking out, in which his own life and Carlo's would be at stake. And if they were to kill Tasavaltan border guards, how could they approach the Princess afterward with a claim of peaceful intentions? But neither could Murat surrender and allow himself to be disarmed.

Once again, with a reluctance as great as on the first occasion, but now feeling a fatalistic acceptance also, he drew his Sword. Uppermost in Murat's mind as the dazzling steel cleared leather was the thought that he could not allow his own son to die in his defense.

This time the Crown Prince felt even less of the shock of unleashed magic than when he had first drawn this Sword. But this time, as on that first occasion, every other human being within a hundred meters was engulfed, overwhelmed by the Mindsword's influence.

In the matter of a few moments, the once-arrogant officer of the patrol had joined his men in abandoning their sworn duty without a qualm, and proclaiming their undying devotion to Murat. The Crown Prince, observing their behavior as disinterestedly as possible, thought the scene was very much like that of the bandits' conversion, except that this time the bandits were on hand to welcome their new comrades to the fold, and make them feel more comfortable with their new status.

And this time Murat found himself able to view the matter somewhat more calmly; true, Carlo had now been exposed twice to the Mindsword's power. But there was really no reason to think the experience would do him any harm.

The young lieutenant, as soon as he had regained control of himself, ceased groveling in the dust, brushed off his no-longer impeccable uniform, drew himself up stiffly at attention before the Crown Prince, introduced himself by name and rank, and asked his new lord's pardon for his inexcusable misbehavior of a few minutes ago, when in his confusion of mind he had actually dared to utter threats against his glorious master.

Murat, speaking in a distant voice, pardoned him freely. The Crown Prince, feeling suddenly depressed, was wondering to himself how he had managed, all unintentionally, to land himself in this situation.

One single pardon, in dry words, did not appear to be enough. The lieutenant, stumbling verbally, trying to control himself, and now, despite being forgiven, apparently on the verge of suicidal guilt and shame, explained that he and his men—he asked pardon for them also—had been unable to understand the situation clearly until the Sword was drawn. Its powerful magic had cleared their eyes and their minds.

Murat silently congratulated himself on the graciousness with which he listened to all this and once more granted absolution. This time he tried to sound more concerned, more human, even while concealing his mounting impatience.

Taking a swift visual inventory of all the men around him, the Crown Prince noted in passing that the old beggar, Metaxas, had evidently retreated to a safe distance in the rear at the first threat of combat. One of the bandits was now bringing the blind man forward again to rejoin the group.

Still more patience was required in soothing and forgiving the officer and his troopers. When the Crown Prince had finally convinced them of his forgiveness, he went on to assure them that he and those who followed him meant no harm to any of the Tasavaltan people, least of all the noble and deserving Princess. He, the Crown Prince—as he patiently explained once more—only wanted to be reconciled with Princess Kristin, and with that purpose in mind he was bringing her an impressive gift.

The Tasavaltan soldiers cheered this news—of course, Murat reminded himself, knowing the power of the Swords, these converts at the peak of their fresh-caught enthusiasm doubtless would have cheered their new master just as loudly and fervently had he announced his intention of raping and murdering their wives and sisters.

Eagerly, several of the frontier guards informed the Crown Prince that the Princess Kristin was not currently in residence in Sarykam, the capital city on the coast. Rather, she and her younger son, the only members of the royal family now in the country, were to be found at their summer retreat high in the mountains, some kilometers inland.

"Good! Very good!" Murat found the news pleasing. The difficulties brought on by encountering the patrol had given him pause, and started him worrying seriously about how he was going to approach the city. If the entire Tasavaltan army had standing orders to take him prisoner on sight—and the newly converted officer, reddening with shame, now confirmed that this was indeed the case—then he, Murat, could hardly expect to approach the capital without having to draw his Sword again, and very likely more than once.

But a summer retreat in the mountains was almost certain to be much more readily accessible. On his way there he and his escort would be able at least to avoid the larger population centers. Murat was about to call for a volunteer from among the guardsmen, to ride swiftly ahead carrying an important message to the Princess; but before doing so he had second thoughts.

Taking the Tasavaltan officer aside, Murat patiently explained the difficulty to him. "If I dispatch a man with a message for the Princess, and that man says he comes from me, and speaks only good of me, the Princess and those around her will certainly believe that I have some of their troops under a magical compulsion. Therefore they will credit nothing the messenger tells them. Instead they will dispatch their own messengers to the capital, to mobilize the entire land against me."

The young lieutenant blinked, trying to grasp a point of view he now found so inherently absurd.

"But that would be so foolish of them, Lord! We here, the men of my patrol, are under no compulsion. Quite the opposite. It is only that now our eyes have been opened to your true nobility." And he looked as if he might be considering breaking his stance at attention to make some obeisance, something on the order of casting himself at Murat's feet.

"Yes, of course, you are quite right. Their attitude is foolish," the Crown Prince murmured soothingly. "But send no message for the time being."

"As you wish, Lord."

Murat shook his head, seeing no way at the moment for him to communicate with the Princess credibly. I am one sane man, he thought, for the moment surrounded by those who cannot see straight or think straight. So I, at least, must retain my sanity. Because it is my responsibility to think for us all. And I must decide what will be best for Kristin and her people too.

Murat raised his voice: "We will all of us march together for the time being. Lead the way to her summer retreat."

The cavalry detachment, having been prudently provisioned for a long patrol, carried food enough to feed not only themselves, but the former bandits as well, adequately for the several days it would take for the combined group to approach Princess Kristin.

Further inquiries among his newest adherents gleaned for Murat a welcome confirmation that at least Prince Mark, whose presence might have complicated things immeasurably, was, as so often, out of the country. But Mark was expected back at any time now.

From certain things that the soldiers said, certain expressions that crossed some of their faces when Mark was mentioned, the Crown Prince got the idea that they might retain a high regard for Mark as a fair Prince and a capable soldier. But these indications of regard for Kristin's husband vanished as soon as the men learned that their new master's attitude toward Mark was less than cordial. From now on several of the men had only black looks and dark mutterings at any mention of their former commander. These, Murat decided, were probably men who had nursed some resentment against Mark even before they caught the vibrations of Murat's feelings toward him.

As for the Princess herself, all the troopers were glad to see and hear how highly Murat thought of her. They also continued to hold Kristin in great esteem.

Murat decided that he had learned all he needed to know for the time being.

"Let us march on," he ordered his combined force. "Toward the Princess, in her summer retreat."

6

FOLLOWING the surrender of the border patrol, the Crown Prince and his newly enlarged entourage enjoyed several days of almost uneventful travel. All during this time the Sword remained sheathed at Murat's side. As they traveled he observed his followers carefully, to see how and when the Mindsword's influence would begin to wear off —sooner or later, he knew, it probably would. And indeed, some of the men's behavior did change with the passage of hours and days. The Crown Prince thought that within two days three or four of the bandits and some half a dozen of the troopers had begun to have second thoughts about their quick conversion. The process, unlike that of their metamorphosis into his followers, was quite gradual, manifesting itself only in solemn faces and thoughtful stares; he had no fears of a sudden betrayal.

As the enduring effects of the shock of magic continued to weaken, the undisciplined bandits grew a trifle lax in obeying Murat's orders, and Carlo reported that some of the troopers were beginning to recall their broken oaths of fealty to Tasavalta's Princess. No dramatic event occurred to illustrate these changes, but small signs were visible to one who watched for them as the Crown Prince did. Quietly he asked his son's opinion on what was happening.

Carlo seemed dismayed at the thought of anyone who had once seen the light choosing to turn away from it again. He suggested that his father draw the Sword once more.

But Murat declined to do that. Instead, calling all his followers to attend him, he explained again, as openly and fairly as he could, his reasons for wanting to visit Princess Kristin. He maintained that his goals were just, and that reasonable people ought to be able to perceive them as such without the help of magic. Certainly he meant no harm to the Tasavaltans' beloved Princess or to any of her subjects. Just the opposite, in fact, or he would not be bringing her this great Sword as a gift. This was the first time many of his new followers had learned the nature of his intended gift, and he saw that it made a strong impression.

After he dismissed the meeting, the Crown Prince saw that Carlo was frowning again, and demanded to know what his son was thinking.

"Nothing you have not heard before, Father."

"Then tell me again."

"I am worried," Carlo said. "Worried by the idea of power such as the Mindsword's being simply given away. If someone other than yourself possessed it, such magic could easily convince people to follow the wrong leader."

"I'm sure it could. But Princess Kristin is hardly an evil leader. And the Sword is mine, to do with as I will."

"Yes, of course, Father. But is it in your best interest to have such a treasure pass completely out of the family? The ruling family of Tasavalta are practically strangers to us. And how do we know that they will always want to behave in a friendly way toward us in Culm? In the wrong hands, your Sword's magic might—thoroughly confuse people."

Murat took thought, and smiled. "Well, Carlo, as things have worked out, you and I are seldom in Culm anyway. I doubt that either of us has much future there. And I think what the Princess might choose to do with the Sword after she has it is beside the point. The point is that I owe her restitution for a great wrong, and I intend to give her this Sword to make up for the one I took away."

"As you say, Father," agreed Carlo dutifully.

But, once out of his father's sight, the son shook his head, still worrying. It did little good to keep telling himself that anything and everything his father did was right, and therefore Father must have a good reason for what he wanted to do with the Sword.

"Are you troubled, young Master Carlo?" The old blind man, sitting as usual on the fringe of the camp, raised his sightless face as Carlo approached. Evidently the beggar had sensed that something was wrong.

Carlo's feet slowed and stopped. He sighed, wondering if the beggar had recognized him by the sound of his footsteps. He wished he could confide in someone.

"Is there trouble, then, young Master, between you and your esteemed father?"

"I don't know," answered Carlo soberly. "I hope not. No, I don't really believe there's any trouble."

"Something, perhaps, concerning the Sword he carries?"

"Tell me, Metaxas—you say you have known the Princess—?"

"Years ago," returned the beggar cautiously.

"Tell me, what is she really like? What would she do with the Sword of Glory if she were to possess it?"

The old beggar heaved a wheezing sigh. Sounding worried, he suggested that it might be better if the Sword were not given to Kristin, nice lady though she was. Metaxas thought it would be much better, for all concerned, if the Crown Prince could be made to see that he should keep such a superb weapon for himself.

"As long as the Sword of Glory rests in the noble hands of the Crown Prince, we can all feel safe. Whereas, in any other hands . . ." Shaking his head, Metaxas let his words trail off.

"That is my own thought." Carlo sighed in turn. "But how can I persuade my father to do anything?"

"It is not for me to intrude between the two of you."

"Of course not. But . . ."

"But—sometimes—I feel it is my duty to make at least one small suggestion."

"Do so."

"It is just this. Blind agreement, blind obedience, is not always the greatest, truest loyalty."

"Blind—?"

"I mean, young man, that if there is some real danger to your father, and he is unable to see that danger clearly, it becomes your duty—and mine, of course, and all his followers—to help him. Even if what we say, or do, should anger him at first."

"I'm not sure I understand, Metaxas."

"Perhaps I have already said too much, young master. Anyway, it is my opinion that if your father feels he must give the Sword to someone, it should be you."

"Me!"

"That is not so surprising, is it? That such an inheritance should pass to a faithful, loyal son?"

"No—" said Carlo, then fell silent. Then he turned and walked away, not knowing if he was angry with the blind beggar or not. To have the Mindsword in his own hands . . . no, he told himself firmly. He did not wish for anything of the kind.

* * *

Later that night, with everyone but a pair of patrolling sentries fast asleep, Vilkata lay rolled in a borrowed blanket on the edge of camp. Choosing a time when both sentries were well out of earshot, he muttered certain antique words into his blanket, meanwhile holding the fingers of his left hand contorted into an unusual position.

Within the space of a few breaths he became aware of the silent arrival of an intelligent presence, inhuman and invisible.

"What news, Master?" inquired the demon's voice. The dry leaves seemed to be swirling right in the Dark King's ear, but still they were barely audible.

Keeping his head three-quarters under the blanket's folds, and whispering, Vilkata reassured his partner that he still remained free of the Mindsword's influence. So far, using the demonic vision secretly provided by Akbar, he had managed to scramble out of range of the Mindsword's power each time that violence threatened. On the last occasion it had been close.

"I believe that most of these fools, if they take notice of me at all, think it only natural that a blind man should try to get himself out of danger when swords are drawn. At the same time they assume that the Mindsword must have caught me at some time, and that I am as loyal to their precious master as they are. I act the part, of course."

"And does the Crown Prince too assume you are his slave?"

"He is a fool like the others. I doubt he thinks of me at all, except as a surprise gift for his beloved Princess."

"Ah. Excellent. I have no doubt that you have managed to deceive them all. When will you seize the Sword, Dark Master?" The dry-leaves-and-bones voice of the demon nagged him eagerly. "Tell me, when?"

"I'll grab it from him as soon as I can, fool!" Vilkata in his frustration had to remind himself to keep his whisper low; mere subvocalization was more than ample for the demon to hear and understand. "I do not enjoy this game, as you can understand, but I must play it patiently. Any man who has worn a sword as long as our friend Murat, and faced as many treacherous enemies as he, is always on guard against being suddenly disarmed, just as he is always breathing. And if I should try to get the weapon from him, and fail, I'll get no second chance."

There was a silent pause.

"Of course, Master. Forgive any suggestion of disrespect that I may have given in my impatience."

"You are forgiven." The Dark King had no intention of offending his partner until he felt confident of being strong enough to exercise control.

Vilkata whispered on, venting his frustration, lamenting the fact that he had still been unable to find an opportunity to seize the Sword from Murat, even though in the Dark King's demon-powered perception Skulltwister loomed ever as a brilliant beacon.

He came near suggesting—though he stopped short of doing so—that Akbar have a go at snatching the Sword himself if he thought it would be so easy.

Then the man had a request. "Can you not make my human body younger, swifter, stronger? That would help."

"I assure you, Great Master, matters are not that simple. The man Murat is magician enough to detect any sudden magical alteration in your person. Magician enough to sense my presence should I come any nearer him than this. The instant he grows suspicious he will draw his Sword. Where should we both be then?"

Vilkata grumbled, but forbore to press his partner to give him more help, or to make an attempt to grab the Sword of Glory himself. He really had no wish to see the Sword in Akbar's hands.

Sounding as malleable and cowardly as ever, and repeatedly fretting about the dangers of discovery, Akbar wondered querulously if they were even safe from discovery here on the edge of camp, with almost everyone else asleep.

"There are no magicians here but me—certainly not the Crown Prince. No real magicians at all—well, there is one amateur who might conceivably be dangerous."

"Ah?"

"His name is Gauranga, the bandit with the gray mustache, and he possesses a sensitivity, if no real skill, in matters of magic. I am beginning to fear what he may detect."

"Yes, I see, Master. Such an individual could present a problem—let me try to solve it."

"I trust you will succeed. Without alarming anyone."

It was early on the morning after this conference that four of the converted Tasavaltan guardsmen approached the Crown Prince and asked his permission to speak.

"Permission granted."

Standing before Murat, the troopers informed him timidly, in one or two cases rather sullenly, that they wished to leave him and return to the service of the Princess.

Murat had begun to expect such a request from some of his men, and readily gave those who asked permission to leave his service. They looked somewhat relieved.

He raised a cautioning hand. "I would ask you, however, to delay your return to your former duties until after I have a chance to make contact with the Princess, which should be very soon now. Will you promise me that much?"

Standing as they were, confronting Murat directly, the troopers were unable to refuse him that much, although their Tasavaltan loyalties had obviously regained an ascendancy. The foundations of their conversion, Murat thought, had been built on nothing substantial in the mundane world, and were now eroding swiftly; in another day or two they might be capable of becoming his enemies once more.

The thought bothered him unreasonably.

"Wait another day," said Murat, "and I will put in a good word for you with the Princess. As soon as I have the opportunity."

He had thought that this gracious offer would relieve the men's remaining worry. But to his surprise the troopers looked more uneasy than before.

"Your pardon, sir, but . . ." Their spokesman hesitated.

"Well, what is it? Spit it out. Speak freely."

"To put it bluntly, sir, the Princess doesn't like you." The man hesitated, then plunged boldly on. "I mean, sir, in the case of someone like Princess Kristin, who doesn't really know you yet, who's never had the benefit of your Sword to clear her vision—well, in the light of what happened last year, isn't it natural that she at least *thinks* she doesn't like you?"

"What I believe you are trying to tell me, trooper, is that she won't listen to me, won't give me a chance to explain about last year. You believe that instead of my being able to put in a good word for others, I'm badly in need of one myself, as far as the Princess is concerned."

The soldier was relieved at not having to spell it out. "That's about it, sir. *We'd* be glad to put in a word for *you*, you've sure treated us handsomely. Only . . ."

"Only you will be regarded, at best, as deluded victims; at worst as deserters. Nothing you say will be believed. I understand." Murat paused. "But you are wrong."

"Sir?"

"Not about the kind of reception you may expect when you report back for duty; I'm afraid you're right about that. But you are mistaken about your Princess." The Crown Prince nodded for emphasis. "She'll listen to me. She'll be angry at me at first, over what happened last year, but she will still listen."

"Yes sir. If you say so, sir." And perhaps, Murat thought, the soldier was convinced.

Shortly afterward that man and the three other Tasavaltans who had chosen to return to their original loyalties rode away. Murat made no further effort to delay them; according to the best information his loyal people could give him, the Princess in her summer retreat was now no more than a few hours' ride away.

And scarcely were they out of sight than another small delegation came to report to Murat that the bandit-magician Gauranga seemed to have been overtaken by an accident during the night. He had died of a plunge down a small cliff.

"Walked away in the darkness to relieve himself, it looks like, sir, and just walked a step too far."

The Crown Prince went to take a cursory look at the body. An odd incident indeed, but there was no evidence of foul play, and certainly nothing to connect Gauranga's death with the beggar. If any faint shadow of suspicion of the blind man crossed Murat's mind, he dismissed it in the next instant as preposterous.

That day Carlo reported to his father that one of the troopers who had chosen to remain with them was a veteran of that famous battle of fourteen years ago, when the armies of the Silver Queen and the Dark King had clashed in battle, each ruler armed with a different Sword.

That night, with most of the group sitting around a campfire some kilometers closer to where they might expect to find the Princess, Murat encouraged this soldier to speak to them of those days.

This veteran had served in the Silver Queen's victorious army, and told now how he had seen the great Lord Vilkata's soldiers overwhelmed by the Sword of Despair, many of them slaughtered on the field, but most taken prisoner while in a state of helplessness. There was no humor in the story, and no joy; it seemed that even the victors in that battle still bore the psychic scars of it.

At the beginning of the tale Vilkata had been crouched at the far end of the camp, alone and distant from the fire. But as the story progressed, the Dark King, seeing more than any of the others dreamed, gradually edged his way closer to the storyteller's fire, and listened unnoticed to this tale of events in which he had played one of the principal roles. The veteran, noticing at last the presence of the Eyeless One, remarked that he'd had an aversion to blind men ever since that day of battle, when he had glimpsed the Dark King from afar.

The blind man on hearing this smiled under his bandage, a sickly, unhealthy kind of smile. Several of the former bandits tittered. Murat smiled faintly, with the air of one whose thoughts are far away, but wished to share the general merriment.

A brief silence fell. When Carlo remarked that the Mindsword was the only one of the Twelve to be known under only a single name, Murat commented that he had also heard it called the Sword of Glory. Others in the fireside circle nodded to confirm this.

And the old veteran of that battle between Swords assured his new master and his comrades that the Sword now carried by Murat had indeed been given several other names by the common people in both armies.

Murat raised an eyebrow. "Indeed?"

"Perhaps you won't hear these other titles spoken in the palaces, sir, among the lords. But we used 'em in the ranks."

"We'll hear them now, then."

"Well, sir, there's Sword of Madness, Skulltwister, Brainchopper, and Mindmasher, that I can remember." The veteran frowned, not looking at Murat, seemingly unconscious that such terms applied to his master's source of power might be taken as offensive. "And there were others—let me see—"

Murat was not too pleased to hear his present source of salvation, his future gift to the Princess, called by such derogatory titles. "I think we've heard enough," he snapped.

"Aye, sir." The old soldier accepted the rebuke stoically and without question, as an old soldier should.

On the morning following that fireside discussion, Carlo had a second meaningful talk with Vilkata.

In the course of this conversation the Dark King worked again at planting the idea that it is sometimes necessary to disobey, even to deceive a lord—even a father—in order to serve him properly. He hardly knew himself what profit he might expect to gain from this intrigue; but he knew that time was passing, and he seemed to be getting no closer to his goal.

On that same morning, Murat was pleased to be able to estimate that even now, several days after he'd drawn the Sword for the last time, some four or five of his converts, from the ranks of both bandits and soldiers, and including the officer who commanded the patrol, still remained firmly devoted to him, if their behavior was not quite as fanatical as it had been immediately following their conversion. And the remainder of the men were still Murat's followers, perhaps as trustworthy as most soldiers in most armies.

The Crown Prince, philosophizing on these matters in conversation with his son, supposed that he and his Sword had happened to encounter these men at a time when they were ready to attach themselves fanatically to the first worthy cause that came along.

Carlo, still innocently fanatic himself, argued that on the contrary, these permanent-seeming conversions were a result of their master's own innate leadership and charisma.

The conversation was broken off when Murat noticed the beggar Metaxas hovering near, as if he would have liked to take part in it also. Repelled by the fellow, and yet reluctant to take any notice at all of his presence, the Crown Prince moved away.

Vilkata had been perfectly correct in what he had told the demon. Such was the disregard in which the Culmians held him that it had never yet occurred to either Murat or Carlo to wonder if the old beggar had really been caught by the Mindsword at all.

Murat only shook his head each time he received yet another round of fulsome praise from his most devoted followers. But he had to agree that he had not been without loyal followers at home in Culm, even when he was out of favor with the Queen and her consort.

His faithful Tasavaltans assured him again that the summer residence of their Princess was now only an hour or two ahead.

Now in his own mind Murat began to rehearse in detail the explanations he meant to offer for his conduct on his last visit, the strong arguments that he was going to present—with great gentleness, of course—to Kristin as soon as he saw her.

He sighed, reminding himself that the Princess might well be angry with him at first sight. Yes, her anger was practically certain. Given how he'd offended her, nothing else could be expected. But at the same time, he had faith in Kristin's fairness and justice. She would listen to him when he approached her, deferentially yet boldly, with his apology. With calm speech and concise reasoning the Crown Prince meant to convince that loveliest of women that he had not really invaded her territory with the intention of subverting her army. Despite what the old soldier had said—what did such men, worthy and loyal as they were, know of princesses?—Murat really had no doubt that he'd be able to persuade her when the time came.

He had another discussion with Carlo on this point. But Murat broke off the talk in irritation when Carlo still seemed doubtful—and when, once again, the old beggar hovered near.

And anyway, the Crown Prince was beginning to think it not all that surprising that a number of people, including some of the more worthy Tasavaltans, should really want to follow him from now on, even after their minds were cleared of magic. If that was what they wanted, it would be unjust of him to prevent their doing so.

His mind was running on such thoughts when his confrontation with the Princess came, at least an hour before he expected it. The meeting was sudden, and startling on both sides.

7

ALONG the east side of the mountains, on the long slopes facing the distant sea, it was a day of low clouds, mist, cool winds, and occasional sunlight. The scenery here tended toward the spectacularly beautiful, with meadows and scraps of forest alternating with stark mountain crags. Small streams tumbled and frothed, pausing for rest in green-fringed pools. This was the land of Kristin's own childhood, to which she retreated whenever possible.

Early this morning she had ridden out from her summer residence for a long ride, accompanied by her younger son, eleven-year-old Stephen, and a small handful of attendants. The party was nominally engaged in hunting, but none of its members cared much if game were taken or not. For Kristin the joy of this kind of hunting consisted chiefly in being able to observe the grace and speed of the high-flying hybrid winged creatures, raptors bred to kill small game for their masters, or track larger prey for mounted humans to pursue.

Whatever degree of success the flying creatures might have today, the Princess knew an aftertaste of bitter envy as she watched them soar in freedom.

She was recalled from useless pondering upon her fate when her son rode close to speak to her. Stephen was a sturdy eleven year old, his once-blond hair now turning darker, becoming a good match for that of his absent father. These days, the boy was looking forward to his father's imminent return from another in the long series of journeys and pilgrimages Mark had undertaken in an effort to serve the Emperor.

"Father will be home soon, won't he? In a few more days?"

"I don't know." Then Stephen's mother regretted the shortness of her reply and the sound of indifference in it. She was not indifferent. "Do you miss your father very much?"

"Of course. Don't you miss him?"

Kristin hesitated, brought up short by the sudden look of wonder in her son's eyes. "Naturally I do," she said at last. "I wish he wouldn't go away so much."

"Why does he have to go away so much?"

It was not the first time Kristin had heard that question from one of her sons, and it grew no easier to answer.

"Because he feels he must," was her reply this time.

"Because he wants to help the Emperor; I know that. But why does he do it so often?"

"Because that's what your father feels he must do."

The boy did not reply at once. Then he said: "Father wants to help Grandfather against his enemies."

"Yes. Something like that." Kristin did not doubt that the Emperor's enemies existed, and that they were evil; she could have named a goodly number of them offhand. But more and more it seemed to her that those scoundrels claimed a much larger portion of her husband's thoughts and actions than she did, and more and more she questioned the need for that.

For a short time mother and son had been quite alone, but now a couple of attendants, one of them armed, appeared riding nearby. These days, the summer retreat and its environs were but lightly guarded by troops and magic. One squadron of cavalry had been detailed for protection, and at the moment was supposedly keeping just out of sight of the hunting party; there was no particular reason to expect any hostile incursion.

Meanwhile, young Stephen, as he did with increasing frequency these days, began questioning his mother about his mysterious grandfather the Emperor, and expressing his hopes of being able to meet him someday. The boy sounded keen on the idea, like someone looking forward to a challenge. Part of Stephen's problem, his mother knew, was that his brother Adrian, only two years older, had already met the Emperor, and had even engaged—more or less on the Emperor's behalf—in difficult and dangerous adventures far from home. There was of course some rivalry between the brothers, and Stephen was the one who seemed by temperament more fitted for high adventure.

"When is Adrian coming home?"

That was not a new question either. "Whenever he reaches a point in his studies when his teachers decide he should have a vacation. Magic is a difficult subject, if you're going to do it properly. Even for someone as talented as Adrian."

"Then it could be years."

"Possibly. I know you miss your brother too."

Stephen was silent, while their mounts carried them a hundred meters. Then he announced: "I'm going up on the hill, Mother. Maybe I can see the flyers better from there."

"Bring me back some interesting news, if possible."

Kristin's son turned his mount, and dug in his heels. In moments he was almost out of hearing, and still riding swiftly.

The Princess watched him go. She was now left for the moment practically unaccompanied, the two attendants who were in sight riding at a distance of some forty or fifty meters.

Moments later, in the process of following a tenuous trail around the steep base of a house-sized boulder, Kristin came face to face with Murat, who was riding just ahead of a small advance guard of his followers.

For a long, long moment there was silence. It was Murat who recovered himself and spoke first. "Do not be afraid, my lady. You need never be afraid of me."

"Treacherous villain!" Even as Kristin gasped those words, she took note of the young man riding a few paces behind Murat, who somewhat resembled him; and of the uniformed Tasavaltan troopers just a few meters farther back. These soldiers were not of the troop assigned to protect the summer residence; and the attitude of these men, looking expectantly toward Murat as if for orders, crushed any momentary hope that this hateful intruder was their prisoner.

Princess Kristin's next thought was that the Tasavaltan uniforms must be a trick, and that these were the villain's own men dressed for more Culmian treachery.

But the troopers, seeing their beloved Princess confronting their master, hastened to close in on the pair, showing her every sign of courtesy and respect, and trying to explain. The explanations at first made no sense at all to Kristin, but she could no longer doubt that these were Tasavaltans.

Murat silenced them with a gesture. Urging his riding-beast a little closer to the Princess, he assured her confidently: "You will have no cause to abuse me this time, my lady. I come in peace."

But now a very different-looking crew, a stretched-out file of six or eight men who looked very much like bandits, were coming in sight behind Murat's mysterious Tasavaltan escort. And far in the rear, one last rider, a man who appeared to have a bandage on his eyes, dawdled on a mount led on a long rope by the last bandit.

These matters were of small interest just now. Immediately on Kristin's left, almost close enough for her to touch, was the huge boulder around which circled the path she had been following. The way was open to her right, where at a distance of some thirty meters a screen of lesser rocks and stunted trees blocked the view. In the middle distance there loomed slopes and crags, at the moment looking utterly unpopulated. Nowhere was there any sign of help.

But still the Princess had not yet begun to be afraid; her outrage had not left her time for fear.

Facing Murat, she declared: "This time, I see, you have come as a bandit leader—a more open and therefore less dishonorable appearance than last year, when you posed as a diplomat."

But even as she spoke, fear was beginning to take its place beside her anger; she struggled to keep the change from showing. The most urgent of her silent worries was for her son: Had Stephen managed to get safely away? And where was Captain Marsaci and his troop? For the moment Kristin could do no more than hope that help might be at no very great distance.

Several of Murat's Tasavaltan converts, still innocently wearing their uniforms of blue and green, were unable to keep silent despite their new master's order. Now some of these men burst out with fresh importunings of their Princess, telling her what a great man the Crown Prince was, and how it would be a grave mistake, even a great sin, for her to delay in placing her whole realm at his disposal.

Murat saw her turn pale under her tan on hearing this lunatic advice offered in such a reasonable tone. But a moment later Kristin felt something like relief as the most logical explanation for these defections crossed her mind. And from the first thought of magic it was only a step to the strong suspicion that the Mindsword must be involved.

Now one of the young Tasavaltan soldiers, on seeing the Princess's expression change again, thought with relief that she was on the point of being converted to Murat's cause. At once the youth began explaining earnestly that all the fuss last year about Woundhealer being stolen must have been only a misunderstanding.

One of the trooper's comrades interrupted to remind him, rather hotly, that, after all, if Crown Prince Murat wanted that Sword, or anything else, he had a perfect right to take it. Didn't he?

A word from Murat was needed to put down the incipient quarrel; but that word was instantly effective.

"And do you believe that you have such rights?" Princess Kristin demanded of him. Her only real hope, she had decided, was to stall for time; but nevertheless, she found that she could not contain her bitterness. She was surprised by the depth of hatred the sight of Murat evoked within her. "What have you come to steal from us this time?"

When the Crown Prince, obviously stung by her words and attitude, started to reply, she interrupted him: "You robber, I never thought to see you cross our borders again of your own free will! You must be as mad as these underlings, these traitors, who follow you."

Murat, though he glared at her momentarily, chose his words carefully and kept his voice soft. "I am not insane, Princess, believe me. True, for a long time I despaired of ever being able to enter your lands again. But here I am, and I bring good news."

"The only good news I can imagine hearing from you is that you are departing more swiftly than you came. And this time going empty-handed." *Where is my son? And where my loyal cavalry?*

The man confronting the Princess mastered his own anger and pressed on. "Last year, in the casino where I helped to rescue your older son—"

Kristin knew it was important for her to be clever, to play for time. She knew that she ought to hear out his absurd argument, whatever it might be, with an appearance of patience. But her emotions kept her from doing that.

"You speak of my son Adrian? You, of all people, claim to have *rescued* him? Your thieving treachery only contributed to the danger that he faced!"

Despite the many times the Crown Prince had rehearsed this encounter in his own mind, nothing about it was going as he had planned and hoped. Instead, matters were taking a sharper turn for the worse than he had ever feared. He had expected anger from the Princess, but somehow he had never envisioned such a depth of enduring bitterness. And her last accusation, thought Murat, was completely unfair. He could feel righteous anger at this injustice reddening his face, but still he did not argue. His own real responsibility for this lady's unhappiness was too shamefully clear in his mind to allow him to do that.

Feeling proud of his ability to continue speaking calmly and fairly under these conditions, he replied, "Nevertheless, dear lady, there was a point in Sha's casino when I was trying to help the lad, and I was fortunate enough to have some measure of success. But the point I am trying to explain now is that during that scene of great confusion at the gambling house, the Sword Coinspinner fell into my hands. With such help I was able to get away, bringing Coinspinner with me."

"And I suppose it is the Sword of Chance you wear at your belt now?" Coinspinner's overwhelming good luck, thought Kristin, might account for this villain's having encountered a patrol of cavalry who for some reason were ready to defect.

"Not so, my lady." The Crown Prince paused for a moment, his own resentment ebbing away helplessly as he gazed at the angry face before him. Kristin's blue eyes were even lovelier than he had remembered. To him, this woman at this moment looked no older than eighteen, though he knew that she must be over thirty. And her beauty was not the deceptive glamour some women were able to achieve by means of magic. Murat felt confident of always being able to sense that particular deception, and he detected no trace of it now.

She asked him crisply: "Then are you bringing back the Sword you stole from us?"

"My lady, if ever again I have Woundhealer in my possession I'll bring it back at once. But unfortunately I do not have it now."

"Then what is your business here?" Kristin demanded icily.

"I have come to bring you a gift," the Crown Prince said, and felt profoundly unhappy when his words seemed to make no impression whatsoever upon his hearer.

He continued doggedly, speaking into the strained silence: "Coinspinner eventually took itself away from me, as the Sword of Chance is wont to take itself from anyone who holds it. But before vanishing, it showed me clues by which I might be able to possess a certain other Sword. That is the Sword I am wearing now. It is the Sword I wish to give to you, to make amends in some small measure for my behavior of a year ago." Murat bowed in his saddle, at the same time frowning lightly to himself. Somehow his speech had not come out as abjectly apologetic as he had earlier imagined it would be.

But he thought that Kristin relaxed slightly. He did not know that she had caught a momentary glimpse of blue and green and armor, not far to her right, just behind the screen of rocks and stunted trees. More bewitched defectors? She was going to gamble that they were not.

A moment later, with an abrupt effort that took Murat and his escort by surprise, she was reining her mount sharply, spurring away from them. From the screen of rocks and bushes twenty meters away erupted a rush of cavalry in blue and green, Captain Marsaci and his force, howling in a charge upon Murat and his men. The Princess had not, after all, been caught completely unprotected.

8

EVEN as Princess Kristin, crouching low over the animal's neck, spurred her mount away from Murat, she was shouting orders to her attacking troops. Carlo thought he heard her cry out a command to take the Crown Prince alive. But whatever her order might have been, it came too late to have any immediate effect upon the line of charging mounted men who had now burst out of cover.

Carlo had drawn his own sword and was shouting also, knowing that his words too were useless even as he cried out a superfluous warning to his father. In the next instant he saw his father struck by a slung stone. But the Prince managed to remain in his saddle, and a moment later he had drawn the Sword of Glory again.

A moment after that, the attack by the blue-green guardsmen was aborted. Their charge ended in plunging, rearing confusion, men and animals swallowed in the dust cloud raised by twenty riders simultaneously reining in their mounts.

But the defensive reaction that charge had provoked among Murat's guardians went on for a few seconds longer; it did not stop until the Crown Prince had shouted orders to his men, and in that brief period more than one of the attackers were struck down.

Carlo rode quickly to his father's side. Murat, his face pale, was managing to control his riding-beast with one hand.

"Father—where were you hit?"

"Right thigh. I'm all right. A glancing blow, no more."

Carlo sheathed his own sword and watched the immediate effects of the enemy's conversion. He thrilled with triumphant pride as once more the Mindsword's intervention produced its inevitable result; soon the largest harvest yet of new followers, their weapons discarded, were arrayed around Murat in attitudes of prayer and submission, begging forgiveness from their new master for not having seen him clearly a few minutes ago, for having committed the unthinkable crime of daring to attack him.

Murat, despite his repeated insistence that he was not much hurt, needed help in dismounting. Carefully slitting his right trouser leg with the point of his dagger, he disclosed a great bruise swelling on the outside of the thigh. He could stand on the leg, though at the cost of some pain; it seemed that no bone had been broken.

Obviously the Crown Prince was angrier this time than on the two earlier occasions when he'd drawn the Sword.

A murmur spread swiftly among the men gathering around him. The slinger who had inflicted the injury had just used his dagger on himself, his last breath leaving his throat in a scream of remorse.

Carlo felt a sense of loss; he'd been looking forward to seeing the unfortunate cavalryman cut up into little bits.

But Murat paid little attention to his attacker's fate; even before the attack on him had come to an end in confused, abject, and horrified surrender, he was already looking around for Kristin.

The sight of her mount, running riderless, gave the Crown Prince a sickening moment. But then he beheld his beloved Princess, physically quite safe, kneeling in front of him, her head thrown back, tears in her eyes and on her cheeks. Murat needed a moment to make sure that they were tears of joy.

Sheathing his Sword, and leaning on Carlo, the Crown Prince hobbled to her as quickly as he could.

As he approached she said, in a breaking voice: "My lord Murat, I am now able to see you for the first time as you really are. You must forgive me, I beg you, for what I have done against you in the past, and what I was saying about you—only a few minutes ago. Could it have been only minutes? It seems to me a much longer time, because when I said such horrible things about you I did not understand. I had to be born again to understand."

Murat wanted to kneel down facing her, but his injured leg screamed pain at him. For the moment he could only lean on Carlo. "Princess! Kristin? I beg of you—get up!"

In a moment the lady had sprung up nimbly to her feet. "As you wish, my lord Murat. Whatever you wish, from now on. I am yours forever. Do with me what you will—but you are hurt! Gods, let it not be serious! Say that it is not!"

"It is nothing. I will not die of a bruise." Then, taking both of his beloved's hands in one of his, Murat tried to frame some reply in accordance with what honor and duty demanded. But the shouting celebration which surrounded Kristin and himself made it difficult to think.

* * *

Half an hour after Kristin's conversion, she and Murat were sitting together in front of a newly made small fire, while their armed guardians, now a band some thirty strong under the command of Captain Marsaci, saw to their comfort and safety. Marsaci had guards patrolling a perimeter surrounding the royal couple at a distance of thirty or forty meters.

There was no physician in the Crown Prince's newly enlarged retinue, but several of the troopers were veterans with experience in all kinds of battle damage, and they agreed with Murat's own assessment of his injury: walking and riding would be difficult for several days, but the wound was no more than a bruise, and with rest it would heal.

When Murat at last commanded the circle of worshipful, worried gawkers to stand back, he happened to catch sight of the blind man Metaxas, standing in the background. Impulsively announcing to the Princess that he had a surprise for her, he ordered the former beggar brought forward.

"Do you know this man, beloved?" Murat asked, when the ugly fellow was standing immediately before them.

"No, my lord," Kristin answered promptly. But a moment later a shadow crossed her face, and she shook her head. "No . . . that is, I do not remember."

As soon as she had spoken, Metaxas knelt before her. "I know the voice of my beloved Princess," he murmured, his own voice almost inaudible.

Kristin still hesitated. "I—I don't know." But she seemed upset.

Murat gestured the fellow away, and burly troopers took him by the arms. "Never mind now, my lady. Later we can talk of him, if there is any need. Now there are more pressing problems that must be faced."

"You mean the reaction of my people, when I tell them how my eyes have been opened to your true nature."

"I—yes, that is a good way to put it, I suppose. How can we avert a conflict?"

"I will speak to them. I am their Princess, and they honor me and will listen to me."

"Let us hope so." Murat turned to his son who was standing nearby. "Carlo, take half a dozen men and reconnoiter. See if we are under observation, if you can; at least discover if more Tasavaltan forces are in the vicinity."

Kristin shook her head. "I should doubt that very much, my lord. But by all means send out your scouts. I pray there will be no more unnecessary fighting."

"I share your feelings," said Murat fervently. Then he nodded to Carlo. "Go!"

At midday, Murat was still sitting in almost the same spot, for he had to avoid putting weight on his leg as much as possible. He was now saying to the Princess, for what seemed to him the hundredth time since he had found her: "But I want to help you. I have come here to help you."

Kristin was sitting on the grass a little apart from the Crown Prince now, and gazing at him adoringly. "Help me? But you have already transformed my life. From now on, my lord, I live only to help you."

Perhaps, Murat thought to himself, it was hopeless to try to explain his position to his beloved now. No doubt he would do better to wait until the effects of the Mindsword wore off, or at least moderated to some extent, as he thought they were bound to do. But with Kristin before him, hanging on his every word, her every expression one of perfect trust and contentment to be with him, he was compelled to keep trying to explain.

"Kristin, what I wanted to do was . . . ever since we met for the first time, I have hoped someday to win your love."

The Princess glowed. "Do you mean it?" she whispered softly.

"Yes, of course I mean it. Now I can—I must—openly acknowledge that was my secret purpose in coming here. But—I never wanted it to happen like this! I do not want you as a slave."

The lovely woman drew back. To Murat's astonishment it was almost as if he had slapped her face. She said in a much different voice: "You may call it slavery or not, as you choose. I only know that all the love I have to give is yours. I am sorry if there is something in the situation that does not please you."

He leaned forward, forgetting his injured leg, provoking a sharp twinge of pain. "Don't weep! I beg of you do not weep!"

Moved by the sincerity in her lover's tone and manner, the beautiful young woman ceased to cry. Tentatively she essayed a smile.

But Murat, shaking his head, could not force a smile in return. He could only mutter once again: "I did not want it to be like this."

Kristin's smile lingered. "But this is the way I am, my lord, and this is how things are. I rejoice to hear that you have wanted me for a long time, and I am overjoyed that you want me still; only the thought that one day you might cease to want me brings utter desolation."

Murat opened his mouth and closed it again, remembering how some of his first converts had been ready to kill themselves at the mere suggestion that he was leaving them. He was not going to suggest anything of the kind to this beloved woman. Nor was he going to take advantage of her in her present enchanted condition.

Presently a call from a lookout informed the camp that Carlo and his scouting party were returning. Getting to his feet with an effort, his weight on his left leg, Murat waited for his son's report.

It was brief and to the point. The reconnaissance patrol had discovered no signs of fresh Tasavaltan activity.

As if the sight of Carlo had reminded her of something, Kristin began to look around, her gaze sweeping the distant hills and meadows.

"What is it, Kristin?"

"My son Stephen was somewhere around. . . ."

"Was he—within a hundred meters, when we met?"

"A hundred meters?" Kristin did not appear to grasp the significance of the distance. "No, I don't think so. He may have ridden back to our summer house, before—before you and I met."

The Crown Prince sat down again, with a grunt of relief. "I remember Stephen. He'll be a year older since I saw him—a likely lad, well able to take care of himself, I'd say." But Murat called his own son to him again, and shortly a cavalry patrol was scouring the area for the boy, with orders to bring Stephen to his mother if that could be accomplished without using force.

While the search was in progress, Murat gave orders to set up camp where they were, and maintain a perimeter patrol, to give warning of anyone approaching.

Murat's leg needed rest; even more desperately, he decided, he needed time to think. Where was he to take the Princess now, where to lead his augmented force of fanatical followers? He asked her who else was at the summer lodge, and found there was only a minimum staff.

He also learned from Kristin that she and her party were not expected back there until late in the afternoon, and no one at the lodge would be really concerned about them until nightfall. Probably not until tomorrow would there be any thought of sending out a search party.

Hours passed, and the patrol dispatched to search for Stephen did not return. Again Kristin expressed some vague concern about her son —"He'll think something terrible has happened to me"—but everyone assured her that there was really no reason to be worried about the lad.

"If he did observe our meeting, and saw how you—came to join me, and if he is now raising an alarm—well, in any case, my Princess, someone will do that, sooner or later, when you do not return to your summer house. What are we to do now, Princess?" The Crown Prince was shaking his head. "What am I to do? Believe me, I had no intention of coming here and making you my prisoner by magic."

Kristin blinked at him, and seemed to have trouble grasping the idea. In fact she could hardly believe her ears. "Your *prisoner?* My lord! Am I a prisoner now?" She laughed at the idea.

"Of course you are not." Murat paused. "I mean that is certainly not my intention. I want you to be completely free, my dear one, and you are, you shall be, as free as I can make you . . . but I'm afraid that your people, those who remain outside my Sword's influence, are not going to see the matter in that light."

Kristin was almost indignant. "If any of my people should come out from the city against us, my lord, or if more units of my army appear, be assured that I am their Princess. They will listen to me when I tell them that nothing at all is wrong." She paused, smiling. "I have formed a new . . . alliance. That is all."

"Yes, no doubt they will listen to you, for a time, at least. But as soon as they learn that you have been exposed to the Mindsword's powers they will react differently. . . . Where is your husband now?"

A cloud crossed Kristin's brow. "Mark is where he usually is. Out of the country. Somewhere."

Murat could all too readily imagine Mark's reaction when the news reached him of what had happened to his wife.

The Crown Prince raised both hands to run tense fingers through his hair. "Let me think. I must have time to think."

Everyone respected his wishes.

Limping away to a little distance from the others, he sat on a rock and nursed his wounded leg and tried to think. The Sword in its sheath seemed to weigh heavily at his side.

His latest mass conversion had caught a beastmaster among the Tasavaltan troopers, who had with him a pair of small winged messengers. So it would be possible to send a written warning to whatever authority remained in Sarykam with the Princess gone. . . . Murat tried in his mind, without success, to frame a message—from himself? from the Princess? signed by them both?—which would keep that authority from trying to interfere.

Next he turned over in his mind the idea of sending Carlo on to Sarykam bearing a flag of truce, perhaps with a few converted soldiers, perhaps alone, to explain how matters stood. If he, Murat, were to go there himself, with or without the Princess, he would only be forced to draw the Sword again, and probably more than once. And if Kristin were to go alone, her people—with good reason—would think her possessed, enchanted, and they would keep her there by force.

And naturally he, Murat, would not be able to allow that.

He thought he could visualize the ensuing chain of events, as stronger and stronger forces were sent against him, to be converted in turn; and he as an experienced soldier knew how to force battle if an enemy did not wish to give it.

Could it really be that easy for one man, with the help of the gods' Sword-magic, to bring a whole kingdom to its knees?

The Crown Prince was beginning to think it could. But perhaps the conquest would have a chance of becoming permanent only if the people of the kingdom were in fact dissatisfied with the rulers they now had, and ready to be conquered. Was Tasavalta—perhaps—in that condition?

With a mental shudder the Crown Prince put such temptations from him. He hadn't come here as a conqueror, but to make amends to the woman he loved, and then to try to win her freely given love.

While Murat had sought to be alone temporarily, he had not actually forbidden Kristin to approach him, and it was soon apparent that she had no intention of remaining at a distance. Tentatively approaching her new lord now, she saw from Murat's slumped posture and woeful expression that he appeared to be deriving no benefit from his interval of silent thought.

Advancing more briskly, she broke silence and resumed her efforts to soothe him. "I will go back to our summer lodge alone, my lord, and explain everything to my people there."

Her beloved smiled at her mirthlessly. "But don't you see, Kristin? Your people love you, and some of them would die for you, but they won't accept your explanations for such a sudden change in your behavior."

"I can lie to them about the Mindsword. Say only that I experienced a sudden change of heart."

"I do not want you to lie to them. They wouldn't believe you anyway. And in any case your magicians would soon detect the touch of magic on you."

She sat at his feet. "Then tell me what to do, my lord Murat. I will be happy to do whatever will satisfy you."

The Crown Prince started to stand up, grimaced, and sank back on the rock.

Then with a decisive gesture he began to unbuckle his swordbelt. He said: "Then I will simply do what I came here for. I want you to accept a gift."

The man who now called himself Metaxas was twenty meters away, watching with demon-vision, easily observing all that happened from behind his bandaged, empty sockets. Now he held his breath. Was the Mindsword about to be drawn yet again? He was on the verge of hobbling away from the couple and their treasure at a speed that would certainly raise suspicions.

And where was his precious demon, who ought to be ready to whisk him from the scene?

"What are you doing?" The Princess seemed alarmed at Murat's actions.

"I am giving you this Sword."

Springing to her feet, she recoiled. "My lord! I will be pleased and honored to carry your Mindsword sheathed for you, if that is what you wish. But I will never draw it, never. Not even if you should order me to do so."

He who called himself Metaxas, watching from a distance, began with a hoarse cough to breathe again.

Murat could only ask her, feebly: "Why not?"

"Because, my lord, I could never draw or hold that Sword. I should be terrified of putting you into a situation where you might worship me. I am all unworthy, and such a thing would be utterly unthinkable. Utterly!"

Murat, holding the weighty unfastened swordbelt in his hand, posed slumped on his rock like the statue of a rejected lover, no longer able to think of what to do or say.

The Princess continued, "And besides, my lord Murat, there are practical reasons why you had better continue to carry your Sword yourself. Very likely you are going to need to use it again, perhaps quite soon, for your own safety. It pains me to say it, but having thought the matter over I must admit that here in Tasavalta you are still surrounded by real and potential enemies, some of whom will think I am bewitched and refuse to listen to me. It would be good for you to convince them all as soon as possible of the truth."

The Crown Prince said in a tired voice: "I had hoped that would not be necessary."

"Happily we can still hope, Lord Murat. My people love me, and usually they accept my judgment. It is I, and not my husband, who has inherited the throne."

"I think your husband," said the Crown Prince, "is not the man to accept the loss of his position in meek silence."

Kristin frowned. "No," she said thoughtfully. "No, Mark will not do that. He is basically a good man, you know. I owe him my life, for on the day we met he saved me from the Dark King."

"Someday I must thank him for that," said Murat, dryly but seriously.

"I fear him now," said Kristin suddenly. "Not for myself. I fear what he might do to you."

"As to that, I have a long history of being able to protect myself." Still, Murat was more concerned than he allowed himself to sound. He had nothing against Mark, and no wish to hurt the man, but still less would he care to be destroyed by him.

By mid-afternoon, Carlo and his scouting party had returned from their latest effort, and there was still no word of Stephen. Murat, trying to ignore the undiminished pain in his leg, was sitting by himself, staring at his sheathed Sword, and thinking.

An hour ago, when he had tried again to denounce his own behavior of a year ago, none of these faithful people around him would listen. Respectfully they insisted on howling in protest. And in fact Murat's apologies were now beginning to sound mechanical in his own ears. All these Tasavaltans, from Princess down to private soldier, now saw the matter of Woundhealer's removal from the realm in a much different light. They could marshal arguments that seemed convincing. A year ago the Crown Prince of Culm had only been following his Queen's orders, and had shown commendable loyalty by so doing. He had wanted and needed the Sword of Love only to heal the intolerable difficulties in his own royal house.

Once the subject had been raised, Kristin quickly proclaimed that last year's difficulties over another Sword had been her own fault, and not at all Murat's. There was no excuse, she insisted, for her not allowing this admirable Prince to have Woundhealer, when he had come asking so decently only to borrow it!

The same Crown Prince today was slow to reply. At length he nodded. "I think I must agree with you there, my lady—even if it is only Sword-magic that now compels you to view the matter in so favorable a light." Murat held up a hand, forestalling her objections. "Not that I was right in stealing the Sword when you refused me, but—"

"Please, my lord, don't call what you did stealing! Of course you were right to take the Sword when I so stubbornly refused to lend it. What else could you have done?"

He sighed. "At the time it seemed to me that I was dealing with a bad situation in the best available way. Later, of course, I came to repent my choice."

There was another chorus of objections. Kristin and her compatriots all repeatedly assured the Crown Prince that last year's difficulties were not his fault but hers; she had been very wrong in not letting him have the Sword. Of course she should never have denied him anything he wanted!

Near sunset there came another moment when Murat and the Princess were more or less alone. She took this opportunity to ask him softly: "Is it true that my lord wants me?"

The look in her eyes made it very plain to Murat that he had not mistaken her meaning. When he tried to frame a reply, he found himself stumbling and stuttering like an inexperienced youth.

"I—how could I ever possibly answer no to that?"

Happiness glowed in Kristin's eyes. "Then I am yours. Completely. I hereby divorce my husband."

The Crown Prince looked bewildered on hearing this; but Captain Marsaci and some of the other Tasavaltan soldiers, near enough to the couple to have heard at least part of what Kristin said, were quick to rejoice. They also joined their Princess in explaining to Murat a certain provision in the ancient traditional law of Tasavalta.

By this custom it was in the power of any reigning monarch, be it king, queen, prince, or princess, to achieve a very quick, legal and formal separation from a spouse. The provision had been invoked only two or three times in recorded history, and its use required certain conditions. As Kristin saw the current situation, these conditions now obtained.

Prolonged absence from the realm by the unwanted spouse was one of the conditions.

On every level of his being, Murat was greatly pleased that this woman he loved was ready to abandon everything for him, even though he knew it was the irresistible magic of the gods which made her do so.

But, as an honorable and practical man, he was horrified at the idea of her invoking this old law now. He saw a bloody civil war looming as a distinct possibility.

A new thought struck Kristin now, and she dared to question Murat indirectly, about his own wife. "Lord, does there exist in Culm any obstacle to our union?"

Struggling with the feeling that events were moving too fast, the Crown Prince experienced a certain relief as he explained that he was still married. He hastened to assure Kristin that his wife no longer meant anything to him. They had not truly lived together for many years.

Carlo, who had recently joined the other listeners, was looking very thoughtful now.

Murat said gently to Kristin, "The Queen and those around her have been angry with me for a long time. For various reasons. And our adventure last year did not help matters. You know, I suppose, that after all my efforts, Woundhealer never reached Culm?"

"We have heard as much in Tasavalta—but few details of the failure reached us."

The Crown Prince could not provide many details either. Last year someone else, troops serving a power still unidentified, had ambushed Murat's troops who were carrying Woundhealer toward Culm. The Sword of Mercy had been stolen en route from those who had stolen it from Tasavalta.

"And so," added Murat now, with assumed lightness, "it would seem that all the treachery I practiced here was quite in vain."

"Treachery!" Kristin was truly outraged, really appalled. "I will not hear that word applied, not even by you, to your behavior, to anything you've ever done. Treachery, indeed! Who dares to call it so?"

Not long ago she herself had been using that word, and others just as bad, quite freely. But he was not going to remind her of that fact now.

The Princess also expressed her outrage against the unknown aggressors who had taken the Sword of Love from the Culmians. "We shall see about them! We shall hunt them down, and retrieve your property."

Even as Murat pondered the futility of arguing with Kristin in her present enchanted condition, it crossed his mind—perhaps not for the first time, but for the first time of which he was fully aware—that his own wisest course might be, after all, to retain the Sword of Glory for a short while to use it at home. Kristin would only be the better pleased if he kept possession of the weapon long enough to obtain justice for himself in his own house and his own country. Besides, his position now in Tasavalta looked intolerable; something like a full-scale war seemed inevitable if he were to remain.

And now, as if he'd spoken his thought aloud, the woman he loved began to insist that the wrongs her lord had suffered in his own country took precedence—they must be righted before he and she turned their attention to anything else.

She spoke with an air of simple practicality. "I see now, my dear, how it must be. We—if you agree, of course—will at once proceed together to Culm. There you will straighten out matters with your family, and settle any difficulties that may arise with anyone else whose opinion and goodwill you consider important. You will be appearing among your own people as the new Prince of Tasavalta," Kristin added complacently, "and I think such an accession of territory and population cannot fail to help them see things your way."

Once more Murat stared at the black hilt at his side. Now he began to see the possibility of good fortune in the fact that he'd been unable to go through with his original plan of handing the Sword over to Kristin at their first meeting. For the first time the Crown Prince had to admit to himself that there might be definite advantages in going about things differently.

For one thing, it was plain that Tasavalta could know no peace as long as he was here with the Sword. His presence in their land, and the fact that he had the Princess with him, could not long remain a secret from most of the people. Either he had to leave Tasavalta for the time being, or else prepare to convert the bulk of the population to his cause —and he still shrank from such a conquest. So far he'd used the Sword only in self-defense, and he'd not go a step beyond that if he could help it. He wanted no allegiance that had to be bought with magic.

No, the best thing to do was withdraw from this land, for a time, until Kristin had recovered her own will, and could make her own decisions freely—meanwhile doing his best to make sure that she would still look on him favorably when that happened.

"One day I *will* give you the Sword, Kristin. As you know, it was my intention to do so as soon as we met, but—"

"Please, my lord. If you love me, do not try to force me to accept that gift."

It was more than Murat could do to keep from blurting out how much he loved this beautiful, devoted woman. Loudly he proclaimed that he was as much enthralled by her as she was by the Sword.

"It is not your Sword, my love, that enthralls me. What is the Sword, after all? It is only an incident."

The Crown Prince gave a wild laugh, and made an extravagant gesture with both arms. "How will I ever be able to leave you?"

The Princess reacted with alarm. "Do not speak of such a thing, my beloved. Not even in jest!"

"I will not! I'm sorry, I promise, I will not!"

Trying to ignore the pain in his leg, hoping to get to sleep in his lonely blanket roll, Murat tried to picture to himself their arrival in Culm. He thought the pair of them ought to rate a reasonable welcome —at least he hoped so. With even a minimum of good luck he ought to be able to live there for a time without having to draw the Sword again. There, in his homeland, he ought to be able to keep it sheathed.

In the morning they would have to ride, whether his leg still galled him or not. He did not intend to be in Tasavalta when Prince Mark returned.

Murat was on the verge of sleep when his attention was caught by a figure standing nearby, almost motionless in the light between two dying fires. It was the blind man, Metaxas.

The Crown Prince sat up, conscious of the weighty presence of the sheathed Sword, snugly almost beneath him, as it always was these days when he lay down.

"What do you want, beggar?" he demanded, hearing the words come out more roughly than he had intended. More mildly he added: "Be careful, you'll walk into a fire."

"I thank the great master for his concern, but it is not necessary; I can sense the heat. The truth is that I remembered something that I feared my lord might have forgotten."

"And what is that?"

"Only," said Metaxas, "only that there are still three other Swords, forged by the gods, in the royal Tasavaltan armory in Sarykam."

9

IN the morning, when Murat reminded Kristin of the existence of three more Swords in the Tasavaltan armory, she eagerly confirmed the presence there of such weapons, and blamed herself for not having thought of them before.

When the Crown Prince mentioned the blind man's visit to him during the night, her face clouded, though at first she made no comment.

"Do you remember him now?" Murat asked her. "From your childhood?"

"No. Though there were many servants about when I was a girl, and I cannot be sure. I suppose he had his eyes then?"

"I had assumed so, though I never asked him. Shall we have the fellow here now and question him?"

"Not for my sake," Kristin answered quickly. "I do not like him. The Dark King was eyeless too, and I still sometimes encounter him in my nightmares. The way he looked at me—I know he could see me somehow—while his magicians were—causing me pain."

"I would do anything," Murat told her softly, "rather than cause you pain again."

Kristin gave her beloved an adoring smile. Then, becoming businesslike, she urged the Crown Prince to issue marching orders. If possible they ought to seize the three Swords in the armory quickly, to prevent their falling into the hands of Mark or some other potential enemy. "Of course it may be too late already. But I think that we must try."

Grimacing, Murat thought the matter over. He had hoped to avoid entering the capital, but . . .

He asked: "Which Swords are there?"

"There are Dragonslicer, Stonecutter—and, most important, Sightblinder."

"Then the blind beggar told me the truth."

"Who controls the first two may make little practical difference to us in our situation, but the Sword of Stealth could be a deadly weapon against you—indeed, against anyone."

"How well I know it!" Murat closed his eyes for a moment, wishing for a chance to rest. Events were rushing him into territory he had not planned to enter. Still, that was a common enough situation for a soldier, and no protracted deliberation was necessary.

"No doubt you are right," he said. "We must try to bring that one with us."

Opening his eyes, he added: "I am surprised that Mark did not take Sightblinder with him on his latest journey, wherever he may have gone."

The Princess hesitated before answering, and again a shadow crossed her face. At last she said: "Mark has good qualities. I suppose he thought that Sword might be needed at home, to defend the realm."

Murat grunted something; he did not care to hear about the good qualities of the man who, he had every reason to expect, would soon be trying to do his best to murder him.

Then, turning, the Crown Prince issued orders to all his followers that they prepare to move quickly on Sarykam. In his own mind he proposed to deal with his leg wound by ignoring it—that was a common tactic for a soldier, and in the past it had served Murat well.

Next he addressed the Princess once more. "I had hoped to avoid entering the city, but I must try to get Sightblinder."

"A wise decision, Father," Carlo approved.

An early morning patrol sent out to take a last look around for Stephen returned, before camp was broken, with nothing to report. But the Princess no longer appeared particularly worried about her son.

"He'll be all right. Frightened, I suppose, poor child, that his mother should be missing overnight—but there's no help for that just now. We may find him at the palace in Sarykam."

The Crown Prince shook his head, and his hand touched the black hilt at his side. "I had no wish to draw this weapon before, and I've less inclination to employ it now. But if the alarm's been spread, by Stephen or anyone else, I suppose I'll have to use it at least once more when we reach the city."

"Murat, my love, I fear you are too scrupulous. It is not as if you are hurting anyone when you draw that beautiful blade—I think it should be called the Sword of Truth as long as it is in your hands. While you have it, it will not harm my son, or any of my people, any more than it has harmed me."

The Crown Prince said nothing in reply. Though he had assistance in mounting, it still cost him an effort not to cry out with the pain in his leg. But then he was in the saddle, and he found that he could ride, at least at a moderate pace. In a few minutes everything was ready, and the march to the city got under way, Carlo riding at Murat's left side and Kristin at his right.

Once on looking back, during the morning's ride, Murat noticed absently that the blind beggar was riding in the rear as usual, his mount dutifully following the animal ahead. The man represented a minor mystery to be sometime resolved.

In this way the small procession proceeded for some time, Murat riding in thoughtful silence. As soon as Kristin saw that he wanted to be alone for a time, she dutifully dropped a few meters behind.

As he rode, the Crown Prince was meditating on the Swords. It was true that Dragonslicer and Stonecutter each had very impressive powers, but they were also very specialized, and under present circumstances he did not see that either of those Swords was likely to be of much benefit to him if he should gain it, or much harm to his cause in the hands of an enemy. Nevertheless, Murat determined to take both of those Swords with him if he could, on the grounds that they were really Kristin's, and the general principle that it was almost always better to possess any Sword than not to have it.

But Sightblinder was a different matter, and the more Murat thought of that Blade the larger it loomed in his calculations. The Sword of Stealth could render even an otherwise negligible opponent deadly dangerous; and Prince Mark was anything but negligible. In fact Murat knew him to be strong, clever, ruthless, and determined, and of all human beings perhaps the most familiar with the Twelve Swords' powers. In Mark's hands Sightblinder might well pose a murderous threat, even to one as well armed, experienced, and wary as Murat.

Sarykam, as Kristin assured him, was nearly a full day's ride away, and Murat had no wish to arrive there at night or with tired men and exhausted riding-beasts. Therefore at sunset he called a halt, went through the painful process of dismounting, and ordered his followers to make camp. Murat saw to it that Kristin was provided with her own small tent, one that the troopers had been carrying; he and Carlo lay nearby, under the stars.

The Crown Prince had much to think about before he slept. When he said good night to Kristin, and made it plain that he did not intend to join her in her tent, she had asked him what was wrong.

In answering Murat chose his words slowly, and his voice was grim. "There is no difficulty that we cannot overcome in time. Princess—

there is nothing I want more in this world than to embrace you. And, when you have been three days free of the Sword's power, I intend with all my heart to do so."

"Foolish man," she whispered fondly. "Do you still believe that your Sword there has enslaved me? Is there some magical significance in a period of three days? What I feel for you is not going to change in three years, or in three centuries."

"I'll not wait as long as three years, I assure you. But grant me the three days, for my conscience. It seems a reasonable interval."

"Of course." The Princess smiled, and looked around their little camp. Everyone seemed to be studiously avoiding watching them. "By then, perhaps, we will have found a place where we can be more completely alone." And, leaning forward, she swiftly kissed Murat on the cheek. A moment later she had disappeared into her little tent.

Next morning at dawn, the Crown Prince, his escort, and his close companions resumed their march. Murat tried to convince himself that his leg at least felt no worse than before.

As the city came into view in the distance, then grew closer and bit by bit more distinct, Murat became more intensely alert, and steadily more suspicious. These roads near the capital, which at this hour ought to have been at least moderately busy with all kinds of traffic, were ominously deserted.

Kristin, too, frowned on observing all these empty fields and highways, and spoke of her concern to her lover, who was riding at her side.

Murat only shrugged fatalistically. "I suppose we ought to have expected it. No doubt someone has spread word of what has happened— that you have joined me." His hand was already resting upon the Mindsword's hilt.

Kristin tossed her glorious hair, and smiled with a determined optimism that Murat decided he had not yet—quite—begun to find irritating. She said: "All of my people are going to learn the truth sooner or later anyway; our love cannot remain a secret."

"Of course not."

"Poor Murat. I see your conscience is still bothering you unnecessarily."

The inhabitants were still totally and ominously absent when Murat and his group reached the city wall. The broad gate which normally allowed access to and from the high road was tightly closed. No sentries appeared on the high wall, and only a distant barking dog responded when the Tasavaltans escorting the Crown Prince and Princess tried to hail their countrymen.

At Kristin's order several of her soldiers pushed and pulled on the massive timbers of the gate, but evidently it had been barred on the inside. The obstacle caused only a short delay; a couple of soldiers with a rope, working unopposed, made short work of getting atop the wall, and moments later were able to open the gate from inside.

One of the two troopers, on emerging from the gate, reported to Murat in a puzzled voice: "It looks deserted inside the walls, sir. How can my people fear you that much?"

Murat did not attempt an answer. He only commented to the Princess: "I fear we may find the armory already emptied of what we would like to find in it."

"I share your fear," said Kristin in a subdued and troubled voice. "Are they all in hiding, or in ambush? What can they be thinking of?"

Alertly, the party advanced toward the city's center, traversing one street after another normally thronged with people, but this morning as deserted as the country roads had been. Certainly, Murat thought, someone had assumed leadership within the city, and had acted decisively and effectively during the night. Stout stone-built houses looked down in utter silence on the visitors. Were the folk who lived here all hiding behind their closed shutters and doors, or had they evacuated the city? Murat, riding the eerily quiet street, could not tell which course the populace had taken, and did not particularly care. Well, he could easily understand why these people were fleeing him and his Sword as if he were the plague. But even so, such a welcome was annoying.

The great square in front of the palace was as deserted as the broad streets. Again, somewhere in the background a single dog was barking, a forlorn and frantic sound. The stout doors of the armory, adjacent to the palace, were closed and locked just as the city gate had been, but Kristin was in possession of the keys, both mechanical and magical, that would enable her to enter here.

No human guards had been posted outside or inside the armory. Not one additional recruit, it seemed, was to be left for the Mindsword to enlist in an intruder's cause. But the strong spells of protection woven by old Karel, Kristin's magician-uncle, were still in place, and Kristin warned Murat and his son as well as the converted troopers against trying to enter. Only the Princess herself approached the doorway, through which she was able to pass freely.

The Crown Prince waited nervously, but he had not long to wait. In a matter of moments Kristin emerged again, her expression grim.

"My lord Murat, all three of the Swords are gone."

Under his breath Murat blasphemed various of the long-departed gods. Beyond that there was not much to be said. No doubt someone—whether it was young Stephen or not made no difference—had reached the city long hours ago, bringing an eyewitness account, or perhaps some garbled version of one, telling what had happened to the Princess. Whoever had taken charge here on receipt of that news had issued orders swiftly and forcefully.

"Neatly done," Murat commented. "But I wonder where they can all have disappeared to?"

"To no great distance, I suppose," said Kristin, sadly. She was obviously hurt that her people had run out on her, without waiting to hear what she might have to say to them. "But it doesn't really matter. I'll explain to them."

Finding pen and paper in the deserted office of the armory, she announced her intention to quickly write out several messages, some addressed to various individuals, others to her people in general. Then she would dispatch runners to leave these notes in prominent places within the city where they could not fail to be discovered.

Standing in the doorway of the little office, watching Kristin as she began to write the messages, Murat smiled fondly at her. "What exactly are you telling your people?"

"Simply that I am going to be their Princess, as before—but no, not quite as before. There will be certain changes in the realm, but only for the better, because from now on I will serve in the name of the most glorious Crown Prince of Culm, who is soon to be Prince of Tasavalta also—and tomorrow, perhaps, the Emperor of the World!"

Murat sighed gently. "I think it will be better, my dearest, more conducive to peace, if you do not claim any thrones for me just yet."

The Princess hesitated. "Very well—I suppose you're right." She crumpled a paper and threw it away, picked up a fresh sheet and began again.

Minutes later, the letters having been hastily distributed nearby, the Crown Prince, Princess Kristin, and their entourage were on their way out of Sarykam.

When the city was an hour's ride behind them, the Crown Prince began to see Tasavaltan cavalry in the distance, but so far the uniforms of blue and green were only scouting, warily maintaining a prudent interval of several hundred meters.

Presently there also appeared a few high-flying winged scouts, keeping track of Murat's small moving column from above.

Murat had cursed energetically on learning that Sightblinder was already gone. But the full implications of his failure to seize that Sword were only now becoming apparent to him. The Sword of Stealth in the hands of a determined enemy meant that from now on, he'd have to be agonizingly suspicious every time he saw someone he loved approaching him—and doubly fearful if ever he saw a being he feared too much to face in combat. Not that, in Murat's case, there were many human or inhuman entities who'd fit either category.

Ah, if only he'd been able to get Sightblinder into his own hands! Then he might have been able to enforce peace. That weapon and the Mindsword might well have formed a practically irresistible combination for controlling minds. Besides providing its possessor with deceptive concealment, Sightblinder also allowed him or her a better perception of the true nature of other folk.

Yes, he was going to have to take the most careful precautions against the great and subtle Sword of Stealth.

And not, perhaps, only against that one. To the best of the Crown Prince's knowledge, six more of the Twelve Swords forged by the god Vulcan were still scattered about the world.

Murat had passed almost his entire life not being in possession of any of the Swords, and in that state had never spent much time worrying over what might happen if one were used against him. But on those rare occasions when he had got his hands on one of the Twelve Blades, he always found himself suddenly much concerned about the others.

Of course, anyone having one Sword became a much more likely target for whoever controlled the rest. The titular Crown Prince of Culm as an itinerant and landless nobleman was one thing, and the same man as a Swordholder was quite another. It was as if the acquisition automatically thrust him, willy-nilly, into some great, only vaguely defined game, whose players had each as his object the domination of the world.

The Crown Prince carefully corrected his thought. The other players, perhaps, had such an objective. His own ambitions remained much more modest.

Now moving briskly along toward the frontier that he and Carlo and Kristin must cross on their way to Culm, Murat considered what he knew of each of the other Swords still in existence. The strongest was probably Shieldbreaker, which immunized its bearer completely against the Mindsword's power, or indeed against the action of any other Sword or lesser weapon, whether material or magic. Only an unarmed opponent could—and almost certainly would—prevail against the holder of the Sword of Force.

The great and evil magician Wood had grasped that fact, certainly, a year ago when he had been forced to cast away the Sword of Force to save himself in Sha's casino. Someone else must have picked up Shield-breaker there. But who had done so, and who might hold that tremendous weapon now, were unanswerable questions to Murat. Nor was it likely that anyone in Tasavalta had the answers, as his new ally the Princess had already assured him.

Next on the list, somewhere out there in the world, was Wayfinder. The Sword of Wisdom could help its owner avoid fatal traps, doubtless including the Mindsword's sphere of influence, and could indicate to him or her the proper path to any goal. Wayfinder's use entailed certain drawbacks, however, usually increasing its owner's risks.

Kristin, who shared much of her husband's extensive knowledge of the Swords, had confirmed that no one knew what had happened to Wayfinder either. At least neither she nor her husband had heard anything new of the Sword of Wisdom since it had vanished from the body of the dead god Hermes, some eighteen years ago.

. . . The Mindsword's sphere of influence, yes. What factors set its limits, exactly? Murat had observed that the effective distance seemed to vary slightly from one use to the next, but what caused the expansion or contraction he did not know. Whatever the causes, he knew that his Sword's influence extended throughout a space of about a hundred meters in every direction from the Sword itself.

And what an influence! All along Murat had known, in a theoretical way, what he might expect the Mindsword to do for him, because he knew what it had done for others who'd possessed it in the past. But the actual experience of drawing and using such a weapon had been beyond his power to foresee. He wondered if the previous owners of the Sword of Glory had felt the same way. Who had they been? The most famous of them, of course, was Vilkata, the Dark King whose image still haunted Kristin's nightmares, a man Murat had never met, now missing for fourteen years and presumed dead.

After checking with Carlo on their line of march, the Crown Prince proceeded with his mental inventory of Swords. There was of course Soulcutter—Murat experienced a faint internal shudder at the mere thought of that Sword, though he had never seen it in action, even from a safe distance. He'd heard that the Silver Queen, who'd used it once, had spent most of her years since then on one religious pilgrimage after another.

Murat knew that Soulcutter had beaten the Mindsword at least once before. But on that occasion, an open confrontation between armies, the two Blades had never been brought into actual physical opposition.

The Crown Prince had no idea which might prevail if that were to happen.

—And Coinspinner, which had so recently been his, might one day be his again. That Sword came and went as if by its own random preference, and no human being, it seemed, could do anything to keep it once it chose to leave. The Sword of Chance would probably provide anyone who held it with the good luck necessary to stay out of the Mindsword's sphere of influence; and Coinspinner was also capable of inflicting bad luck, sometimes disastrously bad, upon its owner's enemies.

The Sword of Mercy could give protection against injury or death to anyone who held it. And it could heal even the wounds, otherwise practically incurable, inflicted by the Mindsword when it was used as a physical weapon.

The last of the six Swords still somewhere out there in the world was Farslayer. Enough to say of the Sword of Vengeance that it could unerringly strike the Mindsword's holder, or any other target, when thrown from any distance. No defense was effective—except of course that provided by Shieldbreaker. Neither Kristin nor Murat could guess who now held Farslayer.

Keeping an eye out for more Tasavaltan cavalry, Murat urged his steed to a faster pace. He and his followers still had a considerable distance to go to reach the boundaries of Culm.

10

PRINCE Mark and his single companion were still some hours' ride west of the Tasavaltan border when the small winged messenger from Sarykam, having located the Prince, came spiraling and crying down toward him, a tiny black omen falling out of a vast gray sky.

The Prince reined in.

"Ben!" he called in a cautious voice. At the same time he held out his left arm to make a perch for the small courier.

The huge man who had been riding a few meters ahead of Mark along the narrow trail turned at the call, then tugged his own mount to a halt and watched the messenger descend.

Of the two riders, both still under forty, the Prince was slightly younger, somewhat taller, and much less massive, though certainly robust enough by any ordinary standard. Both men had time to dismount before the spiraling, skittish messenger ceased to fly in circles and came to perch upon the Prince's wrist.

Having alighted at last, the small feathered creature stuttered in its inhuman, birdlike voice that it was carrying a written communication to the Prince from the wizard Karel.

"Mark, Mark, are you Mark?" it demanded boldly of the man who stroked its head, as if it might even now be able to withhold its burden from an impostor.

"I am Mark—you know it, wretched beast—you must have seen me around the palace since you were a hatchling. Hold still and let me have the message!"

And the Prince of Tasavalta reached for the tiny leather pouch and slipped its belt off over the creature's head.

Ben made no comment, but lumbered closer, openly positioning himself to look over the Prince's shoulder and read the message as soon as it should be unfolded.

The written words, in old Karel's familiar script, were few. Mark's magician-uncle urgently and tersely urged him to abandon all other projects, whatever they might be, and get home as soon as possible. The phrasing hinted at tragic happenings in Tasavalta, though clearly reassuring Mark that there had been no death in the royal family. What had actually gone wrong was not spelled out, against the possibility that the message might fall into the wrong hands.

Ben, having read the message, grunted and said nothing.

Mark made no comment either, but folded the paper briskly and stuck it in his pocket. Then he tossed the winged creature back into the air, calling after it: "Tell the old one I am coming, as quickly as I can."

"Pardon, Prince, but I must rest!" the winged one squawked.

"Come back and rest, then, on my saddle, or behind me if you can. It seems that I must ride." And Mark swung himself up into the saddle again. Moving homeward once more, no faster than before upon a mount already tired, he absently dug out food and water from his saddlebags for the messenger.

Ben, silent and gloomy, was now riding close beside him once again.

In half an hour, the messenger suddenly took wing again, squawked a brief farewell, and soon vanished over a hill ahead.

Ben and Mark maintained a steady pace, each man looking ahead to try to spot some source of water and forage for their animals. Their journey, like some others they'd undertaken, had been long and hard but had brought no visible reward.

Now at last the two men began to discuss the message, and Mark speculated on what exactly might have happened to cause Karel to send it.

Ben offered such comments as he could think of that might be helpful; they were not long, or many.

The Prince, his mood growing blacker the more he thought about Karel's note, finally made a bald admission. "Ben, I have long neglected my wife and family."

"Ha. So have I; not that Barbara any longer cares much what I do."

"It's my fault if you have. What have we accomplished on all these journeys?"

Ben could find only a vaguely encouraging answer to that. Which under the circumstances wasn't much.

Next day, as the weary pair were nearing the Tasavaltan border, they were met by a mounted party, including Karel himself, hastening out to meet them. The old wizard had already received Mark's answer and, relieved that he was already so near, had ridden to intercept him. Having the advantage of winged scouts, the magician and his companions had felt confident of being able to locate the returning pair efficiently.

Mark, on first catching sight of the approaching search party, stared intently, shading his eyes with a broad hand, at the figure in its lead. When he spoke, the relief in his voice was evident. "Thank all the gods, Kristin's well. She's ridden out herself to meet me."

Ben opened his mouth, but then said nothing. At the head of the approaching party he beheld not Princess Kristin but a certain red-haired girl. Even at the distance he had no trouble recognizing her, as strong and young and vitally alive as she had remained for many years now in his memory.

Realization of the truth followed only a moment later, though too late to dull the renewed pang of loss. The figure they were looking at was of course neither that of the Princess nor Ben's old love. It was someone else, and whoever it was was carrying Sightblinder.

Mark was not so quick to come to this conclusion—after all, he had good reason to believe that Kristin was still alive.

"Yes, it's Kristin, all right," the Prince announced. Then he glanced at his old friend, away, and back again.

"Why are you looking like that?"

"Because that's not who I see."

The Prince swung back to face the approaching party. "Kristin, certainly. Or . . ." He looked at Ben again, and in a moment understanding came. "Yes . . . yes, of course."

Actually it was stout Karel himself riding at the head of the welcoming delegation, with the Princeling Stephen close behind him. The old magician entrusted his Sword to an aide as he approached, turning a young officer temporarily into a figure of fantasy whom the others present, all more or less inured to Sightblinder's effects, generally managed to ignore.

Stephen, spurring his mount forward, was the first of the approaching party to reach his father. Clinging to Mark's arm, the lad began at once to pour out a tale of magical horror and outrage.

Reporting loyally to Mark in turn, Karel confirmed the bitter story, adding some details. Then he informed his Prince that General Rostov had already taken one of the other Swords, Stonecutter, from the armory into the southern mountains, where an effort was under way to cut off the road that would offer Murat his most direct route back to Culm.

"Then there can be no doubt it is Murat again."

"There can be no doubt."

Next Karel and Stephen between them related, more or less efficiently, more details of what had happened to Kristin.

The Princeling in a strained voice told his father once more what he'd seen with his own eyes: his mother encountering that evil man who'd been here last year, the Crown Prince of Culm, who had turned out to be such a thief and traitor.

Stephen, watching that encounter from a distant hill, had been too far away to be sure of the stranger's identity at first. He had seen the blue-green uniforms riding with the unknown man, and so had not taken alarm immediately. He'd watched with curiosity, thinking that possibly a squad of cavalry was bringing in a prisoner, or else escorting some visitor of importance.

And then, riding a little closer to see better, Stephen thought he had recognized the evil Crown Prince. He had seen the man drawing a Sword, and had observed by its effects the otherwise invisible wash of magic from that weapon, felling or stunning everyone within about a hundred meters.

Mark was staring intently at his son, hanging on his every word. "And your mother? What more of her could you see?"

"She did not fall from her mount, Father, but she dismounted of her own accord. And then a moment after that, the villain dismounted too —I think he was hurt when our men charged, because he needed help afterward to get off his riding-beast—and then it seemed to me that Mother went with him willingly after that." Stephen's voice faded almost to inaudibility on the last words, and he bit his lip.

It all sounded very convincing, and Karel, looking as grim as Mark had ever seen him, could do little more than confirm the essentials of Stephen's story. Murat of Culm, at the head of a small armed party— but nothing like a real invasion force—had ridden into Tasavalta carrying the Mindsword. First he had ensorcelled a whole patrol of cavalry, and then had taken Princess Kristin hostage—Karel's own arts now told him that she was thoroughly under the Sword's spell. If there were any doubt remaining, she had left written messages proving as much.

The Prince, listening, felt numb and hollow, an empty man going through motions because it was his duty. "Messages?"

Karel dug into a pocket and pulled out a folded sheet of paper, which he handed over to Mark.

"This one is addressed to you, sir."

Hastily Mark broke the little seal, unfolded the paper and read it, first silently and then aloud. There, in what was undeniably his wife's familiar handwriting, were words telling him that he had been divorced and deposed as Prince. The message concluded with good wishes for his future welfare. It read, thought the Prince, rather as if he were some senior official being nudged firmly into retirement.

Mark started to crumple the paper to hurl it from him, then thought better of the gesture and instead handed the document back to Karel's reaching hand. Any token from Kristin might possibly give a great wizard some magical advantage when the contest for her will was fought—as it was going to be—and in the circumstances every possible advantage would be needed.

"But she is physically unharmed?" The Prince marveled at how calm his own voice sounded.

The magician bowed his head slightly. "So it would seem, sir." Everyone else was gravely silent.

"Then we must do our best to see that she stays that way. Where are they now?"

Karel described the place where Murat and his enthralled followers were currently encamped, then detailed the military and magical steps he and General Rostov had already taken. Besides dispatching a force to cut the southern road, Rostov was deploying chosen units of his army on the home front, while a reserve of troops had been mobilized and stood ready for the Prince's orders.

Mark, listening, put aside grief and fear and began to grapple mentally with the practical difficulties of attacking an opponent armed with the Mindsword.

"Any word from Murat himself? Is he asking for negotiations?"

"No, sir."

"Then we'll not give him the satisfaction of asking for them either."

Quickly making decisions, the Prince formally assumed command, then sent a small detachment of men under Ben to take over the efforts being made with Stonecutter to close the mountain passes and high trails leading toward Culm. Rostov, once relieved from duty there, would be free to oversee a general mobilization.

Having dismounted to sketch a couple of crude maps in the dust, Mark wiped them out again with his boot, and climbed back into the saddle, this time on one of the fresh mounts brought out from the city by the welcoming party.

He announced: "We'll concentrate first on keeping the villain in our country, until we can plan how best to attack him."

Ben saluted and rode off quickly on a fresh mount, taking with him a few picked men from the small escort of troops who had come out with Karel.

Everyone else soon set off at a brisk pace, in a different direction. On

Karel's advice the Prince was leading them in the general direction of Sarykam.

Mark as he rode soon issued more orders. A messenger was dispatched to his older son Adrian, giving the facts of the incursion and kidnapping, and such scanty reassurances as were possible. Karel had been reluctant to send word to Adrian until he could talk to Mark.

Mark was anxious to take the field against Murat, but Karel thought it would be best for the Prince to meet first with the Tasavaltan Council. That body was already in session, considering whether to depose Kristin at least temporarily as Princess, since she had demonstrably taken leave of her senses.

"What good will that do us? The point is that we must get her back, do you not agree?"

"Wholeheartedly, Prince. But the Council is involved. If they should depose the Princess Kristin, it would become the duty of your son Adrian to assume the throne. And I fear your own formal authority as Prince Consort might be undermined as well."

"My friend, if I have any authority in my adopted land at all, it is only because you and the other Tasavaltan leaders choose to give it to me. Our son Adrian is still too young to rule, and in any case he's too far distant to be brought home in a few days. The Council must see that the problem can't wait for that."

Karel, announcing confidently that he was able to speak for Rostov and the other military officers, confirmed that they wanted no one but Mark as their Prince.

Mark doubted that the sentiment was quite as unanimous as Kristin's uncle made it sound; but he could not worry about that now.

"Then let us send a messenger ahead, to try to stop the Council from taking action until we talk to them. Or let them send some representative to meet us in the field."

Hurrying eastward, the Prince of Tasavalta made plans for his attack on Murat.

11

At twilight on the second day after the conversion of the Princess, as Murat's party halted to make camp, he again dispatched his son, along with a few chosen troopers, on a scouting mission to see what Tasavaltan forces might be in the vicinity. The Crown Prince was sure that Karel and other enemies had his party under surveillance now, and it was only to be expected that they were planning some kind of counterstroke. The reconnaissance ordered by Murat was a routine precaution.

Carlo, full of unhappy presentiments before riding out of camp, grumbled to his father about Fate.

After a full day in the saddle, the Crown Prince's leg was aching like a broken tooth. His response to his son's philosophical bitterness was not sympathetic.

"Let us create a new fate if we do not like the one that confronts us. Anyway, to me, our current situation does not appear so bad."

But at the last moment, struck by a foreboding of his own, Murat called his son back and handed him the sheathed Mindsword.

"I need not tell you that you must use it only to defend your life, and those of your men."

Carlo accepted the gift automatically from his father's hands, then paused, holding the heavy weapon gingerly, as if he were on the verge of refusing the loan.

"Take it," Murat urged him tersely.

"Thank you, Father," Carlo acknowledged quietly. In a moment he had buckled on the gods' Blade, on the opposite side of his belt from his own sword.

As soon as the scouting party had ridden out of sight, Murat entered his tent, seeking such privacy as he could manage, and did his best to assess his situation.

Though he had no real belief in Fate, he had to admit that a number of factors seemed to be conspiring to keep him from getting his band of followers out of Tasavalta as quickly as he'd planned.

To begin with, there was his wound, which was not improving as he'd hoped it would. Forcing himself to ride had only made matters worse. The injured muscles in the limb had stiffened, the swelling was refusing to go down, and the pain had if anything grown worse. Sharp knifeblade pangs ran from knee to hip whenever the Crown Prince tried to move in certain ways, or alternately if he held the leg in the same position for any great length of time. The few troopers in his band who claimed some knowledge of healing could only shake their heads and offer the opinion that perhaps a nerve had been damaged by the unlucky slinger's hit.

Riding for another full day with such an injury might well prove impossible, and he had the feeling, perhaps irrational, that it might cripple him permanently as well. When he made an announcement to this effect, some talk sprang up among the master's worried devotees of rigging a litter in which he could be transported. But the Crown Prince refused categorically to consider using any such device. He wasn't dying, he snapped at his subordinates, nor was he helpless; after a day or two of rest, he should be ready to ride on. Meanwhile, alertness by all hands, combined with his enemies' knowledge that he possessed the Mindsword, ought to render the camp secure against attack.

It was well after dark when Carlo and his men returned from their scouting trip, which had proven uneventful. They had seen no Tasavaltan military people anywhere, though several flying scouts had been observed. Carlo dutifully handed the unused Sword back to his father.

Next morning at first light, Murat on peering out of his tent was slightly surprised to discover the familiar, repulsive figure of Metaxas squatting patiently nearby, at a little distance from the nearest sentry. The Crown Prince ignored the beggar's presence at first, but as the day wore on the visitor continued to hover in the vicinity of the injured man. Murat had the impression that Metaxas managed to grope his way a little nearer, and again a little nearer, whenever a likely opportunity arose. Drawing almost no attention to himself, and managing somehow to keep out of everyone else's way, the blind man appeared determined to maintain his presence near Murat.

But Kristin, who arrived at Murat's tent at dawn to spend her time with the Crown Prince, trying to do something for his wound, soon became irritated by what she considered the beggar's intrusive presence, and told the fellow to take himself away.

Metaxas at once obediently arose, turned, and started to move off, tapping his way with a crude cane someone had provided for him. But before he had gone half a dozen steps he turned back, pleading.

"Your pardon, my lady. Pardon me, Great Lord. But in my youth I possessed some small skill in the healing arts."

Murat and Kristin both looked at him doubtfully, then at each other. Nothing else was doing the injury any good.

Evidently encouraged by silence, the beggar made the most of his chance. "With your permission, I would like to try to alleviate Your Worship's pain, to make it sooner possible for Your Worship to ride again, and lead us where you will."

"What manner of treatment do you have in mind?" Murat rasped at him, his voice half-suspicious, half-contemptuous.

Metaxas launched into an excited plea. "Oh, the master need not be concerned! I will not ask for hair, or fingernails, or any substance proceeding from the great lord's body. Not a scrap of his clothing will I require, nor even a pinch of dirt from his footprint. It should be enough, with your permission, for me to chant a few words from afar."

Murat stared doubtfully at the wretch for a few moments, then shrugged. "Chant, then," he agreed. "Preferably from the greatest possible distance that will allow you to remain within the camp. Or go farther, if you will; suit yourself about that."

The eyeless man bowed, muttering words of gratitude. By this time a pair of half-suspicious Tasavaltan guards, taking their cue from their master's attitude and tone, had come to flank Metaxas, and they guided him in his withdrawal to the other side of camp.

Murat engaged once more in conversation with Kristin, and promptly forgot about the former beggar. But a few minutes later the Crown Prince, happening to move his leg, noted that the pain was much diminished. The improvement had occurred with magical suddenness.

Soon he had to admit to himself that Metaxas had demonstrated his ability to work a minor healing spell, even while not being allowed to touch the patient.

When Murat called Kristin's attention to this fact, she was delighted at the improvement, but at first unwilling to give credit to the eyeless man. Murat, however, insisted that he knew the touch of healing magic when he felt it, and the Princess was forced to admit that the great bruise on his leg now looked better. The swelling in his thigh had clearly started to diminish, though the leg was still too painful for him to consider riding except in the most immediate emergency.

Despite Kristin's continued antipathy to the beggar, Murat had him summoned again and thanked him. Then, in response to a pleading look from the Princess, he banished his benefactor once more to the far side of camp.

Even had Murat been ready to ride at once, still there would have been delay in getting on the road to Culm today. The men in charge of the riding-beasts and loadbeasts came to report a newly discovered problem. A swarm of mice, which everyone was sure must have been produced or at least mobilized by Karel's magic, had appeared overnight to devour and scatter much of the grain in camp. Feed would have to be carried for the animals on a trip across the badlands. It would be folly to trust to forage on the journey; there were certain to be long barren stretches where the grazing was inadequate.

Nor were mice the only new difficulty. Harness kept breaking, every second or third time an animal was saddled or loaded. And the sky to the south was leaden, shot through by flickers of distant lightning, indicating that a savage storm was brewing.

Murat was well aware of Karel's reputation, and had had no wish to make an enemy of such a powerful magician. But, as he reflected in conversation with Carlo and Kristin, events had swept him along, and there had really been no alternative.

His listeners slavishly agreed.

The rest of the day passed fairly uneventfully. During the following night, Vilkata as usual stretched out at full length on the earth beyond the firelight, at the extreme edge of camp. Lying so, and mumbling into his blanket, he was soon engaged in another secret conference with his inhuman partner.

As soon as the demon arrived, it began lamenting—almost silently— Vilkata's continued failure to seize the Sword.

In a whisper almost choked with anger, the man sternly ordered his subordinate partner to stop whining. He, Vilkata, could now report that he seemed to be gaining the Crown Prince's favor, and could look forward to playing a larger and larger role in service as Murat's magician— since the removal of Gauranga, there was no one else among the converted bandits or soldiers remotely qualified to play that part. But patience was essential; he, Vilkata, might have, could have, done better with the healing had he been granted the boon of hair or fingernails or spittle. But the royal couple were still suspicious of him, and he had not dared to seem to want such powerful tokens.

"And were you, Master, able to make the injury worse from a distance, before you promised to try to make it better?"

"Actually I was. You see, the fellow continues to assume that I have been caught in his Sword-magic, like all the other members of his entourage."

Akbar rejoiced fawningly in his master's success, and praised his farsighted wisdom. He, the demon, devoutly wished that he had been able to do more for their common cause. But alas, Fate as yet had not seen fit to decree him any opportunities.

Vilkata delivered a cold judgment. "You and the young Prince both seem to believe in Fate."

"Alas, it may be that we are both seeking to avoid responsibility. Master?"

"Yes?"

"If I may dare to ask—what *are* the prospects for your snatching the Sword?"

The Dark King sighed. "As I have said before, I am waiting for a good chance, in fact an excellent chance. Because I am unlikely to be granted a second one should the first effort fail. And while we are on the subject," Vilkata added, "let me say that the eyesight you have given me seems not altogether reliable in imaging the Sword itself. When I can get a clear look at the weapon at all, the shape of the handle seems obscure."

"I am doing the best I can, Master."

"Try and do better," Vilkata snapped—or came as close as he could to snapping without speaking the words aloud.

"I will try." Akbar sounded exceedingly timid, if not actually frightened.

"And more than that is going to be required of you. I will have to rely heavily on your help to make me look good as a magician. My own powers are still weak, although with exercise, and with your help, my faithful Akbar, they are beginning to revive."

"Of course, Master! Call upon me at any time for assistance. Does your vision continue to be satisfactory, other than the difficulty with the Sword?"

"In the main, satisfactory, I suppose. Somewhat less garish colors would be preferable. And the difficulty with the Sword, as you put it, threatens to undermine our entire plan."

"That is too bad. I can only do what I can. No doubt the trouble arises because of Skulltwister's own powerful magic."

"Perhaps. In the old days, with others of your kind assisting me, I never had any trouble seeing this Sword or any other."

"I will do what I can."

By the time another day had dawned, Murat's leg felt almost well enough to let him ride. But experience counseled another day of rest. Once more Carlo, again carrying the Sword on loan, took a few men and went out scouting.

The pair of winged scouts were sent out also; and in a couple of hours came back to their Tasavaltan-defector handler with the unwelcome news that the main road leading toward Culm, really little more than a trail, had been cut.

"From what the beasts tell me, the road's completely gone, sir," the converted beastmaster reported.

"Gone! An entire road?"

"Wiped out, at a couple of really narrow places, in the passes. Lord Murat, from the description my little flyers give me, it looks like some heavy magic's been worked against us there. Something's cut away limestone and even granite there, like so much cheese."

"Stonecutter's work."

"I should say so, sir. Very likely."

By now Murat's three days, his self-imposed waiting period before he should accept Kristin's love, had passed. But he found himself making no move to enter her tent. It was as if he were really waiting for something else—perhaps, he thought, a time when they could be truly alone with each other, and at peace. The Princess gazed at him lovingly, and was content to accept what he decided.

With the benefit of Metaxas's healing efforts—the beggar made sure to claim credit at every opportunity—Murat's wound continued slowly to improve. But though this afternoon he was able to walk with only a slight limp, and ride almost normally, he was hardly conscious of relief. The Sword of Stealth was looming ever larger in his thoughts. His fear of that weapon and of Mark's revenge was increasing.

Vilkata, observing the behavior of the Crown Prince intently, and keeping mental notes of all that happened in camp, made a shrewd guess at what these fears were, and considered exerting subtle efforts to exacerbate them. The Dark King wanted the conflict with Mark to go on. Ideally Murat, instead of retreating peacefully to Culm, would stay here until he had enslaved or defeated the Emperor's son. But still Vilkata kept silent on the subject, fearing that any effort he made to influence the decisions of Murat and Kristin might have the opposite effect.

And Vilkata wondered how much longer it would be before the woman recognized him, despite his altered appearance. He discussed this point with the demon when they had another conference.

Still the Dark King feared at every moment to be caught by the Sword's spell if Murat should once more draw it suddenly; some provocation might arise at any time. For this reason Vilkata welcomed the intervals when Carlo took the Mindsword with him on patrol. On these occasions Akbar, taking no chances, continued to spend almost all his time at a safe distance.

During each of his clandestine conferences with Akbar, Vilkata reminded his demon to be ready to whisk him away to safety at a moment's notice.

"I shall certainly do so, Master," the dry voice always soothed him. "Have no fear on that account."

Vilkata even considered trying to browbeat the demon into attempting to seize the Sword—but the man shuddered and again rejected the idea, whose success would be worse than failure. He could not bring himself to contemplate a future in which he would be required, without hope of release, to offer lifelong worship and obedience to a demon. That was one of the most hideous fates that he as an experienced torturer was able to imagine.

During the remainder of the day Murat limped about his camp—the last increments of pain and injury in his leg were stubborn—alternately trying to use and then discarding a cane whittled for him by the cunning fingers of the eyeless man—who else? In the course of his restless movement the Crown Prince reminded his perimeter guards at frequent intervals that they must challenge anyone, no matter who it might appear to be, who approached the camp from outside. Murat also saw to it that everyone in his band was thoroughly briefed on Sightblinder's powers, and made them all swear solemnly that they would allow no outsider into camp without their master's approval.

For the past several days Carlo had been watching and listening to his father with growing fear and dismay. The Crown Prince, rather than looking better with the healing of his wound, now appeared haggard, with dark circles under his eyes. Over and over Murat declared his determination not to be swayed from his planned course of action whether by fear of his enemies, bad luck, or Karel's magic. He meant to take the Sword of Glory on with him to Culm, and there to utilize it—

as sparingly as possible, of course—to regain his rightful place in his own land.

Murat vowed that Kristin, who would stand beside him from now on, deserved no less than a new kingdom in addition to her own.

Several times he assured Kristin that, once having accomplished his own rehabilitation in his own land, he would present the Sword of Glory to her, and from that moment he, Murat, would be her faithful servant—as well as her lover, if she would still have him.

She answered quietly: "I already worship you, my love. I think no magic is capable of changing that."

Murat was too deeply moved to reply in words.

And the Princess Kristin, also silent now, vowed to herself that if her lord ever forced her to accept the Sword as hers, she'd only keep it for him, undrawn, until he someday had need of it again.

12

TOWARD the middle of the night, Kristin, unable to sleep, was wandering restlessly around the camp, wrapped in a soldier's borrowed cloak. The mind of the Princess was in turmoil, seeking some way to help Murat, and at the same time struggling against the sadness that engulfed her with every thought of her lost children and her estranged people.

In her pacing she frequently passed the tent wherein Murat was resting. Each time the sentry looked at her with sympathy.

"He sleeps?" she asked the man quietly, pausing for a moment.

"I do believe so, Princess." The reply was almost in a whisper; no one wanted to disturb the great lord, to deprive him of a moment of his well-earned rest.

The Princess took another turn around the camp. As she was considering whether to try once more to sleep, she heard a sentry call, and a quick answer; it was Carlo and the men of his patrol, returning to the camp at last.

The Princeling, looking tired, rode slowly straight into the center of camp and dismounted near the small watchfire, where he spoke a few words with Captain Marsaci. Then Carlo turned and walked toward Kristin, who stood between him and his father's tent.

Only now did it register in Kristin's consciousness that one or two members of the patrol appeared to be missing, and another had been slightly wounded.

"What happened?" she asked Carlo hesitantly as he was about to pass her. The Princess was well aware that this young man had no great liking for her.

The look Carlo gave Kristin as he paused confirmed that idea. Coldly he said: "A skirmish. Such things happen in war. Don't worry, the precious Sword's all right."

Then the Princeling moved on, muttering over his shoulder: "I must report to Father." Carrying the unbuckled Mindsword in its sheath, he went into his father's tent.

Kristin, following slowly, was able to see past the young man through the open flap. Inside, Murat was dimly visible, stirring uneasily on his simple roll of blankets.

Leaving the tent flap open, Carlo put the Sword down gently at Murat's side, and started to shake the older man.

"Father! Wake up!"

Suddenly Murat started up. His eyes glittering in firelight, he stared at Carlo for a moment as if he did not recognize him.

And then, before anyone could utter a word of caution, or otherwise react, the Crown Prince had grabbed the black-hilted Sword and drawn it from its sheath.

The faint firelight entering the tent through the open doorway fell upon that bright steel and rebounded, striking the eye like an explosion of live steam. Carlo, inside the tent, fell to his knees, covering his eyes. Kristin, standing just outside, heard herself cry out the name of her beloved.

From all the other men in the encampment, sleeping or waking, a muttering went up, a sound compounded of joy and resignation.

Inside the tent, the Crown Prince had leaped to his feet beside his blanket roll, newly drawn Sword once more in hand. His clothing was disarranged, the expression on his face wild and confused.

Then he bent uncertainly over his kneeling son. "Carlo—is it indeed you?"

A pale, drawn face turned up to him. "I'm here, Father. It's really me."

"Then who intruded?" Murat looked bewildered.

"Intruded, Father?"

"Someone was here . . . just now."

The eye of the Crown Prince fell on the smiling figure of Kristin, waiting outside the door, and terrible suspicion overcame him.

"Is it Mark, then—?" Murat murmured. In another moment, feeling himself hampered in the awkward space of the little tent, he hurled the scanty camp furniture aside, and waved the Mindsword at her as if in exorcism. Then, pushing his son aside, he leaped out toward the Princess, getting within striking distance, raising the keen, heavy blade.

The face of the cloak-wrapped apparition before him paled. The slender figure confronting Murat recoiled from the bright steel, as that god-forged Blade flashed in the air.

A voice indistinguishable from Kristin's burst from her shrinking image, pleading: "My lord—what is wrong?"

Knowing only an inner certainty of treachery and betrayal, Murat raised the weapon in a two-handed grip. The Crown Prince shouted at the one who now faced him: "If you, whoever you are, are carrying Sightblinder, I command you to throw it down immediately!"

He stared expectantly, but no other Sword appeared, and the woman's image did not change in the slightest. Other figures, in the background, were huddling in frightened silence.

Slowly the realization came that he had been dreaming of horror and betrayal. It was only Kristin, the real Kristin, who faced him now. Kristin, empty-handed, white-faced, wrapped in some soldier's cloak, her slender body trembling with the knowledge of how close she had come to being slain by her lover.

All around them, the camp was silent. Somewhere in the distance a nightbird called.

Murat, fully awake now and suddenly stricken, stumbled a step closer to the Princess on his wounded leg.

"Oh—my dear—my love—I was afraid that it was Mark. I feared to let him come near you—"

Kristin raised her eyes. Wistfully, fearfully, she said: "I do not think that Mark would ever hurt me."

By now a newer and uglier murmur of noise was going around the camp. Men were glaring at one another in mutual suspicion. Their lord had mentioned Sightblinder. Had someone entered the camp by means of the Sword of Stealth? Rumors, challenges, and speculation flew back and forth, hands gripped weapons, and several fights were only narrowly averted.

Suddenly a new noise rose above the rest. It was the eyeless man, screaming unintelligibly about something. For the time being everyone ignored him.

Murat began shouting orders. In the matter of a few moments, fights had been averted, something like calm had been restored, and Carlo could begin to give the report for which he had awakened his father. For this purpose the two men reentered the tent.

The Princeling, setting up the small folding table that had been knocked over, reported in a distant voice that his patrol had been forced to fight a skirmish with a small Tasavaltan patrol. The fight had been brief but savage, and the enemy had withdrawn before Carlo had been compelled to resort to the Mindsword.

Murat was now fastening the sheathed Blade at his own side again, and trying to concentrate on what his son was saying, even as he listened with half an ear to the screams and moans of the blind beggar in the middle distance. Someone was shouting threats at the wretch to shut him up, and the Crown Prince devoutly hoped that they succeeded.

He said to Carlo: "Would that you had used the Sword. I gave it to you for your protection."

"I realize that, Father. But I did not need the Sword of Glory to survive. And I could not in any case have saved our two men who fell, the fight began so quickly."

"Very well, I'm sure you did the best you could."

After answering a few more questions, Carlo left the tent. As he pushed aside the flap to go out, Murat was moved by the sight of Kristin, her slender figure still muffled in a cloak, waiting just outside.

She came in, without waiting for an invitation, as the young man left. The tent flap closed her in, with darkness and her lover.

At first no words were exchanged. For once casting his own Sword carelessly aside, the Crown Prince for the first time embraced his beloved unrestrainedly.

Kristin responded with passion.

For the time being they were secure against sudden interruption; there was a sentry just outside the tent to see to that. Murat's lips sought Kristin's mouth, and then her throat. His hands explored her body freely. Somewhere in the back of his mind, almost obscured by the rising torrent of madness in his blood, was the thought that if he took her now, just after he had once more exposed her to the Sword, he would be violating his own self-imposed pledge. But just now one more broken promise more or less did not seem of great importance.

He had lifted the maddening, enchanting woman in his arms and was on the point of lowering her to his humble bed, when they were, in spite of sentries, interrupted.

It was the eyeless Metaxas, struggling now with the guards at the very doorway of the tent. The man was still screaming, or trying to scream though he was almost out of breath. Between his howls of sheer emotion he pleaded with the men who held him back and threatened him. He begged that someone must hear his confession, and his words had a coherence and an urgency that made it impossible to simply banish or ignore him; the soldiers were arguing among themselves now as to whether they should disturb the Lord Murat.

With a groan he set down Kristin on her feet, and turned to deal with this disturbance.

* * *

As Murat appeared in the doorway of the tent, Vilkata tried to throw himself on the ground before his new master. The Crown Prince signed to the soldiers to release his arms.

"Great Lord Murat!" the beggar wailed, from the dust.

"What is it, man?"

"Can you possibly be merciful to me? I am the most wretched, treacherous—"

There was no mercy in Murat's voice. "Get hold of yourself! Speak plainly, and be brief, or by all the gods, I'll—"

Some of the soldiers standing by voiced their readiness to kill this confessed traitor out of hand.

Murat ordered them to wait until they had heard what the fellow had to say.

Meanwhile, he who had been called Metaxas rolled on the earth, still beating his breast and proclaiming his guilt, tears running down his bearded cheeks.

"Forgive me, Lord! I would destroy myself now, to expiate my sins— except that now you truly have terrible need of help, help that only I can give you!"

The Crown Prince, losing his temper, savagely kicked the prostrate form before him. The impact sent waves of renewed pain up through his own leg, but at the moment he scarcely noticed.

"Are you going to tell me what the matter is, or not?"

"Yes, Lord! I am—I must confess that from the beginning I have been in your camp under false pretenses. Even before we met, I was plotting to do you harm."

Kristin had now quietly emerged from the tent, her borrowed cloak discarded, garbed in the dress that she had worn beneath it. She was staring past Murat at the eyeless man, and her face was frozen in an expression of horrified fascination.

"Oh?" Murat, bringing his concentration back to Vilkata, could not at first take seriously such a confession from such a source. "You? Plotting how, against me? With whom?"

"With Akbar—does Your Lordship know that name?"

The Crown Prince stared at the strange figure huddled on the earth before him. "Akbar? No. I have heard no one in this camp called that. Is he a Tasavaltan?"

Once more Vilkata screamed in remorse, even more terribly than before. "Alas! Lord Murat, it is not the name of a man!—but of a demon." And with those words he melted entirely into sobs.

13

A DEMON," Murat repeated in a whisper. On legs suddenly gone weak he retreated, one step, two steps, getting out of reach of the shaking, pale-skinned, black-haired hands that would have clutched his ankles seeking forgiveness. The Crown Prince knew a sensation as if a lump of ice had suddenly, by some enemy magic, been made to materialize inside his stomach.

Clinging with one hand to the tent pole just inside the open flap, Murat bent forward, eyes fixed on the crumpled figure before him.

"Who are you, then?" he demanded, in a terrible whisper.

In the course of the eyeless man's convulsions of repentance, the bandage that had covered the upper portion of his face had fallen off, and as he sat up he turned his horrible empty sockets toward the Princess.

"I am Vilkata," he rasped. "I was once the Dark King."

Kristin screamed.

The wretch who huddled on the ground before her shrank back. His speech failed him completely for the moment, and he confirmed his confession with a spasmodic nod.

The Princess slumped, and might have fallen had not Murat quickly moved to support her. Lifting her tenderly, he turned and carried her back into the tent.

He was out again in a moment, ignoring the small gathering crowd of puzzled troopers and converted bandits. Bending down to seize the helpless, hapless Vilkata by the front of his garments, the Crown Prince hauled him to his feet.

"A demon, you say." This time the word was heard by most of the onlookers, and an abrupt silence fell among them.

"Alas, sire, yes—"

"Where is this alleged demon now?"

Vilkata swore he was ignorant of the whereabouts of Akbar. "But I do know, Master, the trick of summoning the foul thing."

"You know the trick? You tell me that a demon is under your control? Or are you babbling, old man, are you utterly mad?"

The Dark King screamed again. "Alas, no, my master, I am not mad. Would that I were!"

Controlling himself with a great effort, he who had been calling himself Metaxas went on to explain.

"Until a few minutes ago, my lord, I had managed to avoid the power of illuminating, healing magic in the Blade you carry. Wretch that I am, I deceived you, having in mind only my own advantage. I only pretended to be convinced of your perfection—I only feigned loyalty, while at the same time Akbar and I were plotting to seize Skulltwister as soon as a good chance should present itself."

Murat's interior lump of ice was, if anything, growing larger and colder. His hopes that the eyeless man was no worse than mad were fading rapidly.

"We'll deal later with whatever crimes you may have committed. Are you telling me the truth now, you offspring of diseased demons?" And again Murat seized the hapless villain, this time brandishing the Sword right under his victim's nose. Again the Blade glowed with unnatural brightness in the muted firelight. "I want the truth!"

Utterly collapsing, the beggar swore over and over that he was now telling the complete truth. The demon had provided for him, was still providing, a kind of vision that functioned despite his lack of eyes; the demon and he had plotted together to do the master harm.

Under the circumstances, with the man subjected now to the full glowing power of the Mindsword, the Crown Prince at last was forced to believe him. Conviction in the matter of demonic vision was reinforced by an impromptu test; when Murat silently brought his Swordpoint close to the eyeless face, the cowering one tried to draw away, as if in fact he could see the danger.

After ordering several troopers to keep a strict watch over the confessed partner of demons, Murat drew Carlo a little aside to confer with him.

Murat started to speak to his son, then paused, staring at the weapon still gripped in his own fist. Then he demanded: "You say there was a skirmish, but you did not draw the Mindsword? Did I hear you truly? Or were sleep and nightmares still ruling my brain, when you came in to report?"

Carlo stared at him. "Yes, Father, that's what I told you. We had to fight a skirmish."

"Good. Good, then I can trust my memory. In these last few days there have been times when my life seems to be turning into the stuff of dreams. Or nightmares." The Crown Prince heaved a great sigh. "I'll hear the story of your skirmish in detail later. Tell me now, what are we to do with this ragged wretch who claims to be a king, and own a demon? Do you believe his tale?"

Carlo gestured helplessly. "I cannot doubt that the man is now telling the truth. Or at least that he believes his own story. But I don't know what to advise you, how best to deal with him."

"Let us be rid of him, as quickly as we can." This came, in a quiet voice, from Kristin, emerging from the tent. The Princess looked pale, but had otherwise recovered from her faint.

"A demon," Murat repeated distantly. Now something in the two words seemed to grip his imagination in an unhealthy way, almost to paralyze him.

"Be rid of him, I say," Kristin repeated urgently. "What other choice is there?"

And Carlo, overcoming his own indecision, seconded her advice. "I agree with the Princess, we must be rid of him, and of his demon."

Murat, shaking his head as if to clear it of some unwanted presence, had to agree with their point of view.

"Yes, I suppose we must. But first there are some things that I must find out. I'll see if he's able to summon this demon before us, and make sure of the truth of the matter."

"No." Kristin shook her head.

"This Blade I hold will protect me during the summoning, and no one else need be present. For your safety we—this beggar—or king—and I—will go outside the camp to do what we must."

Carlo looked agonized, but he had learned to tell when arguing with his father was certain to be futile.

Kristin said to Murat: "I see you are determined."

"I am."

"Then promise me at least one thing, my lord—do not sheathe your Sword again, at least not until you are safely out of Tasavalta. And free of demons."

Murat looked at the Sword, and back at his beloved. Once again, for a moment, he seemed afraid.

The Princess went on. "Your safety, my Lord Murat, is the most important consideration for all of us. And for you to keep the Sword of Glory always in hand is now the best way—nay, the only way—to ensure your welfare."

The Crown Prince nodded slowly. "You are all depending upon me now. I know that."

The Princess took him by the arm. "One more thing—I'm sure that man is the Dark King."

"Sure?"

"I recognize him now, from the day long ago when—when he almost killed me. And I pray you to get rid of him, because I fear him now just as terribly as I did then."

"I have the Sword, and—"

"Even so, Sword or no Sword, what I most dread now is that this evil counselor's presence will be harmful to my most great lord. I would not trust the man the thickness of a knifeblade, regardless of any magical protection. Regardless of how he may swear, and protest, and what he may do to demonstrate his loyalty."

"Father," said Carlo, swallowing. "Let me repeat, I think the Princess is right."

The Crown Prince looked at them both, then at his Sword once more.

He said: "I like the idea very little. But—as a temporary measure only, until we have reached a place of reasonable safety—I'll carry this tool with me naked, and even sleep with it at night."

For a moment it seemed that Murat would say more. But his next thought, unspoken, only hung in the air as he looked at Kristin. And she thought that she could read it: *That means that for the time being, no one is going to share my bed.*

The low-voiced conference among the three was at an end. Now, determined to test the eyeless man's confession by having him attempt to summon the demon, the Crown Prince, with Carlo and the Princess looking on in horrified fascination, once more confronted the wretch who had called himself Metaxas.

The beggar's eye bandage had been restored to its proper place, and he squatted on the ground under the suspicious stares of a pair of guards, standing over him with weapons ready. Other men nearby had equipped themselves with torches.

No, the crouching man admitted, he had never bounced the Princess of Tasavalta on his knee—that had been only a near-blasphemous pretense. Yes, he had once been the Dark King, and yes, the horrible accusation hurled at him by the blessed Princess was quite true—he had once been prepared to torture her to death in an effort to increase his own magic powers. Only the interference of the man who was later to become Prince Mark had kept him from committing that hideous crime.

Murat's anger blazed at the bald admission. Caught up in a holy, murderous fury, the Crown Prince extended the naked Sword in his strong arm toward his victim's throat, until another centimeter's thrust would have drawn blood.

"I'd kill you at once, swine. But I mean to extract more information from you before you die."

This time Vilkata had not cringed away from the Blade. "Certainly I deserve death, Lord. But there are secrets I can tell you first, information I can provide that you must have."

"It seems we are in agreement on that much." Murat pulled back his Sword-point slightly. "And where is your demon partner now? If he indeed exists?"

Before Vilkata could answer, there came a murmur among the onlookers. Kristin, tough lady that she was, could no longer bear this continued confrontation with her former torturer. On the verge of fainting again, she pleaded with her new lord: "Send him away! Or kill him!"

Lowering his Sword, Murat spoke to her in soothing tones. "My love, will you go back to the tent now? Carlo, escort her."

"Let me remain, my lord," the Princess pleaded, "to see the demon if it comes. I want to share your peril if you are determined to face the foul beast, and it should somehow be able to avoid or even overcome the Sword's power."

"Go back to your tent, I say. Carlo, escort her."

Gently but firmly the young man took the Princess by the arm, and led her away. She made no further protest.

As soon as Kristin and his son were out of sight, Murat, after a word to Captain Marsaci, ordered his newly acquired magician to stand and walk. Then he directed the eyeless man, who proved his ability to get around without special guidance, some fifty meters or so beyond the fringe of the camp. There the two came to a secluded hollow in an angle between hedgerows. This was a spot where, Murat decided, any bizarre demonic manifestations would likely remain unobserved by anyone at the distance of the camp.

Vilkata, who for the last few minutes had regarded all his previous schemes with utter loathing, had been examining his conscience to see what additional offenses he might be required to accuse himself of.

He was now on the brink of confessing that he had some days ago made Murat's leg injury worse by means of magic; but before he blurted out another crime, it occurred to him that Murat would be better off without being required to hear such a confession. Indeed, a moment's reflection made the Dark King think that he ought not to have confessed as much as he already had. True, he deserved to die many times over for the harm he had inflicted upon the lord Murat, and upon the woman who had now become valuable and useful to the lord. But confession now would not help that. Above all, Vilkata's death would not help Murat in his present difficulties, but hurt him instead. It was clear to the Dark King that his new master was likely to need all the help he could get in the days ahead.

The master must be brought to trust, rather than hate, his most recently enlisted and cleverest adviser.

A few moments later, in the hollow between hedgerows, Vilkata, muttering and gesturing, went through his brief ritual of summoning Akbar.

Murat, naked Sword in hand, was standing at a little distance from the wizard, inside an elaborated pentacle of magical protection which Vilkata had hastily sketched out on the ground. Not that Vilkata had much faith in the efficacy of such devices against demons, certainly not compared with the protective value of the Mindsword; but he was now determined to take no avoidable chances with his master's safety.

Scarcely had the magician's fingers ceased to move in the gestures of the ritual of summoning, when the creature materialized, startling even Vilkata with its promptness. An androgynous human form, wrapped in dark garments, appeared out of nowhere, standing between the men. The manifestation was accompanied by a drumming or banging sound, which in a few moments trailed away into silence.

Murat, controlling a sudden surge of fear and loathing, firmly stood his ground inside his pentacle, brandishing the Mindsword in front of him.

The demon turned a blank, pale face in the direction of the Crown Prince, then recoiled with a scream of rage when it found itself gripped by the power of the weapon nestled in Murat's right hand. But even demonic rage could not endure the Mindsword's force. A moment after it screamed, the foul quasimaterial beast had assumed a dog-like shape, and a moment after that Akbar had thrown himself down, brutally fawning and cringing, near Murat's feet.

The dog shape did not persist for long. Looking as helpless as any mere converted human, Akbar groveled before his new lord and master, presenting himself in a series of suitably humble and would-be disarming images, some human and some animal. Babies, old women, cuddly pets, appeared and disappeared in swift succession.

Murat, feeling a tremendous disgust, and at the same time exulting in the establishment of his authority, drew back a few paces. Now he felt confident that his safety was assured by the Sword of Glory, and did not depend at all upon the merely human magic embodied in the diagram scratched in the earth.

As in his earlier confrontation with Vilkata, the Crown Prince was holding the Sword level, pointed at the demon, as if he might be required to skewer an enemy physically upon the blade. But this time he felt less of an urge to kill, and greater physical loathing. In fact he felt sick to the point of nausea. Akbar's current display of sniveling cowardice and self-abasement was if anything more repugnant to him than the show of demonic arrogance he had unconsciously been expecting.

Vilkata was watching with great vigilance. Now he made a prearranged gesture to Murat, signifying that the demon was safely Murat's to command.

The Crown Prince called out in a sharp voice: "Foul demon! Your name is Akbar."

"Yes, Master." The demon's voice was unlike any sound that Murat had ever heard before.

"I order you to choose some coherent shape, and remain in it, so a man can look at you at least."

At once the demon assumed a distinct human form, youthful, plump, and eunuchoid. It sat there smiling at its master timidly.

Murat, finding this shape particularly repugnant, quickly commanded Akbar to change to something else. In a moment the eunuch had become a comely maiden, dressed simply and with a fair amount of modesty.

The Crown Prince, even more than most people, had always feared and loathed demons. But tonight, to his great satisfaction, he found himself quickly able to master his natural sentiments and adopt a businesslike attitude.

The demon seemed to sense almost immediately that the worst of the Crown Prince's fear and disgust had passed. The maiden rose lithely to her feet, her peasant skirt swirling lightly, and said in a clear voice: "I am at your service, glorious Master! What are your commands?"

Murat drew a breath of satisfaction. "My first demand upon you—and upon the unfortunate human who admits to having been your partner—is to be told all the details of the plot that you hatched between you."

Both offenders bowed in reverence.

"First, I command you to tell me: Is any other plotter, human or otherwise, implicated?"

Both villains at once began to blubber in unison—even the demon's image seemed to cry. With one voice, speaking with tearful vehemence, they assured their new master that no other conspirators had been involved.

"Very well. I'll take your word on that—for the time being. Next, tell me, what exactly was the object of your conspiracy?"

Akbar stuttered, doing an excellent imitation of an appealing maiden in distress. Vilkata confessed that they had been plotting, of course, to get their hands on Murat's Sword. Both partners wept—Vilkata could still weep, it seemed—and tore their hair—or seemed to tear it—at the mere thought of having contemplated such a crime.

But after a few moments of this demonstration, Vilkata pulled himself together.

"I was—I am—the Dark King." This much was no longer a confession, but had become a proclamation, made with a certain pride. "Like other players in the great game, I wanted to eventually possess all the Swords. Like others, I wanted to rule the world with them."

The Crown Prince glared at him. "And now? What are you now, fallen king, failed wizard? No longer a player in the great game, as you call it. What do you now want?"

"I am—I devoutly hope to be—Your Lordship's magician, and faithful counselor. Certainly I would still be glad to have a Sword, or many Swords. But now, I would want them only as effective tools, that I might be better able to serve my lord."

"Well answered—I suppose." The Crown Prince nodded judicially. "And the demon?"

Akbar, both he and his fellow plotter agreed, was to have been content with the role of second in command when his master Vilkata had succeeded in winning his way back to power.

Murat, suddenly feeling tired almost to exhaustion, lowered his Sword and thought for a moment. Then he made a gesture that was not quite one of dismissal.

"All right, enough. You may spare me the vile details." But his curiosity on other subjects was still unsated, and a moment later he was questioning the scoundrels again.

The next thing the Crown Prince wanted to know was the location of Akbar's life. Everyone knew that the only absolutely sure way of controlling any demon was to have in one's control the object wherein its life was hidden.

Vilkata swore that he had no idea where Akbar's life might be concealed—that was naturally the last thing that any demon wanted to reveal. He turned to his former partner expectantly.

Akbar, who unlike the man seemed to remain in a state of abject surrender—the maiden's head drooped pitiably—proclaimed himself unable to withhold anything from his new master.

"Well, then?"

The demon's slender maiden's arm stretched out, forefinger pointed at Murat's right hand.

Her tender voice murmured: "My life is hidden in the Mindsword itself."

Vilkata's jaw dropped, in what appeared to be genuine surprise. But the wizard-king said nothing for the moment.

Murat gazed at the Blade in his own hand, first with astonishment and then with new calculation. He swished the god-forged steel several times through the air.

At last he looked back at Akbar. "So! Very clever of you, beast. How did you happen to be able to accomplish such a feat of concealment? But never mind, I can hear that tale later."

"At any time my master wishes."

The look of calculation had not left Murat's face. Suddenly he turned to the human magician and ordered him to make fire.

Vilkata blinked at his master. "Sir?"

"It's a simple enough command. I want you to create fire for me, a small flame, here and now. Right here on the ground in front of me. Surely, as you claim to be a mighty wizard, such a feat is not beyond your powers? It seems to me that it might serve as a test for some low-level magical apprentice."

"I fear, my lord, that I can no longer claim to be a mighty wizard. But —you are quite right. Fire ought to be simple enough."

Creeping about on all fours, Vilkata with unsteady hands gathered dried grass and twigs from the fringes of the hedgerows, heaping his harvest into a little pile before Murat. The magician muttered words into his dark beard. A moment later, a small tongue of flame danced forth atop the pile.

Another moment, and the Crown Prince was holding the Mindsword's blade directly in the fire. At the first touch of the live flames the demon emitted a scream of torment. In another moment Akbar was thrashing about on the ground, the demure maiden gone, the creature's apparent body contorting madly as it changed into a bewildering variety of shapes.

The Crown Prince kept at his roasting for a little while, confident that a little heat was not going to hurt his Sword. Rare indeed, he thought, would be the human being who felt any compunction about putting any demon to the torment, for whatever reason; and he himself could feel none now. But for the moment, being under the necessity of holding rational discourse with the thing, he ceased to punish it.

"Very clever," he remarked, when the Blade had cooled somewhat, and Akbar had ceased to scream, now lying huddled and twitching on the sand much as a broken human being might have done. "Very clever, choosing one of the Twelve Swords in which to hide your miserable life. Since the Swords are all but indestructible, there would seem to be no practical way for your life to be destroyed; therefore I cannot reasonably threaten you with extinction. But as we have just seen, your existence can be made hell; and I promise you it will be, if you disobey me."

The demon raised its face enough to peer at him with one clear human-looking eye. "Never again will I even think of disobedience, Lord! Never! My only wish now is to serve you faithfully!"

"See that you do not forget it!"

In fact Murat no longer had the least doubt of the loyalty of either of his new slaves. Before dismissing the demon and his human partner, he formally placed them in charge of the magical defenses of the camp, warning them that they would be held responsible for any enemy success. Let there be no more mice, or other tricks. The pair responded with effusive expressions of gratitude and loyalty, vowing their determination that Karel would be frustrated.

The Crown Prince also ordered his newly allied occult experts to take the offensive as soon as possible against his enemies, Prince Mark in particular. The partners agreed enthusiastically with this objective.

Then, with a gesture of disgust, Murat ordered them both out of his sight for the time being.

In moments they were gone, the demon vanishing as abruptly as it had come, Vilkata trudging back to camp. Finding himself alone in the little hollow, the Crown Prince sat down in the sandy soil beside the dying fire, and threw on some twigs to keep it going.

Bleakly Murat tried to understand the new situation in which he now found himself. At the moment his chief worry was just how he would ever be able to free himself of this demon when the time came, as it inevitably would, to do so.

No matter the degree of loyalty to which Akbar might now be constrained, as soon as the Sword's overwhelming power had been removed from him for a while—a matter of a few days at most—the demon could be expected to strike back at its former master and tormentor more readily, and with a more terrible effect, than even the most revengeful human. In the case of a demon, Murat could see no chance of a conversion becoming permanent, as happened in a certain proportion of the human ones.

Presently Murat, moving tiredly, also made his way back to camp. There he rejoined Kristin and his son, who both expressed great relief that he had come through the ordeal unscathed, and bombarded him with questions about the demon.

Kristin, as soon as she had heard the story of the summoning and confrontation just passed, protested mightily against any alliance with demons, or with the Dark King, who she described as a demon in human form.

But right now Murat felt disinclined to heed her objections on this point.

He returned to his tent, where, alone as before, he tried to get some sleep before dawn.

At dawn some enterprising Tasavaltan commander dispatched winged creatures, not couriers but larger raptors, trained for hunting, in a surprise attack on Murat's camp. These flyers were all but mindless and so all but immune to the Mindsword's power. Their objective, which had obviously been firmly impressed upon them, was to drive off the loadbeasts and riding-beasts from Murat's camp.

The convert troopers standing guard duty at the time, and the remainder who were quickly wakened, sent up a barrage of arrows and rocks, wounding several of the attackers and driving the others off, before the four-footed targets could be stampeded.

Vilkata was at Murat's side almost as soon as the Crown Prince came running out of his tent. The wizard hastened to assure his master that new magical defenses would be promptly put in place, to squelch any future flying assaults effectively.

"Akbar, Your Highness, ought to be particularly good at that."

"So he ought. But perhaps we ought to take some other measures as well."

Murat and his followers had long been aware of the existence, somewhat less than a kilometer from their present camp, of a sturdy farmhouse and its outbuildings. Murat and Marsaci had expected this farm to be occupied as an observation post by Tasavaltan reconnaissance units—or that it would be so occupied if there were any such observers so close to Murat's camp.

Now those well-built walls and roofs were beginning to look inviting, for bad weather was now setting in, summer thunderstorms and hail marching closer from the western horizon. The Crown Prince decided to take a look at the place, and if no disadvantages became apparent, occupy it himself.

Holding his Sword still continuously drawn, and riding at the head of his small force, Murat advanced at a deliberate pace toward the comfortable-looking farmstead.

The farmer and his family could be seen fleeing, mounted on loadbeasts, before the invaders came within two hundred meters. No Tasavaltan troops appeared anywhere, and Murat began to think that they had not after all been using the place as a post for observation or command.

Occupation of the hastily abandoned farm was accomplished without further incident, and provided a bonus. Besides shelter, Murat's party had now come into possession of a great number of fowl, and a dozen or so four-legged beasts that could be killed for food, or put to carrying burdens. Such luxuries as eggs and milk were suddenly available. A good supply of rich cheeses was discovered in the cellar, along with a good stock of salted and dried provender.

An hour after his decision to move camp, Murat sat musing with Kristin in the new comfort of the farmhouse.

"Not a palace, my Princess. But in the course of time we'll come to live in palaces."

"I have had palaces, and I do not need them. All that I need, my lord, is you."

"You will have me into eternity. I swear that."

Murat leaned back and closed his eyes, feeling for the first time in days almost at rest. When he opened his eyes again he admired the construction of the house that they were in, and wondered that mere farmers could afford, or cared about, such pleasant decorations.

The Princess murmured that this was little more than the typical Tasavaltan farmhouse. She mentioned that of course they would leave gold when they departed, or find some other means to pay the farmer for the use of his property and the supplies consumed.

For some reason Kristin's proposal irritated Murat. He was short of ready cash, and doubted that any of the rest of his loyal party had much money with them either.

But the Princess persisted. "They are my people, Lord. It is our custom here to compensate our people, when possible, for losses suffered in time of war." It sounded almost like a rebuke.

"A worthy custom," the Crown Prince said, trying to be agreeable. And in fact he did sympathize to some degree with the abused and evicted peasants; yet he remained irritated. "I have not declared war on these householders, or attacked them. Of course they might have stayed at home and welcomed us; you know, don't you, that I'd have seen the farmer and his people came to no harm at my men's hands?"

"I know that, my lord." The Princess smiled her beautiful smile for him.

"The truth is, Kristin, that I do sympathize with your farmers, and I would like to pay them if I could. But I sympathize even more with my own faithful followers. I think it not entirely Sword-magic that now binds them to my cause."

"Indeed, my lord, I'm sure that it is not."

Murat nodded. "They are, and will be, hard-pressed by the enemy, and I am not about to stop them from eating this farmer's food, or enjoying the shelter of these buildings. Anyway, you are these farmers' rightful monarch, are you not? Surely they ought not to begrudge you and your escort some hospitality."

Kristin meekly bowed her head.

"Anyway," the Crown Prince continued, "I also find it irritating that Tasavaltans like these peasants should not only willfully refuse to hear our case, but actually decline to obey orders given them in the name of their rightful Princess. Remember the messages you were at such pains to distribute? I am beginning to think that it might serve some of these people right if they do suffer a little abuse."

Suddenly the Princess was trying to keep from weeping. But for the time being her lover did not notice.

"Yes," said Murat, "let some of these fat farmers try going on short rations for a while, as our loyal folk have been pleased to do willingly in our service—as even you, my dear, might be compelled to do before we finally succeed in establishing ourselves in Culm."

And why should his beloved Princess and he himself go hungry when these rascal oafs had more than enough for themselves, and no thought of sharing willingly?

So matters stood, or very nearly, when another day dawned. Kristin had spent her first night in the farmhouse in a bedroom alone, and Murat had slept, Sword in hand, in the upstairs hallway just outside her door.

By now Murat's leg had recovered almost entirely; he was even considering that if he should be wounded again, he might allow the magician Vilkata some personal tokens of himself, that the healing spells should be more effective.

He now felt perfectly able to ride again. He decided he was well, and there was probably no more need for Vilkata's healing magic. In this decision the former Dark King now willingly concurred.

The Crown Prince considered taking his Sword and galloping out with a few troopers on a swift reconnaissance, trying to see if a certain alternate route to Culm was clear, or if that way too had been blocked.

But he hesitated. In fact he was coming around to the idea that it would be better after all, in fact it might be necessary, to stay in Tasavalta and conquer it.

14

MARK, after crossing the Tasavaltan border, had changed his original plan and decided to delay his return to the capital—the Council and its decisions would have to wait. Instead he rode directly with Karel and a small escort to join Rostov at the general's field headquarters, hastily established in a farming district four or five kilometers from Murat's encampment.

On reaching Rostov's headquarters, amid a confusion of gathering troops, arriving supplies, and hurrying messengers, Mark learned that Ben had arrived there some hours earlier, and had already gone out with Stonecutter and a small squad of cavalry, to see what additional barriers might be created between the intruder and his native Culm.

Ben returned from his expedition somewhat earlier than expected, only a few hours after Mark's arrival in the headquarters camp. At least some of the Tasavaltan soldiers who had gone out with Ben were missing, and Mark's old friend reported they had been lost in an unplanned skirmish against a patrol of defectors led by Prince Carlo.

The Prince only nodded; skirmishes had to be expected. "Any hope of carving some new barriers with Stonecutter?"

"I don't think so. The terrain doesn't lend itself to that." Ben's huge frame was slumped in a creaking camp chair, as if he were inordinately tired.

Mark nodded. "We've had no indication until now, have we, that Murat's son is with him?"

Rostov and Karel both confirmed this opinion.

"How'd you make the identification, Ben?"

Mark had to repeat the question before the big man seemed to hear him. Then Ben shifted his weight in the chair. "I heard one of our renegade Tasavaltans call him Prince Carlo. Also he was wearing a Sword."

"He wore the Mindsword in a skirmish but he didn't draw it?"

"I couldn't swear it was that particular Sword, but if Murat and his people have others at their disposal, we'd probably have heard about it. And I suppose I might even be wrong about the hilt—there are black hilts in plenty. Still, as you know, the real thing has a certain look about it. . . ."

"I know," said Mark.

"The Princeling and I both came on the scene a little late, after the fight had started. I got my people out of there as quickly as I could once I saw how he was armed."

"Wise decision."

Ben rubbed his eyes. No, he told Mark, he hadn't seen anything of Murat himself, nor, of course, of Kristin.

After answering a few more questions from Rostov and Karel, Ben, who looked worn out, was sent to get some rest. Mark remarked that his old friend didn't seem quite right. Well, losing people in a fight was always a wearing experience.

That night the moon was full and bright, the weather no worse than partly cloudy.

After the Prince of Tasavalta had tried to rest for an hour or two, he was up again, unable to be quiet while Kristin was so near and at the same time so completely out of reach.

Someone had just escorted into camp the displaced and outraged family whose home had just been occupied by Murat, and Mark spoke eagerly to these people, learning what little he could about the enemy disposition. He also had the farmer sketch out for him the floor plan of their house, though at the moment the knowledge seemed unlikely to have any useful application.

After ordering the family to be sheltered in tents for the time being, Mark abruptly decided to ride out by night to take a look at the commandeered farmhouse, accompanied only by Karel.

Mark, as he rode with the ageless magician at his side and Sightblinder sheathed at his belt, turned over in his mind several possible schemes for rescuing his wife. In none of them, at the moment, could he see any reasonable chance of success.

Silently, the Prince recalled how once, years ago, this same Sword that he now carried had been able to protect him to some degree against the Mindsword's force. On that day, too, he had ridden toward an enemy camp in which Kristin was held prisoner, and which was dominated by the Sword of Glory in a villain's hands.

That day marked the first time Mark had met the woman who was to become his wife, and on that day he had saved Kristin from a most horrible and painful death. But, on that distant, marvelous, and terrifying day, Mark's enemy the Dark King had not been holding the Mindsword continually drawn, as Murat was now. And when Vilkata had finally drawn the Blade, Mark had been able to resist its power only partially; and he had realized that he would not have been able to do that much without the Sword of Stealth in his own hand.

Sightblinder's gifts: his eyes are keen
His nature is disguised.

On that far-off day, possessing Sightblinder had made resistance possible—barely possible. Mark was sure that in no very great length of time the Sword of Glory, performing its prime function, would have overcome Sightblinder's secondary attribute of giving its holder enhanced perception.

The Mindsword spun in the dawn's gray light
And men and demons knelt down before.
The Mindsword flashed in the midday bright
Gods joined the dance, and the march to war.
It spun in the twilight dim as well
And gods and men marched off to hell.

Now, as the two men quietly covered the moonlit distance between their own camp and the enemy's, Karel thought the time appropriate to deliver to his Prince a new report, concerning the latest results of his days-long struggle to create and extend a magical domination over Murat's encampment and the people in it.

An early phase of that assault, the plague of mice, had succeeded admirably, but later efforts were having less and less success.

"And during the last few hours the reason has become plain, my Prince. My task has been complicated considerably by a real wizard's opposition."

Mark turned in his saddle. "A real wizard? Whom has he converted now?"

"The news is not good, my Prince. Though there may be some good to come from it in the end—"

"Who?"

Karel told him.

"Why didn't you tell me this at once?"

"I did not want the news to get around our own camp. I am sorry if that was wrong."

Mark drew several deep breaths. "No," he said at last. "You were right. Though of course the troops must be told eventually. When we've had time to prepare them. So, the old bastard's not dead after all."

"Unfortunately he is not." After giving his sovereign a few more breaths in which to digest the disturbing information, the wizard added: "And there is more to tell, almost as bad."

"Then tell it."

"We now face a demon also. Let me hasten to add that Kristin seems to be in no immediate danger from the thing."

Mark, on recovering somewhat from this second shock, felt confident that he could readily drive the demon away if it confronted him directly—at least he had always been able to master such creatures in this way before, through the power of the Emperor's name, though understanding of this power eluded him. But the demon perhaps realized this as well as Mark did, and it might be avoiding him, retreating whenever it sensed the Prince of Tasavalta was approaching.

After a brief discussion of the problem posed by the demon, the two men rode on in silence for a little distance, each busy with his own thoughts.

At last the Prince asked: "I suppose there's no doubt?"

"There is no doubt, sir, that both the Dark King and the demon are now allied with the Crown Prince. But neither Vilkata nor the demon is in command. Rather they seem to be as completely enthralled by the Mindsword as any of the others who now surround Murat."

"Can you overcome them?"

"As for Vilkata, I can, and will, and have, though to beat him thoroughly will take time. His strength in the art is not what it was in the old days; and even then he excelled mainly in the control of demons. Only one of that tribe is in his service now, and that one—its name is Akbar—I consider even more cowardly than most."

"Cowardly, but powerful, I suppose."

The magician nodded. "Formidable, even for a demon. But Akbar I will leave to you, should the foul thing ever dare to confront us directly."

Prince and wizard approached Murat's defended camp warily, climbing the far side of a long hill from which they would be able to overlook the occupied farm. When, extending their view cautiously over the hilltop, they had the house and barn in view below, Karel by his art was able to let Mark see just how far they were from the boundary of the Mindsword's magic. Touching his fingers lightly to his Prince's eyes, the magician rendered that field of force visible to Mark, in the form of an eerie, transparent blue glow in the atmosphere.

"And now, magician? Is there something else that you can achieve in this situation?"

"I can but try, Prince. I am going to try to put everyone in Murat's encampment sound asleep. If that succeeds, we may be able to try something more. Let me have a few moments for silent concentration."

Standing guard while Karel concentrated, cautiously peering over the very top of the hill, Mark gazed down at the buildings and smoldering watchfires of Murat's camp, where a few huddled human figures were discernible in the bright moonlight. The faint bluish haze of Sword-power, visible to his eyes and presumably to Karel's, was centered on the upper floor of the farmhouse, and extended to about twenty meters from where Mark and Karel now sat their riding-beasts. At that point the blue haze faded out abruptly.

Some minutes passed. Then Karel, who had looked as if he were dozing in his saddle, roused himself to whisper encouraging words to his sovereign. The magician's efforts to put everyone in the camp asleep by magic were on the verge of almost complete success.

Mark murmured back: "I don't suppose our friend is likely to sheathe his Sword before he dozes off?"

"I don't suppose so, Prince. But we can hope."

Soon Karel announced that the sleep-pall was even now taking full effect upon all the people in and around the farmhouse. But unfortunately, as Mark was able to see for himself, the Mindsword's influence continued unabated.

"He grasps the weapon tightly even in his sleep, my Prince. Therefore you must not dream of trying to enter the camp to bring Kristin out. We must seek some other way."

Mark was not so easily discouraged. "I have Sightblinder. If I were to try the fringes of this blue haze, test it first with only an arm or leg, and see what—"

Karel was uncharacteristically vehement. "No, you must not attempt it, Prince! Sightblinder will not serve to protect you. At this moment she is still unharmed, except for the spell cast on her by the Sword. We will find another way."

"With a demon hovering near her? We can't wait!"

"I tell you, you must wait! The demon is not near her now. Not anywhere near here—it may have retreated when it sensed the Emperor's son approaching. You'll be no good to her or anyone if you become Murat's slave."

Mark, reluctantly acknowledging the wisdom of Karel's advice, and seeing no other choice, gave in.

In a few more moments Karel was able to assure him that the pall of sleep he had been gradually weaving over the enemy had now indeed taken full effect. The charm had worked so subtly that none of the victims, even Vilkata, had realized that they were being enchanted. To work such magic was comparatively easy at night, because most of the subjects, or victims, would be expecting to go to sleep anyway.

The Prince thought it would be far less easy than Karel made it sound. Then Mark was struck by a sudden hope.

"If I cannot go down to her, can you get Kristin to come out?"

Karel closed his eyes. "The possibility had already crossed my mind. I will do what I can to call her here. But what I can do will probably be insufficient, unless she believes, even in the Sword's enchantment, that she has a reason to come."

Kristin, rousing from a light sleep, had the distinct sensation that someone had just called her name—one of her parents, perhaps, though both her mother and father were long dead. It had been only a dream, then . . . or had it?

She sat up in the unfamiliar farmhouse bed—there was no difficulty in remembering how she had come here—and pulled aside a window curtain. The casement behind stood open to the summer night, and moonlight flooded into the small, neat room which Murat had assigned her. Though small, it was the biggest bedchamber in the house, and the best furnished, with table and chest of drawers and even a little mirror on the wall.

Looking out of the window, Kristin could see a pair of watchfires in the farmyard below, smoldering and dying. There were dim motionless forms of troopers and bandits slumping and lying around them.

It was none of these who had called her.

Raising her eyes and gazing into the moonlit middle distance, the Princess beheld two mounted figures at the top of a long, grassy hill.

Her sense of wonder grew at the strangeness of the awakening call. Unsure at first whether she might not be still asleep and dreaming, the Princess arose from her bed and groped with her feet until she found her shoes. Otherwise she had lain down fully dressed. Opening her bedroom door, she went out into the hallway, partially lit by moonlight filtering through the oiled-paper window at one end. The white walls and coved ceiling, here in the hallway as in the rooms, were neatly plastered as in many prosperous homes in Tasavalta.

Kristin's feeling that she might still be dreaming faded at the sight of Murat, who lay sleeping on the floor just outside her bedroom door. She had to step over him to leave her room. His face was shadowed. The Princess paused to look adoringly at her new lover, who moaned almost inaudibly in his slumber. The Crown Prince was sleeping of course with the Sword in his hand, and she drew in her breath with sudden fear that he might turn over in his sleep and gash himself on that Blade. The Princess knew from old and bitter experience that the Mindsword made terrible physical wounds, almost impossible to heal. Briefly she considered moving the Sword a little, for her lover's safety, but then decided against making the attempt. Tonight Lord Murat might well need the protection offered by that black hilt in his hand, even at the risk of a sore wound.

And besides, she feared to wake her lord just now, lest he prevent her doing something that she had decided must be done—for his sake.

Scarcely had Kristin started down the hall than she stopped again, with a sharp intake of breath. Vilkata was sleeping only two or three meters away, on the floor near the head of the stairs. To her disgust, Kristin found herself compelled to step over his loathsome body as well; and as she did so she considered killing him—for Murat's sake.

The Princess had left her hunting knife back in the bedroom, but there was a dagger in the demon-master's belt that might be snatched away and plunged into his heart. Only two thoughts stayed her hand: this fiend was now sealed in loyalty to Murat, and the possibility was all too real that her beloved might soon be in need of every ally he had. Even this one.

Kristin let the wizard go on living. Stealing downstairs as quietly as possible, she encountered a few more sleeping bodies in parlor and kitchen, but to her surprise no one was awake and on guard. Surely some of these men should be faithfully on duty?

Perhaps, she thought, her lord in his wisdom had stationed the real sentries outside.

Still nagged by the feeling that someone had wakened her by calling her name, but more and more convinced that she had dreamt that much, the Princess went outside, through the kitchen and back door.

The pair of smoldering watchfires in the farmyard seemed to be burning even lower now than when she had glimpsed them from upstairs. Fires or not, there must certainly have been sentries posted out here; but Kristin saw to her surprise that they too, or at least the individuals who might have been sentries, were also fast asleep.

She took one of these men by the arm and tried, without success, to wake him.

Abandoning the attempt, the Princess turned. Peering uphill, into an alternation of darkness and moonlight created by the passage of some clouds, she could again make out the two dim human figures at a distance of something over a hundred meters. Up there on the summit two men were sitting their riding-beasts, at a distance Kristin judged to be somewhat beyond the limits of the Mindsword's invisible power.

It struck her that she was able to see one of those men remarkably well, considering the conditions. Something about the figure's clothing suggested a military uniform, though in the moonlight and at this distance it was really impossible to determine colors. The Princess was suddenly quite certain, without any conscious logic having entered into her discovery, that the man who seemed to be in uniform was a simple military messenger, come under a flag of truce to bring her word of her husband's death in some remote place. In a moment he would ride down the hill toward her, his face grim, shoulders slumped under his tragic burden—

—but wherever the thing had happened, Mark was dead, slain in some stupid combat, or dead in some pointless accident, on one of his hopeless missions attempting to serve the Emperor. And this rider, the anonymous messenger she had feared with all her heart and soul for years, was on the verge of cantering downhill to bring her the word that she had dreaded for so long—

Kristin, knowing in her heart that her doom had come upon her, and moving in a sick, dreamlike calm, observed a path that led out of the farmyard and up the hill. A moment later she was following the path, climbing the hill.

Just as she was leaving the farmyard she took note of a man who ought to have been a sentry, sprawled sleeping at what must have been his post, just inside the fence beside the path. The man moved slightly as she passed him, but the eyes in the upturned face were closed— rather, almost closed—and he snored faintly.

Kristin went on her way. Looking uphill again, she thought that the second man on the hilltop, the one who sat his mount beside the messenger's, looked very much like her uncle Karel.

Mark, straining his eyes, and gripping the hilt of Sightblinder tightly in an effort to enhance his own perception as much as possible, bit back an outcry. He recognized his wife by moonlight almost as soon as she stepped out of the shadows of the farmhouse doorway more than a hundred meters below.

* * *

Murat, after stretching himself out on the floor of the upstairs hall in the farmhouse, had taken no alarm when he began to grow heavily, deliciously sleepy. Such sensations were only natural, considering that his various concerns and responsibilities, together with the slowly diminishing pain of his wound, had allowed him but little rest on several successive nights before this one. He had welcomed the chance to lay his body down, with the black hilt of his drawn Sword still clutched in his right hand, upon a folded rug in front of Kristin's door.

Only in the last few moments before the Crown Prince dozed off did certain unwelcome thoughts enter his mind. Since making his decision to keep the Mindsword continually unsheathed, he had found himself growing more rather than less afraid of Mark. The nets of defensive magic that Murat had woven about his own person with the Sword, and with Vilkata's and the demon's help, was bringing him no increased feeling of security.

Rather the reverse.

And then there was Kristin, and her all-too-justifiable unhappiness caused by Murat's toleration of the foul wizard-king Vilkata. Perhaps worse, in her view, was his new reliance upon an actual demon. Kristin, tender-minded and basically innocent, was unable to face the fact that he, Murat, must now depend upon such creatures.

Well, Vilkata was—or had been—a foul villain indeed, and under other conditions Murat would not have delayed in putting the eyeless man to a horrible death, in payment for what he had once done to Murat's beloved bride-to-be. But the purifying power of the Sword had transformed the foul, treacherous torturer and beggar into a trustworthy servant, at least for the time being. And the fact was that Kristin's own welfare, perhaps her very survival, now required Murat to seek help wherever he could.

That was the last thought of which the Crown Prince was conscious before he fell asleep.

As Kristin climbed the hill, mounting closer and closer to the two men who seemed to be waiting for her at the top, logic suddenly awoke to remind her that Sightblinder, in someone else's hands, might be the cause of her perception of a dreadful messenger. But logic could offer only cold and fragile comfort against the inner certainty of that waiting figure's identity, and the nature of his message. These were horrors that had formed the core of her worst dreams over the past few years. Fatalistically, she climbed on.

* * *

Mark had been sitting motionless in his saddle, gazing downhill with fierce intensity, hardly taking his eyes from that small figure as it approached. He had seen his wife, as if in response to the sheer power of his will, leave the unattainable camp below and come deliberately walking up the hill toward him. Now the Prince feared to move or speak or even breathe, lest he break whatever beneficent spell was granting him his most fervent wish.

Karel, waiting beside the Prince, was silent too, and almost motionless.

Breathing softly now, Mark dared to move, to dismount. Once on his feet he did nothing but stand and wait, while Kristin in the course of her next few steps emerged from the eerily visible haze of the Mindsword's influence. Then, approaching in deliberate silence, she came to stop some four meters from her husband.

At that point she spoke. "Mark? I feel it is really you before me, and not the form I see."

The Prince unbuckled Sightblinder from his belt, then handed the weapon, sheath and all, up to Karel, who still sat mounted. In the next moment the Prince turned and took a swift step forward, meaning to enfold his wife in his arms.

But Kristin stepped back quickly, avoiding Mark's embrace; and as she moved she uttered a strange gasp, partly of relief and partly of something else.

Mark halted himself in mid-stride, reminding himself that the Mindsword's spell could not be so easily dissolved. Considerable time and loving care would be needed to heal Kristin of its effects, even after she had emerged from the field of its direct influence.

There would be no point in beginning with an impassioned declaration of love. "What form did you just see?" he asked his wife, in as calm a voice as he could manage.

She tossed her hair. Her voice was almost bright. "Some anonymous courier, come to tell me that you were dead."

"Kristin!" Again Mark spread his arms, and started to move forward.

Again with a swift, lithe movement she maintained the distance between them. "Mark, I have come up here to tell you, face to face, that from now on you must allow me to go my own way."

Mark managed to edge a half-step closer without provoking a reaction. Silently he cursed all Swords; he cursed Murat. He could see now that he was probably going to have to seize Kris bodily, if he could, to keep her from darting back into the Mindsword's sphere of magic. He could see the blue haze flickering almost at her heels.

Of course he should be subtle; but at the moment he could not.

"Kris, that Sword, *his* Sword, is making you go away from me."

"No!" Her denial, though forceful, was calm and matter-of-fact. "The Mindsword shocked me at first, but—no. Do not think, my former husband, that I am its slave. Or Prince Murat's."

"I am your husband, now and forever—but later we can talk about that. Right now—"

"We must talk about it now. Or rather, I must convince you now that our marriage is at an end. You no longer have any right to command my people, my armies—or my magicians."

Here she swung her gaze abruptly toward Karel. And Mark could see her pause, as if in renewed horror, at whatever image she saw in her familiar uncle's place.

Since Kristin's arrival the old wizard had waited in his saddle, silently and patiently. He was holding Sightblinder now, and when Mark glanced his way he saw instead a second image of Kristin, this one mounted, gazing reproachfully back at him.

When Karel spoke, he did not respond to what Kristin had just said to him. Instead he said: "Holding the Sword of Stealth, I can see more than I did. I see the two of you—"

His words broke off.

"Well?" Mark cried impatiently, at his wife's mounted image. "What is it, old man?"

Kristin too was staring at her uncle, but Mark could not guess who or what she might be seeing in his place.

"Never mind," said Karel at last. For Mark, his voice was Kristin's too. "Never mind. Let us finish our business here."

For Mark, it was, as usual, easier not to look at whoever was holding the Sword of Stealth.

And it was foolish, thought Mark, as he faced back to Kristin, for him to stand here arguing—because he was arguing not with his wife, but with the powers of Murat's Sword. Kris in her present state was no more than a puppet, compelled to say these awful things.

As if determined to prove that the bond between the two of them might after all, when put to the test, be stronger than all magic, the Prince extended a hand toward his wife.

"Come with me, Kris."

Without moving, she gazed back at him. Her expression, clear in the moonlight, was one of calm, patient rationality that chilled him more than any rage or venom might have done.

After a brief pause Kristin spoke. "I tell you, Mark, that you are my husband no longer. Do not blame the Sword, or any magic. That only helped me to see the truth. And the truth is that, even if no one had

brought the Sword of Glory near me, I was ready to leave you anyway."

Kristin glanced toward her uncle once more, and this time recoiled
noticeably, closing her eyes for a moment. Evidently this time she had
seen the old man as someone or something very terrible. When her eyes
opened again, her gaze stayed averted from him.

Then with an effort she said: "Uncle, I know that it is you."

"My Princess," said the wizard heavily, while Mark, glancing sideways, now saw him as Murat, with half a dozen Swords hung from his
saddle. "My Princess, you are not yourself."

At that Kristin dared to look back at Karel again. "But I am myself,
Uncle. More so now than—"

Mark broke in. "Kris, no one in the world outside that camp behind
you really believes that we two have been divorced. Our children certainly don't believe it. Nor does anyone imagine that I have really been
deposed as Prince of Tasavalta."

For the first time since she had climbed the hill, Kristin seemed
shocked. "The messages I left in Sarykam—"

"Have all been read. Everyone understands that you were not in your
right mind when you set them down."

"I was completely in possession of myself."

Kristin had raised her voice a little now. She still spoke with a deadly
certainty, her eyes locked on Mark's. "And every word I wrote in those
notes was true." Now she turned to cast a quick glance back over her
shoulder, into the great web of the Mindsword's magic, still invisible to
her, at whose center Murat was sleeping deeply.

Then, once more meeting Mark's gaze firmly, his dear wife said to
him: "The simple truth is that I have found one who matters much
more to me than you do."

The Prince could feel his scalp crawl with shock and anger, though at
this stage the words should have come as no surprise. He said in a weak
voice: "Kris?"

Her fists were clenched. "I tell you, Mark, that the Sword in my Lord
Murat's hand really had very little effect on me. It provided only a
momentary shock, a stimulus to help me see things as they really were.
Only Murat himself do I now see in a new way; it did not make me see
anything new about you at all—"

"It is useless for the two of you to argue these matters now," broke
in Karel in a dull voice, this time recognizably his own. Perhaps,
thought Mark, the old man, feeling secure in the knowledge that the
three of them were quite alone, had dropped Sightblinder to the
ground.

Mark edged another half-step closer to his wife.

"You say that Murat's control over you is not absolute?"

She shook her head impatiently. "You persist in misunderstanding, despite all your knowledge of the Swords. Murat does not control any-one—except by being the glorious person that he is, so anyone who sees him for what he really is must serve him faithfully from that moment on. He does not know that I am here now, talking to you, and he would certainly not approve—but I have come here anyway, because I hope that I can serve his interests, by persuading you to let us alone."

Karel grunted as if with satisfaction. "I did not expect that his fol-lowers would necessarily obey his every wish—as long as they are convinced that by disobeying, they can more truly serve him. Well, that is reassuring."

Mark, ignoring the magician's comments, said to his wife: "Our son is waiting in my camp to see you."

A shadow that might have been guilt crossed Kristin's face. "Then Stephen is safe. Very good. I was sure he'd be able to take care of himself under the circumstances."

"He saw what happened to you." Another half-step closer. "He was not happy about that."

"He did not understand."

"Oh yes he did. That's why it was so terrible."

Mark's last half-step had been too much. Kristin let out a small cry and turned to dash back into the Mindsword's zone of domination.

But the Prince, who had been shifting his weight forward and mak-ing every other subtle preparation he could contrive, was a shade too fast for her. He had no need to turn before he pounced. His left hand caught her by the arm in a crushing grip, and yanked her back from the fringes of blue haze.

Kristin, who had come unarmed, tried to bite, and screamed, and struggled, but her husband held her now in both arms and swung her off her feet, toward his waiting mount. Karel, having wisely maneu-vered himself into the exact place where he was needed, leaned from his saddle, Swordless, wheezing, recognizably himself. The wizard's large right hand, pale and gemmed with rings, moved out to palm Kris-tin's forehead softly. In the next instant she went limp.

Murat was awakened by the sounds of distant screaming. Not quickly wakened, for it seemed to him that he spent endless time strug-gling toward consciousness from a slough of oblivion. But at last he was conscious, sitting upright on the floor of the upstairs hall in the expropriated farmhouse, the Mindsword's hilt still grasped in his right hand.

He shouted for Vilkata, but at first only a sleepy mumbling answered. In any case it was now too late. He needed no wizard or demon to tell him that Kristin had somehow fled or been snatched away.

15

Kristin came drifting upward out of oblivion, joyfully cradled in a small canoe wrought from the stuff of dreams, borne by this craft with no volition of her own into a beautiful dim grotto that reminded her of someplace, sometime long ago. This was a condition of great happiness but it proved transitory. The Princess yearned for the enchanted canoe to stop at this point but it would not, instead carrying her along a stream that flowed with increasing swiftness.

And then her canoe jolted against reality, and turned abruptly into a plain field cot. With the sudden arrival of full wakefulness the blessed environment of watery dim stream and grotto transformed itself into the dim interior of a military field tent, where a single candle on a map table was all that held back darkness.

And Kristin knew that something horrible had happened. . . .

Her eyes wide open now, the Princess lay without moving on the field cot, covered by a brown army blanket. The desolate rush of returning memory confirmed her fears; Mark and her uncle had captured her, seized her violently just outside Murat's encampment. They had dragged her away by force, detached her from the one being in the universe who now meant more to her than all the rest. . . .

Yet her separation from Murat was not the mortal pang it might have been. A pleasant haze of dulled perception, relaxed indifference, kept her from feeling the full pain that ought to have come with such a loss.

Turning her head, Kristin saw that she was almost alone inside the tent. A woman soldier of the Tasavaltan army, uniformed in blue and green, was dozing, her head nodding, in a camp chair almost within arm's reach of the cot. The woman in the chair roused herself as soon as Kristin stirred, and a moment later had hurried to the doorway and was passing word to someone outside the tent that the Princess had awakened.

Kristin remained inert, trying to marshal her strength, for what kind of effort she was not sure. After the passage of an interval, which to the Princess seemed neither short nor long, her uncle Karel's face appeared above her, swimming dimly in a pleasant haze of lethargy; and soon, beside it, the familiar countenance of Mark.

Speaking tenderly, and as calmly as they could, the two men took turns explaining to Kristin that she was safe and secure in Mark's camp, surrounded by her own loyal soldiers.

Looking from one face to the other, she asked in a small voice: "Loyal to whom?"

The two men exchanged glances. Then he who had once been her husband said quietly: "To their land, and to their Princess."

"Is Rostov here?"

"He is."

"Then kindly convey my compliments to the general, and tell him that I wish to see him."

Another interval went by in the dim tent without looming faces; when they returned, Rostov's steel-stubbled black countenance was there between the other two.

"General, I have orders for you," Kristin murmured sleepily. Somehow she was having trouble calling any authority into her voice.

Rostov nodded. It had never been his fault to waste much breath in unnecessary speech.

"You are to accept no further orders from this man"—the Princess indicated Mark—"who was formerly my husband. Instead you are to send messengers to the Lord Murat, and place yourself and your armies entirely at his disposal. Is that clear?"

The general must have been warned, before he came into the tent, to expect something of the kind. He only bowed lightly, and responded calmly enough.

"As I love you, my Princess, and as I would serve you, I cannot accept such orders from you now."

Mark was silent, but Kristin's uncle standing on the other side of Rostove said to her: "Your soldiers will obey you gladly and most lovingly, Madam, as will I, once you are thinking clearly again."

She shook her head, back and forth on the flat pillow. "I am thinking very clearly now—or I was, until you befuddled me tonight with your magic, Uncle. What kind of enchanted existence have you condemned me to?"

With an effort the Princess sat up, shaking her head some more and trying to clear it. She saw when the blanket fell back that she was still wearing the clothes in which she had joined Murat two days ago—

could it have been only two days, or was it longer? For a moment the grief of separation threatened to overwhelm her.

Karel said: "I am sorry to befuddle you, as you put it, Princess. But you must be allowed a chance to rest." And the wizard made another magical pass or two.

The Prince realized that Karel was allowing Kristin to drift up slowly out of her enchanted sleep. But the old magician did not allow the young woman to return all the way to full awareness, holding her rather in a state of soothed tranquility, numbed enough so that her sadness at being separated from her new lord was quiet and gentle; not the violence of rage and hate that, as he had assured Mark, it would otherwise have been.

Mark, in whom strong feelings of relief and rage contended each time he looked at Kristin, now had a new idea. Drawing Karel away from the cot for a moment, he whispered to the old wizard that they might try giving his wife Sightblinder to hold, in hopes that she would be enabled that way to perceive the true state of affairs.

Karel, after some hesitation, agreed.

Mark sent for the Sword of Stealth, which one of his officers was now guarding. While they were waiting for Sightblinder to arrive, Rostov excused himself and left the tent.

When the black hilt was at last presented to Kristin, she refused to touch it, withdrawing her hands under the blanket.

Mark had reclaimed the Sword Sightblinder, and was about to leave the tent with Karel when, to his surprise and momentary delight, Kristin called him back.

She gazed at him, her eyes luminous with the haze of Karel's relaxing magic. But there was urgency in her voice. "There is something that I must tell you."

"What?" Putting the Sword of Stealth aside again, Mark knelt beside the bed. He reached automatically for Kristin's hand, but she pulled it away from him.

Shuddering, the woman on the cot said: "In—in Murat's camp—there is now a demon. And also a man—if you can call him that—who is the demon's master. The Dark King himself. I saw him."

Mark and Karel exchanged glances. "We know about the demon, and the magician," said the Prince, trying to make his voice confident and soothing. He paused. "Did either of them harm you?"

The luminous blue eyes flickered. "Harm me? No, they would not have dared do that. My gracious Lord Murat has ordered all his followers to honor and serve me. But—for *his* sake I must warn you about the demon, and about its keeper. Because I fear that in the end such servants and counselors will destroy him."

Mark paused. "I will destroy the demon," he said, "if I can. Or I'll send it hurtling to the ends of the earth." Then he patted Kristin's hand gently, touched her hair once, and got to his feet. Then impulsively he started to bend over her, meaning to kiss her on the cheek. But again she shrank away.

He straightened up.

"As for the Crown Prince Murat, I can promise you nothing. I am glad you told me about the Dark King, and the demon," he assured her quietly. "Will you tell us anything else—about Murat's intentions, for example?"

"His intention was to leave Tasavalta quietly, before you began to attack us."

"To leave, taking you with him."

"Of course."

"To Culm?"

"That I will not tell you."

Mark turned away and started to leave the tent.

Then he halted as Kristin spoke again.

"I say again, to you my uncle and you my former husband, that I wish neither of you ill. But it is not for your sake that I warn you about the demon—and about the other, the man who sees with demon's eyes, and who is worse than any demon. What I tell you is for my lord's sake."

"We understand that," Karel murmured.

"If I do not hate you, who are his enemies," she said, "it is only because *he* does not. I tell you that my Lord Murat wishes no one any harm—not even you, who are now bent on killing him."

Mark stared at her. Before he could answer, a guard put his head into the tent to whisper that young Stephen had wakened, learned his rescued mother was now in camp, and was demanding to see her.

"Let him come in," sighed Mark. Earlier he had spoken to his son about the possibility of frightening changes.

When the boy entered, a few moments later, Kristin stared at her son, then held out her arms to embrace him.

Leaving mother and son alone for the time being, Mark and Karel walked out of the tent. When they had gone a few paces, and were out of earshot of the sentries, they began conversing in low tones.

Mark asked, "How long will it be, magician, before she's my own wife again?"

"That I cannot say, Prince," Karel answered heavily. "We may hope for some favorable change in a few days."

Before Mark could speak again, Stephen, on the verge of weeping, came bursting out of the tent. The boy walked quickly away, avoiding his father when Mark would have spoken with him.

Mark let him go. After a final word with Karel, he retired to his own tent to try to get some sleep, leaving word that he wanted to be called as soon as there was any sign that Murat had awakened.

Sleep came quickly to the exhausted Prince, but his rest was soon troubled by strange dreams. It seemed to Mark that he was wandering, fully armed, but with only ordinary weapons, in a strange countryside. His path led him beside an unknown stream. Eventually it came to him that this must be the Aldan, the small river on whose wooded banks he had grown up. Having made this discovery he tried to walk faster, in hopes of catching sight of the mill operated by his foster-father, Jord, or hearing the familiar groaning of the wheel.

The stream might have been the Aldan, but every detail about its banks remained stubbornly unfamiliar. At last, on rounding a bend, Mark came upon his father the Emperor, leaning against a flowering tree with his arms folded, and regarding Mark as if he had been waiting for him to arrive. The Emperor looked no older than the last time Mark had seen him, and now for the first time it struck Mark that this man, his father, looked somewhat younger than himself.

Standing a little behind the Emperor was Ben. Ben's massive arms were folded like the Emperor's, and he was regarding Mark with a strange solemn silence.

The Prince did not hesitate, but strode toward the Emperor in an angry mood, ready to challenge his assumed authority—as indeed he tended to do in waking life, on those rare occasions when he actually saw the man.

Mark halted two paces away from the waiting, imperturbable figure dressed in gray.

"You are my father," Mark said. The words came out like an accusation.

"Yes."

"Very well, then, I need your help."

The middle-sized man in gray looked sympathetic. "What kind of help?"

Mark had not realized until this moment what kind of assistance he meant to ask for. But now he did not hesitate. "I want you to lend me Soulcutter. I know you have it."

The father who appeared to be no older than his son now seemed to be regarding the younger man with disappointment if not distaste. "How do you know that?"

"Because that Sword was in your possession when it was last seen, years ago. You picked it up on a battlefield and carried it away. Who else should have it now if you do not? Did someone take it from you, or have you given it away?"

"The answer is no."

"No?"

"No. I did not remove the Sword of Despair from that field only to give it back again. Besides, that weapon does not belong to me. But even if it were in my possession, I would categorically refuse to loan it to anyone, especially my son."

"Why?"

"I need give you no explanations, Mark, but I will. The best way to put it is that you don't know what you're asking for."

Ben, looking gloomy, having nothing to say, remained standing in the background. Mark understood that this dispute was to be only between father and son.

The Prince moved a step closer, looming over the smaller man in gray. "Will you for once give me a straight, complete answer when I ask you a question? Will you for once admit that I might be right?"

The Emperor smiled faintly at him, and said nothing.

Groaning, muttering in exasperation, Mark moved to seize the Emperor by his garments and shake him. But somehow it was hard to obtain a solid hold.

"You are a bothersome son, sometimes," his father said. And Mark himself, to his surprise, was grabbed in a grip of incredible strength, and jerked about until his teeth rattled.

At that point he came struggling out of the dream to reenter the real world, to find that someone was really shaking him, albeit much more gently than the Emperor had done.

The eastern wall of his campaign tent was glowing in the rays of the newly risen sun. An officer had come in with an urgent report: Ben of Purkinje was unaccountably missing from the camp. Missing with Ben were two riding-beasts, an undetermined amount of supplies, and the Sword Sightblinder.

16

SOMETHING—he had an impression of distant shouts or screams—
awakened the Crown Prince well before dawn, and he could see by
moonlight that the door of Kristin's bedroom was standing ajar. Only a
quick look at the empty bed inside was needed to confirm that she was
gone. Had intruders, treading in supernal silence, stepped over him as
he slept? There were no signs of struggle in Kristin's room. And it
ought to be impossible for anyone, here in the central glare of the
Sword's full power, to intrigue against Murat, to kidnap his beloved.
But still the bedroom window was wide open. . . .

Trying to think clearly, but still fighting a hideous drowsy lethargy,
Murat struggled to his feet, stepped over the still-inert form of Vilkata
farther down the hall, and began to stumble downstairs, leaning on the
farmhouse wall to keep his balance. In the process of making his way
down the narrow stair, the Crown Prince shifted the Sword very carefully from one hand to the other, being very careful lest it fall from his
cramped fingers. With the transfer he felt only the slightest alteration
in the effortless flow of magic. But not for an instant did Murat cease to
hold Skulltwister. There was no moment in which even the swiftest
enemy might have been able to penetrate his defensive field and strike.

Except, of course, by some other magic, operating from a distance.
Now he understood that the slumber from which he struggled to extri-
cate himself was certainly unnatural.

Having reached the dark hall at the foot of the stairs, Murat turned
toward the kitchen, passed through it and went out into the night. But
when he found himself outdoors he was unable for the first few minutes to do much more than stagger about the farmyard like a sleep-
walker. Groggily the Crown Prince strove to free himself fully from the
toils of Karel's slumber-inducing enchantments.

And it was in the farmyard, before he was fully awake, that he heard for the first time eyewitness testimony of Kristin's departure. One of the sentries, seemingly the only man in camp who had not been entirely overcome by sleep, swore that he had watched her go, alone.

Swiftly mounting anger helped Murat break free of the clinging tendrils of soporific magic. And as soon as he felt confident of being able to think coherently, he strode back into the farmhouse, climbed to the upper hall, and in a cold fury started trying to rouse his supposed magician.

He went at the job with ruthless energy, but still it took him a few minutes to get Vilkata fully awake. When the Crown Prince was satisfied that the man could hear him, he informed his vanquished wizard that the Princess was gone.

"One of the sentries," Murat grated, "reports that she walked out of the camp alone, apparently of her own free will. Up the path toward two mounted men who appeared on that hill."

The wretch who had once been the Dark King, now sitting on the floor in a moonlit corner of the little upstairs hall, pressed his pale albino's hands, incongruously backed with dark hair, over the bandage that crossed the upper portion of his face.

His voice sounded muffled. "You say the man reports her leaving, my lord? Why didn't he stop her?"

Murat could answer that, having already briefly interrogated the sentry who had witnessed Kristin's departure. The soldier swore that he had been in a helpless state that kept him from doing anything about Kristin's departure—or would have prevented his interference, had he considered it his duty to interfere. Actually, as the shaken trooper had pointed out, the sentries had been given no orders to keep the Princess in the camp. Rather, everyone had been commanded to grant her every wish. Murat, raging in the farmyard, had been forced to realize that in justice there should be no punishment for the sentry.

Indoors he continued his dialogue with Vilkata, but, as it seemed, to little purpose. When presently the two men descended into the farmyard again, Murat vented his anger on other people. He beat one man with the flat of his Sword when the fellow could not be awakened by less violent means.

And he continued to be angry at his magician for allowing Karel to prevail and put them all to sleep.

"Scoundrel, charlatan! Where is your demon? I suppose the vile beast is sleeping too?"

"I do not think so, Great Lord." Vilkata's tones were full of misery. "But where he is at the moment I do not know."

"Then summon him, and let us see!"

With this end in mind, Vilkata and Murat went alone behind some outbuildings, so that the simple soldiers should not be unduly terrified, and there the Dark King went through the brief necessary ritual.

Akbar when summoned appeared promptly, a blurred and shifting figure in the center of a muffled glow that soon outshone the moonlight and then quickly died away. An almost-convincing human shape was left: the simple maiden's form which Murat had seen during the previous manifestation.

On being informed of Kristin's departure, the demon professed surprise, and started trying to console Murat for her loss.

"Ugly monster!" the Crown Prince roared back hoarsely. "I do not want your sympathy! What I want is to know where you were at the crucial time!"

Akbar, cringing again, replied in a small maiden's voice, explaining his absence by saying that he had wanted to keep out of the way of Mark, whose approach to the encampment he had detected, and who was known to have a knack for dealing ruthlessly with demons.

"I thought this was in accordance with your orders, sir."

"Could you not at least have warned us that we were all being put to sleep?"

The demon cursed and groaned, hoarse tones and coarse words dimming the illusion of maidenhood, admitting that Karel must have been too subtle for it.

"I failed to understand what was happening, sir. I thought the two men were only scouting."

Soon Murat ordered Vilkata to dismiss the useless creature. There was no sleep for anyone in camp during the remainder of the night. By dawn Murat's rage at his enemies, his sleeping sentries, his incompetent wizard and cowardly demon, and at Fate, for failing to prevent Kristin's departure, was threatening to become irrationally, murderously violent.

At last the sight of his son, who was watching him with frightened eyes, sobered the Crown Prince somewhat. Carlo was the only one in his company at whom he had not grown angry.

The royal anger persisted, though over the next few hours it tried to fix itself upon serious targets and grew more calculating. The Crown Prince was now in the process of consciously deciding that whoever was not firmly with him was most definitely against him. By degrees he was coming around to the conviction that whoever did not support him without reservation really did not deserve to live.

He told a small worried gathering of confidants, including his son

Carlo and Captain Marsaci, that almost anything bad that happened to such people could be regarded as a just punishment for their wrong attitudes and willfully bad behavior.

Again and again during the course of the morning, while Marsaci, Vilkata, and others waited for meaningful orders, the Crown Prince called the unfortunate guard, now completely wide awake, back into his presence and demanded to be told all the details of Kristin's departure.

The formerly somnolent sentry, his nerves dissolving under the barrage of repeated questions, informed his master over and over that he had been unable to see any details of what had happened up on the hill. But he had heard several screams from up that way, a few minutes after the Princess had walked out. Yes sir, those yells could have been made by the Princess; it had sounded like a woman's voice.

By now it was thoroughly confirmed that all of the other sentries—indeed everyone else in camp—had been sound asleep at the time. Murat suspected that some of them might have been inclined to deny it, except that any who admitted to being awake when the Princess was spirited away feared being held culpable for having failed to prevent such a calamity.

Around noon Vilkata, on being asked by the Crown Prince for his advice, urged strict enforcement of the military code concerning simple soldiers who slept on sentry duty.

"It will be easy for my lord to replenish his ranks, should they be depleted in the course of justice."

Murat, looking at the other sourly, declined to follow his advice. "Perhaps recruiting more soldiers, even if that were my object, would not be that easy. Think about it. The enemy, fearing to come near my Sword, will certainly retreat in haste from any offensive move we make. They'll run away swiftly, and leave me to waste my energy and scatter my forces into uselessness if I am so inclined. No. No, thank you. When I order a march at last, I'll move to better purpose than that."

Adding to Murat's difficulties of the day was the fact that now his pair of flying scouts, who were too unintelligent for the Mindsword to have any effect on them, had somehow been lost. It was not surprising, when he thought about it, that the beasts should have been lured away or killed by other flyers, or by Tasavaltan handlers, beastmasters more skilled than the lone expert in the small force of his defectors.

But the loss of the beasts was a substantial blow. Murat saw that without good scouts he should have no chance of catching up with

Kristin, or Mark, or any other well-informed and well-mounted individual. He hesitated to send out any more human scouts; it would be a waste of time, now that his camp must be surrounded—at a prudent distance—by numerically overwhelming Tasavaltan forces.

Shortly after midday, Vilkata timidly informed his master that he suspected Karel had found some way to make visible the field of influence of the drawn Mindsword, at least to some of the enemy, including of course Mark himself.

The Crown Prince cursed fluently. It was truly maddening to have the power of the Mindsword in hand, and be unable to strike with it effectively. But the most tormenting aspect of the situation was Kristin's behavior. In truth, he had been hesitating in camp for more than half a day because he was endeavoring to make up his mind about Kristin.

Try as Murat might to disregard it, an unquenchable suspicion had begun to gnaw at him. His doubts had begun the moment he heard that she was gone, that she had evidently walked up the hill to meet her abductor willingly.

Her chief abductor, of course, must have been her former husband. The Prince of Tasavalta, armed with Sightblinder, had dared to approach the camp of the Crown Prince closely. Perhaps the Sword of Stealth had shown him to the Princess in the guise of Murat, presenting an image that she might not have been able to distinguish from Murat himself . . . that was a comfort to the Crown Prince, to think that his beloved had remained loyal, but had been treacherously deceived.

Carlo, when consulted, argued in favor of this interpretation. But as much as the Crown Prince wanted to believe it, he suffered persistent doubts.

Vilkata, in his sincere desire to serve his master, was permanently suspicious of all other servants and advisers, including Carlo. Perhaps these others meant well, but what did this youth and these ignorant soldiers know about intrigue, what understanding did they have of the great game played with Swords? Only he, Vilkata, the wizard and former king, had the experience and foresight to offer proper guidance.

Therefore, the Dark King, in a mode of thought as natural to him as breathing, mentally prepared ways in which he might discredit other advisers. In his heart he was firmly convinced that the dear and glorious master really would be better off if he came to rely on the Dark King above all others. . . .

* * *

And Murat, as the hours of the afternoon dragged on with no orders given, no decisions made, could not get the suspicion out of his mind. Could she, could she, after all, have been lying to him all along? Only faking her conversion by the Sword?

Kristin's uncle, after all, was a mighty wizard; those versed in such matters counted Karel one of the world's best, though he did not seek fame and seemed to care little for his reputation. Might Karel have been able to provide his Princess with some special help, some protection that would grant her immunity even to the Mindsword's powers?

But no, no such magic existed anywhere. The Crown Prince was ready to stake his life on that.

Except, of course, in the Sword Shieldbreaker.

Kristin, while she was with him, had not been carrying any Sword. But for all he, Murat, knew, Mark or Karel might possess the Sword of Force. And if they could somehow have transferred the power of that mighty weapon to her—

No. Kristin would have told him if Shieldbreaker was somewhere in Tasavaltan possession. No, Murat would not, never could, never would, believe that his beloved had been lying to him about her love.

Vilkata, when Murat again questioned him closely, assured his beloved master that yes, years ago, Prince Mark had seemingly defied the Mindsword's power for a time. Oh, for a matter of minutes only, an hour at the most. Vilkata's only explanation was that, somehow, on that distant day, Sightblinder's power of allowing its holder to see things and people as they really were had worked as an effective antidote to the force of Skulltwister.

Murat growled. "And what the Sword of Stealth has accomplished before, it might be able to do again."

"No one can deny it absolutely, my lord. But I think it could not have enabled Mark to enter your camp last night, and go away again."

Murat thought the situation over, and suffered helplessly, and thought some more. His men continued waiting anxiously for orders, but in his uncertainty he let them wait. His intellect assured him that Kristin's conversion to loving him must have been genuine—hope whispered to him that such a transformation might have, must have, would have taken place, even without the Mindsword's power to assist.

But he found his intellect essentially helpless against the seed of doubt, once planted.

A cunning and evil turn of his imagination showed him the Princess and her husband, even now, embracing each other, slyly laughing at him together.

After a few moments of that tormenting vision, Murat took himself firmly in hand, telling himself that there was no reason to suspect, let alone believe, anything of the kind. For a time he managed to put his doubts aside.

But whenever the Crown Prince tried to bring back in memory those predawn screams, supposedly Kristin's, heard by himself as well as by the sentry, they persisted in turning into shrieks of joyous, spiteful laughter.

Calling the abused former sentinel yet once more before him, Murat questioned him for what seemed the hundredth time.

"You say she went out from my camp willingly?"

And for the hundredth time the frightened soldier gave essentially the same answer.

"Yes, my gracious lord, willingly as far as I could tell. But then when she had joined the two men up on the hill—"

"Never mind. It is enough. She went out willingly."

17

As the hours of the afternoon passed and still no marching orders were given by the great Lord Murat, no definite decision of any kind announced, Carlo grew increasingly worried about his father. And the Princeling became to some extent concerned about his own safety as well. He considered his own safety vitally important, and not for purely selfish reasons. The truth was that none of the others in camp knew Carlo's father as he did. And, Sword-magic or not, none of them could be expected to serve the Crown Prince as well as he, who understood his father's every mood and whim, who knew when the Crown Prince really meant an order and when he spoke only out of anger and might soon regret his words.

Certainly no evil magician, and no demon, could be entrusted with the responsibilities of acting as second in command. Carlo meant to do everything he could to minimize the influence upon the great Lord of such unworthy ones.

Vilkata spent most of the afternoon alone in an upper room of the farmhouse, engaged in deep thought. Though he realized intellectually that his bondage of helpless service to the Crown Prince had its roots in magic, still he was conscious of no slightest wish to escape that bondage.

Now established in a more or less honorable and trusted position, he was dutifully doing his utmost as a schemer and intriguer to make plans in Murat's favor, to ensure that no one else did anything to harm the lord. And one person in particular soon claimed the burden of his thought.

Before the Dark King had been many hours a faithful servant of Murat, it had crossed his mind that Kristin's eventual removal from the scene might be required. When, before dawn this morning, he had discovered her flight, his first thought was that the departure of the Princess was likely to prove a blessing in disguise. Might Kristin, as Murat's consort, have been ultimately a harmful influence upon the lord, bad for his career?

The Dark King pondered long upon this question, but the more he pondered the less certain he felt of the answer. Many rulers benefited from the presence of a faithful, loving consort.

Perhaps things would have been different in his, Vilkata's life, his own period of real kingship much prolonged, if he had possessed such a dependable helpmate in the days of his own glory. . . .

. . . but all that was ancient history now. Shaking his head, he who had been the Dark King brought his thoughts eagerly back to the present. His present career, in the service of the One True Lord, Murat, was far more glorious and important than anything he might have achieved in promoting any other cause, including his own.

If Princess Kristin was, or would have been, of doubtful value to the Lord Murat, then what of his son?

Carlo, now . . . the presence of a grown and potentially rebellious son . . . it was hard to discover any positive value at all in that. Of course Carlo, while gripped in the Sword's power, would find it impossible to be openly rebellious against his father. But in the future, someday when the Sword had been sheathed again, or the son had been allowed to travel for some time outside its influence . . .

The Dark King's head ached when he thought of the possible risks to Murat's power in such a situation. Coldly he pondered. Sooner or later, he decided, Carlo would probably have to go.

Meanwhile, Murat was nursing some new suspicions of his own. He wondered whether Vilkata had been able to resist Karel's sleep-making magic, but had for some reason pretended otherwise. And had the cunning Eyeless One somehow induced Akbar to go along with that pretense? The possibilities for intrigue seemed endless.

The Crown Prince tried his best to put these new worries out of his mind, telling himself firmly that they were nonsensical for any holder of the Mindsword. But despite his best efforts he could not entirely disregard them.

While Murat and Vilkata brooded separately, one of the converted troopers was asking Carlo, in genuine puzzlement, why his royal father had not taken the woman to his bed when he'd had the chance. Why should any woman believe that a man really wanted her when he'd refused to do that?

Carlo could find no good answer.

Indeed, Murat himself had now begun to think along the same lines. What a chivalrous fool he'd been! But never mind, he'd get Kristin back. And if—*if*— her loyalty had been fraudulent the first time round, well, it wouldn't be on the second.

He'd find a way of making sure.

There was no reason why the holder of the Mindsword should be forced to endure treachery.

Vilkata, still closeted in the small bedroom he had been granted as his own, weighing as best he could the benefits and problems attendant upon each possible course of action, was coming around to the conclusion that Kristin would be, at least for the time being, a desirable mate and ally for his lord. Every great lord should have a queen, or empress, and no one more fitting than the Princess of Tasavalta was likely to become available to Murat in the immediate future.

The next problem, of course, would be to get her back. The Perfect Lord would no doubt soon declare that as his objective, and Vilkata began racking his brain to find the best way to accomplish the goal.

Later on, of course, Princess Kristin could be replaced if, for reasons of state, a different consort should become more desirable.

Vilkata did not mention this last consideration when, late in the afternoon, he was again called to consult with his lord.

But the former Dark King, speaking from experience, did repeatedly urge deviousness and caution in moving against Mark and the other resistant Tasavaltans, even though it was also necessary to avoid prolonged delay.

"As I see the situation, sir, it will be best if we can somehow lull the enemy into thinking that we are ready to talk peace. Then, advance upon them quickly, strike like lightning with the Mindsword!"

Murat shook his head gloomily. "Mark will not be lulled so easily. Nor will his chief advisers."

"True." Vilkata thought a moment longer. "An alternate plan would be to occupy the enemy capital, then negotiate. If we move quickly enough into a heavily populated region, particularly Sarykam, all of the local people will not be able to avoid your Sword. You will acquire a great number of hostages."

Murat rubbed at his once-neat beard, now grown untended. There were specks and small streaks of gray among the black.

"When I entered the capital a few days ago, it appeared to be completely deserted."

"Indeed, sire. But Your Highness did not use the Sword when you were there." The wizard's tone was gently chiding.

"True, I didn't want to use . . . yes, true. There might have been people, many people, hiding within its range. At that time I didn't want . . ."

Murat's words trailed off, as if he had now forgotten what he had then been trying to avoid.

"But this time you will enter with Sword drawn, as swiftly as you can ride."

The Crown Prince sighed heavily. He squinted in the direction of the other man, as if at something difficult to see. "It might work, but—hostages?"

"Hostage-taking can be a very effective measure, when properly carried out. I myself have on a number of occasions—"

Murat blinked. He appeared to rouse himself from a dream. In a changed voice he demanded, once more: "Hostages?"

Vilkata blinked also. Sensing unwillingness in his master—worse than unwillingness, a rapidly growing anger—he tried to change his approach.

"They are forcing you to such measures, Master," the Dark King murmured defensively. "What the enemy forces you to do is not your fault."

Murat, grieving for his lost Princess, suddenly found himself plunged into horror at the very sight of this man whom she had so violently hated and feared. This man who *had once even tortured her.* Who—

The Crown Prince had a sudden thought: Perhaps it was the very presence of Vilkata and his demon that had forced Kristin to desert his camp.

He roared at the wretched demon-handler: "I will answer for my own faults! I find your advice distasteful. More, I find the sight of you disgusting!"

"Sire, I only—"

Lunging forward impulsively, striking hard with the black hilt, Murat knocked down the object of his wrath. Then the Crown Prince stood over Vilkata, shouting at him, while the fallen magician, his forehead bleeding, struggled to regain his senses.

"In fact, foul man, I find you and your schemes inhumanly repulsive, and I wish to see you no more. Out of my sight!"

* * *

Vilkata crawled, then stumbled to his feet. More shocking than the blow itself was the realization that he had so angered his beloved lord. In the face of such wrath the Dark King did not dare to argue, or to delay his departure; he simply ran, as fast as aging legs could carry him, while turncoat troopers and former bandits stared. Vilkata's first thought in this emergency, reeling and weeping at rejection as he was, was that he must not allow the master to kill him—because if that should happen, how could he serve his faultless master anymore?

Reeling past the barn and the adjacent corral, with blood from a forehead wound still trickling into his empty sockets, the Dark King made no effort to claim a mount, but stumbled out on foot into the lately unworked fields surrounding the farm buildings.

Even now, from the very beginning of this unhappy exile, even before he began to consider where he himself would find his food and shelter, Vilkata was planning ceaselessly for some way to continue to help Murat—and of course to win himself back into Murat's favor, so that he could serve to much greater effect.

About a kilometer from the farm, in the steep side of a narrow creek's tall earthen bank, the wizard found a kind of cave, recently abandoned by some small animal, and in imminent danger of complete collapse. Here was immediate shelter. Here, he thought, his arts and a minimum of practical craft should enable him to keep himself alive and free for the time being. Soon, in no great number of days and hours, his master was going to have grave need of him again. All the strength that the Dark King could muster was going to be needed, he was sure.

Forcing his body back into the tiny cave as far as possible, Vilkata muttered spells meant to conceal himself from discovery, and to strengthen the crumbling earthen roof through which the pale roots of wild grass depended. That he might have warning of any approaching danger—or opportunity—the Dark King spent his next half hour in the summoning and deployment of a score or so of minor powers, half-real and insubstantial beings that were at the command of any practicing magician.

In Vilkata's endless concern to be of service to his incomparable lord, it had not yet crossed his mind that in a few days, now that he had left the Mindsword's field of influence, he would begin to recover from its effects.

That point had already occurred to Murat, and within an hour after the departure of the Eyeless One; but such was the ruler's contempt and hatred for the magician that when the realization came, he did not consider trying to get the foul one back.

Another and more sobering realization, coming to the Crown Prince only after Vilkata had departed, was that he, Murat, did not possess anything like the magical knowledge he assumed would be necessary to summon his demon of supposedly constrained loyalty.

At that point Murat did briefly consider trying to get his magician back. Probably, he thought, the man would show up in a few hours on the perimeter of camp, begging to be reinstated. Should he be allowed to return?

After a little thought the Crown Prince shuddered, and permanently rejected the idea.

Shortly after sunset, the Crown Prince went strolling a little apart from his men, outside the boundaries of the farmyard, his Sword in hand as usual. He had not gone far before, to his considerable surprise, he beheld the demon quietly, almost unobtrusively manifesting itself in front of him.

Murat halted in his tracks, warily twirling Skulltwister. Addressing the slight image of the maiden who now stood before him, he said softly: "I had thought that I would have to summon you."

"It is my experience, Great Lord," the image replied modestly in its young girl's voice, "that anyone who really wants to meet a demon on friendly terms is likely to get his wish. Or hers. In one way or another. Whether magic is employed or not."

The maiden did subtle things with her eyelids and lashes, and briefly showed her pearly teeth. Her dress this evening was somewhat disarranged, even slightly torn, so that it threatened to fall away completely from one fair, rounded shoulder.

The Crown Prince, gazing at Akbar in this guise of a simple young girl, knowing well what it was that he really gazed upon, still found himself, to his own disgust, being aroused by the sight.

With an inward shudder, and a violent effort, Murat put such thoughts and feelings from him.

He said: "Wretched One, I have dismissed your partner, Vilkata. What have you to say to that?"

The girl made a point of rearranging the dress that still kept slipping —oh, quite unconsciously—from one shoulder. She murmured: "Only that I am not surprised, Great Lord. In my own humble view, that man was far from being satisfactory in his capacity as your adviser. Certainly he was not worthy of preferment by a ruler as glorious as yourself."

"Why do you say that? What did you see wrong with him?"

The maiden's eyes twinkled. "I express my opinion, Lord, only because I have been invited to do so. As to the Dark King's deficiencies, evidently you have discovered them for yourself—as I was confident you would, in your great wisdom."

"Then I take it you are not of the opinion that I should try to get him to return?"

"Your Lordship will be the best judge of that. I await your commands." And the demon-image curtsied deeply.

"You know where the Eyeless One is now?"

"I believe, Great Lord, that he has concealed himself. And he is a magician of some accomplishment. Still it is possible that I might find him if I searched."

"Does he still enjoy the vision that you provided for him?"

"He does, and will, until I seek him out and darken it again. Shall that be my task?"

Murat found himself heartily tired of the subject of Vilkata. He hesitated, and sighed.

"What that man does now, or what he sees, is not a matter of the greatest importance. But should you, while carrying out your other duties, happen to discover his whereabouts—let me know."

The maiden waited, poised, hands gracefully clasped in front of her. "It shall be as you say, Master."

Silently Murat took note of the fact that Akbar was now beginning to assume a rather different personality than the one he had presented in Vilkata's presence—calmer and less terrified. Less—*pressured,* perhaps.

That wasn't all. It seemed to the Crown Prince that there was now something vaguely—*larger*—about the demon. Not an increase in physical size, no, the image of the maiden looked much the same, slender and delicate. But . . .

Murat found it almost impossible to define the difference, even to himself. But it was there.

"May I inquire, Master, what strategy you now intend to adopt?"

"I have not yet decided. Before the vile Vilkata left, he suggested a lightning attack, directed at the city. . . ." Murat, with an ambiguous gesture, let his words trail off. Despite his own reaction to the idea of taking hostages, when the Dark King had suggested it, he now found himself admitting inwardly that there was some merit in the plan. Either Kristin had left him willingly, or the Tasavaltans had kidnapped her. In either case, someone in this land deserved to be punished.

Akbar persisted gently. "I take it the plan is not merely for a lightning attack with thirty cavalry, against the city walls?"

"Of course not. An attack with the Sword, in my own hand."

"Despite its source, Your Majesty, the suggestion may have some merit." The demon seemed to be echoing the man's thoughts. "May I ask how such an assault is to be accomplished, according to that lately banished one?"

"I hadn't really thought about it. I suppose, by riding swiftly. . . ." Then Murat, noting the amused expression on the demon's girlish face, allowed his words to die again. After a pause he asked: "You have in mind some means better than an advance by riding-beast? I suppose Vilkata must have meant something other than that."

The demonic maiden moved a step closer to the man, spreading her open hands in a kind of invitation. Her dress had slipped again, her shoulder was bare, her full bosom rather more than suggested.

The girl said: "I myself will be honored to carry you, Master, you and your Sword together, swiftly as the wind. No one in the city will have a chance to flee your righteous wrath before we are upon them."

"Swiftly as the wind, you say?"

"I understate my capabilities, Master. We might travel more swiftly than that, by far."

Murat, despite his innate dislike of this creature, found himself tempted by its suggestions. "And what of Mark's power to banish you, that you feared so greatly?"

"I can smell that one at a good distance, and I'll stay safely away from him. While at the same time I'll drop you and your Sword close enough to bother him a great deal—till the Prince of Tasavalta becomes your worshipful servant. Trust me, Master!"

Carlo, looking for his father, caught up with him shortly after the demon had been dismissed.

"Father, who—what was that, that fled just now when I came up?" The youth sounded horrified.

Murat was annoyed at his son's reaction. "One with whom I had business."

"Father—"

"You will tell me not to deal with demons. I tell you that they are no worse than people."

Carlo had nothing to say to that.

Slowly making his way with Carlo back to the farmyard, the Crown Prince also came back to his bleak thoughts of Kristin. Tenderness had been replaced by wounded anger. He'd have this enigmatic Tasavaltan woman yet, whether or not she was really laughing at him now!

In his heart Murat knew that the most decent and trustworthy adviser remaining to him was his son—but he had to admit that Carlo was perhaps not the most competent.

When the two men were back in the farmhouse again, and the demon, as far as they could tell, was well out of sight and hearing, Carlo engaged his father in an urgent discussion.

"I am worried that you dismissed the Eyeless One."

"Really? I thought you had no liking for him."

"I hadn't. But at least he stood between you and—that other."

To himself, Murat thought that his son really had no idea what the Dark King had been, or what he very well could be capable of being once again.

The Crown Prince said: "You need not worry about that man. We shall manage quite well without him."

"What I worry about is you, Father."

"The Sword keeps me safe."

Carlo did not seem reassured, and Murat was irritated. But the Crown Prince, still full of tender feelings for his son, considered sending Carlo home to safety before launching his swift attack on Sarykam.

He made a tentative suggestion along this line, but it was swiftly rejected.

"No, Father, my place is here with you."

Murat rejoiced inwardly to hear those words, and immediately decided to entrust his son with some key role in the coming attack. On making this decision the Crown Prince realized that he had now already, perhaps unconsciously, decided to follow the plan of attack suggested first by Vilkata and then by the demon.

Murat in starting to elaborate these plans at first considered marching his men away from the farmhouse, to get a little closer to the city before he struck at it like lightning. But before long he came around to the view that it might be wiser to stay encamped as long as possible where he was, amid plentiful supplies and with good shelter for people and animals.

Ominously, he had received no communication yet from the Prince of Tasavalta.

It would seem that Mark had no intention of arranging a parley, or Murat would have heard from him long before now; but perhaps it would be wise to take the initiative in that regard himself? He could send Carlo to talk to the Tasavaltans under a flag of truce. He'd not go himself to any meeting without the Mindsword, and as long as he had that the other side would not care to come close enough to talk.

That night Murat got but little sleep. At first light, having made up his mind to his proper course of action, he ordered his men, just for practice, to break camp at once.

In the midst of the flurry of activity produced by this command, the

Crown Prince, Sword still in his hand, stalked about among his troops, looking around him sharply, wondering if any of his men were laughing at him when he wasn't looking. They could very well be laughing at the way he'd been cheated out of his woman. To his face the men all seemed overtly sympathetic, but—

A new suspicion had been born. Murat couldn't help but wonder.

. . . and then, after he'd had her, enjoyed her fully, or perhaps even before he'd done that, would come the punishment of Mark. That punishment would consist of, or reach its climax with, the obliteration, or at least the removal from the Great Game, of the stubbornly undeposable Prince of Tasavalta.

Having countermanded his order to break camp, Murat looked once more with affection upon Carlo.

"You, my son, are the only person with whom I really enjoy talking anymore."

"I wish I could be of more service to you, Father." It seemed a heartfelt hope.

"You are. And you will be." Serenely, and without transition, the Crown Prince went on to ask: "Tell me, am I the one who is destined by the gods to gather all of the Blades of Power into my hands?" The question seemed to have come into his mind from nowhere.

"The gods are dead," his son commented, after a pause, in worried puzzlement.

18

VILKATA, dozing uneasily in his cramped earth, was awakened by a little occult thing, a messenger invisible to ordinary eyes, come gibbering in terror to whisper an urgent report into the magician's ear. This creature was one of the tiny powers he had set to guard him as he slept, and the burden of its whispered, fearful message now was that a strange and utterly monstrous demon, far more terrible than Akbar, was lurking near the wizard's hideaway.

Whatever personal anxiety the Dark King might have experienced on receiving this intelligence was swallowed up in an awful concern for the dear Lord Carlo. Immediately Vilkata, his body stiff and bent, muscles aching from yesterday's unwonted exercise, came creeping out of his small mud-walled cave to investigate. The bruised scrape on his forehead still throbbed faintly. He emerged into a dull sunless morning of thick mist and beaded moisture everywhere.

Hastily applying several tests, the wizard, somewhat to his surprise, could detect no traces of a demonic presence in the immediate vicinity. He considered calling his other sentinel powers to him for interrogation, but soon discovered they all had fled beyond his reach—in itself an ominous sign, to say the least.

Climbing the creek bank with some difficulty, then walking warily in the direction indicated by his small frightened sentinel, Vilkata had not far to go before his demonic vision showed him a rider in the mist. The man was moving slowly, wrapped in a dark cloak to suit the weather, and leading a spare mount equipped with its own saddle.

"A demon? Hardly that!" Vilkata breathed, studying the rider's figure from the rear with a demonic intensity of perception. In another moment he had let out a little cry, surprisingly childish, and was hurrying forward to overtake the mounted man.

Actually running again despite his aching limbs, the wizard as he approached the other called softly: "My lord! My lord, am I forgiven? Do you come seeking me?"

The rider halted his mount and swung round in his saddle, presenting to the approaching magician's keen demonic vision the noble, thoughtful visage of Murat. But for a moment the Crown Prince did not reply to his banished servant.

"My Lord Murat! Forgive my offenses, and allow me to be of service to you!" Then Vilkata paused, staring in belated realization. "You have sheathed the Mindsword again!"

There was the black hilt at Murat's side, the bright steel muffled in dark leather.

"I considered that I did not need such protection at every moment," the Crown Prince responded at last, allowing his right hand to rest briefly on that hilt.

The Dark King had now caught up, and stood gasping after his brief run.

"I trust Your Majesty will not have cause to regret the decision. I fear that you have many enemies. Only a moment ago I had warning of a tremendous demon in the vicinity."

"Indeed?" But for some reason Murat did not appear to be impressed. In a moment he had dismissed worrisome demons with a careless toss of his head.

"As for your desire to be of service, magician, why, I accept it gladly. I suppose our falling out was not entirely your fault."

Vilkata, his heart pounding with joy to hear these words, bowed deeply. "I rejoice to hear you say it, sire, but I must insist that all the blame was mine."

The wizard was now standing close enough to his master's mount for him to be able to cling to the other's stirrup, and he longed to do so. But at the same time he feared another rebuke. Instead of clinging, he clenched his hands together.

"Master, what plan have you decided on? Have you marched your handful of men forth from the farm yet?"

"Not yet."

The Eyeless One breathed a sigh of relief. "Then what of the plan that I suggested?"

The Crown Prince, looking thoughtful, once more shifted his position in his saddle. He said: "Explain to me once more the advantages of your suggestion."

Rapidly Vilkata rehearsed the advantages of surprise, of striking rapidly with the Mindsword at the enemy heart.

"Yes, of course. But how did you intend that I should transport myself and my Sword to Sarykam?"

"Riding on the demon, Majesty!" the Dark King explained triumphantly. "Naturally I will accompany you to make sure that nothing goes wrong. Together we can reach the enemy capital from here in only minutes, instead of days or hours!"

"That mode of transportation would never have occurred to me." Murat's expression was solemnly guarded.

Terrified lest he might have offended again, Vilkata hastened to offer reassurance.

"Of course it will be necessary to control Akbar sufficiently to make our passage absolutely safe—I can see to that—and with your Sword it should present absolutely no problem anyway. . . . Has Your Highness seen anything of the demon since I—since I left camp?"

"No. No demons at all."

"That's good, sire, very good. As I mentioned a moment ago, very recently I have received a warning—one cannot be too careful with demons. I should be present at your next meeting with Akbar—shall I return with you now to camp?"

Murat evidently found that this question required some thought, reinforcing Vilkata's growing impression that the master today was in a strange, new, preoccupied mode.

"No," the Crown Prince said at last. "I can manage whatever demons may appear for myself, with the Sword. But managing the creatures is one thing, and . . . and the truth is that I have a special mission for you elsewhere."

"Sire, with all due respect, and having your own safety always foremost in mind, I must protest. The management of demons is—"

The Crown Prince, looking haughty, cut him short. "Do you wish to continue in my service or not?"

"Of course, Lord, of course I do! Tell me of my special mission. Where am I to go? I'll go anywhere! And to do what? Anything my lord commands!"

"Calm yourself. The task I require of you is a simple one, though I suppose it will not be easy. I want you, somehow, by your art, to destroy the demon Akbar."

"Ah!"

"You seem surprised. You should not be. When you ruled as the Dark King, you were a powerful magician. Are you still great enough to find this horrible creature's life and snuff it out?"

"To find—" Vilkata goggled.

"To find its life. And put an end to it. Any idea how to go about that job?"

"But—but—in your Sword, Great Lord!"

"My Sword? What do you mean?"

"Is not the foul beast's life still there, where Akbar himself confessed that it was hidden?"

Murat, face turning blank again, cast a long look down at the black hilt by his side.

Then he turned an unreadable gaze back at Vilkata. "I suspect," the great lord said at last, "that the beast has relocated its life elsewhere since it made that confession."

"Ah—or that the demon—lied to us about it?" Silently Vilkata cursed his own gullibility. Even a man could lie, under the Mind-sword's power—provided the motivation were to help his lord. And if a man, certainly a demon. Or might there be some other possibility . . . ?

"All I know," said the Crown Prince, "is, somewhere, somehow, there has been deception." He paused as if considering weighty matters. "Can you still see well enough? I mean—despite Akbar's absence, you are still managing to function without eyes? You found me, and recognized me, without much trouble."

Vilkata raised a hand to his face-bandage. His fingers felt that the cloth was in place, but it was not apparent to his own sight. "Yes, Master. Once granted me, the demonic vision is quite independent of Akbar's presence."

"Then take this mount," ordered Murat decisively, shaking the reins of the spare that he was leading. "There are food and other necessities in the saddlebags. Also an edged weapon or two attached—though one of your talents will probably prosper better by not relying on such crude implements. Go where you want, do what you will, take as much time as necessary. Only locate the demon's life and slay him."

Almost unconsciously Vilkata accepted the offered reins. "Perhaps I will be able to find where his miserable life is hidden now. Perhaps I know a way. . . ."

"You will find it!"

"Yes, Lord!" Under the piercing gaze of his Master, the Dark King straightened up. "As you command. And when I have slain Akbar, Lord? What then?"

"That's better. That's what I like to hear, confidence." Murat smiled and nodded. "Accomplishing such a task should keep you busy for a while. When the demon's dead, and not before, come look for me again."

"Let it be as you command, Master."

Under that commanding gaze Vilkata mounted quickly, and rode off in the general direction of Sarykam; before the mists swallowed him, he turned for one more brief look at his beloved Lord Murat. Then he was gone.

Waiting quietly in his saddle until the other was out of sight, Ben of Purkinje released a long breath, and slowly sheathed the great Sword Sightblinder.

Around midday, Crown Prince Murat, who had not left his camp for a moment during the misty morning hours, was again closeted in consultation with the demon Akbar. For this purpose Akbar had been allowed inside one of the upper rooms of the farmhouse. So far the demon's indoor manifestations had been restrained, though not entirely without effect upon the people in the other rooms. Once the sounds of distant retching carried into the conference chamber.

Today's discussion between slave and master had not made very much progress before Akbar respectfully inquired of the Crown Prince whether the great lord had had any contact with the villainous Vilkata since dismissing him.

Murat was only slightly interested. "No, I still consider myself well rid of that scoundrel. By the way, does he still enjoy the eyesight that you provided?"

The demon's imaged maiden had seated herself on the edge of a narrow bed. Her peasant skirt was creeping up toward her knees, and today her form was a little fuller and more provocative than yesterday. The changes had been subtle, but Murat had noticed them, though he had not yet decided whether to remark on them or not.

In answer to the question about the banished magician's eyesight, Akbar temporized. It was, he claimed, not easy to reclaim such a gift.

"Unless the miscreant himself should fall into my power, and if that happens I will do with him whatever Your Majesty might like me to do."

Murat frowned. The whole subject was still distasteful. "Never mind him for the moment."

The discussion moved on to other matters. Murat, before finally committing himself to the plan suggested by Vilkata and now enthusiastically seconded by Akbar, was trying to anticipate any problems likely to arise in its execution.

One thing in particular bothered him.

"But when it comes down to you, or any other demon, actually carrying me, and perhaps my son—"

"I pray you, Master, do not consider any other member of my race for the job."

"—what I want to know is, are you going to assume some solid form, capable of flight? Take the shape of a great bird, I suppose? Or what?"

"A bird, yes, if that should be the master's preference." The maiden paused, smiling. "Would you like to see?"

"No, never mind." The Crown Prince brooded for a few moments. "The important thing is, you are certain of being able to transport me—or us—in safety?"

"Absolutely certain! If you do not like the idea of riding on a bird, you—we—could be invisible in flight. I can carry several people, or a number of objects, about with me at any time, in secrecy. Trust me, Lord!"

"I think we understand each other on the matter of trust—exactly where is Princess Kristin now?"

"I cannot be entirely sure, Master, but Prince Mark has—I think almost certainly—taken her back to the palace in Sarykam."

Murat took thought for a while, shifting his Sword from one hand to the other as he did so. By now this action had become habitual, automatic, almost unconscious.

"And," he asked at last, "if I decide to bring Prince Carlo with me to Sarykam?"

"I can carry several persons, Great Lord. As I have said. In perfect safety."

"I know that human wizards, even those powerful enough to control demons, are not wont to ride upon demons. Griffins are the magic steeds of choice, for those who can obtain and master them."

"I believe the reason griffins are preferred is, as Your Majesty so wisely points out, that great wizards are inclined to be distrustful of my kind. Because, my lord, those inferior people lack the means that you possess, of enforcing trustworthiness."

The Crown Prince nodded; that sounded only reasonable to him. He muttered, so quietly that even Akbar had to attend carefully to hear him: "I trust no human being any longer, even if their intentions are good toward me."

"I am overwhelmingly honored, Master, to think that *I* am now the one to be so honored, so—"

"Cease your babbling! If I trust you at all, fiend, it's only because you're much simpler than any human being. Pure malignance—but channeled by the Sword now, so all the ill intentions must flow away from me. What do I trust? This Sword, as long as I can hold it in my own hand. And that's about all."

The maiden bowed silently, even while remaining seated on the bed, making her figure an archetype of humility.

Murat told the pretty image: "I have decided that I will probably bring my son with me when I attack. And I will certainly go with the Sword sheathed, when the time comes, because otherwise Karel will be able to track me by the radiant magic of this Sword, and will know at once where I am going, and when, and probably by what means of transportation. Do you concur with my decisions?"

"Regrettably, Master, as regards the need to muffle the power of your Sword, I fear I must."

"But then, when I sheathe the Sword, Karel may very likely know that too."

"It does not seem possible to conceal very much from that one, sire, when his full attention is upon us, as it is now, and we are the focus of all his skills."

Murat considered whether to try to make the sudden quenching of the Mindsword's magic, from the view of watching Tasavaltan wizards, less suspicious by deploying his handful of cavalry in a deceptive sortie at the same time. Give the enemy something else to watch and wonder about.

He wondered whether the best deployment, in such a scheme, would be in a number of small groups, sallying out quickly in several directions from a center.

"The enemy," Murat explained to his son and Captain Marsaci an hour later, when starting to reveal the plan of his attack to them, "will think I am still with you, marching with my Sword sheathed, hoping to keep the identity of my particular group a secret."

"And where will you really be, sire?" asked the captain.

"I'll explain about that a little later. At the last minute."

"It's true," agreed Marsaci, "that if our little band is split up into small groups, the enemy can be expected to waste time trying to avoid the Sword. They won't know which groups are safe to attack. They may well retreat in all directions."

"What would your orders be, Captain, were you commanding the other side?"

"Against the tactic we just discussed, sir?" It seemed that the captain had already given the problem some consideration. "I'd most likely retreat from all these small forces, and let them do what ravaging of the countryside they might. I'd have massed archers and slingers ready, at a distance. That's what I'd say ought to worry us, sir. Bows and slings don't need accuracy as individuals if they come in thousands. I imagine General Rostov must have some such plan in place."

"Very likely, Captain, you are right."

*   *   *

Murat waited until he was alone with his son, before he confirmed his decision about the attack.

"You are actually planning to ride the demon, Father?" Carlo had trouble believing it.

"I see no reason why I shouldn't. The Sword will keep the foul one loyal to me. Only, when I am in Sarykam, surrounded by enemies, I'll need one person with me whom I can trust, even without the Sword. Now there is only you."

Carlo was stunned, and turned pale at the mere thought of being carried on Akbar's back, but he could not refuse. Only for his worshiped father would he agree to be transported by a demon. Despite his loyalty, he feared that the experience when it actually came might be too much for him.

Murat and the demon had agreed between them that Kristin's exact location should be easier to establish than Mark's. She had left several tokens of herself, including a hunting knife and even strands of hair, in the farmhouse. With such aids to magic Akbar felt confident of being able to locate her quite handily.

At the end of his conference with Akbar, Murat dispatched the demon on a reconnaissance mission to make the attempt, if it should be possible without alarming the people in the city.

The demon, in the course of carrying out this mission, happened to observe Vilkata, riding well mounted and equipped, and by now halfway to the city.

His interest awakened, Akbar drifted closer, curious as to how his former partner had managed to outfit himself so quickly and so well, and what his current goal might be. Obviously banishment by the master had not brought about collapse.

The demon thoughtfully observed the wizard's steady progress. At first he was content to watch the man from afar, but soon decided to draw nearer, feeling almost careless as to whether his presence should be detected or not.

On the first part of his journey toward the capital, Vilkata had been busy formulating new plans to help Murat. But gradually those efforts had ceased. A day had now passed since he had been dispatched on his secret mission by Murat, and two days since he had last been exposed to the power of the Mindsword. For the past several hours the old wizard had been experiencing strange and frightening moments, mental flashes and foretastes of thinly disguised malignant hatred and contempt for his great lord.

These fits, moments when the Dark King hovered on the brink of forbidden guilty anger, so far had departed as quickly as they came, leaving him feeling shaken, trembling in horror. Each time he forced the incident out of his mind, until the next occasion came. So wrapped up in his calculations was the Dark King that the true explanation of these terrifying episodes had not yet dawned on him.

But whatever his feelings now toward Murat, Vilkata's suppressed hatred of the demon Akbar was coming to the fore. All of the magician's art and all his instincts insisted that his best chance of finding this hated demon's life lay in proceeding to Sarykam. Sooner or later, whether the foul creature still labored faithfully in Murat's service, or now sought to disrupt his plans, it was sure to leave its traces there.

Frequently during the past few hours the Dark King's concentration had wandered from his assigned mission. The Dark King became aware of Akbar's surveillance almost as soon as it began, though at first he pretended to have noticed nothing. He was not particularly surprised by Akbar's interest; no doubt the demon, whether faithful or treacherous toward their common master, was as suspicious of him, Vilkata, as he was of it. Nor did he allow himself any false hopes that this encounter might provide a chance for him to destroy it; the thing's life still might be hidden almost anywhere.

At last Akbar, giving free rein to his curiosity, and believing that by this time he had probably been observed anyway, openly approached his former partner.

Vilkata raised his eyes, and reined in his mount, as if only at this moment had he become aware of the other's presence.

"Well met, partner," he said at last.

"Well met, as you say." The demon paused. "It seems, great magician, that you are prospering in exile."

"Fate has not been unkind, so far."

"So I see. . . . Tell me, former partner, has our glorious master's glory begun to dim for you as yet? You have now been for some days out of the reach of his Sword."

Vilkata pretended more shock than he felt. "For me the glory of the great Lord Murat will never dim. Is it not the same with you?" And even as he spoke Vilkata felt one of the twinges, a moment of rebellion, coming on. Whatever he felt, he was going to conceal it from this beast that faced him now.

"Of course. Great is our lord." To the magician the words sounded rather perfunctory. And the demon hovered, in the form of a small black cloud, as if it were uncertain of what action to take next.

"Yes, great. I . . ."

Vilkata suddenly fell silent. He stretched up in the saddle, pale hands raised to cover the eyes that he had not possessed for many years. His mount, sensing an abrupt change in its rider, came to an uncertain halt.

"Is something wrong?" Akbar's voice was innocence itself.

"The Mindsword . . ." whispered the man. His tone, and attitude, suggested terrible pain.

This time the demon answered nothing, but only waited silently.

When at last the man brought his hands down from his face, he seemed to have weathered a crisis. His next words were spoken almost calmly.

"You are with me now, Akbar, because I summoned you."

"Indeed?"

"Indeed. It was a subtle summoning, and I am not surprised that you may think you sought me out of your own volition. But here you are, in nice accordance with my latest plan."

At some point since its arrival the black cloud had settled to the earth, where it now assumed the form of an inoffensive dwarf. As the dwarf seemed to bow, something of the old fawning attitude came back into Akbar's manner.

"What, mighty Dark King, does that plan involve?"

"You told us once, the master and I, that your life is hidden in the Mindsword."

"Indeed."

"Well, I am absolutely certain that it is there no longer."

There was a silence. The dwarf was staring, with penetrating, very human-looking eyes, up at the mounted man.

"If it ever was there," continued the Dark King. In a moment he added: "Are we going to reform our partnership?"

At last the demon answered. "Are you on your way to Sarykam?"

"Perhaps."

"The glorious master will soon be there."

Moments after delivering that somewhat enigmatic statement, the demon had departed. And Vilkata, the last shreds of his loyalty to Murat gone, a slowly building rage giving him new strength and new confidence in his reborn abilities, took the first steps toward summoning some other demons.

He was the Dark King, and enslaved no longer. And now he meant to sate himself with power and revenge.

19

O N the morning after recapturing Kristin, the Prince of Tasavalta
had withdrawn temporarily to the capital, bringing with him, under heavy escort, his estranged, mesmerized, and captive wife. The
Princess, making the journey in a covered wagon, was kept under observation day and night by teams of magicians, nurses, and armed defenders. Mark established this strict guard not only to forestall any
further attempt by Murat to communicate with the Princess, but because he feared what she herself might do under the lingering pressure
of the Sword of Glory.

The day-to-day management of military affairs had been left in General Rostov's hands. Mark's concern continued to be more for Kristin
than for the country whose rule he shared with her, though he well
understood how inseparable the two were. He wanted to keep his wife
with him, and at the same time was eager to remove her to a place
where she could get better care, remote from the dangers of the battlefield. Violent conflict now seemed unavoidable.

Also, as Mark confided to his friends and aides, the farther Kris was
kept from Murat, the more she would be spared continual reminders of
her lover's presence nearby. And the less likely that—Ardneh forbid—
she would ever be exposed to the Mindsword again.

Another need, in itself enough almost to compel Mark's return to the
capital, was his postponed meeting with the governing Council. He had
to admit the Council was right in demanding to see him soon.

The royal couple and their party traveled swiftly, but by the time
they came in sight of the capital, it seemed to him that Kristin's affliction had already lasted an eternity. The Prince found it necessary to
keep reminding himself, as the wagon bore his wife in through the
great city gates of Sarykam and toward their familiar quarters in the
palace, that three full days had not yet passed since Kristin had walked

away from her lover, taking herself out of the range of influence of the Sword of Glory.

Only when at least that length of time had elapsed, so Karel had repeatedly warned Mark, would he have any right to hope that his wife would begin to show some basic change in her attitude of utter devotion to Murat.

Another major concern for Mark was Ben. Nothing had been heard from the huge man, or of him, since his disappearance from Rostov's headquarters encampment, at the same time that Sightblinder vanished. He would have had unchallenged access to the tent where the Sword was kept. The only reasonable assumption that could be made was that Ben had stolen Sightblinder and carried it away.

Almost no one who was even slightly acquainted with Ben would have questioned his loyalty in ordinary circumstances, and Mark had often enough trusted him with his life. The inescapable conclusion was that Ben, in the course of the skirmish fought during his last patrol, must have fallen foul of the Mindsword.

"Therefore," said Mark to Karel, as they were entering the city of Sarykam, "the report he gave us on his return from the patrol must have been all lies."

The old wizard shook his head. "Perhaps not entirely lies."

"Meaning?"

"Well, for example, it might very well have been Carlo and not Murat who was really leading the enemy squad—just as Ben reported. Information from the other survivors of the patrol confirms that."

"Then Ben would have become enslaved to Carlo—but do you think Murat would have entrusted his son with the Sword?"

"It's possible. And consider, Prince—if it were Murat to whom our comrade became bound by the Sword's magic, then Ben's first act on returning to our camp would most likely have been to attempt your murder."

Mark, considering, had to admit that that seemed probable.

"But in fact," Karel continued, "Ben attempted nothing of the kind. Which would seem to mean that he does not consider you his master's most important enemy."

"Then what is he doing, to serve Carlo?"

"I have been pondering that. Were I fanatically devoted to that young Culmian's welfare, I think I should consider either Vilkata or the demon his worst enemy—with his own father perhaps not far behind."

"Ah. Yes." And Mark rode for a little time in silence. Then he said: "At least Ben's three days should be up—very soon, if not already."

"My Prince, there is no magical significance to that precise period of time. Recovery from the Sword's power may come more quickly for some people. Or it may not come at all. But at least after about three days we may begin to hope."

Once it became apparent that Ben must have fallen victim to the Mindsword, Karel had hastened to make sure that none of the other loyal Tasavaltans in Ben's patrol had been similarly affected. The wizard had tested these men carefully for indications of Skulltwister's influence, with negative results. Those surviving troopers had been questioned closely before the royal couple and their escort started for the capital, but they were able to add nothing substantial to the information they had already provided.

Ominously, all the men involved agreed that Ben had been separated from them for a considerable period during the skirmishing. For all they knew, their leader during that time might very well have encountered someone armed with the Mindsword. What little information they could offer about the commanding officer of the enemy patrol indicated he might very well have been Carlo and not Murat.

Karel and Mark speculated on the possibility of taking advantage of divided loyalties among the foe, if Carlo as well as Murat was making personal recruits with the Sword. But so far no way of exploiting the division had suggested itself.

Ben of Purkinje, his mind in turmoil, was riding methodically toward home.

He had accomplished something, with Sightblinder, setting a powerful and dangerous wizard the task of killing a—possibly—even nastier demon. One of those enemies would surely destroy the other, and whichever perished, the blessed Lord Carlo would be more secure.

Beyond that, Ben wasn't sure that he had achieved anything at all for his great lord.

There had been moments during the past day—moments coming more and more frequently—with the grip of the Sword of Glory beginning to loosen from his mind, when he was not quite sure, not only of his loyalty to Carlo, but of who he was himself. Such uncertainty of his identity was no great novelty for Ben, who'd been a foundling. Even the last part of his name didn't really belong to him; the "Purkinje" had somehow become attached when, as a youth, he began to rise out of the obscure poverty of his beginnings; no one of any importance could be called simply "Ben." The extra name had stuck, and after years of desultory efforts to disown it, he'd given up.

Today, brooding Ben was riding almost careless of any danger he might encounter on the road. His way was guarded by Sightblinder, his huge right hand resting on the hilt of that sheathed weapon. Steadily toward Sarykam he guided his mount, through farmland and over pastures, threading narrow strips of forest. Mentally he was free to concentrate upon his problems.

Today there were stretches, some of them hours in duration, when the obligation of devotion to Carlo still held sway. Magnificent Carlo, the Princeling of Culm, that young lord unequaled in his glory, who'd drawn the Mindsword only when Ben, encountering him alone in the field, had tried—crime unthinkable—to kill him or compel his surrender.

Then magnanimous Carlo, with the mandate of the gods flashing in his hand, had spared Ben's life, and ordered him to serve the great Crown Prince Murat. Ben had tried at first to persuade the Princeling to pursue his own advantage. But very soon it had become obvious that Master Carlo was under some kind of an odious enchantment, which compelled him to serve his unworthy father.

And today there were other stretches of time, each so far no more than a few minutes in duration, when he was assailed by doubts as to whether he should be serving Carlo at all. Terrible, grave doubts . . .

With an inward shudder he put such frightening uncertainties aside. How, Ben had wondered, was he truly to serve a master so afflicted by bad magic as Carlo was? Certainly not by simply following orders. No, in a case like this, one nodded and smiled when the master gave orders, assenting to all that was commanded—and then one went and did what was obviously best for the glorious lord, who in his present state could not be trusted to know that for himself.

It seemed to Ben that the most immediate threat to his glorious master Carlo was neither Mark nor the master's overbearing father, but the demon Akbar. That creature now, according to Karel's best intelligence, seemed to be gaining some kind of ascendancy in Murat's camp.

Once that demon had been eliminated, Ben decided, Carlo would also be well served by the death of both Murat and Mark—Carlo's father now presented, in Ben's judgment, at least as great a threat to Carlo's success as did the Prince of Tasavalta.

Besides . . . Ben's ugly, deceptively stupid-looking face grew sad at the mere thought of having to eliminate Mark. He could see, though, that such an act might well become necessary at some point, since Carlo's welfare was at stake. Ben had known Mark and counseled him and fought beside him for many years, since they were both boys, long before either had seemed likely to amount to anything in the world's affairs, and therefore Ben was sad about the situation. Not, of course, that such considerations would keep Ben from killing the Prince, if glorious Carlo might benefit from such an act. Naturally, no personal attachments could be allowed to count for anything against the master's welfare or the advancement of his marvelous career.

Naturally . . . though once more doubts arose. . . .

The idea of eliminating the demon, of course, engendered no sadness in Ben. Nor would he be sorrowful to see Murat depart. Once the Crown Prince could be put out of the way, Carlo would not only be freed of his ridiculous enslavement to his father, but ought to inherit his father's claim to the Culmian throne—and if either Sightblinder or the Mindsword, or preferably both, could then be put into Carlo's hands, he should be able to make that claim good.

But any Sword given to Carlo under present circumstances, as Ben realized perfectly well, would be quickly passed on to his megalomaniac father. Therefore, Ben had made no effort to enter the enemy camp and place Sightblinder in his glorious master's hands.

Besides . . . he was beginning to have doubts.

Murat, keyed up by gradually heightening excitement as the hour of his planned attack drew near, was keeping firmly in mind the necessity, at all costs, of maintaining his control over Akbar. From the moment he, the Crown Prince, sheathed the Mindsword, that control would inexorably weaken. For the rest of Murat's life, or until he could find some way to destroy the beast, he would have to draw that Blade again at least every couple of days, or risk having Akbar escape from his control.

And in his darkest dreams Murat could hardly imagine any outcome worse than that.

The Dark King was raging quietly as he rode at a steady pace, continuing his methodical progress toward Sarykam. He fingered the sore place on his forehead, still raw and throbbing despite his magical efforts to heal his own flesh. He knew how poisonous the Mindsword's blade was said to be; even the hilt, it seemed, was capable of causing a particularly nasty wound. An injury that cried out, with every throb, for special vengeance.

The last vestiges of Vilkata's magical enslavement to Murat were now dissolved, and he was trying en route to decide on the best way to strike at his enemies, the Crown Prince now definitely included among them. But Vilkata's anger did not cause him to forget his enemies' strength. Ideally, he would destroy them all by getting them to eliminate each other. Obviously that was easier said than done.

Vilkata's most recent encounter with the demon had done nothing to help his composure. Whether the renewed contract would facilitate his plans remained to be seen. His difficulties were compounded by the fact that in attempting any intrigue against Akbar he risked the loss of his demonic vision. For this reason, the wizard had already summoned other demons to his aid; but how many of their number were going to arrive, and how much help they would be when they did, was, to say the least, still problematical.

Murat felt confident that he and his son, riding aboard the demon, would have an excellent chance of taking the defenses of the Tasavaltan capital completely by surprise. Of course, the Crown Prince reminded himself, Karel's cunning should never be underestimated.

Having been a guest in the Tasavaltan royal palace a year ago, Murat had the general layout of that edifice clearly in mind. Originally he had hoped to have Akbar carry himself and Carlo to some point actually inside the palace, but the palace was not huge, as such constructions went. Logic and memory combined to assure the Crown Prince that no point within the building could be more than a hundred meters from Kristin's bedchamber.

Murat had therefore considered several alternate landing places, but none of these would offer sufficiently quick access to the Princess—not even if he were to use his Sword at once on landing, establishing for himself a zone of dominance inside the very heart of the enemy head-quarters. Still, physical obstacles in the form of walls and locked doors would intervene between him and his goal.

No, he must command the demon to bring him very close to Kristin. But he was determined not to draw his Sword, this time, until he had an opportunity to speak to her. And Kristin had a chance, a final chance, to answer him freely. . . . Of course, it was possible that circumstances should once again compel him to draw his Sword at once when he arrived.

Murat stared bleakly into the distance for a moment. Then his thoughts moved on.

As soon as Akbar had delivered his two passengers, he was to hasten away to a safe distance from Mark, who would very likely be some-where nearby, and stand by for another summons.

As for Murat himself, once he had spoken to Kristin, she would grant him—he devoutly hoped—her free devotion.

Only after she had done that, and with her blessing, would he once more draw his Sword.

On the other hand—

There was still the possibility—

If she *should* refuse him—not likely, granted, but just suppose—if this time the Princess refused him, thereby confirming his worst suspicions about her treachery . . . but no, she was not going to refuse him.

No, she would not.

Murat smiled to himself. It seemed that one way or another, under conditions of acceptance or denial, he would be drawing the Mindsword again shortly after his arrival in the palace. With that act he would inevitably assert his power over a large number of people, including a good fighting force of soldiers—just as in his dream.

Some of that herd of new supporters, the Crown Prince thought, with stone walls between themselves and him, wouldn't even realize at first that he, their new, glorious leader, was nearby. But he had no doubt that their conversions would be just as thorough.

Not only would his new followers be eager to fight for him from that moment forward, but perhaps many of them would prove very useful as hostages. Willing hostages, people who would never try to escape . . . yes, there were many favorable possibilities.

Presently Murat's thoughts turned to his son. Exactly what task he would assign to Carlo when they had landed was, Murat now decided, impossible to determine until the time arrived. Suppose they should encounter a sentry in a corridor, or some servant or official, on the way to Kristin's chamber; why, two men armed with ordinary weapons—Murat meant to bring along his battle-ax as well as his Sword—had a much better chance than one of removing the difficulty silently and with dispatch.

And what if on the way they should encounter Mark? Or if Mark should be in Kristin's chamber when they arrived?

Murat looked forward to that meeting.

Alone in the farmhouse bedroom that had briefly been Kristin's, the Crown Prince, alternately sitting, lying down, and pacing, dreamed and planned through the slow early hours of the night. As the time approached for launching his attack, Murat over and over again imagined himself entering Kristin's room in her Tasavaltan palace. Most particularly he imagined her reaction—delighted, perhaps just a little frightened—at the moment when she saw him come in.

Immediately he would assure her that she had no cause to be frightened. Not if she were loyal.

Sometimes, in Murat's imagination, the Princess was alone and asleep when he entered, and he had to touch her bare shoulder to awaken her.

Again, Kristin would be wide awake despite the lateness of the hour, sitting with her candle at a writing table, and her eyes when she raised them to behold her lover's entrance were filled with the most exquisite joy. . . .

There was another version of this scene that Murat did not welcome to his imagination, but which still would not be denied: one in which Kristin was in bed, but not alone. . . .

Several violent conclusions to that version ran through the mind of the Crown Prince, but for the time being he refused to allow himself to dwell on any of them.

He had thrown himself on the bed, and his waking dreams soon faded insensibly into those of slumber. Troubled sleep brought the Crown Prince visions quite different from the scenarios constructed by his anxious waking mind. Here were experiences of orgasmic glory, in which millions of people gathered to worship him. Yes, millions, hordes beyond counting, joined by other beings who were more than human—joined perhaps by the gods themselves, returning to earth. They had all assembled to give worship to Murat, as it was said that once even the gods had come to give adoration to the Dark King.

The Crown Prince groaned in his sleep. He had never known the Dark King in his days of glory. Vilkata, that filthy beggar? That debased and terrified old man? If the gods themselves could be made to worship *that*—

Then Murat's dreams turned more closely to his own situation. He'd completed his demon-flight to the palace in Sarykam successfully, and a sizable, no, a huge military force in the palace and the surrounding portion of the capital had been caught and converted. His only problem now was that these most recently converted troops could not be made aware that their master was actually present, within the very walls they guarded. Murat shouted and beat with his fists on the stone walls of the palace, to no avail.

Of course, once his new worshipers knew how close to them their glorious new master really was, they would defend him to the death. More than that, they'd fan out eagerly beyond the hundred-meter limit to conquer a whole kingdom for him. And in the future, when the Crown Prince had sheathed the Sword again, the great bulk of these converts would of course remain his loyal subjects. And most of the Tasavaltan leadership—all those who survived—would do the same.

Meanwhile there was a new threat, the stone walls of the palace seemed to be closing in—

* * *

In the deepest hour of the night Murat was awakened, just as his dreams were starting to go bad, by the demon, returning from a final reconnaissance flight. To deliver his report Akbar had assumed the by-now familiar form of a young maiden, who sat provocatively, wearing tighter and scantier clothing than ever before, on the edge of Murat's simple borrowed bed.

Akbar in his report now confirmed that Prince Stephen, as well as Mark and Kristin, was among the members of the royal family on the scene in the palace in the Tasavaltan capital.

The Princess herself had been located with quite satisfactory accuracy—she seemed to be spending most of her time in the bedchamber which she shared, in more ordinary times, with the Prince. This chamber was located high in the palace on the eastern side, overlooking the city and the harbor.

Murat was impatient. "I know where her rooms are. And are they sharing one bed now?"

Akbar considered the question carefully. Slyly he seemed to take his time. "That I could not determine, Master, being mindful of your warning to avoid discovery."

Mark, having seen Kristin settled as comfortably as possible into their old quarters, was sleeplessly working alone in a room just down the corridor. In more peaceful times he used this chamber for a study; just now it was something like a command post.

The Prince was standing at a map table, poring over some documents by lamplight, when there was a knock at the door.

When he barked an acknowledgment, a sentry, his face wearing an odd expression, put in his head. "Someone to see you, sir."

"Someone? Who? What do you mean—"

Then Mark fell silent, staring with wide eyes. The door was pushed in farther. Just behind the sentry stood the Emperor, smiling at his son.

Slowly Mark turned to face his visitor.

"Leave us," he told the sentry in a low voice.

"Sir—"

"Leave us, I say."

The soldier backed out. The Emperor came in, and closed the door. He stood with hands clasped behind him, and his gray eyes moved past Mark to the table.

"Is that an accurate map?" he inquired.

Whatever opening statement Mark might have expected from his father, it wasn't that. He could only gape for a moment in astonishment. "The map? I suppose so."

Turning back to the map, gazing helplessly at the documents spread out on it, the Prince was astonished when in the next moment a sheathed Sword appeared, flying through the air almost over his shoulder, to crash down in the middle of the map.

The Prince spun around—to behold not the Emperor but Ben, Swordless and grinning at him heartily, his huge hands spread in greeting.

At that same hour Kristin, sitting in her chamber alone save for an ever-watchful nurse, was greeting a less surprising visitor.

It was Stephen, come visiting in his nightshirt, hopefully, wistfully, to see if his mother was getting better.

"How are you, Mother?"

She held the boy and stroked the rough texture of his hair. "I'm quite all right. I'm going to be quite all right."

"Are you—are you and father still—?" Stephen couldn't quite manage to get the terrific question out in any form.

"I'm here now," Kristin answered at last, softly. She held her son and rocked him, back and forth. "And your father's here too. No one can promise you anything about tomorrow."

"Mother—"

"No one ever can do that."

The boy seemed about to speak again, when a muffled commotion erupted somewhere out in the corridor. There were distant cries, and running feet. Kristin sighed, and kept to her rocking chair. Stephen hurried out to investigate, to return in a few minutes with the good news that Ben was back, and unharmed, and that he had brought Sightblinder.

"Isn't it good news, Mother? Isn't it?"

The Princess was standing now.

"Yes," she said. "Of course. It's good news, Stephen."

In another moment Karel, accompanied by a physician, was coming in to see her.

"Gentlemen, you still hope by your arts to keep me pleasantly controlled?"

Her uncle bowed sadly. "Madam, we want nothing but your own best good."

Kristin was weeping.

An hour later, and once more after that, Mark too looked in on his wife. The first time he found her sleeping, and he retreated patiently, eager as he was to speak with her joyfully of Ben's return.

At the time of her husband's second visit Kristin was awake, and as they conversed she held Mark's hand and gazed at him ambiguously, as if she were trying to communicate something beyond the limited power of words.

Once or twice she also snarled at him in anger.

20

At the hour when Murat was receiving from the demon his last scouting report before the flying attack was launched, Ben, sitting in a high room in the palace in Sarykam, was describing to the Tasavaltan leaders his encounter in the field, several days ago, with Carlo, and his more recent meeting with Vilkata.

Vilkata, when Ben had seen him last, had been mounted on a riding-beast, headed in the direction of Sarykam.

Given this information, Karel decided to establish a watch for this evil wizard at the city gates. So far the gates were still being kept open on a normal schedule, despite the general state of readiness imposed on the capital. But the watch at each entrance would be doubled.

Mark, before leaving for an extensive tour of the gates himself, commented: "The Sword's effects on our friend Vilkata will be wearing off, as they did on Ben. We can't be sure he'll still be trying to serve Murat."

"We can be sure," said Karel, "that he means us no good."

As for Murat and Carlo, Ben could tell his comrades no more about their plans than could anyone else in Sarykam. He could only suppose that the Crown Prince intended some bold stroke, and that the Princeling, under continuous pressure from the Sword of Glory, would still be slavishly following his father.

Murat, immediately after receiving his last briefing from Akbar in his lonely farmhouse bedroom, began his final personal preparations for the attack. The Crown Prince armed himself with a knife, in addition to his Sword, and stowed in pockets and pouches a very minimum of other equipment. He thought not much was necessary. He meant to conquer the palace and all the supplies it contained, or else die quickly in the attempt.

Putting on garments and taking them off without for a moment ceasing to hold the Sword was something of an accomplishment, but by now the Crown Prince had had several days in which to practice. For him the necessary maneuvers had already become something like second nature.

Only when Murat was fully dressed and ready did it occur to him that the time had come, according to his own plan, for him to sheathe his Sword. After a momentary pause he did so. Though there was no one in the little room to see him, he performed the act with a ceremonious gesture.

Then the Crown Prince at once left his room. After a perfunctory tap on the door of the adjoining chamber, he entered quickly. Inside he found a sleepless Carlo already up and armed.

The lad looked tired and pale, but bravely he announced his readiness to go.

In the upstairs hallway, father and son encountered Captain Marsaci, who had come for them, bearing a torch, promptly at the appointed time. With the captain lighting the way, all three men proceeded downstairs.

Some hours before Murat had decided that to launch their flight from inside the farmhouse would be impractical. He had chosen the hayloft, in the barn, as offering the best security from observation.

The demonic maiden, who had disappeared from Murat's room a few minutes earlier, sat waiting upon a bale of straw for the three men as they climbed a wooden ladder. Behind her the big doors through which hay was normally loaded were standing open to the night.

Marsaci sneezed, on entering the dim, dusty space. Then the captain started to sneeze again, but the spasm was aborted when he belatedly caught sight of the demon waiting for them. Despite the demure appearance of the image, Marsaci did not for a moment mistake it for a real girl.

"Are you ready, my lord?" the maiden asked, addressing Murat as she got to her feet.

"Ready."

In an instant her form had swollen to several times the maiden's size, and changed into the shape of a giant, winged reptile, crouched on two hind legs that looked too heavy for anything that could fly. A wicked head, armed with long yellow fangs, turned on a long neck to grin at the waiting men. The torch shook in Marsaci's hands, and he mumbled something.

Blaspheming various gods, Murat clapped his hand on his Sword-hilt and snarled an order.

"A bird! Let us have a bird, vile creature!"

"As you say, Master." And in a twinkling rough scales were replaced by sable feathers. A giant black bird, with yellow eyes and curved raptorial beak, crouched ready to be mounted. No saddle or bridle were in evidence; perhaps that meant none would be needed.

Boldly Murat stepped forward, and without hesitation straddled the creature's back. He turned his head to stare at his son.

Reluctantly Carlo clambered aboard behind his father, clutching the older man around the waist with both arms.

There was no delay. The Crown Prince barely had time for a last word to Marsaci before father and son were swiftly carried into the air.

Carlo groaned and gasped.

Murat gasped too, a sound of triumph rather than of fear. Then he let out a loud yell of exultation. They were being borne upward at breathtaking speed, into an aerial realm of clouds, sluiced with cool mist and shot with intermittent moonlight.

The night air howled past the travelers at a terrific velocity, but the Crown Prince soon discovered that his journey was not, after all, going to be swifter than the wind. Carlo behind him was suffering a fit of terror, and came near plunging to his death and dragging his father with him.

His father, getting little or no help from Akbar, was forced to struggle awkwardly to hold his son on the bird's back.

Shouting at Carlo did no good, and Murat directed his yells at the demon. "Stop! Return to the earth! Land, I command you!"

At last, in response to bellowed orders from the Crown Prince, the rush of air diminished. The dark earth rose to meet them, and a landing was effected in some farmer's field.

Disembarking from his black, feathered mount, Murat dragged Carlo whimpering and almost sobbing aside, the pair of them trampling waist-high corn. In the distance, toward the city, thunder grumbled and rain was threatening.

The Crown Prince shook his son, and cursed him.

"What are you afraid of? Not heights, don't tell me that. I have seen you stand on a clifftop without whimpering, and climb a castle wall where there were no stairs."

"It is the demon—the demon, Father—the touch of it is horrible—"

"Nonsense. The touch of defeat, of failure, is the only real horror. Pull yourself together, be a man!"

Carlo managed to establish some measure of self-control. "I can only try, Father."

"You can do more than that. You can succeed!"

They were on their way back to where they had left Akbar, when Carlo suddenly put a hand on Murat's arm.

"Father, I have a confession to make. Something you must know, in case I die before I have another chance to tell you."

Murat stopped in his tracks. "What is it?"

"Once, on patrol—the time we fought the skirmish—I once used the Mindsword."

Stopping in his tracks, the Crown Prince stood for a moment as if paralyzed. Then he screamed: "How could you lie to me? How many converts did you make? Where are they now?"

"Only one—only one, Father. The man they call Ben of Purkinje. I do not know where he is now."

Murat started to choke out more abuse, then paused. "There is no time now to settle this. How could you betray me in such a way?"

"No, Father! There was no betrayal! I swear it! I ordered him to help you."

"To help me? How?"

But his son did not answer. The Crown Prince could see Akbar, at a little distance, still in bird-form, crouched and undoubtedly listening.

"Later we will settle this," Murat grated at his son. "Mount! We are going on."

Carlo, almost fainting, once more climbed aboard the silent demon. In moments they were airborne again. This time the Princeling did not struggle in the air, or show any signs of terror. Rather he rode as an inert weight, as if he were already dead.

The rushing flight continued, in darkness and near-silence. Presently Akbar turned back his bird's head to announce that they had almost reached their destination. Neither of the human passengers was quite able to believe this. But before either of them really thought it possible, the city appeared.

"Sarykam," the demon informed them, its voice a guttural grinding through the rush of air.

Indeed, there lay ahead, still far below the sable masses of those mighty wings, a vast sprawling darkness beneath the clouds, a region vaguely distinguishable from the ocean to the east, and from the fields and farms and orchards to west and north and south, picked out by specks of random firelight.

The distance to the capital was diminishing at a speed that seemed incredible to Murat. Already individual structures could be distinguished. Lower and even more swiftly flew the demon. The walls of the city took shape out of the darkness and rushed beneath the demon's wings. And now more stone walls, even higher barriers, loomed just ahead.

These, unmistakably, formed the south flank of the palace.

Both passengers flinched involuntarily as the massive construction hurtled closer. The ramparts were marked with a few high narrow windows that looked too small to admit their flying bodies. One moment a violent crash seemed unavoidable. In the next—Carlo closed his eyes and did not see how the trick was done—the outer wall and its open windows were behind them, and he and his father were enclosed within a high and otherwise deserted corridor. Already they were on their feet, staggering to establish their balance upon a solid floor as the great black shape of their carrier dissolved to nothingness beneath them.

Murat barely had time to deliver a last command, in a fierce whisper, before the demon vanished utterly.

The two Culmians were alone in a long hallway of wood and stone, lighted at intervals by high lamps. The palace was quiet around them, and it seemed that their arrival must not have been observed.

Murat, hand on Sword-hilt, needed only a moment in which to get his bearings. "This way!" he muttered, and directed Carlo with a nod.

But the Crown Prince and his son had taken only a few steps in the indicated direction before a door opened ahead of them, and they stood face to face with a maidservant, her arms piled high with linen. Her eyes opened wide, enormously, and her mouth worked as if she might be about to scream.

Murat backed up a step, ready to draw his Sword at once. "If you are holding the Sword of Stealth," he growled at the maid, "drop it at once, or—"

Before Murat could finish speaking, Carlo reacted more practically, stepping forward and striking the woman down with the butt of his own sword.

The two men stared at the maid, who now lay dead, or unconscious, on the floor.

Then Murat pulled his suspicious gaze away from her. "Come!"

Father and son moved on toward Kristin's quarters. Then, peering warily round a corner, Murat discovered guards posted in a place that would make a final approach through the corridor impossible.

When he relayed this information to his son, Carlo whispered: "Father, now is the time for you to draw—"

"Quiet. This way."

Murat pulled his son down another angle of hallway, then through a door, into a room which proved dark and untenanted. In another moment they were leaving this room again, through a window opening to a balcony.

From this balcony others to right and left on the same high level were visible, and accessible, if one was not discouraged by the need to cross sections of sloping, slate-tiled roof.

"The Princess's suite connects to at least one of those balconies," Murat whispered. "Follow me."

The passage across the slippery roof had to be carefully negotiated, but it was quick. Then Murat and Carlo were on another balcony, then boldly entering what the Crown Prince proclaimed to be the Princess's room.

It was a large, well-furnished bedroom, simply decorated, well lit by several candles. The bed was empty, though covers had been turned back, and Kristin was not to be seen. A middle-aged woman dropped her knitting and rose from a rocking chair to stare at the intruders.

She had time to utter only a slight preliminary noise before Carlo was beside her, holding his knife to her throat.

The Crown Prince, hand on Sword-hilt, stood frozen, gaze focused in the distance, obviously listening for something with a full intensity of concentration.

Carlo heard a small noise, as of a hastily closed door, from one of the connecting rooms.

"Kristin?" Murat, calling the name softly, lunged through a curtained doorway toward the sound.

Carlo suddenly found himself holding the body of an unconscious woman; the attendant had fainted. He lowered her body to the floor, and leaped to bar the door that he assumed led from this bedroom out to the corridor. A moment later he had followed his father into the next room. This was another bedroom of some kind, too dark for him to be able to make out much of its contents. Here a door stood partially open to another balcony, and to the summer night.

The young man hastened to bar the hall door of this room too; almost immediately afterward the handle was tried from the outside, and immediately after that someone out there began a heavy pounding on the door. Now the alarm was being raised in earnest.

Murat was looking warily out onto the balcony of the darkened bedroom. Now he stepped out onto it.

"My love," his son heard him breathe.

In the next moment the Crown Prince began to draw his Sword. Carlo, approaching his father from behind, saw with astonishment a half-grown boy, wearing only a long nightshirt, step from behind some draperies beside the doorway and hurl his body on Murat's right arm.

The Crown Prince was taken by surprise, and the Sword of Glory, glittering faintly in the light of candles in the room, escaped from his grip.

Immediately magic informed the air. The voices of a multitude, inspired and invisible, sounded in the mind of every human near. Murat could only watch as the naked Mindsword described a smooth arc, clattered briefly on the dark slates of the nearby roof, and then went sliding swiftly down out of sight.

Before the Sword had struck the roof, Murat went lunging after it. The unreal voices, chanting glory, mocked him. His convulsive effort to catch or retrieve Skulltwister knocked the night-shirted child aside into a corner.

The Princess Kristin, dressed in a delicate robe, stepped into Carlo's field of vision, clutching at the arm of the Crown Prince. But Murat, groaning and muttering, thrust her roughly aside too, and in the next moment had vaulted lithely over the balustrade. There he crouched, in an exposed position on the roof's edge, staring intently down into the near-darkness of a courtyard, trying to see where his Sword had fallen.

The Princess, murmuring and crying, would have climbed after him, but Carlo stepped forward to hold her back. Then for a moment neither of them was able to act effectively. Both were stricken, stunned, half-entranced by the wordless, soundless flow of the freed Sword's magic.

Others, all around them, were affected too. And the mundane silence of the night had been irretrievably shattered. Whether from one source or several, the alarm against intruders was spreading.

Carlo, holding the Princess with one arm, looked around and drew his own sword, momentarily expecting a rush of guards from somewhere. But as yet nothing of the kind materialized.

In the next instant Kristin, with a surprisingly strong effort, had broken free from Carlo's grasp and was bending over her son. The bare-legged boy in the nightshirt lay moaning, half-stunned, his upper body leaning against the wall in a corner of the balcony.

Murat, maintaining his precarious position a few meters away, at the very edge of a section of roof, had just turned his head to call to his own son, when a crackling noise and a brief glare of light roiled the air eight or ten meters above their heads.

Carlo looked up to see an image of the wizard Vilkata, borne in midair amid a small swarm of half-visible demonic shapes. These descended with their burden, as the Princeling watched, to deposit the Dark King upon an angle of roof. The Eyeless One's landing place was one level down from where Carlo and his father were watching, that much closer to where the fallen Sword had lodged.

Having conveyed their wizard-master to the place of his choosing, the demonic forms melted away into the damp air.

Vilkata—there was no doubting the solidity of his body now—straightened up, his fists on his hips in a royal pose. He called out mockingly to Murat: "Have you lost something, Great Master?"

There was no answer.

A moment later the eyeless man went on: "My ethereal servants, who dwell in air and darkness, inform me that within the last minute a certain treasure has ceased to belong to you, Crown Prince." The magician laughed, and made a pretense of peering around him. "Where can it have gone, I wonder?"

Before Vilkata had finished speaking, the rain that had been threatening broke from low-flying clouds, a steady downpour certain to make the footing on slate tiles even worse.

"Don't fall, Murat! Careful, glorious Master! Ha ha!"

Murat, hanging awkwardly at the brink of the perilously steep and slippery roof, finally answered his quondam magician—with a curse.

Then, for the moment ignoring the wizard's threatening presence as if Vilkata did not exist, he turned back to his son. In an almost conversational voice he said: "I can see the Sword, Carlo! It's only a little way down. Guard me while I climb down and claim it."

"Father, don't—"

"I can reach it, and I will. None of these swine can keep me from it."

But Vilkata, starting from his lower level, was already moving toward the prize, and was plainly in position to reach it first. The man descended carefully, with a certain unnatural slowness in his downward movements, as if he had provided himself with magical protection against a fall.

The Crown Prince looked up at his son again, in desperation. "Carlo, your sword! Throw it! Stop him, kill him!"

Abandoning the Princess, whose attention was still focused on her son, Carlo obediently climbed over the balustrade. He had no particular fear of heights.

"Stop him!" It was a scream of agony.

Carlo, only having got down a meter or two, stopped where he was, clinging by one hand to a drainpipe, his feet braced precariously on small stone knobs he could not really see. With his free hand he drew his sword, and hurled the weapon at the Dark King five or six meters distant; a drawn blade was one of the strongest moves any nonmagician could make against any magical operation in progress. But either Vilkata's magical protection was equal to the challenge, or else the missile simply missed him. In any event it fell harmlessly. And for a long time. They all heard it strike, at last, on pavement far below.

Vilkata was within two meters of being able to grasp the Sword of Glory when the demon Akbar appeared, standing on another balcony, on the far side of the fallen Sword from the magician, but as close to it as he was.

Murat, slowest of the three active contenders, remained hopelessly distant from his prize. Now the Crown Prince paused in his slow progress, just as he was about to lower himself from a roof drain, to see the outcome of this new confrontation. In a moment Murat had hurled his own knife in the direction of the wizard, with no effect. His shouted orders to the demon were ignored.

Now Murat, gesturing fiercely, shrieked again for his son to go and seize the Sword, to sheathe it and bring it back to him, to fight the demon, to do something.

Carlo smiled vaguely, nodded his perfect obedience to his father, and moved as quickly as he could toward the Sword. He could see Skull-twister, caught from its fall by a small projecting cornice, leaning hilt uppermost against a wall in a precarious position.

In the next instant his feet slipped from an impossible foothold, and then his grasping fingers slid from the edge of the slick roof.

Falling, he had several seconds in which to think, to fully realize his failure.

Murat, as if he were not yet aware that his son had plunged to the ground, still barked orders at Akbar, commanding him to put the sheath back on the Sword. "Then bring it to me, to me, your master!"

Akbar, posing on the balcony in the form of a maiden, sent an amused glance toward Murat.

"I have decided," said the maiden, "that someone besides you, my Lord Murat, should bear the Mindsword from now on. I'll carry it myself, for the time being, though I don't look forward to all the attention it will bring me."

The Crown Prince, unbelieving, made a strange sound in his throat.

Akbar continued: "Because you—you, my gr-r-reat Master!—live increasingly in a world of your own megalomaniac fantasies. Therefore, in my judgment, you are becoming undependable."

"You are to serve me! I command you—I charge you—"

"Yes, yes. I know you are convinced you are my master. Most humans who deal with me willingly are under some such illusion. But very few indeed can keep the relationship in those terms. Very few. And you are not one of them."

"—by the Sword's power, I command—"

"Fool. What are mere Swords to me?"

Mark, who had been in a distant part of the city when he was alerted to what was happening in the palace, was hurrying desperately in that direction now. As he passed, he could see swarms of troops and magical assistants gathering, torchlit ranks forming, at somewhat more than a hundred meters from his invaded quarters. These defenders, under good discipline, were deploying somewhat outside the range of the Mindsword's effective action.

At least no one who now held the Mindsword within the palace would find there an army ready-made to fight for him.

"Such delusions are very common when one of my kind—forms a relationship—with one of yours," said Akbar—the maiden was sitting now on the balustrade, modestly swinging her shapely legs.

The demon was obviously toying with his enemies before he reached out to pick up Skulltwister.

Meanwhile Vilkata, only five or six meters from the demon, was almost gibbering at it, plainly trying one spell after another. Plainly none of them were working.

Akbar went on, speaking in leisurely tones: *"After* I pick up this weapon—*after* that, I say—you will, each and all of you, be delighted to serve me, for the rest of your miserable lives. And I intend to see to it that—at least in your case, great wizard, and your case, glorious Master —those lives are very long. But, sadly, it is only now, beforehand, that I can enjoy your anticipation of that prospect."

Fuming and raging, now standing recklessly on a minute ledge in a position where moments ago he had been clinging with both hands, the Crown Prince would not listen, would not understand.

Angrily, with demented determination, he once more ordered the demon to crush Vilkata, and to properly sheathe and deliver the Sword of Glory.

"I think not, Master—but no, it no longer amuses me to call you by that title. I am wearying of this game. 'Fool' is a much better name for you, I think. I am not, and never was, compelled to take your orders. What is the power of a mere Sword, to *me?"*

Murat's speech was becoming unintelligible.

Akbar went on: "The fact is, I do not want to crush the man you call

Vilkata just yet. I may well find some better use for him." And the maiden cast a speculative look in the Dark King's direction.

Vilkata was about to say something, but before he could speak the maiden's slender hand gestured in his direction.

"There. I withdraw my gift of vision. You, my dear Vilkata, shall be blind—for the time being at least. You must be made to understand what the true nature of our partnership is to be."

The Eyeless One clapped hands to his face. Now truly blind, he groped and whimpered helplessly on his slippery roof.

"Be of good cheer. If you were to grovel properly in supplication, I might be willing to shorten your period of darkness."

But instead of groveling, Vilkata ceased to whimper. Drawing himself up, he regained and maintained some dignity in the face of this threat.

He muttered a few words in a low voice.

"Calling for help, great wizard? Feel free to do so. I can repel your—" Akbar's voice broke off.

The Dark King had risked all, diving bodily forward, over empty space, in a blind lunge aimed at the Sword he could no longer see; his right hand and arm, groping, grasping for treasure or for a life-saving grip, made violent contact with the razor-keeness of the Blade. The impact gashed Vilkata, and knocked Skulltwister from its perch.

The Sword fell again, once more passing out of everyone's immediate reach.

Vilkata, his gamble lost, clung blindly to the cornice for an instant, with his uninjured hand. Then he fell—but not to his doom. The shape of his newly summoned demon blurred through the air, catching him in mid-tumble.

The maidenly human shape of Akbar was leaning over the balustrade, watching the Sword fall, when a bulky man burst into view behind it on the balcony and grappled the demon from behind.

Murat, still single-mindedly intent, resumed his infinitely determined, crawling descent. He could still see Skulltwister, which this time had come to rest point uppermost, hilt and pommel stuck down into a drain on a roof's corner. Again his Sword had not fallen far, and he thought he could quickly get within reach.

In the instant of being seized by human arms, Akbar the demon let out a little sound of genuine fear. The maiden's shape vanished in an eyeblink, to be replaced by the semblance of a great ape. A violent struggle began.

* * *

Murat, his immediate enemies vanished or distracted, had needed only the space of a few breaths to get within reach—or almost—of the Sword. From the wall to which he clung, the man, stretching his right arm out to the uttermost, might have barely touched Skulltwister's point. It was impossible to clamber any closer, without going an impossibly long way around.

Drawing in his body, pressing himself against his own wall once again, the Crown Prince took a moment's rest. If only Carlo could help. But Carlo . . .

Concentrating totally on his goal, working as swiftly as he could, Murat unhooked the long empty sheath from his belt. As when he had once before picked up and claimed the naked Sword, he would now have to work the sheath onto the Blade before he dared try to seize the god-forged thing, whose unstemmed tide of magic now bathed him at close quarters.

Sheath in hand, Murat stretched out again. One last effort brought leather sliding over steel. But in making that effort he had reached too far, and felt his supporting fingers slip.

He fell. No intervening cornice here.

The last clear thought of his life was that the sheathed Sword was tumbling after him, and that he might still have a chance to catch it in midair.

Kristin screamed. She had been out on the roof, trying to make her way closer to the scene of action, and at the same time trying to compel her son to stay back on the balcony, to save himself.

Karel had at last appeared inside the royal quarters, and then upon the balcony; the old man was in time to keep Stephen from rushing out onto the roof after his mother, but not in time to hold the Princess back.

Madly scrambling over the wet tiles toward the place from which Murat had fallen, she did not stop at the roof's edge, but plunged down after him.

21

DESPITE warnings to depart, given by Karel and others, a few servants and a handful of soldiers had gathered and were still gathering on nearby balconies and in windows, to watch the struggle for the Sword of Glory.

Stephen and Karel watched from their balcony, the old man's powerful grip restraining the boy from rushing out on the roof after his mother.

Upon a balcony in the next wing of the palace, the dark and apelike shape of the demon Akbar struggled desperately, but to little avail, as if the strong man who had seized it were really more powerful than any mere human could possibly be. The combatants swayed back and forth.

Karel had no trouble recognizing Ben, who was not only maintaining the solid hold he had obtained at the start, but was gradually improving his advantage.

It was not long until Karel, at least, understood what must be happening.

"Shieldbreaker!" he muttered to Stephen, who still struggled in his grip. "The demon must have it!"

The moon emerged briefly from behind rain clouds, and swiftly retired again. For long moments the struggled was conducted in darkness and near-silence. A faint glow of light, from distant windows and courtyards, still made shapes and movements dimly visible. The hideous demon thrashed about and made noises as if it were trying to scream. But the human limbs that held it were tightening inexorably.

Now those who watched could see that something was wrong with Akbar's right hand, or with the image of a right hand that the demon flailed ineffectually at his opponent.

Moment by moment the image of that bestial hand and arm became a little clearer. There was a solid object at its end.

Presently it could be seen that Akbar was gripping a bright-bladed, dark-hilted Sword. With this weapon he attempted to punish and to slay the one who wrestled with him, but the slashes and thrusts directed at an unarmed foe accomplished nothing.

Again and again that shimmering blade and point penetrated the clothing and the flesh of the man who wrestled with the demon. But no blood was drawn, and the wrestler remained uninjured.

Karel muttered again: "The beast indeed has Shieldbreaker! But it must rid itself of that Sword, or lose this fight."

Ben had come to the same conclusion earlier, on seeing and hearing how the demon defied the Mindsword and Vilkata's spells. Now the huge man steadily increased his advantage—as he had expected. He knew the demon would lose this match against even the weakest barehanded human opponent—unless Akbar could manage to rid himself of the pernicious Sword of Force before it was too late.

Once he, Ben, had outwrestled a god under similar circumstances; no mere demon, handicapped by Shieldbreaker, was going to defeat him.

The demon gurgled, a hellish sound, as if the foul thing were being forced to try to breathe. And waved its right arm frantically—no longer slashing and thrusting. Now it was as if the demon strove to free its hand from the bite of a clinging serpent.

And at last—to Ben's horror and surprise, well after he had thought the feat impossible for Akbar to achieve—the Sword of Force flew free.

Vilkata, bleeding and weakened by the gash inflicted by Skulltwister, had been forced to withdraw temporarily from combat. Now, somewhat recovered, his vision restored by a new demonic partner, he came rushing back, borne through the air again by captive powers.

The sheathed Sword of Glory in its last plunge had fallen all the way to the ground, landing not far from the inert bodies of Murat and Princess Kristin.

A few people, emerging from doors at that level of the palace, had just started out into the paved area, heading toward the bodies and the Sword. But the sight of Vilkata and his onrushing escort drove them back inside in panic.

The demon Akbar, in the next moment after ridding himself of Shieldbreaker, had regained strength enough to hurl Ben aside.

Then Akbar gathered his energies for an effort to beat Vilkata to the Sword of Glory. But he saw that he was going to be too late.

Karel was and had been doing his best to repel all demons, but edged weapons had been drawn, and at the moment the old wizard's best was not going to be adequate. Vilkata, stooping from the back of his demonic mount, had just scooped up the Sword of Glory in his uninjured hand—

At that moment Mark, gasping for breath, came running out onto the balcony where his son and Karel stood.

"In the Emperor's name!" the Prince of Tasavalta bellowed hoarsely at his foes—and had to pause to gasp again.

In fact no more words were needed. A swirling blast, as of a hurricane, erupted out of the steady rain and darkness. In a moment the storm had gathered around all the demons, Vilkata caught up in their midst. Nor was Akbar spared. In the matter of a few heartbeats the whole roaring, twisting mass of air and cloud, now shot through with lightning, had mounted high above the palace, then whirled away. Before Karel could draw a deep breath, it was gone, vanishing at last far out to sea.

Silence fell on Sarykam, broken only by a distant rumble of thunder. Then another roll more distant yet, and beneath those sounds the steady plash and drip of rain.

The invasion had been repelled. The demons, including Akbar, were all gone. So was Vilkata. And so was the sheathed Sword of Glory, which the Dark King had just picked up.

Karel feared that, sooner or later, in one pair of hands or another, Skullwarper would be back again to plague humanity.

Right now the wizard, at the moment feeling very old indeed, was confronted by more immediate problems.

Prince Mark, leaning on the balustrade, slowly regaining his breath, was looking around for Kristin.

Tentatively he called her name.

Stephen was already gone into the building, running for the stair that would take him down to where his mother had fallen.

Karel could see (though not with his aging human eyes) how her body now lay there, twisted, resting partly on stone and partly on softer matter. On another body, whose heart no longer beat.

The right hand of the Princess moved, as if it sought to grasp something. Then it was still again. Of the three who had fallen, she alone still breathed.

"Prince," the magician said softly, "she fell from the roof. She is still alive, and she may live. But—there are terrible injuries."

Before Karel had added those last words, Mark was already gone, racing after his son.

Left alone, the old man was in no hurry to run anywhere. Ignoring the rain, he let his body sag on the stone railing. His eyes were closed, but lids could not shut out the visions of his magic.